I0590495

THE NANOBOT TRILOGY

THE COMPLETE SERIES

ROBERT JYSTAD

THE NANOBOT TRILOGY

THE COMPLETE SERIES

ROBERT JYSTAD

Flathead River Publishing

FLATHEAD RIVER
PUBLISHING

To my family past and present

Know that you are loved beyond measure

"How often have I said to you that when you have eliminated the impossible,

whatever remains, however improbable, must be the truth?"

Sir Arthur Conan Doyle in Sherlock Holmes, The Sign of Four

ABOUT THE AUTHOR

Robert Jystad is a California attorney living and working in Southern California. He focused his legal career on wireless communications and founded and served as President of the California Wireless Association for three years and on the Board of Directors for 18 years. Prior to law school, Robert was an editor in New York City working first as a production editor for Plenum Publishing and then as a managing editor and administrative director at Columbia University Law School. He has graduate degrees from Princeton Theological Seminary, Columbia University School of International and Public Affairs, and UCLA School of Law. Robert had success with his academic writing, winning top awards at both Princeton and Columbia. In New York City, Robert explored writing fiction and penned several short stories mostly as a writing experiment. Many years later, moved by the terrors of the Covid-19 pandemic, Robert began a new journey into the realm of techno-thrillers and produced the three novels that comprise *The Nanobot Trilogy*. He lives with his beautiful wife, Konnie, and his two bougie terriers, Fendi and Prada, aptly named by their fur mom.

ACKNOWLEDGEMENTS

I cannot thank my wife, Konnie, enough for the vision and support she has provided me during this journey. She has encouraged me when I was down, celebrated my victories when they came, and kept me steady and in the center of the path when creative impulses might take me down diverse and unproductive trails. She is a rock and without her Van would never have existed.

A special thank you to my sister, Sharon Diekman, an avid reader who has lived and worked for many years in the Silicon Valley, and who offered great suggestions and encouragement. I want to thank my illustrator Kim Peasley for her beautiful and artistic maps and her trained eye. Thank you to my aunt, Carolyn Erickson, also an avid reader and history buff, who gave me honest and compelling guidance. Thanks to Barbara Andrews, a good friend and a reader who knows the genre very well and was not afraid to force me to think. Barbara offered several key insights into the story line.

My daughter Kaia Jystad graciously took the time to read the books despite a rigorous and heroic medical residency throughout the coronavirus pandemic. COVID-19 was not her first experience working with patients that contracted a terrible infectious disease. She also happened to be in Yosemite Valley working as a medical intern when the hantavirus hit, a virus with a mortality rate almost three times that of the coronavirus. This book is a shout out to her personal and professional courage.

Our Westie terrier Prada continues to keep me company as I write, while her Norfolk terrier partner Fendi is out chasing crows and continuing his this-side-of-the-fence standoff with Max, our neighbor's German Shepherd, despite his having sadly passed away. I often find myself identifying with Fendi's delusions.

I am so grateful to my editors, Kim Peasley and fellow golfers Brian and Krista DeWitt, all of whom know how to point out silliness without making the writer feel silly. Long time Red Hill member Mark Monniger took me to the Paramount backlot to view in real life the setting of Book 2. Kim has been with us from the beginning contributing her artistic talents as well as her great mind. Brian and Krista are new team members and a brilliant addition to the story of this effort.

Special thanks to Derek and Shelisa Williams, who both completed careers in the military and as leaders in the Ontario Police Department. They gave me a real view into the workings of the police academy and the politics of law enforcement.

CONTENTS

PREFACE

Detective Van Eng is assigned to the Cold Case Homicide Special Section of the Robbery-Homicide Division of the Los Angeles Police Department. Insiders call it "CHESS." Van also happens to be hearing impaired. Despite her condition, she realized her dream of being promoted to detective because of the unique investigative skills and raw courage that she displayed while working as a medical examiner in the Forensics Services Division. *The Nanobot Trilogy: The Complete Series* assembles the three books that comprise the Trilogy into a single exciting read.

In Book 1, *The Cytokine Plurality*, we learn of Van's background and the events that lead to her unique path to promotion as detective and assignment to CHESS, the Cold Case Homicide Special Section. Her new boss, Detective Paul Young, has a problem with Van. He opposed bringing Van Eng into the Bureau without going through regular channels. He knew that, had she gone through those channels, she would never have qualified as a detective because they would never send a deaf person out in a squad car with another officer as a partner. He considered himself sympathetic to Van's situation as a human being, but he would not be the one to risk the lives of fellow officers because he felt sorry for Van. She didn't belong there. The problem was that Van was proving him wrong – at every turn. Now, in a direct affront to his authority, Detective Van Eng reopened the case on UCLA medical student Marley Dakota and stumbled into her first encounter with a petri dish containing toxic nanobots.

Dr. Belinda Armendariz started as a top engineering student at the Massachusetts Institute of Technology. Shortly after graduation, she moved to Silicon Valley in California and joined the emergent Ragnar Willowbrook Laboratories as Chief Scientist. Belinda was singularly responsible for building RW Labs into a world-class institution. During her years at the helm, the Ragnar Willowbrook stamp of approval became a necessary precondition to gaining access to vast sums of capital needed to bring new products to market. However, the Silicon Valley elite conveniently overlooked the darker side of RW Labs, which had been taking certain ethical shortcuts.

In Book 2, *Resonance,* Dr. Brian Johannsen hesitantly takes over the helm at Ragnar Willowbrook, attempting to resurrect what Belinda in her greed and recklessness had all but destroyed. Belinda, for her part, had left Ragnar Willowbrook far behind. She always believed that she served a deeper and historic interest in the resurrection of her own people back in Northern Spain. She would take any steps necessary to advance her goals, and she held in reserve the wealth she had accumulated at Ragnar Willowbrook for that singular purpose. The same petri dish that nearly destroyed Belinda's accomplishments in America, now opens a door for Belinda in Spain where she develops an arsenal from a new type of weapon and looked to unleash it on the world. That her victims might be entirely innocent and her dream pathological meant nothing to Belinda as she played out the role she knew was meant for her. In the meantime, Detective Van Eng continued to impress the people around her as she followed her own path as an LAPD detective solving crimes hidden in the dark underside of Hollywood.

In Book 3, *The Nanobot Wars,* Van faces her biggest test yet as that same dark side she encountered in Book 2 comes to roost in the very Bureau she calls home and forces pull her into yet another engagement with Belinda. Readers learn of Belinda's background and the circumstances behind Belinda's assumption of the top post at Ragnar Willowbrook. In this finale, Belinda plans to resurrect the Basque Kingdom using her weaponized nanobots are coming to fruition. Meanwhile Brian and his team find themselves assigned to invent the countermeasures that might contain the deadly effects of Belinda's nanobots. In a desperate attempt to locate Belinda and immobilize the new threat, Washington turns to both Van and Brian to drawn on their talents and special skills.

BOOK 1

THE CYTOKINE PLURALITY

MAPS

Map 1. Bainbridge Island, Puget Sound, Washington

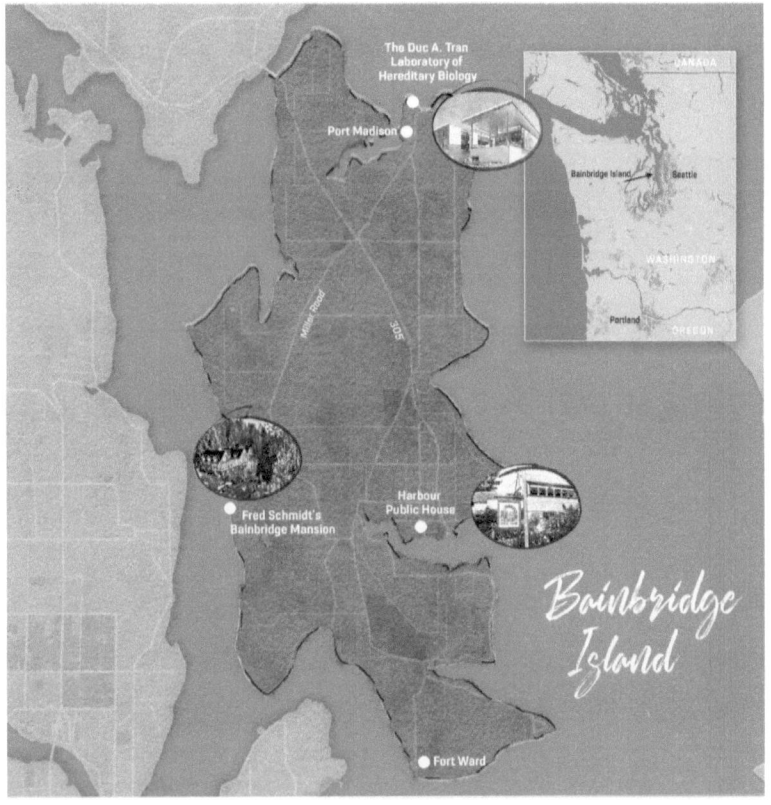

Map 2. Tajikistan, Central Asia

Chapter 1.

Butterflies Are Not Always Free

Imagine the world without sound. No sounds of birds chattering in the trees. No hum of summer cicadas as the hot night drops into darkness. Raindrops do not tap the window. Waves do not roar as they pound the sand. The tea kettle blows steam but does not whistle. There is no music.

But imagine if you were able to make a deal with God. He will take your hearing, but in exchange, he will transform your vision so that you capture the brightest reds, yellows and blues in a home garden or in your classroom, and you will learn to distinguish rose, fuchsia, watermelon, salmon, and other varieties of the color pink in the blink of an eye. In addition, you instinctively sort out the scent of wet leather from fresh leather, candle smoke from fireplace smoke, and grass that is wet from rain versus recently watered grass. In short, every other sense that is essential to experiencing the world as a human being will be amplified, and you will experience reality from a fresh and entirely new point of view.

Is it a fair trade? Hearing matters, and as a child, your ability to relate is what is affected and what ultimately matters when your senses are compromised. Van Eng wasn't thinking about any of this as she ran out the front door to greet the summer breeze, the wet grass and the bright dandelions. To a six-year-old, deaf or not, the front yard is its own universe and full of opportunities for delight, surprise and just fun. She ran and felt her heart beating and lungs pulling for air. She ran until she was exhausted and fell into the fresh, wet grass that captured her nose and tickled her exposed arms and legs. Mom stood at the door admiring her daughter and stifling the pangs of sadness she felt whenever she thought about what Van was missing by being deaf.

Van was not born deaf. She was a healthy 8 lb. and 4 oz. baby girl reaching out for life with her screams and coos and tears. But when Van was barely a year old, and still not able to walk, the family accepted the generosity of a rich uncle, grabbed only what they could carry, and in the dark of night, ran for the boat that would take them away from a frightening, despotic government. They bounced through overhead waves in a small dinghy and then accepted the help of anonymous hands, who pulled them onto the gangway and shepherded them into the bowels of a large freighter. Wet and tired, they huddled together that night and the many nights to come until Van became sick with fever and dysentery. Fearful for their daughter's life, Mom forced her way to the boat deck to get sun and scraps of food. She found pain medicine and crushed it into powder to add to the little bit of water that now was all that was left in Van's bottle. It calmed the fever and helped Van and her parents sleep just a bit despite their exhaustion.

One morning, after a few weeks of this harrowing existence, men with guns boarded the freighter and found the huddled mass of refugees in the hull. They pushed and kicked them into several small boats, and the refugees who thought they were going to Australia and expected to hear welcoming words in English, found themselves yelled at in Khmer in open pens in Cambodia. Who would have thought that their plans for escape to a better life would go so far astray? But at least the food there was better than on the boat, and there was medical help from a volunteer group called Doctors without Borders, and Van began to recover.

Except that she did not completely recover. Mom noticed that Van seemed to be staring a lot and was not responding to her words. She took the child back to the makeshift clinic and presented her to one of the young doctors. That doctor had a worried looked and took the baby to discuss with her team. When she returned with a steely expression, Mom knew not only that something was wrong but exactly what it was. In addition to having a fever, Van's eardrums became infected and had swollen and burst, coating the inside of her inner ear with scar tissue and Van was no longer able to hear.

Months later, the family found a sponsor and flew to San Francisco, where they settled in a Vietnamese community and began to build a new life. Dad became a chef, Mom found work at a garment factory, and the community supported them and played Mahjong regularly together. Eventually, they found a small house with a nice front yard, where now a spry six-year-old Van rolled in the grass and pulled up dandelion stems to see the milky liquid from the flower's stem flowing into the palm of her hand.

Unlike Mom, as soon as Van ran out the front door, she immediately detected a few minor differences from the day before. The rain from yesterday was gone, and today, the sun baked the grass even though it was still wet from the morning dew. The mailbox had been left open, suggesting that Mommy had run into the rain to retrieve the mail but rushing to get back inside and out of the rain, she had left the box open. Daddy's car was gone, which was odd since Daddy worked very late hours and often slept in until lunch. Maybe they needed him for a special breakfast. Down the road was a single car. It looked old, and the front bumper, instead of bright chrome seemed to be a reddish orange, unlike dirt but not clean and new. The car was running, which Van knew because white steam was coming from the tailpipe.

But none of this information meant much to Van. After being locked inside for two days of rain, all she cared about was running and rolling and smelling and looking at the sky. She glanced over at Mommy in the doorway, and felt her love, and watched as Mommy's head spun back towards the house and then, looking quickly back at Van, she held out a flat hand as if to say, "do not move—I will be right back." Van had no intention of moving. The grass was cool, and the sky was full of cottony clouds telling stories of rabbits and elephants.

Which is why what happened next caught no one's attention. Van smelled the smoke of an old cigarette, much like Daddy's brand, only this man was not Daddy. He had mean eyes and dirty khaki pants and one of his new boots was coming untied. But it hurt when he grabbed her arm, and she quickly looked back to the front door— Mommy had not yet returned. She screamed as best as she knew how to, but she was quickly bundled up and pushed into the car's back seat. The cracked leather of the seat scratched her face, and she could smell the old empty cigarette packs that were strewn on the floor. She tried to get up, but another pair of hands pulled her deeper into the back seat and leaned over her to lock the door. She watched as a woman grabbed her hands and pushed them into a hooded sweatshirt that was pulled over her head and her hair tucked into the neck of the sweatshirt. The sweatshirt was soft, like velveteen, and smelled like it was brand new. She felt the car accelerate and a deep uncertain fear made her shake and start to cry as she knew what was now happening was not right. Who were these strange people and why did they take her from Mommy and the beautiful sky?

The car ride seemed go on forever. The smoking man was talking constantly but Van heard nothing. She was learning how to read lips, and he seemed to be asking her name, but she was too scared to try to respond. She didn't trust her voice anyway. He quickly gave up, and the woman sitting with her in the back fastened her seatbelt and let her look out the window. The sky had grown dark with the onset of another rainstorm, but this one felt menacing and dangerous. She saw some squirrels scamper off the road and felt the urge to run herself.

The woman sitting next to her was pretty and was trying to be nice. She had lipstick on her teeth and her cheeks were flushed—they resembled the color of Mommy's makeup. Her perfume smelled strong, like rose perfume. But no... it was lighter and sweeter than rose, more like the gardenias in Mommy's garden wet with rain. The woman kept reaching out to Van as if she wanted to hold her, but the effort made Van angry, and she pushed her hands away and leaned toward the door. The pretty lady was wearing thick heels that made Van think she was pretending to be grown-up. She seemed very young to Van, much younger than Mommy. On another day, she might have even liked her. But not today. Today was wrong and these people were wrong for taking her with them.

Van saw a flash in the mirror and looked back to see red, white and blue lights approaching very fast.

"Shit," said the smoking man, beginning to accelerate and then realizing that that would be a bad idea.

"Honey!" shouted the pretty lady. "What do we do? Oh no! God, what are you doing? Don't stop!"

"Got to babe. Stay calm. He won't know anything and this one," he said, pointing to Van, "doesn't talk."

"I don't think that's nice" said the pretty lady pouting. "What are we doing?!"

"Look. You need to calm down and you need to do it now!" he glowered, with his voiced rising in a controlled anger.

Smoking man pulled the car over. The patrol car slowed and parked directly behind him and the officer walked up to the driver's window and tapped. "License and registration, please."

"Certainly officer," he said, giving a seasoned smile. "What seems to be the problem?"

"There's been an incident. We just doing a little investigating."

He smiled and looked in the back seat. "Howdy, ma'am," he said to the pretty lady. The lady smiled at the officer, tight-lipped and said nothing. He looked at Van. "Beautiful little girl," he said, and immediately Van felt that he knew she should not be there. "Do you always ride in the back with her?" the officer asked the lady.

Smoking man immediately interceded, "The girl's not feeling well, and it helps her when her mom sits with her." This response caused the lady to try an awkward smile.

"So pretty," the officer said, pointing to Van. "How old is she?"

"She is almost eight years old," said the man, "but she looks younger."

The officer said, "Looks to me like she should be in a car seat, but I guess if she is eight…" he said, with a hint of skepticism.

He looked back at Van and asked slowly and carefully. "How… old… are… you?" Van said nothing and started grabbing her hands as if she wanted to make them work. "What… is… your… name?" This time Van made out the question watching his lips. Smoking man barked a bit too quickly, "Her name is Mary." Van didn't hear smoking man's response but said as loud as she could, "I'm Van," although as it blended with smoking man's answer, it sounded more like "I'm fine."

Van's effort at a response clearly unsettled both smoking man and pretty lady who quickly confirmed, "It's Mary, yes it's Mary, that's right."

The officer furrowed his brow, and said, "Okay. Please sit tight. I need to run these," shaking the documents, adding, "and I'll be back."

The officer walked to the patrol car and got on the radio. Smoking man noticed that he kept his lights flashing and it made him edgy. Luckily, he thought, the officer did not tell him to shut off his engine, so he kept it running. The officer stayed on the radio a long time. Too long. This time, when he got out of the car, his partner got out as well and rested his hand on his firearm. As they both approached the couple's car from each side, smoking man got spooked, slammed the car into drive and punched the gas. The car took off weaving, showering the officers with rocks from the road. Neither of them fired, and both ran back to the patrol car and took off after the speeding car.

Back in the patrol car, the officer had been able to call in a blockade as a backup. The blockade waited down the road—three patrol cars with armed officers crouched waiting for the couple's car. Its lights appeared at a corner up ahead as the car barely in control sped toward the blockade and then slammed on its brakes just before hitting the lead patrol car sitting in the middle of the road. The first patrol car quickly appeared behind the couple's car and blocked it in from the rear. Officers jumped out and aimed their weapons at the couple's car. "Do not shoot," said the lead officer. "There is a child involved," he added, as if to remind everyone what they already knew. The couple slowly emerged with their hands up. "On the ground! Both of you! Hands above your head!" As they laid down, officers raced forward and restrained the couple. Van was suddenly alone in the car with her seat belt on. She had hit her head on the door when the car first took off and was thrown forward almost out of the seat belt when the car skidded to a stop. A small cut appeared on her temple. Hands reached into the car and pulled her out. People were talking but she heard nothing. All she saw were people dressed in different colors of blue with badges holding different kinds of pistols and rifles and lights flashing everywhere. Someone wrapped her in a blanket. It was scratchy but made her feel safe and it smelled like a pet dog. She saw lightning flash on the horizon as raindrops began to fall.

The officer returned Van to her parents, who were weeping and beside themselves with both grief and relief. Mom had stepped inside to take a call certain she could walk with the handset and cord back to the front door to continue watching Van. Her husband had called to say he was on his way home, and as she walked back to the front door, she saw the vehicle race away and Van was nowhere to be seen. She called the police screaming, and within 15 minutes, a car was there with officers asking questions and getting details about Van's dress and shoes and hair. Mom's English was not very good, but she told them Van was six years old and was deaf and that she was learning to read lips.

Chapter 2.

Smart Dust

Stress is as essential to life as oxygen. The Buddha told us the key to happiness is the recognition that "life is *dukkha*," usually translated as *suffering*. But *dukkha* is more nuanced than simply the idea of pain or emotional suffering. *Dukkha* is about the pain that we feel and experience as we navigate from moment to moment, unable to predict the future but aware of everything in our life experience that might eliminate this moment's experience of pleasure or happiness. As our consciousness shifts toward that unknown future and away from the present moment, it embeds itself in the vast array of terrors that await all of us—such as loss, failure, abandonment, pain, illness, tragedy, or death. It pulls us away from the present and into that next unknowable moment. The pull is unopposable—a basic element of our evolutionary fitness. It is a biological rule of existence, the demand that we survive whatever we might face, never actually knowing what we will face. What and who we are as identities exists only in the space between a present that cannot be grasped and a future that cannot be known. And we know that we cannot change that basic fact of existence—and that knowing is *dukkha*.

It was not, therefore, without irony that the University of Washington's microbiology lab on Bainbridge Island was called the Duc A. Tran Laboratory for Hereditary Biology, after its most famous geneticist. The lustre of his impact had long worn off, and the Lab had had few accomplishments of note since. Lab technicians who worked there now jokingly called it the "Duc and Cover" lab, as senior faculty scratched and clawed for an idea that might be the next big idea and might restore not only the University's fortune but their own as well.

Fred Schmidt, billionaire CEO of the Silicon Valley-based tech giant Grindle, capitalized on desperation. He knew it increased the resolve to succeed and at the same time, weakened the resolve to demand, and for that reason had inherent value. Fred loved inherent value. His latest foray into health care, self-serving though it was, introduced him to the wider world of desperation where a cutthroat competition had developed among university laboratories for the enormous bequests of large pharma and bio-tech companies. He discovered the Tran Lab after reading Dr. Tran's ground-breaking research on biological predisposition. He also knew that since Dr. Tran's unfortunate passing over fifteen years ago, the Lab was struggling. No new ideas were brewing, and no new superstars were emerging.

But there was talk about a young assistant professor, who after four short years of post-secondary education had a BA in microbiology and an MA in genetic engineering, and then flew through a doctoral program at the University, completing it in just two more years. Fred knew, of course, that the shelf life of genius was never predictable. The quick burst of scholarly success often ended in depression and self-loathing, if not psychosis. He had seen it too many times to trust it. This kid might show some promise and then—blam!—he goes looney or, even worse, off the grid. Fred hated off the grid. He saw it as the modern version of Luddism. Anti-technology for anti-technology's sake. But if the kid had promise, and he did, at least there would be good reason to test it, conduct a trial, give it a shot and see what developed.

The phone rang. Fred picked up and said nothing. He enjoyed the tension that he created when a caller who reached him for the first time didn't know how to respond to silence. He knew immediately when a caller did not know him, and he could determine quickly whether the call was worth his time or not. Those friends and colleagues who knew him began speaking immediately and the efficiency of that interchange also pleased him.

"Hi Fred, it's Derek. I am heading over to Labs now." Derek Whitestone was Fred's lead investment banker. Fred's account had grown under Derek, and Fred had come to trust him with his money, which was more than he could say about almost anyone else in his life. The business relationship developed into a friendship and their families often dined and traveled together. The tightness of that relationship kept Derek close by, and Fred not only could track his investments first-hand, he also often used Derek to explore some of his crazier business ideas, like getting into health care.

The "Labs" to which Derek referred was a local engineering laboratory called RW Laboratories—the RW stood for Ragnar Willowbrook. Also situated in Silicon Valley, Ragnar Willowbrook Laboratories was known for taking certain ethical shortcuts to speed up time to market for new products, a characteristic common to most businesses in the Valley, albeit veiled by a leftward-leaning political face. RW Labs did not develop much on its own. It was better at reverse engineering new inventions and capturing intellectual property rights faster than most inventors, and it paid a lot of money to the top legal talent from Harvard, Yale and Stanford to harvest those rights. Labs also had a tight relationship with the scientific community in China and exploited that relationship when necessary to bypass outdated regulatory restrictions in the United States.

The latest craze at RW Labs was "smart dust." Based on the principles evolving from the developing field of Micro-Electro-Mechanical systems or MEMS, smart dust in its early development had been viewed as a threshold advance in the fight against cancer. Unfortunately for its proponents, opposition to smart dust developed and slowed the technology on the grounds that it was fundamentally contrary to established norms of privacy, and conspiracy theorists proclaimed it as a new form of mind control. Several top names in technology had come out opposing its use in medicine. Smart dust was perfect for RW Labs, which could not care less about any flimsy political opposition. If the introduction of smart dust into chemotherapy regimens could take a minimally effective and brutal form of fighting cancer and produce spectacular results, it would be worth trillions of dollars worldwide.

Fred had been diagnosed with a form of lung cancer called non-small cell squamous. Doctors had caught it in the occult stage—its earliest stage. His prognosis was positive although not certain, and he had been undergoing treatment for the past six months. But it was this diagnosis that had introduced Fred to the intricacies of the health care system and triggered his investigation into new medical technologies. He was particularly interested in smart dust and its applications in medicine. Derek set up a meeting with RW Labs to look at opportunities for Fred to invest in smart dust.

Cheryl Brown was Derek Whitestone's top assistant. She was intelligent and sexy but mostly street-smart. Her father was an alcoholic and her mother a manic-depressive ex-actress. Growing up, she was left alone for long periods of time. But she did well in school and found respite from an unloving family life in books. She was a history buff and in high school won an award for a paper she had written on the stock market crash of 1929 and how its mismanagement led to the Great Depression. That award and her report card got her into UCLA, and she quickly enrolled in the three-two program under which she would get both a BA in the subject of her choosing—history, as it turned out—and an MBA from the UCLA Anderson School of Business in just five years.

When she was first accepted to UCLA, she was given a scholarship that helped cover her dorm expenses and tuition. The scholarship lasted only a year, after which she was expected to find money to cover her schooling, mostly through loans. She liked to party with her good-looking friends and one of them told her that stripping was an easy way to "make bank." Cheryl was skeptical and was not willing to hook for money, but her friend told her of a particular club near the 405 Freeway that was good at protecting its star performers, many of whom were UCLA undergraduates. She gave it a month, and after pulling in $5,000 in four weeks working just two nights a week, Cheryl knew that she had found her ticket. She gave herself the name "Stormy," even though the other girls thought it was "so negative." But she committed to herself that no matter how much Stormy could make from pole dancing, she would never hook.

"Grab your stuff," Derek commanded, as he rushed past Cheryl's nondescript office cubicle. Cheryl knew that Derek preferred quick reactions and got irritable when an assistant was unable to keep pace. She snapped her laptop closed, grabbed her coat and purse, and popped up behind him at the elevator.

"Do I get to know where we are going?" she asked, batting her eyes and flirtatiously trying to get Derek to laugh and relax. Derek enjoyed having Cheryl with him because she made him look good both by being a looker herself and by softening his intensity. He gave her a Harrison Ford smirk, and said, "Get in the car."

The black Lincoln Navigator Reserve pulled up. Gerard, the company chauffeur, hustled around the back and pulled the back door open. Derek motioned for Cheryl to slide in first and stepped in after her. She knew to slide all the way over. The flirty card only worked before real business would start, and the back seat of this car was considered sacrosanct—a holy space for the most important business discussions, second only to the conference room connected to Derek's office.

"You ever heard of smart dust?"

"I have not."

"It's colloquial for something called MEMS or microelectromechanical systems."

"I have heard of nanobots."

"Exactly. These devices are like molecule-sized sensors and if injected into someone who is sick with cancer, for example, they can be programmed to target and kill cancer cells or paint cancer cells to be killed by other systems that work in conjunction with MEMS."

"Are you sick?"

Derek gave her a "please don't be stupid" look but then softened. "All you need to know is that this technology is ready to explode and is only waiting for someone to set the trip wire. We are heading to a lab that is working on smart dust and could use Fred's money to help them along. Fred is keen on it."

The SUV jumped onto 85 South and merged onto Highway 17 south, that treacherous windy route over the Santa Cruz Mountains past Scott's Valley to the City of Santa Cruz and the University of California there, which, contrary to its reputation of being a hippy party school, had one of the most advanced biomolecular engineering programs in the country and was one of the key universities around the world working on genetic sequencing for the human genome project. The SUV turned off 17 onto Graham Hill Road, passed Pasatiempo Golf Club, a golf course designed by the famous golf architect Alister MacKenzie, whose other golf course masterpieces included Royal Melbourne in Australia and Augusta National in Georgia, home of the Masters. The car continued down Graham Hill, passing dense groves of redwood trees, and just past Felton, it turned right into a gravel road that looked like the entrance to a Napa winery. After about 20 minutes of windy gravel road, the view cleared to expose the entire Valley dropping away below and a tall glass building popped into view behind a massive steel guarded gate.

The security guard, who bore the air of someone who had served with black ops in the military, approached Gerard. Gerard was no slacker. He rolled down the window and said with grave authority, "I am here with Derek Whitestone." The guard looked in the vehicle and responded, "One minute, please." He checked the register, and, peering out of the doorway of the guardhouse, he waved to Gerard and motioned for him to enter as the gate slid open, revealing tree-lined ponds with fountains and huge metal artwork positioned, it seemed, haphazardly around the open entrance to the glass building.

Derek waited for Gerard to open the door, and he and Cheryl emerged to see a tall, slim woman in glasses, and a doctor wearing a lab coat waiting for them outside the entrance to the Lab. The woman approached first, clearly a senior executive at the Lab. She said with a European accent, "Mr. Whitestone. So good to see you."

"You as well, Belinda. I hear some interesting things are happening here."

"Always. Please come in."

Cheryl and Derek entered the large lobby with marble floor and columns and large paintings, designed to impress and somewhat inconsistent with the idea of the place being a laboratory. It felt to Cheryl more like a mousetrap for the Valley's unsuspecting nouveaux riche than a laboratory. Two 10-foot copper-cast letters RW stood behind the security desk, which was framed on both sides by metal detectors. Belinda and the doctor handed Cheryl and Derek badges with their names pre-printed and pulled out their own badges. Cheryl and Derek handed the guard their bags and the guard opened the gates to allow the foursome to pass through the metal detectors.

They were ushered into an ornate conference room with water and diet cokes placed on a credenza. Belinda and the doctor, who seemed ill at ease and was very quiet when they met, now became talkative as the discussion moved onto smart dust. A PowerPoint slide deck popped up with glass screens that appeared through slots in the conference room table, and he spoke through the slides in words that meant little to Cheryl, as he grinned and peered lasciviously at her over his glasses. Cheryl knew this look too well, and she knew too well how to play it. She smiled back at the doctor, looking impressed by his words and giving a hint of interest. Derek said nothing and ignored the play as if he was not aware it was happening. What Derek was really interested in was the Lab and the progress the Lab was making toward a marketable product.

"What's the timeframe?"

"You know this product has its detractors," Belinda responded with gravity.

"Let's pretend it doesn't," Derek replied.

"Okay, but we need to take the detractors seriously. Senators Windell and Leumann have mounted an anti-smart dust campaign, and the social media misinformation train is in high gear."

"Mobile phones face the same issue with 5G, right? Those companies are smart enough to know anti-technology conspiracy theorists carry no weight with the American majority. The more important question for the people I represent is—is this stuff real, or are we still in the science fiction phase?"

The doctor grew irritated and with an air of authority responded, "It is definitely real."

"So, then, Herr Professor, what is the timeframe?"

"Microbiology is the foundation of all life, and we take it very seriously."

Belinda frowned at the doctor and jumped in, trying to rescue the conversation.

"The fact is, we are making progress, but it is slow. There is AI technology being developed at Providia that could shift us into much higher gear, but they are not releasing prototypes of that technology without co-licensing, and the cost of license is significant."

"What difference can the prototypes make?"

"It will bump us up by 18 months."

"What is the cost of the co-license?"

Derek knew ahead of time this discussion would be about money, and it didn't bother him. Belinda began to explain the details to Derek, and the doctor made his way to Cheryl and started talking about his latest skiing trip to the Bugaboos. Shortly afterward, the party of four left the conference room and was ushered into a decontamination zone, where they put on sealed hazmat suits and gloves that were designed to keep the workplace sterile. They entered through an airlock door and walked into a large warehouse-sized room full of white light. Bodies in white suits bobbled around the room.

"There are two different processes for nanomanufacturing," the doctor said through his suit-embedded microphone. "Simply put, we call them top-down and bottom-up." He glanced at Cheryl smiling when he said this. "Top-down fabrication starts with large materials and reduces them to nanoscale. Bottom-up starts at the atomic and molecular level. Bottom-up assembles nanoscale devices by combining molecular material. The latter process is tedious and more expensive, but the devices are more reliable and seem to operate longer than what are basically shrunken devices. More importantly, we are beginning to detect self-assembling characteristics of molecules. This could take nanomanufacturing into an entirely new realm."

The group wandered around the room and Belinda introduced them to several scientists whose smiles and nodding responses seemed comical or oddly forced. One section was cordoned off, but Cheryl split off from the group and managed to follow a group of scientists into an area marked "Biological." She approached a younger lab technician.

"Hi," said Cheryl. No response.

"Umm, excuse me." She tapped him on the shoulder.

He looked up from his lab desk and it took him a second to realize someone was talking to him.

"What are you working on?" Cheryl asked.

"Who are you?"

"I'm with Derek Whitestone. We're investors." She smiled her cutest impishly sexy smile and the scientist almost fell out of his chair.

"Pleased to meet you," he stammered. "Uh, I don't think I am at liberty to discuss…"

Cheryl moved closer and leaned lightly on him as she studied the plexiglass window at which he had been staring. "Looks fascinating."

With very little additional prodding, he started into a discourse on virology that she didn't follow. But she kept him talking and began to look around the room. Suddenly his phone buzzed, and a text message popped up. "I'm sorry. I will be back in just a second." He jumped up and sped off at an awkwardly fast pace.

As he stood up, he inadvertently knocked a tightly sealed petri dish off the desk. Cheryl reached down to pick it up and give it to him thinking it might be important, but he was gone so fast that he didn't see or hear it fall, and she was left standing there holding the dish. It was sealed with red tape and labeled "Risk Group IV," which meant nothing to her. Why she did what she did next even she didn't know, but instead of putting it back on the desk, Cheryl placed the petri dish in a side pocket slit in her hazmat suit.

She left and found the original group moving back to the airlock door. Derek saw her and gave her a stern "why did you leave the group" look. She smiled without any hint of shame, and they went back into the decontamination room.

Chapter 3.

Sense and Senselessness (Part I)

The history of forensics combines scientific brilliance with the macabre, a deeply disturbing 19th century criminality that is captured compellingly in Caleb Carr's historical fiction, The Alienist. The science of fingerprinting, based on the assumption that each individual person has a unique set of prints, was not yet accepted as standard practice. But it caught the public's attention when several brutal New York City murders were solved by a young "alienist," a term in vogue at that time for forensic psychiatry. The alienist who solved the cases did so in part by proving that the fingerprints he identified were reliable markers of a specific individual and were remarkably well-preserved on smooth surfaces like glass and gun metal.

The modern form of fingerprinting, which by no means has replaced its progenitor, is DNA sampling. In cases where the oil of fingerprints is undetectable, the "oil" of DNA can be found at virtually every crime scene through bits of hair, skin, fingernails, blood, or semen. Like fingerprints, DNA sampling is a study in probabilities. But unlike fingerprint readers, which used probability theory to identify a "match," DNA decoders only approximate a match. Still, DNA sampling has been added to the list of evidentiary options selected to prove or to disprove guilt beyond a reasonable doubt. But what DNA sampling does much better than fingerprinting is support doubt about guilt, and by that doubt offer a means of proving innocence long after a judge or jury made the decision that no reasonable doubt existed and convicted some poor innocent to a lengthy prison term or even a death sentence. Accordingly, years and even decades after guilt had been established, it might be shown that the likelihood of a DNA match was so low as to be unsustainable. Even those convicted of the most heinous crimes and buried as it were on death row might find themselves in the now growing class of wrongly accused and returned to freedom.

The trauma of her childhood, and the oft-repeated thought as she grew up that she might have become a victim of an unsolved crime, led Van to develop a deep interest in police work. Even as an adolescent, she watched the news about local crimes with acute interest, and she was a voracious reader of detective novels and true crime stories. When she got to high school, she excelled in science, and in particular chemistry, proving wrong the educators who originally placed her in special education classes as a young child only because of her impaired hearing. In college, she majored in chemistry and completed her education with a dual masters in biochemistry and criminal justice. But when she applied to the San Francisco Police Academy, her deafness interceded again, and she was refused entry not because of some absence of skill or intelligence, but rather because of the risk that her deafness allegedly posed to herself and officers in the field.

Acknowledging her education and skills, members of the police academy selection committee suggested that Van consider forensics and even recommended a couple of forensic labs. She applied to a lab in downtown Los Angeles that had a reputation for excellence forged after the O.J. Simpson trials and the public and highly visible claim made by O.J.'s Johnny Cochrane-led legal team that DNA evidence had been mishandled by the LAPD. Van was pleased to hear that she had been accepted and that it was a well-paying job. Van's parents didn't like the idea of her living so far away, so they sold the small Bay area house for an obscene amount, and moved with Van to Monterey Park, a largely Asian suburban town near downtown Los Angeles. Monterey Park was a good choice. Several of Van's relatives, who had also escaped from various terrors in Southeast Asia, happened to live in the same area, and they helped Van's parents find a suitable home for a good price.

Dr. Frank Weatherby was the lead forensic medical examiner in Los Angeles and ran the City of Los Angeles Science of Justice Laboratories located in one of several nondescript multi-story buildings clustered around City Hall in downtown Los Angeles and within walking distance of the new police department. Frank had been a young chemist working at the LAPD crime lab during the O.J. trials and watched in horror as several honorable and highly qualified senior chemists had their lives destroyed by the criminal trial. He survived because good people in the lab and in the department protected him and he had helped solve numerous murders and had cemented his reputation as a careful and methodical scientist. Almost 30 years later, Van found herself as one of several assistants who supported Frank in his on-going effort to address crime in the City of Angels.

"What do you think?" Brad Jones leaned over Van's shoulder to see her notes. Brad was cute and gregarious. Everyone liked him, including Van. Brad had completed an internship with the NYPD in New York City and had been accepted along with Van into the current class of Weatherby assistants.

"Ow!" Van winced. Brad heard a small whine as he put his head too close to Van's hearing aid and caused feedback. Brad jumped back and Van turned with a smirk as she put her hand over her notes.

"Not yet," she said.

"Sorry," said Brad. "I keep forgetting you wear those things."

Van mouthed, "It's ok." She had gotten used to the feedback from her hearing aids and acted like it hurt more to mess with Brad than anything. But it was always irritating—a reminder of an unwanted disability. She turned to focus on the task at hand. Frank wanted a timeline work up on a domestic abuse case that resulted in the death of a young Colombian woman in Baldwin Hills. She was working from emergency dispatch recordings and police notes from interviews and phone recordings made at the crime scene although she had never seen it. So far, the timeline looked as follows:

5:00 pm — husband has verbal fight with boss at work site.

5:15 pm — husband and co-worker meet at bar.

6:00 pm — husband leaves bar after two beers

6:20 pm — husband arrives home.

6:30 pm — husband sits down to watch TV, baby begins to cry, wife asks husband to check on baby

6:40 pm — baby still crying, husband dozes on couch, wife wakes him up and asks him to tend to baby and husband goes to baby's room

[missing data]

7:05 pm — husband hears wife scream and finds her stabbed multiple times and bleeding from stomach

7:08 pm — husband dials 911 tells operator, "My wife has been stabbed and is bleeding."

7:23 pm — police arrive. Husband answers door with shirt indicating blood stains and appears distraught. Wife is lying on living room floor unconscious and bleeding from stomach. Husband claims he was trying to stop bleeding. Baby is lying in crib in her bedroom crying.

7:29 pm — ambulance arrives from County General Hospital. Wife is taken by ambulance to emergency room.

8:36 pm — wife is pronounced dead.

9:15 pm — wife's parents arrive at hospital and take baby. Police handcuff husband at hospital and take him to station for questioning.

11:45 pm — husband is booked on suspicion of murder and remanded to County Jail

Van turned to see Frank approaching quickly. He looked at Brad and motioned for Brad to join him. "Let's hear it," he said. Van grabbed her notes and read through the timeline.

Frank looked at Brad and asked, "So what's missing?"

He answered, "So far, it sounds like the only compelling evidence is the bloody shirt."

Van shook her head. "We have stabs wounds and a dead body, and we have no weapon."

"What else?" Frank asked.

Van responded, "We are missing 25 minutes."

"Ok, you both need to keep thinking about this. Grab your notepads and follow me."

Frank headed toward the door and Van and Brad followed closely behind. They boarded a white Suburban marked 'Forensics Official Use Only' and, within 15 minutes, they pulled up to a small light blue house surrounded by police tape. Frank grabbed the evidence case and all three put on blue gloves and booties. Inside, there were Post-it notes sprinkled around the rooms. The back yard had flags stuck in the ground. Frank and Brad stood over a taped outline of the body. The floor still had blood stains and there were blood stain splashes on the couch and on a counter chair. Unlike Frank and Brad, as they crossed the front yard, Van had taken a mental snapshot and quickly memorized it—something she had done since childhood whenever she encountered a new location. She noticed on a bush on the side yard under an open window that seemed slightly bent. Then, as they entered the house, underneath the overpowering smell of dried blood, she picked up the scent of baby powder. She left Frank and Brad studying the floor around the body tape and walked into the baby's bedroom and looked around. It was neat and organized, almost as if someone had just cleaned it. The changing table was covered with a fresh cloth, and new diapers, wipes, baby powder and a tube of Desenex were neatly arranged in preparation for the next use.

She looked at her notes and tried to envision the husband's movements. He falls asleep on the couch watching TV and maybe is a little drunk. His wife wakes him to go change the crying baby while she is cooking. Does he resent her for waking him up? If he came home intending to murder his wife, it is hard to imagine him falling asleep on the couch at all unless maybe he was so drunk that he simply passed out. Maybe he flew into a murderous rage after she tried to wake him to deal with the baby. If so, rather than carefully attend to the baby, he would have ignored the baby's cries and would have started pushing her or hitting her until he found a knife to complete the act and satisfy his blood lust.

It was true that he had alcohol in his blood at some point in the evening, as indicated by the breathalyzer test given by the police at the station. But the blood alcohol content level from that test was too low even to be admissible, and they were still waiting on the blood test reports. If the breathalyzer's low reading was accurate, it would be unlikely that he was heavily intoxicated, let alone blackout drunk just a few hours earlier. Besides if he indicated heavy intoxication at the home, why would the police not test him then and take him into custody immediately? They asked him if he had been drinking and he gave them the timeline in her notes. Van was beginning to believe that he was distraught not drunk. In addition, if he had been that drunk, why would a caring mother trust him with her baby? Assuming he is raging mad at being woken up as well as drunk and she just wanted his help, the best he would have done is stumble into the kid's bedroom, rip off the diaper, shield his nose, wipe the baby quickly, and then dump a load of baby powder onto the baby's butt, slap on the new diaper and put the baby in the crib still crying and leave baby powder trails on the changing table, all over the room, and in the crib. But there were no baby powder trails, and the strongest scent of the baby powder was coming from a small, covered trash bin in which the last pad from the changing table was neatly folded and placed on top of other dirty changing pads. The room bore the signs of a caring father, not a raging and possibly murderous drunk.

Frank called to Van to come back to the living room. "I need you to work with Joe and capture all footprints in the blood and develop a storyline from the footprints. Brad is working the knife angle."

"Of course."

"Anything from the bedroom?"

"Nothing yet."

Van saw Joe Warren crouching with his digital camera and studying the floor. Joe was the lab photographer and a recognized expert in crime scene investigation.

"What do you see?" she asked respectfully.

"I'll tell you what I see when we are done," he said patiently. "You need to draw your own conclusions first."

Van studied the floor. She noticed immediately that there appeared to be no bloody footprints leading toward the baby's bedroom. They all seemed to be concentrated in the living room and in the kitchen as if whatever happened in the bedroom, if anything, happened before the murder. She asked Joe to take a shot at an angle toward the baby's bedroom. Joe downloaded the photo and together they studied the shot on an iPad Joe had set up on a stand in the center of the living room. Van moved the photo around with her fingers. To the naked eye and to the camera's eye, she was right. No footprints led to the bedroom—all of them were directed to and from the body tape or congregated around in the kitchen and dining room where the phone was located. The floor still needed a chemical wipe, which was technically not a wipe but a spray that turned a light green when it came into contact with blood.

She asked Frank, "Any word from the coroner?"

"I haven't heard back."

Brad was carefully dusting the kitchen for evidence of a struggle or some desperate search for a weapon. The kitchen was clean and the prints he was finding were almost all the wife's prints. There were a few of the husband's prints on utensils and dishes in the dishwasher and a couple on plates in the cupboard where he might have been unloading the dishwasher but otherwise nothing. His prints largely corroborated his story. Brad found them on the TV in the living room, near the phone in the dining room and in the baby's bedroom, the last of which Brad dusted after Van had studied the room.

Van continued her review of footprints. Most of what she was seeing suggested but did not prove that the husband did not commit the murder. Her instinct said they had the wrong guy, but she knew not to lean on her instinct alone. There needed to be something supporting another suspect. She made copies of several of the footprints using contact paper that she sealed in separate plastic baggies, taped them shut, and put a number on each. Her note pad listed the numbers and described the precise locations of the print. Later she would use Joe's photographs to identify further using those evidence tags to show which contact sheets came from which footprints. She took a moment to study the prints and saw no indication that there was a third set. One very troubling thought occurred to her—that it might be possible the wife was suffering from post-traumatic stress and had perhaps stabbed herself. There were several problems with that theory, but the most obvious problem with that was that there was no knife. If the husband found her cut open, he presumably would have no reason to dispose of the knife and would have told the police she killed herself. She made a quick note and set that idea aside for later review. Van studied the footprints and kept looking for a third set of footprints, but nothing suggested a third set. The chemical wipe added nothing new to her findings. She talked to Joe and they agreed on several key points that Van noted.

There appeared to be only two sets of footprints in the blood. There was no visual evidence of a third set. One set came from large feet wearing work boots, presumably male and the husband's prints, and the other set came from small flat-soled shoes, presumably female and the wife's prints. No footprints led to the baby's bedroom although a set of male footprints appeared to have come from the bedroom. Most footprints, both male and female were in the living room around the body tape, suggesting that whatever struggle occurred, if any, it took place in the living room around the body and nowhere else. There was a line of footprints to the phone and back to the body and then to the front door.

"Anything else?" Van asked Joe.

"Nothing I can see at this point," said Joe. "Good work," he smiled.

"Let's go!" shouted Frank from the front door. Brad and Van gathered their cases and met Frank at the front door. As they walked down the steps, Van remembered the bush. "Give me a second," she told Frank and walked over to the side of the house. The bush, which was under a window next to the dining room, was a hibiscus bush that had started to flower. It was intact except for a section of branches growing toward the rear of the house that looked freshly broken.

"I think you should see this," she shouted to Frank and Brad. Brad was tired and looked irritated. Frank squinted against the setting sun at the back of the house and set down his forensic bag. He grabbed Brad's arm and marched him over to Van. "Be careful," Van said to Brad as he started to walk around the bush to look at the broken branches. At that moment, Van picked a scent. "Stop," she said to Brad. She leaned in and picked up a sweet muskiness that was not from the flowers. It smelled almost like blood, and for a second, Van wondered if the blood smell from inside the house was lingering in her nose. But this was more than blood. It was faintly industrial—like a solvent. Then she saw it, a small rectangular piece of brown fabric was caught in the bush. She put her gloves on and took tweezers out of her case and placed the fabric to her nose and winced.

Frank looked at Brad. "Did you dust this windowsill?"

"No sir."

"Get your gear back on and dust the area around the window from the inside."

Van backed away from the hibiscus bush and placed the fabric in an evidence bag from her case and marked it accordingly. Frank told Van, "Look for prints or impressions in the dirt around the bush and tell me what you see. I am getting Joe."

The sun was setting, and the natural light would soon be gone. Van carefully approached the bush on her hands and knees and saw two definite impressions of boots very similar to the boots inside and then saw a hand imprint in the grassy dirt near the bush that would be roughly where a hand might be if someone had jumped from the window over the bush, landed on both of their feet and then used their hand to keep from falling. The team set up lights, marked the area with crime scene tape and placed flags next to the prints in the ground. They collected samples from the bush and from the grassy ground around the handprint and the footprints. They also took molds of both sets of prints. Joe flashed several shots.

Two hours later, Frank, Van and Brad returned to the lab. "I want you both to know you did great work today. Stow your gear at the lab and get a good night's sleep. We can talk in the morning."

Van was tired but invigorated. The discovery at the side of the house had opened the door to another theory. Brad had been getting sullen, feeling Van stealing the limelight, but he noticeably cheered up at Frank's words.

"Feel like a beer?" he asked Van.

"Not tonight—I have a competition next month and I am laying low."

"Competition?"

Van shrugged. "Fitness—Venice Beach. You should come. It's fun."

"Thank you," Brad flushed. So did Van, and she peered sideways at Brad and smiled.

"See you tomorrow."

* * *

"So, what did we learn?" Van loved these conversations and felt a deep admiration and devotion to Frank.

Brad said, unusually humbly, "Maybe Van should start."

"Ok. Hmm. Wow. Well, in my mind, as I approached the house, my first thought was about the baby. In the middle of what must have been an extremely violent and chaotic situation, I wanted to know what happened to the baby."

"Interesting," said Frank. "Different angle. It is not uncommon in domestic abuse cases that result in murder for there to be multiple victims, often the children."

"Yes, but my interest was not in what did not happen to the baby, but what did happen."

"Explain."

"The baby's diaper was changed—or at least the husband claimed to have changed the diaper, and the smell of baby powder was strong enough to match the smell of blood."

Brad said, "Not to diminish your point but houses that have babies usually do smell of baby powder—or you hope they do."

"I don't disagree but there is a difference between baby powder as a residual scent and fresh baby powder. There had been recent activity in the bedroom and the top diaper in the trash bin still smelled fresh."

"Does that lead somewhere?" Frank pressed.

"It does. It suggests—doesn't prove but suggests—that the husband was not contemplating murder when he came home and crashed on the couch. It also suggests that the wife's effort to rouse him to change the baby was not a rage-triggering event and that the husband had a routine with the baby that he followed despite being groggy and possibly a bit inebriated. If all that is true, then two things are possible. One, the husband did not commit the murder and his story checks out. He changed the baby and came out of the bedroom to find his wife already bleeding. Two, he is a cold-blooded killer, who had carefully planned the murder and executed it in a calculated manner that included faking a snooze. But the course of events doesn't really support that."

"Ok. There are a few holes, but I like where you are going. Brad?"

"There was a lot of blood."

"You've hooked me," Frank's sarcasm was not subtle.

"What I mean is there was a lot of blood, but it was not spread all over the house as if the wife was defending herself, fighting back and running for her life from someone she knew could get violent. It was concentrated in one area."

"Okay good—what does that tell us?"

"That she was caught unaware and that her attacker was swift and knew what he was doing. I agree with Van. I don't think this was a rage event. I think it was planned and committed by someone who knew what they were doing."

"Do you make the husband for it?"

"I don't know. The knife is missing. There is no evidence in the kitchen that suggests the knife even came from the kitchen. No fingerprints on other knives or utensil drawers or the dishwasher. The husband could have brought a knife home and then disposed of it, but where? The team checked the garbage and the yard and the house and did not find anything related to the murder."

"I don't know," said Van. "This is not a domestic abuse case. Something else happened here and I am willing to bet someone else was involved."

"A love triangle?" asked Brad, trying to get Frank's attention.

"Except that your own theory doesn't support it," Van answered, now feeling competitive.

Frank ignored it. "We don't have much time," he said, bringing the mood back to somber. "They will arraign the husband tomorrow. Homicide wants to know our take. Let's go visit the coroner."

The coroner's office was a tough place to visit, even to the most seasoned detectives. The air was full of formaldehyde and after even a few minutes, which was rarely the case, the formaldehyde stuck in your nose and stayed with you for days, infecting everything you tried to eat. For Van, it was doubly so, and the worst part of her job.

"What's going on, Frank?" Dr. Gilford von de Grassy was a long-time friend of Frank Weatherby and a unique character in his own right. He wore ear spacers in both ears, and as a younger man had been a tattoo model. You could see that both of his arms were covered as well as his neck and jaw, long before boxer Mike Tyson jumped on that crazy train, as everyone thought at the time. You could not see that Gil had 90% of his body covered and had been on the cover of several tattoo magazines along with his wife, also a tattoo model. But Gil was chief coroner of the LAPD for a reason, and he and Frank trusted each other, and had a deep admiration for each other's work.

"Back again, Gil. Seems like no matter what we do, we never seem to work ourselves out of job."

"Ain't it the truth. You are here on Baldwin Hills?"

"Right."

"I got to tell you this one is unique."

"How so?" Gil walked over to the drawer containing the wife's body, opened the drawer and folded the coroner's sheet back to reveal the head of a youngish Latina. Van, Brad and Frank stood respectfully near the body's head. The skin on her face was light brown with the greenish hue of death. It was passive, without emotion. Her lips were blue. As Gil pulled the sheet back further, all three examiners were startled. The stab wounds looked surgical and not what you would expect in a crime of passion. Whoever cut her knew precisely what they were doing and did it with swift precision. The cut pattern resembled a capital H lying on its side with one horizontal cut just below the navel and the second horizontal cut from hip to hip with a single almost perfectly vertical cut midway between the two.

"Cause of death?" Frank asked methodically. Van and Brad glanced at each other.

"Yes," said Gil. "But that's not all." Frank looked up. Gil went over the cuts and with a gloved hand pulled back the cuts on the right side of the body. "She is missing something." All three examiners looked at the body and then each other. "It appears that the murderer took an ovary."

"Damn," mumbled Brad. They stared at Gil as a new realization began to creep in.

Van said it first, "We may have a serial."

"Yah," said Brad. "They got the wrong dude."

Frank looked troubled, "We got a method guy, I agree. Whether or not the husband is the perp, this was not a crime of passion."

Gil closed up the body. "One more thing. We swabbed the nasal passages and found traces of chloroform."

Frank looked at Brad and Van. Van answered his unspoken question. "Nothing was reported, sir, and we found nothing." Brad concurred.

Frank looked back at Gil and repeated, "Cause of death?"

"You're careful, aren't you, Dr. Weatherby?" Gil joked, trying to lighten the mood. "By the time the paramedics got there, she had lost so much blood, she should have been DOA. She wasn't. The paramedics' efforts to stop the bleeding kept her alive a few minutes longer, but they didn't see that internal cut. She died from an internal hemorrhage."

The team returned to the SUV. "I am not making the husband," Brad repeated.

"And I'm not ready to release him," Frank responded. "I can't risk releasing a potential serial killer just because his first victim is his wife."

"That's a hard call," said Van, "but I agree for the moment." Her mind was spinning. The footprints on the ground outside the window were an almost perfect match to the footprints inside but if there was a third person in the house, there had to be three sets of footprints. As much as Van's Buddhist culture supported a belief in ghosts, she refused to consider the killer floating out of the house. Besides, something had happened at that window, and her hope was that the small bit of evidence they did find might be a lead.

Chapter 4.

Sense and Senselessness (Part 2)

The next morning Van woke up early and hit the road for a quick three-miler. When she got home, the sun was still hidden, and she ran through a quick routine of band work and floor exercises finishing with a 10-minute plank. Dressed and ready for work, she made herself Vietnamese coffee and scrambled eggs from four egg whites. She loved the hot richness of the expensive Weasel coffee blend that her parents bought for her, especially with a touch of sweetened condensed milk. The condensed milk was a delicacy she allowed herself to enjoy only on rare occasions and never when she was competing. Her strict workout regimen excluded all dairy except eggs, her primary source of non-vegetable protein.

The sun was only beginning to rise as she wished her parents good morning and drove into the LA traffic. The drive from Monterey Park to downtown was only a few miles but it was a slow haul. Van had found a few back streets that at least distracted her if they didn't speed up her commute time. As she drove, she thought about the homicide and found herself agreeing with Brad more than Frank. The husband would have to be both calculating and mentally ill to have planned such a cold-blooded murder. He took time with the baby. He cleaned the baby and set up the room as a courtesy to himself or his wife, whichever would have been called on for the next diaper change. Then he casually walked out to the living room where he clinically dissected a living being who was the mother of his child. It just didn't ring true. And there was no knife and there was no excised body part.

The problem was the complete lack of evidence of a third person in the house. There had to be something. She thought about the bush. It was damaged, and if she remembered correctly, the damage appeared to be fresh. She needed to review Joe's photographs and look for DNA and any other chemical substrate on the torn fabric. She was concerned that the bush evidence was just a distraction and that the husband might have launched himself out of that window and inadvertently damaged the bush for a hundred reasons. She didn't believe that, but the truth might simply be so. After all, the footprints were basically the same.

Frank was impressed with Van's acuity at the crime scene, both her unwavering focus on finding a rational storyline supported by the evidence and her heightened visual and olfactory sensitivities. He had a gift for locating talent and he did not hesitate to encourage it. He saw her enter the lab, remove her coat and replace it with a white lab coat. He could tell she was thinking and probably too hard.

"Good morning, Van."

"Good morning, Dr. Weatherby. Have we submitted the fabric for DNA?"

"Not unless Brad submitted it."

"If not, I would like time with it."

"Let's let Brad get the DNA results first before we handle it anymore. I'm a bit sensitive on that one."

He smiled. "Do you have a minute?"

"Of course," she said quickly, a bit startled by this unusual display of early morning courtesy.

"Follow me," he said.

They left the lab and grabbed an elevator that took them about three stories below ground. The light on the floor was hazy, and Van noticed the air had a scent of mildew from old books and wet paper. The linoleum on the floor was worn and dusty, as if the cleaning crew rarely made their way down here, and the lights would make you go mad if you had to spend much time down there. It occurred to Van for a brief instant that Frank's motives might be suspect. He quelled that thought immediately.

"I am troubled by the body we reviewed yesterday."

Van grimaced. "That's an understatement."

Frank laughed. "Sometimes I find that the best way for me to process something troubling is to get away from it. Not a lot of times, but sometimes, just for a morning."

"I like the idea that your brain works whether or not you are actively thinking about something."

"That's a point. It's a remarkable organ. It works all day and then keeps working while we sleep. It works when we want it to work and then works when we stop. There are some who believe it works to fool us into thinking we are making it work. They believe that there is no such thing as pure conscious thought, which they assert is only a neurochemical reaction. Rather, our only true thoughts emerge in the unconscious."

"I don't think I can go there. Sounds as if they think that, without our unconscious mind, we are nothing more than robots. If that's true, then why do we choose when and where to focus our thoughts?"

"Point taken. It's more about philosophy than neurobiology but no question we are thinking even when we are not thinking." He grabbed keys out of his coat pocket and opened a gray door with mesh covering the window and flicked on the light. Inside were rows of boxes and files.

"Come here often?" Van flirted just a bit. Frank gave her a look that told her that wasn't funny. She flushed.

"These are cold case files. Any effort to solve them was abandoned after no suspect was found or, even if they identified someone, nothing turned up to support an indictment."

Van looked at the size of the room, which was not small and appeared to be packed. "Does this happen often?"

"Our job is to ensure it doesn't, and unfortunately, we are not perfect. But there is a lot to learn here. Very few cases go cold because a criminal is a mastermind. Most criminals become criminals because crime is easy, and they are too dumb to find a legitimate way to live. Some criminals want to be caught. For whatever bizarre turn of events that occurred in their lives, crime and punishment is a comfort zone for them. A small percentage of criminals are just plain evil, but it is remarkable how many of them want to be caught. Bottom line, there are a few masterminds, but it is rare that cases go cold because we are outsmarted. Most cases go cold because mistakes are made by the police, by forensics, by investigators who miss obvious clues. Sadly, some cases should go cold that don't—innocents can become victims of a system looking to lay blame. Study the mistakes of others and maybe you can learn to avoid them."

Van was reflective. "I bet a lot of cases involving prostitutes go cold."

"A fair share I imagine," Frank answered as he pulled the door closed.

"I think about them sometimes."

"You do?"

"Sure. I wonder how they decide that selling their bodies as a way to make a living makes any sense. It's like they tried and failed at a couple of alternatives and then just gave up."

"There are a lot of sad stories to be sure, but they call New Orleans 'the Big Easy' for a reason."

"Yeah. Easy doesn't work very well. I find that living your life trying to avoid the pain of failure becomes the most painful kind of life. You have to find a way to move forward. You can't give up."

Van's spontaneous reflection struck Frank, and he reflected on the Simpson trial and how few of his damaged colleagues ever recovered. "This culture is so focused on success that many of us never learn how to manage failure."

"I discovered failure at a very early age. I was six when they put me in special ed. I couldn't hear and the school thought I was slow. When they finally figured it out, they put those giant hearing aids on me and everyone treated me weirdly. I hated them and didn't care if I couldn't hear. I forced myself to learn to read lips."

"You are remarkable, Van. I brought you here because I like the way you think and how you approach your job. Spend some time here. Let me know what you find."

Frank handed Van the keys and left. She walked into the room. It smelled like old, wet cardboard. She wandered around the stacks to see if there was any order or if it was simply old in the back and new in the front. She found the room divided into sections. Each division had a section. Robbery-Homicide, Gang and Narcotics, Vice. The largest section was Commercial Crimes (White Collar). Not a surprise. There was a cage in the back that was labeled Homeland Security. She found the letters R-H and pulled down a few boxes, grabbed a chair and started digging. There were a lot of gruesome photos. One picture showed headless bodies. Another showed a woman cut in half. The file said Dalia. Van knew that one and was tripping to be in the basement of an LAPD building reading about it. She looked to see if there were any boxes that linked murders. She didn't see anything immediately. That was not surprising. Serial killers seemed to fall into that category of evil criminals who wanted ultimately to be caught. She found one file about a murder in Hollywood. She read through a couple of files. The coroner's report made reference to semen found on the body of the victim, a young girl. The file contained a sealed bag with pieces of cloth, sheets, underwear. Written on the bag were notes of a lab technician that included the word "contaminated." She thought of the fabric she found on the bush and started to panic. She quickly reassembled the boxes and returned them as she found them, headed out of the room, locked the door, and ran to the elevator.

She found Brad in the lab, intently studying fingerprint scans.

"Where did you send the Baldwin Hills evidence?" she asked.

"I had Karen take it to DNA, Sixth Floor."

"Thanks."

Van found Karen Wasserman in a small cubicle at the back of the lab. Karen was a lab technician who got her forensics science certificate from a local trade college. She was good at her job, recognized by the school with a special award for being the top student in her class. She was also a single mom, trying to work and raise two kids on her own.

"Brad told me he gave you the Baldwin Hills evidence to have analyzed."

"Yes, he did," Karen replied, with a look of concern as if she had done something wrong.

"You followed protocol, correct?"

"I did."

"Good. Who got it?"

"I double bagged it, labeled the outer bag and dropped it with Sam on the sixth."

"Great, Karen. Thank you."

Van rode the elevator to the sixth floor. The floor that handled DNA was reinforced with heavy steel doors and looked more like a mental ward for the criminally insane. Exiting the elevator, she found herself in a small lobby at the end of which was a heavy secured door and a wall with a thick plexiglass window. She peered through the window. The old backroom kitchen look of the 1990s had been replaced by stainless steel and hazmat suits. Once evidence entered that room, everything that could be done to prevent contamination had been done; the setting calmed Van's surge of panic. She hit a buzzer and a masked attendant appeared at the window.

"Is Sam here?"

"Just a second."

A tall, lanky African American popped into view. "Van!" She had met Sam a few times. He was a young to be leading a key subdivision of the Forensics Science Division.

"Hi, Sam. I am here to follow up on the Baldwin Hills sample."

"Yes. I have been working with it myself. I'm sorry, Van, but I am not detecting any measurable DNA."

"Are you still working with it?"

"Probably not."

"Can you have it bagged? I'll wait."

"Sure." Sam was gone for about 5 minutes and brought it back. "Always a pleasure to see you, Van."

"You too, Sam."

Van signed out the bag and returned to the lab. She gloved up and opened the bag carefully. With sterile tweezers she lifted it out and dropped it into an open petri dish. It looked to be cotton, which if there had been DNA, would be good and bad. Cotton was a great repository of DNA but also could make DNA very difficult to identify because cotton, relative to polyesters or silks, had a very uneven surface.

But she knew she wanted time with this fabric. She stared at it for a few minutes, looking at the shades of color and tints. Someone without Van's perception might call it light brown but Van could see a variety of tans and even some orange caused, it seemed to her, by a very light stain. She snipped a small piece of the fabric near the stain and placed the snip with tweezers in a separate dish. She placed that dish in a vacuum chamber alongside a small dropper containing disilane. Disilane was extremely unstable and flammable when exposed to air, specifically oxygen. But one if its key properties was that it caused residual chloroform to glow. She turned on the chamber and placed her hands in the rubber gloves that allowed her to work in the chamber. Very slowly she opened the disilane, constantly checking the vacuum gauge. She touched the tip of the thin glass dropper to the fabric and immediately it started to glow. Even though chloroform evaporates almost instantly, there was enough residual to react. Not conclusive, but more evidence supporting the husband's innocence.

She then took the remainder of the fabric and held it closely to her nose. She knew the chloroform was not sufficient to hurt her and unlikely there would be any scent left at all. But she closed her eyes and focused on her nose, taking slow deep draws. At first there was nothing, but soon she began to pick up hints of rubbing alcohol along with diesel, fertilizer, eucalyptus and lavender. It was an odd combination of scents, and she couldn't place it. She looked up and Brad was standing next to her as he seemed to be doing more regularly lately. It was a little disturbing, but he was trying to be polite and not interrupt her focus.

"Brad?"

"I think I found something," he said.

"Go on."

"There is a third set of fingerprints."

Van's jaw dropped. "You sure?"

"Let me show you."

Van carefully placed the fabric back in the evidence bag and sealed it. As they walked over to Brad's lab, Van asked him, what places would have rubbing alcohol, diesel, fertilizer, eucalyptus and lavender?

"Don't know about the alcohol but sounds like a farm. Maybe a flower farm? Why?"

"Any flower farms you know of?"

"I have seen orchid farms in Oxnard and Mendocino, on the way to Santa Barbara. Could be a nursery."

"Maybe."

Brad brought up the prints on his screen. He explained to Van how his program worked to identify common point on prints to detect positive matches and fails. Van knew a lot about fingerprint software, but she enjoyed listening to Brad. His way of describing things was both simple and smart. He got to the point quickly.

"Most of the prints in the kitchen and dining room area were her prints. I found his prints on the phone and in the living room, consistent with his story. But there was a thumbprint I pulled off the dining room table that does not match either his or her prints."

"Odd that a killer would be so careful and methodical and leave a print."

"It is, but I think he did."

Van got home around 6:15 p.m. Mom was there and preparing dinner. The house smelled fresh, as if there were new flowers. She walked into the kitchen, and said, "Hi Mom, I'm home."

"Hello, Daughter." Her mom rarely called Van by her name when she addressed her directly.

"Smells good, Mom."

"Yes. Nice. Very cheap."

"Did you go to the Dollar Store?" The Dollar Store was her mom's favorite place to shop other than the fashion district in downtown LA.

"No, no. Your father and I drove to Olvera Street. They have a market."

Van looked at the table. Mixed in with the daisies and mums was fresh eucalyptus. "What kind of market?" Van had assumed it was a grocery store.

"Outdoor market. You know it. For farmers."

"A farmers' market?"

"Yes. Farmers' market."

Van saw Brad as she walked into the lab the next morning. "I need to know where there are farmers' markets around Baldwin Hills."

"Farmers' market." Brad picked it up immediately. "Right. I know there is one on Grove Street in La Brea—that is a famous one. There is also one on Olvera Street. Historic."

"My mom went there yesterday. Want to take a ride?"

"I'm in."

Olvera Street had been a Los Angeles icon since the 1930s. The "street" was a brick walkway for pedestrians only and replicated an outdoor Mexican mercado, with small stalls and restaurants. It celebrated Latino heritage and evolved from a small outdoor market into a downtown Los Angeles museum and tourist destination. Some stalls remain owned by the same families that started them nearly a century ago. But Olvera Street also represented the complicated cultural relationship between Los Angeles Latinos and other LA cultures. Under the veneer of merchandizing and good food was a history of conflict and a battle for recognition and respect that stretched from Mexico down through the Central and South America.

Van and Brad parked at the rear entrance and made their way to the street. Van had never seen Olvera Street even though she worked just a few blocks away. The reds, yellows, pinks and blues of blankets, hats, toys and pottery spilled out of the small stalls, and the smell of carne asada and frying breads overwhelmed the market. Brad entered the street mesmerized by the smell and contentment of Mexican comfort food, but Van's attention was focused elsewhere. She saw the colors and the merchandise and the clerks and managers hustling new business. She saw tourists and the families and older folks out for an enjoyable stroll. She also saw mostly men lurking around shops. Some of the men were probably shop owners overseeing the work, and they seemed to have small entourages. She saw some younger men enjoying the view, potential suitors looking for pretty girls. And she saw others lurking, trying to appear distracted but obviously with more questionable motives.

They walked together casually down the street past stall after stall of the same touristy kitch. "This is not really a farmer's market," Van observed. "More like an open-air pop-up mall."

"Right, except that it's been popped up for 90 years," Brad noted. Behind the stalls on both sides was a row of mostly two-story buildings. Most of the lower stories were restaurants. Some of the first story rooms were recreations of small 19th century offices, giving Olvera its museum effect. Van studied the buildings, looking for signs of a doctor's office or a medical clinic but the smell of the restaurants was so powerful she thought it unlikely that the fabric evidence spent any time there. She also wondered if her mom really knew where she had been when she bought the eucalyptus.

She walked back to the car with Brad, feeling let down but resolved to go to every farmer's market in LA. Then, as they turned the corner, she noticed a flower shop that was not actually on Olvera Street. It was a good-sized shop with a large selection of mums, daisies and roses set out on the sidewalk. There was a small feminine looking gift shop on one side and a two-story office building on the other side.

Van smiled at Brad. "Check this out," she said, as she grabbed his hand instinctively and started pulling him toward the flower shop. He responded by giving her hand a light squeeze, which startled her, and she realized how inappropriate it might have felt to Brad. She dropped his hand and with her hand to her mouth, said, "Oh my god, I am so sorry." He smiled and, in that moment, Van looked at Brad's eyes and felt her stomach drop. "No worries," he said. "I get that all the time." He laughed. She blushed and smiled. "The flower shop," she said determined and turned around this time, letting Brad fend for himself but wishing just a little that she was still holding his hand.

They walked inside and although the roses, gardenias, and jasmine scents seemed everywhere, Van quickly picked up on the strength of the eucalyptus branches that were used to adorn arrangements alone with baby's breath and ferns. She walked to the counter to see an older Latina cutting stems, and from behind a door a small Asian woman appeared. She saw Van and said in slightly forced English, "Hello, may I help you."

"*Ni hao,*" Van responded, hoping to put her at ease. The woman fired back in rapid Mandarin, which, even though Van spoke Cantonese, she understood well.

"I was wondering if you knew of a doctor in this area."

"Doctor? Are you feeling sick?"

"No, I am sorry, but I am from LAPD Forensics, and I am looking for a doctor's office or clinic in this area."

The woman smiled. Her business needed the protection of the police, and she was a frequent caller of 911 when her cameras caught homeless people or other vagrants sniffing around her store. "Very good. I like the police. Very helpful," she said. "Maybe you come back into my office?"

Van turned to Brad, and said, "I'll be back in a minute," and left Brad feeling out of place looking around the flower shop. The older Latina picked up on it and began to engage Brad, asking him if he had a girlfriend. Van followed the shop owner into her office. It was neat and organized but there was nowhere for her to sit.

"May I offer you some tea?" the shop owner asked.

"That would be nice," Van replied, "but my friend is waiting for me."

"I will get him some tea too," she answered and headed to a small kitchen. "Why are you looking for a doctor's office?" she asked from the kitchen.

"We're investigating a homicide."

"Oh. You think a doctor did it?"

"Maybe."

"Why?"

Van wanted to be courteous, but she was wary of the shop owner's curiosity and concerned about interfering in the Department's separate investigations. "I'm sorry but I shouldn't be discussing details."

"Sure. Sure. I'm sorry. I do not know of any doctors here."

"The building next door. Do you know who lives there?"

"Nobody lives there. Been empty for many years."

"Does anybody stay there?"

"No. No. Nobody stay there."

"Have you ever thought about buying it?"

At this, the shopkeeper hesitated. "No, I no buy. Very expensive." Van sensed something off about the response. It wouldn't be unusual for a successful business to consider expanding or simply investing in other assets. Downtown Los Angeles was growing, and multistory condos were springing up all over. Loft style apartments were especially popular and expensive. The land alone under the building would be valuable. But as an empty building, it also might be hard to keep out vagrants who were looking for free shelter.

An Asian man entered through the back door and saw his wife speaking to Van. She saw him, and said, "I must get back to work. Please let me know if I can help."

Van thanked her and walked back out front. Brad was holding a large bundle of flowers. Van thought he might be offering them to her, which would have been very strange, but Brad said, "She told me I need flowers to get the girl. I couldn't say no." They both laughed and walked out the front door. Van wandered over to the front door of the building. She tested it and it was locked. The windows were dusty and had not been washed. She tried to look inside but there was paper covering the windows. She looked up to the second story, and an old shade was pulled down but not all the way. She knocked on the front door but there was no response.

"What did she say?" Brad asked, shifting the flower bundle from one arm to the other.

"Nothing. She did not know of any doctors in the area. But this building is strange, and her reaction when I asked about it was odd."

They returned to the lab. Frank was still there and asked what they had found and why Brad was holding a large bundle of flowers. Van smiled at Brad and said they brought them back to spruce up the office. Brad quickly concurred. Frank furrowed his brow but shifted to the investigation.

"Anything?"

Van described the trip to the market and the flower shop. Frank was encouraging. "Good to follow your hunches. Even if nothing turns up, it expands the window of your investigation. Just be careful of rabbit holes."

"I think it is more than a hunch," Van replied. "I want to test out the florist's claims about that building."

"Fine. If you go back there, take someone from homicide."

* * *

Charles Darling was a senior detective in the Robbery-Homicide Division of the Detective Bureau. He had been at the Bureau for 25 years and was starting to think about retirement. His approach was old school, and he had been somewhat successful at solving crimes, successful enough to be kept around. He was never a star in the making, and he had seen many stars come and go. He had been passed up several times for chief despite working many more late hours than others and often being the first to arrive. He lived by himself, did not smoke and kept his drinking to special occasions. His one vice was reading, and his small home was lined with full bookshelves. Charlie was getting on, but to say he was losing his touch would be wrong. Charles loved being a detective. But he also liked the company of young women, and when Van reached out and the other detectives on the case declined, he offered to help.

They pulled up to the corner across from Olvera Street, and Van pointed to the flower shop and the office building. Charlie turned at the first corner across from the flower shop, pulled a U-turn in the middle of the road, and parked on the spot closest to the corner. The sun was setting and traffic was beginning to die down. It was the perfect time to start a stakeout. Nothing unusual about a 2010 tan Ford Taurus parked innocently but directly across from your place of business. Van looked at Charlie, as if to say, "Are you serious?" but said nothing. Charlie noticed and smiled at the rookie.

"A bit too obvious?"

"I wouldn't know," Van replied. "I've never been on stakeout."

"Sweetheart," he said, a bit too condescendingly. "I've been on so many of these I can't tell the difference between sitting here and in the office. But one thing I have learned—you don't catch any more criminals hiding two blocks away than you do sitting directly across the street. It is amazing how people fail to see the things directly in front of them."

Charlie didn't know Van was hearing impaired, and therefore that noticing the things in front of her and to the side and sometimes even behind her was how Van lived every moment. Van understood conceptually that people were easily distracted and often missed the details staring at them directly, but that was not her experience and the idea of testing that assumption seemed ludicrous. Still Van was bred to respect others, especially those who were her seniors, and she forced down the complaint just as she slid lower in the front seat.

Charlie pulled out a paperback novel and a pen light and began to read. Van stared at the building. Charlie didn't question Van's intuition about the building. He had learned early on to have an open mind about alternative theories of a crime. It was a key Holmesian principle, as in Sherlock, to allow for alternative theories and not get locked into a specific set of facts. His partners back at the Department were making that mistake now by focusing only on the husband and treating the case as a case of domestic abuse however gruesome. He knew they were making fun of him following the hunch of a first-year forensic assistant, but he also knew they would not mind sitting in his place.

The red-orange hue of a Pacific Ocean sunset slowly faded as the new LED-based streetlamps popped on and began to take over as the primary force pushing back on the darkness. Van noticed that several people walked by the car and were startled to see two people sitting there, but they all gathered themselves quickly and moved on either because it was normal, or if it wasn't, they didn't want to know. Then she saw a man step to the building, stop, look around, unlock the door and walk inside. In the darkening evening, it was becoming hard to see detail, but Van saw enough to know she recognized the man, and it was precisely because Charlie had parked so close. It was the same man she saw enter the back of the florist's shop, who, at the time she had assumed was the florist's husband.

She poked Charlie who clicked off the pen light and looked up. "I know him," she said urgently. "I saw him in the flower shop this afternoon."

"Any reason to suspect him?"

"I don't know. Not yet."

Ten minutes went by. Fifteen. Van thought it odd that even though it was dark and the man entered the building, he didn't turn on any lights, at least nothing she could see. Then another man appeared. He was wearing glasses and a tight jacket and carrying a small case, like an old-style doctor's case. He looked around and then knocked on the door. It seemed like forever to Van but eventually the door opened, and the second man went inside. Van looked again at Charlie.

"Something is up."

"Maybe, maybe not," he answered. "Let's see if we can get a closer look."

Van's heart was pounding as she stepped out of the car. She was both thrilled and scared at the same time. Charlie took the lead and they crossed the street. They were careful to stay away from the front door in case either of the men decided to leave. Van noticed a light coming from a window at ground level. The window was lined by brown paper on the inside, but a small part of the paper had pulled back from the window leaving a slight opening. She walked by the window nonchalantly to see if there was any kind of view and when she looked down through the opening, the light was shining on a white table that appeared to be part of a lab. Charlie had pulled his gun just in case. She motioned to him and pointed to the window at her feet. He stepped to the side and looked down. He saw what looked to him like a sophisticated meth lab. Van leaned forward for a second look and stared directly into the eyes of the florist's husband. She froze. Oddly, the husband returned his focus to the lab without any reaction, as if, as Charlie had described earlier, he just missed what had been staring at him right in the face. Charlie motioned Van to return to the car. He had to think, and he didn't want Van in the middle of something undesirable.

When they got back in the car, Van said to Charlie, "She told me there was no one in the building."

"She the shopkeeper?"

"Yes."

"You think she was lying?"

"I do now."

Charlie made a call back to a friend of his in Narcotics. "Got anything about a meth lab near Olvera Street?" He waited and got a response. He looked at Van impressed. "Well, you might have found something, Van, whether or not it's related to the murder."

"You think it's a drug lab?"

"I don't know but it seems fishy."

"What's next?"

"Let's talk to Narcotics. They know how to handle this. Let them do their job first and see what happens. They will set up a full surveillance team to check it out. No sense rushing in and ruining an opportunity. They call it a stumble and bumble. Let's not do that."

Van didn't sleep well that night. She was proud that Charlie had complimented her but deeply unsatisfied. What if the second man was the murderer? Had they lost a key moment in the case? What if he disappeared and the case went cold, or worse, the husband was unjustly charged with the murder, or worse still, what if other murders took place that they could have stopped? She knew it was useless to speculate, especially on dire outcomes, but it was hard not to.

The next day, Charlie brought Van to meet the commanding officer of the Detective Bureau's Gang and Narcotics Division, Detective III Elizabeth Sampling. Detective Sampling was not afraid of a fight. She was renowned for her aggressiveness throughout the Bureau and many saw her as a shoe-in for the next chief of the Bureau.

"One of Frank's bright new forensics stars," said Detective Charles Darling, introducing Van to Detective Sampling.

"Okay," said Sampling, looking toward Van. "What do you think you have found?"

"We were on a stakeout for a murder that happened in Baldwin Hills. Detective Darling recognized a lab setup in the building basement near Olvera Street that we were watching and thought it looked like it might be a meth lab. But I was interested in two men we saw entering the office building or lab, whatever it is."

"Do you think they are connected to the Baldwin Hills murder?"

"Hard to say. The facts of the murder are unique. It looks more like surgery than murder, and one of the men was carrying a medical bag," Van explained to Sampling.

"You said she is in Forensics?" Sampling looked at Charlie curiously.

"Right," he responded. "As to the lab, we will follow your lead. But on this murder case, I think we should be listening to her."

"It is possible there is a connection," Sampling offered. "Thank you, Detective, Examiner Eng."

Charlie and Van left Sampling's office.

"What do we do now?" Van asked Charles.

"Wait," he responded. "Detective Sampling will support us, but we need to support her right now."

Sampling called a briefing and invited Van and Charlie. They detailed the events, and Van described the forensics team's findings and initial investigations. Narcotics set up a stakeout, only this time the stakeout involved multiple cars and officers located at several angles to the office building. The stakeout team had planted cameras and recording devices around the florist shop and the building. Sampling confirmed that in recent months, the Unit had been picking up noise about high volume meth activity in East Los Angeles but had not yet pinpointed a lab until Charlie had announced Van's Olvera Street discovery. Three days after the stakeout, they noticed a white moving van that arrived at around 4:00 am and circled the building several times before parking at the rear loading dock of the office building.

Sampling called Charlie, and Charlie called Van. "It's going down now if you want to get out here," he told Van.

Van was already awake and training. She grabbed her LAPD Forensics Team jacket and left for the Bureau. Forty-five minutes later Charlie and Van arrived at an empty garage set up as a staging area about two blocks from the Olvera Street florist shop and alleged meth lab. Sampling motioned them over. She noticed Van wearing jogging shoes. "Official Forensics gear?" she queried. Van blushed. "No worries, hun," she said. "Probably appropriate if we get a runner." She looked at Charlie. "Does she know how to handle a weapon?"

He looked at her. Van said, "I have been shooting at the range." They got her a Glock-9. She had fired one before but only a couple times.

Charlie whispered, "Watch out for the slide action. It'll tear your thumb apart if you hold it wrong." He showed her how to keep her thumb low. They headed for the cars. "Stay close to me," Charlie said.

They arrived at the office building and placed two cars at the front door and three cars at the rear, pinning down the moving van. Two officers approached the front door, weapons drawn, and banged on the door. Four officers watched the rear loading area. No one was in the van. Charlie and Van watched the front door, crouched behind the open doors of their car. The front door opened, and the officers began yelling, guns drawn, before they entered the building. Three Asian men wearing lab coats came out with their hands on their heads and one officer behind them. Then a fourth man appeared wearing glasses. "That's him," said Van, recognizing the one they saw with the medical bag. Charlie and Van stood up as the officers cuffed the group, but as the officers started to approach the doctor, he suddenly bolted, directly in Van's direction. Several officers yelled stop and pulled their weapons. Van stepped out from behind the car door directly into the path of the fleeing suspect and pointer her Glock-9.

"Stop or I'll shoot!" she yelled.

The man froze, just long enough for officers who had started to give chase to catch him and throw him to the ground and cuff him. Sampling came over and stood by Charlie. "Nice work, this one," she said to Charlie. Van found herself shaking a bit but exhilarated. Several officers came over and patted her on her shoulders, and said,

"Good job." Charlie smiled. "She never ceases to amaze," he said to Sampling.

About a dozen more people were still at work inside the lab when the police first arrived. As the suspects were rounded up, Van called Frank and, shortly thereafter, Frank and the Forensics team arrived and began setting up for analysis of the crime scene. She heard Frank say, "What do we have here?" and she joined him to watch an officer break open a locked freezer. Inside the freezer were plastic containers heavily taped, but Van and Frank could see that the contents included body parts that looked like human organs. They taped off the freezer and called in a police van to carry the freezer back to the lab.

When they finally were able to explore the freezer's contents, Frank's team found a frozen ovary the blood type of which matched the victim's blood type. In addition, Brad's latest print from the house's dining room matched with the doctor, who eventually confessed to having connections to illicit sex organ sales, although he continued to deny any connection to the murder. He was tried and convicted of the murder, and during his trial, witnesses from the lab testified, giving details about his unrequited fetish for surgery and anger at the institutions that failed to acknowledge his brilliance, which had led to a slew of victims, not all of whom died, but who unwittingly lost testicles and ovaries that ended on the black market. How the doctor snuck in and out of the house without being seen was never revealed, but in this case, he had made two critical mistakes, one discovered by Van and the other by Brad. Van felt great relief that the perpetrator had been caught, but to her, the most important outcome was that the grief-stricken husband and father was allowed to return to the baby he so carefully had taken care of that terrible night.

Chapter 5.

The Immoral of the Story

Hans Christian Anderson wrote fantastic children's stories. His first popular work, Fairy Tales, which like Dickens he wrote and dramatized episodically, developed enduring characters that resonated beyond the confines of culture and class. A beautiful mermaid willing to sacrifice herself for the ideal of love. A tiny child whose unselfish care for others ended up rescuing her from a terrible fate. A misidentified duckling who endured harsh criticism, only to rise above the gaggle around him. A haughty emperor blinded by the flattery of sycophants into playing the fool. Anderson's art was like much art. It was more than the simple emergence of a natural talent. It was an art born of pain. Like Van Gogh, Anderson peered through a dingy window into a better world, a world where a child of poverty would no longer be discounted among the masses, a world where beauty belonged to and was recognized in everyone, not just a small elite.

Cheryl Brown wanted to be part of that new world. Although already a stunning beauty, Cheryl carried with her the burden of a miserable childhood that she endured first by burying herself in books and then by earning the praise and recognition of academic success. But, like Anderson, it was her books that saved her. That one of those books was Fairy Tales didn't matter—any story that drew her in and caused her to forget the yelling and harsh words of her early reality was a lifeboat—a safe and secure vessel to carry her away. As they emerged from the decontamination room at RW Labs, Cheryl Brown slipped the petri dish into her purse. Derek said good-bye to Belinda and the doctor indicating he would be in touch. Gerard pulled up the SUV and sped them back to Derek's office.

"Any impressions?"

"Yes. Seemed sloppy for a high-end technology lab."

"That's perceptive, Cheryl. They talk a good game, and they have the important contacts that can help them get out quickly, but it is still a question whether they can produce or not."

"Do you think the Providia software is as important as they claim?"

"We need to find out. I want you to go there tomorrow and see what you can pick up."

Cheryl blushed. It was a high compliment for Derek to send anyone out on their own, and it meant he was thinking about grooming her for a promotion. She thought about the petri dish. She knew it could go very poorly or very well if she disclosed it to Derek. She resolved to hold onto it for the time being. If he was already happy, no reason to risk it.

Derek called Fred as soon as he was back in the office. "They need money."

"Of course they do. Do I need to be the one to give it to them?"

"I have my doubts, Fred."

"Good enough for me. What do we do?"

"I am sending Cheryl to Providia. Possible building block there if we can find the right lab."

Cheryl asked Gerard to pick her up at her home in Redwood City. Redwood City had always been a bit on the lower end of the economic scale in Silicon Valley, and despite a handful of teardowns, the homes remained mostly World War II prefabricated homes built for military personnel working out of Alameda Bay in the 1940s and 1950s. Even still, the market in the Bay Area turned the smallest Redwood City shacks into million-dollar homes and many of these homes had been renovated using pools of equity, so that, even if they were small, they were now suitable for the rising class of upwardly mobile engineers, salespeople, managers and lawyers of the region. Hardwood flooring, crown molding, elaborate landscapes, and stone chimneys transformed the drywall and pine-framed two- and three-bedroom dwellings into craftsman type homes, almost, but not quite, worthy of the price.

Gerard jumped on the south 101 Freeway that ran through the middle of Redwood City and headed toward San Jose. If Redwood City was on the lower end of the economic scale, San Jose was on the bottom of that scale, at least relative to the cities around it. But even San Jose enjoyed the boom that hi-tech brought to the Valley, and many of the marshes at the foot of the San Francisco Bay between Sunnyvale, Santa Clara and Milpitas, just north of San Jose, had been drained and developed into multi-story glass-covered business complexes, one of which housed Providia within the triangle of freeways formed by the 101, the 880 and the 237.

Cheryl arrived at 8:50 am, in time to freshen up and meet with Providia's leadership team, led by the Chief Financial Officer Christopher Deckwalder. Christopher studied computer science at Stanford but, drawn to the success stories of Steve Jobs at Apple, Larry Page and Sergei Brin at Google, and Fred Schmidt at Grindle, he added an MBA from Stanford Business School where he specialized in technology and finance. He was considered one of the top financial minds of the region, which given the setting, was a remarkable accomplishment.

"Good afternoon, Ms. Brown," Christopher welcomed her into the boardroom. "How can we help you?"

"I will come straight to the point," Cheryl responded. She knew credibility mattered in these high-level discussions, and that fools were not tolerated.

It made her proud to know that she learned how to conduct herself in these meetings from one of the best, her boss Derek.

"We are exploring investments in smart dust."

"Interesting. I understand we are still years from a marketable product," Christopher responded. "Why now?"

"Perhaps you can answer that better than I can," Cheryl retorted. "We have been investigating the technology for a client and have been told it is not science fiction and that it is coming and perhaps you have an artificial intelligence product under development that might get us there more quickly. Is that true?"

Christopher looked at his team and smiled. "Maybe," he said. "Let's talk about smart dust."

He turned to his team, who, for the next hour, walked through their view of the challenges and opportunities of MEMS, including the political landscape and growing hostility toward MEMS, which they found to be troubling and problematic.

After that discussion, which Cheryl found to be rambling and highly speculative, she turned to Christopher.

"Do you have it?"

"We do."

"It is ready to implement?"

"As soon as we find the right match."

"What are you looking for?"

"There are production performance indicators that matter to us, but in fact there are two things that matter most: (1) do we believe in your goals, and (2) do we believe in you."

Cheryl smiled. "Seems a bit light for the Valley's most brilliant financial mind."

"They're team goals but I agree with them. I think we are done, Ms. Brown. Thank you for your time."

Cheryl grabbed her coat and bag and was politely ushered out of the boardroom. She was not concerned about how the conversation ended. Providia was not a charity and would be smart about how they packaged and sold an AI product that could revolutionize nanomanufacturing. She jumped in the back seat of the Lincoln, and as Gerard was about to close the door, a young man slid into the back seat.

"Here is my card, Ms. Brown. Don't be disheartened. I am certain we can find a way to do business."

She smiled at the young man, not surprised by the olive branch but that it had been offered so quickly.

"I hope we can," she said, and motioned him to leave and Gerard to close the door.

Back at the office, Cheryl was excited to share the Providia discussion with Derek. She tried to stay cool. He was busy and would ask her for details when he was ready. In the buzz of this excitement, she completely forgot about the petri dish, still lodged in her purse. Derek emerged out of his conference room. He noticed Cheryl was back and moved intentionally toward her cubicle.

"I spoke to Christopher," he said. "You did well—held your ground."

This line of discussion took Cheryl by surprise. She expected to be reporting to Derek, not vice versa.

"Did he tell you what his criteria are for using the software?"

"He didn't need to. I know Christopher. He acts like numbers don't matter, but in the end that is all that matters to him."

Cheryl grabbed her purse. "A member of his entourage reached out to me just before I left." She reached into the purse to get the card left by the young man when the card snagged on the petri dish and pulled it out of her purse, plummeting onto the industrial carpet lining her cubical floor.

Derek initially ignored it, assuming it was a makeup compact, and he graciously leaned down to pick it up for Cheryl, who was impressing him more every day. It felt oddly heavy and it was strange to him that a compact case would be made of glass. He turned it upright to hand it back to her and then he saw the label: Risk Group IV.

"What is this?" he asked.

Cheryl didn't mince words. This moment, as she knew, was about to go very well or very badly. "It was on the floor at RW Labs. I thought it might be something we should look at."

"Look at? Do you know what Risk Group IV means?"

"I don't."

"Jesus Christ, Cheryl!" Derek put his hand up to his forehead and squinted like he was trying to hold back very bad news. "This dish probably contains a pathogen like Ebola or Bubonic Plague, and if there is any leak...oh my God."

Derek ran back to his office. He shut the door and picked up the phone, but he didn't call the Labs or a hazmat or poison hotline. He called Fred.

"We have a problem."

"Go on."

"I don't know what I am holding, but my assistant took it from the Labs. Risk Group IV."

"Risk Group IV? That is a little risky, don't you think?"

"A little? I sure as hell don't want to get whatever is going on in this petri dish."

"Find a biohazard case asap, seal it and bring it by. I'm not sure what they are doing at the Labs but if they are too stupid to let something like this get away, then they deserve losing it. And fire Cheryl."

"I thought about that. But shit, she was doing so well."

Derek found Cheryl sitting quietly in her cubicle. She was running scenarios though her head.

"This is a problem, Cheryl."

"I appreciate that."

"Grab your stuff and go home. I need to think about it."

Without any reaction, she picked up her coat and bag and left. As she passed the reception desk, she turned back to Derek and mouthed, I'm sorry. He looked back, watching her go. His face steeled and she left assuming she would not be back. Derek called a reliable contact at Stanford's principal microbiology lab and asked for an RG IV biohazard transport case. They delivered it immediately. The metal carrying case was lined with rubber and foam and held a dense carbon fiber container that was also lined with rubber and foam. The glass petri dish fit snug in the inner container. Derek programmed a code to lock the case and called Gerard. He thought about Cheryl for a quick second and headed to see Fred.

On his end, Fred knew two things about the petri dish. First, whatever it contained probably had been stolen from another lab, which is why he was not concerned that RW Labs would contact the police and accuse Derek of the theft. If anything, they would try to steal it back and may even come after him, which felt to him like more of a game than a threat. He also knew that it had to be important. RW Labs, if nothing else, did their research before trying to claim a reengineered invention as their own. Risk Group IV was not something to be played with. Not only was it dangerous, but it was highly infectious, and the likelihood of an effective treatment or vaccine was so low that if it were released, a widespread pandemic was not out of the question.

But what could it be? He wondered if it might be a form of nanotechnology but dismissed the thought. Why would it be labeled Risk Group IV? Perhaps it was a genetic experiment and maybe even cancer related. Maybe it was a weaponized form of a bacterium or virus. The RW Labs had made a lot of money finding and reengineering military technology, and not always for the United States.

As he thought about it, he began to get a picture of an opportunity. He needed a high-quality lab that could handle dangerous substances but also was desperate enough to work with him in secret. Bainbridge came to mind, and the young genius he had heard about could be tricky to manage if the curiosity of the genius began to give way to moral qualms. But to Fred, in this case, *tricky* only meant the experiment would fail and the opportunity might be lost. At the very least, he would learn whether the Duc A. Tran Laboratory of Hereditary Biology was willing to work with him or not.

He watched Derek arrive through his massive office window. Fred's secretary held the door and showed Derek into Fred's office. Fred stood there waiting for him with a trusted executive assistant. Without saying anything to Derek and before Derek could speak, Fred told the assistant to take the metal case to the hanger at Moffett Airport where he kept his

Gulfstream 6 or the 'G-Wagon,' as he liked to call it. It didn't bother Fred at all that he spent as little time as was absolutely needed with the dish. He didn't need to see it himself. He knew enough for now.

"Time for a quick trip?"

"Always," Derek said. He glad to be relieved of the metal case. He knew Fred would find it important, but it scared the hell out of him.

"Send Gerard home. I'll get you back."

"Will do. Thank you."

Fred texted his driver and told him to bring the Bentley and to make sure it was "loaded."

Derek smiled. "Loaded" was a good sign that Fred was excited about a plan. They jumped in the back and Fred poured an old Laphroaig for each of them and began the story of Dr. Duc A. Tran, PhD. His capacity for detail was remarkable and when he started one of these stories, Derek knew he was witnessing Fred's real genius.

"You remember the Vietnamese boat people?"

"Yes."

"Well, several remarkable people made their way out of Vietnam and eventually to the United States. One of them was a young biochemistry student who ended up at the University of Washington in Seattle in the early 1980s. His English was poor, but his handling of complex chemistry was remarkable. He flew through a Ph.D. program, and the University hired him immediately as a research professor. Duc Tran had grown up in Vietnam during the war and escaped having to serve in the military only because he was a few years too young. But as he grew older, he watched how the influence of the Chinese cultural revolution under Mao Tse-tung impacted the beliefs in his own country. One of the principal concepts of Mao's revolution was that human nature could be molded, that behavior was not innate and that what they viewed as rigorous education could transform an entire nation into becoming a disciplined and highly productive but subservient people. Nurture could defeat nature, and cultural evolution could be controlled so completely by humans that biology was eliminated as a factor in behavior. Tran questioned that premise and built his entire career around proving it false."

Fred looked out his window and saw the airfield come into view.

"It made him famous. He focused on DNA and called his analysis "biological predisposition." His work laid the groundwork for the Human Genome Project. He won a Nobel Prize in biochemistry, and he used the money to set up an independent lab that was eventually acquired by a public university. Then he got sick, but the therapies that emerged out of his research were too far in the future to help him, and he died when he was only 40 years old. They named the lab after him, but nothing significant has come out of it since."

Fred went on to talk about the Tran Lab and his confidence that they could handle an RG IV dish but, moreover, the possibility that they may have a unique angle on the contents of the dish. He also wanted a test for the new young genius. Derek was concerned that Fred might be more interested in testing out this remote lab for purposes other than exploring the contents of the dish and its opportunities, but he trusted Fred, and more importantly, he served Fred and Fred's money. They boarded the plane, with Fred still holding his glass, and headed to Seattle. He buckled himself into a plush captain's chair and turned toward Derek.

"By the way, Mao proved he was right at least to some degree. He was able to eliminate gender distinctions in the low ranks of the military, and his female foot soldiers became every bit as technically proficient and savage as his male foot soldiers."

"Is it nature or nurture?" Derek asked.

"Exactly," Fred smiled and poured another glass.

The jet landed at SEA-TAC 90 minutes later. A car pulled up to the plane, picked up Fred and Derek, and sped north to a ferry that shuttled them over to Bainbridge Island. The Puget Sound ferry boat system was unique. It originated as an uncoordinated fleet of privately owned boats that served the inhabitants of the islands and connected them to Seattle and the mainland. Starting with a sternwheeler from London and then an American manufactured steamer called the Fairy, the fleet grew into a mass of boats that was nicknamed the "mosquito fleet." Ferry traffic today is managed by the Washington Department of Transportation (WDOT) and, more specifically, the Washington State Ferries System. The hop from Seattle to Bainbridge Island is a mere 35 minutes. Fred and Derek relaxed in the back of stretch limousine as they crossed Elliott Bay to the landing dock where the ferry left them to continue down Highway 305 north through the heart of Bainbridge Island to the Tran Labs.

Derek had never been to the Island, but what he saw looked like a wealthy bedroom community combined with a nature lover's travel destination. He watched as they flew past walking and biking trails and chain bridges in multiple nature preserves containing cedar, pine, Japanese maple and birch trees. Fred told him of a small mock Norwegian village called Poulsbo holds a Viking Fest every year in July. On the north end of the Island, just off Highway 305, they reached a large irregular bay called Hidden Cove and glided along the Cove up to where Dr. Tran built his lab looking north out onto Port Madison Bay and the Sound.

A team of scientists was waiting outside the Tran Labs for Fred and Derek. Derek was holding the metal biohazard case, which he quickly handed to one of the scientists. It was breezy and cold, and the group hustled inside to a modest lobby and elevator bay. It took two elevators to carry the group up to the third floor, where the main offices and conference room had large windows looking directly out onto the Sound.

Dr. Stanley Meisner welcomed the two men to the Tran Lab. He gave a brief history of the lab and a summary of their current projects, which Fred and Derek patiently endured. He looked at the metal biohazard case and concluded with a question. "So, what do we have here?"

As Derek opened the case and carefully placed the petri dish on the table in front of Dr. Meisner, Fred responded, "Our hope is that you can tell us. All we know, as you can see, is that it is labeled Risk Group IV."

Dr. Meisner studied the two men and then looked at his colleagues, who had been quiet but now focused intently on the dish. "It's likely to take some time, Mr. Schmidt."

"Not a problem. I am certain you can handle it." Fred studied the group. The young genius was not present. "By the way, how is Dr. Johannsen doing?" The group looked at Dr. Meisner, who smiled. "He is coming along quite well. We are very proud of him, thank you for asking."

"Very good." Fred smiled graciously. "We'll wait for your results."

Fred liked Bainbridge Island and its nature preserves and had envisioned spending several weeks and possibly months at the Tran Labs. In advance, he purchased a large estate on a remote portion of the island in a community called Westwood, just off Crystal Springs Drive. No one at the Lab knew that he would be staying around. He invited Derek to stay as long as he liked or to take the jet and return home. Derek had much to do and he felt the need to address the Cheryl Brown issue as quickly as possible. Fred would respect his decision on Cheryl one way or the other, but Derek knew that he could not make the decision from Seattle. "Thank you but I must return," he told Fred, and Fred immediately called the jet hanger and instructed them to fuel up for a return trip.

The Tran scientists returned to the boardroom.

"What do you make of it, Stan?" asked Dr. Leonard Whisk, head of the lab's biochemistry unit and Brian Johannsen's immediate senior.

"He wants something else here," he responded. "I don't think it is about the box."

"I feel the same. I'll leave it with Brian. Let's see what he comes up with."

Dr. Whisk had very little time for curmudgeon billionaires. He was chasing his own vision and had been for many years. No one was going to distract him, not even the CEO of Grindle. He took the petri dish over to Brian's lab and set in on the floor next to his desk and walked away.

Derek landed back at Moffett and Gerard was there to pick him up. They drove directly to Derek's business park and Derek raced in through the front door and up to his office. It was 10:00 pm and no one was around. He called his Stanford connection.

"Do you have it?"

"Yes."

"And it is secure?"

"Yes. We placed it in the same type of metal casing that we gave you. It is in the safe."

"Very good." He disconnected and set his phone down. Derek had spent a lot of years in Silicon Valley, and he saw the many ways in which the game was played. Before taking the dish to Fred, Derek had had the foresight to have the microbiology lab at Stanford split the contents of the dish and hand just a portion to Fred. He now had a lot of options. If RW threatened him, he could return it. Like Fred, he too knew, if they did anything, it would be covert and designed to avoid public display. But it could be nasty and that was not a preferred outcome. He also could take it back, plead innocence, throw Cheryl under the bus and possibly use it as leverage to gain a better foothold in a partnership with Belinda. Derek not only had money, but he had connections in the Valley beyond Fred Schmidt. It wasn't out of the question that he might facilitate a deal between RW and Providia that didn't involve Fred's money.

He called Cheryl. She was at a club, drowning her sorrows and trying to find a way to get a cute boy to take her home.

"You realize how stupid that was?"

"I'm listening," she said, trying to maintain her composure.

"The people at RW are snakes. You saw the security there? There is a reason they prefer black ops to off duty cops or ex con security detail. They would not hesitate to kill you, Cheryl. Or me."

"If you are trying to scare me, you're doing a good job."

"Yeah. Okay. Meet me in the morning. There is work to do and I don't want to talk about this anymore."

That went well, he thought. She will be a star if she finds a way to stay alive. He needed to find a way to stay alive, and it was quite possible Cheryl Brown would be the key.

Chapter 6.

The Theranos Syndrome

Washington D.C. was in chaos. A ragtag New York billionaire playboy with an ego the size of Manhattan had won the presidential election and had become the forty-fifth President of the United States. The liberal media was in utter shock at his victory, having battled claims of fake news for the past two years of his campaign, and their heroine, wife of a former President and the brains behind that effort, had just been swept away by the playboy. The conservative media was overjoyed and stunned themselves. The shock jocks who had been riding on an anti-establishment and pro-capitalist wave, suddenly found themselves a legit and a startlingly credible voice for the new establishment.

The new President started right out of the gate. "We are going to change America and restore its pride. We are going to stop being fodder for the world's anti-American rhetoric and we are going to stand up for ourselves and the capitalist power that we have become. No more apologizing for the wrongs of history. And we are going to clean up Washington, dredge the swamp. Eliminate the stupid laws that keep our companies' brightest minds from shining and taking America way over the top. That is exactly where we are going. Way over the top!"

The world didn't know how to take this new leader. A leader of a global power who had no fear. A leader who would look them directly in the eyes and say, "You don't think I have the balls, do you? Try me."

Washington didn't know how to take this new leader. Regulatory department heads and their reports all gathered up their belongings, called their private sector counterparts and fled the Beltway like rats off a sinking ship.

Wall Street did know how to take this new leader. They knew this guy personally. He lived Wall Street and had played Wall Street many times, and they knew that he was someone to be taken seriously. Crazy? He was a little. Just crazy enough to keep everyone around him off balance, and to keep himself in control. They knew that if he set his mind to something, nobody could stop him—nobody but himself. The word went out. Buy! Buy tech! Buy health care! Buy natural resources! Buy media! Buy telecom! Buy commodities! Buy! Buy! The stock market exploded and climbed close to 50% in a few short weeks. And then, despite a massively powerful liberal media and long entrenched liberal left out for revenge and fearful of losing its own credibility, the stock market held its gains and the playboy president had just what he needed to do exactly what he wanted.

What he didn't want was, in his estimate, to subject the American economy to the restraints of the Paris Accords and the pressure of an unrealistic reduction in the country's carbon footprint while other superpowers paid lip service to the effort to make rapid gains in the global economy. Environmentalists under former administrations had won the regulatory battles only to risk losing the war. He believed the Paris Accords were a fraud on American labor and American-based business, and his proof was that the largest of American companies had not only gone multinational, they staffed down their American presence and setting up shop in countries where light regulation and a cheap labor force allowed their returns to pop. He believed he could convince these companies to return to American soil, but he could only do so if he eliminated the harsh regulatory climate of the country, chief of which was environmental regulation.

To succeed, his first step was to debunk the belief that the climate was out of control, and that the rise in the earth's surface temperature was a danger caused by human activity. He went on the attack, calling climate change junk science and defunding and even dismantling the departments like the EPA, which under federal law had become the single most challenging impediment to economic growth. Moreover, it was not lost on him that environmental controls had also boosted the authority of local government, which used the power to withhold or delay environmental permits as a corrupt means of securing political influence over and benefits from business, most of which were small local businesses. The president knew this impact only too well, having battled local government on his own hotel and casino projects across the country. Environmental protection was, in his mind, the giant curtain behind which not only the Washington regulatory complex, but also all state and local regulatory authority in the country hid and pretended to be the Grand Protector of the American Preserve. If he could tear that curtain down, expose the regulatory complex for the hoax that it was, he would end the giant sucking sound and American labor would love him, American business would love him and the American public would fawn at his feet as the Great Savior of the Dream. In short, he would become the greatest president that ever lived.

He was remarkably close to succeeding. But a series of his own ego-driven missteps looked to be his undoing. He refused to cater to the liberal left and called out American media at every opportunity whether his ideas were being opposed or not. He was comfortable only when he was at war, and he delighted in not only making enemies but in baiting his enemies to confront him or risk looking weak. Some might say he was caught up in the very same game that he rose to power opposing. But if he made enemies intentionally or as a byproduct of his own radical pro-American ideals, they came at him and they were relentless. He spent all his time swatting at his opponents like mosquitoes, rather than creating an effective shield by enhancing the credibility of his original position. He was having some success, and to a degree, Washington politics was shifting, and the regulatory complex did fall to one knee, but it was not going down and only history would tell whether what he was doing would hurt or help the country. For the moment, the jury was still out, way out.

Marshall Turner loved Washington, and he knew how to work Washington regardless of who was in office. He was enjoying the chaos and hysteria caused by this new president, and his firm, Blue Ridge Consultants, was doing better than it had been doing in many years. Companies saw the new president as an opportunity to reduce and possibly eliminate the high costs of regulatory compliance, and Marshall had deep connections not only to office holders but also to almost every agency in the city. His firm doubled in size in the first six months of this president's first, and as it would turn out, his only term. Many of his new employees were former regulators and although they disagreed with the new president's view on climate change, they enjoyed the money. They knew the Washington regulatory maze well, or what was left of it, and how best to navigate it.

The key to standing in line with the new president was, as some thought with no small irony, a belief in science. But he refused to believe in just any science, his knowledge cult was new science. "Set the inventors free" was one of his favorite new mottos, and anyone with a direct line to the Environmental Protection Agency, the Food and Drug Administration, or the US Patent and Trademark Office found themselves in huge demand.

Marshall's phone played a short Aerosmith sample, and he clicked on it to answer. Sandra Wellington, an older EPA recruit whose not so hidden agenda was still to fight climate change said, "Good morning, sir."

"Hi, Sandra!" Marshall answered brightly. He was always positive with his employees. There was no reason to be otherwise. If they screwed up, they were fired and replaced—simple as that. Sandra was anything but a screwup. She was a scarred warrior, and unlike many of her former colleagues who became disgruntled and had abandoned Washington, she chose to stay and keep fighting. Sandra was not a believer in regulating as an end in itself and, if regulations needed to be sacrificed to make way for advances in technology that might become potential solutions to the challenges of the age, then so be it.

"Providia is talking about MEMS again."

"Really? Not a surprise I suppose but I thought the last administration pretty much killed it. What do they want?"

"They want a lock on all artificial intelligence rights related to MEMS."

"Good God. Not asking for much."

"A lock on all AI related to MEMS won't work. But it might be possible to secure special rights to most aspects of AI supporting nanomanufacturing."

"Smart, Sandra. Call Senator Quibley. He is one of the few who never gave up on MEMS. We might be able to build a wall around nanomanufacturing that gives Providia what they want. But it'll be a tough battle, and it is going to cost them."

"They'll pay."

"Of course, they will." Marshall smiled. He had endured some tough losses and difficult times, but this was not one of them. He loved it when money came easy. In this case, very few in the old or new Washington establishment would have any idea what Providia was even asking for. The naysayers could be bottled up and discarded as conspiracy theorists. This was exactly the kind of new science this president would support, and the only ones that mattered in the final decision tree would fall in line. Would it be a tough battle? Possibly. There were always surprises, but he doubted it.

Aerosmith played again and he answered. There was a pause, but it was not the pause of a robocall. He heard the sigh of exasperation and recognized it immediately. "Hello, Fred. How is my second favorite billionaire?"

Fred Schmidt burst out laughing. "Not as good as my second favorite lobbyist!"

"What can I do for you? Legalize meth?"

"Definitely not that! You'd break up my monopoly!"

"Can't have that." Marshall chuckled. He enjoyed messing with Fred and pretty much anyone he knew to be powerful. It was part of his charm and a key to his success. "What's up?"

"What are you hearing about bioterrorism these days?"

"It's a dark path, Fred. I wouldn't go down there."

"Actually, I am quite serious. Are you aware of anything the Pentagon is working on?"

"Nothing out of the ordinary. They'd be violating dozens of international treaties."

"Any we care about?"

"Let me put this way. There are a couple of companies allegedly working on antidotes but it's no secret that you can't develop a cure without a disease."

"Risk Group IV?"

"Well, that would be very dark because, as you know, by definition there are no cures, only quarantines."

"So unlikely."

"Yes. Very unlikely."

"That's what I thought. Thank you."

"Fly low my brother." Fred hung up. Marshall blinked back any ideas that Fred was walking down a dangerous path. Fred was too smart for that. At least Marshall hoped he was. He turned back to Providia. He could not help them without getting greater clarity on what they were doing. He called Sandra. "Been to San Francisco lately?"

* * *

RW Labs' Chief Scientist and CEO Belinda Maria Armendáriz gazed through the rain at the massive grounds at the entrance to RW Labs. She smiled at the hidden design created by the iron sculptures and gardens that from her angle resolved itself into the heart-shaped image of her Basque Country. Joan Miró, her favorite Spanish artist, would have been proud. She turned to face the large gathering in her boardroom.

"You think Schmidt is really interested in MEMS?" asked the doctor, who had made the presentation to Derek and Cheryl.

"The better question is whether or not you are really interested in MEMS," she replied. "You need to be more subtle, Leonard."

Dr. Leonard Freund huffed and shrugged his shoulders. He couldn't care less about what Dr. Belinda Maria Armendáriz thought about his dalliances with young female interns. He styled himself as a ladies' man, albeit a late bloomer, and truth be told, he was far more interested in his sexual escapades than MEMS, which wasn't going anywhere anyway. If Belinda could get money out of Fred Schmidt to support MEMS—and she seemed to be able to get money out of a dry turnip—then good for her. Leonard already had more money than he could spend in a lifetime, and pretty much everything other than sex bored him.

At that moment, one of the interns pressed herself into the room and motioned to Belinda. Belinda walked over to the door, and the intern whispered in her ear. Belinda's eyes narrowed and she nodded to the intern who left.

"We may have a problem. Biology is missing a dish."

The group acted shocked and angry. Surely their protocols were so advanced that stupid accidents could not occur.

"Have they been looking for it? Are they certain it is missing?"

"I need the details," Belinda retorted. "Sam Waterford had it last. Find a secluded office and let's have a little discussion. Leonard, I want you in on this."

They pulled Sam out of the lab and into a small empty intern office. Sam knew it was over for him. He would cooperate with Belinda and Leonard, only because he knew they could kill his career, but he was so depressed it almost didn't matter. He had been waiting about 20 minutes when Belinda and Leonard walked into the office with Belinda's assistant who was holding a note pad. Belinda started off as gently as she was capable of.

"I take it we have a problem, Sam."

"Yes, I think we do," he answered dispassionately, his eyes gazing at the table.

"What can you tell us?"

"I've explained it already several times but here it is again. I came back to my desk and found a petri dish labeled Risk Group IV. It was sealed tightly, and I was preparing set up. I assumed Dr. Stein had placed it there, and I didn't know what it was. I got an urgent text to go to the vacuum lab. They needed my help immediately. I dropped everything and ran to the vacuum lab. When I returned, the dish was gone. My first thought was that it had been placed there inadvertently and that whoever set it down had come back to retrieve it. I went over to Dr. Stein's office and asked him if he had removed it, and he told me he did not know what I was talking about.

"Did you find out how it got there?"

"I did." He looked up at Leonard. "I believe it was one of Dr. Freund's technicians."

Belinda looked at Leonard. "Do you know anything about this?"

"Nope. But I will find out."

She looked back at Sam. "You asked around and nobody knows what happened to the dish."

"Yes. If it is still here, we can't find it. That is what I reported to Dr. Stein."

"Ok. Anything else?"

"Well..." He paused. "I had a strange interaction before I ran to the vacuum lab."

"How so?"

"A young woman came up to me in the lab and asked me what I was doing."

Up to this point, a missing Risk Group IV was a serious matter, but it was more likely a failure of protocol and a stupid mistake than corporate espionage. Belinda knew corporate espionage well and her skin started to prickle.

"Did she tell you her name?"

"No. She said something about investors."

Belinda felt herself go hot. She thought about her interactions with Derek and didn't think it was his style. But she didn't know Cheryl Brown.

"Did you tell her anything, Sam?"

"Absolutely not." He looked directly into Belinda's eyes, as if to say you can't doubt me on this.

"Okay, Sam. You can go."

Sam walked out of the room quickly. Leonard looked at Belinda, and said, "He'll be terminated in the morning."

"Not yet," Belinda replied. "We might be able to use him."

Belinda and Leonard returned to their offices. Leonard shut the door and walked over to his window. He knew that his office was probably bugged so he didn't take out his phone, but he thought about calling General Warner at the Pentagon. The dish that was left with Sam had been created in Tajikistan. Its contents were still unknown but had something to do with a mechanical virus directly in line with Leonard's work on MEMS. He had it placed in Biological as a screen and wanted to see if the lab could identify it as a virus or as smart dust. His hatred of Belinda and the control she exercised over the lab justified his keeping it a secret from her, at least for now. But he was upset that it was missing, and like Belinda, Leonard was willing to do anything to find it. He thought about making a visit to Derek Whitestone's office, but he was concerned that word of the missing dish would leak. Belinda was smart to keep Sam around if for nothing else. Even if Sam had not explored the contents, he was more likely to stay silent while he was still here at the labs. He thought about Cindy, the cute intern that had come into the boardroom to report the dish. He sighed. He needed a good distraction right now.

He called her, and said, "I could use some good coffee."

She perked up and whispered, "You mean the rich and creamy type?"

"You got it, fair lady."

They met at the entrance and jumped into Leonard's Porsche Cayman GT4. Belinda watched from her office as they drove away. She turned back to the large screen monitor in her room. A new story was breaking about a Silicon Valley company in biotech that had allegedly defrauded investors out of $11 billion dollars by claiming they had developed a new machine capable of diagnosing blood disorders. Belinda knew about Theranos. They had approached the RW Labs for assistance and for a short time, the Lab had investigated the technology choosing, in the end, to let this one go. It had been Dr. Stein's group who helped make the decision, and Sam Waterford had been part of the team. She remembered with some disgust the pathetic look on the two Theranos representatives' faces when she announced her decision. She had thought to herself, "Do something else. Your leaders are smart. Some ideas are just not worth it." Of course, they refused to abandon their dream. But they chose the wrong path—in the battle for Silicon Valley supremacy everyone steals good ideas but even if outside investors can be dumb, the Valley is way too smart to accept falsified results. Fake it until you make it works in Hollywood. But the wolves of the Valley will tear you to pieces, and that is exactly what happened to Theranos, and it was not unexpected and not pretty. Belinda mused on her own good fortune: Lying about results in the Silicon Valley kills the golden goose every time.

Chapter 7.

A Cold Start

The road to success is rarely a straight shot, and when success comes, it often comes in unexpected ways. The story of Lebron James is instructive. Everyone knows that no team in the NBA can win a championship without a superstar but having a superstar does not guarantee a championship. The New York Knicks have not won an NBA championship since 1973, almost a half century ago, despite attracting multiple superstars for, in part, being in the same sports market as the New York Yankees. They made it to the finals twice with Patrick Ewing in the 1990s but ran into the buzzsaw of the Chicago Bulls under Michael Jordan and missed out on NBA glory. Since then, the tale has been mostly sad and disappointing.

Owning a superstar and trying to win is one thing. Being a superstar and expecting to win is something completely different. Many acclaimed high school and college superstars have gone down in flames in professional sports. The world, as commentator Jim Nantz likes to say, is littered with wasted talent. Lebron James burst into the League in 2003 and was so confident in his abilities that he made a big show of signing with the downtrodden Cleveland Cavaliers and promised to bring a championship to his hometown team. For eight years, he battled management and the press but was unable to get the job done. In 2010, without a championship and fearful that he would have no enduring legacy, he made one of the most controversial free agent decisions in sports history and signed with the Miami Heat. The move worked out and in joining Miami, Lebron helped form the dominant 'Big Three' in combination with Dwayne Wade and Chris Bosh. By 2013, the Big Three already had won two rings. But despite the wins, Lebron was jeered in his hometown as a sellout and the drama prompted ESPN to produce a special about the move called The Decision. The challenges and painful years that Lebron faced in the glare of the public eye in Cleveland honed Lebron and, in another remarkable move, he returned to Cleveland in 2014 to bring them their first championship in 2016 and then earn another with the Lakers in 2020. He is widely recognized in the NBA as a championship machine but the road he took to get there was extremely rough and anything but predictable.

Frank Weatherby called Van into his office.

"Detective Darling was very keen on your work in the Baldwin Hills case."

"I've been hearing a bit. Thank you."

"Well, you not only uncovered a massive drug operation, albeit inadvertently, you saved an innocent man and kept a case from going cold."

"Thank you, sir. Would not have happened without you and Brad."

"Well, I have some good news for you, assuming you think it is good news." Van leaned forward. "Does the Detective Bureau interest you?"

Van felt her stomach leap. Becoming a detective had been a dream of hers since she was a little girl.

"But I didn't even qualify for the police academy? They thought my deafness would be a risk in the field."

"Apparently, they are admitting that they made a mistake. But they don't want to send you to the Academy. They want to bring you in immediately as a Detective 1."

"What about the detective tests and the interviews?"

"Bypass. They will put you in special weapons training. They also have advanced courses in investigative analysis and scientific investigation, but my guess is that you would be able to teach those courses."

Van winced at the compliment. Suddenly, she felt like she would be getting in over her head, that she knew nothing at all about being a detective and would look foolish. Frank could tell she was getting scared.

"Van," he spoke encouragingly. "Your insights in Baldwin Hills far exceeded the insights of the detectives we have on the beat now, even some senior detectives. You will be a great detective. If you have any concerns, I am here. Come by any time. Do not pass this up. You were meant for it."

"Thank you, Frank. I am a little overwhelmed. Are you sure?"

He smiled. "Collect your things. You'll be meeting with Detective Darling tomorrow morning and he will introduce you around. Congratulations."

As he watched her leave his office, Frank had his own mixed emotions. He loved watching his young stars grow and develop, but it was hard to let quality go, and he could see in Van great promise and a great loss for the Lab. He walked to his door and leaned out. "Brad!" He shouted. Brad came running over. "I have something I need you to look at."

* * *

"Good morning, Van!" Detective III Charles Darling welcomed his new protégé.

"Good morning, sir," replied Van not certain what to call him. She wasn't even certain what to wear when she woke up that morning, if that is what you call not sleeping all night and then getting out of bed in the morning.

"Charlie, please. You know me, Van."

"Good morning, Charlie."

"Better. Welcome to the Bureau. I have something for you." He reached into his pocket and pulled out an LAPD Detective badge and handed it to Van. "Congratulations, Detective. Now, follow me."

Van stepped in line behind Charlie, as he made his way across a sea of desks. Van noticed detectives gathered around in clusters drinking coffee and staring at her. A few seemed friendly but most just stared. He stopped at an empty desk surrounded by other desks. "Here is your new home."

Van looked at the desk, then looked back at Charlie and forced a smile. She immediately felt homesick for her desk at the Lab and the freedom and respect she felt under Frank. She started to panic and think again this was a huge mistake, but she remembered Frank's words to her and forced herself to calm down.

"You'll be fine," Charlie whispered. "If you need anything at all, my office is right there." He pointed to the door at the end of a long row.

Van's first day flew by. The Chief held a daily briefing and introduced her and then added ominously, "No shenanigans." Van had no idea what shenanigans he was talking about, but chose to ignore the comment, smiled and nodded. She went to HR and completed a ton of paperwork. They gave her a fob and a parking space. They said she was eligible for a handgun but not until she completed special weapons training, which would start the next day. "They don't fool around here," she thought to herself. Charlie took her out to lunch and invited a few of her new colleagues. They found an Italian restaurant near the Bureau. It was dark with red carpet and dark brown leather booths and framed photos of downtown Los Angeles in the 1930s. As they slipped into one of the booths, Van leaned over to Charlie, and asked, "A bit stereotypical, isn't it?"

"What do you mean?" He looked at her and smiled.

She bit her tongue and replied, "Come here often?"

Charlie laughed. "Actually no. This place is expensive. This is a treat in your honor."

Van blushed.

"And if you don't like it, I promise we will never come here again."

They ordered drinks, no alcohol, and Charlie began, "Boys. I want to introduce you to Detective Van Eng."

"Welcome to the Bureau," they said in near unison. They lifted their glasses in her honor.

"Thank you," replied Van cautiously.

"You are going to learn some things about Van that will amaze you, just as they amazed me," he said. "I want her taken care of, if you get my drift."

"Absolutely, Charlie," the team responded. "Anything you want."

"So," Van leaned in. "Thank you all but I am starting to get the impression that I need to be taken care of. What am I missing?"

Charlie looked at her very seriously. "This is a great opportunity for you. But do not be fooled. Every single detective in this Bureau fought for recognition, and each of them guards it very jealously. Many of them do not understand how you got here through back channels. They will not be so supportive. I am confident that you will do very well here, but it is not an easy job, and it is not an easy atmosphere. When we offer to watch out for you, it means we have your back. Whatever you need, you can come to us." Everyone at the table looked equally serious and nodded their heads.

"Okay, I will. I am grateful."

"Now, I usually order the eggplant parmesan. It's to die for." He looked at her and winked.

"Charlie," she said. "You're killing me."

The next morning Van drove out to the LAPD weapons training facility in Granada Hills. The training lasted three days. She spent the first day in classes and on the range, trying out various pistol styles. She didn't like the Beretta or the Glock. They both felt too heavy and were harder to aim than the lighter Smith & Wesson. But she fell in love with the Kimber Classic bone handle .45 caliber. It was relatively light and she could control the kick. She learned how to load, how to shoot and how to carry, and most importantly, how to avoid having to use it. Charlie called her and complimented her on her choice. He also told her that given her background in Forensics, she would start her training in the Cold Case Homicide Special Section.

"You know a lot about DNA, right?"

"So I have been told, Charlie," she responded, barely holding back a smirk. "Good. Have great weekend and report to Chess on Monday."

"Chess?"

"That is what they call it. C.C.H.S.S. right? It's where all the smart people start. Anyway, great place for learning about detective work." His comments reminded her of Frank and her experience in the cold case files over at the Lab.

On Monday she showed up bright and early and brought coffee with her as much to blend in as to enjoy it for breakfast. When she arrived, there was a large stack of files on her desk with a Post-it note that said, "Take copies to Detective Young." She set her coffee down and asked about the copy machine and proceeded to copy the files and create duplicate folders. She carried the originals and copies over to Detective Young's office. He was a Detective II in Robbery-Homicide. He barely looked at her and told her where to set them down. When she got back to her desk there was another stack of files with a note, "Please copy and return to Detective Black." She suspected something was up but took the files, made copies and carried them to Detective Black's office. She returned to her desk and this time it was empty and she grabbed her notebook and went up to the sixth floor where Chess was located. As she walked out of the elevator, Charlie was standing there and he looked at her a bit cross, and said, "It's 11:30. Where have you been?"

Van was confused by the question but before she could respond, he said "At least you are here now. Follow me." She walked with him down the hall and into an over-stacked and disorganized file room. There were multiple carts overloaded with file folders. They pushed past the folders and found an office at the back. Inside the office sat a bored-looking detective staring at his smart phone.

"Detective Broad, let me introduce you to one of our newest in the Bureau." He motioned to Van and she reached out her hand. He looked up without reaching back, and said, "I've heard of you. Thanks, Charlie." Charlie left Van in the office with Detective Alvin Broad. Alvin Broad had been at the Bureau as long as Charles Darling—same class even. Like Charlie, Broad was nearing retirement but, unlike Charlie, Broad was never even considered a candidate for chief. He was a good detective, quiet, reserved and unambitious. He became a detective not to be a hero but to solve puzzles. Tough puzzles. He had a reputation for cracking more cold cases than any other detective, and when Broad decided that he had seen enough of the street, he requested Chess, and as a courtesy and out of respect, the Bureau put him in charge. Broad was also a teacher, at least philosophically. He enjoyed working with new recruits, and Charlie had placed Van with him partly because he knew she would learn from him but also to protect her. Broad would not be threatened by Van like the other detectives.

"Charlie tells me you have a hearing issue," he said to Van, when they were alone.

"I hear fine with my hearing aids," she said. "But I lost my hearing due to illness when I was an infant."

"Can you read lips?" he asked.

"I can," she replied.

"How many languages?"

"My parents speak Cantonese, and I was exposed to a lot of Vietnamese, so my lip reading is limited to Vietnamese, Cantonese and English. But I speak Spanish fluently and I am decent in Mandarin."

"Incredible," he said. "What do you know about cold cases?"

"Forensics has a cold case filing section and Dr. Weatherby introduced me and required me to spend a lot of hours reviewing files. He told me that a lot of cases that go unsolved are not complicated cases. Rather, a detective or cop or lab technician made a mistake and overlooked something obvious."

"Very good," Broad answered impressed. "Sounds like you are ahead of the game."

"What would you like me to do?"

"Well, for now, just acquaint yourself with what you see around you."

The first thing Van noticed about the room was that, unlike the Lab where everything was labeled and the files were organized by Division, there was no order other than a loose association with dates. The oldest files were on one side of the room and the dates progressed as you made your way to the opposite side. The newest files were lying on carts and it seemed that when detectives downstairs found their file cabinets overloaded, they would simply identify a younger detective to pull all their older files and leave them in Chess, which really meant dump them in a cart in the Chess file room. She asked Detective Broad if she could organize the room and if he had any objection to a more systematic arrangement. Broad didn't care. His activities in Chess were not guided by the files, but by detectives who might stumble across a new fact in an old case and would call him to check in and see if the information rose to the level of pulling the case out of Chess for further review. It wasn't always easy to locate the original files and what Van was proposing might make that easier.

Van got to work organizing the room. She spent several weeks on the project. Occasionally Charlie would stop by and ask Van to accompany him to a crime scene and Detective Broad never objected. Charlie was often impressed with Van's insights at a crime scene, but he was careful not to compliment her in front of other detectives and soft-pedalled her ideas when sharing them with others. Hiring Van had been a bit of an experiment and Charlie was smart enough to keep Van out of the limelight, and quite literally, given her placement in Chess, in the dark. But Van didn't mind.

Detective Broad was very friendly and helpful, and she was not in any rush to show off her skills or to show anybody else up. Besides, the cases she was coming across were fascinating. She decided to organize the files by type of crime—similar to the Lab but not, like the Lab, strictly by Division. It wasn't easy because some cases involved multiple crimes and, in those cases, she selected the most serious crime as the principal category and developed a color-coded Post-It system to show multiple crimes in a single file. She started with all the homicide files and divided them up between gang-related, drug/alcohol-related, sex trafficking, robbery, prison, domestic and other interpersonal, juvenile, domestic and international terrorism and espionage, and then subdivided them into first degree, second degree, manslaughter, negligent homicide, suicide, and finally, cases that were simply accidental deaths. She developed similar systems for robberies, mayhem, assault and battery, white collar and financial crimes, computer crimes like hacking and piracy, etc.

Detective Broad enjoyed watching her develop her system. Sometimes she would ask him where he thought a case belonged, and he began to own the new system as his own. But Van had another idea that was bigger than simply organizing the file room. As she was doing that, she was also building a database that not only would help her locate specific files, it also was grouping the files and connecting them by type of crime, type and name of victim, location, property, details about suspects, evidence, and anything that drew her attention. She had IT help her assemble the database and she started running cold case reports identifying number and type and frequency. Her capacity for remembering detail stunned Broad and they spent long hours sitting and discussing cases from the 1930s and 1940s. She also was able to sort cases by types of forensic or investigative errors that allowed cases to remain unsolved. After several months of work, Detective Broad began to share some of the reports Van was generating with the Bureau Chief, who shared it with the Chief of Police. Van was invited to top-level meetings to share the data, and she noticed, with some concern, that internal affairs started to attend some of those meetings.

She never took seriously the taunts she got from other detectives and the games they played trying to get her to do grunt work. Most of the time, she took the steam out of the joke by simply taking care of what was asked of her. She got coffee, ran errands, made copies, wrote up reports, and did so without complaining, and after a while, most of the detectives began to give her some respect. Then one morning, she came in and someone had placed a single bullet on her desk. She took it to Charlie, who got very serious and said he would find out what was going on. She told Detective Broad, and he suggested she start carrying her Kimber with her all the time. It was unnerving to her. She had noticed that fewer files were being left at Chess.

Van started spending less time with Detective Broad in Chess and more time at her desk, almost as if she were taunting the person who threatened her. She went over to Detectives Young and Black and asked if they needed any assistance with anything. They both shrugged, looked disinterested, and said not now. She wandered into the kitchen and made coffee that she pretended to drink, starting up conversations with other detectives lounging there and chatting. She went outside and relaxed at the rear door near the parking lot where the smokers liked to hang out. No one she talked to gave off any strange vibes, and she began to learn more about the variety of cases that were being investigated but picked up nothing that would expose the person who had threatened her. She asked Charlie if he had uncovered anything, and Charlie had nothing to report.

One day, one of the young detectives who joined the Bureau around the same time that Van joined, invited her to ride along on a stakeout. The detectives were investigating a new Vietnamese/Latino gang called 'The Rush' that was making a play for the Macarthur Park side of Koreatown. They had made a lot of money in human trafficking all around Los Angeles and were headquartered in a couple of karaoke bars off Wilshire Boulevard around Sixth Street. They drove hopped up Camrys and WRXs with green neon lighting on the undercarriage and used Hummer limos to shepherd gaggles of young Vietnamese girls to parties in Hollywood, Malibu, and Marina Del Rey. They had been linked to a couple of brutal murders of other gang members and had developed a reputation for being ruthless. The Gang and Narcotics Division tagged a 25-year-old Vietnamese immigrant, Danny Kang, as the self-appointed leader of the gang.

The detective's name was Robert Johnson. Robert made detective as a police officer in Rampart Division and had been reassigned to Downtown. He knew Koreatown and spent his first three years as a police officer patrolling MacArthur, Rampart and Koreatown. Many of the local business owners knew Robert well, and his ability to get information impressed his commanding officer enough to suggest Robert apply for detective. He did and passed the test with flying colors. They pulled him in under Detective

Young in the Downtown Gang Unit. Young had taken to calling Robert "BJ." Now he was back in his old hood chasing a new gang that was making a lot of noise. He had heard Van spoke Vietnamese, and asked Detective Young if he could bring her along. Young didn't hesitate. "Pull her in, BJ," he told Robert.

Wilshire Boulevard was not an easy place for a stakeout, and the karaoke bar where

Danny Kang ran his operations was a multi-story mall with an underground garage, so sitting out on the street was not very effective. Still Robert pulled into a space across from the garage entrance and down the street about a block where they could see fast cars and limos entering the garage. They sat there for an hour.

"Does this feel like a good location to you?" Van asked Robert.

"You can call me BJ, everyone else does," Robert answered.

"Ok, BJ, does this feel like a good location to you?"

"As good as any."

"What are we looking for?"

"Waiting to see if we see Danny Kang or his chief lieutenants leave the garage. Then we will follow them."

"Ok, but maybe we should get a bit closer."

"We can't be obvious, Van."

"We won't be," she said. "Do you mind pulling into the garage?"

"Are you out of your mind?"

Robert, or BJ, had not had the benefit of working with Detective Charlie Darling and learning the "they don't look at you anyway" approach to stakeouts. Van had been on several stakeouts with Charlie and every time they went out, Charlie had successfully unnerved Van by where he positioned the car. Van wanted to be respectful of Robert and his knowledge of the area, but she now knew this was a rookie mistake. Besides, she didn't want to waste time waiting for an imaginary car

to pull out of the garage.

"Just drive in and around the garage. If it feels uncomfortable, we can drive out. I want to take a look."

Robert looked at Van at first irritated but then he smiled. If she wanted to know his moxie, he would show her his moxie. "You got it," he said. He pulled the car out, narrowly missing a gold WRX that was speeding up the street. He followed the WRX into the garage and, as they pulled in, they saw the WRX stop at a valet station next to a bank of elevators, and Danny Kang and an unusually tall and beautiful Vietnamese woman stepped out of the car, flipped the keys to the valet along with a large bill, and headed to the elevator bank. The valet played cool and crawled into the WRX. Robert and Van passed the valet and drove around the garage acting as if they were looking for a parking space.

"That was Danny Kang," Robert whispered.

"I wondered," Van replied. They turned down another lane, and Van said, "Pull in right here." He slowed the car. "You want to stay here?" he asked incredulously.

"Yes, we can see the elevator bank and the valet." Robert looked a little scared but backed into the space. "It's ok," Van replied. "If anyone gets suspicious, we can act like we are making out." Robert looked at Van wide-eyed. "I am not saying we will make out, Robert," she chuckled.

"Of course not," he said. "I knew that."

They sat in the space for two hours undetected. A couple of people walked by the car and didn't even notice they were sitting there. Robert secretly hoped something would force them to play act a little, but at the same time he didn't. Van pretended to be playing with her phone and took several photos of the incoming cars and drivers. Robert started doing the same. She also made notes as she watched the cars pull in. She saw five lime-green WRXs, an orange Mustang GT, two cherry red Nissan GTs, an old, refurbished Porsche 911, a black Acura TLX and six BMWs, one M4, four 3 series, and a 750i. Most of the drivers were young men in their 20s and 30s. The orange Mustang was being driven by a young woman. She saw an older gentleman get out of the 750i. Many of the drivers were high fashion. A few were dressed in all black. All of them went to the elevator. She looked up karaoke bars and discovered that there was a bar located on the third floor of this mall. "I'll be back in a few minutes," she said.

"You sure?" Robert looked at her and then scanned the garage. He wasn't completely certain they were not being watched. She removed her blazer and unholstered her Kimber. She unbuttoned a couple of buttons on her blouse and got out of the car. She walked toward the valet nonchalantly. The two young guys at the desk gave her a quick look but were distracted by a black Hummer limousine that pulled into the garage right after she passed them. The Hummer and two young men jumped out of the driver's seats to open the side doors. Fifteen girls who looked to be in their late teens piled out of the car. There were all wearing K-Pop gear and too much makeup. Van picked up various perfume scents: Marc Jacobs, Cloe, Dolce & Gabbana, and Chanel. They laughed as they crammed themselves together into the elevator. The men watched them emotionless, and Van strolled forward as if she was simply going to the mall. Inside the mall were several Asian shops, similar to the shops that her parents liked. There were two escalators that carried her to the second floor, where it was mostly clothing stores. Back in the corner, she saw a neon sign and a single slightly heavy-set young man standing next to a gold stanchion with a red velvet rope and an elevator door. There was a poster set up next to the elevator showing someone singing. She went up to the young man who smiled at her. She asked in Vietnamese how to get to the karaoke bar, and he pointed to the elevator. He pressed the button and when the door opened, the elevator was empty, and he directed her to enter. She smiled and nodded at him, which drew a quick smile and nod in return, and walked into the elevator.

The elevator opened into a dark but colorful lobby. There were two velvet couches, and a Chinese coffee table to Van's right. On the left was a cashier behind a chrome counter. Disco lights were running, and a heavy door stood at the back of the lobby.

She walked up to the cashier and said in English, "Hi. I have never been to a karaoke bar like this before. I would like to bring my friends. What is the arrangement?"

He looked at her as if to size her up, and responded, "This is a good karaoke bar, one of the best in LA. We have rooms here that you rent for an hour or more, and each of the rooms has its own hi-def sound system with a monitor that has many catalogues of music." He pointed to a bank of black microphones. "We will give you microphones and take you to the rooms. We have a great menu of foods, and if you like alcohol, we have a nice collection of vodkas, gins and whiskeys as well as beer and wine."

"Would you mind showing me?" she flirted with the young man. He looked up at a camera and a green light flashed on the desk behind the counter.

"Sure," he said. "Just a minute."

He disappeared through a door, and when he returned, he brought a young woman who was wearing the same uniform as him—black jeans and a black button-up Oxford shirt. Van noticed that it was the same woman who had been driving the orange Mustang.

"Follow me," he said.

She walked through the door into a hallway lined with black glass and metal doors with small windows. She could hear various songs being played at the same time and different voices screaming out old rock songs or Chinese melodies. A couple of the rooms had small parties going on and food spread out on the tables in the middle of the rooms. She caught a glimpse of a few rooms in which there were older men sitting and drinking but not singing. As they turned the corner, two young men passed her, and behind them was a line of girls from the Hummer. They stopped at a door with one of the older men, knocked, opened the door and brought in the girls who stood in front of the men.

The host was quick to explain, "The girls serve the men and help them with the sound system. It can be difficult to operate."

Van leaned forward to the host who was taking her around, and said, "This looks like a fun place."

He turned and smiled, "Just one big party!"

Van thanked the host and returned down to Robert, who was not too happy.

"They know me here. This was part of my beat."

"Do you think anyone recognized you?"

"I don't know but we are done here," he said, almost pleading.

Back at the Bureau, Robert and Van stood in Detective Young's office. "Did you follow Kang?" Robert answered, "No sir, but we scoped the garage and took an inventory of cars and drivers." "Good," Young replied. "Put a report together. She can draft it." He looked at Van and said, "She is good at reports." The comment was directed at her, and to Van, it seemed loaded. She noticed that he did not say "reporting," and she thought to herself, if he is involved in the bullet threat, he is not being very careful.

Robert left the office, and Van turned back to Detective Young. "I think I should go back," she said.

"Back where?" he asked.

"To the stakeout site. I think I can get more."

Young looked at her, slightly impressed. "What is your plan?"

Van closed the door. Robert could see that they were talking and was worried that Van might be throwing him under the bus or, alternatively, encroaching on his turf. As she opened the door, Robert could hear Young say, "Be careful, Detective."

Van waited a couple of weeks before returning to the Koreatown mall. In the meantime, she and Robert collected their photographs and descriptions into a report and hijacked a conference room to serve as a war room. They tacked photographs to the wall and created a test hierarchy. BJ and Detective Young downloaded all the intel they had gathered on The Rush mostly through stakeouts. In recent months, Rampart Division had apprehended a couple of gang members for petty theft, and obtained warrants to search their homes, where they found guns and narcotics. The possession charges added leverage, and through those interrogations, they learned about Danny Kang and a couple of his top lieutenants. In exchange for the information, the members served a few months' jail time and were released. The murders that had been attributed to the gang were not simple drive-by executions. The gang kidnapped leaders of a rival Latino gang called El Muerte, tortured them before they executed them, and left the bodies in public view. The Gang Unit had interviewed El Muerte, and they pointed the finger at The Rush. Van needed support, and Robert was too well known in the area to go undercover. She enlisted three officers from the Asian Crimes Unit in the Narcotics Division, two women and one guy. They agreed to play it as Friday night clubbing and dress the part. Van had explained that the look of the bar was high end, and she convinced the Bureau to pay for wardrobe, hire a limo and give them cash for the night. She called the karaoke bar and reserved a room and ordered food.

The limo she hired was a black executive sedan, but it served the part. Van knew she did not want to overdo the look. If it were too rich, she might artificially distance herself from the bar's operations. They pulled up to the valet, who opened the door and saw four Asians laughing and ready to party. They stumbled out of the car and were shown to the elevator. The men at the elevator door told them to raise their arms and did a quick pat down. When they emerged from the elevator, Van went to the counter and saw the young man who had hosted her when she toured the bar. She smiled and waved at him. He recognized her and stepped to the counter, motioning the others to let him check her in. She was giddy and couldn't wait to start singing and flirted mercilessly to send the message that she was single and not involved with the guy in the group.

He led the group to the heavy door and as they walked to the room, he looked at Van and said, "My name is Jack. Anything you want, please ask for me. I can get you anything."

She giggled and thanked him. He led them into the room, where there was food already set up. He gave Van one of the microphones and turned on the monitor. He asked if they wanted English or one of a handful of Asian languages and they agreed on English. He showed them how to use the catalogue to pick songs, and as he left, Van tried to hand him a $20 bill. He looked at her for a second to see if she wanted something, then when it was clear she didn't, he shook his head "no," smiled, bowed, and left them in the room.

They played around in the room for the next couple of hours. Jack came by after about 20 minutes to check on them, and they said it was fun singing rock classics from Abba and Journey and the Stones. They ordered beer and vodka but drank very little. After about 45 minutes, Van walked out of the room and looked around. She saw the young men leading the girls around to different rooms. Typically, one or two would stay in the room. She walked back out to the front lobby and flirted with Jack barely nursing a vodka tonic. She saw the green light flash several times, and when it did, one of the staff would run into the back room. She was able to see a half dozen staff dressed in black working back there. She noticed the woman who drove the orange Mustang acting as if she were a manager. She returned to the room. The group had agreed to play their roles the entire time they were there, cognizant that they might be being watched through hidden cameras. They said nothing about what they were seeing and acted as if they were simply partying the night away.

After about 90 minutes, Jack returned to the room. He motioned to Van. "Come with me," he said. He took her arm gently and led her to another elevator door at the rear of the bar. She was concerned that he might be making a move on her and strategized how to play it lightly and discourage him, but he made no moves. They emerged from the elevator into a lavish almost overdone loft studio with sateen couches and chairs, and a plush white carpet. There were green neon lights in the corners, and a fully loaded kitchen at the back right corner. In the back left corner, where the dining room might have been, was a large mahogany desk with two black leather chairs.

The tall Vietnamese woman whom Van had seen in the garage, was sitting on the corner of the desk, and Danny Kang sat in a large leather chair behind the desk. A half dozen men and women lounged in the room.

Jack brought Van to the center of the room directly in front of Danny Kang.

Danny gave her a stare, and then smiled, and said, "Welcome to Oasis."

Van looked back at him and stood her ground. "Thank you. My friends and I are having fun. Did we do anything wrong?"

"No. No. Not at all. Jack here was telling me you are an interesting person."

"I suppose that is a compliment," she replied. She smiled at Jack. "I think he is interesting as well."

"Yes. I would agree that Jack is very interesting." As he said this, he stood up and came around to the front of the desk. He sat on the edge of the desk next to his Vietnamese companion and studied Van.

"Are you a cop?" The room became very quiet.

"Excuse me?" she said. "Why would you think…"

Danny stood up slowly and leaned forward. "If not, then, my darling," he said very quietly, as he grabbed her ear, "what are these?"

It hurt her and a small whine pierced the air. She jerked her head away from him

and stepped back. "I am deaf," she responded angrily. "You never met a deaf person before?" She pulled them out of her ears and held them out in her hand. "These are my hearing aids," she said, disgusted. "Here. Check them!"

He glanced down and then back at her face, assessing her reaction. Then he backed away and held up his hands in mock surrender. "My apologies. You can never be too careful."

Van was shaken up but gathered herself, only not too quickly. Anybody would have been upset by the aggression. She took a deep breath. "Yah, I understand," she said, as if she was biting her tongue.

"Well then. Please, accept my apologies. Jack," he added, "what is our lovely friend's name?"

"My name is Van," she said, not letting Jack answer for her.

"Well, Van, pleased to meet you. Please join me and my friends for a drink."

"I think you need to work on your charm," she answered, and he laughed out loud. The room relaxed. She took her time, considering the offer. "Thank you," she finally said. "But my friends are waiting, and I don't want them to worry." It was the same line she planned on using with Jack if he got frisky. "Maybe another time?" He smiled and handed her a card.

"Call me," he said. The card had one word on one side and a number on the back. The word was "Oasis."

She took the card. "Have a nice evening," she offered to the room and then to Danny she said, "It's been interesting." She motioned to Jack, who looked at Danny. Danny nodded and Jack escorted her back to the elevator door and down to the bar.

"I'm sorry," he said as opened the door to the room. "It's okay," she responded. "You have interesting friends."

Van and the team gathered their things. The two female cops made a show of being concerned, and Van pretended to waive them off. By the time they got downstairs, the limo was waiting for them. They jumped in acting boozy and were dropped off in Downtown next to a converted loft apartment building where one of the team lived. As the car drove away, Van said to the others, "Let's discuss Monday." "In the meantime," she added and patted her purse. "I'll submit the card for prints."

Van called Charlie on Saturday morning and walked through the events of the evening. Charlie was scared for Van but knew she would do what she felt was necessary. She also told him about her interactions with Detective Young, and he told her that if she sensed anything was wrong to contact him immediately. She called Broad and told him about the night as well. She opened the cold case database and searched for Kang and Vietnamese and Koreatown, and a few cases popped up. One case caught her eye that involved the execution-style shooting of a young Vietnamese couple that was survived by two children—a boy and a girl. The family had not been cooperative, and the police were unable to identify suspects, so it was determined to be a family dispute and not pursued. The city placed the children in Child Support Services and there were no additional notes.

On Monday, Van reported to Detective Young. She had already sent the card to Forensics for prints. Young continued to be impressed by this rookie detective. They agreed that her hearing aids were an unfortunate and probably dangerous mistake, but now that Kang had seen them, that she should continue to wear them. Van asked if any hearing aids had ever been developed that functioned also as two-way radios but Young had never heard of anything like that. "The Detective Bureau doesn't hire many deaf detectives," he acknowledged. He suggested that she talk to the Department's Technology Division and see what they had. "Have you been to FBI and met anybody there?" "Never." "Check with Technology first."

Forensics recorded the clean prints on the card and confirmed they belonged to Danny Kang. They returned the card to Van and Young handed her a new phone.

"Use this." Van called Danny. The Division recorded the call.

"Hi."

"Yeah? Who is this?"

"It's Van."

"Van? Oh, yeah. You're the chick from Oasis."

"You gave me the number. Did you not want me to call?"

"Maybe. What's going on?"

"I'm in the mood for singing again."

"I see. You need someone to hold the microphone?"

"Or maybe just sing with me."

He paused. "All right. I'm busy until about six. Can you get here?"

"Of course."

"Okay, Van. See you then."

She hung up and looked at Young, who was nodding. "I am putting a couple of cars nearby. Anything gets uncomfortable and you call. Got it?" They set up '9' as a speed dial or as the code to text to Robert, who would be in one of the stakeout cars. Van took an Uber to the garage. She dolled herself up enough to look interested but wore jeans and a loose sweater. When she arrived, one of the valets walked her to the elevators but rode with her to the penthouse where Danny was waiting. The same supporting characters were there including the tall Vietnamese woman.

Danny smiled when he saw her. "Welcome back to the scene of the crime," he said extending his hand to take hers and gallantly bowing and kissing her hand.

"Well, I would say this is much better than last time," she smiled.

He looked pleased. "What are you in the mood for?" he asked, motioning toward the alcohol at the bar.

"Diet coke is fine. Are we going to sing?"

Danny furrowed his brow, "You were serious?"

"Well, it is a karaoke bar."

"So it is." He motioned to one of his lieutenants, who opened a cabinet to reveal a PA system and a monitor. They turned on the system and Danny handed Van a microphone. Van loved music and had spent long hours listening to all types of music, sometimes with her hearing aids and sometimes without just to feel the music. She knew her voice was a bit off pitch, but she didn't care. Danny was amazed by her total fearlessness as she belted out Dancing Queen by Abba and a sultry rendition of Toxic by Britney Spears. She gave Danny the microphone and he sang a favorite Vietnamese song, the only song he ever performed at karaoke, just to show that he could. Van smiled and laughed. "You aren't half bad."

"Yes, I am," he confessed. "You want to take a ride?"

"Sure, but please introduce me to your friends."

"You are right," he responded. He went around the room naming everyone there, and they were gracious to Van as Danny would have demanded. "And last but never least," he said, leading her to the tall women posing at the desk, "this is my sister, Min." Van studied her and could make out that Min had reservations about her.

"Your sister?"

"Yes."

"It's an honor." Van dipped lightly. Danny seemed pleased but Min rolled her eyes.

"Come on." Van grabbed her handbag and followed Danny to the elevator. Downstairs the gold WRX was waiting. The valet held the door and Van got in. It smelled like smoke and new car scent combined. "Are you a smoker?" she asked.

"Nah, that's Min." He pulled out onto Wilshire and gunned it. The car took off and sucked Van back into her seat. He turned up Vermont and headed up through Rampart to the 101. He got off at Mulholland and whipped around the corners until he reached the top of Runyon Canyon. He pulled onto the dirt on the side of the road.

"Are we hiking?" she asked.

"Follow me." he said.

The trail was crowded with a mix of locals and young starlets walking their little dogs and aspiring actors showing off their bodies and hoping to meet someone famous. They started down the main trail and then Danny took Van's hand and climbed a small hill where he found a knoll next to an abandoned home and sat down. The view looked right down on Hollywood Boulevard and a building the entire side of which was covered by a six-story rendition of Lindsay Lohan. Beyond Hollywood Boulevard in the distance was downtown Los Angeles, beginning to glow golden in the sunset. Van had to remind herself what she was doing. It felt incredibly romantic and Danny was being surprisingly gentle and not aggressive.

"My favorite spot in LA," he said.

"Why is that?" She pushed back at this point knowing that he liked that in her.

"I've always been in love with that picture of Lindsay Lohan," He looked at her and grinned.

"Right."

"Not really," he said, almost sheepishly. "That's not it. I just find it comforting to get above the fray. I imagine its mine and I rule it and I am king."

"You realize you are sitting on a throne of dirt, Mr. King?" she poked him. He laughed and took her hand.

"You want to be my queen?"

Van blushed. "You need to do a lot more to win this queen," she said.

"How about ice cream?"

"Yes, that might be enough."

He jumped up and they went back to the car. As he was getting in, he got a call. He took the call outside the car and Van could hear him shouting as another side of Danny began to emerge. "Fuck 'em," he said. "Fuck 'em good." When he got in to drive, Van looked at him a little scared. "What was that?"

"Just business."

"Some serious karaoke business?"

She tried to calm him down, but he wouldn't look at her.

"We have to go back."

He punched the gas and after weaving through traffic, they got back to the mall. "I'm sorry," he said as they pulled up to the valet.

"Get her a car," he told the valet and then looked back as he headed to the elevator. She could sense he was torn. "I'll be in touch," he said and disappeared.

The next morning at the Bureau, Van, Robert and Detective Young all stood in the war room that Van and Robert had assembled. Van pinned the picture of Danny at the top and a picture of his sister Min next to him and slightly below. She began to sort the remaining photos of Danny's team according to an order that in her mind reflected the hierarchy she saw in the loft office of the Oasis.

"We didn't know you were in Kang's car, but one of us followed anyway," Robert said. "We followed the car up Mulholland to Runyon and thought he might dump your body in the canyon."

"Right," she said. "Right in front of all those hikers." But she wasn't irritated and appreciated that she had back-up so close. "Did anyone follow him after he took me back?"

"We tried. But we lost him in Silverlake."

"Any gang news?" she asked.

"Nothing concrete. A neighbor reported shots fired but could not identify where and no one reported any crimes."

"I think I need to show you guys something," she said. She went to her desk and pulled out the cold case folder of the Vietnamese couple and brought it to the war room. I don't know if this is related," she started, "but this murder left two orphaned Vietnamese kids, a brother and a sister." Detective Young looked at the file and said, "Seems like a stretch but I'll go with it. What do you think it might mean?"

"At this point, I don't know. I just thought you should see it," Van replied.

"Okay," he said disinterested and laid the file on the conference table. "But remember we are chasing a gang that is known to have tortured and murdered their victims. Whatever you do, Detective, do not take Danny Kang lightly. We don't need to lose a valued member of the Bureau."

She thought his tone was off a little, like he meant it, but didn't really mean it. "Thank you, sir. I'll be careful."

Danny called Van a couple days later. They met at a coffee shop downtown and he took her to Bar Marmont, a high-end restaurant connected to Chateau Marmont, a famous boutique hotel frequented by Hollywood A-listers. He asked about her life and background, and she explained that she was a biochemist who worked at a lab. She talked about her family and the journey from Vietnam when she was young and how she had lost her hearing. They ordered diver scallops and halibut and a Stag's Leap chardonnay. She asked about his family, and he told her it wasn't very interesting and didn't seem to want to discuss it. They walked on Sunset and held hands. He talked about his dreams of running an empire, how he wanted to buy a mansion and have his own helicopter and pad. She asked how he would make his money, and he told her it was easy to get people to pay for stupid things. For example, he said, his team liked to recruit beautiful Asian women and take them to fancy parties in Hollywood. He said it was amazing how rich Hollywood elites, young and old, would pay thousands of dollars just to have beautiful women attend their parties. "I'm not a pimp," he said. "I don't care what they do on their time and we don't control what they do. We just round them up and bring them to the parties and get paid." He laughed. "It's ridiculous but it taught me a lesson. People will pay for stupid things."

"Do you want me to go to parties?" Van said with a bit of an edge.

"Oh my God, no," he responded. "I want you to be my queen." He leaned down and kissed her, and Van's first thought was that she had made a terrible mistake and was getting in over her head.

As they headed back to the car, Danny got a call and as he listened to the voice on the phone, Van could see a dark cloud start to come over him. He got cold and angry and again said they needed to get back to Oasis. But this time when they returned, he took her with him up to the loft. Danny's sister Min was talking to two of Danny's chief lieutenants. They turned when he entered and were surprised to see Van with him. "Help yourself to a diet coke or whatever," he told her. He approached Min and they started talking rapidly in Vietnamese. Van could pick up something about a fight and heard one of the lieutenants mention El Muerte. She watched Min whisper in his ear and could pick out her lips saying, "You want her here?" Danny turned and looked at Van, and said, "I am going to be busy for a while. You probably should go home."

"Whatever you need me to do, Danny," she said.

He paused, wanting her to stay with him, but he knew he didn't want her where he was going. "Go home," he said gently, and walked her to the elevator. He called the valet and told one of them to take her home. Van gave him a hug and left.

She reported to Detective Young her impressions of the night. When she revealed that Danny said he wasn't a pimp, Young laughed. "Right. And BJ here is the president. Christ. Are you the president, BJ?" Young was a hard guy. Van had seen it often and wondered where that came from.

Van continued and described the conversation back at the loft. "They talked about El Muerte." "They did?"

"Yes. I am certain the problem Danny was dealing with had something to do with them."

He looked at BJ, who had been keeping the stakeout going. "Did they go out after Van left?" "Yes. We followed them through MacArthur Park and Filipino town and then up to Mulholland but all they did was drive."

"Something is about to happen," Young said. "We need to pull you out Van."

"No, don't do that. I am close."

Young paused. "Ok, let's give it time. But don't take any unnecessary risk. I have a feeling I am going to regret this."

Danny pulled up on Flower, and Van jumped in. "I've got some business and then we can head out."

"That's fine, whatever you need to do," she said.

They sped down Olympic and turned left on Normandie. As soon as they passed Venice, Van saw several Rush cars pull in behind the gold WRX. Danny slowed and turned into a cemetery called Angelus Rosedale Cemetery. It was an old school cemetery with headstones so close they seemed to be stacked on top of each other. They drove near a large cannon and pulled over and stopped. The cannon was set up on a large, white, carriage-shaped pedestal, and on its base inscribed were the words, "With Malice Toward None." It seemed eerily out of place.

"Wait here," Danny commanded and he and about six of his lieutenants all got out and gathered next to the cannon. Van looked in the side mirror and saw Min pull up behind the row of cars and jump out. Two of the lieutenants, whom Van knew as Tak and Toshi, started smoking. A line of smartly outfitted 1950 Chevy pickups pulled up on the cemetery road opposite the cannon. A group of Latino guys all wearing black jeans and multicolored bandanas got out. Danny stepped away from his group and the leader, an older male in his forties, approached Danny. He smiled and said, "*Olá vato*, my Asian brother, whazzup?"

Danny looked back without reacting and said, "We gonna fix this or do we gotta fix this?"

"Fix what, my friend? There ain't no problems. *Todo está bien!*" As he said it, his members gathered closer around him.

"Yes, there are problems," Danny said, and stepped closer to the leader. "*Todo no está bien.*"

At that point, the guns and knives came out on both sides. Danny looked at the leader and said, "You got two options" and added "*vato*" sarcastically. "We kill each other," he said. "Or we become one."

The gang leader laughed. "Kill each other? You mean you die."

"You think so?" Danny responded. He motioned to Tak, who pulled two bandanas out of his pocket and handed them to Danny. Danny held out the two bandanas. The leader raised his gun and turned it sideways, execution style.

"You motherfucker," the leader said, and spit on the ground. "Now you die." He looked back for support, and he noticed that his members had all lowered their guns. "Shoot these *putos!*" he shouted, but before he could fire his gun, one of his own gang members pulled out a burlap bag and pulled it over the leader's head and shoulders. Two others quickly wrapped him in duct tape and as he was screaming, they took him behind a large gray headstone and shot him. They carried his wrapped-up body to one of the pickups and threw it in the back. Another member walked forward to Danny and reached out with a closed fist. Danny bumped the fist, and when he gave a signal, around the corner came a new lime green fully loaded WRX. It stopped, and Danny pulled a set of keys out of his pocket and motioned for the member to accept the car as a gift. The other members came back from the pickup. They smiled and patted the guy on his shoulder as he took the keys and strolled over to the car. Danny turned and headed back to Van.

Van in the meantime watched the entire scene in horror. She knew something like this was coming, but to be there felt entirely different than what she imagined. Danny was unmoved and emotionless the entire time. The execution was quick and vicious. She had started punching the number '9' into her phone to get Robert's attention but he had not yet responded. As Danny returned to the car, she turned off her phone, fearful that Robert might call her or text her, and Danny might detect that something was up. As Danny came toward the car, one of the other El Muertes caught up with him and said, "See you soon, brother."

Danny nodded, and the guy looked over at Van and his eyes grew wide. "Who is she?"

Danny looked at him like it was none of his business, and the man said, "She's a cop, bro! I seen her at the station!"

Danny turned and grabbed him by the throat. The man held his hands up and shook his head furiously, and gasped, "I'm serious, man. I'm sorry."

Danny dropped his hold and looked back at Van. The cloud came back over his eyes. He jumped into the driver's seat.

"What did he say Danny?" she asked quickly, panic rising.

"He said you're a cop," Danny replied. Then grabbing her purse, he opened it, rifling through it for a gun or a badge. Van knew not to bring them, and they weren't there.

"Danny. He doesn't know what he is talking about. Maybe I look like somebody," she said, starting to shake.

"Well, babe," he said, coldly, "we'll see." He reached back in her purse and pulled out the phone and held it up. "Yeah. We'll see."

She could tell as they drove back that he was betraying that same conflicted sense she had felt before, and that helped her to relax and act like she had no idea what he was talking about. They got back to Oasis and instead of taking her to the loft, Danny took her to one of the karaoke rooms and locked her inside.

"What are you doing?" she asked.

Danny said nothing and disappeared. She waited, wondering if she had made a fatal mistake. She heard a tap on the door. She walked over and looked out of the small window. The door unlocked and standing there was the woman who drove the orange Mustang.

"You gotta get out of here," she said, almost mechanically. "You must leave. Now."

Van didn't hesitate. She grabbed her purse and followed the woman to a stairwell. She turned, said thanks, and then ran down the stairwell, which opened onto an alley adjacent to the building. She looked around and ran to the backside of the mall and then turned down the street and walked quickly away from the mall, trying not to be conspicuous. She was about a block away when Robert pulled up beside her and urged her to jump in, which she did.

As he drove, she asked, "Are you being followed?"

He kept driving and looked back. "I don't see anything and nothing like a Rush car."

Van looked down. The trauma of the moment overwhelmed her. "Don't take me to the Bureau," she said. "Can I borrow your phone?" She called Charlie and explained what had happened. They agreed to meet and Van asked Robert to take her there.

"Who is she?" Van asked Robert as they drove on.

"She is a plant. FBI. It's a joint operation."

"You didn't tell me?"

"You didn't need to know. You were too close to Danny Kang."

Van was unhappy but what Robert said made some sense. "Is she going to be okay?"

"We don't know that yet. We are watching."

In fact, the joint operation had been in place for over a year. The woman in the orange Mustang's name was Mindy Wong. She worked for the FBI as an undercover agent, and had been planted in the Oasis, and through that, the Rush for the entire time. But she was not getting close to Danny Kang, although she had gotten close to Min and through her adopted as a part of the gang. Min bought her the orange Mustang.

Shortly after Van witnessed the execution, and Mindy rescued Van, the FBI raided Oasis and what remained of El Muerte. They found what they considered to be evidence of human and drug trafficking, and arrested Danny Kang and his lieutenants including his sister and several members of El Muerte. Van filled out an affidavit describing the scene at the cemetery. She added to the affidavit the possibility of a connection to the cold case file of the murdered couple.

Danny was convicted on several counts including conspiracy to murder and sex trafficking. His crimes were considered aggravated because of his affiliation with a gang, but his sentence was reduced after it was learned that the couple in the cold case were his and Min's parents. Van went to visit him in prison.

"You got a lot of nerve," he said, through the bulletproof glass that separated them.

"Something about you, Danny," she said.

"Yah? Like what?"

"Don't give up on your life."

"I am a fucking felon, and anyway who are you to tell me...?"

"I am serious. You are an empire builder. Get through this quickly and do it right next time. You can still be the King of LA."

He laughed. "Still wanna be my queen?"

"Get out of here quickly and look me up," she said. "You never know." Six months later, Danny Kang was murdered in jail. Old school El Muertes found him and hung him in his cell with a twisted sheet. Min Kang was released after two years in the Century Regional Detention Center for Women in Lynwood, California, just southeast of downtown Los Angeles.

Chapter 8.

The Cytokine Singularity

Between 1990 and 2010, the computational speed of computers doubled every 14 months. Computer memory capacity doubled every 18 months. Computer storage capacity doubled every three years. These hyper-rapid advances in computer technology were the result of human intelligence. Computers did not make themselves smarter. Humans made computers smarter. But as computers continued to become smarter, the distance between human intelligence and machine intelligence narrowed. Enter artificial intelligence or AI. AI is a quantum leap advance in machine intelligence. The difference between pre-AI software and post-AI software is the ability of AI-driven software to adapt and recode itself in response to new stimuli, a change in circumstances, or a logic problem not previously encountered. In short, unlike operating systems before AI, post-AI operating systems have the capacity to learn. This capacity accelerates the advance of machine intelligence toward human intelligence, and when the distinction between the two evaporates—when that line is crossed—that is the moment of singularity, the moment when human intelligence loses control over machine intelligence.

Fred Schmidt looked out over the bay. The sky was gray, as it usually is in this part of the country. But it was a quiet morning. The water was still, and dark green islands dotted the horizon. He stared at his multiple monitors for just a few seconds, enough time to get a snapshot of the markets. The country was in an upswing, buoyed by the new president's anti-regulatory posture. Fred's personal fortune increased $20 million in the first three minutes of open. If it were that easy, he thought to himself, then why waste time and energy on yet another new venture? He knew the answer before he asked the question—because otherwise he would be bored, and he hated the feeling of being bored almost more than anything. Of course, his personal health crisis had ratcheted things up a notch. Finding some way to stay alive captured his interest, and combining a new scientific discovery with solving his own personal cancer riddle was, in a kind of perverse sense, the best of all possible worlds.

He called Derek. "Good morning, Fred. How's the weather?" Fred knew he wasn't asking him about the actual weather. He liked that about Derek—very few people really knew how to communicate with him. "Calm," he said, "but I could use a good storm."

* * *

Dr. Brian Johannsen loved Bainbridge Island. He often thought of it as its own petri dish. Unique flora and fauna dotted the island, battling invasive species brought by birds and bicyclists and hikers, who thought they were simply enjoying the views. He found a small apartment in Fort Ward, as far away from the Duc A. Tran Laboratory for Hereditary Biology as possible, and he rode his Honda Gold Wing through the back roads to work every day. The traffic on 305 had gotten oppressive, even for a small island, and he could relax and think as he rode on Fletcher Bay Road past Port Orchard and then through Grand Forest West on Miller Road up to Hidden Cove. He parked his bike and pulled off his helmet. As the sun was creeping up and through the thin line between the horizon and the gray sky, an orange light lit up Tran Labs and the pines and lush vegetation that surrounded it. He took a deep breath and walked to the back entrance that he preferred to use. By the time he got there, the sun had disappeared, and the morning returned to its standard gray. He climbed the stairs to the third-floor laboratory and found his office, where he set down his helmet, removed his riding gear and pulled on his lab coat. He loved this office. He was glassed in from the busy-ness of the Lab and he had a floor-to-ceiling window that looked directly out onto Hidden Cove and Port Madison Bay.

Brian pulled his chair back, and as he was about to sit down, he noticed a biohazard transport case on the floor next to his desk. A note from Dr. Meisner was taped to the handle. It read: "Highly Infectious. Follow BSL IV Protocol." He jumped up, opened his Hazmat case and pulled out a jump suit, booties, sleeve covers, two pairs of surgical gloves, and a Halyard N95 Fluid shield respirator and surgical mask. He put everything on and grabbed the case, walked it to a secure lab that the team used for highly infectious substances, and locked the door. Inside, he placed the case on chrome table and carefully opened it. He noticed that an enclosed petri dish was properly stored inside two watertight containers packaged in black sponge. He reached inside to pullout the petri dish and read the label: Risk Group IV. He gently carried over to a gas tight Class III glove box, one of two at Tran Labs. The glove box had been constructed inside a small, sealed room. He entered the room, placed the dish inside the box, gathered his working materials and set them next to the dish. He snapped down the lid to ensure a tight seal and then sealed the door and went over to the intercom and buzzed Dr. Meisner.

"Good morning, Brian."

"Hi Stan. Saw your message. Nice way to wake up."

"You're talking about the bio case?"

"None other."

"Sorry about that. Couple of Silicon guys dropped it off yesterday. One of them asked about you. You know Fred Schmidt?"

"Fred Schmidt, CEO of Grindle?"

"The very same."

"Never met him. How does he know me?"

"Word's out I guess."

"Word's out?" he chuckled. "Right. What do you need me to do?"

"Take a look. Let's figure it out."

"Thanks, Stan. I'll try not to spread it around."

Brian could sense that Dr. Meisner had very little interest in the case. The fact that he had left it on the floor was a clear signal that Meisner had other concerns. Silicon Valley CEOs were a dime a dozen these days, even Fred Schmidt. Bill Gates wasn't a regular with Meisner, but he had stopped by a few times, and they both were members of the same country club. No reason to get worked up. He sat down at the glass in front of the glove box, place his hands inside the rubber arms that allowed him to work on the dish. He carefully opened it and began to separate the contents into five other dishes. He tested the contents for RG IV's "big three": Ebola, Marburg and Lassa, and the results were negative. He tested for HIV and SARs, just to be sure, and the results likewise were negative. He ran backup tests on all known RG III and IV microbes and could not get a positive result. He isolated a small specimen on a slide, placed the slide in a glass containment capsule and closed up all the remaining samples for storage. He pulled his arms out of the gloves, entered the room and grabbed the containment capsule. The lab he occupied had its own Scanning Electron Microscope or SEM, with which Brian used to view microscopic organisms. The SEM was fitted with a special slot for the containment capsule to handle potentially infectious microbes. He slid the containment capsule into the slot and turned on the SEM.

At first, the images were blurred. He tried several different resolutions before an image began to appear. At its core was a small globe about 0.3 microns in diameter. The globe appeared to be spinning around an axis of two spikes that were north and south respectively, the north spike was the same size as the globe, and the south spike about double the size, more than 0.5 microns. Around the equator of the globe were four additional spikes also measuring 0.3 microns, each at 90°, 180°, 270°, and 360°. The spiked globes seemed to cluster in groups of six. Brian noted the perfect symmetry of the globes. He ran a spectrometer to determine composition, and the globe came back as a mesh composed of carbon fullerenes, and magnesium diboride, which is a key element in ceramics. The spikes appeared to be a titanium alloy. The spectrometer confirmed what he had already begun to surmise—these microbes were not organic. He suspected, though, that that didn't mean they were safe, and whoever packaged them as an RG IV organism was sending the message to be extremely careful. He pulled the containment capsule out of the SEM and stored it with the other samples. He returned to his desk, removed the hazmat gear and put his lab coat back on. Then he went to see Dr. Meisner.

He walked quickly downstairs to Meisner's office. He wasn't there. Brian wandered around the floor looking in the conference rooms without success. He asked Meisner's assistant if she knew where he was working, and she thought he might be in the main lab on the first floor. Brian bound down another flight of stairs and into the Lab. He found Dr. Meisner standing with a group of faculty members from University of Washington Microbiology Department or what he now called U-Dub. They saw him approach, and everyone smiled. "Dr. Johannsen! So good to see you! How have you been! Cooking up anything new?"

Brian smiled back and was cordial. As he approached, the group returned to discussing a proposal put forth by Bill Gates to prepare for a global pandemic. The question was whether they might get a jump on any research by anticipating what the source of the pandemic might be. One of the faculty members mentioned Wuhan and the virology work that was being done there. Another faculty member responded that possibly, but more advanced work was being conducted in Zimbabwe in response to the recent Ebola outbreaks. Brian waited for what he felt was an appropriate amount of time and tapped Dr. Meisner on the shoulder. He whispered that he had information on the package. Meisner looked at him a little irritated, and said, "Thank you, Dr. Johannsen. Feel free to put it in a report and send it to me. I will take a look when I finish here." Brian looked at Meisner as if to say, if you are not interested, why did you ask me to look at it, then shrugged it off, and said "Certainly. Nice to see you gentlemen." He added "…and gentlewoman," to the one female faculty member who was present.

Brian returned to his office and shot Meisner a quick email. "Check again with Schmidt. The microbe is not a biologic." He put his lab coat back on the hook, tossed his leather riding jacket over his shoulder, grabbed his helmet and left for the evening.

* * *

Derek Whitestone mused for a quick minute on the storm that Fred Schmidt either was waiting for or possibly even contriving. He knew the health care industry was in a protracted state of chaos. The last administration, after two decades of political stalemate, had passed a health care bill designed to meet the needs of the 20 million souls that high-cost managed care allegedly had abandoned. In so doing, that administration recast a mostly privatized system as a quasi-governmental program that measured success more by the pool of covered entities than by profit. The new administration now seemed hell-bent on dismantling that system and returning health care to a pre-managed care proto-capitalist state driven by profit. But the administration never actually explained how the existing state would end and how that new state might be resurrected. Tidbits here and there made it look like something real, but the health care battles had morphed into a purely political battle—nothing more than a proxy for one administration's opposition to a prior administration. The back-and-forth whipsaw effect of the political wrangling left the health care industry without clear direction and the scientific community that fed the industry its high-cost cures and treatments and devices found itself floundering.

The pressure to survive by being the first to succeed had grown so great that the same community that once prided itself on its independent objectivity now found itself under the allure of bad science, announcing accomplishments and publishing results prematurely and without adequate verification. Fred Schmidt already had his storm. All he needed was the killer app that would bring him his next billions, and Derek knew he was banking on Bainbridge.

The problem with that strategy was the petri dish. Its actual origins were still unknown, and the question of its ownership was complicated enough to qualify as a law school fact pattern. Derek needed an alternative. RW Labs had the infrastructure. Derek could go hat in hand, as he had already considered. He would have to throw Cheryl Brown under the bus for taking the dish, which didn't really bother him. But if he went that route, he wouldn't be able to predict the outcome—a skill he based his entire career around. Belinda could be vengeful. She would want his money for the Providia AI engineering product, but as soon as she had her results, she could try and cut him out. He knew her legal team to be vicious, but Derek had been down that road, and he knew his way around it. Unfortunately, there was a bigger problem. Derek had already split the contents of the dish, and Belinda's team would figure that out. He needed to look elsewhere and he had an idea.

The Lyndon A. Rutter Center for Cellular Engineering at the University of California in Los Angeles had recently announced a breakthrough in cancer treatments. Using self-renewing pluripotent stem cells, researchers at UCLA successfully manufactured T cells capable of enhancing immunity and fighting cancer cells. T cell therapies had been around for years, but in patients with low T-cell counts, they didn't always work. This new breakthrough allowed for the production of T cells without having to harvest them from patients. Derek had met Lyndon Rutter but didn't know him well. Rutter made his money in the lucrative LA real estate market. Lately his focus had shifted to philanthropy, and he had donated large sums to UCLA for the fight against cancer. Rutter's position reminded Derek of his own client, the one who now lived on Bainbridge Island.

Cheryl Brown sat in her cubicle. She didn't feel particularly well and had not taken her coat off. Derek called her into his conference room.

"I need to know what you were thinking."

"I think it is obvious I wasn't thinking."

"I disagree, Cheryl. You have your weaknesses but being thoughtless is not one of them."

Cheryl looked down and then up again to meet Derek's stare. "If the RW Labs was that careless, then there were two possibilities. One was that the contents of that dish were not really that dangerous, and two, that we didn't want to be working with them. I thought that if the dish had anything to do with MEMS, it might give us a leg up, and I figured you would understand that."

Derek smiled. He knew he would not trust Cheryl with the full story, but he could enlist her as part of his Plan B.

"How would you feel about returning to Los Angeles?"

"I'm not sure I understand. Are you firing me?"

"I'm not, but I gave it some thought. You took a great risk and have potentially implicated me and this company in a crime that could ruin us.

You have also risked the wrath of RW Labs, and that part of the story is not over yet."

"I'm sorry, Derek."

"Well, I'm not. I want to know more about this dish. I want you to take it to UCLA Medical School, and shepherd its review. You might need to stay down there a while. I will arrange for an apartment. You need to address your lease here. Work out an arrangement with your landlord. You have two days to get your affairs in order. Meet me back here on Thursday morning."

Cheryl left, and Derek looked out his window. He told himself, "This is a good idea." He called Stanford and arranged for the delivery of the petri dish first thing Thursday morning.

The UCLA Labs had benefitted greatly under the Rutters' generosity, but in fact, it had struggled over the years since another T-cell-related controversy had smeared its reputation. Decades prior, the UCLA Labs was accused of harvesting T cells from patients who were being treated at the University's medical center and storing them for its own research. When the news broke, utter chaos broke out, senior faculty members were fired, multiple lawsuits were filed, and the University was forced to settle claims to the tune of hundreds of millions of dollars. The only thing that kept the lab in operation was its affiliation with UCLA Medical School, which found itself forced to keep the lab open simply for teaching purposes. It took the school more than 20 years to recover from the debacle.

Cheryl was happy to be back in LA. She still had friends there, and the intensity of Silicon Valley had been wearing on her. It felt as much like a break as it did like another job, and Derek had found her an amazing apartment near the Grove, an outdoor high-end mall in Park La Brea built around LA's historic Original Farmer's Market. She spent the weekend partying with old friends, and the transport case rested under the floor in one of her many empty closets.

Cheryl was not alone with her friends. A nondescript black Ford Explorer had picked up her trail on the way down Interstate 5 as she sped past the fields of grain, hay, cotton, grapes and citrus trees grown in the California's central valley along the California aqueduct. It followed her as she made her way over the Grapevine and through the Tejon Pass. It followed her that weekend as she bounced from La Brea to Santa Monica to Malibu to the Hollywood Hills and back to La Brea. On Monday, the Explorer reported that she had gone to UCLA, parked in Structure No. 2 and carried a backpack into the Biomedical Sciences Research Building just off Charles Young Drive.

Cheryl Brown had seen the black Explorer and reported it to Derek. He pressed her to be certain she wasn't being paranoid, and she confirmed that she had seen the same Explorer in her rearview mirror several times since the Grapevine. She was pretty sure the Explorer had followed her all the way down the 5 Freeway. He wasn't certain but he suspected Belinda, and if so, he would not be surprised if Belinda was having them followed. He urged Cheryl to be cautious but to go about her business in the normal course and not act as if she were hiding something. There was nothing unusual about Derek sending Cheryl to UCLA. He might be exploring the same opportunities for investing Fred's money that took him to the Labs in the first place. UCLA's medical complex housed one of the top microbiology labs in the country and the scientists who worked there had been researching MEMS for years. The California NanoSystems Institute sat directly across the medical plaza from the Rutter Center of Cellular Engineering and Medicine. Derek told Cheryl to use her UCLA backpack, which she still had, to carry the transport case. He called Rutter in advance to let them know she was coming. When she arrived, two students met her at the main entrance and escorted her into a small room off the main lobby, where a team was waiting for her.

"Good morning, Ms. Brown," said Dr. March Fielding, who led the virology team at Rutter. "Derek Whitestone told us to expect you."

"Good morning."

"Mr. Whitestone told us you were carrying a substrate of some kind. He could not tell us what it was, but that it might be highly infectious. Is that your understanding as well?"

"It is."

"Can you tell us a little more about what you are bringing us today?"

"Not much more than what Mr. Whitestone has already told you."

"Do you know what it is?"

"It is a petri dish labeled Risk Group IV."

"Nothing more?"

"No."

"Do you know where it came from?"

"I do not."

"Do you know who might have worked with it?"

"I don't."

"Do you understand what Risk Group IV means?"

"Not entirely but I believe it might contain a virus or something like that that is very dangerous."

The team looked at each other. Either she was not telling the truth, which seemed likely to them, or Derek had entrusted one of the world's most potent and untreatable diseases to someone who had no idea what she was carrying. If so, the possibilities were frightening, and Derek Whitestone was committing gross negligence by placing this microbe in incompetent hands. They smiled at Cheryl condescendingly and took the transport case out of the backpack and took her back to the lobby. She went into the women's bathroom and pulled a folded cardboard box out of the backpack. The dimensions of the box were roughly the same as the transport case. She unfolded it and placed it in the backpack and exited the building. She decided to take a different route to her car. She had lunch at the cafeteria adjacent to the student center. It reminded her of being a student there and how nice it was to be worried about nothing more than finishing a paper or getting ready for an exam. She could almost feel the same comfort just by sitting there and watching the other students. She waited an hour before heading back to Parking Structure 2.

When she got to the parking structure, she climbed the concrete stairs and crossed the lot back to her car. That's when the Explorer rushed up on her and two men jumped out and grabbed her. Almost instantly, she heard a whistle, and a UCLA Security Guard was running toward her. The men ripped the backpack off Cheryl's shoulder and jumped back in the Explorer and took off. The security guard caught up with Cheryl and asked if she was okay and if she knew those men. She started crying and told him they had stolen her books. He took some information from her and said he would report on what happened and would tell the security administration to look out for a black Explorer. She wiped her eyes and told him how brave he had been. She wondered if he had any idea how close he had come to being shot and possibly killed.

She sat in her car for another hour. She was afraid to leave the structure, as if it were watching out for her and keeping her safe. Eventually she pulled out, called her friends in North Hollywood and drove out there to stay with them. They had a joint ready when she pulled up and her hands shook as she lit it and took a draw. Exactly what I need, she thought to herself. Her immediate second thought was—what the fuck did I get myself into?

Derek waited for a call. He expected her to follow up as soon as she left Rutter. When she didn't call, he got concerned but another matter captured his attention and he let it go. Several hours later, his phone rang. It was Cheryl.

"What the hell, Cheryl? Did they get it?"

Cheryl was high. "Man, I got jumped."

"What happened?"

"They stole the empty box, those idiots."

"You delivered it?"

"I did and they jumped me in the parking lot after I had dropped it off. You were right about the box. They grabbed me and a student security guard saved me. They took the backpack."

"You certain it was a security guard?"

Cheryl paused. "Well, he had a yellow jacket on." She started giggling and found it difficult to stop.

* * *

When Brian got home, he pulled a beer and a container of fresh wonton out of his fridge. He heated the wonton on his stove, popped the beer and sat down in front of his computer. He looked up nanotechnologies and started reading. He had studied it in school as a part of his doctoral program, but the field was still in its infancy, and he became more interested in the origins and mutations of microscopic life and focused his research there. The material in the petri dish piqued his curiosity. Why that shape and why did they cluster, and what where they supposed to do? He wondered even more basically how could any device that small perform a function and what type of function would it be? He read that there were four types of nanorobotic devices: switches, motors, shuttles and cars. A 'switch' is a nanorobotic device that changes its shape in response to environmental stimuli in a process that is called "conformational change." The stimuli causing the change might be a chemical reaction or heat or ultraviolet radiation. A 'motor' uses energy derived from the change process to move around molecules in its orbit. 'Shuttles' carry molecular compounds like anti-cancer agents to targeted locations. 'Cars'—the most advanced of the four forms of nanorobots—have appendages that can be used for locomotion and steering. The appendages may be actual wheels, but they also could be tracks or tails or tiny hairs or extensions like arms.

Brian also studied several options for powering nanorobots. Power might come from traditional micro-capacitors and mini-generators that create and store electrical power to a special wrap called a piezoelectric membrane that transforms magnetic fields or Radiofrequency (RF) radiation into electrical power. Nanobots can also be powered by electrochemical stimuli like neurotransmitters in the human body. The earliest proposed uses of the nanotechnology were medical. Tiny drills that would pop cancer cells, isolating and cutting off blood flow to the cells. Nanorobots could "paint" cancer cells and prepare them for targeted chemical and RF therapies. The latter focused heat generated by high intensity RF emissions on painted cells and burned them away from surrounding tissue without harming the non-painted tissue. A newer application destroyed pathogenic mRNA—mutated RNA strands that were giving birth to new cancer cells. Beyond medicine, researchers were looking at environmental applications. Nanomites might be created to facilitate the rapid decomposition of landfills and floating plastic islands in the ocean, eliminating toxic waste and its harmful effects on the environment.

Still, he was beginning to get the same feeling he had in graduate school. The more he read, the more it felt to him like fantasy and science fiction. Perhaps it was possible to build a single nanobot. But the impact of a single or even small number of nanobots would be undetectable in the physical world. For nanotechnology to have any noticeable impact, it would have to scale. Take all the computers and laptops and pads and smart phones that had been manufactured around the world over the past 40 years and reduce them to nanoscale and you could fit them all in the palm of your hand. A strong wind would blow them all into total obscurity.

There could be another option, he thought, allowing his imagination to play, and the fantasy to develop. What if nanotechnology was not the end of the chain, but rather the beginning? What if nanobots merely started a physical process, like the fuse of a bomb. He thought about real world applications. Some cancers, for example, were triggered by the presence of toxic substances, but once the cancer was started, the triggering substance, like smoking cigarettes, could be removed and yet the cancer would still grow and eventually consume its host. What if, when fighting cancer, you could trigger the growth of an anti-cancer agent, like T cells, with a relatively small number of nanobots. Unfortunately, he thought, as he shut off the computer and headed to bed, even if that were true, you still needed to solve the scaling problem for a therapy like that to make economic sense.

He fell asleep, musing on Isaac Asimov's three laws of robotics:

A robot may not injure a human being, or through inaction, allow a human being to come to harm.

A robot must obey orders given to it by human beings except where such orders would conflict with the First Law.

A robot must protect its own existence as long as such protection does not conflict with the First or Second Law.

Back in the office, Brian returned to the SEM lab. He pulled out the non-biologic RG IV specimen and set up to do further work. He divided the sample into several new samples. The first sample he heated over a Bunsen burner and then looked to see if there was any change. Nothing he could detect. He tried a variety of acids and still no reaction. At that point, he heard a knock and looked to see Dr. Carrie Comstock standing at the door dressed in a similar hazmat suit. Brian enjoyed working with Carrie. She was a careful and thoughtful scientist, and she had been very helpful to Brian in the past. He held up four fingers, the sign they used to communicate toxicity levels, and she nodded. He motioned for her to enter.

"You must have found something," she said through a microphone in her suit. "You have been incommunicado for two days."

"Stan left something for me, but I don't think he is that interested. I am still deciding whether to be interested or not."

"Show me."

He pushed back from the SEM and flipped on a monitor. "Doesn't look like a biologic," she said. "Too symmetrical. Is it a crystal?"

"I wondered myself," he responded. "I ran the spectrometer, and it turned out to be a combination of metal and ceramics."

"It's a nanobot?" she responded, picking up quickly on the implication.

"I think it might be. Certainly, it is something manufactured. But I can't seem to get it to do anything."

At that point, almost as if on cue, Carrie and Brian watched as the image started to rotate. As it rotated, the spikes began to move in and out of the sphere, extending and retracting. The effect was mesmerizing.

"Maybe it likes women," Carrie joked.

"Did you bring anything in here with you?"

"Only my phone."

"Can I see it?"

As she pulled it out of her pocket, she noticed it was ringing. "Probably a telemarketer." But when it stopped ringing, the image stopped moving.

Brian said, "Wait here." He ran to get his cell phone and brought it back to the Lab. "Call me," he told Carrie.

"My husband might not be happy," Carrie said, in a light-hearted way—she enjoyed ribbing Brian.

He smiled and said, "Just call me."

She did, and when Brian's phone started to ring, the image started to move again. But as soon as he answered her call, it stopped. He spoke over the phone to Carrie and nothing happened. They tried the experiment several times and the results were the same. As long as the phone was ringing, the image would move. Turn it off or answer the call, and the image stopped.

"Wow," Brian said.

"Well, we know it moves," she noted. "But what does it do?"

Carrie went over to the SEM and pulled out the containment capsule. But before returning it to the glove box, she opened it and started sprinkling it into a new dish. "Be careful," Brian started to say, and then he saw Carrie look at him, her eyes widening. She dropped the capsule into the dish and grabbed her throat. Brian felt his own throat start to restrict. He hit an alarm button and caught Carrie before she could fall to the floor. He laid her gently on the ground. Each lab was outfitted with a medical emergency kit, and the teams there had been drilled "over and over again" on its use. He stood up and stumbled over to the cabinet but as he reached for it, he felt his legs give way and he crumpled down to the floor. He looked up and for a brief second saw several white suits enter the room in a walking bubble and start to pull him and Carrie to the outer door and then he passed out.

When Brian awoke, he felt his lungs burning and started coughing. He looked around and could see he was in an oxygen tent. Dr. Meisner and several colleagues were standing outside the tent along with Fred Schmidt, who was likewise suited up. Hearing him cough, they put on gas masks and entered the tent.

"How is Dr. Comstock?" he gagged out between coughing fits.

"She's alive," Dr. Meisner responded. "But we have her on a ventilator. What the hell happened?"

"Fred Schmidt happened," he responded between coughing jags. He found it increasingly hard to breath and someone gave him a shot to relax him and he fell back asleep.

It took three days for Brian to recover. While he was recovering, the team ran the same tests on him that he had already run and likewise determined that the substance was not a biologic and that Brian was not contagious. Carrie had a rougher time. She went into cardiac arrest twice but pulled through it. By the end of the week, they were able to remove the ventilator. Brian stood by her bedside.

"Do I get a Purple Heart?" she asked feebly, forcing a smile.

"More like a Bronze Star," Brian responded.

Carrie coughed, and Brian said, "Take it easy. It's good to see you on this side still." He grabbed her hand and gave it a light squeeze. She drifted back into sleep. He joined Dr. Meisner in the Lab's main conference room. Fred Schmidt was present.

"Can someone tell me what just happened?" Brian questioned.

"We still don't know what caused it," Dr. Meisner responded, "but both you and Dr. Comstock went into full blown anaphylaxis in a matter of seconds. We pumped you full of epinephrine and slowed it down but as you can tell, it took days for you both to recover. We are not certain that Dr. Comstock is entirely out of the woods."

Dr. Meisner looked at Fred Schmidt. "I think we are entitled to some answers."

"I don't know what it is," he said. "I brought it here for you to figure that out."

"Where did it come from, Fred?"

"I am sorry, but I am not at liberty to divulge, and even if I could, I am not certain I know. The origin is proprietary information. You know how things work in the Valley. Information is siloed. That is how we protect it."

"That is also how you protect thieves," Brian said. He was angry and justifiably so. Carrie was an important member of the staff, and Brian cared a great deal for his colleagues.

Fred grimaced but didn't take it personally. He needed Brian and this group to work though their issues and take the sample to the next level.

"Can you still work with it?"

Dr. Meisner shrugged as if he hadn't made up his mind. "It is dangerous but that hasn't stopped us in the past. We need to develop new protocols with it. Give us a few days and we will let you know."

Fred stood up and left the room. Looking back at Brian, he said, "I am sorry about you and your colleague, Dr. Johannsen. I will make it up to you."

Brian watched Fred as he left. He didn't need or want anything from Fred. But he knew risk was a basic part of his chosen profession, and if Dr. Meisner wanted to keep working with the substance in the dish, he would continue to support the effort.

He turned back to Dr. Meisner. "Anaphylaxis?"

"Right, a full-blown cytokine storm."

"Do you think it was an allergic response?"

"We don't know yet, but it doesn't look that way. All we know is that your and Dr. Comstock's bodies immediately went into shock in response to the substance as soon as it went airborne. It could be weaponized, which might be why Fred Schmidt is staying mum."

Chapter 9.

A Host of Brilliant Ideas

The news of Danny Kang's death hit Van particularly hard. She knew that Danny's dark side, which she had encountered on more than one occasion, should have kept her emotionally distant. She also knew that the good she saw in Danny appealed to her in a way she hadn't felt before. She had her doubts that she could rescue him from the consequences of his bad choices, but she found herself desperate to try. His death ended that fantasy.

Detective Young had been overly complimentary of Van's work following the arrest and conviction of Danny Kang and his associates. Van appreciated it, but it did not feel sincere and did not give Van any confidence in Young's support for her as a detective. The excessive compliments were short-lived. Van found her work being scrutinized in ways it had not been before. Young seemed to enjoy pointing her out at daily meetings and asking for her opinion on matters she knew nothing about. She retreated to Chess and to Detective Broad. Her analytical work at Chess had been picked up by another recruit. Detective Robert "Bobby" Davidson was a recent graduate and had studied statistics and computer science at Cal State Fullerton before entering the police academy. Bobby was proud to be a detective, but he had greater ambitions. He had already applied to law school and hoped to join the FBI. For now, at least until he heard back from law school admissions, he was working with Detective Broad in Chess.

"Quite a stint you pulled off, my dear Detective," Detective Broad said in his most affected British accent.

"I suppose you're quite right," Van responded in kind. They laughed.

"Oh dear," she added. "What must I do now?"

"Actually, Van," Broad said, taking a more serious tone. "I do have an idea."

Detective Broad's "idea" was for Van to get herself better acquainted with a new line of medical and pharmaceutical cases that had become the focus of Charlie's work after the Baldwin Hills case. The cases involved complaints raised against doctors and pharmaceutical companies engaging in behavior that exceeded ordinary incompetence and traditional notions of malpractice. Rather, this borderline criminal behavior ranged from a reckless disregard for human safety to the intent to cause harm. Charlie started asking questions after he noticed that many of these cases disappeared under the veil of civil actions that terminated in confidential settlement agreements. The most egregious claims involved death, recklessly accidental or intentional, but the sheen of the medical and pharmaceutical professions often covered up the crimes, which escaped detection for several years, if they were ever discovered at all. Under that same sheen, doctors with ready access to prescription drugs easily hid their addictions and the occasionally disastrous consequences of those addictions. If a botched prescription or surgery resulted in harm and was discovered, the perpetrator usually got off lightly with suspensions and a stint in rehab. Occasionally, a repeat offender lost a license.

Another even darker level involved the criminally insane, who chose the medical profession as a cover or alias. The prime examples of this class were Nazi concentration camp doctors, like Josef Mengele, who collected their dehumanized subjects and brutalized them for no beneficial purpose but to test useless theories of pain tolerance and physical endurance. Even in 21st century America, you could still find doctors, who on their own or in the service of criminal sociopaths, harvested blood or organs without consent while evading the watchful eyes of hospital administrators and medical boards. Van had already run into this one in one of her early cases as a medical examiner on the forensics team. Criminal medical practices like organ harvesting had been commonly treated as urban myths. But the field of clinical psychology classified these criminal acts under a mental disorder similar to Munchausen syndrome by proxy—a disorder in which a caregiver, even a parent, intentionally harms someone under their care. The industry's standard manual of mental disorders, DSM-III, called it the Frankenstein effect.

Alvin and Bobby were working with Charlie and had assembled a collection of files they called Medical and Pharmaceutical Crimes. It was only a couple of shelves, and it took Van less than a day to go through. The early cases included, not surprisingly, Nazi doctors on the run who came first to Los Angeles before being chased to South

America. These files were thick and identified crimes that mostly occurred in WWII in Germany. There were a handful cases alleging the unlicensed practice of medicine in which a family member complained that someone without a license posed as a doctor or nurse and conducted improper in-home surgeries or treatments, which led to the death or incapacitation of another family member. One file caught her attention. The parents of a UCLA medical student who died in a bizarre accident in a lab on campus had come to the LAPD and asked them to investigate her death. They had already filed a large civil suit against the University and were not satisfied with the University's explanation of what happened. The case was assigned to Detective Young, and he had accepted the University's explanation that the student died from anaphylaxis after an allergic reaction to a substance in the lab. He suspected that the parents were using the LAPD to strengthen their civil suit in order to get more money out of the University.

The file included press clippings from the time of the accident. The student, Marley Jean Dakota, was a member of a prominent Sioux family living in Cheyenne, Wyoming. Her great uncle, Russell Means, became famous in the early 1970s after he led several protests, the most famous of which occurred in Wounded Knee, South Dakota. The standoff with federal agents lasted 71days and highlighted the massacre of 350 Lakota Sioux, capturing the attention of the press and the nation. Means later became a Hollywood actor, and Marley's essay about his life and personal physical struggles helped her get admitted into the medical program at UCLA. Marley's dream was to become a specialist in Native American medicine, exploring crossover treatments using both Western medicine and traditional tribal cures. She had never complained of allergies, and her immune system had shown no indications of being compromised. She was 19 years old when she died. At the time of the press clippings, the school was refusing to release any details other than that she had had a severe allergic reaction to an unspecified substance in a medical lab. The school reported only that the reaction triggered an anaphylactic response, and Marley had suffocated from a swollen trachea before anyone was able to get her any medical treatment. The parents' civil case had focused on the school's inadequate response to Marley, but they had no details around the substance that triggered her allergic reaction.

Van took the file to Detective Young, set it on his desk, and sat down. "How can I help you, Detective?"

"Charlie and Alvin had me go through our records on medical crimes. I came across something recent."

Young looked down at the file. "The Dakota kid?"

"Yeah. Tell me what happened with this one."

"You like digging, don't you?" he asked, sounding irritated.

"I'm a nerd at heart, Detective Young. You know that. Did you know she was related to Russell Means, the actor who led Wounded Knee?"

"I saw something to that effect, but it doesn't alter my view on the case."

"Which is?"

"There is no case. It is sad but she reacted to something in the lab. Could have been anything."

"She wasn't allergic to anything, according to the records."

"She obviously was. Perhaps something new. Something she had not encountered before."

"Do you think we need to be worried?"

"I don't see why. She was the only one. No one else reacted or complained of any symptoms. Look, you understand what this really was, right?"

"What was it?" Van was careful not to sound disrespectful.

"Her parents want to make their civil case against the University, and they want to use us as leverage. I have seen it before a bunch of times. I have a problem with that."

"Ok, thanks for run down. Sorry to pull it up again."

"There are better cases, Detective. Don't waste your time."

Van picked up the file and went back to her desk. She wasn't convinced Young was right, but she wasn't sure he was wrong. She thought that if she could pursue the case further without raising any alarms, it would be worth the effort. Besides,

Detective Broad had exposed her to this line of cases for a reason. Even if that reason weren't clear, she knew she would figure it out in time.

Still, she left the office feeling frustrated and headed to the gym. She had found a women's-only gym near her parents' home in Monterey Park. She liked going thereafter work and sweating out the pressures of the day. The owner of the gym was a small, energetic Cantonese woman named Kimmie Vong. Van enjoyed being around Kimmie for several reasons. Kimmie was very direct and always confident, aspects of a personality that Van respected and tried to emulate. Kimmie was also a great trainer and had studied nutrition and Eastern medicine on her way to getting a Ph.D. in acupuncture. Van had spent many hours with Kimmie learning the nuances of Eastern medicine. It was Kimmie who had convinced Van to up her game with her training regimen and sculpt her body in order to compete in bodybuilding and fitness competitions that were becoming the rage again after steroids nearly killed the sport back in the 1980s. Van was motivated to work hard because her job required that she be in good shape. She knew that she was behind the curve because she had not risen through the ranks as a hardened police officer who became a detective. Van trained with Kimmie for a couple of years before she was able to convince Van to enter a competition. Kimmie had a friend who ran Muscle Beach and had his own entertainment company. She introduced Van to Johnny Bask and his company, JB Entertainment. Van learned from Johnny B that the bodybuilding and beauty contest industry had undergone a sea change in its shift away from human growth hormones and steroids. The competitions now celebrated the variety of body shapes and distinguished what they called a "vintage" body shape from a fitness body shape, and even that from bodybuilding. Kimmie like the vintage competitions in part because the makeup, hairstyle and old-school bathing suits were fashion-centric but also because she could enjoy a normal diet. Both fitness and bodybuilding required extra hours in the gym, and highly a specialized diet that Kimmie had undergone as a younger competitor but that she no longer felt like enduring. Her own feelings didn't affect her read on Van, who she knew was looking for a more rigorous lifestyle, and who she knew could compete at that higher level.

Van had been running her three-mile route almost every morning and going to the gym three nights a week. Kimmie helped her manage her diet and developed a workout routine that varied and prevented Van from focusing on one part of her body to the exclusion of others. Van eliminated breads and meats and began to increase her intake of vegetable proteins and eggs. She learned to make tasty vegetarian dinners and convinced herself that life without wine and red meat could still be enjoyable. She especially enjoyed watching her body tone and firm, filling out with new muscle on her calves, thighs and arms while her core tightened up. Her parents noticed the change and started telling their friends how fit she had become.

Johnny B's competitions almost always fell on holidays like Labor Day and the Fourth of July. It worked well for him because he could get more competitors to participate and more spectators to attend who happened to come down to the beach to enjoy their day off work. Kimmie rented an RV and invited Van to drive down to the competition with her. She parked the RV in the lot behind the pickle ball courts adjacent to the Muscle Beach stage.

Johnny B was good at promoting his events. He had been a fixture at Muscle Beach for decades and personally knew many of the bodybuilding stars of the early Muscle Beach years. He had a troupe of beautiful models who worked his events, directed contestants and handed out trophies to the winners. His competitors ranged in age from mid-teens to 80 years old, and the crowd especially loved watching older competitors whose commitment to fitness showed in their tight bellies and skinny but muscular arms with the extra skin of turkey necks and sagging glutes.

Johnny B's lead judge called the vintage group forward. The competitors emerged from an arched entrance and strode up a walkway, adding their best 1950s pose while wearing full body bathing suits and heels with fishnet stockings and flowers in elaborately styled hairdos. Johnny's models lined them up across the stage and the lead judge walked the contestants through a routine. Van saw Kimmie near the middle of the pack wearing a red polka-dotted bathing suit and a red rose in her hair. Van thought she had never seen such pride and confidence. Kimmie was a pro. After initial poses, the lead judge called out competitor numbers and shuffled the line, moving some contestants from the outer edges to the middle and others from the middle toward the edge. It became apparent to Van that middle was the better place to be. Kimmie managed to stay near the middle to the end and then the judge dismissed the competitors.

Van suddenly felt shy as she heard her group called forward. She stared at the bodies of the women in her class, and they all looked so perfect that she felt out of place. Kimmie came over to her and hugged her, and said, "Kill it babe. You look stunning." Van closed her eyes and, as she walked out on the stage, she could see the judges look at her and start talking to each other. She could not hear them, but she read their lips and knew they were impressed with what they were seeing in her. It gave her a boost of confidence. She walked through a series of poses and moved to the side. Her competitors did the same, gave her a courteous smile, and then showered the judges with little flirty moves as they stood there. Van thought the flirtiness was over the top and not very attractive. They called her number and a model moved her to the middle of the line. Another contestant moved from the other end of the line and then a third. By the time they were finished, Van couldn't tell if she was in the middle or not.

They dismissed the line and as they left the stage, she could see Kimmie carrying a giant smile and clapping for her. They hugged, and Kimmie said, "You did it! Now, let's go get lunch!"

They went back to the RV and Kimmie's parents had prepared a feast. Van tried to eat but the nerves from her performance kept her from having much of an appetite. Kimmie kept telling her how great she did, and, at the end of the day, Kimmie took a second place, and Van, to her shock and delight, left with a first-place trophy. Johnny B made a point of finding Van after the event and congratulating her. He told her the contestants had all been invited to a well-known celebrity's house in the Malibu Hills, and that she and Kimmie "definitely" should join him there.

The house was well lit up, and Van could see it against the night sky as she drove up the curving and never-ending driveway. The celebrity was an A-lister, who loved any excuse for a party, and the Muscle Beach events had such cache that he could be certain his many celebrity friends would join him. Van pulled up behind a line of cars that were parking along the edge of the driveway. She saw a Bentley and a Rolls Royce hanging off the edge of the asphalt as if they were Fords and Chevys. Van was wearing a tight nightclub skirt and heels, but she didn't pull any fashion cards and wanted to be low key. She was looking forward to finding a place to sit and relax— it had already been a long day, and she had been on her feet for most of it.

As she walked onto the circular drive at the entrance to the house, she was struck by two thoughts. The house looked like it belonged in England. The arched entrance was a combination of molded concrete and stonework with sharp spires extending above a steep stone-shingled roof. She also noticed that it seemed small. The house was no more than two stories and the entrance hardly larger than a common house. There was stained glass in the portico and a soft orange glow coming through the windows surrounding the entrance. She made her way to the front door hoping to see Kimmie. An older man dressed like a butler asked her name, checked a list he was holding, and allowed her to enter.

The entrance hall was full of people who seemed reluctant to press much further into the house. She slid past them, peeked into the dining room and an attached kitchen that seemed very busy. The dining room table was covered with a variety of dishes. She saw barbecued chicken and racks of lamb covered in garlic and herbs. Different food rings were pressed tightly against each other—artichoke bread and meatballs and sliders all neatly arranged around bowls of various dips. Smartly dressed waiters and waitresses hustled in and out of the dining room snatching up empty platters and replacing them with new exotic dishes. As she purveyed the foods and the activity, an attractive young man in a tight tweed suit with pointy leather shoes brushed up against her and then turned quickly and apologized. He seemed friendly and nice. She stepped down a couple of hard wood stairs into a living room with several soft leather couches and a fireplace large enough for her to stand in without stooping. The room smelled like a mountain cabin. A small fire was burning in the fireplace, or at least it seemed small. She could pick up hints of hickory chips and cedar notes. A long table with a white tablecloth had been pushed against the wall to make room for guests. On the table stood an assortment of wines on one end, reds and whites combined, and a hard liquor assortment on the other end. Bowls of olives, maraschino cherries and sliced lemons and limes stood next to the liquor bottles. Sparkling crystal wine goblets and hi-ball glasses were neatly stacked in the center of the table between the alcoholic alternatives.

"Van!" Kimmie rushed over to her. "Come! Come! Johnny B is here. Let me get you a drink! What do you take?"

Van smiled. Of course, Kimmie would be running around like she owned the place. She made Van feel welcomed and comfortable.

"Can you get me tonic with a lemon?"

They found a corner in a study near a rear sliding glass door with comfortable chairs, and Johnny B walked over with a couple of his friends. He congratulated both Kimmie and Van on their trophies and introduced his friends. Van noticed a couple of Oscars sitting on a fireplace mantle. She also saw the boy with the pointy shoes lurking across the room and trying to make eye contact. She smiled a couple of times and soon he got up his nerve to come over. Johnny B hadn't seen him come over but when he did, he put on a big smile. He turned, and said, "Ladies, please meet the owner of this fine home—the famous actor Martin Richard."

Martin blushed. "Well, my parents are the famous actors, and still own the home," he admitted. "But they spend most of their time in New York City and the Seychelles."

Kimmie recognized him. "You were in the movie Cat's Last Scratch, correct?" She looked wide-eyed at Van. "I love horror movies, and that was one of the best I've seen." Martin smiled and said thank you. He held his hand out to Van, and said, "And you are?" Van introduced herself. Johnny B boasted on Van's behalf of her victory earlier. Van was careful to appreciate Johnny B and his pride in the competition.

"I am still surprised," she said. "The other girls were amazing."

Martin responded, "I am not surprised." Van blushed. "Would you like to see the back yard?" he asked.

She looked at Kimmie and smiled. "That would be very nice," she said. Kimmie winked at Van and watched as Martin and Van exited the sliding glass doors onto a balcony and down a metal staircase.

The view from the back of the house was stunning. The sun was just setting and the Malibu Hills to the East, loaded with red bark manzanita bushes and coastal sage scrub, were taking on an amber tint. The Pacific Ocean on the West reflected the pinks and oranges in the sky and the dark tips of the Channel Islands fell off the horizon to the North. The balcony was covered in flowers. Pots of blooming azaleas and mums hung from above and the railings were lined with red marigolds. As Van descended the spiral metal staircase, she noticed a small grass area below her with lawn chairs set up to watch the sunset and the lights of a large pool glowed up to the right. She looked behind her into a glassed-in game room with a large pool table, a Golden Tee arcade game and a wet bar. Several olive trees dotted the perimeter of the gardens surrounding the grass area and were lit with small, white light strands. Around the grass and the pool stood clusters of guests.

Martin walked up to a group on the grass passing a joint around. Someone offered Van a hit, and she politely turned it down. Martin, who seemed in need of some relaxation, gladly took a hit and passed it back.

"I noticed the Oscars," Van said to Martin."

He laughed. "Not mine. My parents have had some success."

"Would I recognize their work?"

"Are you a movie person?"

"I actually prefer to read," she responded candidly. "But I have seen a few."

"Well, my father is an actor turned director, and my mother played the lead in one of his better films. That is how they met."

"Kind of romantic."

"For them it was. They had me, and then got married... But they do love each other, unlike so many others out here."

"Are you happy?"

"I suppose. I need to find a way to become my own person. I am known more around these parts as their son and not for my own accomplishments."

"I am sure your time will come," Van offered encouragingly. Martin smiled. A blond with a tattooed arm standing next to him and smoking a cigarette offered them something that looked like ecstasy or molly. Van shook her head and Martin declined, though Van wondered if he were declining on her account. Two forty-ish men saw the blond with the pills and bounced over to the group.

"Don't mind if we do," one of them said, and they took the pills and bounced away.

The tattooed blond looked at Martin, and said, "I am sorry, but I overheard your conversation." She leaned into both Van and Martin, and said quietly, as if to let them in on a secret, "You know that if you want to succeed in Hollywood, there really is only one way." Martin glanced over at Van with a 'here we go again' look but she could tell he didn't want to be impolite so early in the night.

"And what would that be?"

"If your parents haven't told you yet, someone should."

"Go ahead. Please. I'd love to know if there is a formula."

"I wouldn't call it a formula exactly."

"Okay."

"The trick is you need to be a member."

Now, Van thought, this could go several ugly ways. Hollywood had battled a lot of accusations of bias, and this drug-toting blond didn't look particularly intelligent. But maybe she had something to say. Maybe she was into Scientology. Maybe she knew something new about the guilds.

"A member of what?" Martin asked, his brow furrowing.

"You've heard of the Illuminati, I am sure."

"I have but educate me."

She smiled. "Of course, you already know. It's like this secret society of the world's most powerful people. They control Hollywood, movies and TV, and if you really want fame and fortune, you need to be a part of the movement. Everybody who is anybody is into it."

Martin had met many stars, and he had yet to be invited to an Illuminati party. "Is there a cost to join? A membership fee?"

"Oh well, yeah," she said, laughing. "It's dark if you want to know. You have to really want badly to become an A-lister. They have rituals. There is devil worship and orgies. I don't know," she added almost condescendingly, "but you don't look like you would be a member."

"As a matter of fact, I am," he said with a light sarcastic bite, and Van's eyes narrowed. "My great-great-great grandfather, if you really want to know, was a Bavarian nationalist who opposed the undue influence of the Catholic church and its superstitions in eastern Germany. He helped start the Bavarian Illuminati and persuaded the French hoi polloi to revolt against their monarchy." He leaned close to the tattooed blond, and whispered, "He personally knew Goethe, who was also a member." Then to the group who looked both stoned and mesmerized, he said, "Sad to say that eventually the German government quashed the movement and only a few Illuminati survived. I am the only living descendent."

The tattooed blond stood there for a moment with her mouth gaping, not sure how to respond. She gathered herself, took a draw on the cigarette, and under her smoky breath, she said, "I knew it."

"In fact," Martin added, "we have a secret ritual going on right now. I am sorry to have to leave but, you know, planes to catch, people to meet, babies to kill." He winked at the tattooed blond and pulled Van away toward another group up by the pool.

"That was fun," she said wryly.

"I can't stand it," he replied, "but I suppose that's obvious." His smart phone buzzed and flashed, and he turned away as he took a brief call. "I am sorry, but I need to leave." He pointed to the group by the pool, and said,

"Introduce yourself. They are a much more interesting crowd." He turned to leave, and then turned back and smiled, "Very nice to meet you."

The crowd by the pool was more animated, if not more interesting. A heated debate was going on about the new president. "He is a misogynist and a moron," a tall, dark-haired woman was saying.

"First, he is not a misogynist," replied a hefty young man wearing glasses and a bow tie. "Unless you think all men are misogynists, but that would be idiotic, and you do not strike me as an idiot. He gives his daughter a prominent role in everything he does and regularly hires women to lead his projects."

"Those moves are covers for him. He is a playboy and seeks out beautiful women as props to satisfy his ego. You know he had his own beauty pageant, right?" saying this, she turned and walked away in a huff, as if she didn't want to waste her time with someone so uneducated.

Bow Tie looked at Van and smiled. "Most of the misogynists I know hire women as a cover." He shook his head and chuckled. A rather intense-looking young woman, who was standing next to Bow Tie, looked at Van and said, "So what do you think about our new president?"

"I don't think he really knew what he was getting into and I don't think he expected to win," said Van.

"I think you are probably right on the latter part," the young woman responded.

Van shrugged. "My family is grateful to be here and does not take the country and its freedoms for granted. But I don't view that as a political stance. I hope whoever leads us does well."

"That's fair," Bow Tie said, jumping in quickly to keep his friend from pushing Van too hard.

The intense one got the hint but added, "There are a lot of people at this party who would love to see this president fall on his face."

Martin walked back up to Van and the new group. With him was a handsome older gentleman wearing a blazer and jeans with Top Siders and no socks. Van's first thought was East Coast, and she soon found out she was right. Martin introduced him as Marshall Turner from Washington, D.C.

"Good evening," Marshall said to the group.

Bow Tie stepped forward quickly, and said, "Pleased to meet you, sir."

The intense one asked rather boldly, "What brings you to the Left Coast?"

Marshall chuckled. "I am heading up to the Bay Area, but I stopped here first to see some friends."

Van was quiet. She had already decided that she would not tell anyone that she was an LAPD detective. She was enjoying the party and entertained by the conversations—not the usual. She didn't want people to feel reserved around her and she was not there to judge. She excused herself and found Kimmie still hanging with Johnny B.

"I am going to get a drink," Van said to Kimmie. "Want to join me?"

"Absolutely," Kimmie responded. As they walked toward the bar, Kimmie asked, "Are you enjoying the party?"

"I am," Van answered. "Some interesting people here."

"Do you find Martin interesting?"

"Sure. I think he is a busy guy. But he is nice and isn't full of himself."

"Maybe," said Kimmie. "He would be a nice person to know."

"Maybe," Van responded and smiled.

They found a couple of seats by the pool. It was dark by now and Martin had set up a couple of heaters so his guests could enjoy the night comfortably. The crowd was getting loud and two fully clothed women had already jumped into the pool. Van could see a couple of rather serious conversations going on nearby. A tall pretty blond was sitting on a small garden wall wiping tears away. Van hoped it was just a bad audition or romantic sadness and not something worse. As she was thinking about it, Marshall Turner walked by and looked down at Van. "We met right?" he said. "But I am not certain I got your name."

"We did. My name is Van, and this is my good friend Kimmie."

Kimmie said 'hi,' and Marshall said, "Do you mind if I join you?"

"Not at all," Van replied. He pulled up a deck chair next to Van and sat down.

"It must be late for you," Van said.

She looked at Kimmie, and said, "Marshall is from Washington DC."

"It's a bit late," he said. "I find myself on the West Coast quite a bit."

"What is it you do?" Van asked.

"Whatever people need me to do. I suppose I am a political consultant. I don't like the word lobbyist, but I probably qualify. I connect people. Sometimes they are businesspersons, sometimes politicians, and sometimes both." Marshall was anything but shy. "What about yourselves?"

Kimmie jumped in. "I own a fitness resort for women."

Van added, "That is how we met. Kimmie is my trainer."

"Fitness is a huge industry but complicated to manage," Marshall said.

"Exactly," Kimmie replied, pleased that he seemed interested. "You have everything from corporate megacomplexes to individual trainers working out of their homes."

"Do you think the mega-gyms will drive out the individuals?" Marshall asked.

"They certainly make it harder and not just for individual trainers—any small business. But I don't see how the math works for them. They drive the price down to nothing and need to cover giant leases. Doesn't make sense to me."

"Interesting," Marshall said. "What about you?" he asked Van.

"I am undercover cop," Van said and laughed. Marshall seemed startled just a bit and then laughed as well, getting the joke. "Sorry," Van said. "Actually, I am a chemist," Van said, which was partially true.

"Really?" said Marshall. "Biochemistry?"

"Well," she said, getting a bit nervous that she had opened a line of discussion that might be better to avoid. "I work with DNA." Kimmie watched Van and stayed quiet.

"That is very interesting," Marshall said. "Have you done anything in the nano space?"

"Why do you ask?"

"I have a couple of nano clients. They are trying to get it going. Nanotechnology is not fully accepted yet. It will be but the public needs to get comfortable with it."

"You are making it more acceptable?"

"I suppose you could say that," he said. "Actually, I am trying to keep it from dying out before it has the chance to prove itself."

"I know very little about it," Van admitted. "I have heard that there are applications in the treatment of cancer, but not much beyond that."

Marshall replied, "A lot of possibilities as I understand it. It turns out there are many important environmental applications. It can decompose oil spills, plastic waste, landfills. That sort of thing."

"Is that what you are working on?"

"Well, let's save that discussion for another time," he said, grinning.

"Yes," said Van. She looked at Kimmie, "And I need to get going. It's been a long day, and I have a long trip home. Very nice to meet you, Mr. Turner."

Marshall stood and graciously said, "I hope I didn't offend. Very nice to meet the both of you. I do hope we meet again." Van smiled thinking that she could not imagine why or how that would happen.

Chapter 10.

The Star of Bethlehem

Fifty million years ago, a large island north of Australia and east of Madagascar in the center of what is now called the Indian Ocean began drifting north through the equator and toward the southwest coast of pre-historic Tibet. The northeast boundary of this giant tectonic island, now called India, gradually made its way northeast until it slammed into the coast of its northern neighbor. What happened next is a matter of scientific debate, but one theory has the northeastern edge of the island plunging under the coast of Tibet and forcing that coast tens of thousands of feet into the sky, forming what we now call the Himalayas. The term *Himalaya* comes from the Sanskrit word *hima* meaning 'snow' and *laya* which carries multiple meanings ranging from 'residence' and 'temple' to 'tempo' or 'timing' in poetry, speech and music. *Laya* also can mean 'melt' or 'dissolve' and the Himalayas, the most famous, most inspiring and most impressive mountain range on the planet, the result of a journey across an ocean and a massive continental collision, in combination, is perfectly captured as *the temple of melting snows.*

The Himalayan Mountain Range spans 2,400 kilometers or roughly 1,500 miles. The range begins in the southeast in the country of Bhutan and then runs northwest in a crescent shape through Nepal and around Tibet to the several states in northern India, then into the disputed regions of Jammu and Kashmir in northern Pakistan, finally settling at their northernmost point in the Badakhshan National Park in south-central Tajikistan.

Garne "Garny" McDonough, the co-founder of Providia, who broke away after Providia decided its core competency would be video gaming, formed his own electronic medical device company called MetaMed that he set up in Sunnyvale, California, around the corner from Providia. Garny had a long and tortured history with the FDA, and it was only with the help of investment bankers like Derek Whitestone that Garny was able to keep MetaMed operating, drawing its revenue from a small number of myoelectric prosthetics that he was able to integrate into muscle fibers allowing people to control the prosthetic naturally. But Garny's big idea was to push the integration into the Central Nervous System so that motion would be controlled by the brain. Garny's breakthrough came when he discovered MEMS and began using smart dust as a robotic device integrator. He refashioned his prosthetics using robotics and created small chips embedded with nanobots that were receptive to brain waves as a means of controlling the prosthetics. The FDA had not been friendly to the use of electronic brain implants, and most of Garny's ideas ended up in FDA shredders.

The FDA debacles convinced Garny to rethink his business plan, and as he learned more about MEMS and smart dust, he began to envision other money-making applications. One issue that especially caught his attention, and he felt might be susceptible to a MEMS-based solution was climate change. Gary didn't really care whether the apocalyptic scenarios of Senator Al Gore were credible. He didn't care if climate change itself was a problem. What he did care about was that a convincingly large sector of the scientific community accepted the evidence that the earth was rapidly heating up, and that at least one cause of the rise in temperature was waste from primarily human activity. Nanobots were already capable of transporting chemicals, and if there were a cost-effective system that might reduce the volume of carbon emissions from cars, factories, landfills, livestock and deforestation by removing it from the air or converting it into water or some other harmless compound, both the government and the industry would pay enormously for that capability. The problem with "direct air capture" was not only its cost but the amount of energy required to make it happen. Even so, the United States government was willing to spend tens of millions of dollars to support technologies advancing direct air capture. Scientists also were exploring carbon mineralization—a normally very slow process that turns CO_2 gases into solids. By exposing CO_2 to certain minerals, the process of mineralization might be sped up, and the gas that is warming the planet could be converted to crystals and made to fall out of the sky like snow.

Garny decided to educate himself and expand his new business network. He attended a series of climate change conferences sponsored by the United Nations and various universities. He studied the Paris Agreement and the Kyoto Protocol and familiarized himself with the chemical properties of the six greenhouse gases:

carbon dioxide, methane, nitrous oxide, hydroflourocarbons, perflourocarbons and sulfur hexafluoride. He met some of the world's top environmental scientists and paid to bring them to his MetaMed offices in Sunnyvale. He introduced them to the engineers in his office working with nanotechnology and encouraged them to collaborate on the use of smart dust for high volume direct air capture and carbon mineralization. He developed a pro forma that he shopped to Derek Whitestone and his favorite venture capitalists, and he got an initial round of $500 million to begin developing an atmospheric carbon scrubbing technology. He would not make the same mistake this time that he made with MetaMed. This time he would prove his technology works and would share its benefits with countries and businesses operating outside the United States. The regulatory Nazis at the FDA would not be allowed to touch his creation until the demand for the product was so great that they would effectively have no choice but to approve it.

Half a billion dollars gave him a lot of options, and he had only two criteria. First, he needed to be free of regulation. Second, he wanted to be someplace inspiring. Several of his new environmentalist friends had been to Nepal and a couple had climbed Mount Everest. Garny thought of his new venture as akin to scaling his own Mount Everest and the prospect of living and working in or near the Himalayas thrilled him. The fall of the Soviet Union and its breakup into the many separate nations that had once formed the Union created unique opportunities for a Silicon Valley startup to find an inexpensive, exotic and very hidden base of operations. He searched the Himalayan range for a location and drew some quick conclusions. He decided that Nepal was too touristy and that Bhutan and the states in Northern India and Pakistan were too unstable.

But as his finger tracked north, he found Tajikistan, and Dushanbe—the Tajik capital with 800,000 people. He learned that Tajikistan had resisted the Russian Revolution of 1917 and played a central role in the Basmachi Revolt that along with Uzbekistan, resisted absorption in the Soviet Union. Rather, the two countries formed the Autonomous Soviet Socialist Republics of the Soviet Union, which were maintained until the dissolution of the Soviet Union in 1991. The Tajiks had several disputes with Armenia mostly, because until recently, the largest minority in Tajikistan was its Armenian population. But Armenia was more distracted by its neighbor Azerbaijan, and both were a thousand miles away on the other side of the Caspian Sea. Like its southern neighbor, Afghanistan, Tajikistan experienced its own internal conflicts, the results of which were brutal. There were claims of ethnic cleansing, which prompted international involvement, and eventually, the country settled down after it was occupied by an international peacekeeping force comprising American, Indian and French troops. In fact, Tajikistan had become somewhat of a refuge for the embattled residents of the surrounding countries. War weary and scarred by the religious zealotry of its southern neighbors, refugees fled to Dushanbe, the population exploded, and Dushanbe became a thriving metropolis. Thus, though not due to its own will or desire, Tajikistan was growing into a pluralistic society with elements of European, Russian, Indian and Middle Eastern cultures all blending together.

Garny took his two lead engineers and flew to Delhi, and then north to Dushanbe. They spent the next week traveling around Dushanbe and then out to the Nurek Reservoir and the surrounding Districts of Republican Subordination, a political division of land managed by the central government not unlike the District of Columbia. They took a small plane to the Jirgatol airport, where they caught a bumpy helicopter ride over the Himalayan foothills through Pamirsky and Badakhshan National Parks to Karakul Lake, a beautiful horseshoe shaped, glacier-fed lake near the border of Kyrgyzstan, 32 miles across and resting at 13,000 feet above sea level. Karakul Lake was known for two reasons. First, it was the location of one of the largest impact craters in the hemisphere, formed by a meteor 20 million years ago. The lake, at its deepest point was 750 feet. Second, it was surrounded by marshes, peat bogs, and pebbly and sandy plains that were home to a remarkable number of unique bird species. BirdLife International identified it as an Important Bird Area (IBA), and the Ramsar Convention listed it as an important waterfowl habitat. The helicopter landed near a small village on the Pamir Highway that had grown up on the lake shoreline. Once a poor and barely surviving village, a small amount of tourism related to the growth of Dushanbe and the annual Roof of the World Regatta revived the village, and it had a small market and a couple of restaurants. Garny and his team suited up and began a trek around the lake, climbing to about 14,000 feet where they found an abandoned Hindu temple built into the cliffs, a thousand feet above the lake. The temple looked across the lake directly to the Himalayas, and Garny knew he had found his dream location for working on smart dust, away from prying eyes and America's robotic regulators.

Over the next year, he flew in construction materials, set up a solar farm for power that he shared with the village, and constructed a road through the mountains to serve the new lab. He also built a helicopter pad so that he could get quickly to Jirgatol, and from there to Dushanbe. A couple of Hindu priests discovered what he was doing and threatened to start a protest, and he gave them funds to build a separate temple on the other side of the lake and they disappeared. After a year, he had a functioning lab operating literally in the middle of nowhere with heated bunks and a full kitchen and dining area. He set up a company and named it TKP Inc., which stood for The Karakul Proposition. His team initially comprised American, Russian and Swedish climatologists, whom he had met at various conferences in Geneva, Warsaw and Doha, and through Columbia University's collaboration with the United Nations Climate Action group in New York. He added to his own team from Sunnyvale biomolecular engineers from the University of Chicago and MIT. He got them to join him in Tajikistan to develop this world-changing technology, both by convincing them to buy into his vision to develop a technology that might mitigate global warming, and by giving them each a compelling salary and a 0.5% profit share in any products developed out of the Lab. He added the incentive that the profit share would double to 1.0% for any products finalized in the first twelve months. But to be a part of the team, there were two conditions. First, they had to agree to living at the Lab continuously for a year, and second, they had to sign a nondisclosure agreement, which if they violated, they would forfeit any profit share and unpaid salary.

Garny had a singular vision for TKP. Producing a nanobot that could direct air capture carbon dioxide molecules was a first step, but he suspected that would be easy. What he needed, and the specific capability that would launch him ahead of his Silicon Valley counterparts, was a new means of ultra-high-volume manufacturing. He had left his competitors in the slough of impenetrable regulatory hurdles and political and social opposition to MEMS and wanted to prove it made a difference. Garny had read about the possibility of self-replication in Eric Dressler's 1986 work, Engines of Creation, but the actual means to trigger self-replication technology remained elusive and mostly science fiction over the intervening decades. Still, Garny had come up an idea.

The team settled into its remote mountain retreat. Several members made special requests for foods that reminded them of home, and Garny had a supply chain set up to bring special delicacies and supplies regularly to the retreat. He softened on his insistence that his team remain at the retreat the entire time, and he organized special trips around the region for them to enjoy. But the team was aware that they were there to develop something novel and highly challenging, and that they were incentivized to get it done within 12 months. He had a well-known motivational speaker brought in to lead brainstorming discussions that were held in the Lab's ornate conference room, with a marble table Garny had handmade in Dushanbe, and a reinforced plate glass window that looked out over the lake and onto the Himalayas.

Garny stood at the head of the horseshoe-shaped table, framed by the mountain scene behind him. He listened to some good, even brilliant ideas about the conditions necessary for something non-organic to grow—most of which focused on the nature of crystallization inspired in part no doubt by the harsh wintery conditions of the mountain lab. He allowed all those ideas to play themselves out, and then launched into his own:

"So how do you solve the problem of self-replication? You start by accepting that you are not God. You are not being asked to create something out of nothing—ex nihilo. But, in fact, you do not need to be a god. The building blocks of life do not require magic—they only require two things: coincidence and attraction. The right particles must meet at the right time. And they must want to meet. So how do you increase the probability of that combination? That part is easy. You find the elements common to the solution, and you increase them until they reach a saturation point—in short, you increase coincidence to the point where there is virtually no instance in which the elements do not meet. You increase co-incidence to the point that coincidence disappears. The problem then becomes attraction. How do you take elements that otherwise exist completely independent of each other and induce them to combine. How would you take a room full of hydrogen and oxygen atoms and turn that into water?"

"That is nothing new," replied Dr. Sadifur Farroush, one of Garny's key MIT colleagues. "You charge it." He paused. "Very carefully, mind you." The room laughed and Dr. Farroush continued. "Electromagnetism. The right temperature and the right charge and electrons begin to fall like pebbles, and snap! Hydrogen rushes in to fill the gap, and you get H_2O—water, enough of which becomes rain. There it is."

"Okay," said Garny. "Thank you. Simple question, simple answer. But we are not trying to make it rain. So let's talk about something more complex. How does a cell replicate?"

"Cytokinesis," answered one of the biomolecular specialists.

"Talk us through that," said Garny.

"Cytokinesis is the process by which a single cell splits into two cells." He went on to describe spindle apparatus and chromatids and all features needed for cell replication. The question everyone was asking themselves as he spoke was how to take a biological process, the miracle of life, and convert it to a mechanical process.

"Okay," Garny concluded. "We know that life self-replicates. We need something that is not life to do the same. Again, let's return to the question of attraction. Dr. Farroush proposes electromagnetism. No doubt an element. Here is what I propose, and then I would ask you to take it and break it apart and see where it takes us. I have been intrigued recently by viruses. We know that they exist in a passive state outside their host cells as virions—miniature protein packets that have no impact on life. The magic of viruses is that they find a way to fake attraction. They lure host cells into consuming them and that is where their devilish impacts begin, because it is only after they are inside a host cell that they begin to replicate at paranormal speeds. I propose that we find the magic trigger of viruses and convert that into a mechanical process."

His comments started loud conversation as the group broke up and the teammates returned to their labs and cubbies to begin to build a virus-based model of nanorobotic self-replication. Within six months, they had constructed a nanorobot capable of capturing CO_2. The new nanorobot was controlled by a central sphere with spike-like projections that moved in and out around the sphere's vertical and horizontal axes. The vertical spike at the southernmost end of the sphere was slightly larger than the horizontal spikes at the equator, and the northernmost spike, employed a gyroscopic effect to keep the nanorobot vertical. Someone noticed that it appeared to sparkle like a star in the night sky. Garny named it the Star of Bethlehem, after the star in the Book of Matthew that guided the three wise men to King Herod in Jerusalem. As the story goes, Herod called his scribes, who then cited scriptures about the Messiah, and those discussions eventually led the wise men to a Bethlehem stable in which the newborn child of Mary and Joseph lay swaddled in a manger.

Within nine months, The Karakul Proposition's team used Garny's virus concepts, and identified the conditions required for basic self-replication. The problem was that the process was too slow. They needed an engine—a feature capable of driving replication at higher speeds. Someone suggested superconductivity, and the team quickly realized that the solution was not in the process; it was in the materials they were using to fashion the nanorobots. They converted the nanorobots to a superconductive ceramic design, and self-replication took off like a flash. At this point, the only limiting factor that contained the volume of the production was the size of the chamber in which self-replication occurred. Garny was beside himself. His experiment was working, and he wanted to introduce it to the world as soon as possible.

There was another small problem. As with any new technology, accidents occur, and Garny had lost several of his team members to heart attacks and strokes that seemed to be caused by food or other allergens present in the Lab. He suspected that the elevation was a factor, but he also credited the speedy results of his team to the low atmospheric density at 14,000 feet. It was the closest anyone had come to manufacturing in the pure vacuum of space, and to Garny, it was a necessary and acceptable risk. The accidents were unfortunate, and Garny was overly generous to the families of the deceased scientists.

Chapter 11.

A Genuis, A Billionaire and a Lobbyist Walk into a Bar

The shock of the smart dust exposure stayed with Brian for several days. The specific lab he had worked in was still closed, following protocol for spills of any toxic or infectious agents, and the advanced protocol for Risk Group IV contaminants. The Lab had placed Dr. Carrie Comstock on paid leave for 90 days. The Tran Labs was well known for taking care of its employees, and Carrie had already been told that if she were concerned about returning to Bainbridge, the Lab would find her another posting. Carrie came from a military family. Her goal was to advance research on infectious diseases, and she knew the best place to do that was at the Tran Labs. Within two weeks, she was back at work with Dr. Johannsen. He marvelled at her stamina and strength. Carrie's resilience gave Brian courage to resume his review of the nanoparticles in the petri dish. He dug into MEMS and learned the different functions that MEMS devices could perform and the different features that had been built into these devices. He asked Carrie what purpose she thought the spikes served, and they posited initially that the spikes were intended to latch onto and penetrate something like a cell membrane. The spikes allowed the device to act like a virus.

They convinced T cell lymphocytes to consume the nanobots. But at that point, even though the cell itself was reacting to this foreign object, the device would go dormant and seemed to serve no further purpose. One possibility was that the only purpose served by the device was to activate killer cytokines, as if it were a biological weapon. But it was just as likely that the cell's reaction to the device was unintentional, whether anyone else had encountered the same reaction or not. They assumed something somewhere had happened, which would explain why the petri dish was labeled Risk Group IV. Brian and Carrie both agreed that building a microrobot for the sole purpose of eliciting a cytokinetic response was too simple an answer, notwithstanding Occam's razor and the notion that the simplest explanation is usually the correct one. Anaphylaxis might be used as a weapon, but it made no sense to go to the trouble of manufacturing a microscopic robot just to cause an allergic reaction, however powerful.

Brian knew that MEMS engineers were working on a use in the treatment of cancer, and he thought maybe the device could be programmed to target specific cells, and then some other force, like electromagnetic energy from something benign like radiofrequencies, might cause the device to attack and kill the cancer cells, something like a B cell lymphocyte. Or perhaps the EME would simply heat up the device and burn up the cell from the inside out. Brian experimented with various frequencies, but it was the same in every case, nothing happened. It was Carrie who suggested that the purpose of the spikes might not be for penetration and damage, but rather to grab something. They tried mixing the devices with blood. There was activity but it seemed hardly detectable. Carrie thought she noticed an attraction to CO_2 and that triggered the break-though.

Brian had a nurse at the Lab withdraw blood from one of his veins and contain it in a vacuum so it would not become oxygenated. They combined the nanomaterial with the de-oxygenated blood and the little robots went wild, flying around red blood cells that were emitting carbon dioxide molecules and snatching the molecules out of the plasma. Each robot grabbed hundreds of molecules before it went dormant. They decided to try an experiment with gas. They filled the vacuum chamber with carbon dioxide and then opened a container with a minute bit of the petri dish substrate. The devices activated immediately and flew around the chamber like a dust storm and the CO_2 levels dropped rapidly as the CO_2 stuffed devices collected on the bottom of the chamber. Brian and Carrie were amazed at the singular purpose these devices seemed to serve. But they still had no idea what the larger purpose might be.

Brian and Carrie wrote up the results of their studies. When they were done, the report was more than 100 pages long and complete with details not only regarding the makeup of the particles but also their structure and apparent function. The report included images from the electron microscope depicting CO_2 capture. They also found evidence of self-replication but included that in an appendix because the process was not apparent and didn't make sense to them. Brian and Carrie presented the report to Dr. Meisner, who was friendly to Carrie but still angry about the accident and the effect of some of the local press on the Lab's reputation.

He flipped through the report and asked them only "What does it do?"

Brian replied, "It captures CO_2."

Dr. Meisner was impressed, not an uncommon response to his staff's scientific analysis. "But what purpose might that serve?"

"I don't know. Fight global warming?"

Dr. Meisner laughed. Brian looked at Carrie, and they both chuckled as well. "We can't come up with a good medical reason for capturing CO_2. When oxygen levels drop, CO_2 levels increase in the blood causing hypoxia, which can become toxic, but the usual solution is not to try and reduce CO_2. The solution is to add oxygen."

Dr. Meisner crossed his arms and touched his chin. It was one of his typical moves when he wanted you to think he had a brilliant idea. "Industrial applications?"

"Yes. Possibly. If you could manufacture enough of these, they might have some impact on carbon emissions. Perhaps they could be used in some kind of advanced catalytic converter and reduce industrial pollutants. It's a thought. But the volume that you would need to have any real impact is so great, even that application is tough to imagine."

"The problem," Brian added, "whether the application is industrial or medical, is the cytokine storm these particles cause in humans. Whether or not they might perform some useful task, the risk that they would get released to the public is a risk too great to imagine."

Dr. Meisner stood his ground, but his tone became dismissive. "All due respect to both of your frightening experiences, but toxicity is rarely a justification for impeding progress. Give it some more thought. Maybe we should get Fred back and see what his reaction might be."

Carrie was beside herself when they left Dr. Meisner's office. "Can you believe that?"

Brian had seen enough of it to not be surprised. He knew that Meisner needed any ideas coming from the Lab to be his own first, before they would be allowed to trickle down to staff, and if he didn't have an idea, he wasn't interested. He thanked Carrie and told her that without her input, they wouldn't be where they were now. Whether or not it would lead to anything ground-breaking, or at least interesting, was yet to be determined. Brian did not have much interest in meeting Fred, but he acknowledged that Fred was a smart guy and might add something. He took off in the Gold Wing for home. The days were getting shorter now and it was already dark, not his favorite time to ride. But the road was open, and as he was passing through Grand Forest West, his phone buzzed. He clicked on the Bluetooth in his helmet. "Hello!" he shouted, slowing the bike to reduce the engine noise.

"Dr. Johannsen!?" someone on the other end also shouted.

"Yes? Can I help you!?" Brian spoke still loudly.

"My name is Marshall Turner! I am here with Fred Schmidt!"

"Just a minute!" Brian pulled the bike off the road onto a side street and shut it down. "I'm sorry. It sounded like you said you were with Fred Schmidt."

"I am. We are here at the Harbour Public House having a pint. Do you have time to join us?"

"I know the place. I am less than15 minutes away. I'd be happy to meet you guys there." Brian jumped back on his bike and took off down Miller Road, which turned into Fletcher Bay Road. He made a left on High School Road and then right on Madison Avenue, which took him most of the rest of the way. Harbour Public House had a small bar that looked out over Harbour Marina. As Brian rode, he thought about what he might say to Fred Schmidt. He expected it to be a candid night. He shut off the bike and walked into the bar with his full leathers on. Fred noticed him right away and came over to the hostess and motioned him in toward the bar where they had a window view of the marina's night lights. Seated at the table were Marshall Turner, whom Brian assumed had called him, and Dr. Stan Meisner. Brian was surprised although he showed no reaction.

"Stan."

"Hello, Brian. Good to see you."

"And Mr. Turner, I presume?"

"That would be me. I have heard a lot about you, Brian. Dr. Meisner had some remarkable things to say. It's a pleasure."

"You good with Guinness?" Fred started.

"Who isn't?" Brian answered back and sat down.

Mincing no words, Fred started the conversation. "It seems that I am the one responsible for almost killing Dr. Johannsen and his colleague Dr. Comstock."

Brian could see that Fred was not afraid to speak his mind. Even though he still was mad, Fred's candor started to win him over.

"Well, in all fairness," Brian said, "there was a warning label. Once we realized what it was, we let ourselves get too relaxed."

Dr. Meisner jumped in. "And what was it, Brian? What did you find?"

Brian studied the table, gauging to see if he was explaining something they already knew. But their interest betrayed them. They stared at Brian, hungry to hear what he had to say. "Ok. Well, the first thing we noticed was that it wasn't biological. That means the dish was mislabeled. It should not have said Risk Group IV. But in fact, it turned out to be just about as dangerous as a Risk Group IV or Biosafety Level IV substance. It caused an almost immediate anaphylactic reaction in my colleague Dr. Comstock, who, as Mr. Schmidt indicated, almost died from it."

Marshall Turner responded, "Just to keep everything on the right level, because not all of us here are highly regarded members of the scientific community, what did you call the reaction you and your colleague had, and what does that mean?"

Marshall came across as sketchy to Brian. He assumed he needed to be careful around him. "It's nothing more than a severe allergic reaction that causes a lot of problems but the most serious is that your lungs and your throat begin to swell up. You can suffocate if it's not treated correctly, and doctors hate it because it is very hard to control."

Dr. Meisner tried to redirect the conversation back to what interested Fred Schmidt. "That's good, Brian. The nanoparticles—what are they for? What purpose?"

"I guess that's the billion-dollar question" Brian answered with a smirk. Fred chuckled at the joke, but he reminded himself of the uncertainties of working with a wunderkind.

"The most we could figure out in the time we have had so far is that they seem especially attracted to carbon dioxide."

Fred responded, "So would you consider them shuttles?"

"If what you mean is a device that transports some type of medicine to damaged cells, no. Not in the true sense of a nanobot shuttle. They do carry CO_2 molecules but not to any destination. As soon as they acquire as many molecules as they can carry, they go dormant and settle at the base of the chamber."

"Like a decontaminant?" Marshall asked.

"I suppose."

Fred said, "Ok. Let's assume we are looking at a CO_2 filtration system. Does it seem efficient? Can a small amount of these particles filter a large quantity of CO_2? Perhaps on something like a spaceship, where CO_2 filtration might be especially important?"

"Not certain about that application, but it will take more work to figure out. If what we are looking at is an environmental application and not a medical application, my first guess is no. You would need real volume to have any broad impact."

Marshall thought about Providia's request for the rights to control nanomanufacturing but said nothing. Fred's wheels were spinning.

"Let's assume there is something here. How do we deal with the effect on humans? Can we assume this is something we can get a hold of or not?"

"Right now, there is no way to know. Dr. Comstock's reaction was immediate and almost immediately fatal. It's only because we are a Biosafety Level IV lab that we contained it and saved her life. Honestly, we can't take this lightly."

"But you can study it," Fred said. "Let's give it another round. I want to know the use cases, and I want to know if we can make it safe. I don't care how much it costs."

Brian saw Dr. Meisner's eyes light up, but he quickly composed himself. "We'll let you know what we need, Mr. Schmidt."

"One more thing," Fred added, and looked over at Marshal. "I have heard that Providia has AI software that might help with manufacturing."

"One of the few," Marshall responded, keeping his cards close.

"Derek Whitestone sent his team over to gauge how far along they were. His sense was that they were very close. Is that your sense, Marshall?"

"They have spoken with me." Marshall knew this game well. He knew that Fred expected absolute candor, and he knew that they might have told Fred about their interaction with him, but he did not know that for sure. "I would say they are close because they seem to think they need some help in Washington."

"Are they going to get it?"

"I don't know yet. It's not a done deal."

"All right, well, whatever is happening there, if we have something here, we are going to need to be strategic. More to discuss, then. Very good, gentlemen," Fred concluded.

Brian drained the pint in front of him and cordially dismissed himself from the group and headed back to his bike. Dr. Meisner did the same, but he was more of a Jaguar guy. Fred and Marshall sat there a bit longer.

"I like the kid," Marshall said.

"Still to be determined," said Fred. "He has real potential. Let's see what he can do with it."

Chapter 12.

Trials by Ice and Fire

Garny locked himself in his office adjacent to the Lab's main conference room. He removed a picture hanging behind his deck of which he was especially proud. The picture was taken in Warren Buffet's lodge in Sun Valley, Idaho, and showed him standing next to the top CEOs in the country including Jeff Bezos from Amazon, Elon Musk from Tesla, Tim Cook from Apple, Fred Schmidt from Grindle, Larry Ellison from Oracle, Larry Page from Alphabet, and Lloyd Blankfein from Goldman Sachs. He opened the safe behind the photo and pulled out an Iridium satellite phone he had been using to stay in contact with the world while his team labored in the labs below.

"We did it."

Franklin Everhart, billionaire playboy and founder of the philanthropy WeGive.com listened. Franklin was the son of William Everhart, the real estate mogul who built most of downtown San Francisco, and Garny's best friend. He had helped Garny get Providia off the ground.

"What exactly did you do?"

What Garny did was build a massive self-contained vacuum chamber at the foot of the ridge surrounding Karakul Lake. He hired local labor, who willingly dug a giant hole that Garny had reinforced with steel and concrete and covered with a dome the size of five football stadiums. The labor cost him next to nothing, and he imported most of the materials from Russia. Ministers from the Tajik parliament came by regularly to watch the progress of the giant chamber, and to pick up their consulting fees for helping Garny manage through the various departments in Dushanbe authorizing the build. Garny had promised them that when his work was finished, he would turn the chamber over to the Tajik government to be used as a giant stadium. When the dome was complete, Garny installed blowers around the perimeter of the chamber and attached directly to each blower were six Mitsubishi marine diesel engines with their exhaust manifolds connected to the blowers. He set up cameras around the chamber that were tied back to monitors in the conference room and placed sensors in the floor, attached to the beams holding up the dome. The team programmed the sensors to read CO_2 levels.

While the dome was being built, Garny's team worked feverishly to produce as many "stars" as they were now called as possible. They had built several star chambers and over time were able to produce about a 100 billion stars that made up about 1000 pounds of star gel. They discovered that by freezing the goo, the stars remained dormant and stopped replicating. A couple of scientists were suspecting that a connection existed between active gel and the life-threatening allergies their colleagues were developing. Running outside into the subzero temperatures of the Karakul winter had saved many lives, and they noticed that freezing the gel kept it stable and safe to work on.

When the chamber was complete, Garny gathered his top scientists in the conference room. They popped on the monitors and the computer screens reading the sensors. They watched as crews dressed in hazmat suits and oxygen tanks wheeled a dozen large stainless-steel containers into the chamber and placed them on marked locations scattered around the chamber. Each container had a heating coil that was powered by electricity. The containers were plugged in, and the crew left the chamber. Garny pressed the start button and red lights flashed in the chamber. A second switch started the diesel engines in the blower rooms. Sensors started to pick up detectable amounts of CO_2 and gauges on the monitors' screens started to flicker. A third switch started each of the blowers in sequence, and flashing yellow lights attached above the blower portals popped on in sequence around the chamber. The process was impressive and remarkably beautiful like a laser show at a rock concert. The gauges jumped and then slowed as a needle measuring CO_2 density moved from green into yellow and then hovered at the edge of red. Once the blowers were turned on, the containers were powered up, and the heating coils began to glow. When the container's chamber holding the frozen star gel reached 250 degrees, the lids on the containers slowly parted and a small dark cloud emerged at the opening. The cloud dissipated almost instantly, and the team stared at the CO_2 gauges. Nothing happened. If anything, the needle was moving deeper into red. "Maybe it is not enough," Garny heard someone say. It is enough, he thought, making himself believe. The nanobots will self-replicate until they reach a threshold. There is capacity in this chamber for trillions, but Garny knew he didn't need trillions. He needed just enough.

Suddenly there was a pop, and the monitors and screens went dark.

"What was that?" Garny screamed at the team. "What just happened?"

"It's okay," said one of the engineers in the corner. "Give it a second. The servers are programmed to reboot once a day. We should have turned it off but don't worry we are okay."

"Holy shit," Garny heard Farroush mutter under his breath.

Then, just as quickly as they popped off, the screens popped back on. Only now the CO_2 needles had dropped to green. The room held its breath.

"Is that a glitch?" one of the other engineers asked.

"We can check," said the first engineer and he clicked on a time bar to the moment just before the screens went dark. As he pulled his mouse over the time bar, the room could see the needles move into the red as they had at the start of the experiment. Then, at the same moment the screen went dark, the needles dropped to zero, but the monitoring program began to run before the screens came back to life. The time bar caught the needles jumping back up to red, and then, over several seconds as measured by the monitor, gradually move down into green. Garny let the experiment run for a few more minutes to see if there were any changes and then shut down the diesel engines and the blowers and the needles fell to just above zero where they hovered.

"Did we just see that?" someone asked, and, after a brief silence, the room erupted, and the scientists started laughing and dancing and slapping Garny on his back. Someone had snuck in champagne, and they popped the cork and celebrated. Garny smiled, but he wasn't entirely happy. He knew he would have to repeat the experiment and that it might take weeks to get back to where they were today. But it was not a bad start. The hazmat crews moved back into the chamber and began washing all the dust that had gathered on the floor into collector drains. He let the team celebrate that evening before informing them the next morning that it would need to be repeated. No one complained. All of them knew that it had not gone perfectly and that there were still questions, but they were confident they could repeat it.

And they did. Over the next twelve months, the team ran the same experiment four times, and each time the results were the same. They also experimented with "washing" the CO_2 residue and reusing the particles, but the used nanobots did not act as efficiently as new nanobots and they gave up trying, and the disposed the used nanobots as waste.

On the satellite phone, Garny said to Franklin, "High volume direct air capture works."

"Really?"

"Yes. We built a massive domed chamber measuring over 500 million cubic feet in volume, flooded it with CO_2 to just under 4,000 parts per million, the average level of emissions measured from the opening of a smokestack at a coal burning plant. Atmospheric CO_2 levels in this region are under 350 parts per million. Within 20 minutes, the saturation level drops to 1000 parts per million, and in under 45 minutes, it returns to between 350 and 400 parts per million."

"What happens if you do nothing?"

Garny expected the question. Franklin was smart and not someone easily fooled.

"Remember that the drop in saturation occurs even though engines pumping CO_2 into the chamber continue to run. There is no question that something is happening to reduce the CO_2 levels that are present in the air."

He continued, "But it is the right question, and we tested for that. If you shut off the engines and open the vents, it takes five hours for the levels to return to atmospheric levels."

"And how much of the material do you use?"

"We started with about 1,000 pounds of frozen star gel divided into 25 containers, each holding about 40 pounds of the frozen gel."

"And it is dormant as long as it is frozen?"

"Dormant enough. A small amount remains active but not enough to have measurable impact."

"How long does it take to manufacture 1,000 pounds of frozen gel?"

"We have it down to two months. But that is something we need to improve. A thousand pounds may be good for a one-shot treatment in an industrial zone, but nowhere near enough for an on-going application or for anything broad scale."

"We can work on that. Congratulations. It is an amazing accomplishment."

"I think so too. There are some issues with safety, but we think they can be managed. I think it's time to present."

"Ok," Franklin said. "See you in Paris."

The next morning, Garny called his team together. "I want to thank you for the sacrifices you made to make this day happen. I am sorry it needs to come to an end, but I am certain most of you will be happy to return to your families and begin your next journey. No doubt our paths will cross again but for now let me say, well done!" Garny kept a skeleton crew on at the lab. He had not decided to shut it down completely. But it was time now to stop spending money and to sell the product. He also needed to find a place to manufacture the star gel in much higher volumes than he had created for his experiments.

Davik Gregorian joined The Karakul Proposition early on as a construction worker helping to redesign the Hindu temple into what became the Karakul Lab. He had grown up in Dushanbe as an Armenian minority and was fiercely ambitious. He wanted desperately to prove his value not only to his family but also to his Tajik bosses. He watched the parade of international scientists and politicians run through the grounds and dreamed of becoming a central part of its operations. His ambition and his intelligence served him well, and the Tajik bosses quickly promoted him through the ranks to construction manager. Eventually Davik became the lead construction manager and was responsible for managing the construction of the giant dome. He hired all the available crews from Dushanbe and pulled in additional crews from Tashkent, Uzbekistan, and at one point had 1,000 construction workers reporting to him. Davik had studied English in school and often served as an interpreter for Garny during construction meetings. The money Davik made allowed him to build a nicer home for his family in Dushanbe, and when he was able to get away from the job for a few days, he would return home to feasts and joyous celebrations. When Garny closed the Lab, he made a point of seeking Davik out and complimenting him on a job well done. He told him he would pull strings for Davik to find a job with a large construction firm in Dushanbe. Daviik thanked him and politely declined, indicating that he had made plans to start his own firm, and Garny was pleased and offered to point business in his direction should any arise.

Davik was happy. The few years of hard work for Garny and TKP had paid off very well, and he could only see a bright promising future. He drove down to the Dome entrance to watch the crews clean up the residue of the last experiment. He put on his hazmat suit and wandered around the Dome, ensuring the quality of the clean-up effort. He had built a special storage room for the 25 stainless steel containers holding the star goo. The storage room was outfitted with several freezers to keep the gel frozen until the experiment began. As he was chatting with one of the clean-up crew's managers, he saw one of the Lab scientists enter the storage room. Davik knew the scientist was an Armenian software engineer whom he had befriended. The engineer had come from Armenia to join the team, and Davik wanted to say goodbye before it was too late.

As he entered the storage room, he could tell something was odd. The engineer had gone inside one of the freezers and ordinarily would have no business being in the freezer. Davik called his name and got no response. He walked to the freezer door and leaned in, calling his name again. The engineer turned toward Davik, and he saw that the guy had been leaning over an open container and scraping frozen star gel into a small, glass petri dish with a knife. The engineer smiled at Davik and set down the dish on a shelf. Davik looked at his friend, as if the scene made no sense. The man walked toward him, and Davik realized a little too late that he was intent on stealing some of the star gel and getting away with it. The engineer was on him fast and slammed Davik against the wall. Davik saw the knife and tried to knock his arm away but the engineer was quicker and had already planned his attack. He slashed deep into Davik's suit, cutting Davik's belly open and then slammed the blade up through the cut toward Davik's heart. Blood rushed onto the freezer floor and crystallized. Davik stared into his Armenian friend's angry eyes until darkness descended, and he crumpled to the freezer floor. The engineer wiped his bloody knife and gloves on Davik's still body. He closed the blade and shoved the knife into the pocket of his hazmat suit. He then grabbed the dish, sealed it and closed the container lid and exited the freezer, leaving Davik's cooling body inside. Slamming the freezer door closed, he removed the bloody hazmat suit, tucked it under his arm, and quickly left the Dome. At his car, he tossed the suit into a case that he placed in the trunk of his car and headed to Dushanbe International Airport to return to his home in Yerevan, the capital city of Armenia.

Chapter 13.

Marley Dakota

Back at the Bureau, Van decided to take a run over to the UCLA Lab where Marley's accident occurred. She studied a map of Westwood Village and the medical campus and found the lab where Marley had been exposed. It was called the Lyndon A. Rutter Center for Cellular Engineering. She parked in parking structure 2, and walked over to toward the Biomedical Sciences Research Building but was distracted by a sign that said "Bomb Shelter Bistro." It was almost lunch and Van was hungry, so rather than go right into the Lab, she headed for the Food Court and settled down with a Diet Coke and vegetable soup. A few medical students sat across from her, and she heard them talking about a lab, although it wasn't clear which lab they were discussing. She got up to clear her tray and walked by the students.

"I'm sorry to interrupt," she said, "but were you talking about the Rutter Center Lab?"

Somewhat irritated by Van's eavesdropping, one of the female students responded, "Can we help you?"

"I apologize but I did overhear you discussing the Lab. I am an LAPD detective investigating an accident that occurred here about six months ago."

A male student calmly replied, "Don't worry about her. Would you like to join us?"

Van smiled. "If you don't mind." She dropped off the tray and dumped her dishes in a bin and returned.

The male student said, "We are very familiar with the Rutter Lab. What can we do for you?"

"I am here about what sounds like a tragic accident in which one of the medical students working at the Lab died."

"You mean Marley," he said.

"Yes. Marley Dakota. Do you know what happened?"

One of the other students jumped in. "None of us were there, but we knew Marley very well."

"Do you think she was doing anything wrong?"

"As in unethical?"

"Not exactly. Did anyone describe her work as careless? Do you think she died because she made a mistake?"

"Marley was one of our top students and her specialty was lab work. She was given that job and a reward for getting straight As in all her labs."

"You don't think she did something that caused her death?"

"That is a lot of strangeness about Marley's death," another student responded, who had overheard from another table and moved over and stood at the table to listen to the conversation. "I worked in that lab until they shut it down, but they didn't really shut it down. Marley was working on something new that the faculty didn't want disclosed."

"How do you know that?"

Another student, who had joined the growing group, said, "Because she told me."

"She told you?" Van responded incredulously. "Did you ever talk to the police?"

"Nope. No one ever asked."

"What exactly did she tell you?" Van pulled out a note pad and started writing.

"Do I need to be worried about talking to you?"

"As long as you didn't have anything to do with the accident, you have nothing to worry about. If you want an attorney, I can wait."

"No that's okay. I was Marley's roommate. I am still so sad about what happened."

"Can I get your name?"

"Sure. My name is Dawn Bordrider."

"Can we make room for her?" Van asked the group, which immediately slid closer together and allowed Dawn to join them.

"I am sorry for you," Van said to Dawn. "Did you know Marley well?"

"Marley and I were roommates for our entire second year of medical school and the beginning of our third year. Marley was a wiz at the lab and began tutoring a number of first- and second-year medical students who needed help."

"Did she tell you what she was working on?"

"No. She did say that the lab faculty asked her if she wanted to assist, and of course she said yes. They then told her that it was something that required her utmost discretion, and that she could not talk about it with anyone—even her family. She knew that they were going to close down the lab temporarily until their review was completed. She also told me that more than one lab was getting involved."

Van wondered whether what happened to Marley might have been intentional.

"How did Marley die?"

"The official word was that she had a severe allergic reaction and went into anaphylactic shock. We haven't heard anything more. The paramedics and fire trucks came to the lab first, and then some special hazmat van took her body. And they sealed the lab for over three months. It has only opened up again recently."

"You say official word. Is there an unofficial word?"

"We think she came into contact with something lethal. Marley was a fitness freak, and a health nut. She drank a lot of weird teas that she said her Sioux tribe used for medicine and in rituals. Nothing ever phased her. I never even saw her get sick, let alone deal with any allergies."

"Any idea what it might have been?"

"We can only guess. UCLA Medical is a top school and guards it reputation very carefully. Maybe they were doing something for the military, working on an antidote to some weaponized germ warfare. But the truth is, we have no idea. Marley kept it quiet."

"Did Marley ever say what other labs might be involved?"

"No. But I saw her going into this building over here, and I had never seen her do that before."

Van looked at what Dawn was pointing towards. The building wasn't unlike any other around the food court.

"Do you know what is in there?"

"Some nano-something institute."

"Any idea what they do?"

"Not at all. I'm sorry but medical school keeps us busy."

"I understand. Thanks, Dawn, and thanks to everyone. Do you have a number, in case I need to reach you?"

"Sure" Dawn replied and gave it to her.

The crowd, which had attracted several more students only because they saw something happening, began to disperse. Van reached out to Dawn and the male student and said thank you. They asked her if she thought a crime had occurred, and she honestly told them that she didn't know but that was part of what she was there to find out.

The first thing Van did after lunch was go to the building that Dawn had pointed out. The doors were all closed and the lights were out, so whatever was in the building was not active. She saw a bulletin board. Tacked to the board was an announcement about a lecture on the ethics of microelectromechanical systems (MEMS) and medicine. The lecture was sponsored by the California NanoSystems Institute.

Van left the Institute and headed back to the Rutter Lab. As she entered, there was a security guard, and she had to walk through a screening device. She had to pull her badge out, which along with her keys and phone was placed in a bowl and bypassed the screening device.

The security guard asked, "LAPD?"

"Yes," replied Van, candidly. "I am a detective, and I am here to ask some questions."
"Just a minute please," he said, as he handed her badge, keys and phone back to her. "Do you mind waiting over there?" He pointed to a bench against the wall. Van

shrugged and went over and sat down. She could see the guard make a call, and within a few minutes, a tall, bespectacled woman approached her.

"Hello Detective. My name is Dr. March Fielding. I am the director of the Rutter Center. How can we help you?"

"Hello, Dr. Fielding. I am Detective Van Eng of the LAPD, but I gather you already know that. I am here with a few questions about the tragic accident that occurred a few months ago in which one of the medical students died."

"It was terrible, Detective. Very unfortunate and tragic. No one here knew anything about the student's condition."

"Do you mind if we go to your office?"

"I don't have much time right now, Detective. Perhaps you could call and make an appointment."

"This is not optional, Dr. Fielding."

"I figured as much. You are aware that there is an on-going litigation, and I have no way of knowing if you are here to assist the students' parents with their case. I was told by Detective Young that the case would be closed and that the LAPD does not facilitate civil litigation. I am sorry but if you have a subpoena, then I am happy to speak with you in the presence of my attorney."

"Did you close the lab after the student's accident?" Van pushed back.

"We did, as would any University office in a similarly sensitive situation. Now I must ask you respectfully to leave. Present me with a subpoena and I would be happy to answer your questions with my attorney. Good day, Detective Eng," Dr. Fielding said, as she turned and walked away.

Van had not known what to expect from the Rutter Center's leadership, but she wasn't surprised. She wanted Dr. Fielding to know that she would not be intimidated. If Dr. Fielding truly had nothing to hide, then she had nothing to worry about. But Van sensed she was worried.

On the way back to the Bureau, she got a call from Detective Young. "Please report to me immediately when you return," was all he said. Van wasn't concerned or surprised. She expected the University to call Detective Young. She reported to his office as instructed.

"I told you this case is a waste of time."

"I don't believe it is."

"How is that?"

"You trusted the University. I understand that. But the science is incomplete."

"The science."

"Yes. Nothing in the record supports Marley being allergic to anything."

"That is not a surprise. We all have hidden allergies, and we have the ability to develop allergies. I never knew I was allergic to grass until I started golfing."

"What we know is that Marley died from anaphylactic shock. What we don't know is what caused it."

"Some chemical in the Lab."

"Did you know that Marley was a lab tutor for the medical school?"

"I had not heard that."

"That means that she was so skilled at lab work that the faculty asked her to tutor other students."

"Okay."

"You don't develop that skill without spending a great deal of time in the lab. After over two years of lab work, Marley never reported any type of reaction, allergic or otherwise."

"How do you know that?"

"Because I interviewed her roommate. In fact, I interviewed her roommate and several other medical students. Marley was at the top of her class. The Lab even asked her to participate in a study that they wanted kept a secret."

"What was it?"

"I still don't know but I believe that the investigation is not done, and with due respect, I would ask that you allow me to continue it."

"I'll consider it. Anything else?"

"Yes. Two things. First, she apparently was spending time at the California NanoSystems Institute. There is a lecture I want to attend tomorrow night."

"Ok."

"Second, I went to the Rutter Lab, where the accident took place and I met Dr. Fielding. She will not talk to me without a subpoena. She is concerned that our investigation might be used by Marley's parents in their litigation."

"Sounds reasonable on her part. I told you I don't like being put in the position of facilitating someone's civil case."

"Well, I can go get a subpoena or you can convince her to talk to me. I don't care about the civil case and I will agree that our conversation will be confidential—as much as it can be."

"I still think you are wasting your time, but I'll give this to you for now. I'll talk to Dr. Fielding."

Van thought to herself, he has to give this to me. It would look very bad for him if he ignored this evidence.

"Thank you, sir."

Young spoke to Fielding and she eventually agreed to be interviewed by Van, but she wanted assurances it would be kept confidential and she wanted her attorney present. She also wanted one more thing—immunity from prosecution. That last request was a hard pill for Van to swallow, but it also convinced Young to let her continue the investigation. If Marley's death was as innocent as Young was led to believe, why was Fielding so concerned?

The next night Van returned to the campus and found the lecture on ethics and MEMS being held in Boyer Hall, across from the California NanoSystems Institute and adjacent to the Rutter Center Lab. She sat near the back of the room, trying to be inconspicuous. A representative of the Institute opened the lecture and invited a state senator to introduce the speaker. The senator hailed the speaker as a leader in the ethical analysis of new technologies. The lecture was titled somewhat ominously: "The Dark Side of MEMS: Ethics and the Nano Revolution." The lecturer was a short, balding, elderly man from the faculty of the University of Madras in India. He walked through the different types of nanoparticles and some of their positive use cases, like hyper-focused chemotherapies and immunity boosters that might be used in fighting AIDs and other immuno-deficiencies. She was especially intrigued by a line of research in which nanobots were used in the brain to fight Alzheimer's and age-related dementia, but Van quickly picked up on a strong negative bias the speaker had toward nanotechnology. The primary focus of his discussion was the toxicity of various elements used in nanoparticles when they were employed at a nanoscale, and the side-effects of this toxicity on the human body. His list of impacts didn't seem much different than a standard list of contraindications of any medicine or vaccine—stroke, blood clotting, inflammation, arrythmia, high blood pressure, cardiac arrest, cancer, death, etc. Van was particularly interested when he said certain nanoparticles might cause "pseudo-allergy". His explanation of "pseudo-allergy" was complex and involved something called cytokines, which she had learned about in her studies, but she didn't follow the explanation very well. He also discussed the dangers of self-replication, which sounded particularly frightening to Van but also unbelievable. How could a microscopic robot make a copy of itself? In the end, the lecturer advocated for an international oversight body and laws restricting the experimental use of nanoparticles in medicine and other applications like environmental science. When the lecture was completed, the senator approached the lectern and shook the lecturer's hand rather vigorously and posed with a large smile for pictures. The audience stood and applauded, but Van couldn't tell if the excitement was over the remarks or the senator's political future, which seemed very bright.

Van walked outside into the warm night and smelled a combination of brick and jasmine. She was surprised to see Dr. Fielding, who was doubly surprised to see her. She walked over to Van, and said, "Hello, Detective. Did you find the lecture interesting?" Her tone was not as hostile as their first encounter.

"Hello, Dr. Fielding. Good to see you again. To be honest, I know nothing about the subject, and I'm not certain I know that much more now, but I do find advances in technology like this inspiring."

"Do you agree with his concerns?"

"I don't know. I don't know enough to agree or not agree. What about you?"

"Let's hold off on that one until we speak. Have a good night, Detective."

Fielding's response puzzled Van. It gave Van the impression either that Fielding wanted to speak with her or maybe she was sensing that Van was getting close.

Van called Dawn the next morning. She asked Dawn if she had met Marley's parents, and if so, did she know how to reach them. Dawn said they lived in Cheyenne, Wyoming, and gave her their number. She called them, explained who she was, and expressed her condolences over Marley's death. She said she had a few questions and they seemed eager to talk to her. They said that they thought the LAPD had closed the case. Van was careful not to give them any reason to think the case was being reopened or that there were any suspects. She explained that she found the facts incomplete and was performing a Bureau double-check on the case. Marley's parents never viewed Marley's death as anything more than a tragic accident, but they were mad at the way the University had treated them and refused to share a detailed explanation of what had happened. They told Van that they didn't care about the money. They just wanted the University to take some accountability for what had happened, and they weren't entirely certain that Marley's death needed to happen. Maybe if the University had acted more quickly, their brilliant and beautiful daughter might still be alive.

Van asked if an autopsy had been performed, and they said yes, but that it had been closely controlled by the University medical staff and that Marley's body had been placed in a body bag. They were not allowed even to see their daughter's body in person before they buried her—they had to identify her by looking at photographs.

"But she died of anaphylaxis, correct?"

"That is what the University doctors told us. There was no independent verification."

"But I don't understand why they placed her in a bag. Did she have some kind of infectious disease?"

"Nothing they indicated."

"Did they say that whatever she reacted to might cause the same effect in others?"

"I'm sorry, Detective, but we were in shock. We didn't really dig into the details. We thought your police department would take care of that."

"My apologies. One last question. Did Marley tell you anything about what she was working on?"

"No. She told us it was secret and that she had agreed not to discuss it."

"Ok. Thank you for your time. If anything else occurs to you, please reach out."

Before she interviewed Dr. Fielding, Van wanted to know more about the Lyndon A. Rutter Center for Cellular Engineering. She learned that the Lab became famous by being the first to connect cellular engineering, a euphemism for stem cell research, with virology, developing novel defenses against uncontained cell replication. So strange, she thought, that a lab with that level of expertise would allow anaphylaxis to get out of control. She also read about the Lab's T cell research and advances in the fight against cancer. What might Marley have been involved in that needed to be kept secret? Were they doing work for the military? The research did not lead Van in any direction. The only controversial work at the Lab was stem cell research, but the opponents of that effort were fading away as the field shifted from the use of fetal stem cells to manufactured stem cells.

The meeting with Dr. Fielding was set for Friday morning. Van agreed to meet at the University. She thought there was nothing to be gained by interviewing Dr. Fielding at the Bureau except to make her more nervous and probably less candid. She invited Detective Young to join her. When they arrived, Dr. Fielding did not look well. They had an immunity agreement, but Dr. Fielding's attorney insisted that they sign a form he had prepared, which, along with immunity from prosecution included protection from the disclosure of Dr. Fielding's comments.

Van began the questioning.

"Are you feeling ok, Dr. Fielding?"

"I am fine. I will let you know if I get uncomfortable."

"Do we have water?"

"We have a fridge with cold water. Would you like some?"

"If you don't mind."

Detective Young was getting restless. Dr. Fielding looked at him and smiled. "Thank you for all your help, Detective Young. You made a very difficult situation tolerable."

"Thanks. I understand. My colleague here has raised some legitimate concerns that I am certain you can address. I suggest we get through with this."

"Fine with me."

"I don't want to waste your time either," Van said. "Marley Dakota was a student here at UCLA and she worked in your lab, correct?"

"That's true."

"What did she do?"

"Initially, she worked as an assistant to the staff technicians, taking notes, getting supplies, cleaning equipment."

"Was she good at her work?"

"She was excellent and for that reason we found some exciting experiments for her to join."

"Did those experiments have anything to do with the Lab's work on viruses?"

"They did, yes."

"Did she have any difficulty with that work? Any concern about infection or reactions?"

"We taught her Lab protocol, and she followed it perfectly."

"When I spoke to you for the first time, you mentioned that no one knew about the student's condition. Do you recall saying that?"

"I do but it was a misdirection."

"Excuse me?"

"It was a misdirection. Marley did not have any conditions—at least none that I knew of."

Detective Young shifted uncomfortably in his chair. He jumped into the conversation. "But she did have a reaction that led to her death, correct?"

"She did, Detective Young. But not because she was uniquely susceptible."

"Maybe you should tell us what happened," Van suggested.

Dr. Fielding looked at her attorney, and she nodded.

"Marley was a superb student. She had a vision for the work she wanted to do and she was a good scientist. She believed that there was a science behind the tribal cures of her ancestors and she wanted to understand that science. She knew microbiology was the only way to really validate those medicines and cures. She believed that if we understood better how they worked and why, that would advance not just respect for her tribe but also Western medicine. She had the ambition and self-direction of an idealist, and we look for that in our field. So when an opportunity arose to include Marley in something special, we did. An acquaintance of mine, who has been very helpful connecting high level philanthropists to the University, and in particular to our work in medicine, contacted me about nine months ago. He told me he was sending me something that would interest us here at the Lab. He understood that University labs had become highly competitive and that it was new developments that drove not only funding but private sector opportunities. He said that what he had might be a break-though, and that if we were the first to unveil it, it could advance our work here by decades."

"I hope you can understand why I was interested. The pressure here to keep money coming in is intense. We do it well, but it is not easy."

"What was he sending you?" Van asked, trying to keep Fielding on track.

"He sent his assistant who was carrying a Biosafety Level IV case in her backpack. Let's just say, it was not the most responsible method of delivery. We opened it and inside was a petri dish that was labeled Risk Group IV. Do you know what that means?"

"It is a high-level infectious disease," Van said, recalling her own work in the lab. Fielding was impressed.

"Do you know how high level?"

"I don't recall."

"It is a level of disease on the order of ebola and the bubonic plague, meaning if released it can cause a widespread pandemic that has no cure."

"Holy shit," Young responded.

"We understand how to work with Risk Group IV material. It requires highly specialized training, and we have that capacity here. We also believed we could train Marley on how to handle it."

"But you were wrong," Young said. "And she exposed herself." Van was thinking the same.

"That is not correct, Detective. We studied the contents of the dish, and it turned out not to be Risk Group IV at all. Instead, it was mechanical."

"MEMS?" Van asked.

"Exactly. There was no biological material at all in the dish. We sent Marley over to the NanoSystems group that held the lecture you attended this week to see if we could get some expertise. They told Marley that it should not be hazardous so long as she wore protective gear. We were beginning to explore the contents when Marley got exposed and died almost immediately of acute anaphylaxis."

"How did she get exposed?"

"We have different level hazmat suits here. The high-level suits are bulky and difficult to work in and we don't use them unless there is real danger. Marley and the technicians working with her were wearing the lighter suits. They opened the dish and the devices activated immediately, penetrating her mask and causing a severe allergic reaction. She wasn't the only one who died."

"What?!" Young jumped out of his chair.

Van grabbed his arm and pulled him back down. "How did we not know this?" Van asked.

"We buried it," Dr. Fielding responded. Young put his hand to his head.

"How many people were infected, if that is the right term?"

"The two lab technicians with Marley both died. They did not react as quickly and we were able to get them transported to the hospital and ventilated, but they didn't make it."

"Is that why you closed the Lab for three months?" Van asked, and Young shot a surprised glance at Van, not realizing she already knew this.

"Yes, but there is more."

"Christ," said Young, not believing anything he was hearing.

"I was in that lab with Marley, and I ended up in the hospital also."

"But you survived."

"Yes," Fielding sighed. "I was by the door to the lab talking with a colleague. I saw Marley drop the dish and grab her throat. The technicians tried to reach for her but they collapsed as well. I jumped outside and slammed the door closed, but not before inhaling a small amount of whatever it was that escaped that dish. I was allowed to leave the hospital, but my lungs are severely burned, and I probably will need a lung transplant to survive." Dr. Fielding was fighting back tears. "I saw so much promise in Marley. I take her loss very personally."

"Her parents are suffering also," Van said.

"I know."

"You kept them away from her to keep them safe, right?"

"Right, but the University has faced a lot of blows recently, and our attorneys are some of the best in the country. They engineered the University's public response, and Marley's parents got caught in the crossfire."

"Is there anyone who can explain why these nanobots cause that kind of reaction?"

"Honestly, we haven't gotten that far."

"Who was your acquaintance who delivered you the dish?"

Dr. Fielding sighed. "Derek Whitestone. He is an investment banker in the Silicon Valley. His assistant was a young woman named Cheryl Brown. Apparently, she had been a student here at UCLA."

"The dish?"

"We have isolated it in a lab freezer that is locked and coded. We closed the lab for three months to ensure that any remnants of the material in the dish are gone and the lab is safe."

"Ok. That is enough for now. Thank you for your time and candor."

Van drove Detective Young back to the Bureau. He was seething the entire way. Van was concerned that some of it was directed at her. But she knew now that her efforts had been worth it, and there was much more to do.

Chapter 14.

Anaphylaxis

Dr. Aida Barasian dropped into her desk chair exhausted. She didn't remember working this hard since she was in her residency program at Georgetown University Hospital in the United States. She heard a code blue called and waited. Another death, but at least they didn't call her name. Then, just as she was drifting asleep for the first time in 16 hours, she heard "Barasian. Paging Dr. Barasian." Her body fought the fatigue, but she forced herself to stand and head out to the hallway.

Lined against the walls of the hallways in Erebuni Medical Center in south Yerevan, patients laid on cots moaning. IVs dripped trying to keep patients hydrated, and in some cases, anti-inflammatories were being administered through the same IV. Most of the patients had oxygen masks. Dr. Barasian made her way past shouts of "Doctor, please!" to the central desk. The lead nurse practitioner in charge, Nurse Arakelian, reported that the line of cars at the entrance to the emergency room was growing. As each car pulled up, paramedics and physician assistants were interviewing the occupants and deciding whether to allow someone complaining of being sick or having difficulty breathing to be admitted. This triage effort had begun two weeks ago when the volume of new patients skyrocketed. Most patients were experiencing light symptoms, but a handful of those cases inexplicably escalated, and in some instances, the patients died. That uncertainty created a panic in the Greater Yerevan population of more than a million people, and at any indication of the illness, they jumped in their cars and headed to the hospital.

Dr. Barasian shook her head. There was no room at the Republic of Armenia's largest medical institution. Beds became available only as people died and bodies were bagged and removed. She said to Nurse Arakelian, "Tell them to start Level 5 Protocol."

Nurse Arakelian had seen it all and was rarely moved. But when she heard Level 5, she cringed. That meant that Dr. Barasian was rationing care by ordering the frontline staff to reject rather than accept patients in the greatest need, in most cases signing their death warrant. The strain on the staff would be very hard as family members screamed at the staff to let their loved ones into the hospital to get medical care. The situation became so dire that staff started filling syringes with a placebo just to placate family members and pretend patients were getting some care.

The chaos that now reigned in Yerevan was due in part to the unknown source of this strange new illness. Officials were calling it a new strain of flu, and some were claiming it was bioterrorism, and that it originated in Azerbaijan. But, in fact, no one knew the source of the disaster, no one except a software engineer who had spent the last two years in Tajikistan, and he was dead.

Hayk Hovhannisian had battled his way out of poverty in Yerevan. He was beaten regularly by his alcoholic father, whom he hated for the way he treated his mother. When he was 14, he ran away and joined an Armenian gang called the Black Hoods. Hayk knew how to be ruthless and was willing to do any deed called upon by the gang's leadership. He rose quickly within the gang and was made the gang leader after someone challenged him to assassinate his own father. He waited outside his father's favorite bar, and when he stumbled out of the entrance, Hayk walked up to his father's face, stared at him until his father's welcoming smile turned into a frown, and shot him in the face. Hayk spent the next year as gang leader until he was caught and arrested for armed robbery. He had never been named for the murder of his father. No one imagined a deed that heinous was possible. He served three years for the robbery and was released, but only after he had picked up a certificate in software engineering through a collaborative program between the local university and the prison.

After prison, Hayk started his own computer business. Within a year, he was making more money than he did as a gang leader, and this time it was legitimate. He gave money to his mother and expanded his business throughout the city. He began to develop construction management software for the largest construction firms in Yerevan and, at their recommendation, for the companies of the firm owners' relatives in Dushanbe. When Davik came to Dushanbe to sweep up all the construction firms for the TKP Dome project, those companies pulled in Hayk to support them. Davik and Hayk met in the central construction compound situated just off the main road to the Lab. Hayk immediately ingratiated himself to Davik, and they became fast friends.

But as successful as Hayk was becoming, he still wanted more. He watched with jealousy as the Dome was constructed and as Davik grew closer to Garny. Davik tried to pull Hayk into that relationship, but Garny saw something he didn't like in Hayk that he recognized in himself and steered clear. Hayk observed the Lab very closely and realized early on that the focus of the Lab and its wealthy founder was the gel they were testing in the Dome. He learned that it was composed of miniature robots and thought that, if he could get his hands on just a small bit of it, he might be able to reengineer it and become as rich as Garny. When the project was complete and shutting down, Hayk snuck into the Dome's storage room dressed as an engineer. He had secured a petri dish from the main lab and a knife. He knew they stored the gel in a frozen state, and he figured he would need to scrape it into the dish. When Davik stumbled upon him in the storage room, Hayk did not hesitate. He murdered Davik and left him in the freezer, knowing he would not be discovered for a long time, now that the experiment had been concluded and the Lab was shutting down.

When Hayk landed in Yerevan, he pulled his suitcase out of baggage claim and decided to check on the dish, concerned that it might not be intact. The baggage claim was crowded as vacationers heading to the hot spots on the Black Sea and the Mediterranean on the west coast of Turkey stood in long lines with their families waiting for plane tickets. He found room on the ledge of a window and opened the bag. The dish was still intact, but the flight had loosened the seal and when Hayk went to place the dish back in the suitcase, it fell open.

When happened next was a nightmare straight out of a Hollywood horror story. Hayk grabbed his throat as his trachea ballooned and shut off his airway. As he fought to breath, he saw the same thing happening around him. The people right around him were shocked and confused as they also started choking, their eyes popping out of their heads. Parents in the vicinity grabbed their children screaming until they could no longer breath. A few doctors ran to help before they realized they were struggling to breath also. They pulled out pen knives and were performing tracheotomies first on themselves and then on everyone around them, hoping to bypass the swelling and saving their lives. Blood from the tracheotomies spewed everywhere, but the relief was short-lived, and the doctors and their new patients collapsed. The only ones to survive the initial onslaught were able to get to the doorways, and Hayk watched as they ran for their lives away from the terminal. It was the last thing Hayk would see as darkness descended and he fell off the ledge directly into his suitcase and the open petri dish. The heat of his body produced a small black cloud of dense active nanobots that rose around his body and out of the suitcase. The cloud began to move toward the rear of the terminal, drawn to the polluted air near the baggage machine and airport staff unloading the planes. The cloud grew as it moved through the jetways toward the planes and trembling bodies piled up in its wake.

Once outside, the cloud doubled in size and began to rain bots as they grabbed CO_2 coming from the planes' engines and went dormant. The people outside grabbed their heads in pain and started coughing. Some grabbed their chests and sat on the ground trying to breathe, but the effect was not as strong as it had been indoors, and for the moment, they were still conscious. The cloud continued to grow until it covered a sizeable portion of Yerevan. Residents of Yerevan noticed for the first time in years that the air in the city seemed to freshen and they walked outside to take deep draws of unpolluted air. Then the dust started falling, and for a moment, everyone standing outside thought a nearby volcano had erupted, and the streets were filling with ash. Unprotected, these thousands of people began to experience headaches and difficulty breathing as it turned out even the dormant nanobots caused an allergic reaction similar to active bots, if slightly less in intensity. Emergency lines exploded, and police, fire and paramedics found themselves racing all over the city trying to collect people with the most severe reactions and get them to the city's hospitals. Hospital beds filled up within a matter of hours, and nurses and doctors rushed to find mattresses that could be placed in the hallways. The City government called for the military to step in and soldiers began delivering thousands of cots until there was no more room at the hospital. That was when Dr. Barasian made her decision to go to Level 5.

It rained dust for a week. The mortality rate from the new "flu" rose precipitously during the first weeks of the "infection," and then dropped to a manageable number, and the vast majority of the hospitalized recovered and returned home. The City hired hazardous material specialists from England, Australia and South Africa to remove the dust, which occupied half of the city within the city limits. The removal took nine months. Periodically, a pocket of dust would surface and blow about, and a few more serious cases would report to the hospital. But the sun did come out and life in the big city returned to normal. The Armenian Apostolic Church experienced a resurgence, and a new cottage industry of mental health professionals grew and became a credible avenue for help and recovery after the national church embraced it. Dr. Aida Barasian was given a national medal of honor for her management of the health crisis. Hayk Hovhannisian was bagged and buried in a mass grave along with the 356 other victims of the airport massacre, which included in roughly equal numbers both Armenians and Azerbaijanis. His family tried to find him and the general word was that his past association with the Black Hoods had caught up with him.

Back in Tajikistan, Davik's family put out an intense search, engaging the construction firms that Davik had managed as well as the state police. Garny returned to Dushanbe from a highly successful presentation to the Global Climate Change Consortium in Paris, France, and facilitated the search for Davik. Within three days, they found his body in the Dome's storage room freezer. Garny attended the funeral, for which he paid, and deposited enough money into Davik's estate to cover the living expenses of his wife and mother and the education of all his children. He placed the Dome in a trust for the People of Tajikistan and it was officially named the Davik Gregorian World Sport Arena and went on to host multiple international competitions. Garny then returned to France to begin work on a mass production lab. He still was not aware of the cause of the Yerevan Disaster.

Chapter 15.

Honesty Would Have Been a Better Policy

"Explain to me, to us, where we stand now," said Detective Young, as he sat behind his desk at the Bureau. Van stood with her arms folded, leaning against the door jam. Robert Johnson sat across from Young's desk and Charlie stood behind Van listening in on the conversation. Van did not want to offend Young any more than she already had just by asking the right people the right questions, which Young had failed to do.

"Let's start with what has not changed," Van offered. "We know Marley died in the Lab as the result of a severe allergic reaction to a substance she was analyzing for the Lab. We know that Marley's parents do not have any details about what happened in the Lab, whatever their motivation behind their lawsuit might be—money or not. We also know now that it appears that there was very little the University could have done to save Marley's life. She died almost instantly."

"Okay," Young said petulantly. "I can agree that at some level, our analysis was not completely off the mark."

"Good," said Van. "What is new? First, Marley was not the only one who died. That matters for two reasons. One, it confirms that other than failing to treat the substance they were reviewing as a dangerous infectious disease, which it was not, the Rutter Center Lab did not violate any standards or protocols. Marley's death, if we are to believe what we heard from Dr. March Fielding—and my instinct says she was telling the truth—was truly a tragic accident. Two, somebody placed a dangerous substance in the Lab without adequately warning the Lab."

"Yes," Young agreed. "What was his name?"

"We have two names," Van responded. "Derek Whitestone and Cheryl Brown."

"Have we learned anything more about Mr. Whitestone and Ms. Brown?"

"We have," said Van. "Derek Whitestone is the principal in a Silicon Valley investment bank called Red Hawk Investments. Whitestone started the bank about 15 years ago with a single client, whose personal portfolio still constitutes a substantial majority of the bank's portfolio. The investor is Fred Schmidt, CEO of Grindle, who we know is one of the wealthiest people in the country."

"How did Derek get access to such a dangerous substance? Did he get it from Schmidt?"

"We don't know that, yet. But we do know, based on Dr. Fielding's interview, that he gave it to Cheryl Brown to deliver to the Rutter Center Lab, and that she did deliver it."

"So," Young said to the rest of the team, "what does this all mean?"

Robert Johnson, not to be outdone by Van, piped up. "If this stuff is that dangerous, where is it now?"

"At the Lab," Van said, "apparently under lock and key in a freezer."

"Do we want to confirm?"

"Fair point," Young said, "but it's not helping us."

"My question," Charlie added, leaning in next to Van in the doorway, "is if

Derek Whitestone knew this substance, whatever we are calling it, was that dangerous, why did he trust his assistant to deliver it?"

"Maybe he had no idea what it was?" Young said.

"Well," Van added, "except that it was labeled Risk Group IV, which should be an indicator of mortal danger. He must have really trusted Cheryl Brown. Either that, or she was his best option even if not much of an option, because he was hiding something. In any event, we need to get to Derek Whitestone and Cheryl Brown, and possibly Fred Schmidt. My recommendation is that we hit Derek Whitestone first."

"Do we know where they are?"

"Only Whitestone at this point—unless he has already skipped. We don't know if Cheryl Brown is still in Los Angeles, but Whitestone will know."

* * *

The death of Marley Dakota had made life very difficult for Derek Whitestone. Dr. Fielding called Derek from the hospital as soon as she was in recovery, a few days after the incident.

"Derek."

"Hi, March.

"I am in the hospital."

"I'm sorry to hear that. What happened? Are you okay?"

"No. I am not ok. The substrate you sent to us in the petri dish has killed three people and almost killed me!"

"I don't understand."

"Yes, you do. You put my lab at grave risk without any warning."

"What are you talking about, March? I trusted that your lab was one of the most sophisticated infectious disease labs in the country. You knew it was labeled Risk Group IV."

"Yes, but it wasn't Risk Group IV, was it?"

Derek had not known anything about the substrate when he sent it down to Los Angeles with Cheryl Brown. But Fred called him immediately after the meeting with Brian and told him what the Tran Lab on Bainbridge Island had found. He also told him what had happened to Brian and his colleague, and how lucky they were that something worse had not occurred. Derek recognized quickly that it was a mere coincidence that the Stanford Lab that divided the substrate for Derek did so without incident, because they had no reason to determine whether it was biological or not and treated it as a dangerous infectious disease. But Derek had been too caught up in Cheryl's drama to think about warning Dr. Fielding, and the "something worse" that Fred was relieved did not occur on Bainbridge Island, did occur in Los Angeles.

When Dr. Fielding asked Derek if he knew that the substrate wasn't Risk Group IV, Derek lied. But that lie didn't solve anything for Derek. If anything, it ensured that the University would do everything they could to direct blame back to him and Cheryl Brown. Derek said nothing to Cheryl about Marley Dakota. She was being hunted by Belinda's crew, and they had already made one attempt to snatch her. It would do Cheryl no good to know she might be implicated in someone's death. It wasn't doing much for Derek either. His plan to capitalize on the stolen petri dish had sprung a leak and it was only a matter of time before the ship would go down. He needed a lifeboat and the only place he knew to turn to was Fred Schmidt.

But, in fact, Cheryl Brown did know or at least wondered. As she was standing in line for coffee at Starbucks, the person waiting in front of her picked up the Times and one of the lead articles was entitled 'Tragedy at a

UCLA Medical Lab.' She reached forward and grabbed another copy of the paper and stood there trembling as she placed her order. She found a seat and started reading.

AP Wire, Los Angeles -- Tragedy struck a well-known medical laboratory on the UCLA Medical School campus on Wednesday morning. University officials report that a medical student died while she was working at the Lyndon A. Rutter Center for Cellular Engineering. The name of the student is being withheld pending notification of the parents. The school says the student was exposed to material that caused a severe allergic reaction and died within minutes as a result of anaphylactic shock. She was pronounced dead at the scene. Officials provided no further details about the accident.

Cheryl's eyes glazed over the remainder of the article that spoke about the origins and accomplishments of the Lab. The article closed with a reference back to the stem cell controversies 15 years prior. She set the paper down. Her coffee shook as she tried to drink it. She had already narrowly escaped being kidnapped, and now she wondered if, somehow, she might be implicated in the death of this student. She hoped and prayed that it had nothing to do with the petri dish. She got into her car and drove back to her apartment. As she drove, she frantically studied the rearview mirror for signs of the black Explorer. She pulled into the gated garage and ran up the back stairs to her apartment, avoiding the elevator. She got inside, checked to see if anyone had snuck into the apartment, and grabbed her only suitcase. As she pulled clothes from the dresser and the closet and incidentals from the bathroom, she tried to calm herself down. She needed to reach Derek, but she didn't want to call him from the apartment—she wanted to get on the road and back to the Bay Area, where she hoped she could hide and have life return to normal.

But as she gathered her things, Cheryl had a flash of an insight. What was she doing?

She had no idea really about what had happened at the Lab. It was possible, in fact, likely, that it had nothing at all to do with her. But how would she know? She needed to get back there and find out what happened. But she also knew that police might be snooping around, and someone at the Lab might see her and alert the police. She was torn, but it mattered more to her to know that the accident had nothing to do with her. She went back down the stairs with a suitcase and a backpack full of her belongings, slowly opened the door to the garage, looked around and walked briskly to the car, threw everything she had in the back seat and jumped in.

As she pulled up to the campus, she decided to drive around to see if there was any unusual police activity. Every step she took was cautious. She made sure the black Explorer was nowhere to be seen, that there were no stakeouts, and that no one was hiding in a car or at a bus stop waiting for her. She pulled on a hoodie and sunglasses, which on campus made her blend in like a student, and she walked over to the same entrance to the Lab that she had used the first time she was there. She expected to see police tape but there was nothing. She tried the door and it was locked. As she walked to the rear of the building, she saw a group of students laying flowers on the steps to the rear entrance and setting up a memorial. She decided to play ignorant and walked up to the students.

"What's going on?"

They looked at her as if she must be stupid if she didn't know, but one of the students took pity, and said, "You didn't hear about the accident?"

"No, I didn't," Cheryl lied. "What happened?"

"Our good friend died here a couple days ago. There was an accident in the Lab, and she got infected and died."

"We don't know if she was infected," another student responded.

"Well, whatever it was," a third student joined in, "she was working on something secret."

"It wasn't that secret," the second student said. "I was there. Somebody brought in a petri dish in a biohazard case to be reviewed by the Lab. I saw the dish. Maybe I am lucky to be alive."

Cheryl felt her knees buckle. She tried to stay calm. "I am sorry about your friend."

As she turned and walked away, one of the students said, "Excuse me, what is your name?" Without thinking and still in shock, she looked back, and said, "I'm Cheryl." The student responded, "I'm Dawn. Thanks for asking about this." She pointed at the flowers and smiled at Cheryl, wondering if Cheryl was as disinterested as she acted.

When Cheryl got back to her car, she was shaking. The chances of it not being her petri dish that caused the student's death were growing slimmer by the minute. If it was her petri dish, she thought, struggling to control her panic, the same thing might have happened to her while she was transporting it to Los Angeles. For some reason, back then, it had just seemed safe.

As she thought about what to do, she noticed movement next to her door. She looked up to her left, and directly into the open barrel of a very large gun. The man holding the gun ripped open the door and a separate pair of hands grabbed Cheryl and jerked her out of the car. No one else was around. No one else saw Cheryl get stuffed into the back seat of the Explorer with a hood pulled over her head and her hands zip-tied behind her back. The Explorer sped away, leaving the driver side door to Cheryl's car open, and her barely touched extra hot Starbucks latte now cold and sitting in the cup holder. Lying on her side in the back seat, Cheryl tried to pull her wits together. She was thinking that she would do whatever these people needed when she felt a jab in her arm that made her feel dizzy before everything went black.

Rather than call and risk Fred not picking up and possibly shunning him, Derek decided to take the two days it took to drive up to Seattle and give himself time to think. If for some reason Fred was gone, Derek had met people at the Lab there and could stop by and ask how it was going. Fred would appreciate the diligence, which he expected of Derek anyway. The drive to Seattle can be one of the most spectacular drives in the country. Derek took his Tesla Model X fully charged and headed up the peninsula through downtown San Francisco and over the Golden Gate bridge. Not the fastest, but it was the most scenic way north. He passed San Quentin State Penitentiary and thought about it in a new way. It was, for the moment, not just about "them"—the poor evil souls who sat there waiting to die or rotting away the balance of their lives. This time, when he looked over the tall, electrified walls, he wondered how often you can see the sun. He stayed on the 101 North because he knew there were superchargers for his Model X and he drove on through Santa Rosa, passing the giant vineyards that produced the expensive wines his tastebuds had grown fond of. He passed by Humboldt, one of the many clusters of giant redwood trees sprinkled throughout Northern California and thought about how he almost named his company after these beautiful giants. But he knew, for obvious reasons, that it was far too common, and he settled on Red Hawk, which sounded more aggressive anyway. He spent the night in Crescent City, a beautiful coastal fishing village just south of the Oregon border and remembered for the tsunami of 1964, triggered by the strongest earthquake ever recorded in North America, a 9.2 earthquake in southern Alaska that sent out the killer tsunami, which reached 150 feet at its greatest height. The tsunami hit the city at midnight, killing twelve people and destroying much of the town. Derek was excited about the next day's journey, distracting him and keeping his mind off Fielding's call and the tragedy at UCLA. He had a fleeting thought that maybe it would have been better for him to head south and check in on the Lab and Dr. Fielding, out of courtesy, but he knew that, if he had, he would be walking directly into Belinda's trap. He needed Fred right now more than anything, and the spectacular Oregon coast would put a check on the panic he felt rising in his chest.

Cheryl opened her eyes. She was no longer sitting in the back of the Explorer, and she had no idea how long she had been out or where she was. She was still cuffed by the zip tie, but the bag had been removed. She blinked through the blurriness, and the image of a tall, thin woman came into view. It took her a second before she recognized the woman as Belinda Armendariz from Ragnar Willowbrook. She also noticed the flirty professor Leonard Freund sitting next to Belinda and chuckled at her own now very real misfortune.

"You find this funny?" Belinda fired at Cheryl.

"Sure," Cheryl's gallows humor continued.

"Well, I don't because I do not take it lightly when someone steals from me."

Cheryl feigned ignorance, even though she knew it was futile. "What are you talking about?"

"The nano dish, Ms. Brown. You stole the nano dish from me."

"Well, if you are up on the news, it looks like I may have saved your life."

"Yeah, I know about UCLA, and I don't look at it that way."

"What way do you look at it?"

"Your impertinence doesn't affect me, Ms. Brown. I am not the one handcuffed to a chair."

"You are right about that," she said, nodding her head and pretending for a moment to let her guard down. "No, but you are the one guilty of kidnapping and drugging me against my will."

Belinda sighed. "Do you want to know why what you did was simply a stupid act? Maybe you don't, really, but I am going to tell you. Yes, you killed someone needlessly. That is about the absolute height of stupidity. We have protocol here, and unlike the unfortunates at UCLA, we knew what we were dealing with." Her voice rose as she fired at Cheryl, not caring that Cheryl was defenseless. "You and your boss Derek could have been part of a trillion-dollar project to develop nanobot defenses against bioterrorism, nanotechnical solutions to global problems, and giant medical advances in the fight against cancer, cerebral palsy, Parkinson's, Alzheimer's, you name it. Sweetheart, you would have been set for multiple lifetimes. But no. You needed to act on your impulse in the moment and now look at you. You are the captive of an elite black ops squad, who could have snapped your neck in an instant. You are coming out of a drug stupor—not the first time in the banal existence you call life. And you are cuffed and tied to a chair facing me."

"What do you want to know?" Cheryl said quietly.

"Where is Derek Whitestone?"

"I don't know. I was in LA, remember?"

One of the guards raised his arm and Belinda signalled him back. "Is UCLA the only place that has my nanobots?"

"I don't know. Derek was with Fred Schmidt when he talked to me. Fred apparently wanted me fired."

"Yes, Fred is a much smarter guy than the rest of us. But I think he made a mistake with Derek that he will regret. So where is Fred?"

"I don't know." Belinda's hand moved and a fist popped Cheryl on the side of her face. Blood trickled out of the corner of her mouth where her cheek slammed into her teeth.

"Where is Fred Schmidt?!" Belinda's voice grew loud.

"I don't know. I don't know. I promise. Derek left with him. That is all I know." This time a fist hit her square in the face. She lost consciousness for a few seconds.

"Are you with us, Cheryl?" Belinda screamed. "Where did Derek and Fred take my bots?!" she yelled in Cheryl's face, spit spraying from her mouth.

"Go fuck yourself," Cheryl replied. She felt something like a pipe hit the side of her head and she went out cold.

* * *

Derek crawled up the Oregon Coast. But rather than the view calming him down, his anxiety grew. He repeatedly had second thoughts about seeing Fred on Bainbridge Island. But he steeled himself and kept driving. It was midnight when he finally arrived—it had been a long day. The slow trip was worth it. It gave Derek the time he needed to formulate a better story. UCLA was not a back-up to Fred for Derek. It was a back-up for Fred. Fred knew Derek to be a conservative investment banker, and as much money as the latter had made for Fred, he had also saved the billionaire millions of dollars on losses that he might have had with poor bets. UCLA was a savings strategy, and Derek trusted that Fred would see the wisdom of it, even as he dealt with the tragedy of it.

Gerard let Derek into the mansion on Bainbridge Island and guided him to Fred's study where Fred welcomed Derek from his long trip and told him there is much to discuss and suggested after a light aperitif that they retire and commence in the morning.

Chapter 16.

A Journey of Their Own Making

Detective Paul Young had a problem. He had opposed bringing Van Eng into the Bureau without going through regular channels. He knew that had she gone through those channels she would never have qualified as a detective because they would never send a deaf or hearing-impaired person out in a squad car with another officer as a partner. He considered himself sympathetic to Van's situation as a human being, but he would not be the one to risk the lives of fellow officers because he felt sorry for Van. She didn't belong there.

The problem was that Van was proving him wrong—at every point. His strategy with the Vietnamese gang The Rush had barely moved with his team sitting there in their cars surveilling the gang from a safe distance. Van had jumped directly into the middle of things, and brought down two of LA's most troubling gangs, the Rush and El Muerte. Detective Young was fighting with Van and Charlie Darling on his decisions to close cases and they challenged him regularly by bringing them back to life. Now, in a direct affront to his authority, Detective Van Eng had reopened the case on UCLA medical student Marley Dakota and stumbled into what may turn out to be a multiple homicide and who knows what else. Bureau leadership was beginning to measure Van's successes against his credibility, and it wasn't looking good for Young. But he didn't know how to stop her. Every time he challenged her, she rose to the challenge and exceeded it. She seemed to be utterly fearless, and he could not understand it. But Young didn't put a bullet on Van's desk. That was Robert Johnson, who thought that he was backing up his boss by scaring Van into submission. That was a stupid move, and Johnson was very lucky that Van realized early on there was no real threat. In fact, she turned the tables on Johnson by exposing him as a weak link on the Bureau's team. She knew he was Young's protégé, for what it was worth, so she let him be. But she enjoyed forcing him to drive into The Rush's garage and watch him almost pee his pants every time.

The interview with Dr. Fielding was the coup de grace. Van didn't care about Detective Young's ego or his future career, and as she pressed Dr. Fielding for answers, she knew Young was feeling the sheer force of her will to get to the truth. The real test started now. The frozen petri dish in Dr. Fielding's locked freezer was part of a much larger picture, and Van knew it even if she did not yet know what that picture included. Dr. Fielding had been in the dark and yet was willing to take on a grave risk. But for what?

Van talked Detective Young into letting her take Charlie with her up north to Cupertino, Derek Whitestone's Silicon Valley home and the location of Red Hawk Investments. They landed at the Norman Y. Mineta San Jose International Airport and took a shuttle to rental cars, where they picked up a small SUV and a GPS and jumped on the 880 South to the 280 West and exited the freeway at the base of the eastern edge of the Santa Cruz coastal mountain range and into the home of Apple Computers. They arrived at Derek's house, a modest but expensive home on the Deep Cliff Golf Course. Not surprisingly, they found no one home. They wandered to the back of the house and Van shared with Charlie her impressions, which by now Charlie knew to take seriously. What Van saw was a rarely occupied and probably professionally cleaned house with a regularly manicured yard to create the appearance of being lived in. She predicted that Derek was divorced and found the idea of living in a large house by himself depressing. That didn't make Derek a criminal, just a middle-aged male who preferred to be distracted by work, a circumstance that no doubt worked well for his principal and possible only client, a billionaire who demanded his immediate responsiveness 24/7. It also put him in a category of aging single males who tend to make bad decisions, and, whether any of Van's speculations were true or not, Derek was making bad decisions.

They headed back toward the 280 Freeway and parked at a modest business complex across from the Cupertino Hyatt Hotel. Red Hawk Investments was on the fifth floor, Suite 5000. Van noticed that unlike other investment banks, this one appeared to be intentionally low key. Other than the custom sign on the wall above the reception chairs, which combined reclaimed wood and highly polished copper that ornately spelled out the name of the bank, the office was routine and filled with business warehouse furniture and standard cubicles. The lack of a high-end address and décor could mean that the bank was not very successful, but Van doubted that, even if they basically served only one person, Fred Schmidt. She saw the low-key design as intentional—a conscious decision to avoid the ostentatious side of the Valley and appear to be a smart, conservative bank. If Van had not heard about Derek's connection to the UCLA tragedy, the office alone would have left a favorable impression as did the receptionist, who was friendly and cooperative. Van showed her badge and introduced herself and Charlie as Los Angeles-area detectives who needed to speak with Derek Whitestone about events in Los Angeles. The receptionist told them Derek had left the Bay Area and reported to her that he may be gone for several weeks. She did not know where he was going but, in all likelihood, she believed he was heading to see his client Fred Schmidt, who had just purchased a new home on Bainbridge Island. They asked if anyone else worked with Derek on the Schmidt account, and she told them Cheryl Brown had been working closely with Derek on several matters, but she hadn't seen Cheryl for a few weeks, and there was an unverified rumor that she was let go. Van also asked if there was anyone else with whom they could speak who might have some details on what they had been working on, but the receptionist said she doubted it. They asked for Derek and Cheryl's contact information and the receptionist shared it without hesitation. She also asked for Fred Schmidt's contact information and the receptionist said that unfortunately that information was confidential, and that she would be happy to share but only if they had a court order. Van asked if she knew anything about why Fred and Derek had gone up north. She did. Derek had asked her to prepare a file for a Duc A. Tran Laboratory on Bainbridge Island just outside of Seattle. Van asked if they could see the file. The receptionist had left it on Derek's desk and went to retrieve it. Van looked at Charlie.

"Coincidence?"

"Right behind you, Van," Charlie replied. "I would give my right arm that there is a connection back to UCLA."

The receptionist returned with the file. Van took a quick look and saw a business card and flash memorized it—Dr. Brian Johannsen, Lead Scientist, Duc A. Tran Laboratory for Hereditary Biology. She handed the file back to the receptionist.

"I don't want to get you in trouble," Van told her.

"Well," responded the astute receptionist. "I am not entirely sure what is happening here, but if it is not good, I don't want to be a part of it." She handed the file back to Van.

"I can create another. I have copies."

"Thank you. If anything does come of this, we will remember your cooperation."

Van and Charlie went back to the car. They sat there going through the material in the file. In it, among what appeared to be white papers, were a pamphlet and a couple business cards, a handwritten note from Fred Schmidt to Derek. The note was on letterhead with an address on Bainbridge

Island. It read:

> D: It is the middle of the night, and I can't get today's meeting out of my head. I think B and RW stumbled into an invention not of their own making and do not fully understand the effects. Dr. J broke it down. This is big. Take care buddy and get yourself back up here asap. F.

Van looked at Charlie. "I don't think we stop here. I'll let Detective Young know we are heading to Seattle. You good with that?"

"Absolutely."

* * *

Cheryl came to in a basement with her hands tied together to a hot water pipe that emerged from the wall above her head. Her head throbbed and her neck ached from holding her head at an awkward angle. Her lip and cheek burned and felt swollen. She tried to shake off the pain and looked around. The basement appeared to be empty. She saw a washer dryer against the wall next to her. She stood and almost collapsed but leaned back against the concrete wall to stay upright. The paint on the back of the pipe was peeling, and she began to rub the zip tie back and forth over the flaked paint trying to break the plastic.

"It's no use, Ms. Brown."

Cheryl turned around and a light was shining in her face. She could hear Belinda's voice and make out a couple of other shapes, whom she assumed were the black ops guards. The voice had changed, softened but not in friendly way. It sounded resolute.

"I don't really care about you, Cheryl. You aren't the first person to try to steal from me. I can tell you this. No one who steals from me fails to regret it. So whether you find your way out of this very difficult situation or not is totally on you. It is no longer in my hands."

"I can't tell you what I don't know."

"Then tell me what you do know."

She looked down. There was no fighting this. No one was coming to save her. No one ever had.

"Okay. I told you I took it to UCLA. Derek had me over a barrel. Either I did what he needed, or I was out. So I took it. He warned me about you. Said you would not hesitate to kill me. I guess I see that now."

"Can we get it from UCLA?"

"I doubt it. It is the subject of an investigation there. It's evidence."

"Okay. I assumed so. Shit."

"But I think there is more."

"More what."

"More of your bots, or whatever you call it. I think Derek gave some of it to Fred Schmidt."

"When Derek kicked me out of the office, he disappeared for a week. I don't know where he went but I'll bet he went somewhere with Fred and they had some portion of the dish."

"Why do you think that?"

"Because Derek had me go to UCLA for him. He did not once mention Fred although he did tell me while I was in LA that Fred was up near Seattle on some island."

"Jesus Christ." Cheryl heard Leonard's voice. "The Tran Lab. It's on Bainbridge Island."

"I'm thirsty," Cheryl whimpered. "Can you get me some water?"

"Sure," said Belinda. She motioned to one of the guards, who grabbed a glass from a shelf, filled it under a tap, walked over to Cheryl, held the glass for her to drink and then put a bullet in her brain. She died instantly.

"Take care of that," Belinda said to the other guard and left the basement with Leonard, who walked away with Belinda but kept glancing back at the grisly scene.

Chapter 17.

Mr. President

Snow on the ground blanketed Marshall Turner's Virginia estate. An overnight storm had caused a brief power outage and Marshall's back-up generators kicked in, waking him in the middle of the night next to his wife, who he knew would sleep through anything. The wind from the storm howled and he got out of bed and walked to his office, clicked on his desk lamp and sat down in his favorite leather chair still in his pajamas, staring at his reflection in the large window while the heavy white flakes danced in the air, moving left and right at the whim of the wind. He thought of Congress and chuckled. His phone blinked on, and a text came in that he recognized was from the White House. Meeting with Blondie. 9 am. It came from the President's chief of staff. Blondie was their personal code, poking fun at the man who cared more about his hair than his politics. A midnight text, thought Marshall. Something is up.

A black limousine pulled into Marshall's driveway at 7:30 am. As he got in, the driver handed him a hot grande mocha latte, lightly sweetened.

"You are too good to me, Manfred."

"And you to me, sir," responded Mario Benitez, whose name was not Manfred but who tolerated Marshall and his sense of humor. Mario's military background made him especially valuable to Marshall, who sought his opinion on international military matters regularly. Their drives into the Beltway often gave Marshall a new perspective on matters he had to address. Besides that, Mario could step in as a personal bodyguard if ever needed. But other than the initial banter, this ride was quiet. The only other words spoken were "White House."

"Good morning, Mr. Turner," Marshall heard from several young staffers as he was escorted through the West Wing to the Oval Office. He reached the main double doors, where he knew to wait until he was ushered into the room. "Marshall!" shouted the President in his booming voice. "So good to see a truly talented man in our midst. Refreshing, right?" he said, as he sent a scathing look around the room at the generals and cabinet members who were gathered there. "Absolutely, Sir!" said the president's chief of staff with gusto, and the President nodded approvingly in his direction.

"Marshall, Marshall. Please sit down." He pointed at the two couches in the middle of the room that were already full.

"You," he said pointing to Ben Drummond, the Director of the Department of Homeland Security. "Make room for this fine gentleman." Drummond hopped up and the others on the couch moved more tightly together to give Turner the room demanded by the President.

He added, "Would you like some coffee?" and without waiting for Marshall to respond, the President pressed a button and yelled "Bring Mr. Turner some coffee asap."

Marshall smiled and said nothing. A young blond carried in a tray bearing the presidential seal and a cup of black coffee with packets of creamer and sugar, all of which also bore the seal and set it on the table. The President smiled at the blond, and said, "Thank you, honey."

As she was shutting the door, he started: "Okay good. Everyone is here. Looks like we have a major event in Armenia. I got a call from Vlad last night, and it is not looking good there. Director, please brief us." William P. Case, Director of the Central Intelligence Agency, had been standing at the window next to the American flag behind the President's desk ignoring what was going on in the room. He already had two agents in the hospital in Yerevan and was demanding to know what was going on there.

"Here is what we know now. Someone flying from Dushanbe to Yerevan carried a highly toxic substance aboard without being detected. The substance was released in the main airport terminal and killed at least 300 people and sickened hundreds more. Whatever this substance was, it increased in size and spread over a large portion of Yerevan and began dropping toxic dust. The hospitals are being overwhelmed with patients."

"Great," said the President. "Just about what I got this morning from reading the morning paper. Have they identified the carrier? Was he Muslim? Madame Secretary, please." He pointed to Secretary of State Miriam Debourge.

"We don't believe this was an act of terror. Not yet, Mr. President."

"But it is a horrific act," he said too loudly.

"Yes, it is, sir. The problem is that Tajikistan and Armenia do not have a history of enmity. As you may know, that tension is reserved to Azerbaijan."

"It could have been an Azerbaijani, right? Maybe he flew to Tajikistan as a distraction?"

"Yes, it is true that we don't know who did this yet."

"Great. Brilliant," he said with a bite. The President looked at Case. "Contact the KGB. We know you have channels. See what they know."

Case glanced around the room as if the President had just given out state secrets. He looked at the President, took a breath, and said, "Yes, sir, Mr. President."

"What, you think the whole world doesn't know you talk to the KGB? Get your head out, Bill. Hollywood took care of that one a long time ago. Make the call!"

"Understood, sir."

"Marshall, what do you think?"

"We have good relationship with Armenia, correct? We have the world's top toxicologists. Let's send a team as an offer of assistance to the country. Maybe add some doctors."

"God damn, I love having somebody smart in the room! How's the coffee?" Marshall ignored the question, just as he had ignored the coffee. The President looked at Secretary DeBourge. "Can we pull a team together?"

As she answered "Yes, sir, Mr. President," he looked over at Case, who knew exactly what the glance meant. "And Marshall," the President added, "talk to some of your Silicon Valley buddies. I want to know if there is anything screwy going on."

"Yes, Mr. President."

Marshall called Fred from the car. He didn't wait for a response. "Something has happened in Armenia. I suggest you find out everything you can at your end. I will see you at your place this evening."

"Will do." Fred rarely took instructions from anyone, but his respect for Marshall was immense. Marshall seemed to have the ability to talk to anyone of any rank without fear and with candor. It was an ability that Fred admired most in the people he knew. He had believed that Derek Whitestone had that same skill set, only recently Derek had given him reason to doubt. He went into the kitchen and poured himself an espresso from a machine that was timed to run at 5:30 am every morning. As he was sipping the expresso, Derek entered the kitchen.

"Good morning."

"Good morning, Derek. Sleep okay?"

"Not really."

"Want some espresso?"

"That would be nice, thanks."

"Ok, Derek. You look terrible. You going to tell me what is going on?"

"We have a problem."

"And what is our problem?" He emphasized the word "our." As he did so, he handed Derek a small double espresso.

"I took an action that I thought was in your best interest and it hasn't turned out well."

Fred paused and studied the floor as if he were studying it. "You know what, Derek? I don't want to discuss this right now. Marshall just called about something extremely serious, and I need time to think and to make some calls and see what I can find out. What I want is for you to relax. Take the day and wander around the island. Give yourself some time to think about what you need to share with me and what you don't need to share with me. Let's meet again this evening when Marshall arrives. There will be much to talk about. I am certain of it."

* * *

Dr. Leonard Freund sat in his office chair. The cold-blooded murder of Cheryl Brown in the Lab basement sent chills up and down his body. Belinda had made him rich beyond his wildest dreams, but her dark side had always frightened him—but not enough for him to leave, apparently. He reached into a lower drawer and pulled out a single malt Scotch. He threw down a shot and then another and then another. His phone buzzed.

"Leonard, my friend. I have good news." It was General Warner.

"Thanks, General. I could use some good news."

"I just attended another climate change convention in Oslo. Everyone is talking about Garne McDonough's proposed solution to global warming. You might recall that he ran a massive test with bot slime and it worked."

"Remind me," said Leonard, knowing the General had not disclosed what was in the petri dish, leaving that discovery to Ragnar Willowbrook. "What do you mean it worked?"

"According to Garny, the bots self-replicated in massive amounts and eliminated a huge quantity of CO_2 from a giant dome."

"What do you care about CO_2 or climate change?"

"I don't, Leonard. But if what this guy says is even half true and we could learn to program these bots to accomplish other tasks, whatever those are, then we don't need massive quantities. We just need enough."

"The bots are gone, General."

"What are you saying?"

"They were stolen out of the lab."

"How is that possible? Jesus Christ. Are you kidding me?"

"We know who stole them."

"Well, get them back!"

"Not that easy, General."

"Make it easy!" he shouted.

"I'll keep you posted," Leonard said and hung up. Her heard the General's fading screams and turned off the phone. Doesn't get much better than this, he laughed to himself and took another shot of Scotch.

He looked at his phone. Belinda had just texted him "Get up here immediately." Here we go again, he thought. He sighed. Maybe it's finally time for Montana. Mountains, a cabin, a fishing rod, a book. But no thrillers. He had enough of that.

Chapter 18.

Van Meets Brian

Van and Charlie took a bumpy shuttle ride up to SEA-TAC, the Seattle-Tacoma International Airport. Van tried to piece together everything she knew so far. But as she thought about it, she was distracted by the view out of the eastern-facing window. The flight from San Francisco to SEA-TAC ran past the thirteen volcanic mountains that comprise the American component of the Pacific Ring of Fire, also known as the Cascade Arc. These isolated snow-covered peaks start with Lassen Peak and Mount Shasta in California and run north past Mount Hood, Mount St. Helens, and Mount Rainier up to Mount Baker on the stateside of the Canadian Border. Van was struck by their beauty and their isolation, giant lonely monsters whose fearsome volcanic wrath might be completely dead or minutes away. Very few tourists had even heard of Mount St. Helens until she blew in 1980, killing 57 people and destroying 250 homes, 47 bridges, 15 miles of railways and 185 miles of highway. She left several inches of volcanic dust over the entire city of Portland, Oregon, 70 miles to the southwest. Van counted the peaks as they flew past and studied the closest peak, Mount Rainier, as they landed. The plane pulled up and stopped short of the jetway. The ground crew pushed a staircase out to the plane, old school. Van and Charlie emerged from the plane on the tarmac and took big draws of the fresh Pacific Northwest air. Van could smell the rain and the wet tarmac from a recent shower. Van had not expected to stay long in the Bay Area, and now that she was in Seattle, she was running out of clothes. They grabbed another SUV from the car rental and popped into a Target directly across from the airport. They took the ferry to Bainbridge Island and found a couple of rooms at the Marshall Suites. They unpacked and agreed to meet at Jake's Pickup, a small deli café next to the hotel. They talked about what they knew and what they thought they still needed to know. Van glanced out of the window and saw a black Ford Explorer with California plates pull into the hotel entrance. She didn't think much about it until she saw four fit men in black boots and black fatigues jump out of the car.

She asked Charlie, "Is there a military base around here?"

"No idea," said Charlie, "but Maps might tell us." They looked at a GPS mapping tool on their phones and there was a naval base nearby called the US Naval Undersea Warfare Engineering Base. But the base was not on Bainbridge Island; rather, it was across what appeared to be called Port Orchard Sound.

"Does the Navy wear black?"

"Well, I think they call it navy blue for a reason," Charlie chuckled. "It almost looks black."

Van knew navy blue from black and the men were not wearing navy blue. "Okay," she said.

The plan was to go to the Tran Labs first. Van figured that there was no longer an element of surprise with Fred Schmidt or anyone associated with him. Derek Whitestone probably already knew they had been to his office, so there was no additional surprise there. If Derek had decided to run, they would have to start a chase and that would be unfortunate. Hopefully, he was smarter than that. But before she met with Fred Schmidt and Derek Whitestone, Van wanted to know as much as possible about the nano matter and whatever else they were dealing with.

They awoke in the morning and headed back over to Jake's for a quick breakfast. The four men were already sitting in a booth, and Van noticed that they did not seem to talk to each other and that they had no apparent interest in her or Charlie. Not yet anyway.

"Let's rent a different car," she told Charlie.

"Really?" he said.

"I have a hunch."

"Then I am with you."

They stopped and picked up a sedan and drove up 305 to Port Madison and found the Duc A. Tran Laboratory for Hereditary Biology. It was a beautiful building surrounded by pine trees, and the peacefulness of the location struck Van, as if absolutely nothing was happening there, when she knew it was the exact opposite. She noticed a large motorcycle with a gold wing parked next to a Jaguar and wondered if it reflected diversity or division in the Lab. She expected to find out. They entered and told the receptionist who they were. The receptionist rang Dr.

Meisner and Van added that they would like to meet Dr. Johannsen as well. The receptionist ushered them into a conference room that was built more for work than show. The white board was full of marks and several sketches were pinned on the bulletin boards, one of which depicted something that looked like a star or an alien spacecraft. Whoever this team was, Van knew to take them seriously. As the two scientists entered the boardroom, it was readily apparent to Van who the biker was. Dr. Stan Meisner still wore a tie to work under his lab coat and Dr. Johannsen was wearing jeans.

"Good morning, Detectives," said Dr. Meisner. "I am Dr. Stan Meisner, and this is Dr. Brian Johannsen. How can we help you?"

"Good morning," Van said, introducing herself and Charlie.

"A bit outside your jurisdiction, wouldn't you say?"

"It's called the long arm of the law for a reason, doctor," replied Van, standing her ground. Charlie chuckled and bit his lip.

"I'm not interested in wasting your time," Van went on. "We are here on a matter related to an incident in which three people lost their lives, one student and two lab technicians."

"Do we need a lawyer?" said Dr. Meisner.

"I'd heard it was just the student," Brian said without concern about Dr. Meisner's question.

Van looked at Brian and turned to Dr. Meisner. "That is up to you, Dr. Meisner. We are here to gather information and no one at the Lab is identified as a suspect in the events in Los Angeles. But if you would like to wait for an attorney, I completely understand."

"I am fine for now," he replied.

Van looked at Brian. "You know about UCLA, Dr. Johannsen?"

"Brian, please. We do, but what we know about it is from the news. Nothing else."

"Do you have any interactions with the Lyndon A. Rutter Lab at UCLA Medical School?"

Dr. Meisner responded, "The microbiology community is a small community. We all know each other, and the goal is to advance the science, and we all support each other in that goal. We collaborate on multiple projects."

"Well," said Brian. "Don't be fooled. We are as competitive as a pack of wolves. We know we need each other, but we are constantly fighting to be top dog in the pack."

Dr. Meisner glanced at Brian. Maybe we do need an attorney, he mused.

"Ok. The real question is do you know how they died?"

"No," said Dr. Meisner.

"No but," said Brian, "the report was that the student died of anaphylaxis after being exposed to a substance in a petri dish."

"That is correct," Van said. "All of them from the same exposure and the same reaction."

"Well, it is difficult to know whether there is any connection or not," said Brian. "But we had a similar incident here, only we contained it quickly enough, and although a couple of us got really sick, nobody died."

"Can you elaborate?"

"Do you know Derek Whitestone and Fred Schmidt?"

Van and Charlie looked at each other and nodded.

"They dropped off a petri dish that they wanted us to analyze."

"Christ," Van heard Charlie mutter.

"The dish was labeled Risk Group IV. Are you familiar with that classification?"

"We are," Van said. "Ebola."

"Right, or at least that class of pathogen. We are a Biosafety Level IV lab and qualified to handle Risk Group IV, as is, by the way, the Rutter Lab."

"That is how Dr. Fielding described it," said Van.

"March Fielding," said Dr. Meisner. "Very well respected."

"Only you discovered it was not a pathogen," Van said.

Brian and Dr. Meisner shot quick looks at each other. "Exactly," said Brian.

"And you let your guard down," said Van.

"We did and almost paid a steep price."

"Just a question and I still have the same question for Dr. Fielding. Didn't the label Risk Group IV trigger in you some extra caution?"

"The label could have been a warning, and in some sense, it was the best warning available. But it also could have been a misdirection. It could have been a mechanism for hiding the contents and limiting access to a very small group of professionals. Where we being cautious? Yes. What happened here was at least arguably the result of an error in protocol, only we have no protocol in place for the treatment of either medical or non-medical nanotechnology. I am not sure anyone does. It should not have been exposed to the air in any space where people are present. I wish we knew that then. We know it now."

"That drawing over there," she pointed to the sketch of the star/spaceship on the bulletin board. "Is that it?"

"Yes, it is. It is a nanoparticle that was manufactured by a human being, but we do not know the source."

"You don't know who produced it."

"We don't," said Brian. "Maybe we should have inquired further but we assumed Fred and Derek wanted to keep it confidential, proprietary information."

"Have you figured out what it does?"

"We think so," said Brian this time. "At least what it does in part, whether it is what was intended or not. My colleague, Dr. Comstock—she was the one who almost died—noticed that the bot seems to be attracted to CO_2. We ran some small experiments and these bots seemed especially effective at reducing the volume of carbon dioxide in the air. Once they had reached their capacity for CO_2 molecules, they went dormant and fell on the floor of the chamber like dust."

"Sounds like a solution to global warming," Charlie said, and the room chuckled.

"Maybe you are right," said Brian. "The world is full of irony, and it wouldn't surprise me that a planet-sized problem would be addressed by a robot the size of a microbe."

"Well, it is certainly true that a microbe can cause a planet sized problem," Dr. Meisner added.

"Do you know why it causes anaphylaxis?" Van asked.

"Hard to say yet," answered Brian. "The nanobot is composed of a titanium alloy and a type of porcelain that bears an electrical charge. It just may be the case that this combination of metals and electricity is something the human body won't tolerate but it doesn't know how to destroy it and it overreacts."

"Any ideas on how to contain it, if it gets released?"

"We are working on that," said Dr. Meisner.

"How so?" asked Van.

Brian and Dr. Meisner looked at each other.

Dr. Meisner said, "I suggest you speak to Mr. Whitestone and Mr. Schmidt. For our part, I think at this point, we might want an attorney present."

"Absolutely understood," said Van. "Thank you for your time." She motioned to Dr. Meisner and then to Brian, who smiled. Van blushed just a little, and Charlie smiled to himself. Van needs someone special like that, he thought, as long as he manages to stay out of prison.

As they left the building, Van looked around for the black Explorer. She didn't see anything that seemed unusual, and she and Charlie got back into the sedan and headed south to Fred Schmidt's mansion.

"Are they part of this?" Van asked Charlie.

"What does your gut tell you?"

"Dr. Meisner is reserved, but that may just be his manner. Dr. Johannsen…"

"Brian."

"Right, Brian. He is willing to talk and sounds to me like he knows his stuff."

"Anything he say jump out at you?" Charlie said to Van.

"Actually, I am surprised no one seems to know the source. It is a manufactured piece of machinery that came from somewhere. Wouldn't you want to know where? Wouldn't that tell you the answers to a lot of questions, including why it was labeled Risk Group IV even though it wasn't a biological substance? Dr. Fielding didn't know where it came from and people died. Dr. Meisner didn't know where it came from and people almost died. The only thing they did know about the source was that Derek Whitestone delivered it, and Derek Whitestone is neither a biologist nor a chemist but rather a Silicon Valley investment banker, and it is very possible he didn't tell them where it came from because Derek stole it."

"So, you are not buying 'confidential proprietary'?"

"Are you?"

"Nah."

"Well, let's see what Fred says. Are you finding this interesting?"

"You betcha!" Van smiled at Charlie, and Charlie nodded and looked out at the Island greenery. Yes, he thought. This was about as interesting as it gets.

The black Explorer waited in the shadows near the Lab. Its occupants saw Van and Charlie leave and thought they looked familiar, but no one placed them. Their focus was on retrieving the petri dish for Belinda and exacting a small price for the Lab's collusion with Derek Whitestone and Cheryl Brown.

Chapter 19.

The Butler Didn't Do It

Derek was the first to arrive, or, rather, he was the first to arrive back at Fred's mansion. He took Fred's advice earlier in the day and spent the day wandering around the Island and let Fred's reaction to his explanation about UCLA sink in. He realized how stupid it was for him to lie to Fred, that Fred would see through it in an instant, and that Derek's only salvation, if there was any at all, was to be totally candid with Fred. He resolved to tell Fred the complete truth, that is, that it was his greed and insecurity that caused him to split the contents of the dish and have Cheryl deliver it to UCLA.

Fred had given Derek a key and told him to let himself back in if he had gone out. He locked the door behind him and headed to Fred's office to pour himself a Scotch and soda. It had started to rain, and Derek looked out the windows through the pine trees over the Sound. Rain has two effects on the ocean. If combined with wind, the sea gets stormy and hostile with crashing white caps. Without wind, rain turns the ocean into smooth glass and the only way to see the movement of waves is to stare at the white edge of the shoreline. He was briefly mesmerized and, for a fleeting moment, forgot about his problems, and then he heard a frantic rap on the front door. No one else was home yet so he went over and opened it, and there stood the famous Marshall Turner, soaked like a wet dog.

"Derek Whitestone?"

"If you wait a minute, I will get him for you," Derek smiled.

"Well, I'll be goddamned. What are you doing here? No, wait. You and Fred are pretty much joined at the hip, right? Why should I be surprised? Um, do you mind if I come in?"

"Hello, Marshall. Yes, please come in."

Marshall pulled in a suitcase and Derek offered him his room to change in. Marshall joined Derek in the study.

"How are things, Marshall?" Derek asked him.

"Well, Derek, honestly, I might be inclined to say the more things change and so on. But this President is… different. Problem is I can't tell yet whether that is a good thing. But tell me, how are you, and how is our friend, Fred?"

Derek and Marshall chatted amiably for about an hour. For Derek, the distraction was welcome. Marshall had opinions about everything and never hesitated to share them. Had Derek been in his usual frame of mind, he would have recorded the conversation mentally and plotted some of his next investment strategies. But he was not in that state. Rather he was a man standing on the edge of a cliff or a tall building, and an instant away from stepping off. They sipped their Scotch and heard a commotion in the entrance. They heard a voice they recognized as Fred's and another they did not immediately recognize.

"Here let me take that," Fred said to Dr. Brian Johannsen, who had just closed his umbrella but wasn't certain where to set it down.

"Freddy boy!" Marshall shouted, as he emerged from the study into the foyer. Derek followed growing quiet.

"And Dr. Johannsen? What a nice surprise!" he added, when it became clear who had entered with Fred.

"Dr. Johannsen," said Derek. "Good to see you again."

Brian was courteous. He and Fred had spent that last few hours together discussing the nanoparticles and whether there were any safe applications or not, and if not, if they might be modified to be made safe. Brian had pressed Fred on the origin of the petri dish, but Fred redirected the conversation, and Brian figured out quickly that the effort was fruitless. Brian was caught off guard when Fred told him that he had an important conversation coming up, and that he needed Brian to be present and would he mind coming over to Fred's place to meet his guests. Brian agreed, and though Fred offered to drive, Brian was used to riding in the rain and said he would follow. Brian had said nothing about the meeting with Van and Charlie. He figured it was not his place. But they did discuss UCLA and the tragedy there. Brian told Fred that if anything like the dish that he and Derek had delivered to Tran Labs was delivered to another location, the outcome would have been predictable. He told

Fred that once he identified the bot as a non-biological substance, he himself lost his fear of the substrate, except for the fact that it had been labeled Risk Group IV, and for that reason alone he continued to be cautious. He had tried to stop his colleague from opening it, but he had been a bit slow to respond, and it had been near disastrous for them. Fred said nothing about Derek to Brian. He was still considering a response and had pretty much made up his mind but had not come to any final decisions. Brian was already drawing his own conclusions about Fred and Derek's actions. He was not afraid of talking with Fred despite the meeting with the LA detectives.

The four men met in Fred's study. Brian had pulled off his riding gear and was still drying out but the fire in the fireplace and the Scotch made him comfortable. Fred started the conversation.

"Gentlemen. I want to thank all of you for being here, especially Dr. Johannsen. His continued work on the nanoparticles has been very productive, and we are forming the beginnings of a plan. His perspective on how we might proceed is critical and I have invited him to consider joining any program we begin to develop." Brian smiled but said nothing.

"Marshall, your timing is impeccable, as usual, and I am especially glad you are here with us now. At our last meeting, you mentioned Providia, and as I said then, Derek has done some initial investigation there. Is there anything you can tell us about the AI at Providia and how that might contribute?"

"Yes, Fred, and I am glad to be here thank you but before we develop any plans I am here on a mission from the President and it is directly relevant to what you are discussing. Do you mind if I impose for a few minutes and take us in a slightly different direction?"

"Not at all."

Derek was listening to everything quietly. At this point, he was disoriented. Fred was introducing Brian and talking about a joint effort as if Derek would be included. He wondered if his idea of confessing everything to Fred was the right idea, and he found himself backing away from that ledge. However, at the mention of Providia, he began to think of Cheryl Brown and wondered if she was doing okay in LA. He realized that he had ignored her completely as his own issues escalated, and he only now recognized that it had been well over a week since they had spoken. He had expected Marshall's mission to be political and was tuning it out as he thought of Cheryl, and then he heard Marshall say, "...there is a developing toxicological disaster in Yerevan, the capital city of Armenia. Hundreds have died from an anaphylactic pandemic that started at the airport in Yerevan, and the hospitals are overwhelmed. Apparently, a cloud that started building at the airport, has grown immense and is raining some kind of toxic dust on the city. We are assembling a team of experts, and Dr. Johannsen, with all due respect to the ideas that you and Mr. Schmidt might have right now, you might consider joining that team."

"Tell me about the dust," said Brian. "What do we know?"

"Very little," said Marshall. "The Yerevan hospital has not been able to identify any pathogen that is triggering the anaphylaxis. All we know so far is that the toxin is causing a cytokine storm, and some people seem to be able to manage it and others are dying."

Derek said almost without thinking, "The victims at UCLA died from anaphylaxis."

Fred said, "UCLA? Derek? I heard about something at UCLA—a student dying in a lab. You said victims, as in plural?"

Brian said, "That is the same reaction we had at Tran."

Marshall said, "UCLA? Why are we talking about UCLA?"

Derek started to speak, uncertain what words to use, when there was another knock at the front door. "Excuse me a minute," said Fred.

As Fred was answering the door, Brian looked at Derek and Marshall. "Do you know where the nanoparticles came from? Where were they manufactured?"

"I might," said Derek. Brian and Marshall both looked at him and as they waited for him to elaborate, Fred walked into the room with Van and Charlie.

Marshall started to joke about it being quite the assembly when he recognized Van from the Hollywood party. Her presence seemed to him to be utterly out of place until Fred introduced them, "Gentlemen, allow me to introduce Los Angeles Detectives Van Eng and Charles Darling."

Marshall stifled a laugh. "I believe Miss, my apologies, Detective Eng and I have met."

"Yes, Mr. Turner," Van said. "We met and spoke briefly at Martin Richard's after party. Good to see you again."

Fred then said, "The detectives are here on business. I appreciate that the situation in Armenia may be pressing but I suggest we allow them to conduct their business first."

"Ok by me," said Marshall, still staring at Van incredulously.

"Thank you," said Van. "Hello, Dr. Johannsen."

"Detective Eng." Fred looked Brian, and Brian returned the look and nodded. The entire room heard Fred under his breath say, "Okay."

"Do you mind if we talk to Derek Whitestone alone?" Van inquired.

Derek responded, "I will speak with you Detectives, but it would be wise for me to have an attorney present?"

"Then I am afraid we need to advise you of your rights, Mr. Whitestone."

"Wait a minute," said Fred. "I want to know what this is about."

"We think you may know already, Mr. Schmidt. Might be advisable for you to lawyer-up, if that is what they call it. For now, our primary concern is Mr. Whitestone."

"Does this have anything to do with UCLA?" Fred asked, sensing the situation that he had orchestrated was getting out of control.

"It has everything to do with UCLA," Van said as she pulled out cuffs that Charlie handed her and approached Derek

"Wait a minute," Fred said. "Derek, you need to tell me now, what happened at UCLA?"

Derek looked at Fred, feeling helpless. Van filled in the void. "Three people died at a UCLA Lab handling the petri dish that Derek Whitestone allegedly," she paused, "had delivered to the Lab."

Fred looked shocked. Marshall and Brian were quiet. "That's right," said Derek. "It was a backup plan."

"Derek," Fred looked at him pleading and almost hurt. "I don't understand," he said and then added, "And what is the crime?"

"As it stands," said Van, "criminal negligence and involuntary manslaughter." She fitted the cuffs on Derek and read him his rights. "We are booking him here tonight at Bainbridge PD. He will be extradited to Los Angeles."

"Don't worry, Derek. I will get you out. We'll deal with the rest later."

"Thank you for your time, gentlemen," said Van, as they moved to leave.

"Derek," said Marshall. "Where did it come from?"

Derek turned back. "Ragnar Willowbrook."

After Van and Charlie left with Derek, Fred returned to the study.

"That was entertaining," said Marshall. "Did you have any idea?"

Fred was angry. "I did. But only an idea. I had a plan and now, fuck me, it looks like it needs to change."

Brian said, "Ragnar Willowbrook. Isn't that the lab near Santa Cruz? They manufactured the nanoparticles?"

"Yes, it is," said Fred. "They didn't manufacture anything. They don't have the technology. But I'll bet they know where it came from."

"Derek got the dish from Ragnar Willowbrook, and you brought it to us," said Brian, now confused and deeply troubled at the events going on around him. He looked up at Fred and Marshall as if the entire world had gone crazy, and he didn't know whom to trust or what to believe any more. Then his phone buzzed.

"We need to get back to the Lab now. There's been an explosion and the Lab is on fire."

"I'll take you," said Fred. "No need to go back out in the rain."

"I'll wait here," Marshall said, imagining the worst.

"We'll get you a mask," said Fred. "You're coming with us."

Chapter 20.

It's Gone

The black Explorer waited on a side road behind a grove of trees. Clouds were building and the breeze that usually preceded a storm was picking up. A dark gray wall of rain was making its way from the north across Port Madison Bay. Boats raced across the bay to the marina, trying to outrun the storm. The ops team could see Detectives Eng and Darling head out of the entrance and get in a beige sedan. "Find my dish first," the team heard Belinda command. As soon as the sedan was gone, they slipped out of the Explorer with their gear. They set up posts around the perimeter of the building gauging the activity inside. They could see a group of scientists gathered at the window, watching the rain come. "Hold," came the command over the radios. Several staff members left the building to beat the rain home. They then watched as Fred Schmidt drove up, parked and entered the building. The team was disciplined from years in the field. They had waited under much more severe conditions. From the wet heat of southeast Asia to the scorching dryness of Somalia to the icy cold of northern Afghanistan, they had waited for hours upon hours for the right moment to do their duty and follow some command. They were a tight, disciplined unit, always ready to do whatever they were called upon to do. Now they waited and hid outside a modern American laboratory in the thick, green brush of Bainbridge Island in Puget Sound as the rain began to fall. Inside, Fred Schmidt had asked to meet with Dr. Johannsen. He was escorted to Brian's office and stood there gazing out the window at a wall of rain quickly approaching the Island.

"Mr. Schmidt," he heard behind and turn to see Brian removing his hazmat gear.

"Good afternoon, Brian. I hope you don't mind my intrusion."

"What's up?"

"What do we know?"

"Well, we have confirmed self-replication. It's a stunning process, like watching a crystal form."

"It can happen anywhere?"

"We are testing that out, but we are keeping the environment very secure. Even still, it is remarkably fast and it speeds up with the introduction of electrical energy and heat."

"What about other uses?"

"That is more speculative. These nanobots are programmed to harvest CO2, as we have discussed. It does not seem that far-fetched to imagine harvesting other type of molecules, possibly even more complex molecules like hydroflourocarbons or methane. If we could find a way to make it safe, I can imagine uses in a variety of situations, from controlling emissions at refineries and coal-burning plants to improving safety in mining operations. There may be electrical storage applications as well. It is just the beginning."

Fred's smiled and started to glow. "That is what I wondered. We have a lot of work to do. Do you mind joining me with a couple people at my place? I am happy to drive."

"Of course, but I might as well head home from there. I'll take the bike."

Brian packed up and put on his rain riding gear. As they left, the rain began to get heavy. Fred ran and jumped in his car and Brian hopped on his bike and took off. The ops team waited in the rain, quietly. When Fred and Brian were a ways down the road, the ops team heard the command, "Gear on," and they all put on gas masks with special low vision goggles snapped in place. The next command was "Go." Quickly and quietly, they moved toward the rear entrance. It was locked but they easily pried it open with a small black crowbar and moved swiftly up the stairs. At the third floor, they fanned out. Most of the staff had left but a handful remained. The team deployed knock out gas canisters around the floor, and everyone on the floor crumpled to the ground. The team checked to be sure they were out and searched the labs' freezers and refrigerators. Belinda had described the dish in detail including the Risk Group IV warning and a special code that identified it as the dish containing the nano gel. One of the ops members waited in the elevator lobby. Dr.

Meisner and a couple of colleagues were taking the elevator up to the third floor and were casually conversing with each other about golf. When the door opened, the ops member quickly tossed in another canister and as the scientists tried to leave the elevator, he pointed his assault rifle and they backed into the gas, falling to the floor. The door closed and he pushed the button to open it and then dragged out the unconscious bodies, placing them next to each other on the floor of the lobby. He heard someone say, "Got bots," and then the command, "Place charges." The unconscious white coated bodies were all dragged to the lobby area and neatly lined up on the floor. The ops team then quietly exited the building down the back stairs and back into the foliage that surrounded the grounds on the rear of the building facing Port Madison Sound. They made their way back to the black Explorer, jumped in and peeled away with a biohazard case holding the remains of the petri dish. They drove for 10 minutes and then parked. The captain of the unit pulled out his cell phone and dialed a 10-digit number. When he hit send, the charges at the Lab blew and a black cloud appeared on the horizon, but the rain quickly washed it away.

Back at the Lab, staff that had been on the lower level smelled the knockout gas from the third floor, and following Lab protocol, quickly grabbed masks and exited the building. Instead of standing in the rain, they ran to their cars in the parking lot and started calling each other waiting for instructions from Dr. Meisner, but they heard nothing. Finally, someone texted the group and reported that Dr. Meisner and several staff members were missing, and a small handful, including Carrie, who happened to be on the first floor in a meeting in a conference room, put on their masks and ran back into the building. As they were entering, the charges on the third floor exploded, sending a large plume of smoke into the sky and glass and metal and wood chips sprayed into the parking lot. The east side of the building, opposite the rear entrance, collapsed. Several staff members jumped out of their cars as fire engulfed the building and ran to the rear entrance to help those who had just entered. A couple staff in the rescue group stumbled out of the door and fell on the ground coughing. Carrie had made her way to the third floor to discover the unconscious bodies lined up when the explosion occurred that sent her sprawling back into the staircase and she tumbled down a flight of concrete stairs. There was a loud bang as the east side of the building collapsed and all but a couple of the bodies fell into the burning debris two stories below. One of those bodies was that of Dr. Meisner. More staff rescuers came up the stairwell and pulled Carrie, who was bruised and bleeding, out of the building. The lobby floor was slanted toward the collapse, and two staff members were hanging on the edge and the rescue team appeared and pulled them to safety.

But the safety was short-lived. When the ops team recovered the petri dish, they had no reason to be concerned that there might be smart dust remaining in the Lab either from the original sample or from the process of self-replication that Brian and the team there had uncovered. In fact, several containers of the smart dust had been stored in a special sealed locker that burst open when the explosion occurred. The explosion shattered the containers holding the additional smart dust and the heat of the fire caused the nano particles to rise, forming a cloud that dispersed throughout the building and into the parking lot.

All the unconscious bodies that happened to survive the partial building collapse died immediately. But the team members in the parking lot who were following protocol and had their masks on weren't affected. A couple of team members had removed their masks but when they felt the tingle in the back of their throats, they immediately put them back on, and even though they started coughing, they didn't have full blown anaphylactic reactions. Port Madison and surrounding communities were extremely lucky that a heavy and windless rain came through when it did and kept the cloud from dispersing any further.

Van and Charlie were transporting Derek to the Bainbridge Island police station, when Derek's phone lit up with text messages from Fred telling Derek to inform the detectives what had happened and not to return to the Lab. Van told Derek to text Fred and give him her mobile and Fred called Van directly.

"What's going on?"

"Dr. Johannsen is getting reports from his team there. It's still unclear why the explosion occurred but the situation is bad and continues to be extremely dangerous. Several scientists were on the third floor when it exploded, and there have been injuries and some deaths, including Dr. Stan Meisner, the top faculty member there. But there is more that you need to know about. According to Dr. Johannsen, the Lab had been able to replicate the nano particles and was storing a sizable amount in a freezer. Some members of the faculty are reporting reactions but they have masks.

We are picking up gas masks at the hospital before we go up there. I am sure police and fire are on their way. We hope to God they know to mask up before they get there."

"Ask them if there is any concern about other infectious diseases?" asked Charlie. The report from Brian came back that possible SARS containment would be required. Marshall, who was riding with Fred and Brian, mentioned what had happened in Yerevan, Armenia. According to Marshall, a large portion of the city had been infected by whatever had been released. The location would need to be treated as extremely hazardous and contained quickly.

"We can pick up masks at the station," Van said to Charlie.

When they got to the police station, there was a skeleton crew. Several officers had gone up to the site of the explosion. Van confirmed that they knew to treat the incident as hazardous and had appropriate gear, and had informed Seattle's HazMat team, who were on their way. Van called Detective Young in Los Angeles and reported everything that had developed. Young told her good work and said to be very careful. They booked Derek at the station. He was led to a cell to be transported to Los Angeles at the earliest convenience, but with the events unfolding at the Lab, it was uncertain when that would be.

Van and Charlie grabbed masks and headed back up to the Lab. The police had set up a wide perimeter, with an outer boundary two miles wide. They evacuated Port Madison and closed all roads going up to the Lab. They taped up an inner perimeter 500 feet around the Lab, and the Lab staff was asked to wait outside the perimeter. Ambulances were on site and transported anyone complaining of allergic reactions to the hospital immediately. The police allowed Fred's car to enter because of Brian, and Van and Charlie's car was allowed to pass. When they got to the scene, they introduced themselves to the local detective in charge. The fire had been put out with foam, and the HazMat team was enclosing the entire building in a tent. All active responders were wearing full Hazmat gear. Charlie told Van that the scene looked like something out of the movie, Mission to Mars. Van and Charlie had already informed the police department of their presence on the Island and weren't questioned. The lead detective confirmed to Van and Charlie that there were 10 bodies and a half dozen more, who were injured in the blast when they tried to rescue the missing doctors. He also confirmed that they found evidence of explosive material in the debris. Van told the detective about the black Explorer she had seen earlier in the day with California plates. She suggested issuing an all-points bulletin or APB though by now they were probably far south. She also suggested they look for SUV tire tracks, maybe All Terrains, where they might have parked. With no other leads, the detective called in the APB to include Seattle and all highways south into Oregon.

Van found Brian speaking to the fire fighters and putting on a HazMat suit.

"I am really sorry about your colleagues," she said.

"I need to get in there," he told Van. "I need to find the dish."

"Let me join you," she answered him. "Maybe I can help." But Van had her doubts that the dish would still be there.

She asked Charlie to start talking to the staff that remained in site. She wanted to know if anyone had seen anything strange including a black Ford Explorer with California license plates.

They suited up and walked up to the building and walked in through a temporary containment entrance, a long white tunnel strung with lights. The rain had stopped, and the air was misting. The day was growing dark and the lights helped them find their way through the debris. The outer East wall had collapsed completely, and Van could see the partial collapse of the second and third stories. The bagged bodies had been laid out on the ground next to the coroner's van. Brian wandered over to the suited-up coroner and let them know to be careful with the bodies given their exposure to the nano particles. They began picking their way through the debris. There was broken glass and shattered lab equipment everywhere. Brian found his monitor and server, but it was partially melted from the fire. He showed Van and said, "That's three years of my life down the tubes." Eventually, they found the small locking freezer in which Brian kept the original petri dish, and they could see marks from the crowbar that showed it had been pried open and broken into and emptied. Van told Brian it was evidence and pointed it out to the local forensics team that had already arrived. They looked around but there was no sign of the petri dish.

"It's gone," said Brian.

Chapter 21.

Van's War

Brian didn't go to Armenia, as much as his expertise might have helped. The catastrophe at the Lab kept him on Bainbridge Island, and he worked closely with Seattle PD's forensics team trying to piece together what had happened. Van and Charlie went back to the hotel and booked a flight to Los Angeles, where they planned to have Derek arraigned. But before she left with Charlie, and as they were removing their hazmat suits, Brian told Van he would like very much to stay in touch. Van said of course they would be in touch as the case moved forward and as whatever they learned from the explosion might advance her investigations in Los Angeles. Brian pulled his hazmat boots off and walked over to Van in his loose T-shirt and jeans and socks on the wet grass, and said no, that he would really like to stay in touch. Van felt her knees give a little and she smiled.

"I would like that very much," she told Brian.

He blushed and said with some relief, "Okay then."

Charlie didn't waste any time. In the car ride back to the hotel, he said, "That Brian, something about him."

Van blushed and just said, "Charlie," and nothing else. Charlie smiled.

The next morning, they retrieved Derek from the police station, cuffed him, and took him to a special waiting room at SEA-TAC designed for police uses. As they sat waiting for their flight to be called, Derek said to them, "There are some things you should know."

"Okay. Are you certain you want to proceed without an attorney present?"

"Yes. You need to know this now. As for me, it is what it is." Charlie looked at Van as if to say, we need to be careful with this one.

Van turned on the recording feature on her phone. "Okay, tell us what you need to tell us."

"The petri dish was stolen from Ragnar Willowbrook by Cheryl Brown. She hid it from me and then accidentally disclosed it to me."

"Who is Ragnar Willowbrook?"

"Ragnar Willowbrook is the preeminent independent engineering laboratory in the Silicon Valley. Everybody who is anybody developing any biomedical applications tries to get an RW Labs endorsement, except that it is really a false front. The lab has gotten rich off their reputation, but they have not developed anything new on their own. They are known for stealing ideas and then winning the race to patent the ideas as their own ideas, and they buy top legal talent to ensure that they win those patent cases."

"Do you think they stole the dish?"

"I don't know. They have a lot of inside channels. They could have paid for it."

"But you ended up with it and you elected not to return it."

"Right. I was torn but it occurred to me that Fred might be able to do much more with it through his channels than Belinda could through hers. Honestly, I thought Fred would be impressed, and truth be told, he was."

"Fred knew the dish was stolen?" Charlie asked.

Derek stared at the ground. "He knew Cheryl took it from RW. He told me to fire Cheryl. Instead, I used her as my back-up option to Fred."

Van asked, "Who is Belinda?"

"Dr. Belinda Armendariz. Her ruthless tactics got her promoted to Chief Scientist at RW and ultimately CEO. I believe that Belinda figured out that Cheryl stole the petri dish, and I am not only concerned about Cheryl, but what else Belinda would do or might have already done to retaliate for its theft. I asked Cheryl to deliver the dish to UCLA—that was my back-up plan to Fred. Cheryl drove it down there and had a scary interaction with men in a black SUV. I assume they were Belinda's men."

"Explorer?"

"Yes." Van looked at Charlie. Derek continued, "She said it had been following her down the 5 Freeway to Los Angeles. We suspected Belinda might be on her tail, so we set up a decoy bag that they grabbed off Cheryl's back. They would have taken her, but a campus security guard was there and intervened."

"Where is Cheryl now?"

"I don't know. I can't reach her."

"You need to give us her contact information. Does Belinda employ black ops?"

Derek got quiet. "Yes." He said looking down again.

"Do you think Belinda could do Cheryl harm?"

"I don't put anything past Belinda."

"Do you think Belinda will come after you?"

"She might. Especially if she doesn't get from Cheryl what she needs."

"You willing to sign a statement?"

"Sure. Whatever you need. I don't care what happens to me anymore."

The three of them flew to Los Angeles and landed at Hollywood Burbank Airport. Van had police vehicles waiting for them. She booked him into the Metropolitan Correctional Facility, a slightly less hostile environment than the infamous Twin Towers correctional facility. Van reported everything that had happened to Detective Young. He knew at this point he need to support her and provide anything she needed to bring this to a conclusion. Van wanted to hit RW Labs as quickly as possible. If Belinda was as hardcore as Derek led her to believe, Van didn't have much time. Belinda could hit anybody associated with Derek, like Fred or Marshall or even Brian, who had been minutes away from disaster at his own lab.

She and Charlie went to Cheryl's apartment. It had been ransacked. Pictures pulled off the walls, furniture torn apart, dishes smashed and knick-knacks scattered about. She called forensics to see if they could find fingerprints, but she doubted they would have been that careless. DNA was more likely, and whether it helped or not, she wanted it. She studied the room. The destruction and debris were random—not orderly or planned. It seemed more angry than intentional, as if someone was sending a message. Like the explosion at the Lab. What purpose did it serve if they had found the petri dish? Retaliation? A message?

She returned to the Bureau and went back into Detective Young's office. "I want a coordinated assault on RW Labs," she said. I want to fight her black ops with our best tactical assault teams. We need to be prepared, and it could get ugly. If what I am hearing is true, Belinda Armendariz is no better than a domestic terrorist, and the material she probably has back in her possession could be weaponized. We need to prevent that."

"We can get SWAT on it, but you'll want the FBI to lead that effort."

"That's fine. Let's get it together."

The FBI maintained an office on the fifth floor of the LAPD's central headquarters to allow for close coordination where needed. Detective Young took Van to the Office and asked for Agent Henry Sams. The LAPD post was not the worst office an FBI agent might fill, but it was not considered high grade. Henry Sams had been with the Bureau for 20 years and was nearing retirement. He had never been viewed as a climber but had managed to hold his job in part due to his good work on several cross-border gang cases. Detective Young and Agent Sams knew each other well. They had a recurring lunch meeting once a month, where they updated each other on new developments. LAPD leadership had a tense relationship with the Bureau but viewed the lunch meetings as beneficial and allowed Young to keep them. For Sams, it was viewed as part of his duty to maintain a connection to the LAPD.

"Agent Sams."

"Hello, Detective Young. Please follow me."

Van was struck by how plain the agent's office looked. There was a small foyer with a couple of ratty chairs and a cheap coffee table. A coffee machine stood in the corner next to a water dispenser and a trash can that needed emptying. Nothing was on the wall except a small, framed sign that said Federal Bureau of Investigation, Los Angeles Bureau. It was a sign that you might miss if you weren't looking for it. She wouldn't have thought twice about it as an LAPD office, but as the central office for the FBI in downtown Los Angeles it seemed very sparse. They went into a small interrogation room with a white table and metal chairs.

"Let me introduce you to Detective Van Eng."

"Pleasure. What is this about?"

"You might have heard about the explosion in Seattle."

"Yes. It is on the wire."

"Detective Eng was there."

Henry's eyes grew wider. "What do you know about it?"

Van responded deferentially. "It's a rather long story, Agent Sams, but it starts with an investigation into an accident at a UCLA laboratory that resulted in three deaths." She walked through her investigation and ultimate capture of Derek Whitestone, who during his extradition to Los Angeles had confessed to a theft that Van believed was connected to the bombing. More importantly, she said, the material that was stolen was extremely dangerous and Whitestone provided information that she believed placed the material in the hands of the person responsible for the bombing who had yet to be detained.

Sams contacted headquarters and assembled a larger briefing that led to a coordinated effort between the FBI, the Bureau of Alcohol, Tobacco and Firearms, the LAPD Detective Bureau and SWAT Team and the Santa Cruz Police Department. The teams set up a war room in one of the classrooms at UC Santa Cruz, about 45 minutes southwest of RW Labs. Agent Sams took the lead for his team and organized command and control for effective cross department coordination. Everyone agreed the operation needed to be tight and that there was no room for jurisdictional in-fighting. They hatched a plan to send a small team to the Lab. If the Lab cooperated, that team would take appropriate action but at any sign of resistance, one team member would text a code and the force would mobilize at the main entrance. Given that they were dealing with black ops, the team knew extreme caution must be taken, and initial cover would be provided by the SWAT unit. In order to prevent the advance team from being taken as hostages, they would be backed up by a small armed SWAT unit and were to advance no further than the main entrance to RW Labs.

The advance team included Agent Sams and Detective Young, Charlie and Van as well as four back-up agents. They left first in two unmarked sedans. Ten minutes behind them was the LAPD SWAT Special Reaction Team in three Lenco BearCat armored rescue vehicles carrying 15 team members.

Behind the BearCats, the FBI and ATF drove another four specially outfitted SUVs carrying another 20 agents. Two LAPD SWAT helicopters outfitted to carry another four officers externally armed with fast action AR-15s waited at the University for instructions.

The advance team rolled up to the guarded entrance of RW Labs in two cars. Agent Sams rolled down his window and displayed his badge to the guard, "My name is Agent Henry Sams. We are from the FBI and would like to speak to Dr. Belinda Armendariz."

"Please hold." The guard returned to the guardhouse. He spoke on the phone and then came back to the car. "Dr. Armendariz is not available."

This was expected. "Please let Dr. Armendariz know that we have a warrant to search the premises." He handed the guard a copy of the search warrant.

The guard left with the warrant. He got on the phone again. In a few minutes, the gate opened. "We're in," Detective Young radioed to the support team, which instructed them to move forward, keep out of sight of the guards and wait for further instructions.

The two cars rolled up the long and windy driveway to the entrance. No one was outside to meet them. They exited the car and pulled their guns. The front desk and the lobby were empty. Then they heard Dr. Armendariz speaking over a loudspeaker into the lobby.

"Good morning, gentlemen. How can I help you?"

"Dr. Armendariz, I am Agent Henry Sams of the FBI. With me are Detectives Paul Young and Van Eng of the LAPD. We have a warrant to search the building."

"On what grounds, Agent Sams?"

"There is a judge in Los Angeles who believes there is probable cause to connect this lab to the bombing of another lab in Washington State."

"That is absurd, Agent Sams. We are a reputable scientific institution, not a terrorist organization."

"You are required by law to allow us access."

"Then you must allow my men to disarm you." At that point, several of Belinda's black ops stepped from behind the elevator bay and pointed their guns at the advance team, which immediately raised their weapons at the guards.

"Stand down, Dr. Armendariz!" Agent Sams shouted. "Instruct your men to lower their weapons. We will not be disarmed." The guards did not lower their weapons. Rather, they began to slowly move forward toward the advance team. Van felt her heart sink, but she held her ground as did everyone else. Detective Young was holding his push-to-talk phone in one hand and his Glock-9 standard issue pistol in the other. He keyed the phone, sending a signal to the support team. As he did that, a doctor in a white lab coat appeared from behind Belinda's guards.

"Stop this!" he shouted at the guards. "Ignore him!" Belinda shouted over the speaker.

Dr. Leonard Freund stepped forward toward the advance FBI team with his hands up. He told the guards again, "Lower your weapons," and to the FBI team, he said, "Take me into custody. This needs to stop."

He walked forward toward the agents. Belinda's voice became very calm and grave. "He must be stopped," she said, and one of her black ops fired a shot that knocked Leonard to the ground. The agents immediately returned fire forcing the guards to retreat a step backward as the agents likewise backed away from the guards toward the front entrance. Van dove forward and grabbed Leonard by the collar as bullets whizzed past her head. Two FBI agents jumped in front of her firing nonstop at the guards, and another agent jumped in and helped her pull Leonard out the front door and behind the parked sedans. Van looked down and saw blood staining Leonard's coat. He looked at it and then up at her and smiled. "Do you mind putting a little pressure on it," he said and then passed out.

The support team raced up the long driveway. "We're clear," Detective Young yelled into his phone once all the agents had backed out the front door continuing to fire toward the guards. A couple of agents were hit and bleeding, but they had moved outside as well. The SWAT team positioned two of the BearCats in front of the entrance as the third BearCat smashed the front doors down and slid into the lobby. Officers in the armored BearCat began fired toward the guards from gaps in the windows. The BearCat's surprise entrance into the lobby had shocked the guards, as had Leonard's actions. A handful ran up a rear staircase while the remainder laid down their weapons and surrendered. The remainder of the team went into the stairwell, guns drawn, and began a search, floor by floor for the remaining guards and for Belinda. There were a few brief gun battles, but eventually, the guards all surrendered. As the team brought them out, Van shouted to Detective Young that the doctor needed medical. A SWAT team member pulled out a kit and put a pressure bandage on the wound. Detective had radioed for the helicopters, and they arrived quickly. They strapped Leonard into a SKED stretcher and flew him over to Dominican Hospital in Santa Cruz.

"Where is Belinda?" Van asked. No one knew. She grabbed Agent Sams and Detectives Young and Charlie, and they began a search of the building. "She could be hiding in one of the sterile labs," she suggested. They ignored the decontamination units and searched room by room, but Belinda was gone. Agent Sams organized a search of the executive offices, including Belinda's office, for evidence of a connection to the Bainbridge explosion. They pulled out dozens of boxes of materials to review.

Van and her counterparts got in the sedan and drove to Dominican Hospital to check on Leonard. He was still in intensive care and being prepped for surgery, but he was alive. The doctors told them it might be a couple of days before he would speak with them comfortably.

Van went back to her hotel. She was still worked up over the day's events and couldn't sleep. She reflected on Leonard's courage and on the courage of the agents who had protected her. She thought about how skillfully Agent Sams had managed the assault. Her phone flashed. She leaned over and it was Brian. Part of her wanted to resist his advances. The other part wanted to melt into his arms. She realized though that she needed to update him on the day and answered.

"Hi."

"Hi."

"How was your day?"

"Pretty intense. I am still shaking."

"Did you get Dr. Armendariz?"

"No, we didn't. She spoke to us and was able to see us, but we think she was connecting remotely. She must have got word and skipped. Or maybe she was just lucky. Anything new up there?"

"Yes. They are dismantling the tent. There are no active nanobots left. All that was left was the used dust. They cleaned and detoxified the site, but it is still a mess. We have had a couple of meetings with the University about reopening the lab elsewhere. They are talking to me about taking over Stan's position."

"Wow. Congratulations, I guess."

"Yeah. I have mixed feelings about it. Could be a dream come true but it's terrible how it has come about."

"Yeah.

There was a brief silence on the phone.

"Van?" Brian said.

"Yes?"

"I miss you."

Van giggled. "Uh, we've known each other how long? Maybe 5 hours tops?"

Brian sighed. "Too much?"

"No," Van smiled and squeezed the phone. "It's not." They hung up. The call relaxed Van and she drifted to sleep.

* * *

Belinda kicked back in her hotel suite in downtown Seattle, smoking a cigarette, sipping Cognac, and looking out over the night skyline at the space needle. The petri dish sat on the coffee table in front of her along with the laptop that connected her to the Santa Cruz lab. She didn't feel bad about Stan Meisner. His arrogant ass got what it deserved, and the Tran Lab would be in disarray for months allowing her to get a jump on developing uses for the nano gel in front of her. It made her feel powerful to have manipulated the FBI remotely though a secure application on her laptop. She watched as everything played out. Leonard had become a problem now for some time and if he hadn't been taken care of today, he would need to be addressed at some point. The phone buzzed.

"General."

"Doctor."

"Bit of a mess today."

"Don't worry about that. We'll take care of it. National security and all. Of course, someone will need to suffer the consequences.

"That shouldn't be a problem. My team acted on their own."

"I am sure of it. Did you get the dish?"

"Yes, I have it."

"Good. You can fly out here tomorrow?"

"No. I am taking some time off. I'll secure the dish."

"Understood. Stay in touch."

Belinda missed Spain and the Pyrenees. Basque Country. Her family had an estate in the mountains above Errenteria, not far from Pamplona and the Running of the Bulls, her favorite event. She mused that she had "run the bulls" today and won, which like the contestants in that insane Basque contest, meant only to her that she was still living.

Chapter 22.

The Beginning and the End

Leonard woke from his surgery. His hand was cuffed to the bed. He laughed to himself, "I guess I made it." He was still surprised that he had had the balls to walk out in front of Belinda's death squad, but he had grown tired of her hardcore tactics, and blowing up the lab and his colleagues on Bainbridge Island had been the last straw for him. He knew it would be tough, but he wanted to get back at Belinda. He pressed the buzzer on his bed.

Detective Young called Van. "The doctor is ready to speak." She grabbed her badge and gun and said, "Meet you downstairs."

They stood in Leonard's room around his bed. The attending physician told them they could have no more than 15 minutes. Leonard smiled and said to Van and her team, "Take as much time as you want. You are the reason I am here breathing at all."

Agent Sams looked at Van. She began, "Dr. Freund, I am Detective Van Eng of the LAPD."

He smiled. "I remember you. You are the gorgeous young agent who came to my rescue. Thank you for that."

Van smiled courteously. "We have a lot of questions for you, sir. But to start, were you aware of the plan to attack the Bainbridge Island lab?"

"Look," Leonard answered, "I am prepared to talk, but contrary to my present appearance, I am not quite as dumb as I may seem. We need an understanding here. I am not discussing anything without a deal."

Agent Sams replied, "We don't have a problem with that Dr. Freund. I just can't guarantee that you won't serve some time."

"Ok, put it in writing and that will be good enough," Leonard said. "Here it is. I don't know that Dr. Armendariz intended the death and level of destruction that occurred at the Tran Lab, but she did instruct her team to find the dish and she told them to make a statement, and they knew that by that she meant for the team to set off an explosive charge. You are aware that the petri dish was stolen from us?"

"We are," said Van. "Derek Whitestone is in Los Angeles in jail awaiting arraignment."

"He'll probably get released," Leonard mused as much to himself as to the group in the room. "Friends in high places, right?"

Agent Sams said, "That's not how we work, Doctor."

"Right," said Leonard. "So, you know Whitestone had an accomplice?"

"Cheryl Brown," Van replied.

"She's gone," Leonard said, remorsefully.

"What do you mean?" Van asked.

"Belinda had her executed in cold blood, after she tortured her into confessing to stealing the dish and to Derek Whitestone's plans in Seattle."

Van looked at Detectives Young and Charlie and shook her head imperceptibly as if to say I am telling you now, I want her in my crosshairs.

"Do you know where the body is?"

"No, but if you search the grounds and the woods around it, you will find a fresh grave. Of that I am certain."

* * *

"Hello, Mr. McDonough," said General Tom Warner standing outside the conference hall at the University of Paris where the annual Global Climate Change Consortium had just concluded. "That was quite a speech you gave."

"General," Garny responded.

"Can we talk?" asked the General.

"We're talking," replied Garny.

"Let's bring this home."

"To the States? I'm open but I left precisely because I would never have been able to accomplish there what I did here. You think I can do that now? You know what my goals are with the technology."

"I do and I support you. Bring it home and we'll make sure you get what you need."

"How about this instead?" Garny proposed. "I'll provide you with a sample. You have your team analyze it and get back to me. Remember, the sample is still dangerous even in small amounts. You need a team that knows how to handle it."

"It won't be the first time," said the General.

The next morning, a biohazard safety case was delivered to the General's hotel room in Paris. Inside the double reinforced case was a tightly sealed petri dish labeled Risk Group IV to ensure proper handling.

* * *

Brian pulled his bike into a gravel turnout to watch the sunset. He parked the Gold Wing and walked over to a rusty metal railing that kept him from plummeting 150 feet to the crashing waves below. Up and down the coastline it was the same. Giant rock pillars and steep stone-faced cliffs all framed the movement of large dark blue waves slamming into the rocks and spraying foam thirty, fifty and sometimes eighty feet into the air. He heard the bleating of sea lions crying for mates and watched seagulls dancing in the wind as it swirled around the steep cliffs.

The sun dropped below dark clouds on the horizon, the drifting remainder of a recent storm, and suddenly sprayed the coastline and the ocean foam with yellow light that gradually turned orange and then crimson. He loved the colors and the feel of twilight. He wondered if he would feel the same about Van. He knew right away that she was special. It didn't hurt that she was sexy as hell, and he longed to be with her in that way. But she would be more to him. The University had asked him to take the lead in rebuilding the Tran Labs. He didn't say no. But he needed time to think and to recover, and for now, the only thing on his mind was traveling south. He climbed onto his bike and continued the long and beautiful journey down Highway 1 to Los Angeles.

[End of Book 1]

BOOK 2

RESONANCE

MAPS

Map 1. The Basque Autonomous Region

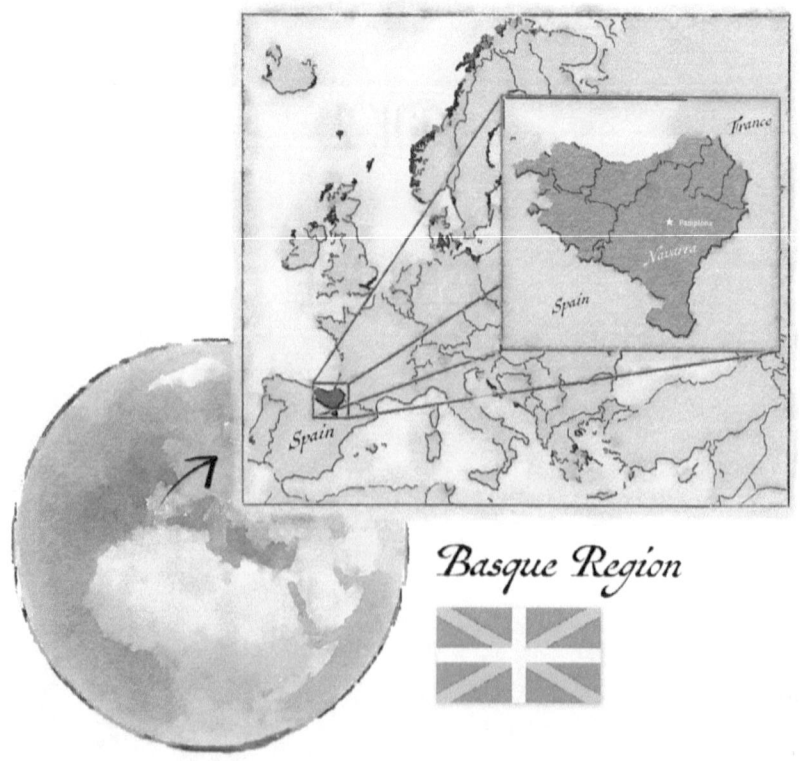

Map 2. The Running of the Bulls

1 Corralillos
2 Cuesta de Santa Domingo
3 Plaza del Ayuntamiento
4 Curva de Mercaderes hacia Estafeta
5 Calle Estafeta
6 Curva de Telefónica
7 Callejón
8 Plaza de Toros

Pamplona

Map 3. Paramount Studios, Backlot

Lucy Park near Sound Stage 25
Paramount Pictures, Los Angeles

Chapter 1.

The Sun Always Rises

It's hard to dispute that life on Earth is a miracle. Whether or not you believe in God or in a *deus ex machina* or even in nothing at all, you must acknowledge that the specific ordering of the universe and this solar system to produce life on this planet was not an inevitability. When the big bang generated the dust particles that eventually made up the sun, the stars, and the planets, the universe did not just snap into place. There was a lot of smashing and grabbing and exploding and battles for position and, in this solar system, Jupiter led the insurrection. The largest of the balls of gas, Jupiter embarked on a massive power grab, consuming all the debris in its path as it made its way closer to the sun. Mars was next in line and should have crashed onto the surface of Jupiter and been consumed by its immense powers. Then, suddenly and without any explanation, Jupiter stopped moving, dead in its path. The giant ball somehow decided it had had enough and settled comfortably into an elliptical orbit around the sun and, as it did, so did Mars and Earth and all the other planets. Had Jupiter engulfed Mars, nothing would have prevented that monster from engulfing Earth or latching onto Earth as another one of its moons and the conditions for life on Earth would never have developed. But, inexplicably, the galactic Game of Thrones ended and life on Earth became a possibility.

There was nothing miraculous about the briefcase, not on the outside. Truth be told, there was nothing special about the briefcase even on the inside, except for the idea it concealed. The crowds around the Capitol Mall were surly. A grand injustice was about to deprive them of another four years of one of the more unique presidents that the country had seen. Whether or not he was very good at the job didn't matter. He was their president, and his time was about to end. The briefcase didn't care about the crowd. It wound its way through the protesters like a leaf floating down a stream, pushing past boulders and branches, hopping through rapids and over small waterfalls and continuing on its way, as if it had a divine purpose. The briefcase's carrier was wearing a trench coat, of course, not because he was a government agent trying to be nondescript, but rather because it was cold. He saw protesters in t-shirts and strange thin costumes and wondered how long it would be before they became hypothermic. He recalled a winter protest from his youth up in Ithaca, New York, years before he joined the same government that he then protested, in which two young women thought shorts and skimpy t-shirts might get them some attention. It got them a quick ride to the hospital and a narrow escape from hypothermic death. He chuckled at the memory. He approached an empty bench, surprising given the number of people around. It was very cold and the bench was metal, so maybe the fact of its emptiness wasn't that surprising. He sat down and set the case next to him under the bench and watched and waited. A nice older woman was feeding birds nearby. She asked if she might sit for a minute, to rest her back. He couldn't refuse, so he scooted over and gave her room.

"Do you think the Potomac has frozen over?" she asked.

"I wouldn't try to cross it today," he responded, smiled, and then stood and left the case under the bench.

A delivery truck waited nearby. It wasn't an easy walk for her, but the case wasn't that heavy. As she approached the truck's cab, the driver's door opened, and an outstretched arm reached down and took the case and closed the door. She felt like coffee and entered a nearby coffee shop to warm up and enjoy a steamy latte.

"Do you mind if I sit for a minute?" she asked an older gentleman in a booth next to the window.

"Be my guest," he responded. She sat, and they waited in silence for her latte.

"Did you make the drop?"

"It's done."

"Good. Now I need you to go to Los Angeles." He handed her a small, folded paper bag. "Tickets and instructions."

She smiled and sipped her latte as she placed the paper bag in her purse. Without anything further, he stood and left the coffee shop.

"Can I warm that up for you?" asked a spry young University of Georgetown waitress.

"Please, dear," she replied and pushed her cup forward. "These old bones need a little extra heat, or they just stop working."

* * *

Dr. Belinda Armendariz awoke in her hilltop villa just outside Errenteria, Spain. Errenteria was a medium-sized town on the coast of Spain, but more importantly to Belinda, Errenteria was a town in her home country, the Basque Country as the people called it, officially the Basque Autonomous Community under the Spanish Constitution of 1978. Belinda believed in her people, fashioned herself their queen, as she dreamed about resurrecting the original Basque kingdom, the Kingdom of Pamplona. She had traced her lineage to the House of Jimenez, the monarchic dynasty that ruled over Pamplona for three centuries beginning in 900 A.D. It was, in her mind, the golden age of the Basque people, and Belinda believed it was her destiny to resurrect the dynasty and bring back the Basque golden age. Her rise to CEO of Ragnar Willowbrook Labs in the Silicon Valley and her growing wealth confirmed her grand destiny, and without telling anyone at the labs, she had redesigned the grounds around Ragnar Willowbrook so that the gardens and sculptures formed the heart-like shape of her Basque Country. From her fifth story office atop the labs, she could swivel her desk chair around and look out her window at the labs' massive gardens and dream of being home.

Now she was home, waiting out the repercussions of her activities in the States, including a battle royal with the FBI and a fatal explosion at the Duc A. Tran Laboratory on Bainbridge Island, an island in Puget Sound nearest downtown Seattle. It was her ops team that had planted the charges causing the latter and—even though it had not been her intention to destroy the Tran Lab—her team got a bit too enthusiastic, and the explosion resulted in ten deaths. Belinda knew she might be hunted if she were tied to the explosion, but she had an ace up her sleeve. General Tom Warner, a five-star general at the Pentagon, knew about the accident and about the petri dish she had back in her possession, and she was certain he would protect her.

She looked at the petri dish and thought about where it had been. General Warner had called her colleague at the labs, Dr. Leonard Freund, and arranged for the delivery of the dish to Ragnar Willowbrook. The general would not divulge its source or contents, although he did warn her about it, and when they received it, the dish had been labeled Risk Group IV, meaning it was not only toxic, but possibly lethal. He wanted Belinda's company to discern its contents and get back to him with a sense of its possible uses, military or otherwise. Belinda knew that the Pentagon was not always interested in military uses of technology. Several prominent examples of modern advances in technology started with the military, and the Pentagon's interest in those advances extended well beyond a simple kill factor. ARPAnet, for example, was a computer-based communications network developed by an arm of the Department of Defense, the Defense Advanced Research Projects Agency (DARPA). The military wanted a decentralized communications network that would withstand a nuclear attack. In the 1990s, DARPA shared the ARPAnet technology with several universities, which converted it into a nationwide computer communications network and renamed it the Internet. Belinda studied the dish, but she was not focused on whether she had possession of a potential weapon or not. What mattered more to her was that she was staring at a watershed advance in technology that she could control.

The question was, what to do with it now? Back at the lab, they had been in the process of formulating the protocol for its handling, but Dr. Freund let curiosity get the best of him and had made the mistake of giving the dish to a highly skilled technician named Sam Waterford for preliminary review. That might have been the first step in the process anyway, but Belinda, who struggled with Dr. Freund's lack of control in several areas, had developed a successful protocol for handling new discoveries and it upset her when her protocol was treated lightly. Water under the bridge now, though. Freund's mistake had led to the labs' likely demise and forced Belinda into hiding. Still, she had it back in her possession and had an opportunity for a fresh start. She would not go back to the States. That would be too risky. She had more than enough money in several offshore accounts and could start up a new lab, here in her home country, Basque Country or, perhaps better, just outside of the City of Pamplona.

Pamplona, of course, has been known around the world for other reasons, principally for its hosting of an annual test of true bravado, the fiesta del encierro also known as the Running of the Bulls, which took place during the mid-summer Feast of San Fermin. The event that started sometime in the 1800s was preceded by a centuries-old practice of herding bulls brought to the City of Pamplona on boats and wagons through the streets of downtown Pamplona into the bullring where they would eventually fight and die. The herd was led by one cowherd who raced ahead of what Hemingway called "the furious energy" of the bulls for the nine hundred meters from start to finish. The foolish test of bravery, the bravado, was started by young men who joined the cowherd and raced ahead of the bulls and risked being trampled, gored, or tossed in the air all to prove their merit as men and win the hearts of the women who pined for their fleet-footed heroes.

Belinda loved the encierro. For her it was a beautiful metaphor, not of grooms chasing brides as many of her compatriots saw it, but of death chasing life, the ultimate race against time. The fear she saw in the eyes of the runners just before the gore or the fall excited her more than anything else. As she watched, she took in deep rapid breaths, almost as if she were running herself, and when the heat became too much for her to bear, she would grab runners off the streets as they moved to the edge to avoid being run over. She pulled them upstairs and into her bed where she ripped off her clothes and made mad furious love usually with some foreign tourist whose delight at his fortune got him slapped and beaten and scratched and used up and tossed back to the street only to avoid the next wave of bulls. She did it repeatedly and found it invigorating, and it restored her and energized her to take the next giant steps toward her ultimate goal. Her latest move had been to target the Silicon Valley in California, which she knew had become the center of the universe, an actual Golden City of El Dorado contrary to the fantasy version sought by Sir Walter Raleigh. She found her way to the Silicon Valley and Ragnar Willowbrook Labs where she eventually connected with a partner in General Tom Warner from the Pentagon, and Belinda began to build her own empire.

* * *

The Gold Wing raced down Highway 1. Occasionally Brian let the bike get too close to the edge of the highway where he could look straight down into the cresting ocean waves that smashed against the cliffs and sent spray almost back on to the highway a hundred feet above. He raced through the winding curves moving in a manner smooth and controlled, not a furious energy but calm and focused. He thought always of Van, the girl detective who captured his imagination. She was right to say that he hardly knew her. But her pull was magnetic, irresistible. Crazy as it seemed, Brian knew that he had no choice but to head south, down to Los Angeles, down to everything he despised about urban life and the vapid Hollywood scene if only to discover whether his heart knew what his head was resisting, that this one might be special.

The highway straightened out and turned east just as he flew past Elephant Seal Vista Point, and the steep rocky cliffs were replaced by large brown fields. He passed signs pointing to San Simeon and glanced up the hills to his left where, in the distance, William Randolph Hearst's castle-styled mansion peered out over groves of birch trees into the small bay below. The castle had been a Hollywood playground in the 1930s and '40s for dignitaries and stars of silent films and the first "talkies." Hearst's closest companion, starlet Marion Davies, developed a reputation for hosting lavish parties at the castle, and her many prominent guests ranged from Charlie Chaplin and Mary Pickford to Calvin Coolidge, Winston Churchill, and George Bernard Shaw. Brian smiled as he imagined a convoy of old convertible roadsters packed with fancy men and women riding up the long windy road to the castle holding champagne glasses and sitting precariously on the top of the back seat or the window's edge laughing and nearly being catapulted out of the car. For some, those few days would be the highlight of their entire lives.

The road veered back to the coast, and Brian stopped for lunch in Cambria at the Moonstone Beach Bar and Grill. He found a booth with an ocean view and relaxed behind a plate of fish tacos and a Diet Coke. He thought about the lab back up in Bainbridge and winced at the heartless destruction and death that had just occurred there. But he paused in reflection at the thought that it was mere coincidence of a sudden downpour that had prevented a widespread catastrophe from the release of the toxic "smart dust" on which he had been working and that, after an inadvertent prior release, had almost killed him and his colleague. Brian didn't believe in divine intervention, but if anything were to convince him otherwise, that would have been it. Now, just days after the explosion, the university already was talking to him about replacing Dr. Stan Meisner and rebuilding the lab. Meisner had been Dr. Brian Johannsen's mentor, and even if Brian didn't particularly like Dr. Meisner, he was deeply saddened and angered at Meisner's death in the explosion. He wasn't ready to consider the university's premature offer. He wondered if Fred Schmidt, the Silicon Valley billionaire who had introduced the lab to the toxic nanobots, was behind the urgency to get the lab back in operation. But for now, Brian didn't care about Fred Schmidt or the University. He needed to get to Van, drawn as if by some irresistible force. He knew it would be foolish to imagine a life with Van, but it was hard not to let his imagination run just a bit. He bristled at the thought that he might be obsessing and maybe even bordering on creepiness, and he fought the urge to let the fantasy run on. Van had her own plans for her life, and whether he might be a part of it was not something he could control. As he finished his tacos, he thought there's nothing wrong with taking it slow. He gulped down the Diet Coke, paid, and jumped back on his bike, racing down Highway 1 and then onto what one 1970s' rock band called Ventura Highway, unconsciously increasing his speed as he got closer to Los Angeles.

Chapter 2.

Uno, Due, Trey

Trey Nguyen stared at the pages in front of him. He hated the title, "The Power of Small," but his opinion had been overridden by the movie's lead writer Peggy Rice and, more importantly, by the movie's producer Jerry Cortez. Jerry knows Hollywood, Trey thought. Who am I to second guess? Trey turned to the script. The storyline was certainly dramatic, and the technology was novel and interesting in its own right, but Trey wasn't satisfied. It needed a tension among the lead characters that was real and compelling.

The movie focused on a young female patient in the intensive care unit of a hospital in Hawaii. She was a brilliant college track star who was preparing for the next Olympics and decided to spend Christmas holidays prior to her last college season with her family in Oahu. Trey knew Hawaii well, and his ability to enhance the scene was easy. The girl, Monica, was on a long training run on the outskirts of Honolulu when it started to rain. The rain was warm, and it was easy to enjoy the run as the streets began to fill up from the downpour. She headed down to a small bay and noticed a sewer pipe extending out from the point at the edge of the bay. Water was rushing full force out of the pipe, but Monica didn't think anything of it as she removed her running shoes and jogged into the ocean. She liked the press of the water against her legs as she could feel it forcing her to use her core as she splashed through the water exhausted but happy. Suddenly she felt pain shoot up her leg, and she got out of the water to examine her foot. She saw a small bit of broken glass protruding from a cut. She pulled out the glass and headed back to the hotel where her family was watching movies and resting. That night, she grew restless in her sleep and noticed that her foot had swollen past her ankle. She woke her mom, and they headed to an emergency room to have it checked. The swelling continued, and the skin on her foot began to turn blue. They drew blood and sent a skin sample to the labs. While they were waiting for results, Monica went into cardiac arrest, and they moved her into the ICU. They were able to stabilize her, and she fell asleep from medication used to slow her pulse and reduce the swelling. But the virus continued to spread, and the swelling moved above her knee.

Trey imagined the panic of Monica's mom and the doctors as they tried to diagnose her condition. He read the scene of the mom calling Monica's coach in California and made some tweaks to emphasize their helplessness. The doctors had called a specialist in infectious diseases at Harvard Medical School, and after receiving the lab results in Cambridge, he concluded that she had a novel form of a flesh-eating virus. He suggested pumping her with steroids, which they did over the next two days without success as the virus took hold and spread. Trey had written the hospital scene in a fever as if it was up to him to cure Monica. The specialists were failing, and Monica was closing in on death when a young doctor named Kate Shaw who was in her first year of residency at the hospital made a startling suggestion. While at Stanford, she had heard of microscopic robots called nanobots that could attack viruses. Trey set the backdrop. Scientists were exploring the technology in various labs around the world, but the world's leading nanotechnologist was hiding at a lab in Bogota, Colombia. The doctors agreed that the young resident should join the Harvard expert in Bogota and see if they could find the nanotechnologist and convince him to come to Hawaii to save Monica's life. Jamie Fleck's's daughter Christy had already signed to play the role of Monica. The casting director was courting Kaitlin Deiter to play Kate Shaw. She had expected to cast Sven Connery as the nanologist, a reclusive ex-patriot from the States who had gone to Bogota to avoid the impact of an accusation that triggered US regulatory interest and had him embroiled in university politics. Unfortunately, the famed actor passed away before shooting began, and they were scrambling to find a replacement. It was always easier to write for a part when the role had been cast. He imagined Bill Brighten in the Connery role given his well-established ability to create an aura of disgruntled brilliance.

The scene that needed the most work was the initial interaction between the American medical team and the disgraced ex-patriot professor. It was too easy to appeal to a vague moral obligation to cure Monica, and there was very little drama in that. The idea of including a sexy young resident on the trip as enticement to come to Hawaii was a bit puerile, albeit a consistent Hollywood tactic, and it needed to be handled delicately so as not to discredit the movie. Trey first decided that the disgraced old professor and the Harvard expert should have a history, something like the distinguished Harvard expert having exposed the other as a fraud. Laboratory circles are relatively tight, and it made sense that the old professor might have become a well-known infectious disease expert himself who, after being disgraced, found himself in Bogota trying to develop a new miracle therapy using nanotechnology. The tension when they meet should be palpable. The presence of a sexy young female doctor should disgust the old professor who would see right through the shallow attempt at using seduction to get his compliance. But she would surprise him with her medical skills and knowledge of the science. He was struggling over a rudimentary problem of quantum physics, and she would recommend a solution that wasn't itself the right answer but that would lead him to an answer. Trey's physics background helped him frame the problem in simple terms, as well as the discussion around a solution to the problem. The young doctor would win over the grizzled genius and convince him to come with her to Honolulu.

The storyline ended with the nanobot invention curing Monica, who would go on to succeed at the Olympics. Now Trey could add to that storyline the restoration of the genius's damaged reputation. It was good, thought Trey. The key to the movie had to be Bogota.

He stopped writing and gazed out the window. It was dark, and the studio park outside his window was lit up by a few small decorative lights. The phone rang.

"Hi, Trey. It's Min. Guess where I am."

"I don't know. Disneyland?"

"That would be fun, but no. I am at Melrose Gate. Can you tell them to let me in?"

Trey smiled. It was a nice surprise. "Let me talk to the guard."

Min handed the phone to the security guard, and after a brief exchange, he handed the phone back and waved her through.

Trey went outside and stood by an old, gnarled carob tree with a large but oddly short trunk. He picked up a faint whiff of chocolate, or maybe he just imagined it. Soon he saw the green undercarriage of the gold Subaru WRX as it pulled up and parked. Min got out of the car. She was tall and had an elegance about her as she locked the car. He started down the path toward her, and she made her way to him. They had only been seeing each other for a few weeks, and both felt the shyness of a young relationship only beginning to give way to confidence and certainty. They didn't hug, but as they turned back to the studio, Trey reached down and grabbed her hand. She leaned into his arm, and it made him happy.

"How's the writing?"

"It was a good day," Trey answered her. "I'm almost done. Do you want to come in and wait a few minutes?"

Min smiled. "That would be nice."

Trey opened the door and let her inside. The room had the disheveled look of a writer's office. Papers were stacked in random places around the room. Books sat on a small dining table, some in stacks and others opened as if the memory of a particular page mattered. There were half-drunk cans of Diet Coke on the desk and coffee table. A small couch with a torn pillow and a stack of manuscripts sat opposite the desk behind the coffee table.

Trey asked Min if she would like to sit, and as he led her to an open space on the couch, she pulled him down and they both fell on the couch laughing, the manuscripts falling to the floor. She wrapped her legs around him, and they kissed passionately as if they hadn't seen each other in years. Trey reached for her breasts and felt the hardness of her nipples through her blouse as Min moaned. He reached underneath the back of her blouse to find the clasp of her bra and struggled with it. "Just a minute," Min whispered breathlessly. She unbuttoned her blouse and pulled off her bra as Trey pulled off his shirt. They wrapped each other up in their arms, now skin to skin, groping and kissing and moaning and breathing, enjoying the full passion of their embrace.

After several minutes, Trey pulled back.

"Let's get out of here," he said.

Min, with sparkles in her eyes, said, "Okay. Meet you in Larchmont?"

Trey's quick imagination put them naked in his bed, tossing and writhing in ecstasy. Then he saw his roommates pounding the door telling them to be quiet.

"Your place might be better. My roommates . . ."

"My place it is."

They got up and dressed. Trey walked Min to the door. "I owe Stan these changes tonight. Let me drop them off, and I'll see you in an hour."

"God," said Min. "Don't wait too long. You'll drive me crazy."

Trey laughed. "We can drive each other crazy." He kissed her passionately at the door. "I'll see you soon."

Min took off toward her car, this time running and carefree, excited about the night ahead. Trey watched her, wondering if he should just postpone the script updates to tomorrow and leave with Min right now. He knew he couldn't, though. The movie was on a tight schedule. He turned back into the room and flipped through his changes. It was good enough for now. He punched the new pages and put them in a notebook, heading to his car. He walked past Studio 25 and heard the late-night shooting of the Bruce Willis remake inside. As he walked around the back corner of the studio, he saw a limousine parked near the stage. Assuming it was an A-listers' perk, he imagined making out with Min one day in the back seat. Suddenly he stopped. He kicked himself as he realized he had left his condoms back at the studio office. As he turned and started to run back to the office, two people emerged from a small door behind him, and he slammed into an older lady who fell and dropped several envelopes. The envelopes opened and rolls of cash spilled across the road.

"On my God," he said. "I am so sorry." He could see that she was hurt.

"You idiot," said the man, whose voice Trey thought he recognized but, in the dark chaos of the back alley, could not make him out. The man scrambled to pick up the bills, and as Trey moved to help the older lady, the man pulled a gun and yelled at him, "Get out of here! Leave us and get out of here." Trey looked at the gun, frozen for a moment in fear, and then he took off running. His mind raced as he got back to the office and sat inside. He couldn't make sense of anything he had just seen, and at first he couldn't remember why he came back to the office. He sat there for several minutes afraid to move, trying to figure out what he had witnessed. He looked at the couch, and images of Min floated back into view, and he thought to himself, Stan can wait. I just need to get out of here. He held on to the notebook but left the condoms in his desk drawer and opened the door. He looked around and saw no one, so he turned and locked the door. When he turned back, there was a gun in his face. "Please," he said, "I didn't see anything."

"Come with me," he heard her say. Trey held his hands up in front of him.

"I don't know anything," he pleaded. They crossed under a lamp, and she pushed him with the nozzle of the gun into the park and toward the old carob tree. As soon as they were on the grass, Trey looked down to the road and thought he saw Min's gold car, thinking she might distract the assailant and maybe he could escape. But there was nothing there.

"Count to three, my dear," she said.

"I don't want to," he responded starting to whimper.

"Count to three!" she demanded.

"One . . ." There was a flash, and Trey was gone. The man appeared, and he and the older woman carried Trey's body into the garden and laid it down carefully at the foot of the carob tree and quickly left the park.

Chapter 3.

Dawn of the New Revolution

In 1972, Stephen Jay Gould, an American paleontologist and biologist, along with his colleague Niles Eldredge, published a landmark paper advancing a new theory of evolution. The theory, called "punctuated equilibrium," was hailed as the most significant advance in evolutionary theory since Darwin first penned it on a small sailing ship anchored off the Galapagos Islands. The new theory posited that evolution is not constant and gradual, as its proponents had assumed for the past century. Rather, Gould and Eldredge claimed that species remain in the same general state for long periods of time, possibly millions of years, before there is a sudden and substantial mutation event in which a single species splits into two or more distinct new species. That major mutation event is then followed by a prolonged period of stasis before the next major mutation event occurs. Gould and Eldredge drew these conclusions only after years of searching for evidence of evolution at the microscopic level. Unlike Darwin, whose conclusions were drawn by inference to the visible world, these scientists captured an alternative evolutionary design floating up from the invisible world—not a peaceful image of gradual and imperceptible change but rather a violent image of change-inducing cataclysms.

Garne "Garny" McDonough had never been afraid of change, even the sudden and disorienting type. If anything, Garny intentionally instigated that more radical change, and his bank account reflected how far he was ahead of the game. He had founded the chip manufacturer Providia on a hunch that video was the next wave in computing and, on that hunch, made his first billion. But he abandoned that effort when the Providia board of directors followed his partner's lead into video gaming systems. Sure, there was money to be made, but Garny dreamed of inventing new life-changing technologies, and entertainment had always bored him. He left Providia and founded MetaMed, a prosthetics company that sought new ways of integrating biomechanics and microelectronics. But there he ran into the American regulatory system and found himself and his inventions frustrated by what he viewed as weaker minds. There was one benefit. The MetaMed experience introduced Garny to a form of nanotechnology—microscopic robots also known as "smart dust" that operated at the cellular and sub-cellular levels. He learned that nanobots called "switches" change shape in response to stimuli in a process that is called "conformational change." A "motor" uses energy derived from the change process to move around molecules in its orbit. "Shuttles" carry molecular compounds like anti-cancer agents to targeted locations. "Cars"—the most advanced of the four forms of nanobots—have appendages that can be used for locomotion and steering. He dug deep into nanorobotics and nanomanufacturing and uncovered what he believed to be a connection between these micro-technologies and the problem of global warming. Garny had always wanted his work to produce something spectacular, and he knew he might be onto something special. He began to attend climate change conferences and symposia and learned that the key contributor to global warming was carbon dioxide but that the focus typically was on reducing the emissions that produced CO_2 rather than removing CO_2 from the atmosphere. Garny heard about a process called "direct air capture" in which excess CO_2 was literally scraped from the atmosphere, but even if the technique worked in small laboratory experiments, no one had advanced the technology to be sufficient to handle the volume needed to have any impact at all on the earth's atmosphere. Garny had an idea, and his Silicon Valley contacts readily availed themselves of his business genius and gave him a half billion dollars to support his new venture. He pulled together an international team of scientists and built a secret lab at the northern end of the Himalayas on Karakul Lake in Tajikistan where his team agreed to be locked down for twelve months to invent a nanobot that (a) could direct air capture carbon dioxide and (b) could rapidly self-replicate so that a large mass of carbon dioxide rich airspace could be swept clean and the elements of the earth's atmosphere could be brought back into balance. He called the venture "TKP," which stood for "The Karakul Proposition."

Garny's efforts in Tajikistan proved fruitful, and after repeated successful testing at a massive indoor stadium he built next to his TKP lab, Garny reported his results at the annual Global Climate Change Consortium in Paris. His report triggered the interest of a particular five-star general at the Pentagon, and he agreed to let the general take a sample of his nanobot gel to be tested in the United States. What Garny did not know was that one of his local hires, an Armenian-born computer software engineer from Dushanbe, had stolen a dish of the gel as the lab was shutting down. He flew to Yerevan, Armenia, with the dish in his suitcase, and after he arrived at Yerevan International Airport, he accidentally released the nanobots in the airport terminal. Garny knew that the nanobots had an abnormal level of toxicity, but he was so consumed by the results of his CO_2 testing that he never developed a method for controlling the toxic impacts of the nanobots when humans were exposed. The accidental release of the nanobots at the airport resulted in a tragedy later described as the Yerevan Disaster, the death of hundreds of men, women, and children at and around the airport and the sickening of thousands more throughout the city. However, the disaster was never explained, and unproven theories of Azerbaijani-based bio-terrorism distracted the investigations into the source of the disaster and exacerbated political tensions between Armenia and its contentious neighbor Azerbaijan.

General Tom Warner, Garny's American contact at the Paris Consortium, ordered the petri dish delivered to a well-known Silicon Valley lab called Ragnar Willowbrook Labs for review. While the petri dish was there, an ambitious intern from a local investment bank picked it up during a visit to the lab. Ultimately, the CEO of the lab used her black ops team to recover the dish, leaving death and mayhem in their wake. That CEO was Dr. Belinda Armendariz. Garny knew nothing of the petri dish drama, and General Warner told him nothing. Belinda was hiding in northern Spain with the petri dish, evading any investigations into the deadly impacts of her black ops team and strategizing her next moves, when General Warner contacted her and proposed to bring her to Paris to meet with Garny. Garny suggested that they meet in the state room of the Napoleon III Apartments in the Louvre. Belinda trusted General Warner not to expose her to authorities, and given the opportunity to meet the eccentric billionaire, she reluctantly agreed.

When Belinda entered the state room, she immediately felt at home. She wondered if Garny knew anything about her and her appreciation of wealth and opulence. The Napoleon III Apartments reminded her of her ancestors' palaces and kingly fortunes as royalty in the time of the Basque Kingdom circa 900 A.D. Every room was draped in burgundy and gold. Every wall held massive stuccoes. The state room contained a fifty-person dining table surrounded by red velvet chairs and gilt bronze decorations on the walls, and every open space, including the ceiling, was covered in detailed oil paintings of the French Baroque. Three huge crystal chandeliers hung over the dining table.

Garny was seated at the head of the table speaking to General Warner. They stood when they saw Belinda enter the state room.

"Gentlemen."

"Garny McDonough, let me introduce you to the highly regarded CEO and chief scientist of Ragnar Willowbrook Labs, Dr. Belinda Armendariz."

"My pleasure," said Garny. "Armendariz. Is that Basque?"

Belinda felt her knees give slightly, but she recovered quickly. Nothing he might have said that day would have surprised her, except for that.

"The pleasure is mine."

A waiter appeared with a tray carrying two bottles of Basque Wines, a Rioja Alavesa and Txakoli *(chacoli)* de Getaria, a soft red wine and a light green sparkling wine, both made from varietals grown in the Basque Country. Belinda looked at Garny as if to say, "You've made your point," but instead she said, "Thank you for your thoughtfulness. Honestly, I prefer Scotch."

"Not a problem at all." Garny spoke to the waiter in French, and the waiter disappeared and returned with a bottle of a single malt Laphroaig and three glasses. The waiter delivered the glasses to the table, poured, and moved to the corner to await further instructions. Garny motioned for him to leave the room.

"I understand you are vacationing in Spain, the Basque Country, I assume," Garny said to Belinda. The question immediately called out Belinda's strategy of escaping detection by hiding in an obvious location, given her nationalist leanings. But she had her reasons and her resolve. "It's my home, and I have returned there for an indefinite period of time."

"Won't Ragnar Willowbrook miss you?"

"They will. But that's not my problem now."

Garny glanced at General Warner. "I heard there was some trouble," he said, eyeing General Warner to see if the statement shook him up. Warner didn't move.

Belinda, likewise, was prepared. "Corporate espionage. I am sure you are aware of it, Mr. McDonough, especially in the Silicon Valley."

Garny smiled. He felt himself cautiously warming to Belinda. "Goes a bit beyond typical corporate gamesmanship when the FBI gets involved, doesn't it?"

"Where there is money, there is always government," Belinda retorted.

"Sometimes, where there is government, there is money," General Warner threw his hat in the ring.

"Well said, my dear general," Garny laughed. "Well, now, let's turn to the real conversation. So, Dr. Armendariz, what do you think of my bots?"

Belinda blinked but not noticeably. "Your bots?" Belinda had turned Ragnar Willowbrook into a powerhouse lab not only by being paid huge sums to assess other people's inventions, but also by grabbing patents and other rights to many of the inventions she secured from naïve and unassuming young engineers who found their way to the valley seeking fame and fortune only to have their ideas absconded by RW Labs and other agents of Silicon Valley giants through nefarious means. Garny knew the game and knew better than all but a small handful how to navigate the battles. But Belinda had already taken ownership of what she now viewed as hers. General Warner never told her where they came from; she assumed the military had developed them. She looked quizzically at General Warner.

"Surprised?" said Garny.

"No," she said settling into her new knowledge. "General Warner here never described the source, but I'm not surprised."

"They are unlike anything you have ever seen," he said. "Wouldn't you agree?"

"I'll be honest with you, Garny. I've never seen them."

"How is that possible?" It was Garny's turn to look to General Warner.

"They were stolen, Garny," Warner replied. "Belinda went to great lengths to get them back, which she did, but she never had the chance to study them."

"I see." Garny paused, several seconds. He looked at Belinda. "You do want to see them, right?"

"Very much so, Mr. McDonough. I understand they are quite remarkable."

"Good," he said, pushing away from the table and preparing to leave. "In the meantime, I would like to see a plan. We are standing at the edge of a vast frontier that we are about to claim as our own, and we are well ahead of any efforts to duplicate what I have already accomplished. That gap is likely to close over time, but, for now, what would you do if you stood in my place?"

Belinda looked up at the fresco behind Garny. The painting showed a beautiful scene of a stag standing in the forest snow and watching a brilliant winter sunset, completely at peace, as its mate pawed at the ground looking for scrub to eat under the frost.

"I don't know that I know yet, but I can tell you this: you won't find me scrounging around for scraps while you stare at the sun."

Garny glanced at the painting and laughed. "Fair enough. We will meet again soon, Dr. Armendariz. The general will set it up."

Garny left the meeting wondering if he had made a mistake to trust General Warner and his mysterious aide-de-camp, Dr. Belinda Armendariz. Certainly, she would have found a way to study the bots, even superficially. Maybe she did, and she was being coy. But he doubted it. There was nothing in her demeanor that suggested excitement or curiosity. He expected to be bombarded with questions, and she just sat there looking at the paintings. Still, General Warner was Garny's key to getting back into the States without suffering at the hands of US regulators. He knew that it was not his invention of a more effective means of direct air capture and a new way to address global warming that mattered. There would be many applications, and those applications would be valuable. He fully expected to expand that business line as far as it would go. It might even get him a Nobel Prize. But the discovery that really mattered, and the key to Garny's real success, was his invention of a process for nanobot self-replication. Garny's bots proliferated at unimaginable speeds, and he knew the secret to that self-replication. It was the process that mattered. It was the process that would bring about a new revolution in nanomanufacturing and, through it, a revolution in the production of everything from soup to skyscrapers. He, Garne "Garny" McDonough, was the sole author of that process, the divine architect of what could amount to the next stage in human evolution.

Belinda left the meeting, but after returning to the hotel, she grabbed her suitcase and went directly to the airport and flew back to Bilbao Airport, the air transport hub for the Basque region. She drew two conclusions from the meeting. First, she needed to be extremely careful around Garny. Garny was both smart and savvy, and he could just as easily use her and discard her as he could anoint her as his second in command. Second, she needed to find a way to get up to speed quickly on the nanobot gel in the dish. She viewed it as an error on her part to have accepted the meeting with Garny so quickly. She not only needed to know what Garny had created, she needed to know how and what he viewed as the significance of his invention. She needed to assess her value to Garny, and she no longer could hide behind the veneer of Ragnar Willowbrook. The FBI would be watching the labs to see if she might attempt a veiled return, and notwithstanding General Warner's assurances that he would protect her under a gloss of national security, returning to California and the Silicon Valley was certainly not an option now and might never be an option. She needed a legitimate establishment in Europe where she could connect to the right minds capable of fully assessing the nanogel. She found it quickly. The University of Navarra in Pamplona not only had an established and respected medical research institute, it also had a small group of specialists in bio-MEMS, a field of nanotechnology focused on the use of nanobots in medicine. The research unit, a division in the university's chemistry department, was called the Supramolecular Materials for Biomedical and Environmental Technologies (SUMBET). The faculty working at SUMBET had received numerous awards and were working on nano-sized drug delivery vehicles and nanocomposites.

Belinda understood the risk of returning into public view. She assumed that she was on several Interpol and CIA lists and was the target of multiple investigations if not a joint operation. But she was here in her home where her neighbors and Basque compatriots knew of her commitment to them and the vision of a Basque Country, and it comforted her. She thought of hiring a go-between, perhaps a student capable of conveying messages and delivering the product. It reminded her of Cheryl Brown, a young aspiring woman whom that bastard Derek Whitestone had hired and used to steal Belinda's nanobots and then to deliver Belinda's stolen nanobots to UCLA and caused a giant mess for Belinda. Belinda had no remorse for what happened to Cheryl. Cheryl got into the game way over her head and lost. It happens. But Belinda didn't like the idea of trusting a go-between to remain loyal, and certainly not someone who would be responsible for a substance that Belinda suspected could be very dangerous. She had to trust that her national identity, a commitment to which was unusually strong in the region, meant more than any mishaps that might have occurred in the United States. Even more, Belinda needed to maintain a firm grip on whatever might happen at the university, and she needed to get to know the university faculty who worked with her so she could assemble her team for a new lab.

She grabbed a scarf and sunglasses and hailed a cab. She wrapped the petri dish in another scarf and stuffed it in her bag. The cab raced down Avenida de Pio XII, named after the tallest building in Pamplona, and dropped her at the College of Medicine. She went directly to the provost's office and asked to meet with the dean, Dr. Eduardo Seguro, a white-haired balding man with a bit of a limp.

"How may I help you?" he asked Belinda after she sat in his cluttered office.

"I know your reputation and the famed reputation of this program," Belinda responded.

The dean smiled.

"I would like to discuss a donation."

"Very generous of you," he responded. "I can connect you to University Foundation."

"I would like to discuss with you first if you don't mind," Belinda replied.

"Absolutely, absolutely," he answered, betraying his nervous habit of repeating the same word twice.

"I understand you have a department that is exploring nanotechnology."

Dean Seguro fumbled for his glasses. "Yes, yes. I don't follow it much. It has a strange acronym, Subnet or something like that."

"SUMBET," Belinda responded. "I believe it stands for Supramolecular Materials, but I don't recall the entire name." She was careful not to offend the dean.

"Yes, yes. Right, right. SUMBET. Hmm. What is your interest?"

"I am interested in endowing a new faculty position, a chair in nanotechnology in support of the work of SUMBET."

"Well, that is very generous of you."

"I don't really care what we call it. We could name it after my late husband, Dr. Leonard Freund. Maybe just call it the Freund Chair in Nanotechnology."

"That sounds fine."

"How much would it cost to endow a university chair?"

"The foundation can help you there, but we are a well-known school. I am sure it is in the range of 500 to 750,000 euros."

Belinda shrugged it off. "Not a problem. But I do have a request for SUMBET. I have materials I would like them to review."

Dean Seguro walked Belinda to the chemistry department that resided in the College of Medicine and the office of SUMBET's lead scientist, Prof. Marta Echeverria. He left them together and assured Belinda that he would have the University Foundation contact her. Alone with Prof. Echeverria, Belinda asked about the safety protocol for toxic substances, and as she handed her the scarf-wrapped petri dish, she pointed out the warning label Risk Group IV. Dr. Echeverria immediately pushed the dish and the scarf back to Belinda. Belinda explained to the professor that extreme care had to be taken with the dish but that the gel contained nanobots and not an infectious disease. Her hope was that the department might analyze the gel but only under strict RG-IV protocols. Professor Echeverria called the dean to discuss and came back smiling, taking the dish but handing Belinda back the scarf, and assuring Belinda it would be handled with the utmost care.

As Belinda returned to her hotel in downtown Pamplona, Hotel Tres Reyes, a wave of relief washed over her. She stood on her balcony overlooking the Taconera Gardens, and felt, for the first time in many weeks, like she was back in control. She ordered room service to bring her a scotch and her favorite cigars, and she sat on the balcony and drank and smoked until the sun set a fiery red over her beloved city.

Chapter 4.

Not Quite Requited

Van looked down at her phone. Brian had just left another text. "Just passed Atascadero. Nice Central Coast town. Heading over to Morro Bay knowing I will see you to Morro. Okay that's dumb." She sighed. The idea of a guy traveling from Seattle to Los Angeles just to see her was nice, but in this case, it didn't fire her romance neurons. She worried she was being careless in her communications with him and should have shut the whole thing down right away, but for some reason, she didn't shut it down. Brian was extremely good looking and a smart and nice guy. Who wouldn't want someone like that? I'm an idiot, she thought as she struggled with her feelings. Detective Charles Darling, Van's mentor at the bureau, hadn't been very helpful. He couldn't stop talking about Dr. Brian Johannsen for the entire journey from Bainbridge Island to Los Angeles as they transported investment banker Derek Whitestone to Los Angeles to be arraigned for crimes that led to the death of UCLA medical student Marley Dakota. She typed back with some hesitancy, "See you to Morro."

She put her phone down and stood to go see Detective Alvin Broad, her first official boss at the Detective Bureau. Alvin ran CHESS, as her colleagues called it. Van spent many hours with Alvin in CHESS and was responsible for cataloguing the files on a database capable of detailed searches for matches. The bureau's leadership was so impressed with her efforts, they ordered Van to attend and report at top-level meetings. Van's reports didn't make her many friends in the bureau as she exposed the misuse of CHESS as a repository for prematurely closing several older, and sometimes not so old, investigations. One colleague she managed to offend was Detective Paul Young, her senior in Robbery-Homicide who also led the Downtown Gang Unit in Gang and Narcotics. Van didn't care if Detective Young was offended or not. Van's respect for Detective Broad was unmatched. Broad was great at his job and had a reputation for solving more cold cases than any other detective or officer in the department. But he was not motivated by ambition; he simply loved solving puzzles, especially puzzles that brought criminals who thought they had escaped the system to justice. Broad saw in Van a peer even though she was still in her first few years as a detective. He admired her doggish and gutsy pursuit of answers, and he refused to allow the jealousies of other detectives to impair her work at the bureau; and for that she trusted him completely. They both liked the fact that CHESS was in a dingy and dusty back room and that no one else wanted to spend time there except the two of them. At least it was a bit better organized than it had been, and for that, Detective Broad gave Van all the credit. She caught him rereading Kurt Vonnegut Jr.'s Breakfast of Champions.

"Have you read this?" he asked as she approached his tiny office at the back of the file room.

"In junior high."

"You should try it again."

"Sure, but why?"

"I honestly don't know, really." He set the book down between the stacks of files and reports on his desk. "Vonnegut has a way of explaining me to myself, I suppose. Might not be the same for you."

"Might be, though, right?" Van said amused at Alvin's effort at appearing disinterested in his own opinions.

"Ok," he smiled, "so check this out." He picked up the book again and turned to a dog-eared page and read:

> And here, according to Trout, was the reason human beings could not reject ideas because they were bad: Ideas on Earth were badges of friendship or enmity. Their content did not matter. Friends agreed with friends, in order to express friendliness. Enemies disagreed with enemies, in order to express enmity . . . They even had a saying about the futility of ideas: [i]f wishes were horses, beggars would ride . . .

"What does that say to you? Does it explain your boredom with normal people?" Van poked at Alvin.

"Normal people don't bore me," said Alvin defensively.

"Really?" said Van. "Is that why you find yourself fascinated with criminals?"

"Well, as far as people go, I do tend to enjoy smart criminals more than most."

"I think what you enjoy is watching smart criminals make mistakes."

Detective Broad pointed to the stack of files on his desk. "Well, speaking of making mistakes, take a look at these cases," he said. "There is an odd symmetry to them but no obvious connection. They appear to be random killings."

If Detective Broad thinks there is a connection, Van mused, there would a connection. Van thrived on the moments when Detective Broad would pull her in to help solve these unusual mysteries.

"Can I ask a few questions?"

"Shoot."

"Similar weapons?"

"No."

"Geography?"

"Possibly but not absolutely. These murders stretch from Fresno to the Imperial Valley."

"Eastern California?"

"No. There is a Bay Area file and a few in metro Los Angeles."

"Age?"

"No, and before you ask, the demographics of age, race, or gender don't tell the story."

"So, it is not a gang initiation rite."

"I wondered that, too, but no. I see a pattern but not a connection."

"Ok, thanks." Van smiled as she grabbed the stack. "You know what they call Cheerios and beer, don't you?"

"Breakfast of champions," they said in unison and laughed.

Van returned to her desk with the stack of files. She opened the database and began cataloguing the contents of the files. The murders had been committed mostly by younger males, and there was no evidence of relationship with the victim where jealousy or control or sexual frustration might have induced the act. Occasionally there were break-ins, but many of the murders took place in the open and some even took place in a public setting in front of witnesses who most of the time refused to cooperate. There was no consistent evidence of insanity or intoxication, but each of the murders had elements of planning. They were not spontaneous. Victims were caught unaware by a killer hiding nearby, or they were lured to a park or into a home. It took several hours to add up the data, and the more data she added, the less likely it seemed to her that Detective Broad had a point.

The facts were all over the place. She had often discussed with Detective Broad how the job itself might induce the best detectives to begin to imagine connections where there were none, the same way that, if you stare at a stationary object long enough, it might appear to move. She recalled how her first boss in LAPD's forensics unit, Dr. Frank Weatherby, had taken her to the lab's file room to get her mind off a case she was working. Sometimes, he had told her, it is important to get away from a problem before you can solve it. In this case, Van wondered if Alvin needed a break and time to realize he was imagining a pattern where none existed. But then Van had been staring at her screen for six hours straight, and it was probably on her to get away. She grabbed her bags and headed for Kimmie's gym.

* * *

Brian sat on his balcony and stared at the ocean. There was a light offshore breeze, and the waves were peaking and breaking to the north off a southern swell, a clean long curl. A couple of surfers ventured out and were enjoying the early morning rides. He stared at his phone and thought about texting Van, but he found her latest reactions to him unsettling. Maybe he was making a mistake. He had been clear with her that he wanted to get to know her on a more serious level, and she initially seemed to be encouraging it. But now he could sense that she was hesitating. Still, he thought to himself, I've got nothing to lose except maybe my self-respect, and at this he smirked. He thought for the briefest second of turning around and returning to Bainbridge Island to face the mess he had left behind: his colleagues dead, his lab and his work destroyed, and a crazy Silicon Valley billionaire who, at least from Brian's perspective, had been the cause of the nightmare. But the pull of Van's appeal was strong. Maybe he was worrying needlessly, fighting a natural impulse to protect himself. He slugged down the last bit of Starbucks and went back into the room to get ready for the ride.

As he was repacking his saddle bags, he noticed a folder that he brought with him, a folder that he had left with Dr. Meisner and that had managed to survive the melee and the fire. It was the report to Dr. Meisner. Stan Meisner had run the Tran Laboratory for over a decade before he was killed by Belinda's black ops team. Brian didn't enjoy working for Dr. Meisner, but he respected him as a scientist and understood the realities that Dr. Meisner faced as the head of a private lab, albeit funded mostly by the University of Washington. Dr. Meisner's death and the destruction of the Tran Lab were a terrible loss to the scientific community of the Pacific Northwest and a personal loss to Brian. Dr. Meisner had a quirky stand-offish personality, but he acknowledged Brian's talent and was grooming Brian for a significant role at the lab. All that said, Dr. Meisner had ignored the report in which Brian and his colleague Dr. Comstock determined that the material in the petri dish was mechanical and not biological and had a curious ability to scrub carbon dioxide from the air. On the downside, though, the material was highly toxic to humans, which they discovered when Dr. Comstock opened the concealment container and almost died when she inhaled the nanobots they had just been viewing in an electron microscope. He flipped through the report and studied the simulations of the strangely symmetrical spiked globe with arms that extended and retracted. He recalled the groupings, the almost family-like nature of the nanobots, how they huddled in groups of six. But the real magic, though not magic at all, was its ability to self-replicate. A group of six became twelve and then twenty-four and so on. He slipped the folder back into the bag, tossed them over his shoulder, and headed out. Soon Morro Bay disappeared, and he floated through San Luis Obispo and down to Pismo Beach. As he approached Santa Barbara, the traffic began to build, and Brian followed a gang of bikers as they split the lanes and raced haphazardly through the standing cars. He followed the bikers all the way into Los Angeles. They noticed him and a few gave him the thumbs up, an invitation to join them. They turned onto the 10 Freeway and pulled into Venice Beach where they found the parking lot of the Rose Café and rolled up together. They motioned Brian to follow them, and sensing nothing that concerned him, he thought why not. They all wore black vests with the insignia Brothers of Sobriety, and as he rolled into the parking lot, two bikers approached him.

"Nice Gold Wing. 750?" the first asked.

"No, it's a GL1800. A little more distance than a 750."

"You come a long way?"

"I suppose. I rode from Seattle."

"Damn. What a ride, though, right?"

"What a ride. I'm Brian."

"Name's Phil, Brian. This is Jaward," Phil said motioning to a large black biker. "He's from Sierra Leone and is the president of our club."

"Very nice to meet you, Mr. Brian," said Jaward, who extended his hand.

"Actually Dr. Brian," Brian reached forward. "Johannsen."

"Dr. Brian, then," Jaward replied. "Please join us inside, Dr. Brian."

Brian learned that the Brothers of Sobriety was not actually a collection of recovered alcoholics as he had assumed. Rather, the "gang" was a collection of former marines turned Hollywood stunt men, and they used the word "Sobriety" to reflect a commitment to professionalism and respect for the dangers inherent in their trade. As they gathered in the bar, Jaward held his beer high and said, "To Sobriety." "Sobriety!" the team responded in unison and clanked their beer bottles. Jaward and Phil were heading to a job on set, and when they learned that Brian had ridden down from Seattle for a girl, they laughed and invited him to join them as their guest.

"I think I should let Van know," Brian said. "She is expecting me."

"Invite her along. We need to meet the woman who has taken Dr. Brian's heart and maybe his manhood." Jaward and Phil laughed and slapped Brian's shoulders.

"Come along," they said. "You don't always get to watch real stunt work."

Brian found a niche in the back of the room and called Van.

"Hi, Van, I'm here in Venice," he said to her voicemail. "I met some bikers who are working in Hollywood as stunt artists. They invited me to watch them work. Call me when you get this. Bye."

Brian laughed to himself as the Brothers of Sobriety rode en masse through the Melrose Gate at Paramount Studios as if they owned the place. The guard smiled and waved as if he were used to the sight. But as Brian approached, he held up his clipboard and motioned for Brian to pull aside and stop.

"Your name, sir?"

Brian pulled off his helmet and suddenly felt awkward. "I'm Dr. Brian Johannsen."

The guard flipped through his clipboard. "I don't see it here. Do you have an appointment?"

"Henry!" shouted Jaward who had turned around from the front of the pack. "Stop harassing the young man. He's our guest."

"Just doing my job, Mr. Kamara. You need to call ahead."

"Of course, you are right. My deepest apologies."

"I'll let this one slide. But please, in the future . . . It could mean my job."

"You're the best, Henry!" Jaward shouted as he turned his bike back to the front and led the group onto the lot, passing the DeMille Building, the famed

Blue Sky water tower, and back to Stage 32 on Leonard Nimoy Way. As they entered the stage, Brian noticed huge green screens with actors dressed in superhero costumes. Jaward led Brian to a director's chair.

"What's the picture?" Brian asked.

"It's another comic book pic, one of those unknown ones. We get to play alien mobsters. There's food and sodas in the back. Help yourself. I'm heading to makeup. It may take some time. Relax and look around; don't think about the girl. You might see someone you recognize. I understand Danny Radcliffe is here today."

"Danny Radcliffe? Harry Potter in an alien pic?"

"Don't tell him that. He can be a bit sensitive about it."

"Mum's the word," said Brian, and Jaward let go a loud laugh as he walked toward the trailers.

Brian looked at his phone. Nothing yet. He headed to the food table and saw a beautiful young woman with a hard hat and a tool belt. She smiled at him and said, "Watch out for the brownies. You never know here."

"Thanks for the warning. You working on the movie?"

"I'm key grip."

"Key . . .?"

"I manage the lighting and rigging crews."

"You work with the stunt teams?"

"Sometimes, where there are cranes involved. Things like that."

"I'm here with Jaward Kamara."

"I know Jaward. He is the best. He takes care of everybody."

Someone shouted, and the woman turned to leave. She looked back and said, "I didn't catch your name."

"Brian." He smiled. "Dr. Brian Johannsen."

"I'm Lily, but everyone here calls me Bess."

"Ok, Lily Bess, very nice to meet you."

She smiled and took off running.

Brian chuckled. If he had known the City of Los Angeles could be so much fun, he might have come down a long time ago.

* * *

"Wake up, daughter."

Van felt her mom's gentle touch and looked up to see her mom's face in the darkness. "What?"

"The detective. He is here. You must wake up."

"Mom, I can't see your face. What did you say?" Van was groggy and wasn't wearing her hearing aids.

Mom spoke louder. "THE DETECTIVE IS HERE!"

Van rolled over to see that it was 2:00 a.m. She'd been sleeping for three hours. "Ok, Mom. I got it."

Van pulled herself up and put on a bathrobe and her hearing aids. She walked into the living room to see her mom hand Detective Charles Darling a cup of coffee. Darling smiled as Van wiped her eyes.

"So, she does sleep," he said and then took a sip. "Boy, I love your mom's Vietnamese coffee."

"It's not Vietnamese," said Van. "It's probably French drip. What you love is the sweetened condensed milk." She looked at her mom and motioned for her to bring another cup. "What are you doing here?"

"We got a call. I was up and figured better for us to ride together late at night."

"Hard time sleeping? You should work out more."

"I got nobody to impress."

"Whatever. Give me a few minutes, and I'll be ready to go."

"No rush. Your mom is taking good care of me."

"Yes, I am taking good care of Mr. Detective," said Van's mom.

"Mom," said Van. "You realize that I am a detective also, right?"

"Yes, daughter."

Darling had driven from his home in San Dimas, and Monterey Park—where Van's parents owned their home—was along the same route to the police headquarters in downtown Los Angeles. Detective Darling didn't stay on the 10 Freeway. Rather, he merged onto the 101 North, the Hollywood Freeway, until he got to Melrose, where he exited and headed west until the Melrose Gate onto the Paramount Studios lot appeared on his right and he turned right up to the guard station. He held up a badge, and the guard directed him to Stage 24 and let them through. There was a lot of activity on the lot even though it was well past midnight. They drove down 3rd Street and Avenue A, and when they turned right, they saw police cars parked in front of Lucy Park with lights flashing.

Darling said to Van, "You ever heard of Lucille Ball and Desi Arnaz?"

"You're kidding, right? You ever heard of TV Land?"

"Actually no. I don't watch much TV. But I did watch I Love Lucy."

"Andy Griffith, I Love Lucy, The Mod Squad—that's the cable channel that shows the stuff that you old people used to watch as kids."

"Ok. Lighten up."

They pulled up and parked in the street behind the flashing lights.

Darling flashed his detective badge, and a young officer let them under the police tape. In the middle of the park was a very old and inosculated carob tree surrounded by neatly manicured bushes and benches. Behind the tree was the Chevalier building on the right and southern wall of Stage 25 redesigned as Lucy's Bungalow. Van picked up a hint of carob and lilac through the freshly mown grass. The stage facade, nicely designed, seemed out of place to her, and the park looked more like a backyard than planned space. There was a falseness about the scene.

"Detective Darling. Detective Eng." Captain Jack Venturi met Charles and Van on the grassy park.

"Captain."

"We have a body: male, twenties, Asian, execution-style shooting, single shot to the back of the head."

"Vietnamese? Japanese? Korean?" Van asked.

"I think Vietnamese, but honestly not sure."

"Witnesses?"

"None yet." "Where is the body?"

"In the garden under the tree."

"How long has Forensics been here?" Van had seen the forensics lab's white SUV parked up by Stage 25 when they first drove up. The coroner was parked behind them. She saw three people standing at the rear door to Stage 25. They appeared to be smoking and watching the scene.

"Maybe two hours."

"Thanks, Captain." Van walked up to the edge of the crime scene. Flood lights surrounded the park and lit up the buildings and the carob tree. Forensics had placed flags around the body and tied police tape to the flags to mark the body and added more borders around the garden perimeter to keep everyone out. Van saw more flags planted on footprints and any other markings that might be evidence. She saw Dr. Frank Weatherby, the chief medical examiner and her first boss at the department, standing over a young woman who appeared to be a new recruit. He looked up and smiled and left the recruit to continue planting flags.

"Detective."

"Frank. It's the middle of the night; what are you doing here?"

"I could ask you the same."

"I can blame Charlie. You have no one to blame but yourself."

"True enough." Frank shrugged as if it didn't matter.

Van smiled. "What do we have?"

"One dead boy. Too young for this."

"Was he shot here? Or was he dropped here?"

"We are putting it together. This park is visited by a lot of tourists. It's a messy crime scene to begin with, and the officers who showed up first were not as careful as we prefer. Thankfully, no one touched the body."

"Find any bullets or casings yet?"

"Tough in the dark even with the flood lights. We are looking."

The LA coroner, Dr. Gilford von de Grassy, joined them. The tattoos on Gil's face and neck popped in the strange light of the flood lights. The friendship

of Frank Weatherby and Gil von de Grassy went way back to their early days in the department, and Gil had been a tattoo model prior to that.

"You remember Van Eng?" Frank said to Gil.

"Of course! She's at the top of the always growing list of Frank Weatherby superstars, and if I recall, she's not a fan of formaldehyde."

"Who is?" said Frank.

"Don't even go there," Van grinned.

Frank asked Gil, "What about time of death?"

"Somewhere around 9:00 p.m. yesterday."

"Any indication of other trauma?"

"Nothing I can see here. When Joe finishes with his photos, we will load him up and take him back."

"Are we certain this is where it happened?"

"He could have been placed here, someone leaving a message."

"Except that we found this in the bushes." Assistant medical examiner Brad Jones was holding a plastic evidence bag. Inside the bag was a black loose-leaf binder full of script pages. Brad and Van had been hired by Frank at the same time. Brad came from the NYPD's Forensics Unit.

"Hello, Brad," Van smiled.

"Detective."

"What do you have?"

"Looks to be a working script. We need to take it back and dust for prints. You'll find the title interesting: 'The Power of Small.'"

"Interesting how?"

"Something to do with nanobots."

Van felt her stomach drop. She had lingering post-traumatic stress from the fight at

Ragnar Willowbrook where she had been shot at by Belinda Armendariz' black ops team after they blew up a lab in Seattle retrieving Belinda's stolen nanobots.

"When you are done with that, I need to see it."

Van excused herself and walked back to Avenue A. Up at Stage 25, the three smokers were still outside the back door. She walked over to them. As she drew near, she could smell pot, but the smokers didn't seem concerned.

"LAPD. Do you mind if I ask you a couple of questions?"

"You mean this is real?" said a tall thin woman. "Or are you playing with us?"

"There has been a murder. It's as real as it gets."

"Oh snap!" said the younger guy, who immediately dropped his joint and stepped on it.

"Stuart," said his friend. "Dude, weed is legal. Why did you waste that joint?"

"Weed may be legal," said Van, "but I'm not sure your boss would be excited to know you are impaired. Are you conscious enough for me to ask you a couple of questions?"

"They don't care," said the woman. "This is Hollywood. Most of the people here are stoned or high on something. Go ahead and ask."

"You didn't know there had been a murder."

"No, we saw the floods and thought they were setting up for a scene."

"Did you hear anything that sounded like gun shots?"

At this the three all laughed. "We listen to gun shots all day long. They're doing a *Die Hard* remake inside."

"I'm Genevieve Sayer," said the tall woman. "I'm in makeup. This is Will Flask and Stuart Brighton," she said pointing to the two guys.

"We're in set design," said Will. "But all that means is we roll stuff around."

"Speak for yourself," said Stuart annoyed. "I'm an artist."

Genevieve and Will laughed. "Maybe a latex artist," said Will, and Stuart immediately punched him in the shoulder.

Will looked at Van. "That's assault, right?"

"Well, it would be battery if Stuart had intent. But, please, stop. I just have a few more questions." She doubted she was spending her time wisely.

"You said you listened to shots all day. Do you think you could tell the difference between a stunt gun and a real handgun?"

"I doubt it," said Genevieve. "After a while your hearing goes to shit."

"Ok. Did you see anything unusual?" At this question, all three smokers grinned a you-have-to-be-kidding grin, and Van was ready to close her book and walk away.

"Actually," said Genevieve, stopping Van, "I came out here earlier, before all the melee, and I saw a really cool car pull a quick U-turn in front of me and peel out of here."

"What kind of car?"

"It was twilight and getting dark, but I think it was an all-gold Honda or Subaru."

"A WRX?"

"Yes, could have been, with green lighting underneath."

"Anything else?"

"No."

"What time do you think it was?"

"It was after eight o'clock last night."

"Did you see anyone in the park? Maybe limping or struggling? No one shouting, 'Help me'?"

"No."

"Thank you, Genevieve. Boys, go easy on that," she concluded, pointing to the doused joint.

As she walked away, she heard one of them say, "Dude, there was a murder. That's crazy." The other said, "Maybe we should go inside."

"Van?"

Van was staring at the pavement as she reflected on the gold WRX. She thought to herself, it could not be possible, but the green undercarriage light brought her back to Danny Kang and the Koreatown gang, the Rush. Danny had died in prison after Van's first undercover beat brought down the gang.

"Van Eng?"

She looked up and saw a face she thought she recognized, but the combination of flood lights and darkness made it difficult to see him.

"Oh my God. Van, it's Martin, Martin Richard."

"Martin?"

"From the party. What are you doing here? Wait. Let me guess. You have been discovered. God, I knew it. You have that look."

"Martin? From the house in Malibu?"

"Yeah. I know. I'm in makeup still. I'm working on this Willis remake in Stage 25. What are you working on? Is it a new police show?"

"I am working a case, Martin."

"I get it." He grinned knowingly. "Still in character."

Van smiled. "I remember you, Martin. It was a nice party. But no, I am not an actor. I'm on a real case. I am sorry I didn't tell anyone at the party. I am an LAPD detective, for real."

"What? Whoa. I need to process that. You win a beauty pageant and you're a detective?"

"That was a fitness contest, but yes. We do have a real case going on here. How long have you been here?"

"We started shooting around ten or eleven last night. I guess they are trying to save money. It is a *Die Hard* remake."

"I heard. You didn't get here until after nine?"

"Right. I entered on the other side. I saw some commotion here but didn't check it out until later. I just walked over to the café. They serve twenty-four hours. There's always something going on. Look, can I call you? Maybe we can get something to eat some time?"

Van thought about Brian and his trip to see her. She felt a tinge of guilt, but she didn't even know Brian. Martin was nice and not assuming. He seemed intelligent even if he was pursuing a career in movies. She'd have to be clear with Brian. "Sure." She jotted her number on a page in her notebook and ripped it out. "Don't wait too long."

Martin looked at her. "Ok. Very cool, Detective." He headed back to Stage 25, and as she turned to see him leave, he turned back as well, smiled and waved, and then headed into the rear entrance.

The investigation wrapped up about 6:00 a.m. Gil had packed up the body and took it back to the morgue for the autopsy. Brad and Frank wrapped up their forensics review and returned to the lab. Detective Darling told Van about the café on the lot, and they headed over for coffee and to mull over the details. Upon discovering the body and after calling the police, Paramount Security called its principal contact for The Power of Small, Jerry Cortez's director Stan Workman. Stan called the lead writer, Peggy Rice. The police took the initial interviews before Van and Charlie showed up around 3 a.m. Rice told the police the victim's name was Trey Nguyen and reported that he had been working on the movie for the past twelve months and was instrumental in working the technical details about nanotechnology into the script. She was not aware of any personal drama in Trey's life and knew of no problems with anyone working on the film. He was a bit of a loner, but everyone liked him and respected his contributions. He recently moved into Larchmont Village, an upscale community in Greater Wilshire just below the Paramount Lot, where he rented a small house with friends. He came originally from the Bay Area where he had just completed a dual masters in English and journalism at Stanford. He had published short stories with a technology bent and applied to be a writer on the film. Peggy hired him immediately, and he had lived up to her expectations. His death was a terrible shock, and it would have an impact on the film.

Charlie and Van laid out a plan for their investigation and then headed back to Van's home in Monterey Park. She had seen Brian's text from earlier in the day but resisted the impulse to respond. Now that Martin showed up on the lot, she was glad she wasn't being too hasty with Brian. But she was too exhausted to think too much about either of them, and she fell asleep as soon as her head hit the pillow.

Chapter 5.

The Price of Progress

The first transcontinental railroad spanned 1,912 miles and connected the western extension of the existing US railroad network in Iowa with the Oakland Long Wharf on San Francisco Bay in California. It was a marvel of human industry, eclipsing the Continental Divide and piercing the Sierra Nevada Mountain range on its journey to the Pacific Ocean. Each mile of rail was supported by 3,250 railroad ties weighing approximately 200 pounds each, which in sum totalled 6,214,000 railroad ties at an aggregate weight of over 1.24 billion pounds. Started in 1863 and completed in 1869, the railroad project became a haven for 15,000 Chinese immigrants, many of whom were escaping the terrors of the Pearl River Delta wars in Guangdong. But it was a brutal respite. They were paid about $1 per day and preferred their own food to the food provided by the Central Pacific Railroad. The death toll was never calculated, but it is estimated that hundreds died from illness, heat exhaustion, dynamite explosions, and other accidents. The rough conditions eventually led to a labor strike that was brutally quelled but that nevertheless increased wages and improved overall working conditions.

History suggests the railroad barons who built their fortunes around these modern marvels had little, if any, concern for the plight of their Chinese labor force. Their attitude reflected that of American high society, which also had a low view of the immigrants and their strange beliefs and culture. These nouveau elite held the false view that the race was weak and frail despite it being responsible for managing to haul and set 1.24 billion pounds of railroad ties over six years, an average of more than 80,000 pounds for each laborer for the ties alone, not including the massive manual removal of rock and earth and the placement of gravel rail bed and steel rails.

Grindle CEO Fred Schmidt studied his oversized photo replication of the Pacific Railroad and the 100 or so Chinese laborers posed for the shot. He thought of the tragedy at the Duc A. Tran Laboratory for Hereditary Biology on Bainbridge Island and wondered if he had been too careless. Derek Whitestone, who was sitting in a jail cell in Los Angeles serving a sentence for criminal negligence, had been candid with him about the source of the dish. Derek's assistant Cheryl Brown, executed by the same criminal who destroyed the Tran Lab, had stolen the dish. Fred and Derek personally transported the stolen dish to the lab on Puget Sound and left it for Dr. Brian Johannsen who was working under the top scientist there, Dr. Stan Meisner. Meisner was killed in the lab explosion. Brian was with Fred when it occurred and, for that reason alone, survived the blast. Now Derek was serving time for his role in the theft and its consequences at a UCLA lab. No one, as far as he knew, was connecting Fred to anything. Fred attributed that anonymity to Derek, who very easily could have pinned some guilt on Fred. But he didn't, and Fred understood and respected Derek's loyalty. There still was the issue of Derek dividing the petri dish and keeping some of the nanobot gel for his own benefit, and Fred had no doubt Derek was acting in his own interest and not Fred's. But he didn't really care about that. Derek's reckless actions led to the death not only of his assistant Cheryl, but also of a gifted student at UCLA Medical School and two others, and Derek was suffering under that knowledge and his current predicament. Fred would get him out, and Derek would feel forever indebted to Fred. Fred could use that, and Fred needed Derek to help retrieve the remainder of the nanogel, which Fred suspected might still be at UCLA.

Derek Whitestone had been in jail for six months awaiting his trial. He bore a mixture of depression and rage. His actions had resulted in the deaths of innocent people including his assistant, who might not have been innocent, but she didn't deserve to be brutally executed by Belinda Armendariz. His cell door opened.

"You have a visitor, Whitestone."

Derek perked up. No one had seen him there for the past six months. He hoped to see someone from his office or his family or maybe even Fred. As he approached the community room, he looked around and saw no one he recognized. Seated at one of the metal tables was a well-dressed older woman. She smiled and stood as if she recognized him.

"Derek."

"Yes?" The guard led him to the table.

"I am Samantha Dash, defense attorney from Rollins Brown. Fred Schmidt hired me to get you out of here."

At that moment, Derek looked up and saw Fred being ushered into the room. He jumped up, but he was cuffed to the table and momentarily lost his balance. Fred came over to steady him and put his hand on Derek's shoulder.

"Fred," said Derek, holding back his tears.

"Hello, old buddy. You've lost some weight. Looks good on you."

Derek looked at the floor and chuckled. They sat down.

"Take these off, please," said Samantha pointing at the cuffs. The officer obliged.

"We'll get you out of here," said Fred. "Sam here is one of the best in LA."

"We have filed for rehearing of denial of bail. We just need to prove you are not a flight risk."

"No, never," Derek said, with more than a hint of desperation. "I love Los

Angeles. Palm trees, beaches, Disneyland. Why would I ever leave?"

"Right. Rest assured the judge will take our word for it, not yours. My firm is well known in the Los Angeles criminal justice system. You just need to say, 'Yes, your honor' or 'No, your honor.' Can you do that?"

Derek didn't respond. Fred looked at Derek and leaned in to speak quietly. "I am going to need something from you, Derek. The dish, the one you secretly delivered to UCLA behind my back? I need you to get that dish back to me."

"The petri dish? Isn't it evidence?"

"It's too dangerous to be used as evidence. They are storing it in a special vault at the same UCLA lab."

"But what if I am out on bail and get caught? That would make it very bad for me."

"You are already charged with an aggravated felony, Derek. It can't get much worse than this."

Sam said nothing.

Fred added, "I need you to figure this out. You have good university connections, and I can't be associated with the retrieval of the dish. That is on you, good friend."

Derek sat quietly. He appreciated Fred as a friend, but he knew Fred well enough to know it was never that simple. He was desperate to get out of jail, but was he desperate enough to take that kind of risk? He had never wanted to kill anybody, and he had trusted the lab at UCLA to know how to manage an RG-IV substrate. What he didn't expect was that the lab would take fewer precautions after they discovered the dish contained nanobots and that mistake would cost an unfortunate UCLA medical student her life. Of course, the lab was no friend of his now that he had caused a tragedy. To retrieve the dish, he would need to steal it, and right now that seemed impossible.

"I can only promise to do the best I can," he told Fred.

"That's my man," said Fred. He looked at Sam. "How quickly can we get this rehearing?"

"It's already on the calendar in two weeks."

"Push it up. I want him out of here immediately."

The hearing went as expected, and Derek was released under Sam's firm's assurances that he would present himself for trial. Derek walked along the Venice boardwalk. The trial weighed on him, but at least he was free again. The ocean never seemed so beautiful. The beach breeze was cool and refreshing. Children were playing in the shower and running and laughing. The odd-ball Venice characters he used to blow off as crazy, strolling guitar players, roller skaters dressed in wild colors, now just seemed to be delighting in life, a feeling Derek now shared. The scene produced in him a sense of hope he hadn't felt since the last time he talked to Cheryl Brown about delivering the toxic dish to UCLA. He stepped into a coffee shop.

Sam Dash was there, sipping a mocha and poring over her laptop. She barely looked up when Derek sat down.

"I'm here," said Derek.

"Are you here?" she said. "Actually here?"

"Come on," responded Derek. "You called me."

"Seems to me you have a problem," she replied, looking up and cutting him a hard stare.

"About a thousand fewer problems than I had in the Towers."

"No doubt that is true, but you have one very large problem right now."

"And you can help me?"

"I think so, but it will cost you."

"Why not just work with Fred?"

"You heard him. He can't know anything or be connected in any way."

"Seems like a stretch to me, but what are you suggesting?"

She handed Derek a card. It read, "Pink House Acupressure."

"Isn't this a massage parlor?"

"Doesn't matter what goes on in front. Take the card and show it to the host. Leave. Wait five minutes and walk around the building to the back door. Someone will pick you up. After that you are on your own. Whatever happens, I had nothing to do with this, and remember, Fred knows nothing about it, either."

Derek took the card. It seemed a bit cloak-and-dagger and not particularly intelligent, but he had no other choices. He'd lost connection with UCLA after he was arrested. His contact there, Dr. March Fielding, the director at UCLA's Rutter Center for Cellular Engineering, had died from a lung infection while he was in prison. The dish that Fred wanted him to retrieve was locked in that lab. Derek wanted nothing to do with it. He knew as soon as it was discovered stolen that he would be targeted and the interrogation would be brutal. But he owed Fred for getting him released and more than likely owed him for saving his life. In prison, he had convinced himself that he didn't have much to live for. Then Fred showed up.

Pink House Acupressure was a small cottage-looking building set back off Wilshire Boulevard in Santa Monica. Perhaps it had been painted pink at one point, but now it was a dull white and badly in need of a paint job. Two expensive cars were parked in the small lot adjacent to the building, and as he entered, he saw an older white male in a suit disappear behind a large door.

"May I help you?" said a small teenage-looking Asian woman standing behind a counter. Derek smelled incense and noticed orchids placed around the room. He smiled because it seemed appropriate and handed the woman the business card he got from Sam Dash. She stopped smiling and said, "Please wait." She took the card and disappeared behind the same door.

Sam's instructions were for him to leave, not wait there. So he did. He walked to the corner as if he were crossing at the light and then turned back and headed to the rear of the building. No one was there. He waited five minutes and started to walk back to the entrance when an old convertible Mustang appeared in the alley. It appeared to be full of college age kids out partying. A young woman was in the front seat, straddled on the lap of a guy Derek assumed was her boyfriend. She had smooth dark hair, designer sunglasses, and was wearing faded jeans shorts and a tank top that was not covering up very much. She jumped up to her feet, more like bounced, and shouted toward Derek.

"Are you the dude with the card?" she yelled at Derek, laughing as her boyfriend tried to pull her back down.

"The what?"

At that point a woman appeared at the back door of the massage parlor and gave Derek back the business card. He pulled out a $20 bill, and she snatched it and nodded toward the kids in the Mustang.

"Get in!" they shouted, and the couple in the front seat jumped into the back as Derek fell into the front seat. The car sped down the alley as Derek was fumbling with the seat belts.

"Don't worry about those," said the driver. "They don't work anymore." Derek grabbed the hand hold on the door and hung tight, certain this would be his last ride and preparing to be catapulted out of the car. The car sped onto an on-ramp of the 10 Freeway. The wind whipped around the front window and, surprising Derek, flowed over the passengers as if they were sitting under a hard-shell roof. Derek began to relax, still unclear about what was happening and how this ragtag group of ne'er-do-wells could possibly help him get the dish. They pulled off at La Brea and headed north.

"Can you buy us some weed?" The dark-haired woman leaned forward from the back seat toward Derek, touched his shoulder, and smiled.

"That's not going to happen," Derek said sternly. She immediately frowned and flopped back petulantly at first and then laughed and kissed her boyfriend.

"Maybe you guys could clue me in."

The driver looked at Derek, as if he were sizing him up. "You need to sit tight for now." They turned right on Wilshire Boulevard, and the driver pulled the car to a red curb in front of LACMA, the Los Angeles County Museum of Art. Derek looked at what seemed to be a small forest of streetlights topped with acorn-shaped lights.

"Get out and wait here. Someone else will pick you up in about thirty minutes."

"Here?"

"Yes. Right now."

Derek climbed out. "Thank you?"

As he stood, the dark-haired woman jumped into the front seat by herself and blew him a kiss, and the Mustang sped away.

I didn't even get their names, he thought to himself. But no doubt that was best. He still was having doubts, and the cloak-and-dagger didn't inspire any confidence, but he trusted Attorney Dash to know what she was doing. He sat down next to the Public Works artwork and waited.

It wasn't a driver who approached him.

"Are you Derek Whitestone?"

The stranger was also young, but he looked more like a graduate student than the kids in the Mustang. Derek stood and brushed the street dust off his pants.

"Who is asking?"

"Please confirm."

"Yes, I am Derek Whitestone."

"Follow me."

They walked down Wilshire Boulevard and turned left at Hauser and headed up past 6th Street. Derek had done a lot of walking while he was in jail, so the stroll didn't bother him. They passed several small apartment buildings on the way. He thought of Cheryl Brown and the condo he had purchased for her before she disappeared. The condo would have been nearby. He saw a sign that said Villas at Park La Brea and followed the young man through the guarded gate and into one of the olive-colored apartments there. The two-bedroom was sparsely furnished. Derek noticed a bookshelf stacked with textbooks, a desk with a laptop and separate oversized monitor. The floor was covered in neatly organized stacks of paper.

"Please wait here."

Derek sat down on the couch and eyed the stacks of paper. Most of the stacks were made up of copies of scholarly articles. He leaned forward and flipped through the stacks nearest to him, mostly biological essays focusing on epidemiology, skin disorders, inflammation, viruses, and topical treatments. He reached further and flipped through articles on allergies and anaphylactic shock. Then he saw a pile of newspaper clippings, and as he looked closer, he realized the articles were about Marley Dakota and the UCLA lab where she died.

The young man who led him to the apartment returned. "I need you to follow me."

"Stop," said Derek. "What is this? What is going on?"

"It's need-to-know, and you don't need to know. Not yet."

"That's where you are wrong."

The man, who at that point was pulling the door open, turned back to Derek.

"Close the door," Derek said sternly.

He paused, then shut the door, turned to face Derek, and folded his arms across his chest.

"Do you know who I am?"

"I've been given instructions. I don't really care who you are."

"Yes, you do," said Derek. "What is this?" he said pointing to the stacks of paper.

"My research."

"You are a medical student?"

"I'm a doctoral student in biomedical engineering."

"Did you know Marley Dakota?"

"Yes. I worked with her in the same lab."

"You know about the accident."

"I was with her the day she died."

"You know how she died?"

"Who are you? Why do you care?"

"Right. I will tell you who I am, but you need to explain to me what is happening here. Deal?"

"Deal."

"My name is Derek Whitestone."

As soon as he said his name, the young man's eyes widened.

"Yes. I am the one who Sam Dash got released on bail. I was charged with criminal negligence for Marley's death."

"The dish is yours?"

"In a manner of speaking."

"You killed Marley?"

"I didn't kill anybody. I trusted Dr. Fielding to handle the materials properly. That's why I had it delivered to her. You are supposed to be helping me get it back. Is that what is happening here?"

"We have it."

"You have it? Forgive me for asking, but why are you doing this? Money?"

"We are getting paid, but that's not why. The university is so concerned about liability that it is doing nothing to find out what is in that dish. My students and I are digging in. We want to know what it is and why it killed Marley and Dr.

Fielding."

"You think it killed Dr. Fielding?"

"We know it did. She was exposed when Marley was exposed. She just happened to be near a door, and when she saw what happened, she closed the lab door and locked Marley and two assistants inside the lab. They died immediately. Dr. Fielding inhaled enough to severely burn her lungs. She was on a ventilator for a week and then released. But the damage to her lungs was too great. Turns out she was a smoker with emphysema. Her lungs were already severely damaged. After the event, she needed a lung transplant but didn't get it quickly enough and died within a few months."

"Christ," said Derek. "So, what have you learned so far?"

"We know these are nanobots. We don't know why they were developed or why they are toxic to humans."

"So why are you giving the dish to me?"

"We want to cut a deal."

"Let me hear what you are thinking."

"We want in on your research. We want to be part of the team."

"That might be difficult. I don't know you. But I was led here by my attorney, so presumably she does. Maybe, maybe not. I do have an idea. What's your name?"

"William Perkins, III."

"Well, William Perkins, the third, let's get going."

Perkins took Derek to another apartment. When he entered, he saw the same gang of kids that were in the Mustang. The dark-haired woman smiled and quipped, "So we meet again," but Derek wasn't feeling flirty. His mind had been racing. Why would Sam Dash connect him with these kids? Was Fred really interested in getting the dish, or was something else going on? He thought that his own defense might rest on the findings of a research team, but he never imagined it would be students, especially students who knew Marley Dakota and Dr. March Fielding. Still, it felt like a gift, like someone was watching out for him. Perkins returned to the room carrying the biohazard case. He offered it to Derek and said, "Do we have a deal?" Derek smiled.

"Keep it," he said. "Keep it, and be extremely careful with it. Take it back to the lab where it can be stored safely."

"We were told to give it you."

"Don't. I'll get back to you, and I'll confirm if my team is willing to work with you. You still have access to the lab, correct?"

"We do."

"And you have the proper equipment there to study it, right?"

"Right."

"Do this for me. Take the sample and divide it into two containers. Separate them, but keep both of them sealed and stored safely."

Now it was Perkins' turn to smile. "You got it, Mr. Whitestone."

"Now take me home, preferably in a car that has working seatbelts."

Derek called Sam Dash as soon as he was back in his apartment. "I met your friends," he said. "I'm not sure all that was necessary."

"Trust me," said Sam Dash. "We are tampering with evidence—not something we can take lightly. Do you have the dish?"

Derek explained that he told the students to take it back to the lab. Sam Dash thought Fred would not be happy, but Derek shared with her the conversation with William Perkins. He explained that whatever Fred planned to do with the dish, it was of no use to him unless he had a place to take it and study it. It was already at UCLA. Why take the risk of removing it? If there was a team there that was willing to study it, Fred could learn what he needed to learn, and no one would be at risk of running afoul of the law, including Derek who was out on bail and at greater risk than anyone. Sam Dash was amenable, but she wanted to know Derek's plan to ensure Fred didn't lose possession. "Let's talk to Fred," he said. "I'm always in favor of attorney-client privilege."

Chapter 6.

The Resurrection of Ragnar Willowbrook

Mary Shelley wrote the novel *Frankenstein* as a teenager. That alone was remarkable, but what also was remarkable was that she wrote the classic on a dare. Her close friends, the poet laureate Lord Byron and Shelley's soon-to-be husband Percy Shelley, challenged Mary to a contest in which each would write their best horror story. Shelley decided for her part to take on the local alchemist society, which believed life could be created artificially in a laboratory. She knew of a castle nearby that happened to be owned by the Frankenstein family, and with a dash of hubris and immense blossoming talent, she produced the story that turned that family's name into the epitome of horror. The story initially came out as *Frankenstein; or, the Modern Prometheus*. The addendum was lost to history. But as Frankenstein, the novel endures today as fresh as it was two centuries ago. The actual story, not surprisingly, is much deeper than the Hollywood version. The creature, whose name is not Frankenstein, had a rough and brutal early go at life but eventually finds a hiding place near a nice farming family where he teaches himself to speak and to read. After realizing that his looks frighten real humans and that humans will never accept him, he returns to his creator, Dr. Victor Frankenstein, demanding that a mate be created for him to cure his loneliness. The good doctor begins the effort but, regretting his original act and believing that what he created was evil, he destroys the mate and drives the creature north into the Arctic Circle to be forever lost . . . or maybe not. Thus, like any good horror story, the Frankenstein monster survives in the imagination to keep us in dread. But Frankenstein is as much commentary on human nature as it is a good horror story. Shelley saw human beings as inherently fearful creatures whose nature it is to conquer or destroy what they do not understand.

Ragnar Willowbrook was too important to the scions of Silicon Valley to disappear, as it were, into the Arctic Circle simply because of Belinda's shenanigans. Any new medical or biochemical invention, no matter the genius behind it, needed the stamp of approval from an independent authority before it stood any chance of mass acceptance. RW Labs provided a seal of approval, and the role made its leadership rich beyond their wildest dreams. Belinda happened to be good at running the lab, but she wasn't unique. With her gone and with the new fame he acquired by his act of bravery in the battle at the lab, Dr. Leonard Freund found himself the billionaire club's latest new buddy. But Freund was smart. He didn't want Belinda's job. The risks of bad judgment in that position were too great, and prior to Belinda's unfortunate departure, he had been planning his own retreat into a comfortable isolation. He accepted the role of returning the lab back to its original state as the Silicon Valley's standard bearer, and the money came easy, but he continued to search for the right replacement.

Dr. Brian Johannsen was enjoying Los Angeles and especially Hollywood. He was young, smart, and good-looking, and his easy-going intelligent style blended well with the Hollywood elite. His attention on Van softened as he found himself distracted by the vixen crowd that attached itself to anyone associated with "the industry." He needed the distraction. He had connected with Van for lunch at a cute little restaurant on Larchmont called Lemonade. The restaurant owners had converted a small bungalow near Paramount Studios into a chic little cafe painted white with yellow trim to match the name. Van told Brian she was busy working a case on the lot and had a minute to meet with him over lunch. He felt the same pull to her as soon as he saw her get out of her car in the parking lot, but when he went to hug her, he felt her resistance. Brian understood it. What right did he have to expect her to be attracted to him the same way he thought he was to her?

They had spent less than a day together in the middle of a tragic scene on Bainbridge Island, and now he had traveled fifteen hundred miles to present her with a giant ball of romantic pressure, pressure he suspected she didn't really like. Still, to see her warmed his heart and, to be candid, other body parts also. He smiled and tried to reassure her that he was not there to interfere with her life. They had a nice lunch together. He shared his stories of Jaward and the production, leaving off his interactions with Lily. Van described a bit of the murder scene and suggested Brian be careful in Los Angeles and especially Hollywood. It was easy to find trouble here, she told him. He knew from that interaction not to ask her out again, but she did let him give her a light hug as they left. "If you need me for anything," he told her, "I plan to be here for a while."

The interaction left him depressed. He called Jaward who invited him back onto the lot to cheer him up, and when he got there, Jaward had a surprise for him. One of the cast members for the alien pic had gotten ill and Jaward convinced the cast manager to let Brian fill in. She directed him to makeup where they found a black leotard that he slipped on that contained hundreds of diodes, a trench coat from the 1930s, and a fedora. They returned to the cast manager who took an iPad and quickly reviewed with Brian several scenes that had been shot. Brian had been on the outside of the production when he first visited the studio. At that point the storyline made little sense to him, and he was overwhelmed just by being on set. Now he needed not only to understand the story line but imagine his own role in it. The aliens had arrived at the scene of a mob execution and had used the skin of the dead mobsters to hide their identities. Their disguises had allowed them to infiltrate the mob and kill all its members except the leaders whose minds they controlled with a kind of mutant telepathy. The aliens looked nothing like Jaward or the other members of Sons of Sobriety, the motorcycle stunt men gang. The cast manager told Jaward to work with Brian to get him ready for the shoot. Jaward took him to the side of the green screen stage where they practiced moving about like aliens trying to be human. Jaward showed Brian a quirky move that exposed them as disguised aliens, and then the director called them to the set. Brian thought his heart would jump out of his chest as he walked under the intense lights now turned on the stage. But he felt a huge relief not to be thinking about Van. When it was over and he was undressing in makeup, Lily came over to him.

"You are a natural," she said, smiling.

"I doubt that very much," he said. "I just hope I didn't mess it up."

"Mess it up? No one knew you were new. You handled it like a pro."

Jaward had said pretty much the same thing, and the cast manager concurred, inviting Brian to stay involved even after the missing cast member returned. She promised to find him a role and told him to head over to the Screen Actors Guild and get enrolled immediately. "We might even get you a speaking role," she told him.

Lily invited Brian to join them at a post-production after-party. Brian smiled and promised to stop by, but he needed some time alone after what had turned out to be a hectic day. He drove his bike past the Hollywood Bowl and up to Mulholland Drive where he leaned into the turns on the unendingly curvy road and let the Los Angeles skyline, glowing in the sunset, slip behind him. He turned north on Coast Highway and headed up to Point Dume where he parked on Birdview Avenue and wandered to the cliff's edge and sat down staring at the darkening waves. He could see couples holding hands and walking down to Pirates Cove Beach, and he chuckled as he imagined the active make-out scene below. The sadness of his encounter with Van returned, but he knew it wouldn't last.

His phone rang. He looked quickly thinking what a fool he was to imagine it might be Van, and it wasn't.

"Dr. Johannsen?"

"Yes. Who is this?"

"Dr. Leonard Freund, Ragnar Willowbrook."

"Should I be speaking to you?"

"That's your call, Doctor. I would like to talk to you."

"I'm listening."

"Dr. Armendariz has disappeared. We suspect she returned to Spain but there's been no word, and she has become a fugitive wanted by the FBI, the CIA, and Interpol among others."

"I have a problem with this call, Dr. Freund. How do I know you weren't involved in the murder of my colleagues?"

"You'll just have to trust me, Brian. Belinda had her own methods, and she controlled them. Perhaps she tolerated me as a cover, but so far, the police have not included me as a suspect, and if I had something to be concerned about, I would not be calling you."

"I suppose. What is it you want?"

"I want you to consider running Ragnar Willowbrook."

Brian shook his head. "No thank you, sir."

"Why not?"

"Because, despite the holy pile of crap you and your colleagues created for me at the

Tran Lab, I know your reputation, and my apologies, but I have no interest in being a hired gun for Silicon Valley robber barons."

"That is precisely why I want you to come here."

"What does that mean?"

"Whatever you think of Ragnar now, there was a time when Silicon Valley engineers and inventors flocked to us because our imprimatur bore credibility. We got fat and rich and, candidly, stupid, and our survival today depends upon recovering that credibility. You can help us. You can turn this around."

"Right. I'm not your guy, Dr. Freund. If I do anything, I need to start fresh and clean and not have to deal with baggage, especially Ragnar Willowbrook baggage."

"I appreciate that, Doctor. Please give it some thought. You can reshape us in your own image and bring your Tran Lab colleagues here. This could be a good place for them to land."

"Good night, Dr. Freund."

The night lights of Los Angeles grew brighter, and Brian headed to Laurel Canyon to find Lily's party. When he arrived, they were enjoying wine and weed. Brian passed on the weed, but he loved California reds, especially Dave Phinney's zinfandel blend called "Prisoner," and when they passed that around, he couldn't refuse. Lily's boyfriend Javier Gartzi was a young brilliant doctor who worked at Cedars Sinai in the neurology department. Brian spent most of the night in spirited discussion about the latest developments in the treatment of dementia and Alzheimer's. Gartzi had some familiarity with nanotechnology but held a common bias about its risks. Lily had several friends who were startlingly good-looking, and they found Brian irresistible and fawned on him as he and Gartzi debated the merits of nanotechnology. When he said good night, Van was far from Brian's mind.

Freund's offer continued to pester him. He knew his gut reaction to reject the offer was the safest course of action and for that reason alone probably the only intelligent response. To accept the offer meant that he would be walking directly into a lion's den, a spider's web, a venomous snake pit that stood against everything he held to be true. His life's goal had been to find solutions. Money meant next to nothing to Brian, and although he did not see money itself as evil, he viewed the desire to accumulate massive wealth itself as a poison. An obsession with wealth fired the engines of the Silicon Valley, and its inventions had merit only if they were scalable and created a frenzied mass appetite among consumers. Ragnar Willowbrook fed on that obsession. Dr. Freund was kidding himself to think Brian might be able to reshape Ragnar Willowbrook into a credible institution. It was a foregone conclusion that the lab survived only with the largess of its billionaire customers, and their continued interest had to be nurtured if not seduced out of them. That was not Brian's game, and he hated it. He had watched with some disgust as Dr. Meisner from the Tran Lab sacrificed his own research and values to the full-time effort of obtaining funding to keep that lab operating. There was a simple reason the lab never recovered the prestige of its original founder, Duc A. Tran. Tran was driven to find answers and to expose the fallacies of his region's anti-cultural culture. Meisner, who took over when Tran died, never adopted Tran's vision or any other vision. He was caught up in the prestige of the Tran Lab, and his efforts to chase that prestige and the money associated with it ended gruesomely.

But Hollywood would distract Brian only momentarily, and eventually he knew he needed to get back to the cauldrons of science, discovery, and invention. Still, for now, Hollywood was a welcome respite from the terrors and trauma of the Tran Lab, and. More importantly, the buried sadness he felt when he thought of Van. He felt like he had made new friends in Javier Gartzi and Jaward Kamara. He called Jaward and arranged for a ride the next morning. The Sons of Sobriety pulled up to Brian's apartment noisily at 6:00 a.m., and Brian grabbed his helmet and roared out of the garage to the hoots of the MC. Jaward led them to an area north of Los Angeles where the state flower, the golden poppy, covered the hillsides like an orange blanket. The air was cool and the cloudless sky a light blue. They pulled their bikes into the Antelope Valley Poppy Reserve, an odd-looking assembly of leather-clad rough ex-Marines admiring the delicate flowers. Some sat on the benches smoking. Others took off on the paths that ran through the flowers. Brian noticed that in some swales the orange was so dense it looked like a carpet. After about an hour there, Jaward asked Brian if he'd like to visit a castle in the desert. They roared out of the flower park on Lancaster Road and turned down an old asphalt road in need of repair and overblown in spots with sand. Brian noticed an abandoned structure off in the distance that looked like a castle. And so it was, and Jaward told Brian it was called Shea's Castle. A New York developer named Shea had the castle built for his wife before the crash of 1929 left them penniless and forced them to sell the property. The castle had a run of several owners before it was finally abandoned. Hollywood had made use of the castle for some marginally popular TV shows like Rat Patrol and Buffy, the Vampire Slayer. A gate at the front entrance did a poor job of preventing trespassers, and the bikers climbed through and wandered around the turrets and through the dusty chamber rooms. One biker found an 8-foot gopher snake that took a defensive posture and reshaped its head to look like a rattlesnake. The biker grabbed it by the neck, shoving the helpless reptile into the faces of several club members. Jaward gave the biker a stare that said, "You need to stop," and shook his head. The biker laughed and strode, full of bravado, to the back door, continuing to pester others with the hapless and confused snake, and then flung it over a rusty chain link fence into the dry shrubbery that made up the desert floor. The animal gathered itself and, upset at the loss of its hunting ground, lurked away from the noise of the gang.

They stayed at the castle all day until the sun dropped below the horizon and the cool night air began to wash away the desert heat. A few hardy tourists stopped by, but when they saw the bikes parked against the front stone wall, they decided a view from inside the car was enough and they drove away. The castle turned out to be a fun place to explore with hidden doors and antechambers and a dungeon-style underground basement that might have been a torture chamber but more likely was used for other types of illicit activities. Jaward began to explore Brian's past, and they spent several hours talking about what happened at the Tran Lab and how special forces subjected to the rigors of armed conflict might be drawn into criminal activities. Jaward shared stories of his friends who turned mercenaries and ran guns into battle zones around the world because the money was good and the jobs weren't boring. Boredom, he said, was the real torture ex-Marines and other combatants faced when they returned home. The thrill of violence was not easily replaced by the mundane events of ordinary life. Brian asked how Jaward managed it, and he responded: "Well, I have this MC and these idiots whose mild insanities keep me from chasing crazy, and then there's Hollywood. If I need to go full gang, I can satisfy the fix by pretending to be crazy in an almost convincing atmosphere. It helps me put my devils back to bed." Brian appreciated Jaward's candor and hadn't realized how much he himself needed to talk, and when he mentioned his friends at the lab, he choked up and had to stifle the tears. His rage toward Fred Schmidt and Belinda Armendariz and Ragnar Willowbrook boiled over, but Jaward's response surprised him and caused him to pause and rethink his opposition to the offer. Jaward said,

"In the same way that the thought about a snake is more frightening than facing a real snake, the fear of your demons will haunt you until you meet your demons face to face. You cannot tame the lion until you enter the lion's den."

The next day Brian called Dr. Freund. They arranged to meet in two days at Moffatt Airfield on the south side of Mountain View directly below Google's massive innovation complex. He also called Van who acted surprised and oddly a little hurt when he told her he was returning north. He didn't explain why. She wished him the best and, in a tone that sounded resigned to losing Brian, she encouraged him to stay in touch. Her response split Brian into two halves, one demanding that he stay and pursue Van, the other demanding that he let her go. If it's meant to be, he told himself half-heartedly, it's meant to be. Then he told himself he was an idiot, and the next day, he jumped on the Gold Wing and used his travel time back north to reflect on Dr. Freund's offer to him to reshape Ragnar Willowbrook in his own image. He also thought about Fred Schmidt, and he found that the anger was beginning to subside. Fred Schmidt needed Brian's talents, and Brian needed a steady source of revenue at the lab. Belinda was another story. Belinda's heartless use of special ops to retrieve the petri dish and destroy the lab was not an act he could ever forgive, ever.

Chapter 7.

Film Noir

The collapse of the global economy in the 1930s, the rise of fascism, and the dawn of a second world war two short decades after the first world war, which had been branded "the war to end all wars," found their expression in an era of Hollywood filmmaking known as film noir. Juxtaposing dark and light and emphasizing shadow, these films, mostly crime-related, reflected a brooding pessimism in the mood of Americans. The soundtracks for these movies employed some of the slower and dripping sounds of jazz that were also becoming popular and reflected the same somber depression as the shadow play. Sometimes referred to as jazz noir, the tracks mixed loud fortissimo almost randomly with soft subito piano bars, adding to the mystery of the film and introducing a kind of chaotic element into the soundtrack for a frightening and disorienting effect that had audiences clamoring for more.

Detective Van Eng had never been a fan of American cinema, in part because she kept herself too busy and in part because, as an unintentional result of her cold case research in CHESS, Van was beginning to associate Hollywood with its more diabolical side. It didn't help that her parents, unlike many of their Los Angeles friends, refused to rely on television to teach themselves English. Television, in their minds, was a needless distraction from work and prayer. Work and prayer, as they had learned through difficult lives, was the only way for the poor to feel secure. Van had incorporated that same rigorous work ethic into her own life.

Martin Richard's interest in Van was heightened by this lack of interest in Hollywood and celebrity. He had grown up with people constantly fawning over his parents, and his parents' disdain for the worshipping masses was on display for all to see, including their only son. In their minds, they were nothing more than the creators of an entertainment medium. That it made them rich beyond their wildest dreams was a coincidence, not a goal, and the only people they cared about were the other artists and creators who shared their own struggles to produce something beautiful or compelling. That shell was itself a significant part of the lure of Hollywood, and tourists and wannabes flocked to Los Angeles by the millions with the hope of breaking in or catching a glimpse of the actual living person whose brilliant performances filled their evenings. Martin had wasted no time inviting Van to dinner. Van accepted because, when she had met Martin at the party he held following the Muscle Beach contest, she saw something in him that seemed genuine and honest. She hadn't made her mind up about Martin, but she had no trouble giving him a shot at capturing her attention. Martin, for his part, put on a good show. He hired a car to pick Van up at her home, something her parents couldn't stop talking about. The driver brought her to his parents' Malibu home. This time they were at the house, and Martin introduced her to them as Detective Van Eng. Martin's father, Director Frank Richard, invited the couple into the living room. Van was reminded of the night of the party, how that was the same room in which she first met Martin, a shy but good-looking young man with pointy shoes. She remembered the oversized fireplace, which dominated the room and was large enough to hold a bonfire. The two Oscars were still there, but she could see that the fireplace mantle had been rearranged and now, instead of side by side, the statues were separated, one at each end of the mantle. Martin's mother Denise asked if Van would like iced lemonade and said they have a special family recipe. Van was thirsty and lemonade, special or not, sounded especially good. Frank enjoyed talking, and he expressed how proud he was of Martin pursuing his own life and career without leaning on his parents' reputation. He also seemed to have a special interest in Van's experience as a detective working with the LAPD. Was she comfortable there? Did she feel treated fairly? The line of questions struck Van oddly invasive, and she tried to be engaging without directly responding. Frank chuckled and apologized suggesting that of course she would want to be cautious on such subjects. Van felt it appropriate to congratulate Martin's parents on their accomplishments, nodding in the direction of the statues, and they thanked her and played it down. Martin's mother called it silly media event, but Frank did seem to delight in the mention of the awards. Martin, slightly embarrassed at his parents' obvious fawning over Van, pointed to his watch and stood, and Frank escorted Van to the door as Martin grabbed her scarf and his jacket. They stood at the door, and Van felt there was something slightly staged about the meeting. Martin apologized for his parents, and the driver held the door as they slid into the back seat.

"Please take us to Mastro's," Martin instructed the driver, and they headed down Mulholland to Mastro's Ocean Club on Pacific Coast Highway, just below the Getty

Villa Museum. Van knew Mastro's to be a high-end expensive restaurant, and she noticed that the maître d' recognized Martin and treated him almost obsequiously as he led them to a prominent table. She watched Martin to see if that recognition mattered to him and helped him to feel more self-important. She wondered if the reason he brought her to this restaurant was because he wanted her to feel special, but given the maître d's response, it wasn't unusual for him to eat here. She knew Martin had grown up in a prominent family and was used to special treatment, but she didn't like it and it concerned her. She was drawn to Martin because he seemed to be humble despite his circumstances. She wasn't entirely certain that his humility was real. But as the night went on, she relaxed and found herself having fun with Martin and enjoyed his stories about his parents' exploits and his own experience working in Hollywood. In the end, Martin was a perfect gentleman and rode with her back to her house and gave her a gentle hug and light kiss to close the night. He asked if he could see her again, and she enjoyed his excitement when she said yes.

Detective Paul Young met her at her desk when she arrived the next morning.

"Any suspects yet in the Paramount murder?" he asked probing, as he often did, for a weakness in Van.

"Nothing yet, Paul." Van had let herself get familiar with Paul. She didn't allow his condescending attitude toward her to bother her.

"What are your next steps, Detective?" he pressed, but at that moment, Detective Charles Darling showed up and terminated Detective Young's inquiry.

"Our guests are here," he said to Van using his fingers to make quotes. "Van can catch you up later." Detective Young was clearly irritated, but Van smiled at him and grabbed a stack of files and followed Charlie to the main hallway where a half dozen people were milling around and whispering to each other. As they approached the waiting group, Van could smell smoke on their breaths and wondered why so many in Hollywood ignored the well-established warnings.

"Thank you for coming," Detective Darling told the group. "We will be asking you to meet with us individually and will call you one by one to come with us."

"Are we suspects?" said a thin young man who seemed irritated to be there.

"We haven't identified anyone as a suspect yet," said Van, trying to alleviate the group's concern. "Our hope is that you might help us get closer to a resolution. We want everyone associated with the film to feel safe."

"You think this had something to do with the film?" said the same young man.

"We don't know if it did or didn't," said Detective Darling. "We do know the Mr. Nguyen was shot at close range and, therefore, that the shooting

must have taken place on the lot. But the sooner we start, the sooner we can let you go home."

"Can you let me go first? I'll convince you I don't know anything and I can get out of here."

"Thank you for the offer, but we have an order already decided. We will try to get all of you home quickly. I would like to start with Tracy Pickett. Are you here, Tracy?"

"That would be me," said a perky blond about twenty-four years old. She followed Van and Charlie back into the bureau's offices and into a small sterile interrogation room.

"Thank you for coming, Ms. Pickett."

"Well, if I didn't, you probably would have subpoenaed me. I didn't need that headache."

"Very smart," said Charlie. "You are the producer's top executive assistant?"

"That's correct."

"How well did you know the victim, Trey Nguyen?"

"I was in many meetings with him," she said. "But I wouldn't say I know him well. Peggy spoke highly of him and often brought him to share his ideas with Jerry."

"Peggy Rice?"

"Yes. She's the lead writer. He worked for her."

"Was there anyone working on the picture who didn't like him?"

"He was a bit of a loner, and sometimes that can be off-putting, but no one I know actually disliked him."

"What about his personal life?" asked Van.

"Like I said, I didn't know him."

"But did you see him hang out with anyone suspicious?"

"There was a tall Asian woman who was allowed to visit him on the lot and who sometimes dropped him off at work. But I didn't see anything unusual, except maybe one thing."

"Yes?"

"She drove an all-gold car. Seemed a bit ostentatious, but I also thought it was cool. It had a green light in the undercarriage you could see at night. I guess I assumed she was rich."

"Did you speak with Trey the day he was killed?"

"You mean night?"

"Yes, the night he was killed. Is that important to you?"

"We didn't start shooting until 10 p.m. We had a writers' meeting, as we usually did, just before the shoot around 8:00 or 8:30. We noticed he wasn't at the meeting. It was highly unusual for Trey. He was always the first one to the meetings. I remember Jerry saying he was going to go far."

"Was it a problem?"

"The fact that Trey wasn't there?"

"Yes."

"Not really. The writers' meetings were rarely about the shoot that day. That team was always five or six shoots ahead of schedule. If Peggy needed something from Trey for that day, she didn't show it. Peggy doesn't display much emotion. That is one reason Jerry uses her so much."

"So why was it noticeable?"

"He just was always there. Many times he was the first to arrive."

"Do you recall hearing anything? A scream or a gun shot?"

"It's Hollywood, Detective. Screams and gunshots are routine."

"You didn't?"

"Not that I recall."

"Thanks, Tracy."

The detectives continued their interviews for another two hours. Peggy Rice was, as Tracy Pickett described, the consummate professional. Trey Nguyen was one in a long list of aspiring Hollywood writers. She considered him much better than average and extremely reliable, which was nice but not expected. Aspiring writers often had issues, according to Peggy. It wasn't particularly surprising that one of them would miss a meeting and then show up the next day a bit disheveled and apologetic. If they weren't particularly good, Peggy would dismiss them immediately. Trey was very good and probably would have gotten away with it. But if Peggy was saddened by Trey's death, she didn't show it. Van had the impression that Peggy was thinking more about the next script revisions than the police interview.

The annoying young man turned out to be a set designer named Tad Brown. Tad was an apprentice journeyman. Both Van and Charlie picked up quickly that his overblown ego and irritability were probably drug induced, most likely cocaine. His responses were not consistent and his memory not reliable. He would say things like, "Yes, I definitely saw him that night, but wait, maybe it was Tuesday."

When they were done, Van and Charlie compared notes. She told Charlie she thought they should take a little more time with Tracy Pickett. She suggested that she return to the lot and shadow Tracy on the job. Charlie knew better than to question Van's hunches. Van found Tracy in her office at Jerry Cortez Films in Santa Monica. The low-profile brick building provided Cortez the anonymity he wanted, and the first thing Van noticed was that no one parked in the spaces in the front of the building, all of which had parking meters. It gave the impression that the building was not occupied. The next thing Van noticed was that all the windows were blacked out with red molding around the sixteen small windowpanes that made up each window, and the front door also was painted red and offset against a black entrance with a single number centered above the door. She parked out front and put a credit card in the meter for an hour. She suspected a camera somewhere was tracking her movements as the only figure out front. As she reached for the bell, she heard a click, and a voice seemingly popped out of nowhere, "Welcome, Detective Eng. Please come in." Van turned the chrome handle and pulled the door open, which was surprisingly light. Behind the first door was a short hallway and a second door, and it was at the second door that she met Tracy.

"Sorry for the elaborate security. We don't encourage too many visitors here," she said. "You can imagine how interested the industry is in knowing what Jerry's latest project might be."

"It looks vacant out front," Van said.

"Another ruse," Tracy responded. "I can assure you it is anything but vacant here."

"This is where you spend most of your time?"

"At least half. We do a lot of post-production here, and it is a good place for me to manage Jerry's affairs."

Van looked closely at Tracy as she said this, knowing the bad boy reputation several Hollywood producers still had. But Tracy didn't budge. "Not those affairs, Detective. Jerry's not that type. Never has been, despite being remarried."

"I see," she said, not entirely convinced. He was a Hollywood icon after all.

"I appreciate you letting me hang around a bit," Van said, redirecting the discussion.

"Well, I imagine I wouldn't have much choice if I did. Truth is, Trey's death disturbs all of us. No one who I know knows why he was shot, and it has us all on edge, given this latest movie. Honestly, it feels a little better to know you are here, and you are welcome to stay for as long as you want."

"Any chance I could move my car?"

"Of course. Let me get you a key fob and you can park underneath the building like the rest of us."

Tracy introduced Van to the others in the office, and Van noticed they all seemed appreciative of her presence, just as Tracy described. The only one who was a bit dismissive of Van was Peggy Rice. Van had not been fooled by the tough facade during Peggy's interview, and she knew not to be fooled by it now. At least Peggy was consistent.

"Tough to lose somebody," she said to Peggy when they were alone in the kitchen.

"I'm not heartless, Detective."

"I never figured you were."

"Fact is we all are still in shock and this damn movie."

"What do you mean?"

"Jerry has his pick. He could do anything he wants to do. But this one?"

"I'm not sure I understand."

"Come into my office."

Van spent the next hour with Peggy. Peggy wanted Van's complete attention as if she finally had someone she could vent on. Van saw stacks of scripts in piles around the room and photos of Peggy with what she assumed were her own two small children. She smelled smoke although there were no signs of cigarettes. Van noticed a lavender book on the shelf with the name "Rice" on the binder.

"Is that you?" she said.

Peggy smirked. "It was me. Not me anymore."

"What do you mean?"

"Words are not the same to me as they were when I wrote that book. Now they are time sequences and frames. Now they are efficient and precise and cost money, and under that pressure, you won't see me trying to pen hundred thousand random words into a story." Peggy's sarcasm dripped through her response deep and heavy.

"That alone sounds like a novel."

"Hah!" Peggy chuckled almost in pain. "You are perceptive, aren't you? I was warned."

"You don't like the movie?"

"No, I hate it."

"Why?"

"To be honest, I'm not entirely sure. I have opinions about the writing, and I have worked with Trey to improve it. But it's not really the writing that bugs me."

"Ok."

"Sometimes you stumble into a bad movie, and there is nothing you can do to fix it. Jerry got all excited about nanobots after he went to a climate conference in Paris. The script seemed to emerge out of nowhere, and then when we hired Trey, Jerry took him under his wing, and the next thing you know, the kid is producing pages and pages of rewrites."

"You got jealous?"

Peggy laughed. "Oh God no. What a bad storyline that would be. Lead writer shoots assistant for being better than her. Maybe CSI or Murder She Wrote but not a movie. Hah!"

Van thought she saw a nervous tick in Peggy's reaction. "But it's a problem, right?"

"Trey was never a problem. Besides, Jerry made it clear to me that I had final say over everything about the script. The problem is that it feels like we are squeezing a concept into a movie and filling it in with a bad story. The Power of Small—even the title sucks. Jerry has done so many things that are so much better than this."

"This can't be the first time you've had to take junk and turn it into fine art."

"That's interesting. Maybe I am just losing my patience."

"But you are not really telling me anything, Peggy. What is the issue?"

Peggy stared at Van and then gazed at the black curtain hanging over her window. "I can't put my finger on why, but it feels like the movie killed Trey."

"Nanobots are hot. A lot of people want in on the gold rush, even Hollywood. Any reason to think someone wanted to kill the movie and Trey was just an easy target? Cinematic terrorism?"

"I don't know. I . . . maybe."

"Are you scared, Peggy?"

Peggy pursed her lips. "It's a brutal industry, this Hollywood thing. There are some brutal people here, and it's not the first time I have been concerned. But I don't see that. I don't think so."

"Just checking the angles. Tell me the story."

Peggy was afraid. Van saw that right away. The other Cortez staff were scared, also. They all seemed to be hovering around Van as if she could keep them safe. She had expected mistrust and maybe some anger at her for invading their sacred space and placing them under a forensic microscope.

She had thought, if she could feel out some guilt, she might be able to isolate it and narrow the search for a suspect. But she didn't see any suspects, and she didn't feel any guilt, at least not in this office—just fear.

Chapter 8.

The Algernon Effect

The 1966 novel *Flowers for Algernon* by Daniel Keyes has an unusual history. First, the novel was written originally as a short story and won the 1958 Hugo Award for Best Short Story. Keyes expanded the same story into a novel eight years later and won the 1966 Nebula Award for Best Novel. Keyes' publishers classified the novel as science fiction, the story about a young man diagnosed with phenylketonuria, a metabolic disorder that impacts brain activity. The main character, a young man aged thirty-two, named Charles Gordon or "Charlie," undergoes experimental surgery to address his brain disorder with the goal of increasing his intelligence. The initial results are dramatic. Charlie's IQ jumps from 68 to 185, and his new-found thirst for knowledge becomes insatiable. He pores through encyclopedias and journals, and his knowledge base grows to exceed all around him. He becomes famous both for having undergone his unique surgery and for his capacity for absorbing information. Then, rather quickly, the effects of the surgery begin to wear off, and Charlie, who now understands his own plight in a way he never could have prior to the surgery, prepares himself to lose everything he has gained. Soon Charlie begins to regress to his old self, but before the process is completed, he pays respect to a mouse named Algernon, the first subject of the same experimental surgery and which, like Charlie, experienced a brief flash of self-awareness before falling back into the darkness.

Garny McDonough enjoyed his newly acquired celebrity. The buzz of his presentation to the climate conference and his novel solution to managing carbon dioxide emissions earned him invitations to several United Nations meetings and conferences, and the leading countries were taking notice. The French president invited Garny to meet with his top climatology advisors, and the United States State Department UN envoy sent him an invitation to dinner. Garny was hardly thinking about the brief meeting with Belinda. What he did think about was that he had expected to be impressed given General Warner's accolades about Belinda's accomplishments. But the meeting did not go as he had expected, and he concluded that he had no reason to view her as a threat to his future success. He especially didn't plan to have much more to do with her after she ignored his invitation to follow up their first meeting. She had simply left without a word.

In any event, his energies were focused elsewhere. He needed a compelling follow-up to his United Nations presentation and his declarations of advances in the use of self-replicating nanobots as a carbon-capture technology. He searched for an enclosed structure similar to the dome he built for the Karakul Proposition at Lake Karakul in Tajikistan. He'd heard of a velodrome he thought was near the Eiffel Tower, called Vel' d'Hiv, short for Velodrome d'Hiver. The velodrome had hosted several events from the 1924 Summer Olympics but became infamous after it was used to detain more than 13,000 Jews who were later deported to the concentration camps at Auschwitz. The French government refused to acknowledge any complicity in Nazi atrocities until 1995 when President Jacque Chirac issued a public apology for the incident at Vel d'Hiv. Unfortunately for Garny, or maybe not, the Vel d'Hiv had been demolished in 1959. So Garny found another structure in Paris that did suit his needs and, coincidentally, was called the Dôme de Paris and, also coincidentally, the very structure that was built in 1959 to replace Vel d'Hiv. The dome was an indoor concert and performance venue in Port de Versailles in downtown Paris. It was not as large as the dome he built in Tajikistan, but at 4,600 seats, it was certainly large enough for a grand display of his air-cleansing nanobot technology.

Located in the 15th Arrondissement on the Boulevard Levebre and just off D50, the dome had hosted the Beatles, the Rolling Stones, the Grateful Dead, and Pink Floyd in the formative years of rock and roll. The French government agreed to let Garny use the dome for his demonstration in exchange for his promise to remodel and upgrade the structure when the experiment was concluded. Garny knew the dome would need to be modified and made plans to replicate his design of the first dome at Lake Karakul. He contacted several members of his engineering and construction team who had worked in Tajikistan on the first dome and flew them to Paris with promises of a share in the company if the experiment was successful. They started by sealing off the entire grounds with a twelve-foot portable concrete wall called a Bremer wall, developed for blast protection by the American Paul Bremer for use in

Iraq and Afghanistan following the Gulf War. Access to the encampment was tightly controlled and created a buzz around Paris, with stories ranging from claims that it was a massive art project to concerns that it was a new type of prison for terrorists. Garny's team then sealed the entire building and built a huge fan complex where they placed a dozen large Mitsubishi marine engines, half of which were a part of the original experiment. He contacted the Karakul Lab in Tajikistan where his imported team of scientists had helped him invent the self-replicating carbon-capturing nanobots. The team at the Karakul Lab had been exploring alternative uses of the nanobots, but nothing they developed compared to the carbon-capture technology that was making Garny famous among the world's climatologists. The Karakul team continued to manufacture the Star of Bethlehem nanogel and now had several tons of frozen goo stored in a secure cave that Garny had constructed adjacent to the lab. He arranged for several tons of frozen Star goo to be transported to Paris using his newly acquired Russian cargo plane. Shortly after the first experiments proved successful, Garny began drawing up his plans for a massive atmospheric release of the carbon-capturing nanobots and purchased an Antonov An-124 Ruslan cargo plane from the Russian government, the largest operating cargo plane in the world. Only twenty-six An-124s were built, and production halted when tensions developed between Russia and Ukraine. The planes were massive and not very expensive. Garny had purchased his first An-124 for $30 million, and he was preparing to buy more planes for a massive release of the Star goo as soon as the right deals were in place. A successful trial of the product would be essential if he was to cut any deals.

Belinda, meanwhile, had been busy. After several weeks and many failed trials, Professor Echeverria's team finally determined that the nanobots were "capture bots" capable of shifting the balance of atmospheric elements. They used a gas spectrometer in an air-tight chamber to determine that, after the introduction of the nanobots into the chamber, oxygen and nitrogen levels increased and carbon dioxide levels decreased. They ran a safety test by placing several mice in the chamber, all of which died from some type of asphyxiation within seconds after the nanobots were released. One student proposed that the mice were going into anaphylactic shock after they autopsied the bodies and found heightened levels of cytokines in the mice's blood. Belinda reported the results to General Warner who claimed to know nothing about the toxic effect. Belinda suggested that it might be capable of being weaponized, and Warner instructed her to explore it further both to determine its potential as a weapon and to identify a method for countering its effect, an antidote or a preventive treatment.

Garny sipped his breakfast coffee and studied the nearly completed remodeling plans for the dome, which he could see directly across Boulevard Victor. He glanced up at the name "Eugene" printed on the green fringe of the patio canopy shading him from the morning sun. He mused whether the famous American playwright Eugene O'Neill night have sat in the same location reviewing his own favorable French reviews.

"Garny." A head appeared in the sunlight creeping over the edge of the canopy. He recognized the voice.

"Good morning, Tom. Please sit." Garny motioned the waiter with his hand.

"Garçon! Un autre, s'il vous plaît."

"Immédiatement."

"How are the preparations coming?" asked General Warner.

"We're close," said Garny. "I am designing a viewing platform for hundred guests. I am concerned that the test equipment is not decipherable for most of the guests. I want the test results to be spectacular, and I need a simple but powerful way of displaying them."

"Makes sense. How about a video showing a daisy growing and blooming against a clear blue sky?"

"No." Garny shuddered, and they both chuckled.

"Seriously though, Garny, any safety concerns?"

Garny stared at the general. "Nothing we haven't already accounted for. We are concerned about a certain level of toxicity that exceeds local environmental standards, and anyone working in the arena will have full hazmat gear."

"You've never been exposed?"

"Of course not. We take precautions."

"Have you tested the toxicity levels?"

Garny started to get irritated. "The suits worked just fine in Tajikistan. What are you getting at? Do you know something?"

"It's just that this is not Tajikistan. It is downtown Paris, and an unfortunate incident would have major impacts and might blow the whole project."

"Typical American."

"What? You now identify as French?"

Garny laughed. He looked back at the name Eugene on the canopy. "No, but they certainly seem to recognize genius more readily than my friends in the States."

"They also are wary of over-flattering reviews."

"I hear you, Tom. It's a fair point. I'll bring in some extra masks just in case."

* * *

Belinda was back on her hotel balcony in Pamplona. She looked down at the two sedans parked near the hotel entrance and imagined she was being watched. So far no one had approached her, and she wondered if she might be paranoid, but she doubted it. The work at SUMBET was proceeding faster than Belinda expected. Her team had already discovered that, in addition to reducing atmospheric carbon dioxide, the bots had the capacity to self-replicate. She knew it was time to collect the original sample and any expanded materials from the newly formed bots and move out of Pamplona to a more secure location. She also knew that she needed support from the right people in Basque Country, a group that would be more loyal to her than to Interpol or to CNP, the Spanish national police. Working with SUMBET and the University of Navarra had been a risk. But given the quick results of their nanobot research, she knew it had been worth the risk. Now, she needed to terminate that effort and not get caught.

But Belinda faced a challenge. Global support for separatist movements was waning. The face of the Basque National Liberation Movement, Euskadi Ta Askatasuna or ETA, lost its hold on the BNLM after a split developed between those who had tired of the violence and who believed Basque self-identity did not require self-determination and those who held on to the dream of an independent state. Several key leaders in the latter group were arrested in 2011. Shortly thereafter, ETA formally terminated hostilities toward the French and Spanish governments in a widely publicized international campaign to end the Basque conflict. In 2017, ETA disarmed the organization and disclosed the locations of several weapons caches in southern France. The Spanish government leaned on ETA to disband completely, and in May of 2018, at ceremonies in Geneva, Switzerland, and in Cambo les Bains, France, the ETA declared itself dissolved. But Belinda believed the conflict was not ended. Just before it dissolved, ETA had endorsed Catalonia's independence referendum, a movement for independence from Spain that the Spanish government sought to prevent through political means and, those being unsuccessful, resorted to violence at the referendum vote.

The move triggered criticism from Amnesty International and Human Rights Watch and rekindled anti-government sentiment among several Spanish ethnic groups, including the Basques. Upon her return, Belinda had been meeting in secret with former ETA leaders, and although not all those meetings went well, Belinda had gathered a small cabal of Basque separatists determined to carry on the effort. They called themselves "The Pamplona Effect." She organized a midnight raid on the university, in which her Pamplona Effect team tore apart the SUMBET lab and stole lab materials including, but not limited to, the dozen biosafety hazard cases containing the expanded nanobot samples that Belinda had lent to the lab for her research. The next morning Professor Echeverria called Belinda in a panic, describing the burglary, the destruction of the lab, and the unfortunate loss of Belinda's nanobots. Belinda expressed her relief that no one was injured or worse, but she did not hold back on her dismay and anger at the loss and insisted that every effort be made to find the nanobots immediately, describing the extreme danger the nanobots posed to the public, a danger Professor Echeverria's own team had uncovered. She recommended that Professor Echeverria warn the police about the dangers posed by the nanobots in detail, a move that she knew was likely to dampen any aggressive efforts to chase down the perpetrators, at least efforts by the local police. She needed time to get herself out of Pamplona and to a remote location in the Pyrenees where she could engage in her more serious efforts at weaponizing the nanobots. Belinda had been searching for the right location for this next stage of her project. She found it near a remote northern Spanish town in central Pyrenees called Ainsa. At the top of a hill overlooking the town of Ainsa and a large reservoir called Embalse de Mediano stood an abandoned monastery and settlement called Muro de Roda. Muro de Roda was an old walled town that had been abandoned after the bubonic plague decimated its residents in 1347. The site had few visitors and had never been formally classified as a cultural heritage site by the World Heritage Fund. The only group supporting the monastery was a group of nuns in Ainsa who formed a Save the Roda fund, but despite their best efforts, Muro de Roda was deteriorating and had turned into a partying hideaway for high school and college kids to smoke weed and do hallucinogenic drugs.

Belinda arranged for the purchase of the property under the name of a faux conservationist group committed to restoring the settlement to its original appearance. She began restoration of the above-ground structures and, at the same time, started construction of a large underground laboratory directly under the settlement. She built an underground helipad that she screened with doors covered in a pattern of bushes and shrubbery, detected only by a special camera she had installed on the helicopter using lasers and speckle-based imagery. The site would be undetectable to satellites or drones. The main entrance to the lab was an elevator concealed in a building she determined to be the old settlement's brothel. She figured that an old-fashioned brothel might be too interesting to visitors, so she refashioned it as a warehouse and constructed another tourist bordello down the street. She made the lab several levels deep. The top level consisted of her office and an adjoining conference room with windows that looked out from the side of the hill onto the lake and the town of Ainsa in the distance. Level 2 was the primary lab with a viewing room, a decontamination chamber, and the main lab floor. Level 3 was a secure level in which she built special chambers for the nanobot research. Level 3 also contained a secret escape route to the underground heliport in the event Belinda needed a quick getaway.

While the lab was under construction, Belinda carefully recruited her team. She needed a team leader who was both a brilliant engineer and in lockstep with her own nationalist ideals. She needed someone who would commit completely to the twin goals of absolute secrecy and weaponized nanobots. She found him in Paris, teaching at the University of Paris-Sorbonne in the polymer chemistry lab. She had met him in Navarra through SUMBET where he was studying at the nanotechnology institute on a paid sabbatical. She had joined the faculty for drinks at the Café Iruna, at a table in a room dedicated to Ernest Hemingway, who haunted the bar in 1920s while he was writing *The Sun Also Rises*.

"Belinda, so good of you to join us," said Professor Marta Echeverria. Still, early in their research on Belinda's nanobots, Professor Echeverria invited Belinda to drinks regularly to get updates on the developing research and to get to know the team she had selected for the work. "Let me introduce you to Dr. Hadj Arkoun, on sabbatical from the Sorbonne."

Belinda smiled. Dr. Arkoun was young and dashing, and her first thought was not directed to his research. But if Dr. Arkoun picked up on any vibes from Belinda, he wasn't showing it. He didn't smile and gave the impression that, if he wasn't focused on his work, he was wasting his time. Marta convinced him to join the party that night by letting him know Belinda was funding their research. But he was not a glad-hander and not particularly social, despite his good looks.

"Arkoun," said Belinda. "Sounds Algerian."

"Trés bon. Very good," responded Hadj. "Paris by way of Algiers."

"I see." Belinda raised her scotch. "Here's to Paris by way of Algiers. Rock the casbah!"

"Rock the casbah!" shouted the others at the table, already well into the well for the night.

"Indeed," Hadj joined the toast but only half-heartedly. "You are aware that Algeria has contributed much to Western science and culture."

"Wouldn't surprise me," replied Belinda. "Americans seem to have the idea that Western history starts and ends in England and that the only good ideas these days are American ideas."

"I can talk all night about Camus, Derrida, and Fanon," said Hadj. "All of them born Algerians, as was Saint Augustine. But you would never guess my favorite famous Algerian."

At this Marta jumped up on her chair and shouted to the entire restaurant, "I bloody love Yves Saint Laurent!"

Belinda looked at Hadj and furrowed her eyebrows. Hadj put his head in his hands.

"You've had this conversation before?"

"Only every night," said Marta, almost falling out of her chair as she tried to sit down.

"That's not true," muttered Hadj.

"What if it is?" said Belinda. "The real question is, how did a sabbatical from the Sorbonne bring you to Pamplona and not take you back to Algiers?"

Hadj looked over at Marta. "It brought me to Navarra and my new beloved friend Marta Echeverria. I have been working in quantum chemistry and superconductivity, and I find myself drawn to nanotechnology. SUMBET is one of the top institutes in the field."

"Have you looked at my nanobots?"

"I have. I have a lot of questions."

"Such as?"

"The composition is strange to me but oddly familiar."

"What do you mean?"

"I mean the elements used to fabricate these bots are uncommon. The spikes are a tungsten alloy. That makes sense because tungsten and carbon are covalent and tungsten acts like a carbon magnet. If your goal is to capture carbon, tungsten is the perfect choice. But the spherical body of the bots, presumably where its 'brain' resides, is made from a unique type of porcelain. I haven't determined it molecular elements yet, but it's not a metal. Porcelain is an element used in superconducting because resistance in porcelain is close to zero. But why would these bots need to be superconducting? It's genius, really. It's almost as if they can draw enough electrical power to operate from the air around them."

Belinda's eyes moved back and forth between Marta and Hadj. She could see in Marta a deep admiration for the younger Hadj, bordering on devotion. Suddenly, Hadj stood and raised his glass to the entire bar, only, unlike Marta, deepening his voice to create an air of respect and honor. "To Yves Saint Laurent." By now the other bar patrons had picked up on the act. "Yves Saint Laurent!" they responded in unison.

Belinda and Hadj began to meet regularly. She pressed him on his explorations into the structure and functionality of the nanobots and their possible uses. His knowledge of nanotechnology was superficial, but she noted how quickly he was acquiring mastery of the subject matter. She also learned that Hadj had a special interest in weapons technology, but whenever she tried to move the conversation in that direction, he shut down. She realized quickly that, if she were to learn more about his knowledge and experience in that area, she needed to allow it to emerge from him and not force the question. But Belinda could tell Hadj found her intriguing. She was the funding source behind the SUMBET research, and he often queried her on her goals. Belinda spoke about practical applications of nanotechnology and its implications in electronics, energy production, and medicine. She said she was particularly interested in atomic precise manufacturing or ATM and the ability of nanobot-based manufacturing systems to eliminate manufacturing defects and reduce the cost of production. But she never disclosed her more aggressive goals, and Hadj knew nothing about the theft of the nanobots, or if he figured it out, he said nothing. When Belinda invited him to join her in the design and construction of the laboratory at Muro de Roda, Hadj didn't hesitate to accept, and more importantly to Belinda, he didn't ask questions.

Chapter 9.

The Show Must Go On

Peggy made her way to her car in the garage under Cortez Studios. She watched carefully for any signs of an intruder and picked up her pace as she approached the Jaguar F-Type P380, her first real luxury sports car. Her thumb rested on her alarm button, ready to push down at any sign of a threat. She climbed onto the driver's seat and slammed the door, heaving a sign of relief. The car started immediately, and she backed out of her designated spot and pulled toward the gate, which was beginning to open as she drew near. Peggy waited while the gate completed its journey across the entrance. She thought she saw movement, but every time her eyes chased the motion, nothing appeared. As she waited, she looked down to see a folded sheet of paper resting on the passenger seat. She stared at it for a moment as if its presence made no sense. In the instant that she accepted it as something real and not imaginary, her hand jumped to the fold and opened it to read, "Your next." Her first thought as she looked at the note was the improper use of "your," but just as her critical grammatical eye found the error, she heard a loud crash, and her driver-side window shattered and her head slammed to the right against the small and mostly purposeless right cushion of her car seat head rest. She slumped forward onto the steering wheel horn, the car screaming its warning throughout the underground garage.

Van and Charlie rested at the studio cafe. Van's interviews at the Cortez studio with Peggy Rice and others suggested a connection to the film, but she was dubious. The murder of Trey Nguyen smelled more like a gang hit than an anti-Cortez conspiracy. Multiple witnesses confirmed that a gold WRX with green undercarriage lighting exactly like the car Danny Kang used to drive had been on the lot, and one witness saw a tall thin Asian woman get into the car, the profile of Danny Kang's sister Min Kang. She wondered if Trey had been dating her and ended up on the wrong side of Min's wrath. Van and Charlie questioned additional movie crew members, and no one had any knowledge of a relationship Trey had with Min or with other crew members. He was very reserved and seemed only interested in his writing and the storyline of the movie. Moreover, the murder had elements of precision like a pre-planned hit: a single shot that caught Trey in the head as he stood in the garden under the trees in Lucy Park just outside the studio office in which he was working. It did not bear the more common random marks of a jealous lover acting out of rage. But Van knew not to rule out the possibility, and she knew also that eventually she would need to confront Min.

Van's phone rang.

"Detective, thank God!"

"Tracy?"

"They've . . . they've shot Peggy!" Tracy burst into tears.

"What are you saying Tracy?"

"In the parking garage," she sniffed and tried unsuccessfully to gather herself. "Someone shot Peggy."

"Is she all right?"

"I don't know. The ambulance is here now taking her to the hospital."

"Which hospital? Did they tell you?"

"I think it's Santa Monica Medical. They have a trauma center."

"Thanks. Can you meet me there?"

"Yes. I will."

Van explained to Charlie what happened and said she would catch up with him later. She jumped in her car and raced down to the freeway. She rushed into the trauma center and, flashing her badge, asked about the status of Peggy Rice.

"Ms. Rice is in intensive care. They just brought her in. She has a bullet in her neck. They are working on her now. You'll need to wait."

Van looked over and saw Tracy walking toward her.

"Thank you. Please let me know if her condition changes."

The nurse nodded her assent. Tracy was visibly shaken.

Van held Tracy for a moment to calm her and asked, "Do you know what happened?"

"Not really," said Tracy, wiping her eyes. "We saw Peggy leave. She seemed nervous. We told her to have a good night, but she didn't respond as she usually does. She just jumped into the elevator, and after about five minutes we heard a crash, like a car accident."

"She was shot while she was in her car?"

"Through the driver-side window."

"Was it close range?"

"I don't know. I found her first. She was slumped over and bleeding."

"I'm sorry, Tracy."

"It's so horrible. Poor Peggy." Her eyes began to tear again, and she wiped them away to no avail.

"I'm so sorry."

Van drove back to the Cortez studio parking lot. The entrance had been taped off, and Peggy's car was still parked at the gate. Police were guiding the remaining cars out of the lot through the entrance gate, which was locked open. Van flashed her badge and quietly observed the scene. She imagined the locations where the shot might have entered the driver-side window. Given a possible correlation with the murder at Paramount, Santa Monica and LAPD units were working together. She noticed her former boss from forensics, Dr. Frank Weatherby, and her former colleague, now Frank's assistant, Brad Jones, standing near the car and plotting trajectories. Brad saw her first and smiled. Frank seemed very focused. She walked over to where they stood, careful not to disturb evidence flags already planted near the vehicle.

"What have you found?" she asked.

Frank looked up as she approached, and Brad shouted somewhat too excitedly, "Van!"

"Good evening, Detective," Frank said in a warm but serious tone.

"Hi, guys. Welcome to Santa Monica. What's your take?"

"We're not jumping to conclusions, yet. We have not seen the victim and must base our assumption on the broken glass pattern. What we understand is that a single shot was fired and that the bullet lodged in the victim's neck. We have searched for the casing without luck and think the shot was taken across the street where the shooter could see the victim as she drove up to the gate."

Van's forensics training began to take over as she surveyed the same area Frank and Brad were reviewing.

"Do you smell burned wood?"

"What do you mean?" Brad asked.

"As I was walking over here, I picked up on the smell of burnt wood."

"I think there is a dump not too far from here."

"That's not it. It's a fresh smoky smell. Did you look at those eucalyptus trees?" She pointed to a row of four mature eucalyptus trees planted directly in front of the building.

Both Frank and Brad knew about Van's heightened senses, the result of her body's response to hearing loss as an infant, and they respected her keen sensitivities.

"Check out the trees, Brad," Dr. Weatherby directed.

Brad and Van walked back to the first tree at the corner of the building nearest the entrance.

"There it is," Brad pointed triumphantly, as the two surveyed a dark straight line cutting through the outer layer of smooth white bark on the tree at about four feet high, the level of Peggy Rice's driver-side window. Brad called over the team photographer and jotted down the mark, its height, length, and direction. He could barely smell the burn even as he placed his nose near the mark.

"You amaze me," he told Van, and she smiled courteously. Brad had always had a thing for Van, and for a short moment, Van had wondered if she felt the same. But that was now two years back and ancient history, at least on her part. Frank walked over to the burn mark and took out a laser pen that he often used for analysis. He lined up the pen with the mark on the tree, and a red line shot across the street to the stucco wall of a garage port. The three of them ran over to the garage, Brad first returning to the car to grab his forensics kit before joining the others as they approached the garage driveway. Frank held out his arms to keep anyone from walking over the spot where the shooter might have hid and set up his gear. Brad taped a wide ring around the wall and the carport. Van walked to the rear of the carport looking for footprints, tire marks, and, most importantly, the bullet casing. She walked to a door at the rear and knocked, but no one answered.

"Get Joe over here," Frank told Brad as he pointed to shoe prints and other marks in the dusty floor of the carport. Van watched from the step, and the glint of a reflection caught her eye. She walked over to the northside wall of the carport and leaned down to see a brass shell caught in a crack in the cement near the wall. She called Frank over, and Frank motioned to Brad to bring his kit. Brad used tweezers to slowly dislodge the shell and place it in a bag.

"I ought to bring you back to the department," Frank said to Van, quietly enough for her to hear him but not Brad.

"I'm not adding anything your team doesn't already do well," she said, and Frank raised his eyebrows and turned back to the crime scene.

Finding the shooter's location yielded a good amount of information that might be useful as the investigation proceeded. The team noted several footprints in the dust, indicating the possibility of more than one person present at the location. They must have waited for a while, because the team found cigarette butts and a ketchup packet carelessly left behind in the stakeout as they waited for Peggy Rice, or perhaps anyone else, to emerge from the studios.

If the goal had been to terrorize the studio, it worked. Two people working for Cortez on The Power of Small had been shot, one fatally. Cortez shut down the building and ordered his staff to start working remotely from their homes, using Zoom and other communications portals to conduct their business. Peggy was placed in an induced coma to allow her body to recover. The bullet lodged in her larynx, and it was sheer luck that her airways were not blocked by the blood and tissue from the wound causing her to suffocate. But her vocal cords were severely damaged, and doctors were not optimistic that she would be able to recover her speech.

Cortez called the bureau, and Charlie and Van drove to his home in the Hollywood Hills near Laurel Canyon to speak with him. They entered behind a large gate covered by several cameras and drove up to the entrance. The mansion was a jumble of rusted iron I-beams and large glass panels mixed in with reclaimed wood with tall lodgepole pine trees dotting the front yard. Van recalled Bainbridge Island and thought the home might look more fitting in the wet woods of the Pacific Northwest. For a brief second, she thought of Brian and wondered what he was doing now.

She rang the doorbell, and it played the theme song from a movie she didn't recognize. Charlie said, "Independence Day," and Van shook her head and muttered, "Hollywood." She expected a butler to open the door to enter a foyer filled with life-size characters from movies, but when the door opened, it was a small energetic girl about eight years old who shouted, "Daddy, the police are here!" Cortez appeared wearing shorts and sandals and holding a coffee mug. The foyer, contrary to Van's expectations, was sparsely decorated. "Sorry about the doorbell," he said as if he was used to saying it often. "We did that for my daughter, Chelsey. Please, come in."

He led them to a family room that felt small and cozy except for an oversized flat screen TV hanging on the wall and a fireplace mantle that seemed a bit too large for the room. He offered them coffee.

"No thank you," said Van. "We don't need much of your time, but we do have some questions."

"No rush," Jerry responded. "Take your time. We're all shaken up about what's happened, and we need to find a way to make it stop."

"Were you aware of Peggy Rice's misgivings about the movie?" Van started.

"I was, but long since the days of Charlie Chaplin mocking Hitler, Hollywood has not backed away from any challenge, despite the risk or the threats."

"This new film you are working on, why was Peggy concerned?"

"Take a look," he responded and handed Van a stack of cards and letters. She flipped over a postcard that had a poison symbol on one side and a cryptic note on the other side: "Kill The Power or you will feel the POWER." She handed the pile to Charlie.

"You didn't think about turning these over to the police?"

"I get these threats all the time. There are kooks out there that can't seem to handle someone else's success, and I can't let it stop me from what I love doing."

"But someone on your set was murdered, and Peggy was tying it to the film."

"I checked into the group that opposes nanotechnology. There's a lot of bluster, but they aren't criminals. Most of them work in the Silicon Valley as programmers or project managers. They claim to be worried about mind control and artificial intelligence and government abuse of civil liberties, but they're not terrorists. They just have a different opinion. If they knew what the film was about, they would see that their opinion is well represented in the movie."

"These notes and cards don't look innocuous, Mr. Cortez."

"That's just because you haven't stood in my shoes. Like I said, this is typical. They're just kooks."

"Have you engaged anyone in the anti-bot movement directly?"

"I haven't. But I have asked my Valley friends to look into it."

"Who, in particular?"

"I would start with a company called Providia. I've spoken with them quite often. Their CFO, Christopher Deckwalder, is as sharp as they come. Providia has been exploring nanobots for a while now and are developing an AI product for that market. They are as familiar with the anti-bot movement as anyone."

"What else? What aren't you telling us?"

"I'm not withholding anything from you, detectives. Just ask."

"If you get these threats all the time, then why was Peggy Rice so scared?"

"I don't know."

Van looked around the study. She studied the understated family room and the famous producer in his shorts and sandals, and something seemed off. She reminded herself that she shouldn't expect normal in Hollywood and thought that maybe the setting seemed a bit too normal.

"Do you mind if we take a look around?"

"I suppose I could ask for a warrant."

"You could."

"Help yourself," Cortez said, but Van could sense some irritation. She studied the family photos on the mantel. There were family photos of three older children standing with their own children. Scattered around the room were vacation photos with someone younger who appeared to be his latest wife. The photos showed them together hiking in Machu Pichu, mountaineering in Switzerland, and scuba diving in the South Pacific. But none of the photos showed Chelsey.

"Chelsey is your granddaughter?" Van queried.

"Chelsey is a foster child. My new wife doesn't want kids, but I like kids and I convinced her to let us bring in a foster child thinking it might trigger some parental hormones."

"How long has Chelsey been in the family?"

"About three months."

"Is it working?"

"Not very well."

"Can we speak with your wife?" Charlie asked.

"She's not here right now. She's out shopping."

"When do you expect her back?"

"Next Tuesday."

"Next . . ." Van started as she and Charlie looked at each other.

"She's in Rio for a fashion show."

Chapter 10.

Ragnar Willowbrook Redux

The windy redwood-lined drive through Scott's Valley up to the labs reminded Brian of the daily journey to his lab on Bainbridge Island. Like the Tran Lab on the island, his ride to Ragnar Willowbrook ended by opening onto a beautiful vista where the sunrise illuminated a spectacular view. On Bainbridge Island in Washington State, he used to slow his bike and watch the other pine-covered islands of Puget Sound emerge floating on the Pacific Ocean. In the hills above Santa Cruz, California, the massive trees along the road suddenly opened onto a view of the entire Silicon Valley with the sun rising in the east over the San Francisco Bay. Despite all his doubts about his decision to run the infamous Ragnar Willowbrook Labs, the setting alone gave Brian a sense of destiny or at least, in this moment, the confidence that he was where he was supposed to be.

Brian pulled up to the gate. "Mr. Johannsen," said the guard, recognizing Brian's face from the memo sent out by Dr. Freund. "We've been expecting you."

"Good morning," Brian responded a little surprised by the recognition. "And your name is?"

"Drake, sir."

"Very nice to meet you, Drake."

"And you as well, sir. The driveway will take you to the main entrance."

Brian wound his way up the driveway to the tall glass structure. He saw statues sprinkled randomly in the grassy yards surrounding the building. He pulled his bike up to a roundabout at the entrance. Immediately another guard approached him and said, "Happy to take care of that for you, sir."

"Is there a better place for me to leave the bike?" Brian asked.

"There is a garage entrance around back."

"Hop on," said Brian. "Might as well learn."

The guard appeared a little confused but climbed on the back of the bike and directed Brian around the building into the gated entrance of an underground parking garage that the guard called ahead to be opened. He then directed Brian to an elevator that the two of them rode to the main lobby. When they exited the elevator, the main receptionist, who had been waiting near the elevator, gave the guard a stern look and then said to Brian, "Dr. Johannsen, I presume. Welcome to Ragnar Willowbrook. Could I get you to go around the security entrance and come over to the reception area?"

Brian walked past several security guards who were shaking their heads and then into the main lobby where Dr. Freund and several colleagues were standing.

"Why am I not surprised that you would not come through the front door?" said Dr. Freund laughing and extending his hand.

"It wasn't intentional, Doctor," replied Brian who turned to the guard and said, "Thank you for the escort, Derrick."

"Not a problem, sir," said the guard. "Thank you for the ride."

Brian looked at the massive entrance and the huge brass letters "R-W" above the reception desk. The ostentatiousness of it all gave him pause, and he wondered if his decision was wise. He picked up a badge and followed Dr. Freund and his team into another elevator that took them to the fifth floor where Dr. Freund showed Brian to his office, also massive, and then into the adjacent board room, which was already filled. As he surveyed the room, Brian saw Fred Schmidt. That didn't take long, he thought to himself.

"Honorable board members and guests," began Leonard, standing at the head of the board room table, "I am pleased to introduce you to Dr. Brian Johannsen." The room erupted in applause, and Brian smiled, thinking, If I have my way, most of you will be gone in six months. But what he said was, "It's an honor to be here and a privilege to be working with my esteemed new colleague, Dr. Leonard Freund."

The introduction of Brian to the board went well, thought Leonard. Fred Schmidt had restrained himself from rushing to Brian and capturing his attention. Most of the board members were relieved to have the problem of Belinda behind them, but they were concerned about the future of Ragnar Willowbrook without her leadership. At least Leonard had been smart enough to know that he was not her replacement. Still, Brian had a lot to prove, and RW Labs had a lot of work to do to restore the Valley's faith in it as the premier testing grounds for new technologies. As the board members were leaving, congratulating Brian and glad-handing each other for at least possibly surviving the past debacle, Fred asked if he could see Brian and Leonard in Brian's new office.

Brian stared out of the massive window from his new fifth story office. He imagined watching the sun rise as he used to from the Tran Labs conference rooms on Bainbridge Island. He stared down at the giant grass yards and the large iron sculptures dotting the yards. He noticed that, from this view, they appeared to be in a poorly formed circle, almost, but not quite, in the shape of a heart. It seemed random to him, and he considered having them relocated, but the shuffling behind his caught his attention.

"Ragnar Willowbrook?" said Fred, assessing Brian quizzically.

"Mr. Schmidt," said Brian.

"Gentlemen," interceded Leonard. "Seems like we have a few things to discuss."

"I don't think I would have placed you here," said Fred.

"Why not?" Brian replied.

"Something to do with Belinda Armendariz, I imagine."

Brian looked down at the desk and then back at Fred. "You think I've sold my soul?"

"No, I don't. My best guess says you think you can change things."

"I don't know if that is true. I don't know what Belinda did while she was here. She made RW a huge success, and I am certain Dr. Meisner up at Tran tried to model what we did there after what she was doing here."

"Is it a model you supported?"

"I didn't, but I wasn't responsible for running a lab. I wasn't a fan of Meisner's desperation, but I also wasn't responsible for salaries, supplies, and rent."

"Why do you think I chose Tran over RW?"

"Fair question, but how would I know? You probably felt you would have more control at Tran. Meisner needed you."

"You didn't feel the same?"

"I didn't care about Meisner's failures or successes. I cared about the science, and the science you brought to us almost killed me and my colleague. Arguably, that same science is what killed Meisner and destroyed the lab."

"I didn't know that would happen. The dish was marked RG-VI, and you obviously had been cautious with it. I didn't know what it was and I wanted

to know what it was, and I chose Tran because I assumed Meisner would put you on it."

"You went to Tran because of me?"

"Precisely, Dr. Johannsen. And I am here now because of you."

"Go on."

"Dr. Belinda Armendariz destroyed the Tran Lab because she believed Meisner was an accomplice in the theft of a petri dish from Ragnar Willowbrook. Your colleague opened that dish and inadvertently exposed both of you to its contents, nanobots that happened to be as toxic to human beings as an RG-IV virus."

"You are not telling me anything I don't know," said Brian getting irritated.

"You also know that she retrieved the nanobots in her raid on Tran."

"Right. Where is this going, Fred?" Brian had begun to wonder if Fred might be working with Belinda.

Fred picked that up immediately. "No, I have no interest in Belinda. I do have an interest in the nanobots, and I don't need what Belinda resorted to murder in order to obtain. I have them."

"You have them what? The bots?"

"I have a sample. I can tell you how, but it's not that important."

"You made that same mistake before. It was not a good call."

"Ok. I'll be candid with you. You need to trust me, and I need to trust you. My colleague, Derek Whitestone—"

"I met him."

"Had the foresight, I suppose, to divide the original dish and have it delivered to a lab in Los Angeles."

"Rutter?" Brian knew of the famous UCLA lab. "Didn't a student die?"

"Yes, and a jury convicted my colleague of criminal negligence. But he is out now, and he is talking to that lab. You'll need to get to know a graduate student by the name William Perkins III. He has the samples, and he wants to work with us. Seems to me that one way to make it up to UCLA is develop something together. I want you in on it, and if you do choose Ragnar Willowbrook, then I want Ragnar Willowbrook in on it as well."

Brian looked at Leonard who smiled. He couldn't believe what he was hearing. It seemed incredible that Fred Schmidt would be the one to offer him a path forward that he could embrace. The resurrection of Ragnar Willowbrook depended on the recovery of its credibility, and there was no better way to begin that difficult journey than in a public collaboration with another highly accredited lab.

"There is one catch," Fred said. Of course, there is, thought Brian.

"The samples, which are being held at Rutter, are still evidence in the case."

"Great," said Brian. "So, we are tampering with evidence? I won't do that."

"I don't expect that. We need a deal with the LAPD. We can divide the sample and work on a portion of it. We also can become special experts who advise the court. These nanobots are not something any average forensics lab can handle. They need our assistance, and we can explain that our work with the specimens will not alter the nature of the specimens and therefore won't change the character of the evidence. If they say no, then we put the dish on the backburner until the case is over."

"What about you? Won't this pull you into the case?"

"I've already passed that test. Civil litigation still may be possible and maybe I have

deep pockets, but my connection even there is remote. I had no idea Derek took the bots to LA."

"How do we get a deal with LAPD?"

"I have my attorneys working on it, but I understand you might know somebody who worked the Dakota case. It would help if we had her support."

"Van?" Brian blurted a little too loud.

"I believe that is her name, Doctor," Fred said, suppressing a smile. "Detective Van Eng."

* * *

Van wasn't satisfied with the Cortez interview. Granted it gave her the Providia lead, and that lead might prove to be useful, but she couldn't accept the anti-bot theory. She couldn't reject it, either. Not yet. She also wasn't accepting the inside job theory either although it seemed the more likely of those two options. Her time at Cortez Studios didn't expose anything that suggested a disgruntled crew member or a love triangle. She was intrigued by the gold WRX and the possibility that Trey's death might be gang related. Van knew that line of thought needed more analysis. But if that were the explanation, then why shoot Peggy? And why leave a note that said, "Your next"? Peggy's frustration with Cortez over the movie had left Van with many unanswered questions, and now that Peggy was in a coma at the trauma center and might not recover, Van might not get her answers.

Still, the gold WRX had an ominous presence over the investigation, and Van needed to nail that element down. It was possible Min Kang had sold the car, and the lead would dead-end. She knew it would be foolhardy for her to go back to the Oasis karaoke bar in Koreatown by herself. She called Detective Robert Johnson and asked if he would join her. Detective Johnson had been jealous of Van's success at the bureau, not unlike several others, and although he could be a bit impulsive, he was a good detective and he knew Koreatown well, having worked it as his beat before being promoted to detective. Together, they drove back to the mall on 6th Street and parked in the underground garage where, together, they had first seen Danny Kang, the leader of the Vietnamese gang The Rush. Min Kang, Danny's sister, had also spent time in jail for her part in Danny's crimes. But unlike Danny, Min survived her incarceration. No doubt she was not happy with the LAPD in general and Van Eng in particular. Van scanned the garage for the gold WRX but didn't see it. She worried that the visit might be fruitless. They took the escalators up to the second floor and met the club host at the Oasis elevator. They flashed their badges, and he led them into the elevator.

The elevator opened onto the Oasis lobby, and Van led Robert to the front counter. They flashed their badges again, and staff, appearing disinterested, asked them to wait in the lobby. Van recognized Toshi, one of Danny Kang's former lieutenants, from her time undercover in the gang. Toshi saw her and smiled.

"Detective Van?"

"Yes, Toshi, that would be me. And this is Detective Robert Johnson."

"Nice to meet you. What is it you need?"

"We have some questions about a case we are working on. Is Min here?"

"She is, but I doubt she'll talk to you."

"We don't want to have to get a warrant, Toshi."

"Am I a suspect?"

Van and Robert spun around to see Min Kang, a tall and strikingly beautiful Vietnamese woman wearing what appeared to be workout gear. Van could tell that she had put on muscle during her time in prison, and she thought about the Muscle Beach competition that she had won with Kimmie, her best friend.

"Not any more than anyone else at this point," said Van. "We have no leads."

"Makes me want to have an attorney present," said Min.

"That would be your choice," said Van. "We can start our conversation now and you can decide how you want to proceed, or we can arrange for you to come downtown and bring an attorney. Your choice."

Min paused, long enough for Van to wonder if Min had reason to be concerned.

"Follow me," she said. She led them back to the elevator and up to what Van remembered as Danny's headquarters. The setting was different now. Min had removed the wet bar and replaced it with a small kitchen. The red velvet and dark leather furniture was gone and replaced with more traditional couch and chairs with blues and whites mixed in a tasteful combination. The curtains were pulled back, and the room was filled with sunlight. There was no sign of the karaoke cabinet that Van recalled with some embarrassment had been her introduction to the gang. As before, they were not alone, but instead of just young men with guns standing around, there was a mix of men and women who looked like they were working. It was more a business than a gang. Danny's desk was still there, but it was clean and empty, although behind the desk was a bank of Apple iMac computers, all active.

"You are here about Trey's death, I assume?" Min said to Van after inviting Van and Robert to sit.

"There's more," said Van. "But let's start with that."

Min sighed. "I blamed you for Danny's death for a long time."

"Danny?" said Van somewhat startled but only somewhat. Danny was the elephant in the room. Danny Kang was Min's brother who died in prison at the hands of a rival Latino gang called El Muerte. Van's undercover work had exposed Danny's crimes as a Vietnamese gang leader and led to his arrest and conviction, and as Min knew, Danny had fallen in love with Van. What Min didn't know was that Van had fallen in love with Danny. She saw him as a brilliant leader and hoped that Danny would get his act together in prison. He didn't make it, but it was appearing that Min was the one who turned her life around.

"I had a job to do, Min," said Van.

"Danny needed to be stopped," said Min. "The Rush needed to come to an end. The violence with El Muerte was escalating, and a lot more people, including innocents, might have died."

"We're not here to talk about Danny," said Robert, and Van held up her hand.

"We'll talk about whatever we need to talk about," she said studying Min.

"I don't want to waste your time," said Min. "Go ahead."

"Ok. Your car was seen on the lot when Trey was killed," said Van. "Were you there?"

"I met Trey while he was writing the script," said Min. "After I got out of prison, I would hang out at this bohemian coffee shop called Primo Caffe on Sunset Boulevard. I had heard it was a hangout for Hollywood writers and, well, you never know, right?"

"You met Trey there?"

"I did."

"Did he tell you he was writing for Cortez?"

"He was very secretive. He just said it was a good story. He called it futuristic."

"Were you dating?"

"Yes."

"What can you tell us about Trey?"

Min described Trey as a quiet, almost shy guy who felt more at home at a keyboard than anywhere else. They were seeing each other when Trey got the word he would be joining Cortez's team on a new movie and he was beside himself with excitement. Min had been candid with Trey about her background and time at the women's prison, but it didn't seem to bother him. But Min did not feel as if Trey was always candid with her. He would tell her he needed to leave for a research trip, which Min never questioned, and he would be gone for several days.

"Where did he go?"

"He never told me, and I didn't press him," she said. "But I did look in his bag and saw two boarding passes for flights to Virginia and San Jose. I knew he was from the Bay Area, so it made sense he might want to go home, and I wasn't hurt that he wasn't ready to take me. I wasn't sure that would ever happen. But I also saw a visitor's badge with a company name, and I looked them up. It's a technology company in Sunnyvale called Providia."

Chapter 11.

Plus Ça Change, Plus La Même Chose

Garny sat outside at Café Eugene studying the Dôme. The Bremer Wall now obscured all but the top of the Dôme. He checked his watch. The convoy carrying his frozen nanobots was late, and he was beginning to get impatient. Garny's guests would be arriving at noon, and it was already past 8:00 a.m. The Ruslan An-24 had landed at Le Bourget as expected, and the three refrigeration semis should have been there waiting. He looked repeatedly down Boulevard Victor. He called his transport supervisor who reported that the trucks had arrived late but were back on schedule and should have been there by now. He called Paris Transit RATP to see if there were any traffic delays. In fact, a large wreck had occurred on the main autoroute around Paris, the Boulevard Périphérique. The truck drivers had tried to contact the supervisor at Bourget who was flying by helicopter to the Dôme to meet them there. Traffic was at a dead stop, and police were clearing a lane to let cars pass and reduce the pressure of traffic. The trucks waited in the outside lane adjacent to a single lane road and an empty office complex. A single white van was parked on the adjacent road. Inside the van, a team of black ops dressed as mechanics began to spill out of the van and walked through traffic toward each of the trucks. The drivers hopped out of their cabs and opened the rear doors to let the ops inside the refrigeration units. Once inside, the ops hid small remote detonators on each of the containers, exited the trucks, and returned to the van. The drivers returned to their cabs and waited as traffic began to roll.

Belinda pulled up on Boulevard Victor alongside Café Eugene. She saw, as she expected, a disgruntled Garny McDonough holding a French newspaper and glancing up and down the road. The driver of the VTC pulled into a turnout parking space and told Belinda, in French, "We are here." She thanked him and jumped out, maneuvering her way past the outdoor tables, and approached Garny from behind.

"You seem jumpy," she said as he spun around and knocked over his espresso with the newspaper.

"Shit," he exclaimed and looked up. "Belinda? I didn't think I would see you quite yet."

"Waiting for someone?"

"No. Please sit."

She sat and ordered her own café au lait.

"Do you feel ready?"

"For the test? Of course. We've run it too many times. We know what to watch out for. I just get a little performance anxiety."

"The great Garny McDonough has human feelings."

"I like to think so, but I wouldn't mind being a bit less human."

"Cyborg?"

"That's fantasy. I can't stand waiting here anymore. Come with me."

Belinda paid for her café and asked for a paper cup. Garny was already standing at the street waiting impatiently for her to join him. She smiled and walked up to him coolly, resisting his momentary intensity. They walked across the two-lane roads of Boulevards des Maréchaux and Boulevard Victor to the Bremer Wall and down to the gated entrance. As they crossed past the guard station, Garny inquired if there was any word from the trucks. At that same moment, the first refrigeration truck appeared at the gate, and soon after, the remaining two trucks pulled up behind. Garny jumped on the cab step and pounded on the window. The driver rolled down the window.

"What took you so long?" he yelled at the driver.

The driver calmly replied, "There was an accident."

"At least you are here now," Garny said with exasperation. Then he yelled at the guard who was getting ready to inspect the trucks, "Get them inside now! We need to get this set up." The guard abandoned his checklist and waved the truck past the gate. They pulled around behind the Dôme and backed into the truck bays. Teams of handlers dressed in protective gear and masks were waiting at the bay. Garny screamed into his phone at the transport supervisor to get the containers unloaded and staged in the Dôme's central arena. Garny took Belinda through the front entrance and up to the observation booth he had set up for his honored guests. He handed Belinda a mask and told her to hang on to it for the test.

"The observation booth is sealed tight. You shouldn't need it but hang on to it just in case."

They watched as the transport team set up the containers around the arena. This team was new to the trial and had no idea what they were handling. They had been told to confirm each container had power, but under no circumstances were they to attempt to open the containers. Garny then excused himself and left to wait at the entrance for his guests.

Belinda waited in the observation booth. She could see the two large screens that Garny had erected on the stage opposite the observation booth and the containers spread out around the arena. Six giant fans were lined up on the front-most walls of enclosed rooms built adjacent to the stage. Inside the rooms sat a half dozen Mitsubishi engines quietly waiting the commencement of the trial. As soon as the arena was empty and the team setting up the test had vacated the area, Belinda sent a message to her ops team, which was gathered in the rear staging dock where athletes and entertainers typically waited before their performances. The message simply said, "Fire." They reached in their pockets and flipped a switch triggering each of the small detonators attached to the containers. The detonators went off quietly with a small puff of smoke, but the nitric acid inside each detonator fused the container lids shut.

Garny didn't see the blasts, but a few members of his staff who were in the arena did and started to move toward the sealed containers. Belinda's ops team quickly disposed of the witnesses and pulled the bodies into a storage unit in the rear staging dock. They pulled on their protective gear and stationed themselves around the arena as if they were preventing anyone from entering. In the meantime, Garny welcomed his distinguished guests, French and other European political figures, the under-secretary-generals of the United Nations, including the executive director of the UN Environment Programme (UNEP), the Special Envoy for Climate Change, and finally General Warner with a small team of U.S. Defense Department officials. He immediately set out to look for Belinda, but he couldn't find her. Belinda used the distraction of all the guests to make her way back out of the Dôme and across to Café Eugene where she hailed a cab. Garny was so busy he didn't realize that Belinda was gone, and General Warner's inquiries about her whereabouts didn't trigger any special concern. Garny geared up for his performance, checking his notes and reviewing the staging area and the pit of the Dôme to see that his team was in place. The guests gathered in the observation booth. A few of the guests noticed the protective gear being worn by the staff in the arena and asked if the test would be safe. Gary entered the booth and took a microphone as he walked to the front of the booth.

"Ladies and gentleman, honored guests," he started. "Thank you for joining us here at Le Dôme de Paris for a demonstration of the carbon-capture technology developed by my latest venture, The Karakul Proposition. First, let me describe what you see before you." The lights in the arena went down. Two large screens on the stage and a handful of monitors in the booth depicted the snow-capped peaks of the Himalayas set against a deep blue sky with the words "The Karakul Proposition" written in various green shades and spinning and then fixing against the blue sky, giving the image the clean and environmentally pure look that Garny intended. Spotlights popped on, directed at the canisters on the arena floor.

"You see the containers set at various locations around the floor of the Dôme. Each of these containers is holding 40 pounds or about 18 kilograms of a frozen mixture of carbon-capture nanobots and hydrolyzed collagen. You also see the large fans next to the stage. Behind each of the fans are several 1500 horsepower Mitsubishi marine engines, the type that are used to power cruise ships and large marine vessels." The spotlights turned off, and the screens then flickered to black. Out of the center of each screen emerged a single Star of Bethlehem nanobot, a white porcelain globe with titanium spikes at the north and south poles and smaller spikes around the globe's equator. The bot spun slowly round its midpoint, and the spikes moved in and out of the globe.

"Let me introduce you to our hero or savior, if I may be so bold," said Garny smiling as if he were the father of a newborn. "We call it the Star of Bethlehem."

As the bot spun, balls of carbon dioxide molecules appeared hovering in the black space around the bots, and as the spikes emerged from the central globe, the molecules snapped onto the spikes, which drew them inside the globe and then emerged clean to capture more molecules until the spikes could no longer move and became overloaded with the molecular spheres.

The guests were mesmerized by the animation on the screens. Questions popped out of the crowd, "How does . . .? and "What about . . .?"

"I'll be happy to answer your questions in due course," Garny responded, basking in the glow of the presentation's impact.

"Carbon capture is not itself all that remarkable," he added. "A fundamental problem with climate change is the magnitude of the problem. We are all aware of the important role behavioral change plays in simply beginning to address the issues raised by climate change. But behavioral change is a long-term solution and may not occur fast enough to prevent the cataclysms we expect with climate change. Our only true hope is technology, and today I will show you a technology I believe could be the very answer we seek. The irony is that the solution we are proposing to you today is a solution using the tiniest machines capable of being manufactured: microscopic nanobots. That is exactly what we are proposing. But there still is a problem. We don't have time to manufacture the billions of tons of these devices needed to address the problem. In that time, carbon emissions would overtake the atmosphere, and our only solution is to escape to Mars or some planetary moon. Of course, space travel may save a few, but it is not the solution we need. The problem is here on this planet, and it is this planet we need to save."

The group nodded in assent.

"But what if the technology had the capability of inventing itself? What if, like a virus-driven plague, these nanobots could self-replicate?"

Garny heard some anticipated chuckles of disbelief.

"Let me show you something I think you will find quite interesting."

A new animation appeared on one of the screens, while the other screen showed lab technicians in white protective gear gathered around a device that looked like a centrifuge. This animation depicted bots colliding and breaking apart and then growing into new bots of the same design. On the adjacent screen, the technicians were viewing a screen from the centrifuge and a video of a clear gelatinous mass inside the centrifuge growing and, in a short time, doubling in size.

"That's not possible," Garny heard someone say.

"It is possible, and I will show you what we have learned over the past year about how nanobots can replicate at high speed. Please look back at the monitors. You now see a gauge that runs from red to green. In a minute, we will start the experiment. You can see the needle is pegged at zero. The number zero marks the point at which carbon dioxide in the air around us is in proper balance with primary elements of Earth's atmosphere, nitrogen and oxygen. We will close the vents and completely seal the Dôme. It becomes airtight. After we close the vents, we will fire up the Mitsubishi engines, and you will see the needle move toward the red zone. When the needle reaches neg-5, the amount of carbon dioxide in the air will bother your lungs and cause you to cough. At neg-10, the saturation level becomes deadly. We will release the nanobots long before we reach neg-10, so do not worry. My point is to show you how effective the nanobots are at filtering the carbon dioxide out of the air. You will see the needle first move into red and then slowly back into the green and to the positive side of the gauge. In case you do not believe the gauge, once the needle has been green long enough for the bots to be saturated themselves with carbon dioxide, at which point they fall harmless out of the air like dust to the ground, my assistants will walk to the center of the stage and remove their protective gear to prove that the air has been cleansed. Let me ask you to take your seats. You will notice that there are protective masks under each of your chairs. We don't expect there to be any problems, but this is an experimental setting, and masks are there as a cautionary measure to help you feel comfortable with the experiment. Now, before we begin, are there any questions?"

The lights went down, and all the guests could see were the two large screens on the stage. The two large gauges appearing on the screens were pegged at zero, the needles pointing straight up. It was quiet in the observation booth. Spotlights lit up the large fans, and the noise of the Mitsubishis exploded into the darkness and quickly became deafening. Garny's assistants handed out ear plugs. The needles fluttered and then slowly, almost imperceptibly, crawled to the left and into the red. Garny's team offered the guests drinks and hors d'oeuvres as they waited and watched the needles move to neg-1 and neg-2. When the needles hit neg-5, more spotlights lit up the stainless-steel canisters with the frozen nanobots. The smoke from the tiny explosions had dissipated and everything appeared normal. Garny pressed a button, and red lights popped on all the canisters. He explained to the guests that the heating elements in the canisters were warming up the frozen bots. The needles moved to neg-6 and neg-7. New spotlights lit up each of the masked guards standing around the arena, fully clothed in protective gear. At neg-8, Garny took a large switch on the main panel and pulled it down. Nothing happened. The needles moved to neg-9. He didn't react except to speak quietly into a com microphone on his lapel.

"Are the lids releasing?" he whispered to the team standing in the arena. There was no response. None of the guards moved. The needles closed in on neg-10.

"Answer me, dammit," Garny said, his voice rising enough for the guests to hear it.

They began to shuffle in their seats. General Warner reached down for his mask and indicated to his team to do the same. Other guests began to copy General Warner. The nanobot gel reached boiling point inside the canisters. The lids remained firmly sealed by the nitric acid. The guards simultaneously pulled the Glock-9 handguns they had hidden in their gear and began firing at the observation booth. The glass panes shattered, and thick clouds of carbon dioxide gas poured into the booth. A lucky few who had their masks on, including General Warner, ran to the rear exit and down the stairway into the main lobby. A few other guests were already putting on their masks when the glass exploded and got out as well. Those who remained screamed in terror and tried desperately and unsuccessfully to pull on their masks as the gas overwhelmed them, and their bodies started to convulse and then dropped comatose onto the booth's floor. Garny had taken a bullet in his side but remained conscious enough to crawl over to his mask and get it on. Bleeding, he pulled himself up to the control panel and shut off the Mitsubishis but in doing so took another bullet in his chest and fell back, lying on the floor with the others. Belinda's team stopped shooting, exited the building at the rear staging area, and removed their protective gear. Then, using the chaos that erupted after the shootings started, they made their way undetected to their vans, which were waiting outside the Bremer wall.

Suddenly the canisters burst open, and black clouds of the white hot nanobots spilled into the arena's gas-filled air space. The clouds grew to fill the arena in seconds, and a dense fog of nanobots entered the shattered windows into the booth. Anyone without a mask who was might still be alive despite the carbon dioxide poisoning went swiftly into anaphylactic shock and suffocated. Within minutes, gorged with cardon dioxide molecules, the nanobots began to fall harmlessly out of the air, covering the booth and arena floors in a fine dust. The main screens on the stage, and the booth's monitors were still active and showing the gauges. The gauge needles, which had pegged past neg-10 at the far end of the red zone, slowly moved back toward center. But no one saw the gauges except Garny. Everyone else who remained in the booth was dead. Garny, having shut off the Mitsubishis, lay on the floor bleeding and watching in shock as those around him without masks died. Then, just as he passed out, he turned his eyes up and watched the needles move into green.

Chapter 12.

The Salt of Ernest Hemingway

The discovery of a new talent always commands our attention. Our reaction is especially magnified when the talent is unusually young. Mozart began writing music when he was five and wrote his first symphony when he was eight. Alexander the Great successfully led the Macedonian Army into his first conquests when he was seventeen. Joan of Arc was seventeen years old when she became a national hero in the battle of Orleans against the English. Lafayette was nineteen when he led his French troops across the Atlantic Ocean in support of the American colonies. Mary Shelly wrote *Frankenstein* as a teenager. Bobby Fisher won the World Chess Championship when he was fourteen years old. There's something exciting about youthful accomplishments that sparks our keenest interest.

Ernest Hemingway was not known as a child prodigy, but he began his journalistic career at *The Kansas City Star* while he was still in high school. He served in World War I at eighteen, and, after his discharge due to a severe battle wound, he worked as a foreign correspondent in Paris. While in Paris, he made his first visits to Pamplona, the setting of his first novel, *The Sun Also Rises*. The same setting inspired other now-famous works including *Death in the Afternoon, For Whom the Bell Tolls, The Dangerous Summer,* and *The Garden of Eden.* In 1953, he wrote, "I will never do more than Pamplona has done for me."

Dr. Brian Johannsen had been a prodigy, but he hated the special treatment as a child and buried himself in science as a way of avoiding the attention. He never imagined himself running a major lab, let alone one with the caliber, and now spoiled reputation, of Ragnar Willowbrook. Belinda's former colleague and new chief scientist at Ragnar Willowbrook, Dr. Leonard Freund, rolled the dice by bringing Brian to Scotts Valley, the home of Ragnar Willowbrook in the hills above Santa Cruz. He recognized that RW Labs needed a new face, one that might cause their major donors and clientele to let go of the lab's tainted past and get back to the legitimate work of certifying Silicon Valley innovations. Brian wasn't completely convinced he could bring the labs back to life and do it in a manner consistent with his own moral code. But Freund had triggered something in him, and if he could be successful, he knew it would make him proud. He also knew it might establish his legacy as a major contributor in his chosen fields: biomechanical engineering, genetics, molecular physics, or whatever. But the latter didn't drive him, and as much as he might want to impress Van, whom he still pined about, he suspected that motivation didn't drive her either.

"Hi, Van," said Brian, standing in his oversized office looking out over the lab's massive gardens, which still had Belinda's footprint.

"Brian?" Van responded, surprised at the call.

"How are you?" he started.

"I'm good, busy, but hanging in there. You?" She couldn't tell if it was a personal call, and she worried a little that Brian might still be pursuing her. She prepared herself to let him down easily.

"Settling in. I understand you know Dr. Leonard Freund."

That name caught her off guard. Van had saved Freund's life in the FBI's raid on Ragnar Willowbrook Labs.

"Uh, I do. Why do you ask?"

"Freund invited me to the Bay Area. He wants me to restore Ragnar Willowbrook."

In Van's mind, Ragnar Willowbrook was synonymous with Belinda Armendariz, the assault on Brian's former lab, and the murder of Cheryl Brown.

"I don't understand."

"I'm not sure I do, either. But Freund needs help here, and it was time for me to get out of Los Angeles."

"I don't know what to say. You're not working with Belinda, are you?"

"Belinda is gone. No one knows where she is, and Leonard is letting me reshape this company into something I can feel good about. He's given me a blank check, and I decided to take it on."

"Well," said Van skeptically, "I don't see you there, but I want you to be happy if you can make it work. Be careful. Ragnar has a dark history."

"Yeah, I know, and I am not entirely certain this is the best decision. But one of my first moves is to align with another reputable lab and work on something that could be game changer."

"Makes sense, I guess."

"Are you familiar with the Rutter Lab at UCLA?"

"You're kidding me, right?"

"I understand you might be."

Van started to put things together. "What are you looking for, Brian?"

"I've been told another set of the bots may be there."

"Safely secured as evidence in the Marley Dakota case, which, as you know, is still ongoing."

"I'm not interested in disrupting legal proceedings. I want to work with you, Van, not against you."

Van paused. She'd felt her heart begin to race in anger but knew better than to let her feelings take over. She wanted to be mad that Brian had aligned himself with an institution that had a criminal history. She also felt hurt that he would allow himself to be manipulated by his colleagues into taking advantage of their relationship. But deep down, she trusted Brian. She knew how much he liked her, and yet, when she failed to reciprocate, he didn't press and try to force her feelings. Maybe that would not have been so bad, but it showed her that Brian had integrity and that he was strong enough not to lose himself in his quest for love and companionship. He was willing to walk away. Still, was he crossing a line by using this relationship? Or was it a bridge, a way to stay connected?

"I'm listening," she replied.

"Those bots are as important to science as they are to the case. They serve no purpose just being locked up. The more we can learn about them, the more likely you are to be able to use them in the lawsuit and the better our mutual chances at locating their origin. In addition, we know we can divide the contents without destroying the evidence and just use a sample."

"You would need a court order."

"That's fine with us. We even could be designated as expert witnesses and you could use our testimony."

"Let me think about it and check around. Honestly, it troubles me, but you might have a point. I'll get back to you."

"That's fine, Van. It's nice to talk to you."

"Right. We'll be in touch. Be careful there, Brian. It could be a snake pit."

Brian hung up. The longer he spoke to Van, the harder it became for him not to express his true feelings. But he held his emotions in check although he knew he would not be able to work. He took off his lab coat and headed down to the garage. He sped through the gardens, and at the gate, his new friend at the front gate, Drake, smiled and waved him through. He shot down 17 to Santa Cruz and grabbed Highway 1 North past Natural Bridges State Beach and then sped north along the grass-brushed coast until he got to Half Moon Bay and Mavericks State Beach. He hiked up the bluff past the radar domes and found a spot on the dirt cliffs overlooking the break. He didn't care that he wasn't alone. It was a good day, and waves were breaking between twenty-five and thirty-five feet out past the point. He asked someone if he could borrow their binoculars to see hardy old surfers throwing themselves and their long boards down the crumbling mountains of water, not always successfully. But the good rides were inspiring. The call with Van had been hard, but Brian steeled himself and firmed up his resolve. He would make the Labs work without sacrificing his moral code. He would set new standards for certification and ensure the safety of his team. Anyone who varied from his directives would be removed, whether it was a night janitor or a top board member. The thought and the setting helped to calm him down. He knew then that it had been a mistake to call Van and use their relationship to get what Leonard wanted. The deed was done, but he would apologize. If what he said about the dish were true, it wouldn't have mattered who called Van about the bots. It didn't need to be him.

* * *

Van was low after talking to Brian. She wondered if she had been too hard on him. Ragnar Willowbrook had reflected Belinda's wicked ambitions, but it didn't have to. If anybody could restore the Labs, Brian probably was that person. He was right about the bots. They weren't doing anybody any good locked up in a lab at UCLA. She would check with Charlie and her trusted colleagues at the Bureau and would support a motion to designate the Labs as expert witnesses for the prosecution so the bots could be released into their custody. Her phone rang again, and this time it was Martin Richard. She liked Martin, although she suspected he liked her more than she did him.

"Hello, babe."

"Martin," she grimaced. "Not babe."

"Okay, okay, lighten up. What are you doing?"

"Right this moment? I'm deep in a good book."

"Well, it might be a hard sell, but the movie I have been working on is having a release party here at the lot this evening. It would be my honor if you would join me."

"That's better. I'd love to. What do I wear?"

"As little as possible."

"Martin."

"Okay, okay. Don't worry about dressing up. It's more of a cast celebration. Just throw on some jeans and come down here. It'll be fun."

"Thank you . . . babe."

"There you go. I can't wait to see you."

The party excited Van and pulled her out of the funk. She showered and pulled out her full makeup kit and finally herself presentable. She grabbed her tight designer jeans, a loose sexy sweater, and ankle-highs and jumped into her car. When she got to the Melrose Gate, one of the guards recognized her.

"Detective?" he asked, looking at her in wonder.

"Yes, Henry," she said slightly embarrassed.

"Making friends on the lot?" he grinned.

"No, Henry, I'm undercover." She flashed a flirty smile.

"Cover girl maybe," he said. "No way undercover."

"Thanks, Henry."

She cleared her throat, and he glanced quickly down at his list. She doubted he was reading it.

"Go ahead, Detective. Have one on me." Van laughed and gave him an air kiss as she drove onto the lot.

When she walked into the stage, she saw Martin cornered by two extras. She could tell he enjoyed the attention. He saw her and excused himself and ran over to her before anyone else there laid a claim.

"Van!" he said as he swooped her up in his arms. "You look stunning!"

She didn't fight him back, more to keep from embarrassing him and because she kind of liked it, even if she suspected he was putting on a show. She gave him a light hug in return.

"What do you want to drink?"

"Lime and soda would be fine."

He disappeared, and in the brief minute he was gone, Van swept the scene. It looked to her like the party was mostly extras and a few lower-level cast members. She figured that any A-listers, if they showed up at all, would make a brief appearance and then leave for some other party where they could hang out with other A-listers and not be assaulted by the extras trying to get recognized or even just another gig.

"I couldn't wait for you to get here," he told her as he handed her the glass.

"Is it a wrap, as they say?"

"Not yet. It goes into post, and if they need to reshoot anything, they may pull us back out. But basically, the camera work is done."

"How do you feel?"

"About my role?"

"Yeah."

"I killed it. I'm an emerging star."

"That is what they tell you?"

"Every day."

"Do they know your parents?"

Martin laughed. "Of course. I don't believe anything anybody tells me."

Van laughed. "I'm sure you did great. I can't wait to see it."

Martin introduced Van to several cast members. Most of them were nice. A few were distracted, waiting for the director and the leads to show. Van detected a sense of self-importance in a few who she suspected were being courted by agents. One particularly cute guy named Glenn tried to move in on Van with Martin standing right there.

"She's cute," Glenn told Martin.

"She's mine," Martin responded, and Van cut him a look.

Glenn ignored the comment. "You want to see my trailer?"

"You have a trailer?" Van responded.

"She doesn't know me, does she?" Glenn said to Martin.

Van pointed to the two extras that had been flirting with Martin earlier. "They look a little lonely," she said to Glenn.

He looked over at the two extras, who were cute but overdone, and they waved back as if they knew him. "Maybe they want to see your trailer?" she said, being a bit too direct, and then she whispered to Martin, but loud enough for Glenn to hear, "Or maybe they've already seen it."

Glenn grimaced. Van squinted at Glenn, and Martin, a little worried by the banter, pulled her away leaving Glenn alone as the two extras jumped him. The director finally showed up and gave a short speech thanking everyone. Martin introduced him to Van, and he was pleasant but he looked distracted. He said to Martin, "Good work out there." Martin thanked him, and he responded, "Please say hi to your parents for me." Van smiled and, holding the smile, glanced at Martin, who she could tell was fighting the urge to say more but left it at "I certainly will." To Van he said, "Can we get please out of here?"

Martin drove Van up to Hollywood Boulevard and then east to the Hollywood Bowl and up to Mulholland Drive. It was dark and a bit dangerous as Ferraris and Lamborghinis rushed up behind Martin and then scooted dangerously around him on curves in the road. They climbed up to an empty cul-de-sac where they could park and see the lights of traffic on Pacific Coast Highway against a dark ocean. Martin leaned over, and Van let him kiss her. The kiss was warm and romantic, and Van relaxed into the moment. Suddenly Martin's phone buzzed, and Van said, "You should get that."

"I don't want to," Martin said, obviously heated up.

"At least check who it is," Van said.

Martin sighed. "Crap," he said when he saw the screen. "It's my parents."

He spoke for a few minutes, and Van could tell he was talking about her.

"They want to know if you want to go to Spain?"

"What?" she said, still a little fuzzy from the romance.

"They want to know if you want to join us in Spain."

"Spain as in Europe?"

"Yeah, there's this thing in Spain they like to attend every year. They are fans of Ernest Hemingway, and there's a group that gets together in Pamplona every year in Hemingway's memory to watch the running of the bulls."

Sounds crazy, Van thought. But she said, "I don't know. When are you leaving?"

"It's next month. July."

"Wow. Let me think about it. Can I tell you tomorrow?"

"She said yes," Martin told his parents, and Van punched him.

"Ow. I mean she'll say yes tomorrow." Van punched him again but not so hard.

Chapter 13.

An Idea Whose Time Has Come (Part I)

The phrase, "Nothing is more powerful than an idea whose time has come," is often attributed to Victor Hugo, author of *Les Misérables* and *The Hunchback of Notre Dame*. He never actually wrote that phrase, but what he did write was close enough to give him some credit for it. What Hugo said was, "One resists the invasion of armies; one does not resist the invasion of ideas." That quote comes from Hugo's *Histoire d'un crime* written in 1852. The quote did not emerge in a vacuum. Hugo had a point to make, and the point was timely. His compatriots were disparaging inequities emerging from the industrial revolution, but Hugo saw it differently. He worried about a new kind of economic despotism that he believed should be opposed by economic and political freedom. Hugo's hope was of a United States of America and a United States of Europe joining hands, exchanging products, art, and works of genius. Its antithesis, the socialism of the moment "would bring about a general bankruptcy. It would ruin the rich without enriching the poor . . . It would convert France into a country of gloom." Hugo's phrase was a first attempt at articulating the power of the marketplace of ideas. But it was the French writer Gustave Aimard who framed the quote: "There is something more powerful than the brute force of bayonets: it is the idea whose time has come . . ."

Belinda took the call from General Warner. She had left the Dôme de Paris on her rented scooter undetected by any of the guests, including General Warner. Belinda figured correctly that Garny was distracted by the magnitude of the event and didn't realize she had left the event. But she also knew General Warner would be attending and would ask about her. She had told Warner that she would be attending the event, but she did not tell him her actual plans. As she made her way north, her team kept her informed of their progress. She asked for confirmation that Garny did not survive, but all the team could tell her was that he had been shot but still was able to shut off the Mitsubishis. Even if he survived, she figured he would be angry and would find some way to come after her, but Belinda had been ready to move past

General Warner for some time now. She had completed the construction of her new lab in the Pyrenees, and her own goals for the use of the nanobots were developing rapidly.

"Hello, General," said Belinda. She found a farm road outside of Paris to relax and smoke a cigar.

"That was slick, my dear," said Warner. "More impressive than Bainbridge."

"You surprise me," said Belinda.

"You assumed I'd be upset about what . . . almost dying? I've almost died more times than you care to know. But I'll admit this one was close."

"You were not a target."

"I was not an obvious target anyway. I assume you recognize that our goals remain aligned. I am still willing to help you."

"I'm not looking for your help anymore, General."

"If you don't want my help, then I'd say you are beginning to make some bad decisions, and that is not good. This stunt you pulled in Paris was not necessary, and it will get you into trouble. Interpol will be on this in a flash. How do you propose to avoid them without my help?"

"That is my concern, General."

"I guess it is, Belinda. But let me tell you this before you leave. You may want to be on your own, but you don't have to be. I am here if you need me. Just call." Warner hung up.

Belinda knew Interpol would throw resources at this new incident, but still, it would take time. She also knew that the events at the Dôme would tarnish Garny's reputation if not shut him down completely. If a small experiment like that could be so easily disrupted, how would he ensure a large-scale deployment on an order impacting climate change event would not be cataclysmic? He would have a lot of work to do to convince any government entity, including General Tom Warner's United States of America, to consider deploying his technology. She finished the cigar and made her way to a small aerodrome outside of the village of Pontoise. Her ops team was already there waiting for her, and together they boarded two small planes for a six-hour journey that took them to the local Pamplona airport where Belinda's helicopters waited to take them into the Pyrenees to Ainsa and Muro de Roda. The helicopters settled down on the landing pad at the Muro Lab, which then sunk into an underground port and disappeared as the camouflage cover closed over them.

Hadj met Belinda below the still rotating blades.

"What do we have?" she demanded from Hadj as she jumped from the helicopter, knowing Hadj was operating well ahead of her expectations. He spoke rapidly as they made their way to the lab.

"We have two major discoveries. First, we have identified the biological trigger for cytokine storms and the anaphylactic reaction in humans. It is related to the carbon-capture mechanism. The body reacts to the CO_2 saturation by flooding the lungs and other organs with oxygenated blood that is rich in cytokines. The blood starts the anaphylactic swelling, and the cytokines get activated to a point where the body loses control and suffocates itself. We believe we have a therapy as well. If you can combine a robust dose of antihistamines with oxygen therapy before the CO_2 hits, you can slow the cytokine storm and prevent full anaphylaxis, or at least that is our theory for now."

"Interesting. What else do you have?"

"Our second discovery is this. We believe Garny solved the self-replication problem and developed a mechanism for high volume manufacturing, but we doubt that he really understands self-replication."

"And we do?" said Belinda. She loved having discovered Hadj and adding him to her team. He had been an amazing discovery.

"We are getting closer," said Hadj. "Garny understood that all you need is a threshold event before the process takes over by itself. We think that Garny used superconducting materials to escalate the pace of self-replication. What we don't know is if he realized that freezing the bots and then heating them to the right temperature speeds up the process even further."

"We can produce larger quantities of bots using that process?"

"Yes. I believe we can."

"Can we control the bots?"

"The only mechanism we have for controlling them, other than freezing them, is to saturate them with CO_2. Once saturated, they become inert."

"But that is not the solution."

"Right. All we have at this point is a dirty bomb. We can do better, but we need a control mechanism."

* * *

Bost Karnivan slammed down his coffee a bit too hard, and the hot fluid burned his hand.

"Shit," he muttered. He shook his hand and wiped the back of his hand on

his pants. "Dammit, guys. We are wasting time," he said to his team of AI engineers sitting around a table in the Providia break room.

"I'll beg to differ," responded Karl Kloust. Karl was Bost's top engineer. They had worked together at Intel's office in Berlin before moving to the United States on green cards and accepting their current positions at Providia on the reclaimed bay north of San Jose.

"Explain yourself," said Bost, frustrated by his sense of their lack of progress.

"The SENSA XO has only been processing for one week. We knew this would take at least thirty days to solve even with that kind of power."

"I know I agreed to this," said Bost, "but the more I think about it, the more it doesn't make sense to me. I don't see our current technology, even if it is highly advanced, giving us what we need."

"You are wrong," said Karl, confident his candor would have no impact on Bost. Bost cared about one thing and one thing only: solutions. How they got there didn't matter. What they said didn't matter. Identifying solutions to problems was all that mattered.

"I'm not wrong, but please, enlighten me."

"It's all about bits, Bost, and how we make them move. The faster the better. You know that. If artificial intelligence has taught us anything, it's that Occam's razor works. Shave off the extremities and whittle the problem down to basics, and you'll get to the best answer. The simple fact right now is that the SENSA XO is the fastest AI supercomputer in operation, other than AURORA at the Argonne National Lab in Illinois. We don't own AURORA. We, and NASA, own SENSA, and SENSA will give us our answer. We need to be patient."

"Karl, I appreciate your loyalty to the technology, but we are getting this wrong. It was our approach that created the problem that SENSA is trying to solve. SENSA is burning through bits needlessly. There must be another approach."

"Gentlemen." Providia CFO Christopher Deckwalder entered the break room. He liked Bost and his team and preferred hanging around these engineers over his own finance team. As brilliant as Deckwalder was known to be in the Silicon Valley financial circles, he preferred the math of engineering to the math of finance, which he views as necessary but boring. He craved the type of mind that was stimulated by the act of creation, and Bost had that type of mind.

"Good morning, sir," piped several voices.

"We are waiting on SENSA to deliver?" said Christopher.

"Yes," answered Karl, eyeing Bost.

"For now," said Bost.

"Can I get you and your team to join me in the executive conference room?" said Christopher. "We have a guest I think you'll want to meet."

Bost and his team made their way to the elevator, a constant gaggle of voices trying to decipher Bost's break room comments. The elevator opened to the tenth-floor executive reception area, and Bost could see a small group seated around the conference table behind the glass doors. He immediately recognized Leonard Freund.

"Hello, Leonard," said Bost. He respected Leonard as a good engineering mind, but he had never liked Ragnar Willowbrook and the presumption there that they were the best lab in the country and the only one capable of validating other people's ideas. He always had been dubious of Ragner's claim of owning certain patents and genuinely feared sharing his ideas with the lab. He wasn't surprised to hear that the lab had run into serious trouble with the FBI and that its outspoken CEO, Dr. Belinda

Armendariz, had disappeared. But at least under Belinda, Ragnar Willowbrook had been a force to be reckoned with. Bost doubted that Ragnar had much of a future under Leonard.

"I'd like to introduce you to a new team at Ragnar Willowbrook," said Christopher. "Of course, you know Dr. Leonard Freund. With him today is the labs' new CEO, Dr. Brian Johannsen. Dr. Johannsen was one of the best minds to survive the incident at the Duc Tran Labs at the University of Washington. I'll let Dr. Johannsen introduce the new members of his team."

"Brian is fine," Brian responded as he stood to address a skeptical Providia team.

Bost sat quietly and observed Brian as he spoke. There was something about his candor that Bost appreciated, but it didn't do much to change his opinion about Ragnar. Then Brian began to explain the process of self-replication that he had uncovered while he was at the Tran Labs. Bost shook his head.

"Self-replication is a fantasy," he said.

"I would have thought the same," said Brian, "until I saw it with my own eyes."

"It violates the laws of physics," Bost said. "Tran should have taught you that."

"Which laws of physics?" Brian queried, pushing back. "The laws of physics change when you get down to subatomic levels."

"I understand quantum mechanics," said Bost. "But quantum is not magic. As hard as you try, rocks do not reproduce themselves."

"Crystals grow, under the right conditions," said Brian.

"And water freezes when it is cold enough," said Bost. "But that is not self-replication."

"We take it for granted that biological structures self-replicate. What is it about the physical world that is any different? At the subatomic level, what is the difference?"

"DNA is the difference," said Bost. "Cytokinetic cell division is the difference."

"All I ask is that you open your mind," said Brian. "We would like to invite you and your team to Ragnar to witness what I am describing."

"You are asking us to validate your work?" Bost said with a hint of sarcasm.

"No," said Brian. "We are here for another reason. It is not a secret to us that you are developing a mass manufacturing process for nanobots using artificial intelligence."

"What is your point?" said Bost. Brian could sense the pressure Bost was under to deliver something quickly.

"We think we can show you that the answer to that problem is simpler than you might think, but you'll have to come see it for yourself," said Brian, watching as the impact of his words washed over the Providia team, quite literally as coffee splashed out of its cups onto several engineers' lapels. Bost sat back in his chair. Karl rose to defend his boss, and Bost motioned him to sit. "But," he continued, "that is not why we are here."

"Why are you here?" Bost responded.

Brian explained his new arrangement with the Rutter Lab at UCLA. He described the Dakota Marley tragedy as well as the near tragedy at the Tran Lab when he first encountered the petri dish with the nanobot gel. He described the arrangement that Ragnar now had as designated expert witnesses for the LAPD in the Marley Dakota case still pending in the courts and how, under his direction, Ragnar was authorized to test and experiment on a shipment of the nanobots that was heading to the labs as they spoke. He explained what he knew about the carbon-capture technology embedded in the nanobots but that he had learned very little about how it worked and what else might be possible with these nanobots, which, as he had explained earlier, were capable of rapid self-replication. These nanobots, he said, are essentially microchips, and they must be capable of being programmed. If that is true, then what would it take to introduce artificial intelligence into the nanobot chipsets?

"We want a partnership with Providia to explore that possibility," Brian concluded and sat down.

Christopher Deckwalder smiled. This was new, and he sensed it might be a watershed moment for Providia. He gave Leonard an approving look. Bost looked at Christopher and back at Brian.

"When can we see this demonstration?"

Brian pushed back his chair, walked over to Bost, and extended his arm.

"Soon," he said, "very soon."

At that moment, Deckwalder's executive assistant entered the conference and whispered in his ear, "The police are here."

Chapter 14.

The Power of Small (Part I)

Hollywood's long-standing relationship with the CIA is well documented, even by Hollywood. Check out, for example, *Into the Shadows*, a documentary narrated by Alec Baldwin. But the dance is a tenuous dance. Hollywood's ability to generate dramatic moments that draw the world to its screens requires a freedom of voice and independence of thought that hasn't always lined up with the Washington propaganda machine. The mistake made by the Chinese government and other countries' centralized media-control agencies is to remove the freedom needed to produce believable storylines. The forced messaging in those products remove an audience's ability to suspend belief and lose themselves in the storyline. All government-driven products are viewed skeptically, and the entertainment value of the piece is lost. In the worst cases, it becomes a mockery of itself. Even in the United States, the political spin doctors that drive the government's voice deplete that voice of credibility. Hollywood profits from this lack of trust and styles itself as the true voice of the people. The trick, and hence the dance, has been to convince a global audience that Hollywood and the American propaganda machine are not the same.

Peggy Rice had been out of her coma for a week. The hospital moved her to a skilled nursing facility to monitor her condition before allowing her to return to her home. Tracy Pickett had visited Peggy every day before and after she came out of the coma. She told Peggy about Van and her colleague's visit to the Cortez home. Tracy, not without some resistance, handed Peggy the screenplay.

"Work has stopped on it?" she asked Tracy.

"For now," she said. "But Jerry has a lot invested in this project, and I doubt he'll kill it."

Peggy gave Tracy a focused look.

"I'm sorry. Bad choice of words."

Peggy shook her head. "Don't worry about it," she said. "That's the problem with our industry. We take words seriously but for the wrong reasons. So where are we at on this?" she said holding up the manuscript briefly and then wincing from the pain shooting through her neck.

"It's where you left it."

Peggy flipped open the first few pages and reread what she had read a hundred times.

FADE IN:
EXT. COLLEGE CAMPUS, EVENING

The dominating spire of an Ivy League university against a bright fading sunset. There's a light on in a window next to the spire against the baroque façade of the building. A shadowy figure is looking out of the window as a student exits the building and walks down the lighted central path to an old Mustang convertible, top down, waiting for her. **DRIVER GUNS ENGINE.**

"Doesn't this sound more like *Animal House*?" Peggy asked Tracy. "Creepy professor stalking sexy co-ed?"

"Jerry likes it," Tracy said. "He wants the storyline to hint at the corruption of genuine academic goals by corrupt corporate interests."

"Call Spielberg. We'll need the rights to *Indiana Jones*."

"You don't mean that," Tracy said.

"What is so unique about this manuscript that Trey had to die for it?"

"Trey loved his work, Peggy. We don't know why he died," Tracy said fighting back the tears.

"Or why someone shot me," Peggy said grimacing. "The answer may be here. We need to find it before anyone else gets hurt."

Tracy reached for the manuscript, and Peggy handed it back. "I think you need to rest," Tracy said and set the manuscript on the breakfast tray next to the bed. "I'll see you tomorrow morning."

Peggy waited for Tracy to leave and reached back for the manuscript. This time the pain was too much, and she gave up and fell back against her pillow.

"You're probably right," she sighed and drifted back to sleep.

* * *

Van and Charlie waited in the lobby. Providia stood in line with a host of Silicon Valley-based companies that had captured the magic of the Information Age and turned it into billions of dollars. The Providia lobby looked like a prepubescent boy or girl's dream come true. The walls were covered with oversized banners advertising Pokémon Go, Mortal Kombat, and Halo, and there were actual video game machines placed strategically around the lobby. Van walked over to one of the machines, and the young receptionist called over to her, "Go ahead and play. It's free!" Van smiled politely and shook her head. She walked back to Charles and sat down.

"What's your take?" he said, always looking to Van for her unique impressions.

"The genius of distraction," she said, and Charlie grinned and shook his head approvingly.

The elevator doors opened, and Brian and Leonard appeared in the lobby with their Ragnar Willowbrook team. They were talking intently. Van noticed Brian before he saw her. Leonard recognized Van at once and paused Brian to walk over and greet her.

"My dear detective," Leonard said grinning from ear to ear. "What on earth are you doing here at Providia?"

"Official business," said Van studying Brian's reaction to her.

"Well, then," said Leonard, "don't let us interfere. But if you don't mind, let me introduce you to our new CEO." Leonard pointed to Brian. "I hope you approve."

"I'm reserving judgment," said Van with the slightest grin. "Maybe we should let him prove himself first."

"He is already proving himself to me," Leonard replied. "But I understand that you might be a different matter."

"You can stop, guys," said Brian. He was feeling proud about the interaction with Providia, and even though Van's presence surprised him, it didn't throw him too much. As he listened to Leonard and Van's banter, he told himself that his mind was focused on larger matters. As for Van, Brian's lack of interest felt oddly appealing.

"Good to see you, Van, even if it is a surprise. Thank you for your assistance. We are eagerly awaiting the bots' shipment."

"Good to see you too, Brian. Congratulations again. Please be careful with the bots. We don't need another accident."

"You haven't heard?" queried Leonard.

"Heard what?" said Van.

"Something happened in Paris. They're saying it might have been a terror attack."

"What do you mean something happened? What does that have to do with us?"

The receptionist called out to Van and Charlie, "Detectives?"

"Hard to say," Leonard said. "Now is clearly not the best time. Can you come to see us before you return?"

"Detectives? Excuse me, but they are ready for you upstairs."

Van studied Brian and Leonard carefully. She looked at Charlie. "Can we make time?"

Charlie nodded but said nothing.

"Fine." She turned and headed for the elevators with Charlie, not looking back.

Brian looked at Leonard. "I heard about an explosion in Paris, but that is all. Is anyone taking credit for it?"

"I have my suspicions," said Leonard.

* * *

Van and Charlie settled into the conference room with Christopher Deckwalder.

"How can I help you, detectives?" Christopher started.

Van responded, "Good morning, Mr. Deckwalder. Maybe we can start with introductions?"

"I know who you are," responded Christopher. "You are Detective Van Eng with Robbery-Homicide at the LAPD. You were recently promoted to Detective II, so congratulations are in order. Your partner is Detective

Charles Darling, same bureau, higher rank. I believe Charles is close to retirement if I am not mistaken. Been with the bureau a while—says a lot. I assume you know who I am."

"Yes, we do."

"So, how can I help you?"

"You are familiar with the Hollywood producer, Jerry Cortez?"

"I am, both because I have seen his movies and because I know him personally."

"You are friends?"

"We've become friends, of sorts. I met him after interest developed in making video games styled after his movies. Recently he asked us to consult on a new film he is working on."

"The Power of Small?"

"Is that the name? I didn't realize they had chosen a name."

"Forgive us our ignorance, but what is it that qualifies Providia to consult on this movie?"

"Providia has been involved in microelectronics for a long time. We were one of the first to explore nanotechnology, although we never developed a product. We got into media and video gaming technology through chipset manufacturing. We realized early on that nanotechnology was not really a viable market until you could mass produce nanobots. Doesn't take a genius to figure that out. It does take a genius to generate the solution. We hired some of the best minds in the world. Our initial efforts were fruitless until we shifted our focus to artificial intelligence as a potential solution. We still are working on the solution to the manufacturing problem, but it is AI now that we are looking at as the product, not nanobots. Maybe it is not our market, but our expertise in the field goes way back."

"What is it you think nanobots can do?"

"It's an untapped market. Hard to say, really. Today, most of the applications are medical. There are also new materials being developed using nanobots, some which may have applications in our semiconductor technology. But the full scope of the technology is still to be seen."

"Are you aware that one of the movie's writers was killed on the Paramount lot?"

"We are. It's terrible, tragic."

"Did you know the writer?"

"Not any more than we knew anyone else working on the film."

"Did he attend any meetings between you and Mr. Cortez?"

"Jerry invited us to his writing sessions, and he might have been there. There were a handful of writers at those meetings."

"Nothing about Trey Nguyen stands out to you?"

"Not really."

"What kind of advice did you give Jerry?"

"We talked about the movie. He was interested both in the story and in the impact of the movie on public opinion. His primary concern was that he did not want nanobots to be seen as magic or fantasy. The movie is not science fiction; it is supposed to be drama. Jerry wanted the message of the movie to support new technology and to battle the fears associated with new technology. He wanted the nanobots to be real, to function as they are capable of functioning. We helped him draw that line."

"The story is about the medical benefits of nanobots?"

"I wouldn't say that, although there are pointers. It's a modern war flick."

"Halo meets Call of Duty."

"I suppose."

"Nanobots as weapons?"

"You'll have to see the movie."

"That's not an answer."

"What I am saying is, it's a matter of creative license. Mind if I ask you a question?"

"Shoot."

"Where are you going with this? Do I need to call my attorney?"

"Cortez suggested we talk to you. He said you know something about antagonism toward nanotechnology. We are exploring. We have no leads on Trey's death, but with the Rice's shooting, it appears that someone is targeting the movie and not just Trey. Why would anyone resort to violence to prevent a movie from being released?"

"Hollywood's an easy target for anyone looking for notoriety. Everyone knows Charles Manson and Helter Skelter. Does the name Mark David Chapman ring any bells? Famous for shooting John Lennon. The violence of Hollywood is pervasive, and it is not limited to the movies. Have you heard of the Black Dalia? She was an aspiring actor. I once met a young director named Adrienne Shelley who was murdered in her office by a studio construction worker who staged her hanging to make it look like a suicide."

"Cortez showed us his collection of threatening postcards. We are going through them now. You think what happened to Trey was a random disturbed movie fan?"

"There is a history that backs up the possibility."

"That's fair. But what about someone with an actual agenda?"

"What do you mean?"

"The movie is about nanobots. What about someone who thinks nanobot technology is evil?"

"That's possible as well."

"What do you know about that?"

"We see it all the time."

"What do you see?"

"We get calls and letters from individuals who are not connected to any group and whose opposition ranges from genuine concern to outright hostility."

"Do you keep records of these communications?"

"I am pretty sure we still have some of the written threats."

"We'd like to see what you have. What about organized opposition?"

"It's there. It's real."

"What does it look like?"

"There are two versions. There's a quasi-legitimate version that tries to get lawmakers to ban the technology. They have whitepapers on mind-control experiments and neo-chemical warfare, and they raise a lot of money and support candidates who share their agenda."

"Would they resort to violence?"

"Not likely. That battle is a battle over public opinion, and it is a battle that the opponents of new technologies always ultimately lose, but they inflict a lot of damage along the way."

"But there are others."

"Yes, there are others."

"What are we talking about?"

"Something along the lines of eco-terrorism."

"Have you actually run into that in this space?"

"Not yet. Not directly."

"What do you know?"

"There is one person up here who has caught everyone's attention."

"Name?"

"His name is Robert Anders, but he goes by Hack."

"What has he done?"

"Mostly property damage, a lot of graffiti, but he is serving time for arson setting fire to some corporate managers' cars. No one here was directly affected, but we lost a good manager over the incidents. He left Providia out of concern for his family."

"This guy, Hack, is serving time?"

"A few years. He burned the cars while they were still in the driveways of the managers' homes."

"I see. How long has he been incarcerated?"

"Probably three or four years. Not certain. He'll probably be out on probation soon."

"Where is he at?"

"Elmwood State Prison. Milpitas."

"Was it just him, or was there a gang?"

"You'll have to ask him, though I doubt you will get much out of him. He is known for having taken the rap himself."

Van thanked Deckwalder for his time. She handed him a card. "You hear anything, please let us know."

"My pleasure, detectives."

* * *

Coming out of Sunnyvale, Van and Charlie drove the back way to the Ragnar Willowbrook Labs through Cupertino, home of all things Apple. Saratoga-Sunnyvale Road terminated at Highway 9, which meanders up to the ridge of the Santa Cruz Mountains. The Silicon Valley fell away beneath them as they climbed the narrow but popular two-lane road. They passed several wineries on the way, not the historic wineries of Sonoma or Napa, but playgrounds of the nouveau billionaire class sprung from the now historic garage labs of the South Bay. They found the long entrance to Ragnar, and for a moment, both Van and Charlie relived the fright of the battle between the FBI and Belinda's special ops team. They pulled out into an opening where they expected to see armed guards and a tall gate, but there was nothing except the remnants of concrete foundations where the guard house stood.

The top of the original glass building was still visible and emerged into full view as they reached the broad circular entrance. Van noticed the garden was overgrown but that the large statues from Belinda's time had been removed and placed in a smaller manicured area on the east side of the building, on the slope overlooking the valley. They parked on the circular drive and entered the building without a guard. The security desk and the lobby furniture had been redesigned and simplified. All signs of the FBI battle had been cleaned up and plastered over. The large ten-foot cast bronze letters had been removed, and a clean-looking sign that said "The New Laboratories of Ragnar Willowbrook" was mounted just above eye level behind the security desk. Brian and Leonard emerged from the elevator bank to welcome Van and Charlie.

"I like what you've done with the place," Van poked fun at Brian.

"The location is ostentatious enough. Belinda didn't need to gild it," Leonard replied on Brian's behalf.

"Just part of the rebranding," Brian responded.

"Listen to the CEO," Charlie winked at Van.

They took the elevators to the top floor, and it was apparent they were still undergoing renovations. Unpainted drywall boards divided up the original conference room and Belinda's gigantic office space. A new conference room looked out over the eastern slopes of the mountains and down into the valley. The floors were covered in cardboard, but the room had nice chairs and a classic conference room table to enjoy the view. Fred Schmidt was sitting at the table with his laptop open. He stood when he saw Van and Charlie enter the room.

"Hope you are not here to arrest anyone," Fred said, recalling the last interaction with the pair of detectives at his Bainbridge Island home.

"Let me introduce you to our new chairman of the board," said Leonard.

"We've met," said Fred. "Nice to see you again, detectives."

Van smiled and sat down. She studied the room and the view and picked up on a sense of relief that she imagined was not present when Belinda ran the labs. Everyone seemed relaxed, and it was not as forced as it was at Providia. She looked at Leonard.

"We are here, Dr. Freund. What is this about?"

Brian looked at Leonard. "Let me start."

"First, you noticed the changes around here. They are not just cosmetic. Ragnar Willowbrook built itself up, with Dr. Freund's expertise, into a patent validation powerhouse. Nothing in the biomedical engineering space

dared enter the market without the labs' seal of approval, and they paid for it. But as you know, that wasn't enough for Belinda Armendariz. She twisted the original mission into her own version and began stealing intellectual property rights from unsuspecting talent, and this place became a very dark place. But no one knew how to compete or challenge Ragnar Willowbrook's authority. Corporate labs catered to R-W and basically looked the other way in exchange for certification. University labs were hungry for recognition and thought what R-W had done was a kind of a model. Moreover, competition among university laboratories became fierce, including the Bainbridge Island lab where I worked when we first met. The quality of work suffered there in the chase for the next big idea, and I think our science itself suffered."

"But she's gone, right?" said Van. "From what I've heard, she's vanished, or somebody influential is hiding her. She committed serious crimes, out of this place, and she needs to be brought to justice."

Brian started to speak in response, but Leonard held up his hand.

"I know how dark this place became," he said. "I was a part of it and I don't make any excuses for what we did. But I want Belinda brought to justice as much as you do. Something happened in Paris, and it has Belinda's fingerprints on it, and I think you'll be very interested in the details."

"What do you know, Dr. Freund?"

"I can't tell you exactly how we got the nanobots that, as you know, were stolen. Suffice it to say there are national security protections around that information. The penalties for disclosing it are something I can't face without sufficient protection that I don't believe you can provide. But there is a lot I can tell you. I've been hearing buzz for a while now about a new method for fighting climate change. It's coming out of Europe, and the American government is too arrogant to believe somebody outside of this country might have a brilliant idea. It isn't getting much attention in this country. But the UN is taking an active interest. That organization is very active on the climate change front, and they host annual climate conferences where they bring the best minds in the world to address the questions that forest fires, drought, desertification, and other global infirmities are raising.

"Recently, a very prominent individual from this area, one of the wealthy original founders of Providia, disappeared after he left the company. We had heard he was messing around in a new type of prosthetics, but we heard nothing more. His name is Garne McDonough. Apparently, through his work in prosthetics, Garne, or Garny as he calls himself, became very interested in nanobots, and while he was working in some undisclosed location, he developed what he is now claiming to be a solution to global warming using nanobots."

"That seems counterintuitive," said Van.

"What do you mean?"

"It's a global problem. How would a microscopic device solve a global problem?"

"Exactly. We thought he was off his rocker and had spun a yarn that somehow got the UN's attention. Well, apparently, he assembled a very prominent display of the technology that was to take place at this year's Global Climate Change Consortium in Paris. Then I found out that the incident that recently happened in Paris is connected to Garny's show."

"The explosion?"

"It wasn't exactly an explosion," said Brian. "We think it was Garny's experiment gone wrong."

"Or sabotaged," added Leonard.

"You think Belinda had something to do with it?"

"Like I said, it has her fingerprints."

"Did you talk to Garny?"

"No. Garny is unconscious in a Paris hospital. He was shot and survived, but only because he was wearing a mask. Several dignitaries died at that incident, a few from gunshot wounds but most of them from CO_2 poisoning."

Van stared at Leonard. "You certain it wasn't a disgruntled employee?"

"No. It was a team effort, like Bainbridge and like the fight we had here. Moreover, it was carefully orchestrated. Garny chose the Dôme de Paris because he wanted visibility. He redesigned the Dôme to work for the experiment, adding what he thought was sufficient security."

"And yet somebody found a way in, and you think it was Belinda."

Fred Schmidt stepped in. "We do. And so does Interpol."

"Interpol? How do you know?"

"They contacted me," said Leonard. "They know about her history here at Ragnar Willowbrook."

"Good to know they know about her," said Charlie. "We appear to have ourselves a bona fide terrorist."

Fred responded, "We don't know if that's her goal, but we do know she is comfortable with violence."

"I want Belinda caught as much as anybody, but what do you want us to do?" said Van. "We are LAPD detectives. We only get involved if the agencies with jurisdiction want us involved. Plus, she's international now."

"You don't need to do anything yet," said Fred. "But this is about the bots, the same bots from Bainbridge Island and the same bots that caused the incident at UCLA that got Derek Whitestone and Cheryl Brown in trouble.

We don't where or when Belinda will show up, but wherever these bots are, she's somewhere in the background. You need to stay alert."

"Maybe it's time to tell us the whole story," said Van.

"I think so," said Fred and motioned to Brian.

* * *

"One last visit," Van told Charlie. "Let's go see our new friend at Elmwood."

"Hack," said Charlie. "Sounds like the guy had mean parents."

Elmwood Correctional Facility in Milpitas, California, is among the largest correctional complexes in the United States and holds up to twenty-six hundred men and six hundred women in minimum- to medium-security cells. The two jails there are the Elmwood Men's Facility and the Elmwood Complex Women's Facility. Until 2016, when California became the fifth state to legalize the recreational use of marijuana, Elmwood was also known as "Weedville," given the number of innates charged with illegal possession and/or distribution of marijuana.

Van and Charlie entered the visitors' center and flashed their detective badges. The guards led them to an enclosed room for private meetings. After about fifteen minutes, a tall and lanky middle-aged inmate in a faded orange jumpsuit was brought into the room. He had a scraggly salt and pepper beard and long dark hair with a bald spot in the center of his head.

"Fifteen minutes," said the guard, as if it were a routine meeting with a defense attorney. Neither Van nor Charlie paid attention to the guard. One phone call and they would have as much time as they needed.

"Robert Anders?" Van started.

"Who's asking?" replied the inmate.

"I am Detective Van Eng, and this is my partner Detective Charles Darling."

"Did you say Darwin?"

"Darling."

"His name is Darling?"

"At least it's not Hack," said Charlie, taking on the mouthy inmate.

"Hacksaw, my friend," replied the inmate.

"Your buddies at Providia called you Hack," said Van.

"No one who knows me calls me Hack. Everyone else is just ignorant."

"So is it Hack or Hacksaw?"

"I don't really care what you call me or what those assholes at Providia think you should call me."

"They also tell us you are a philosopher, Hack," Charlie kept pushing.

"What the fuck does that mean?"

"It means you have a theory that supports protecting the village by torching cars."

"I didn't torch the cars."

"That's not what they tell us."

Van interjected, "Do you like movies, Hacksaw?"

"I don't watch movies," he replied. "Hollywood is a waste of fucking time."

"Do you read, then?"

"Yeah."

"What do you like to read?"

"Pretty much anything."

"Ever read any screenplays?"

"Maybe."

"Ever been to Hollywood?"

"A few times. I took my family to Universal Studios."

"Ever been to the Paramount Studios?"

"Not that I recall."

"Ever read anything by Jerry Cortez?"

"Not that I recall."

"Do you know who Jerry Cortez is?" asked Charlie.

"He makes movies, right?"

"So, you do know something about movies," said Van.

"I know American culture if that's what you mean. Doesn't mean I engross myself in movies like most Americans."

"You are better than most Americans?" said Charlie.

"I didn't say that. I just don't like to waste my time."

"Seems like you wasted several years sitting in here," prodded Charlie.

"Do I have to take this?" Hacksaw looked back toward the guard who didn't respond.

"Tell us about nanobots," said Van.

"What about them?"

"What's your issue with them?"

"They are dangerous."

"Don't they have the potential to help humanity, fight cancer, that sort of thing?"

"What do you think they are? They are microscopic machines that can get in your brain through your eyes, ears, nose, mouth, and asshole. What do you think they do when they get inside you? At the very minimum, they are poison to the body, but that is just the beginning. Have you ever heard of *Sacculina carcini*?"

"No."

"It is a parasite that takes over the brains of certain crabs and turns their bodies into zombie-like hosts. It's a weird aspect of nature but it shows you that our brains are not impenetrable. Why do you think the United States Government is investing so much money in MEMS, micro—"

"Micro-electrical-mechanical systems," said Van.

"Very good," said Hacksaw.

"You think violence is the best way to oppose nanotechnology?"

"A little bit of property damage gets a lot of people's attention these days."

"And you think you need to get their attention."

"I do. Very few people realize what this technology is and what it is capable of. We can't let the government have that kind of power. The power to control our minds, our bodies, our votes, and all through some technology that we can't even see."

"Did you know that Cortez is producing a movie about nanobots?"

"No."

"Ever heard of *The Power of Small?*"

"Is that the name of the movie?" Hacksaw laughed. "So stupid."

"What about Trey Nguyen?" Charlie queried.

"No."

"Peggy Rice?"

"She an actress?"

"I think we're done here," said Charlie, motioning for the guard.

"One last question," said Van. "Do you know anybody who feels the same way you do about this technology?"

"Sure," said Hacksaw laughing. "We're a fucking movement, and we are going to bring this house crashing down."

"Right," said Charlie. "Good luck with that."

Chapter 15.

The Running

Historians do not gift the City of Pamplona with much of the romantic luster painted by Hemingway in *The Sun Also Rises*. Rather, the City of Pamplona's true history is one of repeated destruction and rebuilding after being caught in conflicts between the Franks, Moors, Visigoths, Andalusians, and Vikings. Even during the so-called glory days of the Kingdom of Navarra, Pamplona was not much more than a small fortress occupied mostly by poor and starving peasants who were easily overtaken by marauding hordes from the north or the south. Pamplona's running of the bulls, glorified by Hemingway, was, in its inception, no more than a pre-game ritual played out during the Feast of San Fermin prior to the bulls' eventual destruction in the Pamplona bullring. Even the festival itself has a questionable history. The Feast of Saint Fermin was based on a story about a bishop whose reputation for large-scale mass conversions to Christianity—allegedly forty thousand pagans in three days— appears to have been made up.

Neither the dubious nature of the feast nor the insanity of the event deterred Hemingway from finding in it bravado and romance. It is unique after all. Among the many stories of Native Americans chasing down buffalo on foot or horseback, or of ranch hands guiding large and unruly herds of cows hundreds of miles, there are no known stories of trials or competitions where either young male tribesmen or adolescent cowboys try to outrun or outlast the "furious energy" of stampeding herds of any type. This apparent and highly entertaining lunacy exists only in the City of Pamplona. The unanticipated twist in the City of Pamplona's tortured history is that the city is now experiencing an era of prosperity unlike any in its entire existence, as year after year, driven in no small part by Hemingway's novels, millions of tourists descend on the city to witness the spectacle of the Running of the Bulls.

Martin Richard could barely contain his excitement that he would be spending several days and nights with Van as they traveled to Spain with his parents. His parents noticed the spark in Martin and did not hide their own exuberance that their son might have finally found someone special and worthy of their time and attention, and they were eager to encourage the relationship. Van was excited as well. It was her first trip anywhere out of California, let alone the United States, and she checked out several books on Spain and Pamplona, and she even reviewed some of the distinctions between European Spanish and the local Mexican and Central American dialects she was exposed to in Los Angeles.

But Van's excitement was not focused on Martin, and she felt a bit guilty that she might be taking advantage of him and his family as she prepared for the trip abroad. She shared her concern with Charlie, and he told her she was out of mind even to consider feeling guilty. They invited her because they wanted her on the trip. "Just go and enjoy," he said. "You deserve a break, and who knows, if Martin is not your dreamboat, you might stumble upon some hot Spanish guy."

"I am not going to Spain to look for other guys," she protested. "I will respect Martin and his family, and what happens with Martin happens."

Charlie laughed. "The Spanish have a saying: 'Leave your daughters at home or they will leave their hearts in España Viejo.'"

"That's not a saying!" Van said but giggled in spite of herself. "That's not even good Spanish."

* * *

Van stood at the window staring at the red and white rooftops of Pamplona as they glowed in the setting sun. Martin put his hand on her shoulder.

"I want to go out," said Van. "I want to see Pamplona's streets at night."

"It's our first day," said Martin, whose hormones had been racing like crazy ever since Van had said she was fine staying in the same room with him while they were in Spain. "We need to rest and recover from the time change."

Los Angeles was nine hours behind Pamplona, and even though the sun was setting, it felt to Van like the day was only beginning.

"You should come back to bed."

"Whose bed?" she asked with a mischievous grin. "Yours or mine?" The room they occupied was a small studio apartment with a kitchen, bath, and two twin beds on opposite sides of the room.

"Uh, well, uh, since you asked . . ." Martin stammered.

"Silly," Van laughed. "You know the deal."

Martin looked heartbroken, and Van leaned forward and gave him a light kiss. "Come on," she cooed flirtatiously and pulled him toward the door. "Let's take a walk outside."

The night air was warm and dry and right with scents that Van gobbled up like a banquet feast. The streets where they stayed were like stuccoed canyons dotted with small cafes. Small noisy cars smelling of diesel raced past them as if the streets were empty. Van looked as far as she could see down the narrow *calle*. Everywhere she looked, people occupied stools in front of canopied openings where steaming plates of food were being served. She smelled spicy sausages mixed with eggs and fried potatoes, grilled asparagus, and mushrooms, and it seemed that everyone was drinking beer. She grabbed Martin's hand and ran from café to café, trying to distinguish the subtle differences in the cuisine. One restaurant smelled more like seafood, and she saw pictures of salted cod on plates heaping with steaming vegetables.

"Here!" she shouted over a passing car and found two stools for her and Martin. "Isn't this wonderful!" she said, and Martin flashed an image of himself as Gregory Peck seated with an Asian Audrey Hepburn in the movie Roman Holiday. But Van had already ordered food and two beers for the two of them. He smiled as he watched her eyes flit back and forth at all the new sights and sounds of Spain. Two dark-haired Spanish young men wandered toward the two of them and he saw her flush a little, and it made him feel just a bit jealous.

"Do you think they are running?" she whispered to Martin, pointing at the two men.

"Let's ask," said Martin, emboldened by Van's presence. He jumped up and said, "Excuse me, but do you speak English?"

"Of course," one of them responded. "And we can read English, too," said the other, who looked at his friend, and they laughed at the American.

"I am sorry, no offense intended," said Martin, trying to appear unaffected.

"And who is this beautiful woman who has come to Spain to delight our senses?" the first said pointing at Van.

"This is my girlfr—" Martin started to say but Van cut him off.

"You can call me Van," she responded in perfect Spanish.

"You are from Spain?" he answered a little confused.

"I am here with Martin," she said touching Martin's arm. "We are here from Los Angeles to see the Running of the Bulls."

"Of course, you are," he answered and smiled to show her how charming he might be.

"We were wondering if the two of you are planning on running."

"Yes! We are runners," said the second with great pride. "You have found us out. We just now are reviewing the route. Did you know you were sitting on the Calle Estafeta? This long narrow street is one of the most difficult parts of the running. Runners are tiring by the time they get to this last stretch, and if they have the courage to keep running, this street is where they are most likely to be gored or trampled."

Martin said, "Our room overlooks this part of the route. My parents come here every year and select different locations to watch the running."

Van said, "My apologies for our rudeness, but we didn't get your names."

"I am Mateo," said the first speaker.

"And I am Bartolomeo," said the second. "But my friends call me Tolo."

"Aren't you afraid?" asked Martin. "Things can happen out there."

"Scared to death," said Tolo beaming. "That's why we run fast!"

Everyone laughed. "Can we buy you a beer?" Martin followed.

"No. No. Not this night. But when we are done, we will party like there is no end."

Mateo got serious. "We need to review the route. Would you like to come with us?"

"Yes," Van responded without hesitating. "That would be so interesting."

Martin tossed back his beer, and the four of them took off.

"This section of Estafeta is very dangerous," said Tolo. "This is the final straightaway before the bulls enter the ring, and they are moving very fast here. Their horns are very sharp, and they scrape them along the walls so all you can do here is run and your legs by now are very tired. The doorways are often jammed with runners trying to avoid being gored. You must keep moving forward."

"Yes," said Mateo. "These weigh up to six hundred kilos, or over one thousand pounds each. They are gentle giants unless you make them scared or angry, and the running does both."

The street ended at a larger road called Calle de Mercaderes. A sign on a small shop on the other side of the street read "La Curva de la Estafeta."

"La Curva," Van said out loud reading the sign.

"Si, La Curva," said Tolo seriously. "Dead Man's Curve. This is where many runners get hurt not because they are not fast but because the bulls themselves slip and fall as they make this turn and they fall on top of the runners."

"Seems like you want to be in the inside of the curve," said Van.

"Exactly," said Mateo. "But you must be fast and brave because the bulls slam into the first corner even as they slide into the opposite walls of the Estafeta. Very dangerous here."

They continued left up the Mercaderes onto the Plaza del Ayuntmiento, or Town Hall Plaza. An ornate three-story building stood on the opposite end of the plaza. The face of the town hall building bore four large flags above the second-story balcony where the town mayor would appear and hold court at public meetings. Every balcony was guarded by a light blue wrought-iron railing and bright red canopy, and the balconies overflowed with flowers of all colors in preparation for the feast. At the rooftop stood two large carved stone crowns surrounded by impish figures carrying horns. Just under the roof's peak was a large clock that reminded Martin of the *Back to the Future* town hall clock on the Universal backlot. Van noticed how uneven the pavers were and wondered how anyone could run and maintain their balance. Next to the town hall was the Call de Santo Domingo. Mateo said this first stretch of the run was his favorite.

"You feel light as air as the race begins," he explained. "Your body is shocked by many surges of adrenaline, and you shoot down Santo Domingo like a cannon shot."

"Yes," said Tolo. "But the adrenaline lasts only for a few hundred meters, and you begin to breathe very hard, and then you hear the bulls and the fear kicks in and there is a small surge that passes quickly because now you know you are tired. No one finishes the route before the bulls. The fastest make the dead man's curve just as the bulls reach them. Most of us turn our eyes to see the first bulls pass you at the town square. They fly by like you are standing still, but you are running hard and you hurt and your muscles tighten up, and only then the fear takes over as these giants bang into you and push you down against the brick and stone pavers and they knock you into the walls and you get bruised and cut by the sharp edges of doorways and porches and window frames."

"And you do this why?" asked Martin.

"Because we know that no one else has the courage to do what we do, and for a brief moment we feel like kings."

Van stared at the boys. "I understand," she said. "You are both very brave."

Tolo and Mateo smiled and laughed and bid the couple good night. Tolo turned back as they neared the top of the run. "Enjoy the show!" he shouted.

Van tossed and turned that night unable to sleep. At about midnight, Martin's parents appeared. Van was glad they were in separate beds.

"I am sorry, huns," said Martin's mom. "But we know how hard it is to

adjust to the new time zone and thought you might like something to help you sleep."

"Thank you," said Van. "I normally don't but I can't get the image of charging bulls out of my head."

"And you haven't even seen them yet," said Martin's father. "It is an incredible spectacle. It's unlike anything you'll see anywhere in the world."

"Here you go," said Martin's mom as she handed Van two pills and a glass of water. "Drink up; you'll need plenty of rest while you are here."

The next morning Van awoke refreshed. She glanced out the window and could see that people were already gathering in the streets, many of whom wearing the runners' red and white colors. She shook the sleep clinging on her eyes and smelled fresh coffee and fruit and bread just hot out of the oven. Martin was setting the breakfast table.

"Get up and eat, sleepy head," he said smiling. "The bulls are coming soon. We want to be ready."

Van smiled and replied, "Give me a few minutes." She grabbed some clothes and bounced into the bathroom.

Together, Van and Martin barely fit on the balcony. Martin didn't mind, and Van was so absorbed in the sensory overload, she didn't notice. Estafeta was bursting with red and white: red and white on the plaza, red and white at the cafes, red and white on all the other balconies around her. People everywhere were shouting and laughing, and in the mix of noises she resorted to reading Martin's lips to understand what to expect. At just before 8:00 a.m., the police arrived and cleared the streets yelling for everyone to get inside or behind special fences set up for the race. At exactly 8:00 a.m., she heard church bells, and the crowds on the balconies and behind the fences went silent. Tourists jumped the fence and ran into La Curva to get pictures, and the police grabbed them and pulled them back behind the fences. There was a light roar that grew louder, and suddenly dozens of runners appeared at the corner, and Van could see the bulls in the middle of the pack. The spectacle was just as Tolo and Mateo described. The bulls screamed around the curve, and one slipped on the cobblestones and went down, slamming unfortunate runners on the outside of the curve into the hay bales stacked at the turn guarding the entrance to the bodega operating at that corner. The bulls ran zig-zag down Estafeta, ramming the walls as they ran, and everyone around Van was screaming. One of the runners stumbled and a bull right next to him lowered its head and a huge gash of blood opened on the runner's side, and suddenly Van understood why everyone was wearing red and white. Halfway down Estafeta, the bulls gained momentum, and runners began to pin themselves to the side of the street to avoid being smashed or gored. Six runners were still in front of the bulls, and Van saw Tolo and Mateo race below the balcony still in the front pack. The bulls seemed to be gaining, and she screamed out of excitement and fear for them to run. They reached the end of the Calle still in front and disappeared around the corner into the funnel that led to the bullring. As soon as the bulls and the runners passed, the crowds surged into the street laughing and shouting, and Van felt a mix of disgust and morbid fascination at what she had witnessed. She turned from the balcony and went back inside.

"I hope they made it," she said to Martin once they were back in the room. "That was brutal."

"It's history," said Martin. "Unique in all the world."

"I suppose," she said. "I'm not sure if I liked it."

Over the next few days, Van convinced Martin to leave the city and go into the countryside. They toured the villages surrounding Pamplona and enjoyed relaxing at cafes and found several Navarra wineries where they spent the afternoon hiking through vineyards of Tempranillo, Garnacha, Cabernet Sauvignon, and Merlot. Martin remained a gentleman, and Van felt comfortable flirting and enjoying the moment without concern that Martin might take it too seriously. On the second afternoon, as they were walking through vines as tall as Martin's six-foot frame and talking about Martin's odd experiences with Hollywood A-listers, Van commented, "Martin, why are you so nice to me?"

"You must know the answer to that, Van," he responded.

"I know you are nice to everyone."

"Come on, Van. I like you."

"I like you, too," she said and smiled. "This has been such a wonderful week, and your parents are so nice me."

"They like you. They think you are good for me."

"Look at you," Van said. "You could have anybody you want. Why do you put up with me?"

"Well, you are a little unusual."

"What?"

"You know, you speak your mind. Nobody intimidates you. That's attractive to me. I like it. You make me feel bold."

"You need to feel bold?"

"I'm a dude. We all need to feel bold. Some women pretend to be impressed. They're not honest, just manipulative. They try to get something from you, and it's obvious. Other women compete. They are not comfortable unless you are off balance and they are in control."

"What do I do?"

"You don't do anything. You're just you. It's so great to see you excited

about being here and wanting to take everything in. You're honest, but you're also not afraid. It's refreshing."

"I guess that's a compliment."

Martin took Van's hand. "I like you. I really like you." He leaned down to kiss her, and she let his mouth touch her lips and thought about pulling away. He put his arm around her small waist and pulled her in a little tighter, and she touched his chest and gently pushed back. She saw the hunger in his eyes, but he didn't fight her. He pulled back quickly.

"I'm sorry. I know the deal we made."

"Don't be sorry," she said. "It was nice. I like you, Martin. I do. I just need some time." She looked around and then gazed in the sky. "This place is so beautiful and so romantic."

The next morning Van rose early. She told Martin she was heading out for a run. It was the fourth day of the running, and sweepers were out in mass cleaning up the debris from the night's festivities. She ran down to the bullring and saw the funnel where the bulls and the runners collided before entering the bullring. The air around the ring was not fresh, a mixture of animal blood and sweat and dung. She ran around the ring and back up Estafeta, climbing to the curve and then into the Plaza del Ayuntamiento. As she ran through the plaza, she noticed a group of runners hanging around a doorway. She thought at first they were having a pre-race meeting when the door opened and a runner appeared smiling and raising his hands in what appeared to be a victory sign. The other runners clapped and patted him on the back. She headed in the direction of the group, thinking she might see Tolo or Mateo, when the door opened, and an attractive middle-aged woman appeared in a bathrobe and leaned against the doorjamb. The group of runners standing outside the door all got excited, and Van thought maybe she was witnessing the location of a secret brothel in the heart of the race. The woman lit a cigar and shooed the runners away pointing toward the start of the race. They smiled and waved and blew her kisses and headed back up Santo Domingo. Van thought about turning back to the apartment, but the woman interested her and she slowed her pace to get a better look. As she was approaching, the woman began to watch her and then in an instant disappeared inside and closed the door. Van stopped, recognition seeping in, and she immediately turned around and headed back to Martin and the apartment, her mind racing and her heart pounding but not from the effort of her morning run. Back in the plaza, the face of Belinda Armendariz appeared in a window above the door. What on earth was a detective from Los Angeles doing in Pamplona? In the moment of her brief hesitation, Belinda had very little doubt that the detective recognized her just as she had recognized Van though they had never met each other. Van knew Belinda not from any personal interaction, but because she had seen her face on several police photos and head shots the FBI had taken, as well as in her own online research. Belinda was less certain at what she saw than Van, but she had seen Van on a monitor and had taken some pains to identify the young woman who had saved her disloyal chief of staff at Ragnar Willowbrook. Belinda had very little doubt that she was watching this same young woman walk rapidly across the Plaza and head down Calle Estafeta. She stepped back from the window after Van disappeared and called Hadj.

"Pull the team together," Belinda ordered. "I need you here in Pamplona right away."

Before she got back to the apartment, Van ducked into a pastry shop and called Charlie.

"She's here, Charlie," said Van as soon as Charlie answered.

"Van! So nice to hear from you. Are you having fun?" said Charlie aware of Van's serious tone but keeping it light.

"I'm sorry, Charlie. I need you to listen to me. Belinda is here in Pamplona."

"Ok. What do you want me to do?"

"I don't know. I need someone to tell me what to do."

"Did she see you?"

"I think she did."

"Isn't it likely she will leave the city and disappear again?"

"Maybe I should call the police?

"Don't do that. Let me talk to the FBI first. I'll call you back. And be careful," he added knowing that Van was not likely to take that advice.

Charlie called Agent Henry Sams, the Los Angeles Bureau FBI agent who had led the effort to take Belinda at Ragnar Willowbrook.

"Agent Sams, this is Detective Charles Darling, LAPD. We met on the Cheryl Brown matter."

"Detective Darling, of course. What's up?"

"Detective Eng believes she has located Belinda Armendariz in Spain. Pamplona, to be specific."

"What is she doing in Spain?" Sams asked.

"She's on vacation there with a friend. They are there to watch the bulls run."

"I've heard of that. Seems kind of crazy."

"She's there just to watch, but what do you think? If she is right, we might have an opportunity to catch an international fugitive."

"I'll make some calls. Tell her not to call the police there. If I recall correctly, Belinda Armendariz is Basque, and Pamplona is Basque Country. We'll have to proceed cautiously on this one."

Charlie called Van back and relayed the message. He repeated to her, "Please be careful."

Van left the bakery and watched behind her as she made an indirect route back to the apartment. Martin was awake.

"How was your run?" he said. "You were out for a while."

"I need to change my clothes," Van responded. "I need to blend in better. Do we have anything white and red?"

"My mom might have something," said Martin.

"I'm very sorry, Martin, but something has come up. I may need to find another place to stay."

"What?" Martin said perplexed. "What are you talking about?"

"I swear it has nothing to do with you. This experience has been wonderful. But I have seen someone I ran into in my past and I think she saw me, and I believe her to be very dangerous. It might not be safe for us to be together. I need you to trust me on this."

"I'm not sure what you are saying but let me call my parents. If you want something white and red to blend in, I am sure my mother has something. I'll ask her to bring it over."

Martin called his parents, while Van waited to hear more from Charlie. Agent Sams called her directly.

"Van," he said, "I've reached Interpol. There was a terrorist event in Paris, and they are linking Belinda. Interpol has an office in Madrid. They are sending agents to Pamplona as we speak. Tell me what you saw and where."

Van told Sams about the race route and the doorway on the Plaza del Ayuntamiento where she saw Belinda standing and smoking her cigar. She explained what she saw in detail.

"Very good," said Agent Sams. "I want you to pack up your things and leave Pamplona. If Belinda saw you, it will not be safe for you there."

"I understand," said Van. "But I think I can be of assistance here."

"Let Interpol handle it. I'm sorry to cut your vacation short, but you and your friends should leave at once."

Van hung up. She knew Agent Sams was right, but all she could think was, She's going to get away. Martin's parents showed up, and Denise immediately came over to Van.

"Honey, what is wrong? Are you feeling unwell?"

"I'm fine," said Van. "But I just had an encounter with someone who is not a good person. I really think that, for you and your family to be safe, we need to split up. I'll be candid with you. I have been asked to return to the States, and if anyone connects you to me, then you could be in danger as well. I know it is a hard thing to ask, but you should think about heading back home. Pamplona will be here in the future, but right now it is not safe."

"Nonsense," said Frank. "We are here with you, and whatever you need, we can help you get."

"I don't think that is the right answer, Dad," said Martin. "She is telling us that, for all of us to be safe, we need to leave. If that is the case, I am ready to go, but I won't go without you, Van."

"I can't go yet, Martin. I must help the team. I must be certain she does not get away."

"This is so confusing," said Denise. She looked at Frank who was shaking his head. But Frank knew he couldn't control Denise. Denise looked back at

Van. "I believe you. We'll do what you want us to do, but you must assure us that you will leave as soon as you possibly can."

"I will," said Van. "I am the eyes on the ground for now. As soon as I am not needed, I will leave. I promise."

Denise handed her a white blouse and a red bandana. She looked over to Martin and Frank. "Let's get our stuff together. This is not the time for us to be heroes."

"Put your things together," she said to Van, "and meet us back at the other apartment. You can stay there. I have an extra wig if you think that would help."

"It just might," said Van, grateful for her concern. "Thank you."

"Shit," said Belinda after hanging up with Hadj. She was as pissed about her romantic holiday being interrupted as she was about her unfortunate exposure to someone whom she knew was a relentless bloodhound. She couldn't stay at the plaza apartment and needed to leave immediately. She called a friend of hers who had a place on the other side of town and arranged to have her belongings delivered. She showered and got dressed and put on a blond wig she used for incognito travel. She left the apartment and looked around, half expecting to see Van again but did not, and jumped into a waiting taxi that took her to an airport where Hadj and her team were landing one of the helicopters.

In fact, Van was there in her red and white blouse and wearing her new wig. Belinda mistook Van for one of the many tourists and partiers filling up the plaza before the race. Van, however, watched Belinda get into a taxi and immediately crossed over the Plaza to Calle Santo Domingo and hailed another taxi just as the police barricaded the Plaza for the morning run. She directed the driver to follow the taxi, and they took off up Santo Domingo, passing the pen where the bulls stomped and snorted at the crowd of runners warming up for the run. They crossed over the Arga River and then turned back south along the Taconera Gardens and the Three Kings Hotel near where Belinda first stayed in Pamplona. The taxis turned east on Avenida de Baja Navarra, and Van almost lost Belinda as they merged onto crowded circles with similar-looking taxis. She just managed to catch Belinda as they crossed over to Cntr. Sarriguren and then appeared to merge onto the Navarra motorway but ducked under the overpass and raced east and north into Innovation Business Park. Once they were free of traffic, Van asked the driver to slow down and drop back, just far enough to keep Belinda in her sights. They passed a circular Siemens building, and Van watched as two gold and black painted Sikorski helicopters landed in a field behind the Siemens building. Belinda's taxi pulled into a dirt parking lot adjacent to the helipad field. She jumped out and appeared to glance back toward Van's taxi. Van told the driver to pull forward until they were out of sight and had reached a dead end on a lower road adjacent to the dirt lot. Van told the driver to stop in the parking lot of the lower road and to let her out next to the hill. She told the driver to turn around and retrace his route back to the motorway and waited for his car to clear. Then she climbed up the small hill that separated the two parking areas and hid behind a bush where she could see the waiting helicopters, their rotors spinning and kicking up dust. A team of operatives dressed in black military fatigues stood by as Belinda spoke over the noise of the rotors to a younger man with a dense but short black beard. Van waited to see if Belinda would board one of the helicopters and, if nothing else, she could report their initial direction. She hoped local air traffic control or the military flight operations would see the flyers and track them to their destination.

But Belinda did not board either Sikorski. Rather she walked back to the parking lot where a black Suburban was just pulling up. She didn't act at all like she was concerned with being followed or that she had some idea Van was watching her every move when Van picked up the scent of sweat. Before she could turn around, someone popped a black canvas bag over her head and pushed her to the ground.

He grabbed her hands and cuffed them behind her back and then jerked her up to a standing position. He pushed her forward, and she stumbled over rocks and almost fell as she stepped down off a curb and onto asphalt. She heard a car door open, and the man told her to step up and into the Suburban. Inside the vehicle, Van was pinned between two large men. No one spoke as they drove, and Van could tell that they had merged on the motorway and seemed to be heading west and then north. The ride was eerily reminiscent of Van's experience as a toddler when, at six years old, she was kidnapped from her front yard by a couple that was caught shortly after the abduction. Only this time, her mom was not screaming into the phone at the police and everyone she knew thought she was on her way home from Pamplona and away from Belinda and the danger she posed. Van tried to stay calm. She knew Belinda was capable of anything, but so long as she was alive, she might be able to leave clues or relay something to the international teams that were hunting Belinda. The SUV pulled off the main road onto a gravel roadway. Van could smell the dust and hear the crunch of the tires as they rolled over the loose pebbles. They had been driving over an hour and no one spoke a word, a testament, thought Van, to the team's deadly professionalism. It was possible they thought the same of her, because this time when they pulled Van from the SUV, they were not so rough. Someone was cooking over a wood fire, and Van smelled hickory mixed in with the char or roasted pork and grilled vegetables. She also smelled fresh laundry, and despite her own situation, she had the impression she was at someone's home, perhaps family and maybe, although it seemed unlikely, Belinda's family. But Van knew not to relax, and as they walked away from the smells of home and toward the scent of diesel and sweat, she steeled herself expecting rough treatment. It never came. They took her into a room and closed the door. She heard a woman's commanding voice give instructions to remove the hood. When they removed the hood, the wig Van was wearing slipped sideways and covered the left side of Van's face. Belinda laughed.

"I take it that's not your wig," she said. Van didn't respond, and Belinda motioned to have the wig removed.

"Well, Detective," Belinda said, "I was wondering if we might meet. I didn't expect to see you here."

Van looked back without a word. She had no reason to identify herself or anyone she might have been with.

"Perhaps you can explain what prompted you to follow me out of Pamplona."

"I like your choice of cigars," Van said.

"She speaks," said Belinda. "Well, I have a sense of humor, as well." Belinda motioned to her team, and the tallest soldier approached Van and took her hearing aids out of her ears and handed them to Belinda.

"Let's see how well you function without these." She let the hearing aids dangle and then put them in her hip pocket. Van stared at Belinda without emotion, while she studied the setting and the soldiers in the room with her. Belinda might have thought she was putting Van at a disadvantage, but Van's skills at reading lips had been honed since she was an infant. Without her hearing aids, Van could pretend not to hear and possibly Belinda would let her guard slip.

"Why are you here?" Belinda said to Van, and Van said nothing.

"Why are you following me?" she asked again, and Van said nothing.

"Get her some food," said Belinda to the squad. "And take off the cuffs. Just make sure she can't leave."

They closed and locked the door. Van looked around. The room she was in appeared to be an office with a small bed. She was seated in a chair next to a desk. There were books and papers on the desk and in a small bookcase next to the desk. She could tell that, if this team was responsible for abductions, this was not their normal hiding place. The papers were invoices, and the books were mechanics manuals. It looked to be a business, and by its smells, it must be a repair shop, possibly for farm vehicles. There was a door that led to a bathroom and in the bathroom a small window, too small to fit through, but at least Van could stand on the toilet and see the fields and the sun setting on the horizon. She smelled the plate before it got to the door. The soldier delivering the food set the plate on the desk but kept his hand on his revolver. Apparently, he was told to be cautious with Van. He pulled a bottle of Orange Crush out of his pocket and popped the metal top off with his thumb, a feat that honestly impressed Van. Van was hungry; she hadn't eaten anything all day. But she didn't trust the food. The soldier saw her hesitation and grabbed a handful of pork and shoved it in his mouth. He took a swig of Orange Crush to wash it down, turned, and left, locking the door. That was all Van needed. She finished off the plate in a few minutes and downed the remainder of the soda. Suddenly she got very tired, and she lay down on the bed and, despite her anxieties, passed out.

* * *

Belinda knew she was being reckless. But she convinced herself that she needed a break, just a few days to restore her energy and drive. That break was Pamplona and the running of the bulls. She called Hadj into her office at the Roda Labs and, without offering specifics, instructed him to manage the labs in her absence. Hadj had done great work with the Garny nanobots taken from the University of Navarra. He had successfully expanded the volume of bots through carefully managed self-replication chambers and was in the process of fashioning a variety of hot-cold projectiles that kept the bots inert until a heating element activated the bots into a weapon. His latest effort was focused on precision, narrowing the scope of a bot strike and eliminating the dirty aspects of bot-based projectiles, whether bullets or bombs. Hadj's technical brilliance garnered immense loyalty and respect from his teammates, and Belinda's faith in Hadj as a leader and as her principal lieutenant was absolute. She had no concern about the labs' continued operations if she left to enjoy a few well-deserved days of relaxing in Pamplona.

For her Pamplona trips, Belinda traveled under the Basque pseudonym Elizabeth Elcano, an homage to Ferdinand Magellan's Basque second-in-command, Juan Elcano. Elcano is credited with successfully completing the first global circumnavigation in 1522. Magellan is usually given the credit, but his claim was to find a transatlantic trade route to the East Indies through the passage at the southern tip of Chile now known as the Straits of Magellan. Unfortunately, Magellan was killed in a battle on the Maluku Islands, and it was Elcano who led Magellan's crew back to Spain through the Indian Ocean and around the treacherous Cape of Good Hope. Belinda pulled her falsified travel documents together along with several wads of cash and, in the pre-dawn hours, jumped on her favorite bike, a Harley Davidson Street Glide, and left Muro de Roda for Pamplona.

She always stayed at Calle Mercaderes 6, a five-story apartment complex overlooking La Curva de la Estafeta where the most damage occurred during the running. Her corner room had a balcony that looked over the Pamplona rooftops, and if she leaned out far enough, she could see the Pamplona bullring where the afternoon events were taking place. But the running was a sideshow for Belinda. She positioned herself at an ideal location where she could pick and choose from the young men whose only purpose in facing the bulls was to win the embraces of the many young women in attendance just to witness the heroics. Belinda was not young, but she was beautiful enough and could easily seduce the young and wild runners. No one knew who she was, and her various aliases had kept her anonymous. But she nevertheless was a legend among the runners who gathered early in the morning at her doorway at No. 6 hoping to be one of the chosen few, with "few" in quotes.

That morning Belinda had been inspired, and after the third runner to rip off his clothes and dive into Belinda's warm bed and open arms and legs, she decided it was enough for now and put on her silk robe, grabbed a cigar, and wandered down the apartment stairs to the large walnut doorway to observe the preparations for the morning run. Her final young suitor tossed on his white and red runner's uniform and bounded down the stairs ahead of her, throwing up his arms in triumph as he emerged from the doorway into the small expectant crowd gathered at the No. 6 entrance. The crowd cheered, once for the runner and then for Belinda as she leaned out the doorway, blowing her cigar smoke teasingly at the young men. Out of the corner of her eyes, she detected a runner whose wardrobe didn't fit into the costumery gathering in the plaza. Instead of the white and red, she was wearing a dark blue jogging suit that reminded Belinda of an FBI training suit. But it wasn't her wardrobe that made Belinda turn and look at the runner. Rather, it was the way the runner suddenly stopped and stared at her, as if she had made a snap identification. The young woman was Asian and quite pretty, and as they fixed on each other's gaze, Belinda made the connection. This woman was the same woman she had seen on her monitor when the FBI tried to serve her a warrant to search Ragnar Willowbrook. This same woman had stepped forward into gunfire to pull her ex-colleague, Dr. Leonard Freund, to safety before Belinda's black ops team could take him down. Belinda recalled that she wasn't FBI herself, but in the melee that ensued, Belinda had forgotten about her. Now she was staring directly at her standing in front of her in her home country. The young woman was the first to turn and run, but Belinda knew immediately she needed to do two things. She needed to abandon her love nest immediately, and she needed to hunt down this young woman before she could interfere in Belinda's plans. Kicking herself for being so foolish, Belinda raced upstairs and called Hadj, ordering him to assemble the team and fly to Pamplona. Then she cleaned up and put on a disguise and pulled all her belongings together. She asked the apartment manager to call her a taxi and waited inside the apartment lobby for the taxi to arrive. When it finally did, delayed by the police who were setting up for the running, she jumped through the front doorway and dropped into the back seat of the taxi, throwing her luggage in first and sliding in to make room for herself. She directed the taxi to the heliport where she expected Hadj to be waiting for her, and the taxi took off down the packed street. As they turned the first corner heading over a bridge, Belinda looked back and noticed a taxi that appeared to be following her. She told the driver to speed up and then changed her mind. She told the driver not to be obvious but to let the taxi follow them if that was what it was doing.

As they approached the heliport, Belinda jumped out and walked briskly toward Hadj and the waiting team. She told them she had been followed and directed a small group to circle around the parking lots and position themselves to see who was in the taxi. They reported it was a young Asian woman and watched as she climbed the knoll between the parking lots. They moved in behind her and pistol whipped her, knocking her to the ground. Then they hooded her and cuffed her and marched her to a black SUV waiting at the heliport. Belinda was angered to have her vacation ruined, but she had to admit that she was a bit impressed by the woman's tenaciousness. She had seen it in California and was witnessing it again in Spain. It wouldn't change the outcome, though. Belinda would not tolerate for very long a challenger as aggressive as this one.

Chapter 16.

An Idea Whose Time Has Come (Part II)

Bost Karnivan, from Providia, and Brian Johannsen met regularly. The respect each had for the other developed quickly and a friendship began to form. They spent hours in the labs at both Ragnar Willowbrook and Providia and devised multiple tests for deciphering the full capabilities of the nanobots. Bost was glad Brian introduced him to self-replicating capabilities of the carbon-capture bots. But he was not satisfied that the unique capabilities of these bots could be repeated. The ceramic bodies came from a silicate mineral not common to the United States and seemed to contribute to the heat necessary to cause vitrification, the process by which silicate is melted into glass. What was unique about this silicate was that it contained a small charge that sped up the heating process needed to turn the material into a superconducting ceramic without the use of an external source. Bost and Brian released the bots into airtight vacuum chambers to test the self-replication process and introduced different gases to see if it would impact the process. In some cases it did, and in one particular case, they introduced a small amount of pure hydrogen and created a flash that scorched the inside of the chamber and ruined it for further use.

But the work they did together that energized Brian the most involved the programming of smart dust with artificial intelligence. He expected that the use of AI in nanotechnology would be complicated. But Bost and his team had determined that nanobots can work in combination with each other to increase memory and storage capacity to a point where they responded to advanced programming. Bost was proud of the more creative applications of the platform. For example, he could upload a digital photograph and the bots would organize themselves into an almost exact replica of the image. Brian found a photograph that he and Van had taken together and sent it to Bost, and the nanobots seemed instinctively to recognize the shadowing in the photograph. Bost showed Brian how he could manipulate the image, and the bots refashioned themselves to give Brian large ears, facial hair, and male pattern baldness. Brian joked back it was no wonder Bost hadn't solved the self-replication problem, a point that sunk in a little too deep, and Brian had to calm Bost down with a pat on the back, reassuring Bost that the AI work he had done was incredible. They left the bots in the chamber, thinking the next day they would continue the AI experiments, and as they left the lab, they failed to see the bots continuing to refashion themselves in various images stored in the composite memory of the nanobot gel.

* * *

Van didn't sleep well in the room. She knew instinctively that she was in very deep trouble, and as the night wore on, she drifted in and out of a restless sleep. Twice she awoke shivering at the prospect of Belinda's malicious plans for her. She wandered into the bathroom and stared out the small porthole of a window, testing it but knowing she would never fit through it and escape. She searched for tools or weapons she might use on her guard, tried to pull nails out of the wall and to unscrew the toilet set, but everything failed. She fell asleep and dreamed that her mom and dad were looking for her and that she was trying to reach them but could not move her arms. Suddenly the scene shifted. War had arrived. The sky was dark, and heavy armored vehicles slogged across a muddy battlefield still smoking from the aftermath of an aerial assault. The female battalion leader was shouting commands to units preparing to assault the vehicles with armor-piercing RPGs. Van stood near the elder woman ready to take orders. The commander turned to Van, and Van looked directly into Belinda's face. The distant sounds of explosions seemed to be getting louder . . .

Van opened her eyes still troubled by the dream. Her hearing aids were laid out on the table next to the bed. She heard a muffled pounding and saw the door frame shake. She put on the hearing aids, and immediately the muffled sounds burst into a loud banging as someone yelled, "Breakfast! Get up and get dressed!" Van shook her head awake and pulled her shoes on as a lock turned and the door burst open.

"Jesus Christ!" she heard. "What does it take to get you out of bed?"

Van said nothing, and the guard set down a tray of eggs and toast with some coffee. Van picked up an odd scent from the food, but already having eaten dinner and still hazy from a restless night, she grabbed a fork and gulped down the eggs and toast. As she sipped the coffee to wash down her food, she felt what she thought was the fatigue of sleep and fought against it, willing herself to wake up and face her captors. But the desire to sleep was too great, and she slumped back onto the bed as the coffee fell from her grasp and splashed on the floor.

"Put her in the Escalade," Belinda instructed. The guard, joined by others, tied her hands and feet and covered her head with a black hood. They hoisted her body into the middle row of the SUV and climbed in after. They headed back into the city center to the bullring at the bottom of the running course. They parked at the rear of the ring opposite the entrance, then checked to see that Van was still unconscious, removed her hood and ties, and lifted her out of the vehicle. Following the SUV on a low-profile Ducati and wearing a black helmet, black gloves, and a black riding suit, Belinda pulled alongside the parked Escalade. The guards draped Van's inert body on the back of the bike, lightly secured her hands and legs to make her appear to be riding tandem, and Belinda took off for the course.

At the top of the course, runners were gathering for the last day of the running. Dust rose from the bull pens as the cowherds shouted and smacked the bulls with sticks and whips, working them into a frenzy. At the sound of the church bells, they opened the gate, and bulls poured out of the pen, slipping on cobblestones as they made their escape directly onto the course and in the direction of the red scarves bobbing and weaving in front of them. They recovered their footing and raced at the red scarves, eyes wide with fear and rage at the beatings they had just taken and compelled forward by the blood red in front of them. They raced down Santo Domingo and into the Town Hall Plaza. They caught up with the red scarves and lowered their heads to shred through the runners. Several of the runners jumped aside, and the bulls' momentum kept them racing forward even as the maddening red patches began to dwindle. Suddenly a motorcycle with two riders bounced up an adjacent staircase and burst through a gap in the temporary fencing and appeared at the front of the runners. The bikers raced ahead of the runners down Calle de Mercaderes, and as they sped around La Curva a.k.a. "Dead Man's Corner," to the crowd's horror, the back rider seemed to slip off the back of the bike and crumpled onto the cobblestones directly in the path of the runners and the racing bulls. The driver stopped and looked back and then, to the shock of the crowd, raced away from the scene, leaving the body of the young rider in the middle of the course.

Van's hip and then her head hit the cobblestones hard. The sharp pain lulled her from the silent darkness, and she inhaled a mix of oil and cow dung that made her cough and seemed faintly reminiscent. She lay there lured back into the darkness, and then she felt it: first a rumble and then a thumping that was chaotic and disorganized. She wanted to move, but her arms and legs refuse to respond. Her vision started to clear, and she could see fuzzy faces and wide eyes staring at her behind barricades. The checkered blue caps of the police were pushing through the crowds to get to her. The first runners passed her, and she raised her head to see the bobbing and snorting heads of bulls rounding the curve. One bull went down and slid on its side into the barricades fronting the corner grocery. She smelled the sweat from the bulls, and a few hands reached down to pull her aside but gave up quickly to keep running. The lead bull dropped its head, horns reaching forward to toss her aside. She felt two strong hands latch onto her arms and jerk her out of the bull's path. The runner threw her over his shoulders. Then, reaching the concrete wall, he set her on her wobbly feet, commanding her to stand back tightly against the wall as another bull raced by and grazed them both with its horn, ripping the shirt and scratching the tightened stomach of the hero runner who had abandoned the race to save her.

He spoke to Van, but without her hearing aids, she heard nothing and only now felt the abject fear of the moment, recognizing that she had barely escaped with her life. When the bulls passed, the runner walked her to the nearest barricade. He was about to hand her over to the crowd and then realized that the police were likely to arrest her, thinking that she had recklessly driven onto the bulls' course, endangering both runners and bulls with the motorcycle. He turned her back toward the street and walked her quickly down the rows of barricades and then off the course where he found an open door and pulled her into the foyer. There was a single chair there, and he carefully set her onto the chair. Van's head was beginning to clear, and she pulled her arm from the hero, thinking he had other ideas, and he let go and immediately stepped back.

"I'm sorry," he said.

"Where am I?" Van asked him, straining in the dark to see the speaker and read his lips.

"You are in Pamplona."

"I know it's Pamplona. Was I just on the bulls' course?"

"You were. That was very foolish. Why would you do that?"

"What do you mean? What did I do?" Van was still fighting off the effects of the narcotic.

"You and your friend rode your motorcycle right into the bulls' course? You know that's very dangerous and, by the way, unlawful."

"What motorcycle? What friend? I don't know what you are saying." Her head started throbbing. "My head hurts. I think I need a doctor."

"You don't remember me?"

"Excuse me?" she responded, squeezing her eyes against the pain.

"We met the other day. It's Tolo."

Van looked up through the dusty air and made out a familiar face. "Oh my God, Tolo." Van could barely speak, but she recognized him. "I think I need a doctor," she repeated and then passed out.

* * *

When Brian returned to Ragnar Willowbrook the next morning, he was excited to get back into the lab. Leonard tapped on the door to his office.

"Good morning, Mr. CEO," he said hoping to get a rise out of Brian.

"Leonard!" Brian said a little too loud, still unaccustomed to the size of his office. "Good morning. I have some exciting news!"

"I'm sure you do, but I have some disturbing news."

"What's that?" Brian responded a little annoyed about being distracted from the latest nanobot developments.

"You remember the Los Angeles detective who we ran into at Providia?"

"You know I do." Leonard had his attention.

"She's in a hospital in Spain."

Brian felt a rush of conflicting emotions. "What is she doing in a hospital in Spain?"

"Detective Eng called her office in Los Angeles and said she had seen Belinda in

Pamplona. Apparently, the FBI told her to sit tight and wait for help, but she didn't, and the last word they got, she was admitted into the hospital drugged to the point of overdose."

Brian felt a tinge of jealousy that Van might be in Spain with someone else, but he set it aside.

"Do we have any way of reaching her?"

"I thought you might want to try. Here's the number. She's still in ICU, Ward 8."

Brian took the number and mulled over whether he should call her. He still felt it triggering emotions, but he knew that, if Belinda was still active, Ragnar Willowbrook might be a target. It would help to talk to Van, even if it was difficult, and he was genuinely concerned about her.

"Thanks, Leonard."

Leonard smiled as he backed out and closed the office door.

Brian sat as his desk and stared out the window. Then he reached for the phone. They connected him to Van's bed. Charlie answered the call.

"Is she ok?" Brian asked.

"Brian! Good to hear from you." He winked at Van, who rolled her eyes and adjusted her hearing aids. "Let me put her on."

"Are you ok?" he repeated to Van.

"Hello, Brian," she responded stifling her own feelings. "Are you in California?"

"Yes, I'm at the labs now. Leonard told me what happened. Sounds like a lot of people are concerned about you."

"I know. I am feeling a little stupid."

"I don't know about that. Sounds like you exposed Belinda's hiding place."

"She is here, at least she was. I have no idea now. I still don't remember what happened."

"If I may ask, what are you doing in Spain? Looks like it's Pamplona. Were you there for the bulls?"

"I came here with a good friend. It's my first trip to Europe, or anywhere international. And yes, we came to watch the bulls run. But then I put him and his family at risk. I feel terrible about that. But at least they got out and back to the States."

Brian took a breath. Of course, she would be there with a guy. But that didn't matter.

"I'm sorry what happened, but I am glad you are ok. I know you are still recovering. Let's be in touch in a few days. I'm going to want to find out more about Belinda. I am worried she could show up back here. For now, is there anything I can do?"

"Not now. I'm still a little tired. They are taking good care of me here. Thank you for calling, Brian. It is nice to hear your voice."

"Yours too, Van.

It was hard to hang up. Brian felt an unwanted urge to keep talking, but he pushed back his chair and put on his lab coat. As he left the office, he asked his assistant Bob to set up a meeting in the conference room with his directors, including his new director of security, Jaward Kamara. Brian had called Jaward shortly after he started at Ragnar Willowbrook. He had made Jaward a good offer to run security at Ragnar, and he was pleasantly surprised when Jaward accepted and moved out of the Hollywood scene to join him in the Silicon Valley. Jaward's only condition was that he be allowed to bring a few of his club members to support him, and Brian didn't hesitate. They were all trained Marines and had been part of elite fighter attack squadron. They would make a great security team and a good counter, if needed, to any special ops group that Belinda might reassemble as her new team.

Chapter 17.

General Tom Warner

The Pentagon is that unique five-sided building symbolizing strength and security that houses the top brass of the four main branches of the US military—Army, Navy, Air Force, and Marine Corps—along with the two newest branches including the Coast Guard and Space Force. Contrary to popular belief, the geometric design capable of withstanding the greatest force is not a pentagon but a triangle, although debate rages over whether it should be a circle. The Pentagon was not designed as a pentagon, because it was a strong design. The land on which the Pentagon was built, formerly owned by Confederate General Robert E. Lee, happened to be bounded by five roads that coincidentally formed the shape of a pentagon. Thus, on September 11, 2001, when terrorists flew American Airlines Flight 77 into the southwest side of the building, it was not the shape of the building that protected the workforce of more than thirty-three thousand. Rather, it was a matter of coincidence that the side of the building that was hit was under renovation and therefore was mostly empty, though 184 personnel were killed in the attack. That said, due in part to its unique design and tragic history, the Pentagon has become a National Historic Landmark and a mastery of architectural planning and construction, five layers deep on each of its five sides.

General Tom Warner hated the Pentagon. The building was a maze to navigate, and it felt like he walked several miles every day just to attend mostly useless in-person meetings. Even though the military had installed the best and most expensive firewalls that Silicon Valley geniuses had developed, military brass continued to oppose the use of Google Hangouts or Zoom or any other Internet-based video conferencing technologies. He wondered if they even knew that the Internet was first conceived as a military technology. Military intelligence, as he enjoyed reminding his colleagues, was an oxymoron, and he enjoyed that mostly because he knew most of them didn't know what an oxymoron was. Meetings at the Pentagon were always in person, and to General Tom Warner, that meant little more than a new pair of shoes every six months.

Thus, the general found good reasons to travel and travel often. He was especially fond of the Silicon Valley and had made many important contacts there. He learned several years ago about the work being done at Ragnar Willowbrook, and he knew he had a special ally in Dr. Belinda Armendariz who seemed to have a unique appreciation of the military. He noted that she had an affinity for special ops, and he had helped her assemble a top-notch security team composed of former Green Berets and Navy Seals. He also knew that she liked testing and assessing new military inventions and she was not shy of demanding the highest prices. He suspected that she had millions stashed in unregulated accounts all over the world, and he admired her for it. When he got the chance to have billionaire Garny McDonough's nanobot invention analyzed, which he discovered on a trip to Paris, he turned immediately to Ragnar Willowbrook.

But General Tom Warner walked a fine line. Guarding the security of the United States of America required risk taking, and the persons he worked with to get that done did not always share his goals. Still, he knew the moral high ground was a vulnerable location best suited to religious and political idealists but less than optimum when dealing with the rogues of the world. He didn't even mind the rogues of the world so long as they were his rogues, and in his mind, Dr. Belinda Armendariz was his rogue. He met her on one of his Silicon Valley adventures at a company that was exploring military use cases for a new supercomputer it had built in conjunction with NASA. The supercomputer, the SENSA XO, was the second fastest supercomputer in the world. Initially the SENSA XO was intended for non-military applications, like engineering space flight, but the company was a video gaming chipset manufacturer familiar with the popularity of military themes in video gaming. Exploring actual military applications was an obvious next step. The company had hired Belinda as a consultant on several projects given the rise of Ragnar Willowbrook Labs under her leadership. The theme of the meeting was World War III, and the company had invited Warner to meet with its nascent AI team along with the top minds behind its most popular video games. Warner was especially impressed by the developer of Sim City, but it was Belinda's probing questions that caught his attention and he invited her to dinner. When Garny McDonough first showcased his nanobot carbon-capture technology and offered to let General Warner option the technology to explore alternative uses, Warner immediately turned to Belinda and Ragnar Willowbrook.

Warner maintained his relationship with the video gaming company, a company with a close relationship to several Hollywood producers. Warner's favorite contact there was its CFO, Christopher Deckwalder who, even as a finance wizard, knew a lot about smart dust and the latest applications of nanotechnology. Like Warner, Deckwalder enjoyed good scotch and fine cigars, and Warner used to bring Deckwalder to Washington, D.C., to visit his favorite cigar bar where they pontificated late into the night about smart dust and its potential for military application. They also discussed the debate over the ethics of smart dust and if it would impede the advance of the technology. It was there they came up with the idea for a movie that might counter that opposition and popularize smart dust as an exciting new technology. Deckwalder thought he could sell the idea to Jerry Cortez and, with Warner backing the movie, get it financed. Warner loved the idea, and they discussed storylines and characters and even threw out well known actors' names. Deckwalder nixed it immediately, and they continued late into the night, laughing at their presumption but all the while deadly serious about making the picture. Deckwalder suggested they hire a professional scriptwriter to assemble the storyboard and one of Cortez's favorite agencies to handle the pitch. He knew Cortez received hundreds of manuscripts a month, and even though Cortez and Deckwalder were friends, he knew Cortez would not waste his time on a poorly conceived idea. In addition, the connection between Tom Warner and Jerry Cortez needed to be kept remote, and Deckwalder was more than capable of handling the deal. Warner used a special Pentagon fund for his pet projects and had carte blanche to spend any amount he believed was necessary to guard the country's national interests. Deckwalder and Warner outlined the story and the initial financing details on a single sheet of Pentagon stationary. The opening offer would be $50 million. Warner signed and dated the sheet and sealed it in a manila envelope for Deckwalder to keep in a secure place. As soon as Deckwalder confirmed that Cortez would do the picture, Warner would transfer funds into an account managed by Deckwalder under the name of a new production company that they agreed, after a long conversation, would be called Critical Mass Limited. Although they were prepared to hire the best talent, they expected Cortez to add a handful of additional production companies who would supplement the first $50 million with whatever Cortez needed to complete the picture. Warner's connection with the CIA ran deep, and he had run multiple joint operations combing special ops with hand-selected CIA agents. To prevent the picture from being connected back to the Pentagon, Warner would rely on agents to carry communications between Warner and Deckwalder. Critical Mass itself would be a front, composed of agents with a history in Hollywood. Warner handed Deckwalder the manila envelope. Deckwalder looked at Warner and said, "We can do this."

"We can, Deck, and we will," replied General Tom Warner. "This is the easy part."

* * *

Delta Flight Number 4609 descended onto the tarmac at Los Angeles International, and Aida Godinez looked over the landmark known as the Theme Building. The William Pereira design, which back in 1960 tried to turn Los Angeles International Airport into a futuristic air travel hub, now sat there empty like a dead bug in the middle of a computer chip. I would have enjoyed that as a young child, thought Aida who had never been to Disneyland. She rode the escalator from the departure level down to baggage claim, where a chauffeur stood waiting holding a placard with her last name "Godinez" written on the otherwise blank card. She directed the chauffeur to grab her bags, and they found the limousine parked in a no-parking zone. An airport police officer stood by the limousine. "Jerry Cortez thanks you," said the chauffeur and flipped the officer a $100 bill. The officer tipped his hat and walked off. The chauffeur helped Aida climb into the back seat, a bit of an effort given her age. She pushed herself to the middle bench, in reach of glasses and liquor bottles stacked in a decorative bar. Uncomfortable, she then pushed herself back to the back seat where she could easily watch the driver who seemed far away. As the car pulled onto World Way, the main road serving LAX terminals, Aida leaned forward and shouted, "Excuse me, sir?"

"Yes, ma'am," replied the driver.

"Do you mind if I sit up front with you? I think I might be more comfortable."

"Not at all," he laughed.

* * *

"We got her."

Detective Paul Young leaned smartly against the doorjamb to Detective Charles Darling's office.

"They are booking her now."

Van looked up, irritated at being interrupted. It was one her pet peeves. Anyone who interrupted her while she was speaking demonstrated not just a lack of courtesy, but ignorance. Van wasn't arrogant about her intelligence, but if she made the effort to speak her mind, those around her might want to listen to what she had to say. It didn't surprise her that it was Detective Paul Young. She looked back at Charlie who nodded in assent.

"Go ahead, Detective," Charlie responded.

"Min Kang," he responded as if nothing could possibly matter more. "She is being booked for the murder of Trey Nguyen at Paramount Studios."

Van started to jump out of her chair, but Charlie laid a soft hand on her arm and beckoned patience.

"What evidence?" Charlie queried Paul.

"It seems your little protégé hasn't told you everything she knows," Young replied dismissive of Van's research on the case.

"And what is that?" said Van stifling her anger. Paul Young's jealousy of Van's success in the office was a poorly kept secret. He never passed up any chance he had to show her up and prove that she didn't belong in the bureau despite her record and reputation.

"Relax, Detective Eng," said Detective Young. "You're doing a fine job. You just missed a couple key elements."

"Come on, Paul," Charlie answered, now getting irritated himself. "Tell us."

"Ms. Kang was on the lot the day of the murder."

Charlie looked at Van. "Is that corroborated?"

"It is," said Detective Young. "But there's more."

"We explored this line, Paul," said Van. "Ms. Kang's car was on the lot. That doesn't make her culpable. We also know that Min Kang and Trey Nguyen had become friends and she was getting close to him. That raises the possibility of a crime of passion, but absent more, it is not enough to book her. She knew about the movie script, and she's the one who led us to Providia, a connection we are still exploring. We questioned Cortez's crew about her and Trey's relationship, and nothing turned up anything suggestive of motive."

"Did you search the car?"

"I didn't have probable cause."

"You should have found some. There's a weapon."

Van studied Detective Young. She didn't like this chess match he seemed intent on sucking her into. She turned to Charlie. "That's not a surprise; her brother was killed in prison by a rival gang."

"There's a match."

"The bullets match?"

"We're running ballistics right now, but the shell casings from the Cortez building match the model. It was a 9-mm Glock."

"When was it last fired?" Van pressed, but Detective Young smiled. "We have what we need to book her. We'll get the rest. She is awaiting questioning now. Feel free to listen in."

"Good luck with that," said Van.

Min Kang sat on a steel chair with her hands cuffed to the table. Van studied her through the one-way glass and began to doubt her own premonitions. Min had been very close to her brother, and his death would have been shocking notwithstanding their run-and-gun lifestyle. The years in prison certainly hardened her, and who knows what Trey might have uncovered about her or what he might have done to invoke her wrath. Min Kang was not someone to take lightly. Detective Young

entered the interrogation room with Detective Robert Johnson. He introduced himself and Detective Johnson.

"I remember you," she said to Johnson. "You came to see me with that deaf detective."

"Ms. Kang," started Detective Young, "you are being booked on suspicion of murder. I'm sure you understand the consequences of murder." He emphasized the word.

"There are no consequences if you are innocent," she replied, "even if it is murder," she said mockingly.

Detective Young set the bagged Glock 9 on the table.

"You recognize this weapon?"

"What I recognize, Detective, are my Miranda rights."

"Do you want an attorney?"

"You're damn right I want an attorney."

"That's your call, Ms. Kang. But you should know things here can go very bad for you if you refuse to cooperate. If we can talk, there's a lot we can do to help you."

"You're kidding me, right?"

"I'm not."

Min looked at the one-way glass and then up at the camera. She shouted to the camera, "Can I get a professional in here? Please!"

Van smiled at Charlie who was watching the interrogation.

Detective Young slammed his fist on the table.

"You were there, Ms. Kang, that night. We have witnesses."

Min thought of her romantic interlude with Trey, and it made her sad. But she said nothing.

"Your boyfriend make you mad?"

Nothing.

"You find out he cheated? Was that it? You think you are so hot no one would cheat on you? You got mad and did what your dead brother would have done?"

Nothing.

"Give it up, Ms. Kang. We have you nailed."

"You don't know shit," Min answered quietly but defiantly.

"Book her," Detective Young said to Detective Johnson.

They rose from their seats, and Van entered the interrogation room.

"We're done here," said Detective Young to Van.

Van looked at Min who was raging at Detective Young.

"Your attorney is on her way," she said. "Do you need anything? Water or coffee?"

"Coffee, please," Min responded. "Black with sugar."

Van looked at Robert Johnson. "Get her some coffee," she instructed him. "Black with sugar."

Johnson looked at Young who was intently watching Van. He shrugged and said, "Do what she says."

Van turned toward Min. "One question, Min," she said. "You can answer it or not."

Detectives Young and Johnson stopped by the door.

"Do you know Jerry Cortez?"

"The director of Trey's movie?"

"He is not the director, but his company is producing it."

"Sure. I have heard of him."

"Have you ever been to his production office in Santa Monica?"

"I don't know. Trey dropped off script notes in a lot of places."

"You never met Cortez?"

"I don't think so."

Outside the room, Detective Young approached Van. "What was that about?"

"You should let her go," said Van. "You don't have enough to hold her."

"We'll see what ballistics says."

"I'd wager it's not a match," said Van. "At best, it'll be inconclusive."

"What's the deal with Cortez?"

"I don't know yet. But this is not a gang war or a lovers' quarrel."

"Stake your job on that?" replied Detective Young, with a slight grin.

"If that's what you need me to do, Paul, then yes."

Chapter 18.

Breakthroughs

One nanometer is one billionth of a meter. There are 25,400,000 nanometers in one inch. One sheet of paper is 100,000 nanometers thick. If the diameter of a marble were reduced to a single nanometer, the diameter of the earth would be one meter. Scientists had dabbled in nanoscale experimentation for a hundred years, but the efforts took on a new vigor in 1959 after the delivery of Richard Feynman's breakthrough lecture on nanotechnology, "There is Plenty of Room at the Bottom." It took two decades, but by the early 1980s, researchers produced nanoscale crystalline quantum dots with semiconducting capabilities. Within just a few more years, widespread nanoscale manufacturing was happening all around the globe. The invention of the scanning tunnelling microscope now allowed scientists to assemble compound molecules from independent molecules. Soon thereafter, a variety of novel consumer items with special properties, such as antibacterial socks, appeared on the market. Nanomanufacturing took another leap forward in the early 1990s when carbon nanotubes were discovered. By 2005, researchers were using algorithms based on crystals to induce molecular self-assembly and a year later produced a nanoscale car, the movement of which was controlled by heat and at extreme temperatures moved too fast to be tracked. In 2010, IBM used a nanoscale silicon tip to produce a three-dimensional relief map of the world 1/1000 the size of a grain of salt. The process took 2 minutes and 23 seconds.

Brian Johannsen and Bost Karnivan were spending so much time together at the lab, their colleagues joked about them being an old married couple. But Brian found himself driven in a way he hadn't felt since graduate school, and Bost was the perfect partner to inflame his inspiration. Their initial efforts at blending artificial intelligence with the nanobots introduced an ability to mimic images. These nanobots recognized shadow and gradations of light and dark in images, which allowed the bots to reproduce images, perfect reflections of black and white pictures and photographs. They spent days trying to generate the same results with color pictures and then moved to sounds and music. But these early experiments were no more than preparation for what they knew to be two critical developments in the usability of the bots. First, they needed to eliminate the bots' toxicity to human beings. Garny McDonough, inventor of the bots, never addressed this problem because he never tied the tragic events in Armenia's capital city, Yerevan, or even what had happened at UCLA or the Tran Lab on Bainbridge Island to the bots he had produced in Tajikistan. But Brian knew from personal experience that these bots were deadly. That problem had to be addressed. The second problem concerned the control of the bots. The bots' ability to self-replicate meant that, much like viruses, he and Bost could easily lose control of the bots and their effects if they were not restricted to the vacuum chambers in which the experiments were being conducted. But of the two, which was more important? If he could address toxicity, control was less critical of an issue. But without control, a small accident could be disastrous. He and Bost agreed that it would take longer to address toxicity. They would likely need to find alternative metals and substances that might not be as effective as the existing combination. Control felt like a more solvable problem, and AI might help them get there faster. They spent the next several weeks experimenting with temperature, sound, and light with varying but less-than-satisfying degrees of success.

When Garny McDonough needed to solve the problem of self-replication, he looked to microbiology and studied the behavior of viruses. To solve the problem of control, Brian Johannsen also found his answer in nature. One day, on his way to work on the Gold Wing, he accidentally drove through a swarm of bees and was stung on his wrists and neck. Thankfully, he wasn't allergic to bees, but it hurt like hell and pissed him off. He considered himself unlucky to have driven through the swarm and wondered how the swarm ended up in the middle of the road. That thought led to the next, the cause of the swarm, which led to the next, the role of the queen bee in managing the swarm, and a light bulb went off. What if he could program into one of the bots the attributes of a queen honeybee? If the other bots would follow the directions of the queen, he didn't need to control the mass of bots. He just had to control the queen. Bost was ecstatic and told Brian the idea was almost as good as some of his own. They went about building a queen bot and tried out different types of biomechanical pheromones that the other bots could recognize. Through those pheromones, they programmed a variety of signals like start, stop, huddle, expand, left, right, and so on. They made the queen's instructions primary, and where the queen bot was present, the "worker" bots would not respond unless the queen directed them to respond. Show the queen a photo and instruct the queen to replicate; the bots replicated the photo. Show the queen a photo and instruct the queen not to replicate; the bots would stay dormant. The idea was so novel that Leonard Freund was certain they might win a Nobel Prize and bring glory back to Ragnar Willowbrook. Brian was too caught up in the effort to worry about awards and recognition. Now that they had unlocked the key to control, they needed to solve for toxicity. Brian expected that would take time. He enlisted Bill Perkins the Third and the UCLA research team to study the problem and in particular the methods that pharmaceutical companies use to control or eliminate the toxic effects of new drugs and waited to see the results as he continued to explore more complex control maneuvers through the queen bot.

* * *

Hidden in the underground laboratory at Muro de Roda, Hadj Arkoun felt like he was in heaven. The small town of Ainsa was a short hike from the lab down a steep hill. The town had several bars and small but impressive restaurants where he could relish in the local cuisine. He enjoyed those evenings, because Belinda had given him a blank check to spend whatever he needed to turn the small petri dish of nanobots into weapons of mass destruction. But when he was not in the village, he was hard at work in the lab. He had spent the first several months at Roda growing the bots and now held several hundred pounds of bots in cold storage. His first thoughts on weaponizing the bots focused on the use of heat. The bots seemed to replicate faster in hotter temperatures, and the most effective temperature seemed to be just below the melting point of the porcelain body. He experimented with the toxicity of the bots, subjecting several unfortunate small animals to the shock of exposure and death. He wasn't satisfied with the results. The lethal impact took too long, and he knew that eventually someone would develop a spray or a pill that would protect them from the toxic effects of the bots. In order to effectively weaponize the bots, he needed to increase both the toxicity of the bots and the speed of its effects. He considered forming the bots into a dirty bomb, infecting the bots with active uranium or plutonium molecules. Even though he found dirty bombs to be a highly effective means of terror, he did not like the lack of control. He quickly realized that, like the guided rockets that had destroyed his boyhood village, he wanted to develop a weapon with pinpoint accuracy, immediate in its impacts and capable of focusing in on a specific target. As he reflected on the need for precision and control, he decided to start small and perfect the control mechanism. His first invention was a new type of small arms. When he showed it to Belinda, she asked him how a bot bullet might be any better than an ordinary bullet. Both would kill by sheer impact. Hadj nailed a target sheet at four hundred meters in an underground test range that he and Belinda had constructed. He instructed a technician wearing a hazmat suit to place a cage of hamsters on the floor below the target. He grabbed Remington MSR, a tactical precision rifle with a range of a thousand yards and fit it into a secure port on the firing side of the range. These bullets didn't need to hit a target. They just had to get close. Hadj was a better marksman than Belinda had expected, and he hit just above the bullseye. The cap of the bullet shattered, and a small cloud of bots emerged, filled the space around the cage, and in a few minutes sprinkled to the ground. Hadj ordered the technician into the enclosed range who brought the cage back. Belinda didn't need an explanation. She confirmed the hamsters were dead and then told Hadj, "Go bigger."

* * *

Van was right about the ballistics test. It came back inconclusive even though Min owned the same type of handgun that killed Trey. Detective Young had been forced to release Min Kang, but he let her go with a warning that he would be keeping his eyes on her. Min laughed out loud in a way that she now knew irritated Detective Young and batted her eyes sarcastically. "Oh, Detective," she said, "that's what all the boys say." Van couldn't suppress a chuckle.

Van and Martin Richard hung out a few more times after she returned from Pamplona, but something about the events in Pamplona changed the relationship. Martin repeatedly told Van he should have stayed with her in Spain so he could protect her. But as gentle as she could, she reminded him this was not the movies and that this evil person and her henchmen probably would have killed them both. The conversation made Martin feel impotent, and as hard as Van tried to reassure him that he was the sexiest man in her life, they both knew something had changed. Martin's parents had taken a special interest in Van and invited her to dinner regularly with their Hollywood friends, hoping the luster of Hollywood would improve her impressions of their son. Van enjoyed the dinners and made some new friends, but nothing changed. As the child of Hollywood elite, Martin was never at a loss for female attention, and Van encouraged the distractions by turning her focus back to her work. Detective Young's failed attempt to pin the murder on Min Kang troubled Van. Resolution of the case would have brought a sense of relief, and a part of Van hoped it would have ended there. Instead, she felt growing anxiety of an unsolved murder and an apparently connected and unsolved attempt at murder.

Peggy Rice had recovered from the gunshot wound and was released from the SNF. She still didn't like to go into the office, and her boss didn't fault her and let her work from her home in Malibu. Van walked to the front door wondering why someone would build a home two hundred feet off Pacific Coast Highway, the busiest and probably noisiest road in all of California. Great location for a deaf community, she mused.

Peggy's sister came to the door.

"May I help you?"

"I'm Detective Van Eng of the LAPD. I believe Peggy Rice is expecting me."

"Sure. Just a minute."

She closed the door and left Van on the porch.

Van heard footsteps and a woman who sounded like Peggy yelling, "Jesus Christ, Alex, you can't leave her outside!"

The door opened, and Peggy stood there in a robe with her sister standing sheepishly behind her.

"Come in; come in. I'm so sorry. This whole situation has my sister on edge. She didn't mean to be rude."

Van smiled. "Perfectly understandable. Please don't—"

"Come in; come in." Peggy interrupted. She led Van to a porch overlooking the breaking waves of the Pacific Ocean. It was utterly serene, the exact opposite of the front door.

Peggy was still talking. "Would you like a Diet Coke?" Peggy remembered what Van drank in the office.

"You remembered. Yes, please. That would be nice."

"The bullet messed with my amygdala but thankfully not my hippocampus. My memory skills are fine, but I may burst out crying for no apparent reason."

"I'm sorry."

"Don't be. I'm still here, still tetchy and still working on this damn movie script."

"Tetchy?"

"I'm a curmudgeon. Never mind. Let's get started. Alex! Bring us two Diet Cokes!"

"On it!" Van heard her voice echoing from the kitchen.

"I've been mulling this over now for weeks and I have some questions, but let's hear your questions first."

"Absolutely. Some of these are going to sound like questions I asked you about Trey."

"Hit me."

Van started with the basics. What did Peggy recall about that day? Anything unusual? Did she hear anything in the garage? Did she see anything before she was hit with the bullet? Peggy had nothing to add to what Van already knew. Then she began probing into Peggy's feelings about the movie script.

"We've discussed this before, but you are still describing it as the 'damn movie script.' Do you still think there is a connection between the script and Trey's murder and now your injury?"

"I do."

"Ok, let's start with these." Van pulled out the stack of cards that Cortez had handed her. Each card was covered in plastic. "You are familiar with these?"

"Probably not all of them. But I forwarded to Jerry anything that seemed threatening. Those were his instructions." Peggy flipped through the cards. "I'm not sure all these are real."

Van recalled Cortez handing her the cards and how he had dismissed any connection between them and the murder. She and Charlie had reviewed them at the bureau and had them dusted for prints without success. A handwriting analyst reviewed the cards and sorted them by varying styles. Nothing about them suggested they were anything but the work of kooks, as Cortez described. It had not occurred to Van or Charlie that they might be fakes. But why would someone fake a threat about an obscure technology?

"What makes you think they are fakes? Someone shot you, Peggy."

"Something about the script isn't working for me."

"What do you mean?"

"The movie is about this runner who goes to Hawaii and develops a flesh-eating virus who basically gets saved by nanobots."

"I kind of agree it doesn't sound very plausible."

"Let me get you a copy. Take it home and read it carefully. Let's talk when you are done."

Peggy handed Van a copy of the script. "Feel free to mark it up."

Chapter 19.

Weaponized

There's a long history of commercial products and use cases resulting from inventions originally designed for the military. The Internet started in the United States as ARPANET, a top-secret communications network that would withstand nuclear attack. England and France developed their own versions of ARPANET around the same time, allowing for the possibility of a global Internet. Duct tape was not originally developed for air conditioning ducts – it started as a waterproof sealer for ammunition cases in World War II. Wireless communications, radar for commercial airlines, bug spray, GPS for mapping, superglue, and space flight booster rockets were all initially developed for the military. Perhaps less obvious, tampons likewise were initially a military invention. Cotton menstrual pads had been around for decades, but tampons weren't invented until World War I when a shortage of cotton made it necessary to find a cheap alternative method of managing the flow of blood from battlefield injuries. An American company developed what it called "cellucotton" using wood pulp and sold it to the military for bandages. Red Cross nurses adapted the new material for their own hygienic purposes, and the same company eventually repurposed the material and marketed a new product called "Kotex."

The success that Brian and Bost had manipulating nanobot swarms using a "queen" bot got General Tom Warner's attention. He asked Ragnar Willowbrook to set up a demonstration. Bost pulled in his team from Providia, and Brian brought Bill Perkins and the UCLA team up to the Santa Cruz Mountain Lab. He also called Van and let her know about the demonstration in the event the attorneys prosecuting or defending the case against Derek Whitestone wanted to attend. In order to expand the size of the demonstration, Brian had a special three-story chamber constructed on RWL grounds. Two stories of the chamber stood above ground, and one story remained underground. All three stories of the chamber could be seen from all sides with seating above and below ground. The UCLA team had been working for months on a system for rendering the bots safe for human exposure. All they had accomplished so far was develop a spray with a cytokine inhibitor that if inhaled protected anyone exposed to the swarm that otherwise would put a person into anaphylactic shock. The spray worked well; they had tested it on several different species before human trials, and it worked every time. But they had not been able to produce a single bot with the same functionality and intelligence as Garny's bots, let alone a bot free of toxic effects. Bill Perkins was experimenting with a special molecular "jacket" that had the same effect as the spray, but he was months away from perfecting it. So, Brian built the demonstration chamber. The bots would remain inside the chamber and the audience protected from any impacts on the outside. As a secondary protection, Brian set up an overhead system that would release the spray if any bots escaped the chamber and triggered a special alarm.

General Tom Warner showed up to the demonstration early with Christopher Deckwalder, and Brian showed them the grounds and the new demonstration chamber. Warner, still suffering from the effects of Garny's disastrous trial in Paris, told Brian he would prefer to stay above ground. He added that he trusted the spray would work and the demonstration would be fine, but he had brought his own gas mask just in case. Brian saw Van arrive with Charlie and the attorneys. He welcomed them and directed them to sit in the above-ground seats. Below ground, Bill Perkins' team took reserved seats alongside researchers from Providia that had been a part of

Bost's AI team. Jaward stationed his security team on the perimeters. He had objected to Brian's showmanship and wanted the entire demonstration indoors. As the sun dipped below the horizon, the lights around the demonstration chamber dimmed. Bost had come up with the idea of painting the bots with a phosphorus molecular array, so Brian fitted the chamber with black lights to illuminate the swarm. The chamber filled with a light purple mist as the sky darkened. Brian and Bost took to the stage and explained the theory of the queen honeybee and how they used it in combination with AI to garner control over the swarm of glowing purple bots that filled the chamber. They introduced key supports of the effort including Leonard Freund, Tom Warner, and Christopher Deckwalder. Brian described the work the UCLA team was doing and had Bill Perkins join them on the stage. They thanked the audience for coming and stepped over to a control panel. In the center of the chamber stood a three-sided screen. The screens flashed a large image of the

Labs' RWL logo, and immediately the bots replicated a three-dimensional RWL in front of each screen. The RWL logo dissolved into the name "Providia," and the bots followed suit. Then the screen flashed a series of increasingly complex images of historical figures and Hollywood actors, and the bots responded in kind. Christopher Deckwalder turned to Tom Warner and said, "This is incredible." Warner wasn't smiling. He focused intently on what he saw, and up to now all he had seen was picture painting and nothing he could use. Next Brian introduced sound, and the bots responded to changes in sound with a fascinating display of shapes and pulsating movement. Warner started to get impatient.

The screen went dark, and the bots returned to a purple mist form. Brian began typing in commands, and out of the center of the mist formed a petri dish being held by a giant gloved hand. Next, out of the center of the petri dish emerged the tip of a spear and then its shaft, and the image morphed into an arm holding the spear. The tip of the spear appeared to penetrate the glass. "Here we go," said Warner. The hand spun 180° and launched the spear toward the back screen. Out of the back screen came another hand, and the spear hit the center of the hand's palm and shattered like glass. The audience jumped to their feet and cheered. Brian walked back to the stage.

"Thank you," he said. "Now we have a special part of the show where we invite a member of the audience to come forward. I'd like to invite LAPD Detective Van Eng to join me on the stage."

Van was mesmerized by the display. She wasn't entirely sure what she was seeing. It had the character of a holograph, a three-dimensional movie, but she understood that it was not the production of something being created in front of their eyes. When Brian called her to the stage, she was so lost in her thoughts that she almost didn't hear him. Charlie poked her and said, "Get up there." As she approached the stage, Brian took her hand helped her up the steps. The nanobots visibly pulsed when he touched her, and they both stopped. Brian joked that he did not do that and maybe they knew something he didn't know. But Van saw it in Brian's eyes, the tiniest glint of sadness that he quickly covered up and focused back on the audience.

"I want you to see that there is another level to our work. Recall that I said we are using artificial intelligence. What we have learned over the past months is that these bots have the capacity to learn without additional programming."

He asked Van if she had any photos in her possession. He whispered so everyone could hear, "I really hope you do," and the audience laughed. She said yes and handed him an old picture of her parents holding her as a baby in Vietnam. Brian took the photograph and held it up to a camera mounted above the glass. The bots resolved into a three-dimensional display of the photograph, and the audience responded in unison with an "Awww." Brian handed the photograph back to Van, and as he did, Van picked up a strange sound in her hearing aids. She heard what she thought was her name, slowly

and clearly, "Vaaannn." It sounded like someone speaking for the first time. It repeated, "Vaaann."

She turned to Brian. "Did you hear that?"

Brian smiled. "Hear what?"

"Did someone just say my name?"

She turned back to the glass and watched as a small hand began to form, then an arm, and then a complete and accurate image of her standing behind the glass looking directly back at her. As she moved, the image moved in response. She leaned forward, and the image leaned forward. She spun around, and the image spun around.

Van looked to Brian and giggled. "You did this," she said.

"Scout's honor," he replied holding his hands in mock surrender. Van laughed and bowed to Brian and then to the audience who stood and clapped. Behind the glass a small pair of hands formed and clapped with the audience. Christopher Deckwalder and General Tom Warner congratulated Brian and Bost on an amazing display and on the tremendous progress they had made with the bots in such a short time. As they left the grounds, Deckwalder turned to Warner and said, "That, my good sir, makes everything worth it. Imagine the applications." Warner looked back and smiled. His mind was turning as well.

* * *

"California is making progress," General Warner said to Belinda and Hadj, seated across from him at a Pamplona café.

"Progress?" said Belinda in response.

"I heard they made some nice pictures," said Hadj dismissively.

"Be careful not to underestimate that team," said General Warner.

"That team," said Belinda, "is capitalizing on my efforts."

"You laid the groundwork," said Warner. "I'll give you that."

They sipped their espressos. Hadj looked at the general and wondered if Belinda was making a mistake to trust him. He could easily have Interpol or CIA agents in the shadows watching their every move and preparing to take Belinda into custody or worse. Belinda's only protection, he thought, is the progress I am making toward weaponizing the bots.

"I need you to explain something to me," said the general. "The detective."

Belinda was expecting this conversation. It wasn't the first. Several members of her team had asked her what she was trying to accomplish by leaving Van alive. It would have been simple enough to squeeze her for intel and, whether she capitulated or not, to terminate her. The Pamplona stunt seemed to be just that, a stunt.

"I had my doubts," said Belinda. "She was a nobody in the beginning, and if she had remained a nobody to me, she'd be a gone nobody now."

"You think she is more than that?" asked the general.

"Call it a hunch. When I saw her dive into the bullets to save Leonard Freund, I thought to myself there is something more to her. As she was chasing me toward the helipad in that taxi, I began to formulate a plan. I can't tell you the whole story, Tom. For one thing, I don't think you really care about it. You have other interests, and I can serve those interests if you are willing to let me. But I think I can use this detective. If the bulls killed her, so be it. But I am guessing she is asking herself the same question: why did I let her live? I can assure you one thing. She is coming after me and she will not give up, and I can use someone like that."

"Or get caught, and that is not in my interest," said the general. "But I'll give you this; you are an enigma, Belinda Armendariz. Now what have you got to show me?"

They stood, headed for the car that would take them to the helipad, and Hadj thought to himself, I'm happy to show you, General Warner, but it might be the last thing you see. Belinda picked up on Hadj's lack of trust and stared him down. He knew from that look alone that she had something else in mind and that it was not up to him what might happen next. Hadj took a breath and climbed into the car. When they reached the helipad and climbed into the Sikorski, Hadj sat next to General Warner and fastened his harness. General Warner turned to Belinda and shouted over the noise of the rotors, "I don't care what you do with the detective but stay away from Ragnar Willowbrook."

Chapter 20.

The Power of Small (Part II)

Van's favorite place to work at the LAPD's downtown location was in the storage room office on the floor where all the CHESS files and evidence were housed. She had been instrumental in reorganizing and digitizing the evidence kept in that room, and her efforts helped to solve several cases abandoned in that room. She also exposed an abuse in the department, the common practice of prematurely dumping difficult cases in CHESS. The exposure earned her the confidence of internal affairs and senior department leadership, but also the wrath of several detectives, including Detective Paul Young who had disapproved of Van from the beginning. She liked the solitude of the storage room office and admired her section head, Detective Alvin Broad, whom she turned to often for guidance and insight and who worked out of the same office.

Van sipped her coffee and flipped through the cards all still in their plastic sheaths. She read through the cards several times, trying to pick up on a flaw or hint that whoever wrote these cards was using them as a distraction. The messages were largely the same: stop the movie or there would be consequences. The consequences varied. They ranged in severity from public humiliation to medieval types of torture and death. She studied the postmarks, and as might be expected, several of the cards came from the same post offices. She sorted the cards by postmark, and not surprisingly, the cards from the same post office matched in style, which, Van mused, would make sense whether they were fakes or not. She thought the connection might be too precise, evidence perhaps of some plan although weak. She looked at the report of the handwriting analyst, and whatever similarities existed were not conclusive. Even if one person planned the charade, that person might have enlisted the help of others. Van wondered if more than one person might have been involved in Trey's murder.

She set the cards down and turned to the script: *The Power of Small*. The front page said, "Original Screenplay by" and then listed a small handful of names including

Peggy Rice and Trey Nguyen. She noticed a pattern in the format and, never having written a screenplay, looked up the elements and formatting of a good screenplay. It followed a simple pattern: scene heading or slug line, action, character name, parentheticals, dialogue, and transition. Scene One, for example, started "EXT. COLLEGE CAMPUS, EVENING." The scene described a difficult interaction between two faculty members, one taking the moral high ground concerning school policy and the second arguing about the importance of his research but on the losing side of the argument. The story line pulled Van in, and before too long, she found herself halfway through the script. She set it down and imagined Trey caught up in the story and working hard to give each of the characters credibility. She wondered what might be important to Trey about the script. The technical elements were not overdone, and even the discussion about the effects of quantum mechanics on the microscopic world was handled with a light but compelling touch. Van was drawn into the character of the ex-patriot professor who reminded her of her mentors in the department, Charles Darling and Alvin Broad. She found herself attracted to that character even more than the dashing doctors trying in vain to save Monica's life. She went back and reread the piece where Kate, the young resident, helps the ex-patriot professor solve a physics problem. Something about the interchange stood out. The problem the old professor wanted to solve was how to get nanobots to communicate with each other. He believed that, if he could get the nanobots to work together, they could effectuate a cure more quickly, whether it was fighting cancer cells or flesh-eating viruses. Too much programming was required when the bots followed commands individually. Kate suggested that the bots might talk to each other if they had a link like an electrical bond or frequency. That conversation set the old professor on fire, and the movie did a time lapse of quick images depicting the progress they would make over the next several days turning the bots into a more effective cure. But one line stuck out and didn't really seem to fit. In one passionate exchange, Kate says to the old professor, "Why do you keep pointing at the deck?" The professor had been lost in a discourse on structure and geometry and, in a flurry of scientific mutterings on carbon nanotubes and buckyballs, gave a brief discourse on the relationship between buckyballs and dodecahedrons, which, if Kate had not been aware, were roundish balls produced by fitting twelve pentagons together. He tells her repeatedly to look more closely at the dodecahedron, to which she responds by asking, "Why do you keep pointing at the deck?" The question might be a reference to the dodecahedron, but it seemed insignificant, and that made it odd. Perhaps it was an inside joke and or obscure academic point that Trey simply buried in the conversation like a literary fingerprint.

Van read through the rest of the script. She found the story touching and liked the way the old professor recovered his dignity. But she didn't see anything that obviously pointed to a suspect or to Trey expressing concern about the story line. Even if he did bury a clue to some concern he was having, nothing in the story would have caused so much concern that the solution was to kill the writer.

Then she turned over the script. In the middle of the back page, she saw three dots.

* * *

Brian sat on the cliffs overlooking the giant waves breaking at Mavericks. It was a big day, and at least a dozen surfers were in the water waiting for a tow onto the peaks of the mammoth waves. A lot of them fell, a few taking the full brunt of the heaving lip as it crashed into the stirred-up waters below. Miraculously, or so it seemed, they all popped up after the wave passed in time for the recovery jet skis to reach them, quickly pulling themselves onto the rear safety board of the ski. They waved back at the crowd gathered with Brian on the cliffs as if to say, "Look at me! I survived!" As dangerous as it was, they seemed fearless and hopped off the board as soon as they were past the break, ready for another attempt. Brian didn't surf, and as crazy as it was, these surfers made him want to give the big waves a try. He put that thought away quickly as he watched another surfer get sucked over the giant break. The thought he couldn't put away was the demonstration. He felt lucky for it to have gone so well. He thought of Van's touch when he led her to the stage and the magical effect if had on him. He was certain. or at least he hoped, that it had a similar effect on her, but nothing in the way she responded to him after the event suggested anything more than friendship. Then he thought of the bots and the pulse he saw and felt behind him as he touched her hand. There was no command; the bots either reacted to some stimulus, or the timing of the pulse was merely coincidental. What else could it be? Then, as if that wasn't odd enough, they copied her image without any prompting. The effect on the audience was supernatural. They were certain he had programmed the bots to mimic Van, but he had done no such thing and was concerned that, if he told anybody, he might cause undue concern. Of course, he was concerned. He had to be able to control the bots. He'd had two goals: get control of them and ensure that they were no longer toxic. Van never told Brian that the bots called her name. Afterward, she convinced herself that she hadn't really heard anything, because if she had, it must be that she was going crazy. Brian knew, whatever else was going on, the artificial intelligence that he embedded into the bot logic was taking on a life of its own and the bots were learning. Bost had been just as excited about the demonstration as Brian. As they packed up the show, Bost pulled Brian aside.

"That was awesome!" he said, unable to contain his happiness. "I have no idea what you did with your lady friend, but I'd say our microscopic friends have taken a liking to her." He laughed.

"She's not my lady friend; she's just a friend," Brian replied. "You and I need to study more about the physics of attraction, but whatever the hell happened up there, there was some connection."

"Something," said Bost. "So now what do we do?"

"Talk to your boss. I'll bet Providia has some ideas. I'll try to get Van back up here as well. Whatever that was, we need to figure out what happened and why."

* * *

Van called Peggy Rice.

"What do you think?" asked Peggy.

"What should I think?" responded Van.

"I could be wrong, but I think Trey was in on something or aware of something going on behind the scenes."

"I'm not seeing anything that leads me in that direction," said Van. "What do you think is going on? Do you know something that you haven't shared with me?"

"I might, but I don't think so."

"What troubled you about this movie?"

"I never liked it. It wasn't something that fit Jerry's style. But he's been so adamant about getting it done, despite Trey's death and then what happened to me. He is still pushing it, Van."

"Given the amount of money you've already spent, he might have a good reason."

"It is a common problem in Hollywood. Investors in movies spend a lot of money. The staff and the cast add their efforts. But at some point, you realize this is simply a bad movie and nothing you are going to do will make it better. The tendency is to cut the budget and hope you can sell it to a streaming service."

"I read the script and I don't think it's that bad. I don't go to movies, but it seems like something I might enjoy."

"That's why I write movies and you solve crimes. It is possible to salvage this movie, but it's going to take an act of God."

"You gave me the script, Peggy. Is there a clue in it?"

"Ok. That's fair. So, it's a stretch, but I gave the script to Trey to add technical story line around quantum physics. He was savvy on the science behind the movie. He was especially keen on something called buckyballs and wanted to work the concept into the movie."

"I saw that. That was a strange line about 'pointing at the deck.' I assumed he was trying to get us to focus on the shape of the ball. He called it a dodecahedron or something like that."

"Right. I think there is something there, but I can't figure it out," said Peggy. "I thought you might."

"I'll keep working on it," said Van. "In the meantime, I have a question for you."

"Yes?"

"Do you ordinarily put three dots on the back of your manuscripts?"

"Dots like periods?"

"Right. Three dots. Right on the back."

"Let me check something," said Peggy. She set her phone down and disappeared. Van could hear Alex singing in the background. She wondered if she had earbuds and wondered what it might be like to use earbuds. Her hearing aids didn't allow for it. She thought someone should program hearing aids to store music. It wasn't the first time she had the thought. Peggy returned.

"You're right."

"About the dots?"

"Yes. I didn't notice it before, but there are three dots on the manuscript, the hard copies and the Word version on my computer."

"Do they mean something?"

"Well," Peggy paused, "there is a punctuation mark called an 'ellipsis.' It gets placed at the end of a sentence, and it can indicate that an idea was not completed or that someone was interrupted while still speaking. It could also mean the story line is not finished. But it is unusual to have an ellipsis standing on its own and not at the end of the sentence. In fact, like a period or a comma, you don't even leave a space at the end of the word nearest the ellipsis. It is connected to the word, like a tail."

"I wonder if it is a secret symbol or a code that someone else would be looking for. Whatever you do, don't erase it. Let's keep thinking about it."

Chapter 21.

Critical Mass

Theories about the end of the world garner devout followers even though history repeatedly proves the theories false. Pope Innocent III linked the rise of Islam to the apocalypse and predicted the Second Coming in 1284—it didn't happen. German astrologer and mathematician Johannes Stoffler predicted a great flood would consume the earth on February 25, 1524, when the planets aligned under Pisces. The prediction triggered an increase in boat sales, but the year ended in drought. Revelation 13:18 links the number 666 to the Antichrist, and many seventeenth-century Christians believed that the Antichrist predicted in Revelation would come in 1666. In fact, on September 2, 1666, the City of London was decimated by a fire that destroyed eighty-seven parishes and thousands of homes, but the beast of Revelation failed to materialize. The Millerites thought their reading of the Bible proved that the end would come in 1843 or, after the date passed and their leaders were forced to redo the math, maybe it meant 1844. In 1910, gas masks became the rage after an observatory reported that the tail of Halley's contained a poisonous gas called cyanogen. In 1974, two Cambridge astrophysicists published a book called *The Jupiter Effect* suggesting the alignment of the major planets would trigger earthquakes, including an earthquake along the San Andreas Fault in March 1982—nope. A movement called the True Way predicted that, on March 25, 1998, God would appear on American television, Channel 18 specifically, and announce plans to return to Earth.

There are many more such predictions. Perhaps the closest we have come to realizing a true end of the world scenario is the invasion of Ukraine by Russian President Vladimir Putin. Such a massive breach of national integrity by a major nuclear superpower has not been imaginable since the creation of the National Security Council at the United Nations. Security Council members India and Pakistan have been at each other's throats for decades, but the implications of a full-scale religious war between those two nuclear powers have them locked in permanent stasis. This year, Putin called the bluff and decided it was his destiny to restore Mother Russia even if nuclear war might result. Not surprisingly, with the United States and Russia on the brink of a nuclear war, new apocalyptic theories are making their way back into American religious discourse. Maybe this time they are right. Or maybe not.

Criminal defense attorney Sam Dash, Esq., grabbed her legal pad and stood before Judge Eliza McCracken of the Los Angeles Superior Court, Spring Street Courthouse. She walked to the jury box and smiled. "You have been very patient and carefully attended to the evidence proffered by the prosecution claiming to support the conviction of my client, Derek Whitestone. You must be very tired, and I can assure you this circus is about to end. Whether or not Mr. Whitestone had a petri dish containing nanobots delivered to a UCLA laboratory is not relevant to his conviction. Whether or not he knew the materials in the petri dish were toxic or dangerous is not relevant to his conviction. The container that held the dish was labeled RG-IV, as was the petri dish itself. As we have explained, RG-IV stands for Risk Group IV, and every major university laboratory that handles extremely dangerous biological material has protocols in place for the handling of RG-IV materials. UCLA has a laboratory manual describing those very protocols. Make no mistake, the death of Marley Dakota and the lab assistants who were with her is a tragedy and the loss her parents feel must be terrible. But that loss is not the fault of Mr. Whitestone, and there is no legal way to pin this tragedy on him through a trumped-up claim of criminal negligence." Sam Dash reviewed the elements of criminal negligence with the jury and described how criminal negligence is not supported by a mistake in judgment or carelessness. She argued that the prosecution failed to prove two key elements, knowledge and causation, without which the claim could not stand. Derek Whitestone did not know that the lab would mishandle the petri dish, and Derek Whitestone did nothing other than have the dish, properly labeled, delivered to UCLA.

"There is no other just result here," she said. "Mr. Whitestone's reputation has been destroyed, and he has needlessly served seven months in jail awaiting this trial. He will not get that time back, but even if you can't give Marley back to her parents, you at least can give Derek Whitestone back his life." She looked to the judge, nodded, and returned to her seat.

Van sat in the audience. She looked over at Marley's parents and knew that they were suffering to have to go through this trial. Contrary to Sam Dash's argument,

Van believed Derek had been reckless. She knew the damage the nanobots did at Brian's lab on Bainbridge Island, almost killing Brian and his colleague Carrie Comstock. She believed the RG-IV label was not an effective precaution. RG-IV, she had reasoned to herself, indicated a biological hazard. The key should be whether Derek or his assistant told the lab the nanobots were not biological or gave any indication they were not as hazardous as the label suggested they might be. Derek had not testified on advice of his counsel. Sam Dash was smart enough to leave proving the details of the communications regarding the petri dish to the prosecution, and Dash had been right—the prosecution could not prove anything that Derek or his assistant said about the dish.

It was not a surprise when the jury came back with a verdict of not guilty and let Derek Whitestone go free. But even still, the trial had been worth the effort. Marley's parents' civil trial had been continued until the criminal trial was concluded, and the prosecution unearthed mounds of evidence that the university had not followed its own protocol in handling materials labeled Risk Group-IV. The university eventually settled with the parents for an undisclosed sum, rumored to be in the seven figures. Even though the money could not bring Marley back to her parents, they used the money to establish a medical research institute in Marley's name at the University of South Dakota, fulfilling Marley's dream of a laboratory that blended the teachings of Western and tribal medicine. As they left the courtroom that day, Van approached Marley's parents and apologized saying, "I wish we could have done better." They smiled and told her, "You did your part. The ancestors will serve Mr. Whitestone with whatever it is he deserves. That's not our job. We have a Sioux shaman whom we visit when we need guidance and comfort. He told us Marley was still working in the world and that great things were still to come from her efforts. He also told us that you, Detective Eng, are very special and that we must do everything we can to help you realize your destiny. Please do not forget us. Anything we can do for you, we will. All you need to do is ask."

* * *

Bill Perkins and his UCLA team worked tirelessly in their efforts to reverse the toxicity of the nanobots, and it was not proving to be a simple matter. They conducted extensive research on pharmaceutical methods and learned that those teams with eight-figure budgets did not always succeed. The toxicity of certain compounds resisted mitigation regardless of the solution. But when they did succeed, the solution usually fell into one of four categories: (1) a type of antivenom, a counteragent to the compound's toxicity; (2) an immunity booster that prepared the body in advance for an invasion; (3) a modification of the compound's molecular structure that would preserve its character but would render the compound harmless; or (3) a protective coating around the compound. Options one and two were not viable because the delivery mechanism would be too slow to cover the planet. In addition, there was no way to immunize the world against the toxic effects of these bots. Option four had some promise, but if the coating wore off or was not effectively applied, the toxicity would return and the bots might become deadly again. That left option three. Perkins' team studied the molecular structure of the bots for weeks. The problem with modification of the tungsten-ceramic combination was that it was key to the bots' ability to self-replicate. Any time they introduced an alloy, it muted the superconducting effects of the combination and the bots stopped self-replicating.

It was Bost who suggested feeding the question to SENSA XO, the AI supercomputer co-owned by Providia and NASA. "Do it," said Brian, without hesitation. He turned to Bill Perkins. "You've made good progress," he said. "Work with Bost, and let's find a way to get SENSA XO to answer the right question."

It took time for Bost and Bill to gather and feed the SENSA XO the volumes of data on toxicity that the supercomputer would use to develop a solution to the problem posed by the toxic nanobots. Bill explained to Bost that the inventor of the nanobots must have taken years to discover the right combination of elements that would produce a self-replicating nanobot. As hard as his team had tried, he could not find a molecular solution that would both render the bots benign to humans and preserve the ability of the bots to self-replicate. It was as if that self-replication ability itself produced the toxic reactions in humans. Eliminate self-replication, and the bots would be rendered harmless. But the team knew that was not the answer. Self-replication was essential to the bots' ability to perform. No mass-manufacturing machine could stamp out the trillions of bots needed simply to be visible, the problem that Bost himself was trying to solve before he met Brian. So, the team fed the SENSA XO terabytes of data on toxicity and nanotechnology, and the supercomputer created and ran millions of algorithms on the question, and each time the result was the same: failure.

It was Brian who framed the question that produced the beginnings of an answer.

One day, when he was working with the bots on a complicated color image, he typed in the question: "Why do you follow the queen?" The nanobots went quiet, and Brian waited. After a few minutes he typed in the same question: "Why do you follow the queen?" The bots stirred and vibrated. Then they began to move rhythmically, and small spherical shapes emerged out of the mass. They began rotating around each other, like planets dancing in a gravitational field. The dance went on for a few minutes before the mass flattened into its original shape. The fact that the bots answered questions at all was something Brian discovered at the demonstration. He still didn't understand why the bots had such a peculiar reaction to Van. But he did recognize that he could pose a question, and the bots would try to answer. The little demonstration in response puzzled him until he began to think about the bots not acting in isolation, but rather like a swarm of bees or a colony of ants. The bots operated in isolation, meaning they worked. But as a collective, they were transformed, and with an effective leader or guide, their abilities reached beyond what had been expected. But what was it about the queen? He thought about the dance, and he noticed that the images responded to each other, reacted to their actions, and were uniquely attracted to each other. He shared the discovery with Bost and Bill Perkins, and they fed the data from Brian's research into the SENSA XO. They headed out for beers and waited and hoped for an answer. It was there for them when they returned.

* * *

Belinda and General Warner took the car down to the little town of Ainsa. Belinda was wary of showing herself in public these days. Her stunt with Van in Pamplona won her some unwanted publicity even though very few people knew it was her who had driven into the path of the bulls and disrupted the event by dumping Van in the road. But General Warner wanted to celebrate. Hadj's demonstration had exceeded his expectations and put Brian's accomplishments deep in the rearview mirror. It should not have surprised him. Brian was not interested in weaponizing the nanobots. All Hadj wanted to do was build a new weapon, and he had done just that. As he explained, it started with bullet-sized nano-ballistics, as Hadj now called them, and grew into a single missile capable of spreading a dense cloud of bots over a small town. The missile was impressive on several fronts. First, it could be fired by anything from a hand-held launcher to a fighter jet. Hadj explained that the bots alone were toxic enough to kill human beings but that he had increased the toxicity of the bots by fooling the bots into thinking buckyballs containing hydrogen cyanide were carbon dioxide molecules. The nanobots would attach to the buckyballs, and human beings exposed to the nanobots would die of asphyxiation in the same moment that they went into anaphylactic shock. Hadj told General Warner that the bot cloud from a single missile would immediately disable everyone exposed in a five-mile radius and, in just a few minutes, would cause death and then would fall to the ground completely harmless. Moreover, the missile could be exploded at such a height that there was no destruction to existing buildings. The fear such a device would instil in any local population would ensure quick military victories with no loss of military personnel.

Neither Belinda nor General Warner were concerned that the weapons might violate a global ban on chemical and biological weapons that had existed since 1925. In their minds, the stockpiling of nuclear weapons was far worse and the only factor that prevented their use was the generally acknowledged fear of global nuclear destruction. That strategy, which appeared to work during the several decades of the Cold War, only worked so long as countries continued to agree nuclear weapons should not be used in conflict. But behind the scenes, each country possessing such weapons knew that, if pushed to the brink, they would make the same decision President Truman made to end World War II, notwithstanding the catastrophic results. Every single one of these countries included in their defense plans for the tactical use of nuclear strikes. President Reagan went so far as to develop an anti-nuclear defense force, euphemistically called "Star Wars," even if such a defense effectively promoted the use of the weapons.

General Warner was beside himself with glee. He suggested that they celebrate in town. Belinda showed him to the town bar, which was famous for its *rebujitos*, a sherry-based mint cocktail. They drank late into the night, and Belinda called Hadj to come and pick them up rather than, as she suspected would happen, let the good general drive them off the side of the cliff. Belinda explained to the general that her goal was to produce a stockpile of these missiles. Once her plans to establish the Basque Nation were completed, she would then market her excess weapons to the highest bidder. General Warner, she said, for a price, could secure the weapons for his own country's purposes and capitalize on the sale, which could make them the richest arms dealers in the world.

General Warner had his own idea. It was not a good idea to let Belinda have control of these weapons. Belinda was an international criminal. Even though she used her brilliance to fund the invention of a new weapon and set up a laboratory that was about to become a weapons manufacturing plant deep in the Pyrenees, she was a wild card and unpredictable—in other words, a serious liability. His concern was that Hadj would be loyal to her, but he expected that loyalty could be bought for a price. Certainly, Hadj would have concerns about Belinda's loyalty to him once she had her weapons. What did Hadj care about the Basque Kingdom, anyway? The general knew Belinda needed his money. He could string her along until he was assured that Hadj was willing to defect. No need to rush. General Tom Warner was a patient man.

Hadj pulled up, and they climbed back into the car, laughing and sharing their alcohol-induced flirtation. The general could be a bit handsy when the mood struck him, and the mood was striking him. Belinda laughed and forced down her disgust at romance with older men. She knew with her looks she could have anyone she wanted and usually did, and men like the general did not fall into that bucket. But she could put it on, and as the general fell into the fantasy of romance with Belinda, he had no idea that she was holding a hypodermic, and he barely felt the needle as it plunged into his thigh. He did see it, and rather than being angry, he laughed as he passed out into Belinda's lap.

When the general woke, he was no longer laughing. Hadj had gagged him and bound his hands and feet to a chair with zip ties. He screamed "Belinda!" but all that came out was a muffled noise. Hadj had a gun pointed at the general's head.

"Here is what is happening, General Warner." Belinda leaned close to his face. "You are going to wire $75 million into a special account."

"Never," mumbled the general. "You can kill me first."

"That is not a problem, sir, if that is your preference."

"Let me talk," came the muffled response. Belinda looked at Hadj, and Hadj removed the gag.

"Think about this Belinda," pled the general. "You are alive today because the United States government values your genius. Interpol, MI-5, and the CIA all see you as an international criminal, and yet I have found a way to protect you. Remove me from the picture, and the world will come crashing down on you."

"Gag him," said Belinda, with an icy edge.

"Hadj, Hadj," said the general, spitting through the gag. "You don't want this. You'll be a criminal just like her."

Hadj pulled the gag tight. The general glanced around and now saw that he had been tied up below the target on the driving range. He squirmed to get free as Hadj and Belinda exited the enclosed range and headed the four hundred meters to the tip of the firing range.

"Now you will see," said Hadj as he loaded the Remington MSR, this time with standard ballistics. He fired three shots, each intentionally missing the general who lurched left and right and eventually caused the chair to topple over. Hadj paused, removed the standard cartridge, and inserted a single nano-ballistic bullet into the firing chamber. He hit the target bullseye almost dead center and then watched as the general looked up in horror. Within seconds, his eyes began to tear, and his body jerked spasmodically as he tried unsuccessfully to breathe, finally giving in to the darkness that he knew was unassailable.

Hadj turned to Belinda whom he expected to be satisfied by the result. But she wasn't satisfied at all. In fact, she was raging. She wandered in circles holding her head and talking to herself as if Hadj were not present. Then she pointed to the dead general and yelled at Hadj to clean up the mess, and in that moment, Hadj hesitated. Maybe the general was right. Maybe this was a mistake.

Chapter 22.

Silicon Valley Iconography

Silicon Valley artist and art broker Drue Kataoka believes the distinction between art and technology is blurred. "Art is technology, and technology is art," she explains. The question, seemingly missing from her description, is whether technology can replace art without removing something that is essential to art being art. Digitized music can be made to sound more on pitch than an analog recording, and yet musical purists would prefect the scratching of a needle on a vinyl record to a stream of bytes and bits from a smart phone. When our ears hear what our brain tells us is something musical that we enjoy, it should not matter that the sound is produced by a machine. When we listen to a radio broadcast or a live stream on a laptop, it should not matter that the sound is carried to us as analog waves or digitally encrypted packets. The same analysis applies to the visual arts. Nothing suggests that we enjoy digital art any less than a fifteenth-century oil painting. In fact, science is an essential element in those early masterpieces. The use of convergent lines and linear perspective by Renaissance painters blended the science of those days with the art of those days to create the art at which we now marvel. Contemporaries of the Italian painter and architect Filippo Brunelleschi believed nature could not be realistically portrayed unless it is viewed from a measurable distance and location. Art as a reflection of nature could not be disassociated from science. One could make a convincing argument that it was science that made the art. In today's vernacular, art cannot be disassociated from technology. And yet we are troubled by the inevitable conclusion: art produced by a robot is no less artistic than art produced by a human being.

Brian enjoyed the art his nanobots produced. To him, those reproductions were as remarkable as original photographs or paintings. Even if the bots did no more than capture carbon dioxide out of the air and reflect the images he placed in front of them, Brian felt the pleasure of having created something new as if it were his own. Bost was the more practical of the two. Even if he, like Brian, relished in the remarkable results they had obtained to date, he reported to a boss who cared very little for anything that could not be made into something that generated a return on his investment. But the answer to the question of how to eliminate or at least reduce the bots' toxicity to human beings was not the answer either of them expected. After analyzing gigabytes of data, the Labs team pulled from the Internet and private sources and fed into SENSA XO, including data on the molecular structure of the bots, immunity, cytokines, macrophages, multi-organ failure, anaphylaxis, and related syndromes, the supercomputer came back with a remarkably simple answer: pH. The human body regulates its own pH by converting carbonic acid into carbon dioxide that gets expelled when we breathe. Carbon dioxide acts as a buffer to keep the body's pH in balance. The failure of that system and the change in the body's pH can cause coma or death. The bots were having that effect. The carbon-capture feature of the bots changed the body's pH and triggered the cytokine storm that caused, among other things, hyperinflammation and acute respiratory failure. But what would counter this effect? Brian and the UCLA team spent hours analyzing the SENSA XO results. Now they understood the problem: the bots had been created as a form of carbon-capture technology and that technology, unchecked, killed humans.

It was Bill Perkins who pointed out that the bots go inert after they load up with carbon dioxide molecules. "They fall out of the sky like dust," he said. "What if there is a way to limit their collection capacity? What can we do to reduce the amount of carbon each bot captures?"

"The problem is that they kill before they go inert," said Brian. "What else makes them inert?"

"Freezing temperatures," said another UCLA grad student, the young dark-haired woman who had flirted with Derek Whitestone in the Mustang and who now was sizing up Dr. Brian Johannsen. Bill Perkins knew her well and had given her the pet name "Mustang" and not just because she liked the car.

"Maybe we mix them with liquid nitrogen," suggested Perkins.

"Liquid nitrogen evaporates," answered Brian. "Freezing the bots is a good temporary solution for something like transport. Once they are unfrozen, they are as lethal as if they had never been frozen."

"You said you want to load them up," said Van, who had been sitting on the sidelines watching the interaction. "Restrict their capacity."

Brian looked over to Van and smiled. He had asked her to come up to Ragnar

Willowbrook because he wanted to explore the bots' reaction to her presence at the demonstration. Van, from her end, was frustrated by her inability to solve Trey's murder and unhappy at the outcome of the Derek Whitestone trial. She needed a break. She also wanted more from Providia than they gave her on her first round, so returning to Silicon Valley served multiple purposes. Then there was Brian, whose pull toward Van was something she continued to resist, though her will was weakening.

"That's right," said Brian. "What are you suggesting?"

"I'm not the expert here, and I don't pretend to be," Van responded, playing down her chemistry background in forensics. "What if you created a fake molecule, something that mimics carbon dioxide?"

The team's eyes widened. "That's brilliant, Van," said Brian. "We need to find some way to use the laws of attraction." He cast a quick glance at Van when he said it, but there was no reaction. "I want to enhance the bots' capabilities, not diminish them. That may be a solution."

"How do you fake carbon dioxide?" asked Mustang.

"Let's figure that out," said Brian.

* * *

Christopher Deckwalder studied the imitation Brunelleschi hanging in the wall of his office. It was a 3-D rendition of The Sacrifice of Isaac, one of Brunelleschi's early works. It showed an angel staying Abraham's hand on the altar at the very last moment before Abraham carried out what he believed to be the command of God to sacrifice his only son. Deckwalder liked the piece for several reasons. He wasn't particularly religious, but he believed the story was an early commentary on the practice of human sacrifice as much as it was supposed to be a statement on the depth of Abraham's faith. At the same time, and more importantly to Deckwalder, the piece stood for the importance not of faith but of sacrifice. Even though Isaac was spared, though one might well imagine he suffered serious psychological injury, God provided the ram, caught in a nearby thicket, to satisfy the obligation of sacrifice. Deckwalder believed in sacrifice. He enjoyed his immense wealth and was anything but a miser, and yet, he knew sacrifice was an essential element of financial success and expected his employees to believe the same. Like most of the more successful

Silicon Valley companies, Providia rewarded their employees who showed a willingness to place work above all other activities and literally live their work. They encouraged this behavior by adding fully stocked kitchens, video game rooms, and even sleeping pods to their interior business décor.

Deckwalder's assistant spoke to him over the intercom. His guests had arrived and were waiting in the boardroom. He opened the double doors that connected the board room to his office, a display of his own power as he gave visitors a glimpse into his immense though sparsely decorated office. These visitors had seen it before and shrugged it off. Jerry Cortez sat in the middle of the boardroom table with Peggy Rice seated next to him on one side and his new director, Frank Richard, alongside a well-known actor/producer on the other side.

Cortez introduced everyone, all of whom Deckwalder knew except for Frank Richard.

"What happened to Stan?" Deckwalder asked.

"Stan wasn't buying into the script," said Jerry. This was only partially true. Workman had grown close to Trey Nguyen, and although he did not think the script was great, he believed Trey was making significant improvements in the story line, enough so that his work alone might turn the script into a good movie. Trey's death hit Workman especially hard, and then Peggy Rice was almost murdered. The combination of incidents knocked Workman off his game, and he knew he would not be able to complete the picture and had asked to be relieved from his contract. Cortez was furious. He was now fully invested in the picture and was determined to complete the production. He called his friend Frank Richard who had just returned from a harrowing experience in Pamplona, and Frank was ready to get back to work and get his mind off the trip. He reviewed the script and found it sound enough to support and, with Jerry's assurance that they would get the money they needed for a high-end production, signed on to replace Workman. "Frank, who you know is an Academy Award-winning director, loves the script and believes in it completely. Right, Frank?"

This also was only partially true, and Frank was not a kiss-ass. But he also knew his moments, and this was not one of them.

"It's a great script," said Frank, unflinching. "We can make this happen."

"And how are you feeling, Ms. Rice?" Deckwalder asked. "I heard about the parking lot. I might be afraid to go back."

"I'm fine, thank you, and you are right. If I am not on set, I am working remote these days. Technology lets me do that."

"Any word on the investigation?" Deckwalder persisted.

"Nothing yet," said Jerry. "We are talking to the LAPD. The detectives working the case are intelligent. I'll give them credit, but nothing moves fast with that group."

"Are we worried it will go cold?"

"I don't know. All we can do is trust the experts. But let's move on to something more positive. We have a movie to make."

"Yes, we do."

"That said, movies require money. Frank, can you share with Mr. Deckwalder our latest budget calculations?"

"Call me Chris. Enough of this mister stuff."

"Okay, Chris," Frank said, and he launched into a detailed explanation of the revised costs of production. He assured Deckwalder that they would minimize location shoots, which were more expensive, and spend as much time in the studio as possible. Still, even after working in shortcuts, talent remained the biggest factor, and the best talent was not cheap. In the end, the $50 million that General Warner provided would only cover about half of the budget. The team would need to find another $50 million. Deckwalder was not fazed. He knew General Warner would pick up the balance, and even if that proved to be an issue, he could turn to his Silicon Valley friends who generally thought about money in the billions and could pull that money together quickly.

Cortez took Deckwalder aside after the meeting. He instructed everyone to meet in the lobby in a few minutes, and the two of them disappeared into Deckwalder's office behind closed doors. "Have you spoken to the general recently?" Cortez asked.

"Not for a couple of weeks. I hear he was going to Europe, but I'm not certain why. He has a lot going on."

"I haven't, either. Our friends at the agency are putting on additional pressure to get the script completed for their review. I support national security, but I'm not a fan of their censorship team."

"Is Peggy in shape to pick it up?" asked Deckwalder.

"I think so. She is returning to her normal self as quicky as anyone might expect."

"Can she handle the technology?"

"The latest script, which we found in Trey's room, has a lot of it done. But we probably need someone closer to the source. You have any good writers on your team?"

"Probably not of your team's caliber. My guys are wonks, not literary geniuses. Let me ask around. How much time do we have?"

"We should have been done by now, but as long as we can get the funding we need, we'll be fine."

Chapter 23.

Resonance

Why do we like music? It can calm us down, make us feel happy, or even heighten a sense of outrage. We know how it works. Music triggers the release of dopamine in the brain. Dopamine is a neurotransmitter that enhances learning, pleasure, memory, sleep, and motivation. Dopamine played an essential role in our evolution as a species. Activities that are essential to our survival trigger the release of dopamine, like eating and sex. But the human species didn't need music to survive, so where did it come from and why would it have the same effect on our brains as essential survival skills? One theory is that, as the human brain evolved, it developed patterns to communicate with other human brains, and it relied on dopamine to recognize the incidence of patterns. This makes some sense, because humans understood early on that survival was not simply a matter of fight or flight. They learned that the collective made them stronger, smarter, and better able to resist danger. But the ability to function as a collective required that they communicate. This theory suggests that the brain's use of dopamine to trigger attention to pattern didn't draw a distinction between the patterns that form speech and the patterns that form music. There's more to this story for sure, especially when one considers musical genres and the presence of music in the animal kingdom. But at the bottom of it all, evolutionary theory has a hard time explaining the origin of music. Maybe it was an accident of nature, the incidental result of an otherwise essential skill. Or maybe it was a divine gift, God's way of saying, "You are working hard to stay alive. Here's a little extra to help along the way."

Van waited outside Brian's office. She was enjoying an avant-garde jazz group out of Paris, and her latest hearing aids had added digital Bluetooth technology so she could listen to music through her smart phone. Brian peeked through the door. Van didn't notice him at first, and when she saw him watching her and smiling, her heart skipped, only in part out of embarrassment, and she fumbled to turn off the phone. She gathered herself quickly and walked in.

"I know I poked fun at you last time," she said. "But seriously, this is an impressive gig you have here."

"I'm still settling in, Van. You know the history here. I run into it all the time. But we keep finding a way, so we'll see."

"Do you ever hear from Belinda?" Van asked. It was a double-edged question, but Brian had nothing to hide.

"I doubt she would expose herself that way," said Brian. "If anything, she might attempt some kind of subterfuge, and I have our security team on high alert for anything unusual."

"I like your security team," said Van. "Curious how you met Jaward."

"Have dinner with me, and I'll tell you."

"Brian," said Van patiently, preparing to discourage the advance. Then she hesitated. "Maybe some other time. Right now, I am here to get some answers, and I think the same goes for you."

Brian put on his lab coat and handed Van a new monogrammed lab coat, size small, that he had delivered for her. Above the check pocket it read, "RW Labs."

"I hope you don't mind," he said.

"No," Van replied. "It's nice, and it fits. Thank you." But as they headed to the elevator, she grimaced just a bit.

Down in the lab, they entered the sterilization room and put on sealed hazmat suits before walking through the sealed doorway into the main lab. As soon as they entered, several lab assistants looked up from their work and smiled at Brian, and he acknowledged each of them by name. Bill Perkins and his team were working at the far end of the lab.

"You remember Van?" said Brian.

"How could we forget?" responded Bill and extended his hand.

"Any luck with faking carbon dioxide?"

Bill looked at Brian and smiled. Brian turned to Van. "It was a great idea," he said. "Hence the new lab coat. We may make you an offer."

Van laughed. "You can stop the BS."

Brian frowned. "I'm not really joking. It was a good lead, and here is what we found. Go ahead, Bill."

Van could tell Bill Perkins was very proud of his discovery.

"It wasn't that we could build a fake carbon dioxide molecule, as if we could build it out of other molecular substance. That didn't work. But we stumbled upon a theory in physical chemistry that is rarely discussed in organic chemistry. Do you remember ever hearing about 'resonance'?"

"Not in chemistry," Van replied. "I am familiar with the effect of resonance on hearing aids, like when similar frequencies crash into each other and cause vibrations or harmonics."

"Interesting," said Bill. "But no, this resonance is not about vibrations. This resonance is about relocating electrons so that the bonds of a molecule are not the same, even if it is effectively the same molecule. Our smart little nanobots do not appear to be able to distinguish resonant carbon dioxide from actual carbon dioxide. When we apply resonant carbon dioxide to the same airspace occupied by our nanobots, the bots eat it up just as fast as the actual molecule. We think—hope—that, if we can coat the bots with a thin film of resonant carbon dioxide, we can eliminate their toxicity or at least reduce it to a level barely noticeable."

"That is absolute genius, Bill," said Brian, and Van could sense that Bill took Brian's opinion very much to heart. She could sense the loyalty that he was developing around him. "When do we start testing?"

"We have been working with inert materials with positive results. We are moving to organics and then live specimens."

"Godspeed, my friend, and to your team." Brian slapped Bill on the shoulder. "You are doing amazing work."

Brian and Van moved over to a large, sealed room, and Van noticed the chamber that was used at the demonstration in the center of the room. They entered, and Brian flipped on the light. The chamber was connected to several tanks of liquid nitrogen, and a thermometer read –210°C.

"We'll need to warm them up a bit," said Brian. "We keep them frozen when we are not working with them." Brian flipped a switch, and a red lamp came on in the chamber. "It'll take about ten minutes. We can wait over here." They found some chairs. "So, how's it going in Los Angeles?"

"It's going well," Van replied. "You hear about the case against Derek?"

"I did. Must have had good lawyers."

"He did. Fred Schmidt paid for his defense."

"I don't know what else we could have done. He was so reckless. He got his assistant killed and your lab blown up and colleagues killed and injured. But I am not a lawyer and never want to be one."

"But if none of that had happened," said Brian, "think of where we might be today and what Belinda might be doing here with those bots. Yeah, it was terrible, but at least she's not here."

"I'm not ready to credit Derek for that," Van replied, and Brian quickly apologized.

"It's ok," replied Van. "That's a situation that still scares me. But I'm not thinking about it as much. I wish I could figure out what is going on with that movie that people got shot and a young writer died."

"Do you think it's something to do with Providia?"

"I don't know. But I need more time with Mr. CFO over there. I think he knows something he has not yet divulged."

A short burst alarm sounded, and Van winced at the noise.

"I'm sorry," said Brian, "but we are ready."

They moved over to the bot swarm, and Van could see the bot swarm moving rhythmically inside the chamber. Brian had Van go to the light switch as he carried an open laptop to the side of the chamber and plugged it into a dock on an elevated desk. He motioned for her to turn off the room light as he flipped on the blacklight inside the chamber. Then he flipped on a small light over the laptop. Van watched from a distance, still wary of what had happened at the demonstration. Brian ran through a series of images, as he had done before, and the bots responded in kind.

He noticed she was hanging back and urged her to come forward. As she moved toward the chamber, the bots began to change colors from purple to blue. The closer she got to the chamber, the lighter the blue became until it almost appeared white.

"When do I freak out?" asked Van.

"They are contained," said Brian. "No reason for fear. But they are reacting to you despite my commands. Let's explore it."

They ran through several different maneuvers. Each time, the bots responded to Van. When she touched the glass, they formed an image of her hand. If she held her hand on the glass long enough, they reproduced an image of her in the hazmat suit. At one point Brian took her hand, and they both saw a pulse run through the swarm.

Later, after they had removed their suits and desterilized and were back up in Brian's office, Brian offered Van a Diet Coke as he sipped at a scotch.

"I can't get over it," he said, "the reaction to you. It's as if they are reading you."

"It's strange," said Van. "It's almost hypnotic. I watch them and I want to move in sync with their movements, but I don't know why. Surely, it's not just me."

"I haven't seen that reaction with anyone else here," he said. "Maybe they are picking up on brain wave patterns, but if that is the case—and it seems remote—we are talking about something almost telepathic, some kind of communication."

"When you added AI to the bots, what did you expect would happen?" Van knew enough about Brian's research to wonder where that was going to go.

"I wasn't certain anything would happen. But it is clear now that they have formed something like a neural net that is functioning as an operating system."

"Are they teaching themselves?"

"They must be. They are doing much more than my commands direct them to do."

"What does it mean, Brian? Aren't you concerned?"

"Not yet. We are on the verge of something very new, and I need to see where this takes us. Now, what do you think about dinner?"

"I am hungry," she said sounding resigned. "Let me check on my parents, first. Then we can get a bite."

In fact, Van felt her pulse rise. She called her parents, but her mind was on Brian. She thought about Martin, and she knew she was ready to move on. Martin had continued to reach out even as he was dating other women. It was tough for him to let go, and his spoiled Hollywood upbringing made it even more difficult. But Brian? As much as she found his advances irresistible, something inside told her to resist. He was a good person, and she had no doubt that Brian would do what was right. Unlike Martin, Brian had let her go. He moved away. He took a job she probably would not have approved of, if she had any input. Now he was making scientific advances no one anywhere in the world was making. Or at least that was what it seemed. How could she be so stupid not to at least try with him? She hadn't given him a chance. But even still, the power of his feelings for her scared her. Then he surprised her. At dinner, the conversation was almost bland compared to the day. He talked about what he wanted to do at Ragnar Willowbrook. They chatted about the criminal case but without any insight. He drove her back to her hotel to drop her off, and in a moment of weakness when she thought about inviting him in, he looked at her like a father or a good uncle and said, "Thanks for dinner. Good luck tomorrow at Providia. Let me know how it goes."

She snapped out of her momentary fantasy. "It was nice, Brian. I'll let you know." She reached out and grabbed his hand. "Good night."

* * *

"Back again?"

Christopher Deckwalder walked into his boardroom to see Van sitting there by herself. He was irritated, both by the unexpected meeting with a police detective and by his inability to reach General Warner.

"My apologies, sir."

"Oh, please. Do I need an attorney?"

"You're not a suspect, sir. You may be a witness. But if you feel like you need an attorney, I don't have a problem with that. I'll wait."

Deckwalder took a seat across from Van and took a breath. "You need a Coke?"

"No, thanks. Water would be nice."

Deckwalder hit a button on an intercom near his seat. "Bring in some water for the detective." He stared at Van and let it linger. She ignored the power move.

"What are you looking for from me?"

"You are involved in this script, 'The Power of Small'?"

"You know I am."

"Tell me more about that."

"It's just a movie. I happen to be an expert in the subject matter. Jerry brought me in to advise his writers."

"But you are more involved than that, aren't you?"

"I am, a bit. After we met and my interest in the movie because I recognized it might help the public image of our product, I offered to help. Jerry made me an executive producer."

"The movie wasn't your idea?"

Deckwalder shifted in his seat and cleared his throat. "No, it wasn't."

"Whose idea was it?"

Deckwalder tapped his fingers on the table. "I don't know, really. What difference does it make?"

"I'm trying to solve a murder that, candidly, could be a serious problem for the movie, assuming you really want it made."

"Of course, I do. We have a lot invested."

"So then help me. Why would anyone want to murder a writer?"

"You're assuming the murder has something to do with the movie."

"I am."

"Why?"

"Nothing leads anywhere else."

"His girlfriend?"

"She's checked out."

"The crew?"

"That I don't know. Nothing yet, but have you had interactions with anyone that you might question?"

"Did you know the director resigned after the murder?"

"No. I didn't."

"Stan Workman. He claimed to be too affected by the violence to continue with the project."

"He told you that?"

"No. Jerry told me."

"Did you replace him?"

"We did, a new guy named Frank Richard."

"Frank?"

"You know him?"

"We've met."

"He is supposed to be very good."

"What happened to Stan?"

"That I don't know, and no, I don't how to reach him. Jerry probably does."

Van closed her notebook. "Thank you for your time. And if you do figure out where this movie idea came from, please let me know." Van paused, long enough to watch Christopher Deckwalder shift uncomfortably in his chair. "I will find out."

Van left, and Deckwalder immediately called Cortez. "She wants to know who brought us 'The Power of Small,'" he told Cortez.

"Tell her," Cortez replied. "It's not a matter of national security. It's a movie. What does Warner think?"

"I can't reach him. I've been trying. I am starting to get concerned."

"He's been involved in some dark stuff; he's probably in deep cover."

"What should I do?"

"Tell her."

Van rode in an Uber back to the airport in San Jose. She thought about her evening with Brian and realized how much his respect for her mattered to her. She was irritated by the interaction with Deckwalder, but she was more troubled that no one told her Workman had left because of the murder. She needed to find him. Her phone rang.

"Detective?"

"Mr. Deckwalder?"

"I can explain why I hesitated to tell you, but the idea for the movie came from the Pentagon."

"The Pentagon?"

"Yes. I've been working with a five-star Army general over there. His name is General Tom Warner."

"Is that who is funding the movie?"

"Yes."

"Any reason the Pentagon would want to murder Trey?"

"I don't know."

"That I believe. Thank you, Mr. Deckwalder."

The car pulled up to the airport drop-off zone. Van sat unmoving, a thousand images through her brain. But her main thought was, what was General Warner up to? "We're here, Ms. Van," said the driver. She shook herself out of the stupor and headed into the airport.

Chapter 24.

The Director

Stan Workman sat in his small office at Paramount. He had explained to the studio executives about his decision to leave The Power of Small, and they concurred. He told them the incidents had left him unable to focus and effectively lead the crew. He also told them that he was still mourning Trey. They had worked very hard together, and he had high hopes for the prodigy. So Stan was off the project. He stared at the stacks of manuscripts around him. Others had already reached out for his services. He still was viewed in the industry as a brilliant director, someone who had the capabilities of reaching the pinnacle of his craft.

He heard a knock. As he reached for his coffee, he shouted, "Come on in. Its open."

Van and Charlie pushed the door open. "Mr. Workman?"

"Yes, please come on in."

"It's the LAPD."

"Come on in and have a seat. Sorry for the mess."

Stan got up quickly and cleared several manuscripts off the couch. Van picked up the mixed scents of old coffee and fast food. A stack of empty bottles of Orange Crush stood in the corner. Fresh cut flowers were laid down on a cheap credenza near the door.

"You have fans," said Van pointing to the flowers.

"Those are for my wife. She's been unhappy recently."

"Do you want to tell us why?" asked Charlie.

"Sure, but you are the detectives looking into Trey's murder? I remember seeing you on set."

"Yes, sir. I am Detective Eng, and this is Detective Darling."

"Stan Workman. Call me Stan.

"Ok, Stan, tell us about Trey."

"Trey was a newcomer to Hollywood and sharp as a tack. We worked together building out the screenplay that he and Peggy Rice put together, though it was mostly Trey."

"How long did you work with him?"

"Initially it was about four months, to hammer out stage directions and dialogue. I know enough about the business to know that, if you try to shoot and write at the same time, which is somewhat inevitable, you jack up the cost of the picture, and it can and often gets out of control. I like to start clean and make sure that change only occurs when necessary. It's also my way of controlling the cast. Once these projects begin, everyone thinks they are a writer, and I made certain the only writer on that set was Trey. Anyone who questioned him, questioned me."

"You said Trey, right?"

"Right."

"I thought Peggy Rice was lead writer."

"Peggy is Cortez's lead writer. But the lead writer on the movie, as far as I was concerned, was Trey. Peggy is good and all, but I needed Trey's special skills. Not only that, I think he had a better imagination than Peggy."

"Ok. Trey was the lead writer. Let's talk about what happened. First, where were you the night Trey was shot?"

"I was here, in this office, waiting for Trey to bring me his latest updates."

"Can you corroborate that?"

"I'm sure I can. There were people in and out all evening. I even had dinner ordered in."

"Do you have a receipt?"

"Probably. I'm sure I can find it."

"Do you have a weapon?

"No. I don't like weapons. People get hurt. I never saw a need."

"When did you hear about the shooting?"

"I don't recall a time, but it was late in the evening."

"How did you hear?"

"It was Peggy. She ran over here pounding on my door and screaming, 'It's Trey! It's Trey'! I opened the door and she was crying. She told me what happened, and I ran over to the park with her. I asked if someone called the police. The first cops showed up shortly after. They got my name and details."

"Why would anyone want Trey dead?" asked Charlie.

"I really don't know. He was a good, smart, hard-working young writer, a huge talent that I thought would go a long way."

Van then pressed the director. "Do you think Trey had any suspicions? Did he ever question anything about the movie?"

"We had long discussions. Cortez showed me some of his hate mail, raised some interesting questions about nanotechnology." Van noted Stan emphasized "nano."

"What's your opinion?" she asked.

"I'm not a Luddite," he answered. "That's not to say the topic isn't worth some analytical care."

"What about Trey? Was he having any moral qualms?"

"Not at all. Trey was an avid supporter. He kept describing all these amazing new inventions that would come from nanobots that would transform medical care, industry, even the climate."

"The climate?"

"Yes. Trey knew a lot about climate change. He told me he read about a guy from the Silicon Valley who thought he could use nanobots to change the climate. He said there were amazing reports coming out of a climate change convention in Paris.

That's what I liked about Trey. His interests were diverse, and his knowledge was expansive for as young as he was."

"But the movie—did you get any sense that he embedded something like a code into the script?"

Workman laughed. "If he did, it was beyond me. I suppose he could have. Like I said. the guy was remarkable. But I am close to the script; I didn't see anything."

"Do you have a copy?"

"I do. Let me find it."

Workman stood and walked to a low-level bookcase against the wall. Van studied the room. She saw pictures of a vacation trip and two dusty Emmys sitting on a shelf. There was no smell of cigarettes, which she had come to expect in Hollywood offices, despite all the warnings. She didn't see any alcohol. The guy seemed to be clean.

While Workman was looking, Charlie asked him, "Were you disappointed to leave the movie?"

"Yes and no. I like Cortez, and this wasn't a typical Cortez film. I would not have taken it on if it were. I felt like Trey was getting close to making it a great movie, rather than sheer propaganda."

"Did it feel like propaganda?"

"It was certainly borderline. That guy Deckwalder, whatever his name, from the company? Never liked him. But he's the money guy, so you kiss up."

"What do you know about the funding for the picture?"

"Just that. Some rich Silicon Valley billionaire asshole wants to make himself richer. I mean I suppose there are real medical breakthroughs, and they may be important. I don't want some idiot who opposes the technology just because it is new to prevent that. Maybe we were doing something important. But I don't care about making rich guys richer. Here it is." He dug the script out of a stack he found on the bookcase and handed it to Van. She flipped through it to the dialogue that she found odd.

"They are talking buckyballs and things I know nothing about. Then they have this conversation. The young doctor, Kate, says: 'Why do you keep pointing at the deck?' The old professor tries to get her to focus on the ball, this geometric ball he is holding. But the doctor asks again, 'Why do you keep pointing at the deck?' Does this mean anything to you?"

"It is interesting. That scene was one of our hardest scenes to develop, and in Trey's mind it was critical. But this is new. This was something he wrote that night. I'd been so upset with everything that happened that I never really studied his latest edits."

"Does the deck mean something?"

"I don't know what he meant in the context of the scene, but the deck is the area reserved for me and the other executives while we are shooting the film. It's a naval term, like a ship's deck."

"Who was on the deck the night Trey died?" Van asked.

Stan studied Van and Charlie as he dredged up the memory. "Just me," he said, "and Peggy."

* * *

Van knocked on the Malibu front door. From inside she heard a yell, "Alex! Get the door!"

Alex peered through the spy hole and disappeared for a minute. She soon returned and opened the door. "Detective!" she said. "Nice to see you again!"

"Hello, Alex," said Van. "This is my partner, Detective Darling. Can we come in?"

"Sure!" said Alex, a little forced. Peggy appeared in her bathing suit and a robe.

"Detectives," said Peggy, looking like she applied her makeup a bit too quickly. "Van, I didn't know you were coming. Detective Darling, please, come on in."

They entered the front room and could see that the tide was up and larger-than-normal waves were crashing and running up just below the footings of the house.

"Can I get you something to drink? Maybe some gin or, uh, Diet Coke, right, Van? You guys look a little tense."

"No, thank you, Peggy. We have a few more questions, if you don't mind."

"Absolutely, whatever you need. Did you find anything in the script?"

Alex brought over bottles of water and Diet Coke and set them on the table.

"Possibly," said Van. "If there is something there, it is subtle. Let's go back to the night Trey was killed. Can you walk us through that night?"

Peggy glanced at Alex, who looked concerned, and said to Van as she pointed to an unopened bottle of water, "Do you mind?"

"Of course not."

"Where do you want me to begin? We had been shooting for about six hours. It was the scene between the young doctor and the old professor. Trey and Stan had been talking a lot together, as they usually did. The scene, like a lot of scenes in the movie, wasn't working very well. I suggested to Stan that we needed some edits. Trey came to me and asked me what I thought. I told him it was too technical, that he needed to dumb it down. I told him to remove the stuff about dodecahedrons and quantum physics. It was too much, and it wasn't necessary to the script. He disagreed with me, but he said he would take a look. I told him, 'You need to do more than take a look. You need to fix it.' I could tell he was irritated, and he marched off, like he often did, in a kind of childish tantrum."

"Did you talk to him after?"

"He went over to Stan to complain. At this point I knew that's what he would do. It had become an MO for him. He pretended to check in with me and then would convince Stan to side with him."

"Sounds like that upset you."

"It did. No boss likes to be second-guessed all the time. But it didn't upset me enough to kill him."

"Ok. What was your relationship like with Stan?"

"I've worked with Stan before. He can be overly controlling, but most directors are. You get used to it."

"Did you talk to Stan that night, after the spat with Trey?"

"I did. I told him he coddled the boy, built up his ego too quickly. He told me I should listen to him. Stan thought the boy had a bright future."

"Stan didn't take your side?"

"He had an opinion. We differed. It happens. Two professionals."

"What happened after?"

"What do you mean?"

"Trey went to his office to write, I assume."

"Right. Trey went to his office. I went to the commissary to get dinner and to get away from the set for a moment."

"You went alone?"

"No. The casting director and costume designer are friends. They joined me. We ate and didn't get a call back from Stan, so we went out to have a drink on Melrose. When we got back it was dark, but there was a lot of commotion on set. Someone said, 'Trey's been shot.' I ran over to his office, and there was a crowd in the park. That's when I saw him." Peggy's lip started to shiver, and she put her hand to her mouth as if to get control.

"What did you do?"

"I asked if anyone called the police. One of the bystanders said they were coming. I asked if Stan knew and no one said anything, so I ran to his office and told him. He came back with me, and we waited for the police."

"Let's shift a bit. What do you know about the funding of the movie?"

"Anything specifically?"

"Who are the primary investors?"

"There's Providia under a production company called 'Critical Mass Productions.'"

"Providia is an investor?"

"Deckwalder writes the checks."

"Anyone else?"

"Jerry has a small group of local investors. Some of them are actors. He turns to them often, and they make a good bit off his movies."

"What about mob money?"

Peggy laughed. "Mob money?"

"Sure. That can't be a surprise."

"I've seen some shady characters hanging around but not mob."

Charlie asked, "What shady characters?"

Peggy froze for a minute.

"You ok?" asked Van.

"Yes, I'm sorry." She took a sip. "You know LA and Hollywood. We seem to attract the worst of humanity, prostitutes and drug dealers looking for extra money. They come in droves and sign up as extras. We have security when there's a problem, but we don't discourage it. We need the bodies."

"Ok, that's interesting, but I doubt many of them are funding your movies."

"You want rich shady characters?"

"Tell me about Deckwalder."

"That guy gave me the creeps."

"Why?"

"I'm not sure. He had an agenda. He kept asking for copies of the script. He'd given them back to me redlined. I asked him, 'What is this?' He told me, 'Some suggestions. Take it or leave it.'"

"He was editing the script?"

"I don't think it was him."

"Why?"

"Because I have been around, and I can tell when someone's silent hand is in the mix."

"Like . . . what? The government?"

"I'm not very comfortable answering that. Are we about done?"

"Sure. Do you own a weapon?"

"No. I wouldn't know how to use it."

"Thanks. We'll be in touch."

Van and Charlie stood, and Alex said, "Let me get the door." Van detected an odor that smelled like fear. She looked at Alex, and Alex was sweating profusely. She kept wiping the underside of her arms. Just as they were about to leave, Van turned to Alex and said, "Just out of curiosity, Alex, where were you the night Trey died?" Alex looked back at Van dumbstruck. She tried to speak, but she could only mumble. Peggy tried to calm her down. "It's ok, honey; don't be afraid. Just tell them you were here." Charlie gave Peggy a harsh look, and Peggy said angrily, "What? She was." Then for no reason, Alex turned away from Van and ran out the door. Van jumped out after her, and then Charlie. She got to her car and fought with her keys to open it. Van reached her just as she unlocked it and tried to crawl in.

Charlie was there right after, and the two of them wrestled Alex to the ground, while she screamed, "No! No! It wasn't me! It wasn't me!"

Peggy ran after Alex and screamed, "Alex! What are you doing?" She kept telling Van, "She doesn't know what she is doing!"

They put Alex in the back of their car. At first, she was hyperventilating, and Van helped calm her down. Charlie called for backup just in case. Then he walked Peggy back to the front door. "We need to take her down. You don't need to come with her, but it might calm her down." Peggy said, "You don't need to take her. She is just sensitive. She didn't do anything."

"It's up to you."

"Yes. Ok. I'll need to change. I'll come down after."

Chapter 25.

Toxicity

American culture has become toxic. Back in the post-Stalinist, post-World War II days when the Soviet Union attempted to redefine itself on the global stage, they sold the world on the idea that American culture was inherently toxic. Americans are selfish, greedy, racist, colonialist, and imperialist. As the country entered the Vietnam War, supported internally by the spun-up fear of Soviet domination, American's youth said no to both spin doctrines and rebelled, promoting a new communal individualism that included brain-expanding drugs, free love, and opposition in any form to the "establishment." As that youth movement grew, another more insidious movement gained momentum. Starting in the early 1930s as a reaction to the economic crises of the early twentieth century, that movement reflected the rise of populist-driven fascism in Europe and crypto-communist fascism in Asia. It was built on a pseudo-scientific view of ethnic superiority and combined nationalistic zeal with xenophobia, the belief that another nation/race might supplant your nation/race as its superior. In the 1930s and '40s, the political leaders of Europe, in short order, capitalized on this movement and spurred it on for their own political ends. In the 1960s, American political leaders viewed the neo-fascist movement as a distorted resurrection of a pre-Civil War era mentality and focused their efforts on delegitimizing the movement.

In 2016, one presidential candidate, to the astonishment of many, made it to the White House on an America First platform. That platform started out as a strictly economic platform and was initially based on a "Hail Mary" attempt to discredit those currently occupying the seats of power. The new anti-establishment sentiment underlying that election brought a non-politician to the highest political office along with the hope that it would trigger change in the very nature of American party politics. It did not. Instead, it cemented a rigid party division that had been developing since the late twentieth century. This division highlighted the extremes and gave birth to the renewal of a populism born of those extremes. Those extremes now dominate American public discourse, and the new question for American culture is whether the level of toxicity that we have now reached will stabilize at a level considered tolerable or will lead to an even more serious division.

The UCLA team moved forward quickly in its attempts to address the toxicity of the bots. Resonant carbon dioxide was working on trial levels and demonstrating itself as a potential antidote to the shock of untreated bots. Tests on live human cells and then on small mammals were producing startling results, and it was finally determined that first human trials might move forward. Bill Perkins presented himself as the first test subject.

"Absolutely not," said Brian. "You are the lead on the toxicity team. I can't have you out of commission, even for a short time."

"I know it will work, Doctor," said Bill. "The results are conclusive."

"You know as well as I do that human complexity makes this a giant step. I don't want you as the test subject. I want you running the test."

"Who are you proposing we start with?"

"Leonard!" Brian shouted into his intercom. "I need you in here."

Dr. Freund popped into the office immediately. "What do you need?"

"I need a test subject."

"For what . . . the bots?"

"We need to know that resonant CO2 is the answer we've been searching for."

"I can line up some interns, see who has the nerve."

"I was thinking that you might step up."

"Me?"

"Do you trust us?"

"Well, of course, but . . ."

"Good. Thank you for volunteering. I think we need two test subjects. We will go in together, you and I."

Bill looked at Brian shocked. "If you think I am important, surely you can't place yourself at risk."

"You are running the test. Leonard and I will be your first test subjects."

"Doctor," said Leonard, "can you give me a minute to think about it?"

"It's about leadership and credibility, Leonard. This move is ours to make." He turned to Bill. "Put together a plan. I want sufficient safeguards in place. We don't need to be reckless. I want to be ready to go tomorrow."

The next morning, Brian and Leonard found blue surgical gowns waiting for them in the decontamination chamber with instructions to remove their clothing, shower, put on the gowns, surgical slippers, surgical gloves, and a tight cap to cover their heads. Two attendants met them after they dressed and walked each of them into adjoining chambers. The chambers were separated by a large window, and in the center of each chamber was a surgical chair capable of being converted into a flat surgical bed. Next to each dentist chair was a standing surgical table holding a container filled with liquid nitrogen that contained two syringes and a hot pad. One syringe contained untreated bots. The second syringe held bots coated with resonant carbon dioxide. Each station was fitted with an oxygen mask and O2 tank. A second surgical table held a bottle of Benadryl and two EpiPens, filled with epinephrin, and capped blood vials. At the head of each chair was an EKG monitor that also displayed blood pressure, pulse, and blood oxygen levels.

The attendants led Brian and Leonard into the two chambers. Leonard looked wide-eyed at Brian, and Brian spoke through the room monitor: "Are you ok, Leonard?"

"My pulse is rapid, my blood pressure is spiking, and I have a splitting headache. But otherwise, yes, I am fine."

Brian laughed. "Give him a sedative," he said to the attendant. "We need him relaxed."

The two test subjects sat in the two chairs, and the attendants partially reclined the chairs, and each was fitted with an IV with a saline drip. Leonard got a shot of Midazolam in his IV and immediately relaxed. The attendants fitted the oxygen masks on both subjects, moved the trays into their proper positions, and left the room. Two members of the UCLA lab team entered each chamber wearing full hazmat gear. They had miked the suits and the two rooms so that everyone could communicate.

Bill Perkins, who was also in full hazmat gear and in Brian's chamber, started the test: "Are we ready to go?"

Brian nodded immediately and turned and looked at Leonard who was staring at him through his mask and the window. "Leonard?" he asked. Slowly Leonard nodded and resigned himself to the trial, lying back into the reclined chair.

Perkins then instructed the assistants: "Apply the benadryl." They unclipped a small bag with a Benadryl solution that fed into the IVs. "Remove the red syringes."

The two syringes were taped with red and blue duct tape: red for the untreated bots and blue for treated bots. A lab assistant in each chamber lifted the red syringe out of the liquid nitrogen with forceps, looked across to the other assistant to confirm they had the correct syringe, and both placed the syringe on the hot pads. As the frozen gel in each syringe began to melt, it turned from a gray paste into a black cloud. Perkins monitored the transformation.

"Administer the untreated bots," he instructed, and the assistants injected the black cloud into the IV. Within seconds, both subjects began to strain, struggling to take in the rich oxygen in their masks. With the benadryl in their systems, neither of them went into full anaphylaxis, but their bodies nevertheless strained again their immune systems trying to inflame their organs. Leonard began to panic, the sedative notwithstanding, and tried to pull off his mask. Brian, despite his own struggles, commanded Leonard to relax. While this was happening, the assistants removed the blue syringes and placed them on the hot pad. The treated bots turned from light grey into purple, and once Leonard stopped struggling, Perkins instructed the assistants to administer the treated bots.

Within just a few second, both Brian and Leonard began to relax and breathe slowly and evenly.

"Draw the blood now, please," said Perkins. The assistants removed the IVs and connected each blood vial to the needle that was still in the subjects' arms. Rich red blood poured into the vials.

Brian was watching his arm, and when he saw the blood spill into the vial, he said, "That's a good sign."

The two subjects were disconnected from everything except the oxygen and helped into two wheelchairs that were standing in the two chambers. Mobile beds had been set up in the main lab, and each of them was helped into a bed. Bill Perkins took the blood vials into a room with a scanning electron microscope, or SEM. He placed a vial into a sealed container and inserted it into the SEM. On the screen set at low resolution, he saw red blood cells floating in liquid hemoglobin. He increased the resolution until he could detect the bots. The treated bots were slightly larger than the untreated bots and easy to tell apart. But he noticed that the bots were behaving in a way that he had seen in other test animals. Rather than floating independently, the bots were clustering. The untreated bots seemed to be more attracted to the treated bots than any other elements in the blood, and in combination, they were forming small bot chains that went inert and floated harmlessly to the bottom of the vial. He took a snapshot of the chains and printed the image. Then he ran out into the lab to Brian and Leonard.

"It worked just as we expected," Bill said, his covered face beaming through his mask. "The untreated bots are linking to the resonant bots and turning into harmless microscopic chains."

* * *

Christopher Deckwalder looked at his phone. Multiple calls to General Tom Warner resulted in nothing. He understood that Warner could very possibly be on a secret mission that necessitated his temporary disappearance. But in all the time they had worked together, nothing like that had happened. Deckwalder also thought that, if this were the case, Warner might at least alert him to the need to disappear without explaining why. He hadn't said anything. Given the importance of the movie project, the disappearance of General Tom Warner made no sense. Deckwalder decided to call the Pentagon directly.

"I need to speak with General Tom Warner's assistant," he told the Pentagon operator.

"I'll need a code," said the operator.

"I don't have a code."

"Then the best I can do is take a message."

"Then please take a message and have his assistant call me back."

"Go ahead."

"This is Christopher Deckwalder. I have been working with General Tom Warner for the past year. It is urgent that I reach him, but I have been unable to reach him now for two weeks, and we were talking almost every day. Please contact me immediately."

"I will pass on the message."

"Thank you. It is very urgent."

He hung up and called Bost. "What's the latest?" he asked Bost.

"We've had a breakthrough."

"What kind of breakthrough?"

"Brian has found a way to eliminate the bots' toxicity."

"How does he know?"

"He tested it on himself."

"He did what?"

"I know. Crazy. But it worked."

"What does it mean?"

"It makes we can work with the bots without being concerned."

"It's a good step. Now we need applications, use cases. We need to find ways to monetize these buggers."

"We are looking into it. The most obvious are medical uses; we should coordinate with biotech. What about Garny's operation? What was it called? MetaMed?"

"Garny? That SOB. I have no idea where he is."

"Let's find him. Can you find him?"

"I can try."

Deckwalder hung up. He still felt abandoned by Garny. Providia was making great strides when Garny left. Granted the video game market didn't satisfy Garny's moral compass, but it was exploding, and Providia's control over the chipset market had it in a great place to capitalize and then move on from there. Garny hated it, though. He took his billion dollars and left Providia and Deckwalder in his wake. He never called back and then disappeared.

As he was pondering this next move, his phone rang.

"Christopher Deckwalder?"

"Yes?"

"This is the Pentagon. My name is Lieutenant Colonel Mark Blankfard. I am General Tom Warner's assistant. We haven't spoken before, but General Warner has mentioned you."

"Great. Thank you. I need to find him. How can I reach him?"

"We are having the same problem."

"Excuse me?"

"General Warner flew to Spain two weeks ago. Shortly after he arrived, we lost contact with him."

"What was he doing in Spain?"

"He didn't explain. He just had me book the flight."

"Let me know if you hear anything."

"Will do, sir."

Deckwalder looked up MetaMed. The company had been shut down for at least two years. He found some old numbers for Garny, but as he expected, none of them worked. He called a handful of Garny's executives from MetaMed, but none of them seemed to know anything, except that Garny had disappeared to some remote place in Asia. They told him that Garny had enlisted several scientists to go with him, but everyone who had gone with him was sworn to secrecy, so they never knew exactly where he went or what he was doing over there. As he ran through his lists, he recalled that General Warner had an old connection over at Ragnar Willowbrook, Dr. Leonard Freund.

"Leonard!"

"Hi, Christopher," said Freund, with a slight cough. "What can I do for you?"

"You feeling ok?"

"I am ok," he said. "What do you need?"

"I think I heard some good news."

"You did?"

"Yes, from Bost."

"What did Bost tell you?"

"Leonard, you had a breakthrough, right? Just tell me."

"I'm not feeling great, Christopher. Can we do this later?"

"Of course. I just wanted to know if you'd heard about Tom."

"Tom?"

"General Warner."

"No," Leonard said, hesitantly. He knew Warner and Deckwalder had a relationship, but he wasn't certain what Deckwalder knew about the source of the bots. "What about General Warner?"

"He's missing. I can't find him. I've called the Pentagon, and they are reporting that he is missing. Have you heard anything from him, at all, recently?"

Leonard paused. "It's been a while, honestly. Nothing since the demonstration."

"They said he went to Spain."

"Spain? That's where Belinda was hiding."

"Belinda? Your boss?"

"My former boss. You remember that detective from LA? She found Belinda in Pamplona. She ended up in the hospital there."

"Belinda?"

"No, the detective. Belinda apparently roughed her up."

"Leonard," said Deckwalder, "is Warner working with Belinda?"

"They knew each other. But what they have to do with each other now, if anything, I have no idea."

Deckwalder called Bost back. "Pack your bags," he said. "We're going to Spain."

Chapter 26.

The Cost of Making Movies

Actor Willem Blanche glanced at his mark to be sure he was in the proper position. He looked up slowly at his young beautiful counterpart, Rachel Scott, and took his time responding to her, given his age and the weight of his sadness. She repeated the question. "Will you come with us?" Blanche looked over at Harry Bleland, another established actor playing the part of Blanche's former colleague at Harvard. Blanche measured his resentment. Bleland's character had played a central role in ostracizing the renegade faculty member from the scientific communities connected to Harvard. He focused his response on Bleland.

"You," he said, emphasizing the subject, "want me back in the States?"

"Charles," said Bleland, with a light touch of paternalism befitting his role as the established and highly regarded Harvard professor, "we need you, and we need you now."

"And you thought that by bringing her, I'd be more inclined to come?" the old ex-patriot responded, his pitch rising in anger as he pointed at the young doctor. "You think I am that pathetic?" he answered, his pitch rising to a roar.

"Stop it, Charles!" Bleland said forcefully. "This is not about you. It's not about her. And it's not about me. It's about saving a life. Now either you get your bags and come with us and give us a shot at preserving a young athlete's life, or don't. I don't care anymore. Just stay here and live out the rest of your pathetic life!" Bleland turned as if to leave.

"Stop it! Both of you!" said Scott with an intensity beyond her youth. Bleland froze.

"Charlie," she said, "your work means nothing if you don't put it to use. Forget him." She pointed to Bleland. "Forget Harvard. Forget the regrets. This is your moment, this moment, right here, right now."

The camera pans from the young doctor's face to Blanche. A small tear forms in the corner of his eye.

"Cut!"

"Okay, people," said director Frank Richard, "nice job. Rachel, that was beautiful. One thought, if you don't mind, I'm not buying the pointing. You're not accusing him. You're trying to get Charles to ignore him. Make a move. Just make it more subtle. Tilt your head. Extend your fingers slightly in his direction. But keep your focus on Willem. Got it? Good. Let's go again."

Van watched from the deck. Even with the tensions surrounding the movie, she found herself mesmerized by the highly acclaimed actors performing in front of her.

Cortez approached her. "What do you think?"

She looked up at him. "Trey would have been proud."

"Trey will get credit. We wouldn't have this without him."

"I'm sure. I am here to talk to you if you have time."

Cortez looked at Van. He took a breath. "Certainly. Can we go to my office?"

* * *

Alex sat alone in the interrogation room. She tried to light a cigarette, but her hand was shaking so badly, she couldn't light it and set down the lighter in frustration. Van entered the room with Charlie. They sat across from her, the cigarette still dangling from her lip. Charlie reached over and grabbed the lighter. He flicked it on and held it for her. Alex took the cigarette in two fingers and took a draw from the light. "Thank you," she whispered, almost inaudibly.

Van watched Alex. Her reaction back at the Malibu house was certainly dramatic, but it didn't fit.

"Are you ok, Alex?"

"Would you be?" she responded testily, out of the character that Van had come to know.

"Ok. That's fair. I need to give you your Miranda rights. You know what those are," she said.

Alex smirked. "Sure," she said, still with an edge and then tapped the cigarette's ashes on a tray on the table.

"Tell us how you met Peggy."

Peggy arrived shortly after the interrogation started. They led her to the room from which other detectives observed the questioning.

"Doesn't she need an attorney?" Peggy asked.

"She's been Mirandized. She didn't ask for an attorney."

"She didn't even ask?" Peggy shuffled uncomfortably.

"She was mad," said Alex in the room.

"Mad at what, exactly?" asked Van.

"She was mad at Workman. Workman and Trey were spending all their time together. She even claimed Workman was diddling Trey."

"Diddling? As in sexually?"

"That's what I understand diddling to mean," said Alex.

"Did she have any proof?"

"No. None at all that I am aware of."

"Did she suggest she would accuse him?"

"She didn't."

"How did Trey die, Alex?"

"I don't know."

"Then why did you run?"

"I ran. I got scared, and I ran."

"What scared you?"

"She did."

"Peggy scared you?"

At this Peggy began to mutter to herself, "No. No. No."

"Why did she scare you?"

"She wanted me in on it."

463

"In on it?"

"She knew if I was in on it, I would keep it secret."

"Stop!" Peggy yelled from the observation room. "She needs an attorney!" She pounded on the window. At that moment, Detective Paul Young approached Peggy Rice from behind. She pounded the window again, and he grabbed her arms as his colleague Robert Johnson put on the cuffs. She struggled against them.

"What are you doing? Stop that!"

"You have the right to remain silent," he started.

"You're an idiot!" she yelled at him. "You got nothing!"

In the interrogation room, Van continued with Alex. "Did Peggy kill Trey?" she asked.

"No," said Alex, looking down. "She didn't."

Peggy looked back at Paul Young. "Hah!" she said. "Take these off!"

"Did you kill Trey?"

"No. But I'm not going to say any more. I am ready for an attorney."

"Did you hire someone to kill Trey?"

"Get me an attorney."

* * *

As they headed to Cortez's Paramount office, he asked Van about her background. She shared with him how she had always wanted to be a detective and how disappointed she was not to get admitted to the police academy due to her hearing impairment. She credited several mentors of hers who had helped her become a detective through back door channels and how now she simply wanted to be good at her job.

"It's an interesting story," he said.

"It's my story and I'm happy. I've met good people, and I am grateful."

They entered his office. It was cluttered with memorabilia from many of his movies but otherwise was organized and clean. Van sat on a fancy leather couch, and Cortez pulled up one of his desk chairs and sat across an ornate coffee table.

"Nice office," said Van.

"My wife decorated it. It's a bit much for me."

"She back from Rio?"

"You remember? Good. Yes, she's back. She got a good tan."

"So, I'm not certain you have heard, but Peggy Rice has been detained along with her roommate, Alex."

"I heard."

"What can you tell me about Peggy?"

"She's been with me a long time. I hired her as a writer directly out of film school."

"She went to film school?"

"She did. It's where she started honing her craft. She joined me just before Armageddon and Coyote Ugly. She was great! We have been a great team for a lot of years."

"She was instrumental in hiring Trey?"

"She was. She wanted to train Trey, bring him up the same way I brought her up."

"But Trey didn't seem to need her?"

"Peggy was losing her edge. I didn't need to tell her; she knew. Stan Workman knew, too, and he began working directly with Peggy."

"Did you sense that was a problem?"

Cortez looked at the coffee table. "I didn't. We all have our glory moments, and we all lose our edge at some point. Some would say I've lost mine."

"But Peggy didn't just lose her edge. If she killed Trey, she went over the edge."

"I can't explain that. I do know that she was feeling our downturn and was getting frustrated, maybe feeling somewhat responsible for it. Then

Workman began to substitute Trey in for her and ignore her. I wasn't paying attention. I had my own issues. I can see it upsetting her."

"Thank you, sir," said Van. "There will be a criminal case. You can expect to hear from us."

"Anything you need."

"Thank you. I can help myself out."

* * *

Alex got an attorney and worked out a plea deal with the district attorney to turn state's evidence against Peggy Rice. Peggy, as it turned out, was not handling her declining position with Cortez very well. It was her idea to fake the terrorist threats and discourage Cortez from making the movie. She had written enough CSI episodes to know how to imitate actual threats. She used Alex to hire two drugs addicts who worked as extras for Paramount, one of whom worked on The Power of Small. The addicts were dealing on set, and Alex, who had come out of that same Hollywood subculture, presented them with an opportunity to expand their operation in exchange for the murder. She suggested that they get into costume, and the young woman found a friend in makeup who redid her as an old woman. She bought vintage clothing from a thrift store for the night of the murder. Trey was unlucky on two counts. He came upon them in the middle of a deal and accidently knocked the young woman to the ground. He then inadvertently led them back to his office, and the young female addict confronted him in costume and shot him. She and her partner then dragged Trey's body to the garden in the park. Peggy's criminal genius didn't stop at the murder itself. She realized that she could deflect attention away from herself if she was also the victim of a similar crime. So it was that Peggy arranged for the parking lot shooting, only it went far worse for her than she expected. The same couple who murdered Trey was supposed to shoot the car window as she was leaving. Being generally incompetent addicts, they accidently shot her in the head and would have killed her except that she survived. Alex knew the couple, and she was able to direct the police to them in short order. They were arrested in the middle of a back lot drug deal, and the police were able to get one of them to confess to the murder for hire. Peggy continued to protest her innocence. The court sentence was lenient and gave her life with the possibility of parole after twelve years. The civil case for wrongful death brought by Trey's family against

Peggy Rice, Jerry Cortez Productions, Critical Mass Productions, and Paramount Studios was dismissed as to the latter three defendants and was still pending against Peggy.

Chapter 27.

Van's Dreams

In traditional Chinese custom, the dead speak to their living relatives through dreams. In those dreams, the dead convey needs: I need money, I need a house, I need clothing, I need hair, I am hungry, I am cold. These expressions of need are converted into duties that the living have to the dead. In the service of those duties, a cottage industry has grown that prints and sells fake money, paper houses, paper clothing, etc., and that has developed the means to convey these items to the dead by burning them near a deceased relative's grave.

There is little debate among Buddhist philosophers as to whether these material needs are real in the land of the dead. But if you believe the dead have self-perception, then you also may believe that this self-perception can concern itself with material need. Those impressions of need can be satisfied by an offering that is reflected in the burning of representative items like fake money. For the living, these acts of giving ameliorate the anxieties of the dead, and for that reason alone, despite the absence of actual need, the dead bless them for the offering.

Van's family conducted these rituals in service of their dead. Try as she did to convince her mother and father that these were simple superstitions, the rituals stuck. Van understood their history. She knew that they were driven by the concern that if you did not address the needs of the dead, they would suffer needlessly. Moreover, it took very little effort or cost to alleviate that suffering. Eventually Van gave in, and she found her own her dream life enriched as she paid it the same attention that her elders paid to their dreams. In one such dream, she saw Brian fighting against what appeared to be a large black cloud. But as he swung what seemed to be a large bat, it had no effect. The black cloud swirled around the bat, completely unaffected. Brian swung harder, to no effect, except that the cloud appeared to be wrapping itself around Brian and lifting him in the air as if to swallow him whole. Van ran to the cloud yelling for it to stop, but Brian was disappearing into the cloud as it lifted him higher. She jumped to grab Brian's foot just as it disappeared, and she hung there screaming, "Let him go." The cloud stopped. She thought she heard it speaking to her, but what it said made no sense. The cloud relaxed its grip and let Brian go, and as they fell back to the earth, Brian turned and wrapped his arms around Van, floating softly to the ground and nestling on the soft sand of a beach, Brian on top of Van. She woke up, sweating and trembling with excitement.

Van checked the time. Her alarm was just about to go off. She rolled out of bed, grabbed her workout gear, and walked softly downstairs to not wake her parents. She used a French press to make her Vietnamese coffee, and while she was sipping the hot brew, Mom appeared.

"Your father is making me crazy."

"What this time?"

"He wants to go back to San Francisco and see his friends there."

"Why is that so bad?"

"We don't have time to go to San Francisco."

"You do if you make time."

"How am I supposed to make time? I am working. We have a party this weekend, and I am cooking for the party. You should meet my friend's son. They say he is a genius."

"Mom," said Van appealing, "you need to stop that. Every mother's son is a genius."

"Honey, you need a man in your life."

"I have a gun. Why do I need a man?"

"Don't talk like that to me."

"I'm sorry."

"You need a man like every woman needs a man."

"Well, honestly, Mom, that's a little old school."

"You kids."

"I'm almost thirty, Mom. I'm not a kid."

"And I'm a mom who knows her daughter."

Van finished her coffee. "Ok. I need to run. I'll be back in an hour. Love you!"

Van took off. She started with a light jog. She could feel the caffeine kick in and her brain clearing from the morning fog. Then she remembered the dream. I should have asked her, she thought, her mom's image fading and replaced by the Brian of her dream. Maybe I can take Dad, she thought. Maybe it is time to see Brian again.

* * *

Bost called Brian. "I need you to know something."

"Sure. Let's get together," he said. "We haven't celebrated yet."

"Sorry, bud," responded Bost. "The boss had other plans."

"Tomorrow then?"

"I can't. Deckwalder flew me to Spain."

"Why Spain?"

"Because General Warner is missing, and he thinks he can find him."

"Isn't Belinda in Spain?"

"That's why he thinks Warner is here."

"That's crazy. What does he want to do, walk into a trap?"

"I don't know. He's like all the other Silicon Valley geniuses. Ordinary rules don't apply."

"You're the genius, Bost, not him, and you need to get out of there."

"I can try. We are meeting with the chemistry department at the University of Navarra later today. They have a unit there called SUMBET, Supramolecular Materials for Biomedical and Environmental Technologies. It's the university's nano-tech group."

"Cool name. Sounds like AlphaBet, Google's new name. Some bet, get it?"

"Only you would draw that connection."

"I don't know. Maybe you'll learn something, Bost. But for God's sake, be careful. Don't search out Belinda. She's bad news. You saw what she did to Van."

Bost hung up. He never liked Deckwalder's obsession with the general. At first it was about video games and teaching kids how to fire weapons with their computers. Deckwalder had always wanted a Pentagon deal. Never having served, he was seduced by the might of the military. Bost missed Garny. He realized only now that Garny had the sense to leave at the right time. He wished he knew where he was. He wanted to tell him how AI was transforming the nanospace and how the new team at Ragnar Willowbrook had figured out how to detoxify the bots. But Garny had been gone for years. Bost knew it was just fantasy. Deckwalder called and told him the car was waiting. Bost slurped down his espresso and left the lobby to join him. As he crawled into the car, Deckwalder handed him a bio sheet. "This is our contact at SUMBET," he said. "Her name is Professor Maria Echeverria." Bost read through Professor Echeverria's accomplishments in nanotechnology, which were impressive. But her title jumped out at him, and he looked at Deckwalder as if he were out of his mind. Apparently, Professor Maria Echeverria was the first person to hold the Leonard Freund Chair of Microelectronica. Deckwalder looked at Bost and smiled. "I think we have hooked our fish," he said, in a way that confirmed to Bost his boss's sheer lunacy.

Chapter 28.

The Briefcase

They had called it the War Room Annex even though the United States was not a combatant in any war. The War Room Annex or WRA was operated by the Air Force in a joint conference room at the center of the Raven Rock Mountain Complex. Raven Rock was one of several deep underground nuclear bunkers constructed in the 1950s to ensure the continuity of the American government in the event of a nuclear attack. The joint chiefs of staff viewed Raven Rock as their primary emergency deployment center, and the War Room Annex replaced the Situation Room at the White House and became Command and Control. In case of certain select national emergencies, the country's political and military leaders would be called to the WRA at Raven Rock. These emergencies in the past had included the Cuban Missile Crisis, the assassination of John F. Kennedy, the impeachment of Richard M. Nixon, the attempted assassination of Ronald Reagan, the destruction of the Berlin Wall, 9-11, and the so-called January 6 insurrection. The leaders taken to the WRA included the president, or whoever was in the position of the president if incapacitated, the secretary of state, the speaker of the house, the senate majority and minority leaders, the directors of the CIA, the FBI, the NSA, and the Department of Homeland Security, and the joint chiefs of staff representing each branch of the military. One might think it would be the White House or the Pentagon where such meetings would take place. But in fact, intelligence reported that those locations were the favorite targets of multiple nuclear powers and known terrorist organizations. So, the meetings were held elsewhere, and in many instances, the meetings were held at the WRA deep under Raven Rock Mountain.

Nothing was happening that constituted such a national emergency, as far as CIA director William P. Case was concerned. But at least once a year, the Air Force oversaw a special security drill that altered the routine schedules of these leaders and scrambled off a dozen military helicopters to bring them to Raven Rock. In those instances, when the leaders were pulled out of their routines and forced, as a matter of practice, to fly to Pennsylvania, the WRA would be stocked with the best champagne, the oldest scotches, and the finest cigars and the atmosphere, devoid of actual national crisis, would devolve into a party, a "thank you" to the leaders for their participation in the drill. Case knew this time he would not be enjoying a good scotch as he jumped off the helicopter steps and jogged to the Raven Rock entrance where a special elevator would take him into the WRA. Most of the leaders around him were laughing, assuming it was just a drill. But there was no champagne, scotch, or cigars.

"Gentlemen and gentlewomen, could I have your attention?" said Case as the room began to quiet down. "I have called you here because a new threat has been brought to our attention, and we believe its implications could be global."

"Is it considered a military threat?" asked Admiral Marcia L. Wolfenden, chief of naval operations.

"We believe it is," said Case. "You may recall an incident that occurred about two years ago in Yerevan, the capital city of Armenia." He flashed a photograph of the Yerevan International Airport, showing bodies scattered in the main airport lobby, and then additional photographs of Erebuni Medical Center, patients stacked on gurneys in hallways.

"Looks a bit like Wuhan at the outbreak of COVID-19," said Bernard McKillen, speaker of the house. Several people laughed. Case stared them down, and they quieted.

"I can assure you it is not," said Case. "At the time, we suspected it might be a terrorist attack, something involving a chemical or biological weapon.

The victims all showed acute anaphylaxis, a hyperallergic response to a foreign agent. The CIA had two agents, one of whom took these photos, who ended up in the hospital owing to their own exposure."

"If it is not chemical or biological, what is it?" asked the new president.

"We believe it to have been the result of exposure to microelectronics. Some people call it 'smart dust.' The more common name is nanotechnology or nanobots," said Case.

"Do we think Yerevan is connected to what happened in Paris six months ago?" asked FBI Director Jason David Snell.

"We do," said Case. He flashed a photograph of the Dôme in Paris. "The attack that took place in Paris disrupted what was supposed to be a demonstration of the special capabilities of these nanobots to rebalance carbon dioxide in the atmosphere. The toxic effect of the nanobots was not entirely understood, and a terrorist group exposed dozens of officials to the unfiltered nanobots, and fifteen people died, including the organizer of the event. The biological reactions to these nanobots were the same as the reactions in Yerevan."

"Do we have any details on the group who caused the tragedy?" asked Admiral Wolfenden.

"We don't," said Case. "But we have reason to believe that the Paris event was only the beginning. We believe that someone associated with the event may be weaponizing these nanobots and may be making plans to start a serious conflict."

"How do we know?" asked the president.

Case reached for a briefcase lying on the table. He pressed a code, and the briefcase popped open. Inside the briefcase was a movie script entitled "The Power of Small." He passed around the script.

"Take a look at the script. The story line concerns the medical benefits of nanotechnology, but that is not why I am sharing it with you. Turn it over and look on the back page. What do you see?"

The leaders passed around the script and noticed the three small dots in the middle of the back page.

"We didn't think anything of the dots," said Case. "But just before he left for Spain, one of the Army's generals, a General Tom Warner, sent us this manuscript under top secret cover and told us to note the ellipses. We sent the script to our forensics lab, and they looked at every ellipsis in the manuscript. When they put the dots on the last page under an electron microscope, they saw these three images."

He flashed the first image on the screen. The first image on the single tile was a detailed map of Europe. The northwest section of Spain was highlighted and annotated with the words, "Basque Autonomous Region." It also identified the cities of Errenteria and Pamplona. He flipped to the second image, and it showed handwritten notes from a notebook describing a method for weaponizing nanobots. The final image was a photo of Belinda Armendariz standing in a doorway.

474

"We can recognize Belinda Armendariz in this photograph, but we have not yet identified where it was taken," Case explained. "We have shared this intel with our counterparts in Europe, who have been chasing down leads from the Paris incident."

"Are you talking about the Belinda Armendariz from California?" said Snell.

"We believe we are," said Case.

"We ran into her in the Silicon Valley," said Snell to the larger group. "We did not apprehend her, but we did capture several former service members who appeared to be functioning as a black ops team. We believed this team was responsible for destroying a lab outside of Seattle. We ran an op to apprehend her at her lab in the Silicon Valley, but she wasn't there."

"We are aware of what happened in California and in northwest Washington," said Case. "We believe her to be in Europe, but despite the coordinated efforts of Interpol, MI6, and the CIA, we have yet to locate her."

"Is she on your most-wanted list?" the president asked Snell.

"She's been identified as a criminal at large, but not 'most wanted.'"

"You might think about that."

"There is someone you should talk to," said Snell.

"Who is that?" asked the president.

"She's a young LAPD detective. She was a part of the FBI operation in the Silicon Valley, and more recently, she had an unfortunate run-in with Dr. Armendariz in Spain. The run-in almost killed her. Her name is Detective Van Eng."

"Bring her in," said the president. "We need to know what she knows."

Postscript (Book 2)

Belinda called her team together in the conference room at Muro de Roda. She closed the screen covering the panoramic windows overlooking the valley and the Embalse de Mediano, a reservoir near the town of Ainsa. A large panel TV descended from the ceiling.

"The world as we know it is about to change," she said. "The modern military is not prepared for the destruction we are about to wreak. Dr. Hadj Arkoun, our chief scientist, will explain."

Hadj took control of the screen and popped up an image that looked like a cross between a ballistic missile and the lunar module from NASA's early moon missions.

"What you are looking at is what we call a nanobomb. The nanobomb is like a neutron bomb, a tactical nuclear weapon, the primary goal of which is to kill rather than destroy. Like a neutron bomb, a nanobomb does not leave radioactive waste that takes decades to clear for human occupancy. With a nanobomb, the environment returns to normal in a matter of hours, and we can deploy troops to an area almost immediately. But unlike a neutron bomb, our nanobomb has no known defense. We have designed our nanobots to penetrate any standard hazmat material. Only material specifically designed to prevent penetration of these nanobots will work against them. The nanobomb is also as effective at ground level as it is from the air. Our nanobomb can be planted in a disguised form and detonated remotely. We have produced two dozen of these nanobombs and are in the process of developing dozens more."

He showed a close-up of the modular cap.

"These modules hold about hundred pounds of nanobots in a frozen gelatinous form. The module contains a heating element. The missiles carry the modules into the air as high as a mile, and as they rise, the gel is heated up. The heat converts the gel to a gas. A small charge explodes and releases the gas-filled nanobots, which forms a cloud that rains down on the targets below. The nanobots are deadly to all human life, and within a few minutes, an entire town can be decimated. Then, in just a few hours, the bots evaporate and disappear."

Belinda took over.

"This is a new form of war, gentlemen. Let me explain. Standard military strategy starts a campaign by targeting key infrastructure and munitions depos. The Japanese in World War II hit a naval base in Hawaii and destroyed the destroyers stationed at that base. That strategy will no longer work. Just as you cannot attack a nuclear power plant and expect the country you are invading to be habitable, if you destroy these weapons simply by targeting munitions storage facilities, you will cause the very damage you are seeking to prevent by releasing the nanobots into the atmosphere. The power that only we control is the power we need to accomplish our goals, whatever we decide those goals to be."

The faces in the room nodded.

"This is not just a new class of weapon," said Belinda. "It is a new kind of weapon. It is as important as Alfred Nobel's invention of dynamite 150 years ago."

"The Nobel that started the Peace Prize?" asked one of Belinda's deputies.

"The same," said Hadj.

Belinda looked over at Hadj. He studied her eyes. This peace, he thought, will be painful.

[End of Book 2]

BOOK 3

THE NANOBOT WARS

MAPS

Map 1. The Basque Autonomous Region (*See* Book 2, p. 232.)

Map 2. Pamplona (*See* Book 2, p. 233.)

Map 3. Muro de Roda (from Google Maps).

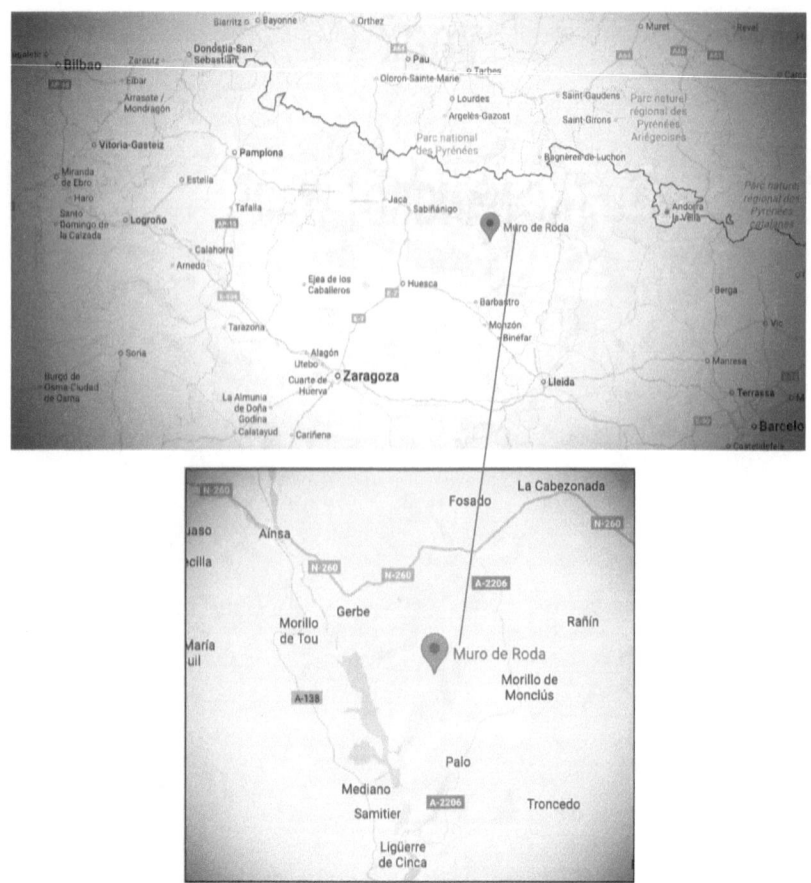

Chapter 1.

Realpolitik

Socialist ideologies gained their foothold in the late 1800s by calling out the crude and abusive labor practices of capitalists during the industrial revolution. The exciting advances born of refined gas and electricity in that same time promised a modern life of convenience. That promise collapsed under the grim realities of mass production and an impoverished labor class. Enough evidence supported the claims made in socialist tracts like *Das Kapital* that the rich were getting richer and the poor were getting poorer to give socialist ideas momentum. Under the thought leadership of Karl Marx and the actual leadership of his adherents, the now-educated poor were mobilized to get justice and economic fairness. But the leaders had a secret. They knew the only path to change was violence and they embraced it wholeheartedly and led the believing masses directly into brutal and sadistic wars which, to the surprise of many, they won.

Then, after rooting out the monarchists and capitalists who allegedly had made everyone's lives miserable, rather than fairness, the poor got dictators who covered up their new-found power and wealth with military costumes and racial hatred and propaganda machines. The dictators solidified their power and wealth by eliminating dissent and rewarding loyalty. Under those regimes, survival of the masses was not based on merit or talent or accomplishment but simply support for the regime and its entrenched propaganda.

If the obvious problems were not enough, like the Death Star in *Star Wars*, socialism had a hidden flaw in the design. Adherents failed to acknowledge that the economic policies of universal if rudimentary housing and 100% if uninspired employment killed any initiative not borne of political ambition and ultimately ground the system's economic engine to a halt. Today's so-called socialists seem oblivious to this inevitability. They either never learned of the images of bread lines, toilet paper scarcity and actual poverty of living in a late-twentieth century socialist country, or they choose to ignore it.

Belinda Armendariz' parents were not socialists and did not believe in the principles of the Socialist Workers' Party running the Spanish government. In fact, they opposed socialism of any form in any government. At six years old, Belinda didn't care one way or the other. Her focus was on her pretty dresses and her dolls and preventing her brother from messing with them. She didn't follow dinner table discussions of Mahatma Ghandi and his ideas like *satyagraha* and nonviolent civil disobedience. She ignored the lengthy discussions of the many meetings her parents had attended and the many scholars who spoke at those meetings and shared their views on economy, ethnicity and nationalism. She wasn't impressed by the wonders of Basque history and its unique culture, which were being suppressed yet again by a government fearful of the loss of control over a large heart-shaped piece of land covering northwest Spain. As her parents grumbled about the negative publicity that the violent Basque nationalist movement called the ETA was having on their nonviolent campaign to free the Basque nation from Spanish domination, Belinda would sneak a peek under the table trying to feed their miniature French poodle. She just wanted dinner to end so she could play with her dolls for a few minutes before her bath, which she hated, and bedtime.

Then, on one fateful evening in the middle of a robust dinner discussion, Belinda heard a knock at their front door.

"Daddy," she said and pulled on his sleeve.

There was a louder knock and this time her parents heard it. Belinda's dad, Mikel, rose from the table and walked toward the door, finishing a thought in the conversation. He looked out the eyehole in the door, and then turned to his family and said, "Stay seated at the table." He opened the front door to a bevy of police officers, more than necessary for any routine inquiry.

"Are you Dr. Mikel Armendariz?"

"I am. How can I help you?"

"Please step back, Dr. Armendariz." The officers entered and pulled his arms behind his back.

"Why are you in my home? What right have you to be here?"

"We have a warrant for your arrest."

"On what grounds?"

"Criminal association with the ETA."

"I don't have any association with the ETA. I detest what they do."

"You can raise that with the Court. Is your wife home?"

Belinda's mom rose from the table. Her hands were shaking as she watched the police handcuff her husband.

The officer called her over. "Please join your husband. The arrest warrant covers you as well."

"You can't take us both," she said. "We have young children."

Belinda started to cry and ran to hug her mother, Amaia. "Mommy," she said between sobs. "Are they taking Daddy?"

The officer added: "You can help your children pack. Social Services is here to attend to their needs."

"We have relatives. Can we make a call?"

"You have five minutes to pack the children's things. I suggest you move quickly."

A young woman in a uniform entered the home. Belinda's mom looked at her husband and shrugged. What do I do? she mouthed.

"This is all a mistake," Mikel said. "Do what they say. We will get it fixed by tomorrow. I know someone we can call from the station."

"Oh, my God," Amaia said, fearing the worst. "Oh, my God. Oh, my God."

She hustled into the kids' bedroom and dragged out their suitcases. She threw piles of fresh clothes into the suitcases. The children followed her. Belinda grabbed her dolls. "Mommy, where are we going? Can I take my dolls?"

Amaia grabbed the dolls and put them in the suitcase. As she pulled things from the bathroom, she started sobbing.

"Mommy, Mommy, don't cry. It's ok," said Belinda wiping away her own tears.

Belinda's 10-year-old brother, Zor, turned toward his mom, holding his suitcase in silence.

When the family was finally assembled in the living room, Amaia grabbed both her kids and told them she loved them and not to worry. She would talk to them as soon as Daddy got things fixed. The police took Mikel to the car and sat him in the back seat. They returned and handcuffed Amaia, and the Social Services agent took the suitcases and told the children to come with her. Belinda watched through the window in stunned silence as the police car with Mommy and Daddy pulled away and as an unknown officer exited the house carrying away their little dog.

The social services agent said nothing for several minutes as she drove from the children's home. The children sat in the back seat and said nothing. Belinda's brother had said nothing all night as if he were mute. Finally, the driver looked over her shoulder. "What are your names?" she asked, trying to seem motherly. Belinda looked at her brother. For a minute, they didn't respond. "That's fine," said the woman. "You don't need to speak. My name is Clarice. My friends call me Clare."

Zor remained sullen. "Where are you taking us, *Clare*?" He emphasized her name in disgust.

"We are going to a place that is warm and friendly," she said, "just until your parents work things out with the police."

"You are lying," said Zor. "They are taking our parents away."

"They are not!" shouted Belinda and began to cry again.

"Be nice to your sister," said Clare. "Stop scaring her."

"You are not my mom," said Zor, but he added nothing more.

Clare stopped the car in front of the House of Angels, a local orphanage and adoption support group run by the Catholic Church. A nun met them at the door. Clare left them with the nun and turned and headed to the car, wiping a small tear from her face. Once inside, a priest approached Zor and instructed him to follow him to the boys' dorm. Belinda ran and grabbed her brother, scared that he would be leaving her also. The nun tried to calm her down.

"Now, now, dear," she said. "The boys' dorm is down that hall and the girls' dorm is down this hall. He is not leaving. You will see each other for breakfast. I promise you."

Zor pulled his sister's arm off his leg.

"Go with the nun," he commanded. "I will see you at breakfast."

The nun led Belinda to a large room with a dozen beds. Girls of varying ages were goofing off and the nun, ignoring the playfulness, said, "We have a new guest, girls. Her name is Belinda. You must welcome her with the love of Christ Jesus."

The morning came and went. And the next day and the next. No word came from her parents. Clare never came by to check on the children. The nuns quickly grew tired of Belinda's incessant questions about her parents. Did they call? Did they stop by? Did you see their car driving past the orphanage? She refused to stop asking even when the questions triggered punishments. As she grew older, the nature of her questions changed. Have you heard from the Court? Has there been a decision? Were my parents in the paper? Every time the ETA committed another act of terror, Belinda wondered, were they there? Is it their fault? Then, eventually, the multiplicity of questions merged into a single inquiry – Are they dead?

Chapter 2.

Originality

Wassily Kandinsky has been heralded as a pioneer of modern art. He assembled his most recognized abstractions in his mid-60s, explosions of color and geometric design based on biblical stories of the Apocalypse and the Flood. As a young man, Kandinsky began his training at the Odessa Art School and, at the same time, earned a professorship in law and economics at the University of Dorpat (now Tartu) in Estonia. At the age of 30, he abandoned his professorship and enrolled in the Munich Academy of Fine Arts where he initially was refused admission. He studied art on his own and, on one visit to a Monet exhibit, found himself transfixed by Monet's impressionist painting *Haystacks*. The lack of a distinctive object in the painting seemed improper to Wassily but the painting stuck with him. He explored color theory and uncovered a connection between color and music and eventually he found a spirituality in painting or what he called *inner beauty*. His analytical mind led him to view in music a similar kind of abstraction, and he began to think of that abstraction as a door to the soul. Painting became a kind of spiritual expression for him, and he leaned on his orthodox Christian training for themes in his work. Music would play a dominant role in his art theory, and he even titled his paintings with musical terms *improvisation* and *composition*. Kandinsky's thought experiments and spiritual journeys found their deepest expression in his abstractions, where he found refuge from the harsh realities of war and the rise of fascism and revolution in the early twentieth century.

Belinda Maria Armendáriz clutched her books tightly to her breasts as she climbed the steps below the massive ionic columns that fronted the Massachusetts Institute of Technology's School of Engineering. It was her first day of classes and, excited as she had been to be admitted to MIT, she now faced the frightening reality of the immense brain power of the student body. She fought against a growing conviction that she did not belong, and it took all she had not to turn around and leave the campus. She forced herself to keep moving forward and was heartened as young men smiled at her and held open the massive doors that led to the lecture hall. The lecture began. The school president was there to welcome them and congratulated them for being the brightest students of their generation and for being admitted to the most prestigious engineering program in the country. He concluded by saying, "Now that the niceties are out of the way, allow me to introduce to you my fellow faculty member and Nobel laureate in physics, Dr. Andrzej Abramowitz, whom we affectionately call 'Double AA.' You, however, will call him, Professor."

Belinda opened her notebook and pulled out a pen, but as she popped off the cap it flew out of her grip and hit another student sitting in front of her in the back of the head. He turned and looked at her shocked at first and then amused, and several students around her laughed as she tried to apologize. The old professor looked in her direction and said, "Maybe we should start with theories of propulsion," and the entire class of 200 students erupted in laughter. Belinda fought back the urge to bolt and buried her head in her notebook.

But the feelings soon disappeared and, as the lecture continued, she found herself drawn to the wide scope of engineering subjects the professor began to lay out, including biomedical engineering, chemical engineering, electrical engineering, and especially nuclear engineering. As she left the lecture hall, committed only to getting out of the lecture hall as fast as she could and over to Hayden Library where she could bury herself in her books, she felt someone tap her on the shoulder.

"I think this is yours," said the young man whom she accidently had hit in the head with her pen cap.

"I'm so sorry," Belinda muttered as she took the pen cap from his outstretched hand. "I am such an idiot."

To her surprise, his face went ashen, and he stood there paralyzed. Then, without saying another word, he abruptly turned and left, leaving Belinda standing and holding the pen cap with a confused look on her face. She shrugged and headed to the library, pondering the interaction and realizing that he hadn't even asked her name.

As the weeks passed, Belinda began to get her footing. The Hayden librarians knew her by name because she spent so much time there and, after scoring the highest marks in her class on her first exams, even "Double AA" smiled when he saw her. She continued to avoid the young man though she couldn't understand why he seemed so ashamed every time she caught him looking at her.

She made a few friends in her dorm who invited her to join them for late night snacking sessions and old movies in the student lounge. Her best friend, Betsy Hargrave, stayed in the same suite of dorm rooms as she did but catty-corner to her room.

Betsy was from a wealthy family who lived in Manhattan on the upper East Side. Betsy's goal was to become a doctor, but her math scores were so high that her family convinced her to go to MIT and then decide from there what to do with her life. Betsy was popular and boys regularly showed up to her dorm room, but Betsy had a serious boyfriend in New York City who went to NYU to study acting and theater. Still Betsy got invited to many dorm parties and she always brought Belinda along as a buffer to the more aggressive boys.

As the term approached the holidays, Betsy asked Belinda if she planned to go home for the holiday break.

"I need to get ready for finals," Belinda told her.

"Doesn't your family want to see you?"

"They will understand."

Betsy knew that Belinda did not like to talk about her past and, ordinarily, she let it go to talk about something fun. This time she persisted.

"How could they understand you missing the holidays? My family would go nuts if I told them I wouldn't be around for Christmas and New Year's. We even have family members from England who fly to New York just to be with us at the holidays."

"It's hard to explain," Belinda responded and looked down.

"Can't be that hard," said Betsy. "I have several rich friends whose parents paid for nannies and boarding schools and distant college campuses just so they could run around and pretend to be single."

Belinda sighed, warmed by Betsy's smile. "Definitely not that."

She shrugged.

"There is no one for me to go home to."

"What do you mean? You mean…you don't have family?"

"I have a brother but he…" Belinda struggled to complete the thought.

"Your parents?" Betsy asked. "Are they still living?"

"It's hard for me to talk about it," said Belinda.

"Time for coffee, then," said Betsy spryly. "I have a pot in my room."

She took Belinda back to the dorm, pointing out cute boys and laughing infectiously. By the time they got there, Belinda was relaxed.

"My family is Basque, and my parents joined a liberation movement when I was five years old."

"Basque? That is a Spanish ethnicity, right?"

"If you asked my parents, they would tell you it's more of a nationality than an ethnicity. But yes, there's an ethnic component and it's unique. It's a combination of Spanish and French but neither also. We used to have our own kingdom a long time ago. We were very poor and looked down upon by the larger and wealthier Spanish monarchies. Eventually we were absorbed into Spain, but we preserved our Basque identity. My parents believed it was time for the Basque people to be free to control our own destiny. My father was arrested several times by the Spanish government for protesting."

"Sounds very commendable. But something happened. What?"

"I don't know. I never knew. I was a child. I heard someone in the Spanish government died in a bombing. My parents were arrested, and my brother and I were taken to an orphanage. We never heard from our parents, and no one would tell us what happened. The kids at the orphanage told me my parents were killers. They taunted me and no one stopped them. My brother tried to protect me, but they beat him up, every day. I hid in the school library and read books."

"My god, Belinda. That's terrible."

"It was my life, I suppose, for better or worse. I read a lot of books. I became the top student in all my classes, and the director of the orphanage took me under his wing and prepared me for university.

My brother fought back against the bullies and eventually became the leader of the orphanage gang. He got into trouble all the time. The staff wanted him kicked out of the orphanage, but the director protected him because he was my brother. Finally, one of the kids in the gang died in a terrible accident. They blamed my brother and sent him to a juvenile detention center. I saw him a few times, but he was bitter. He was mad at my parents for leaving us alone and mad at the orphanage for making him into a criminal. I decided to research the bombing that led to my parents' arrest. It turns out my parents were part of a group that followed Gandhi and believed in nonviolent protest. They didn't set the bomb and there is no evidence to support that claim. The government set them up as scapegoats and tore apart my family."

"Oh, Belinda," Betsy said sadly and then brightened up. "Ok, look, you need to be with someone at the holidays. I am taking you with me to New York."

Belinda cracked a smile. "I suppose, if you insist," she said. "That might be nice."

The holidays turned out to be much nicer than Belinda could have expected. Betsy's parents were at the center of the Manhattan elite and every day they either entertained a visit from a someone influential or attended a party hosted by a politician, a celebrity and even a member of the United Nations. They lived in a two-story condo on Manhattan's upper East Side, a huge corner condo with a view to the Queensborough Bridge to the southeast and the Central Park on the west, directly over the top of the Metropolitan Museum of Art. The weather was warm for December and piles of snow from a recent storm were melting. The streets reflected the season and were decorated with scores of holiday banners and wreaths and lights.

Every day, Betsy took Belinda to a different City landmark. They rode elevators in the Empire State Building, took a boat to the Statue of Liberty, rode bikes over the Brooklyn Bridge, watched the chess players in Washington Square Park and even walked through the ashes at the tragic World Trade Center Memorial. Belinda couldn't remember a time in her life when she was that happy, except maybe the day she received the package from MIT acknowledging her acceptance.

Every morning, she and Betsy found a streetside cafe where they enjoyed bagels and coffee. But Belinda's favorite spot to visit was directly across the Fifth Avenue entrance to Betsy's residence, what Betsy told her locals called "The Met." The Met had dedicated a wing to famous Spanish artists and included a life-size reproduction of Pablo Picasso's *Guernica,* a large gray-scale painting that stood 12 feet high x 25 feet long. *Guernica* represented Picasso's protest of the Spanish government's bombing of a small Basque town of the same name. The wing included celebrated works by Salvador Dali and Joan Miró and made Belinda feel at home and proud.

Betsy's parents, Paul and Mary, were intrigued by Belinda's Basque heritage and they spent long hours drinking spiked eggnog and talking about Belinda's parents and Basque history. They offered to Belinda that they would work their connections at the UN and in Washington, D.C. to find out what had happened to Belinda's parents and sparked the tiniest glimmer of hope in Belinda's heart. Belinda's brains and good looks also won her some attention from Betsy's male friends. One, a young graduate student at Columbia named Sergio, took a liking to Belinda and spontaneously showed up on several of Betsy and Belinda's outings.

At first, Belinda assumed he liked Betsy and told her she didn't want to interfere with Betsy's social life, but Betsy laughed and told her he was like a brother to her. The three of them bounced around the city in taxis, Belinda pretending not to notice Sergio's focused interest on her. Classes resumed in January and Belinda found herself inspired by the New York City experience with Betsy's family. She dove into her studies and Double AA asked her to join an elite student group that was working on new developments in robotics and competing in an international robotics competition called Robot Wars. The boy, with whom she had the encounter on the first day of classes, also was invited to join the robotics squad. The interaction helped him get over his shyness and they often worked together, joking about the incident. The simplest robots were remote-controlled circular saws or sledgehammers. Belinda and her team constructed robots out of high tensile steel to protect their robots' bodies and brains from the standard pile driving robots that usually won those competitions.

It was Belinda's idea to attach a tungsten composite arm extender below the robot's chassis that could reach under a bot to flip it over before a scorpion-like stinger would slam into the underbelly of the unfortunate competitor and attack the motherboard that served as its brains. The MIT team made it all the way to Nationals and the Final 16 that year, when the competitions were abruptly cancelled over a trademark dispute. The MIT team was devastated until they got a call from the Stanford team that was ranked as their top competitor.

The Stanford team had decided to form their own competition and told the MIT group that if they could pull together the top 16 finalists, Comedy Central might be interested in airing the competition on cable television. They changed the name of the competition from Robot Wars to BattleBots. Belinda and the MIT team, with the support of Double AA, heartily agreed to fly to Long Beach, California, for the competition. They scheduled the competition for May, which left the MIT team one month to prepare.

Late one night, two days before the competition was to start, Belinda and Harry, the shy boy, were resting on a couch in the student lounge when Sal Pinsky, the so-called genius and leader of the MIT team, approached.

"You guys should see this," he said. "Follow me."

Belinda and Harry obediently jumped up from the couch and followed Sal out of the lounge. They walked a couple of blocks when Sal grabbed Belinda and pulled her into a bush, or at least that is what it felt like. It turned out to be a hidden gap in the hedge. Belinda reached back to pull Harry through as he hesitantly peered through the hedge.

"Shhh," warned Sal, his finger to his lips. Then he pointed to a lit window and inside the trio could see students working. "That's the Stanford team," he said. "Watch."

Belinda knew right away what they were witnessing. "We shouldn't be here," she said.

But she could not look away and watched with growing interest as, inside the lab, the students were experimenting with a robotic device that looked like a mobility platform. They thrusted broken broomsticks at the platform and as soon as the device detected the thrusting broomstick, the platform made a swift lateral move, evading the stick. As hard as they tried, the students could not get their sticks under the platform.

"Oh, no," whispered Belinda to Sal. "They'll kill us in the competition."

"Yah," said Sal. "I thought you'd find this interesting."

Harry watched with the same concern. "What should we do?"

"Let's wait," said Sal. Belinda was already thinking. "We need a way to block to device's ability to anticipate the thrusting arm. We need a cloaking system."

"Like what?" said Sal. "We're not dealing with radar. We can't stealth our bot."

"What are we dealing with?" Belinda asked. "Is it radio frequency or laser? There must be a way to block it."

"We can't block it," said Sal. "We don't have time. The competition is in two days."

"We can't just capitulate," said Harry. "Maybe we can outsmart it. Speed up the thrusting arm."

"It's already too fast," said Sal. "Watch what they are doing. I have another idea."

Belinda and Harry looked at their leader. "We need a virus."

"Oh," said Belinda. "I get it. Trap and inject."

"No," said Sal. "We need to sabotage the bot."

"Whaaat?" responded Belinda and Harry in unison. "I don't think that is smart," said Belinda.

Sal ignored her. "Let's get out of here," he said, "before someone sees us."

Back at the lounge, Sal pulled the team together and began to formulate a plan. "First we need code – something interferes with movement, that freezes the bot in place." He pointed out the two best coders and instructed them to get to work. "You have 24 hours. It doesn't need to be perfect; it just needs to work." Then he looked at Belinda and Harry. "You two," he said, "are the saboteurs. Tomorrow night you will find a way to break into the lab. It must be clean. We can't leave a mess. I will arrange a pre-competition meeting tomorrow between MIT and Stanford leadership and suggest rule changes. They'll think I am trying to get an advantage and push back, but I don't care about rules. I just need to give you time to get in, upload the virus, and get out."

Belinda and Harry didn't respond.

"I know you think this is wrong but let me explain something to you. This is not just a college competition. This is war, and, in this war, rules don't apply."

Chapter 3.

A Foolish Consistency

W. Sommerset Maugham, a well-known and highly regarded 20th century British author and playwright, lived a conflicted life. Unable to follow his father's footsteps into law due to a life-long speech defect, he chose medicine but, in the end, abandoned medicine and opted to write instead. He was recruited by the British Secret Service after serving as an ambulance driver in World War I and hid his homosexuality by marrying and raising a daughter. The marriage lasted 12 years during which Maugham maintained a gay relationship with a younger man named Gerald Haxton, with whom he traveled the world and held lavish parties in the French Riviera. His early writings were not well received, although his first novel, *Liza of Lambeth,* drew from his experience working as a doctor in the London slums and was praised for the quality of writing but criticized for its content and support of an adulterous lifestyle. Despite the criticism, the first printing sold out and convinced Maugham to focus his career on writing.

He wrote several plays before producing his masterpiece, *Of Human Bondage,* about the struggles of a young man bearing life with a club foot as a handicap that many likened to Maugham's struggles with his speech and his homosexuality. He was highly regarded as well for *The Moon and Sixpence* and *The Razor's Edge.* He wrote the latter during World War II, in which his lead character, traumatized by World War I, rejects the East Coast wealth of the 1920s and finds new meaning through his travels and studies in India.

Maugham had tremendous success as a writer, was highly honored and lived what anyone might think would be a charmed life. But despite all the wisdom contained in his many writings, he died at 91, having succumbed to the conflicted nature of his life and rejecting those who loved him the most.

Van looked down and noticed she was holding a folded piece of paper. She carefully unfolded it, curious at what it said. The page contained a list of items and at the top of the page it read, "To Do List." The list briefly confused Van – she didn't recall having written any to do list and certainly not this one. But the handwriting did look a bit like her handwriting. Then she read it:

To Do List

1.   Meet Brian at the beach.

2.   Bring a blanket and wine and cheese.

3.   Wear a sexy blouse.

4.   Let him kiss me.

She felt the buzz of romantic excitement at the prospect of meeting Brian and dropped the list on the front seat of her car as she entered the beach parking lot. She grabbed a blanket and wine basket and saw a figure on the beach. Spreading out the blanket and falling on her knees into the sand, she pulled out the wine and felt a hand on her shoulder. Suddenly the thought of Brian felt strange. "Why Brian?" she wondered. "I haven't seen him since the nanobot demo." The hand ran down her arm and she rolled over and opened her eyes.

"Good morning."

"Huh? What?" Van stirred. She leaned up on one arm and realized she was drooling. She quickly wiped her mouth.

"Martin!?"

Martin Richard was sitting up in bed, his shirt off and wearing only underwear.

"Hi, babe. Sleep well?" He wore a devilish grin.

Van's mind began to focus. It wasn't her first dream about Brian, and the dream left her feeling strange. But here was Martin mostly naked and in bed with her and she was not dreaming.

Van felt a tinge of regret. She remembered Martin coaxing her into his bedroom and making out with her and she had just enough wine in her to allow things to happen that she might not otherwise have allowed.

Martin, on the other hand, was happy. He leaned in to give her another kiss, and she gently pushed him away with her hand and said, "My breath must be terrible."

Not discouraged, he laughed and said, "Do you want some breakfast? I think my mom is making it."

Van cringed at the thought of Martin's parents and answered, "I am not really hungry," and, trying not to be rude, she quickly added, "but coffee sounds nice."

Breakfast with Martin's parents turned out to be enjoyable. They asked a ton of questions about Spain and Pamplona having left there under Van's direction, acknowledging her acute sense of the danger that they might have faced if they had remained in Spain. She tried to avoid describing the incident at La Curva, where Belinda had dumped her in front of the runners and bulls, but they pressed hard enough and eventually she described the scene. She justified it to herself thinking the more they know about Belinda the more aware they might be of the danger they faced with her in Pamplona and, maybe, the less inclined they would be to push Martin in her direction.

She doubted it worked, though, when Frank made the comment, "You're like a real-life female James Bond."

"No, I'm not," she replied, not having seen any James Bond movies. "But thanks, I think." Martin walked her to her car and asked about seeing her again. She smiled and kissed him on the cheek. "I'll call you," she told him. "But that," she said pointing back to the house, "that is not happening again." Martin took it in stride and grinned. "We'll see," he said and laughed. Van smirked and fell into the driver's seat. *He's right*, she thought. *Who knows?*

Back at the Bureau, Van ran into Charlie.

"My dear," he said.

"Come on, Charlie," she replied with a smile. "I am not your 'dear.'"

"Of course," he said. "I meant to say, 'my dear Detective.'"

"Ok, enough. Any news?"

"Nothing here except the usual – gang warfare, mob hits, corrupt cops."

"Welcome to Tuesday."

"There is someone waiting for you at the front desk."

"Me?" An image of Brian flashed in her mind, but she quickly set it aside.

"I don't think you know this person," Charlie said. "He is very patient. He's been sitting there for 45 minutes."

"That's odd." Van called the front desk. She looked at Charlie. "He's with the federal government but not FBI apparently. They are putting him in a room. Do you want to come with me?"

Charlie and Van found a young man in an interrogation room. He was smartly dressed and carried himself with an air of importance. As they sat down, Van noticed other detectives walking by the window and peering in.

"How can we help you?" she said.

He pulled out a card that read, *Office of the President of the United States, White House.*

A black SUV was waiting for her at the airport curb. Van was tired but exhilarated. The first rush of adrenaline that accompanied an invitation to meet the President of the United States had long worn off, but the waves of excitement persisted. Charlie stood next to her only because she had insisted that he be invited to come along. The black SUV was exactly what they expected, but Charlie looked at Van and said nothing. He could tell by the look on her face that they were thinking the same thing. What is it about people in positions of power and the need to ride around in black SUVs?

As the secret service ushered her into the Oval Office, Van was overwhelmed by the thought about her parents' treacherous journey to freedom in the hull of an old freighter. She knew the stories her father told her about how her mother had kept Van alive by risking ridicule and derision and going to the top deck to plea for food and medicine. The ship's crew had laughed at her and mocked her and threatened her with their rifles and yet she continued to press her luck and ask for assistance. They rolled their eyes and said, "Here's comes Momma again." But someone always took pity and found something to give to her for her baby.

While on the plane, Van had read up on the White House and its many renovations, including President Teddy Roosevelt's addition of the West Wing and President Taft's expansion of the same and construction of the Taft Oval Office. She noted the three windows that looked out on the White House lawns, and she wondered if you could see the Rose Garden. But she was especially fascinated by the story of the President's desk.

When she entered the strange round room, she quickly took in most of its details. In addition to the President, she noted four men and a woman, two generals, the President's chief of staff, the Secretary of Defense and the Director of the CIA. Charlie was not permitted in the Oval Office and waited in the lobby for Van to return. Her eyes fixed on the desk.

The President welcomed her and introduced her as Detective Eng to the room. He beckoned her to sit on one of the cream-colored couches. The woman, the CIA Director, sat next to her.

"You're not the first person to stare at my desk," said the President.

"My apologies, Mr. President," said Van and looked at the carpet as if she had breached some protocol.

"None needed," he said. "I shouldn't say it is my desk. It belongs more to the office than the position."

"It's just that I know the story," she responded, "and I am a bit overwhelmed to be here."

The others in the room stopped talking and looked at Van.

"So am I," said the President and smiled. "No matter how many hours I have spent in here."

He looked around. "Do any of you know the story of the desk?"

"Didn't it come from a ship?" asked the Press Secretary.

"Yes, it did." He looked at Van. "Care to enlighten them?"

Van looked around. She was not interested in showing off and it felt odd to her to be put in the spotlight. She spoke quietly.

"The desk was a gift from the Queen of England. Its wood came from the H.M.S. Resolute, a British Navy ship that had been trapped in ice in the Arctic Circle and rescued by Americans."

"She is exactly right," said the President. "Do you know what it is called?"

"It is named after the ship."

"It sure is," he replied and looked around to see that everyone in the room was impressed by this child of Vietnamese immigrants who knew American history so well. "It is called 'The Resolute.' Appropriate for a sitting President, don't you think?"

Van heard the murmurs of assent. "Interesting also how a ship named the Resolute might get stuck in the ice," Van added risking a moment of humor. There was a moment of silence and then the President laughed out loud, as did everyone in the room.

"I think they call that a foolish consistency," said the President smiling. Then he became serious. "Do you know why we asked you here?"

"I don't, not really."

He looked around. "Nobody briefed the good detective?" The room didn't move.

"Well," he said, knowing his instructions had been to keep her in the dark and basking for a moment in the power of his new Office, "I understand that you have some familiarity with Dr. Belinda Armendariz."

* * *

Dr. Brian Johannsen headed on his Gold Wing down Highway 17. The misty rain collected on his face shield, and he had to wipe away the drops to see the road. Driving his bike in the rain never bothered him though. The whole point of traveling by motorcycle was to be exposed to the elements, sun, wind, bugs, dirt and even rain. He liked how it made him focus on exactly what he was doing in the moment even though there was so much else on his mind. Soon thereafter he pulled up to the entrance of Providia and parked. He grabbed a leather satchel out of one of his saddle bags and made his way to the entrance. Bost Karnivan, chief engineer in Providia's nanotechnology division, waited by the door.

"How was the ride?" he asked Brian.

"Wet," said Brian smiling, always happy to see Bost. Bost and Brian had been working together regularly ever since Brian demonstrated to Bost how nanobots could self-replicate. Brian did not invent that process, he uncovered it and learned how to create the conditions for self-replication.

The genius behind self-replication had been "Garny" McDonough, former billionaire founder of Providia who left after his partners at Providia voted against him to get into video gaming. Garny had been missing for over a year and was presumed dead after a terrorist event in Paris took the lives of several prominent environmentalists. They entered the lobby at Providia, adorned with banners and posters of prominent video games and movies about video games. Brian noticed a large poster announcing the premiere of a new movie from Paramount, *The Power of Small*. He recalled Van's involvement in the backlot murder and wondered if he should be impressed with Paramount's resolve to bring out a movie despite the murder of one of its writers. He figured Providia's interest in the movie was its focus on nanobots. He thought about seeing it.

"They're waiting," said Bost, picking up on Brian's momentary distraction. "You still feel the same?"

"Pretty much," he responded. "We'll see what they say."

Bost escorted Brian to the top floor board room. The windows overlooked the south end of the San Francisco Bay. Brian noticed the tide was out and he could see clammers walking around in thigh high mud boots poking into the mud for clams. A collection of individuals stood at the opposite end of the board room conference table. Brian recognized most of them. He of course knew Christopher Deckwalder, founder of Providia. Standing around him were Frank Stafford, founder of Microsystematics, Bill Bodrogian, founder of American Biogen, Thor Johnson, founder of Johnson Robotics, and Keith Lucerno, founder of Cryptocoin. They all stopped talking when he entered. Brian wondered if he'd ever seen so much wealth gathered in one room before. Deckwalder moved toward him and extended his hand. One individual, whom he didn't recognize, was seated and remained seated. Unlike the others, he was not smiling.

"Quite a gathering," said Brian.

"Let me introduce you to a few friends of mine," said Deckwalder.

Brian was courteous and shook everyone's hand.

"Last but not least," said Deckwalder, "I want you to meet Sam Cook. Sam's family goes back to Captain James Cook. You might have heard of him."

"Hawaii?" queried Brian.

"Hawaii made him famous," said Sam Cook, staring intently at Brian. "Hawaii also murdered him."

"Well," said Brian. "Sounds like he was a brave guy."

"Fearless," answered Cook. "Pathologically." He smiled.

"So, gentlemen, it's my honor to be in your presence. But why am I here?"

"Brian," answered Deckwalder. "I mean Dr. Johannsen. We've been watching what you are doing with Ragnar Willowbrook. Very impressive."

"Thank you."

"But he is not Belinda," said Cook looking at the others.

"Belinda is a criminal," said Deckwalder. "We aren't looking for a criminal."

"We are looking for a leader," said Cook. "Is this laboratory technician a leader?"

Bost spoke up in Brian's defense. "He is the smartest one here. People look up to him. He is restoring Ragnar's reputation – something very few people could do."

"That's our concern," said Cook. "These gentlemen of business have been very patient. But their patience is running thin."

"What is the problem?" said Brian, although he already knew the answer.

"Well, for one, I have five patents waiting to be cleared," said Bodrogian. "Belinda would have had those turned around months ago." The other billionaires murmured assent.

"You have work to do," said Brian. "Your patents won't clear with bogus studies."

"That's outrageous," said Bodrogian, pounding his fist. "Those studies have the backing of the best pharmaceutical scientists in the country."

"Your anti-Alzheimer's compounds cause cranial bleeding, and you propose to manage the bleeding with a clotting mechanism that causes strokes. Solve those problems and you'll get cleared. But not until then."

Deckwalder interjected. "What are you looking for Brian? Money? Funding? You need more support for your nanobot studies?"

"I don't need anything," said Brian. "You want a clearance from Ragnar Willowbrook to mean something? You need to let me do my job."

"You need to take care of this," said Cook, "or you may not have your job for much longer."

Brian watched Sam Cook. He had the look of a mob don but who was he? Was he deluded enough to think the legacy of a colonialist ancestor gave him leverage?

"My board decides my fate," said Brian. "Not you."

Thor Johnson had been staring at the table during most of the interchange. "Last time I looked," he said, "I had a seat on your Board."

"I know you do, Thor," said Brian, forcing himself to stay calm. "But what would you have me do?"

"Right now, in this moment, I believe your job is to listen. You don't need to react. You don't need to make a hasty decision. Just listen to everyone. This is not bully politics."

"I might beg to differ, but I hear you. I appreciate everyone's concerns, and I promise I will take it under advisement." He looked at Deckwalder, "I think this discussion is over." He turned to the group, "My best to you all."

Chapter 4.

Ambivalence

In 1936, F. Scott Fitzgerald wrote: "The test of a first-rate intelligence is the ability to hold two opposing ideas in mind at the same time and still retain the ability to function. One should, for example, be able to see that things are hopeless yet be determined to make them otherwise." He penned the line in his short story "The Crack-Up," a semi-autobiographical story tracking Fitzgerald's late life battle with depression. The story was not published until after Fitzgerald's death and received critical acclaim. But one wonders what opposing ideas an American intellectual in the 1930s might hold. There were several big themes dominating the 1930s. Fascism and communism were on the rise simultaneously. In the United States, the fight between interventionism and isolationism gathered steam with the latter temporarily holding sway. In 1936, Congress adopted the Neutrality Act, forbidding the President from making any American contribution to the fight against Nazi expansionism. Disregarding calls for boycotting the 1936 Summer Olympic Games in Berlin, the United States brought the competition's second largest team. Hollywood executives, despite Hitler's documented abuses of Jewish citizens, peddled lightly on anti-Nazi interventionist themes, influenced in part to stay out of the conflict by the Los Angeles German consulate, specifically Georg Gyssling. But in an era of financial suffering when belief in ideologies dominated public discourse, Fitzgerald's idea that intelligence might be better indicated by uncertainty rather than certainty had a revolutionary tinge. At the very least, it made for good dinner conversation.

"This is not war," Belinda said. "It's a game."

"It is a war game," Harry answered.

"That's not the point," Belinda replied. "I'm not a saboteur and I'm definitely not breaking into a university lab even to win a war game."

"You are probably right," said Harry. "But we are talking about a national championship."

"One that we win by cheating?"

"I can guarantee you that Stanford is not above a little friendly espionage."

"We can win this without cheating."

"How?" asked Harry, who had already committed to the bold move and was fighting to keep his nerve up.

"I don't know, but I believe we can."

Sal walking into the lounge. "You two have a plan?"

"Belinda has doubts."

"Really? Moral qualms?"

Belinda was silent. She had no interest in debating Sal – he'd make her feel foolish. She wanted to win the competition, but not at any cost. *We can be smarter than them,* she thought to herself.

"Let's be calm and try to act rationally," she said to Sal and Harry. "What are we up against? Stanford knows they need to evade our probe, and it looks like they figured out a way to do it."

"Pretty damn good way too," said Sal, thinking he would entertain Belinda but certain he would not change his mind. He wanted the Stanford battlebot sabotaged.

"Well, what are our options? First, we could ignore the problem and hope their solution doesn't work."

Harry jumped in. "You saw it, Belinda. It's effective."

"Right and ignoring it would be dumb. The bot darts left every time. What if we recalibrate the stinger to aim to the left. Our probe shoots straight at the bot, it jumps left and BAM! The stinger hits it as it moves left."

"You are forgetting at least one thing," said Sal smugly. "The effectiveness of the stinger depends on the extender arm flipping the bot. It can't reach the motherboard through the top of the bot."

"True," said Belinda. "I agree. The stinger is not the solution. We need a way to fake an attack so that it looks like the probe is extending. A feint. Like a boxer."

"Well, these bots are not human beings. They don't anticipate moves. They react to moves. You can't fake a move. Either you move or you don't."

"So, we move," said Belinda. "Twice. We add a second probe. We program the bot to detect the bot's reaction to the first probe, spin in that direction and shoot out a second extender."

"It's possible," said Harry. "There is room for a second attachment."

"I don't know. They were throwing a lot of broomsticks at that bot, and it evaded all of them," said Sal.

"Then we need a backup," said Belinda. "The virus."

"Now you're talking," said Sal. "When are we breaking into the lab?"

"We're not. We are not committing sabotage," said Belinda. "We will hit them at the event."

Comedy Central confirmed they were cablecasting the event at the Long Beach Convention Center. Students lined up for several blocks to be allowed into the show. Racks of lights lit up the room in the center of which was a fenced-off battle square.

The floor of the battle square was made up of concrete tiles designed to protect the hard floor underneath. A large flashing sign that read "BattleBots" hung high over the center of the square, well out of the range of any combatants. One camera stood on each side of the square attached to heavy duty mobile tripods. A third camera was attached to a boom that could extend into the center of the square without falling over. Unmanned cameras were positioned to view the competition from the floor level, presumably connected to the control booth where a director would make calls to flip to camera A or B to catch bots in action from the floor as if you watched at eye level.

The Stanford team entered the gym, and the students erupted in applause and shouts. They pushed a dolly holding two different bots and supporting gear. Belinda and Harry stood by the battle square going over last-minute adjustments to their bot. A crew member walked over to Belinda.

"Would you like a little makeup, dear?" she asked Belinda. "You look a little flushed."

"No, thank you," said Belinda. "I'm fine."

"Are you sure? The cameras can get a little warm and make you look ruddy."

"Go ahead," Harry told Belinda. "Enjoy the moment."

Belinda recanted and followed the crew member to a makeup stand.

"Harry!" Belinda shouted back as she made her way. He looked up. "Your lips are a little washed out. You want some lipstick? Bring out the red?"

Harry looked for a moment as if he was considering it. Then he smiled and shouted back at Belinda, "Make me!"

Belinda grabbed a lipstick container and started drawing in the air. The crew member told her to sit still. They laughed.

The event opened with a demonstration. Teams with bots that had not made it to the finals were allowed to display their technical prowess. They introduced bots with legs that walked and bots that rolled. One bot slithered like a snake. The crowd was impressed. The announcer said, "Now for a word from our sponsor."

Belinda joined Harry at the south entrance to the battle square. Sal wandered over after an on-camera interview in which he praised his team members for their brilliance. They lined up the bot they called "Mustang Sally" and closed the gate. Stanford was ready at the opposite entrance. Both teams closed the gate and went to their respective control posts. The lights came on and flooded the square. For a brief few seconds, the lighting blinded Belinda and she could not see the bot. The blindness made her panic, and she almost dropped her control unit.

"Here we go," she heard Sal behind her. "Stay steady and remember the plan."

Belinda heard something like a horn sound and saw the Stanford bot racing to their corner. Belinda's first thought was to run, and she turned the bot left and headed it for the adjacent corner. She saw the Stanford team laugh and give chase. The crowd roared. She pivoted and raced back to her gate and Stanford moved to cut her off. She slammed into reverse and, just as the bots were about to crash a chrome ax popped up out of Stanford and slammed several times into the concrete tile at Sally's front end.

Belinda pivoted again trying to get behind Stanford, but the bot seemed to have eyes as it spun in time with Sally. The ax slammed again trying to make contact. Belinda tried to back away and, in the moment, it took to change direction, the ax clipped Sally's corner and made a large dent. The crowd cheered. She saw Stanford pump their fits in the air after the hit.

"You're ok!" she heard Harry yell.

Sally spun in the direction of the ax and, as it reloaded, she hit the probe button and the extender flashed out toward Stanford, but as expected, Stanford deftly moved to the left and evaded the thrusting arm. For the next several minutes the two bots continued this dance. Stanford chasing Sally with an ax and Sally attempting in vain to flip Stanford over. A horn sounded and the parties were instructed to bring their battlebots home. The score showed Stanford 1, MIT nothing.

Harry told Belinda she did great as she handed the controls to Harry. Sal said nothing but looked at Belinda with pride. She had executed the plan perfectly.

A sign flashed "Round 2" and the teams returned to their control ports. This time Harry took over. Stanford was more cautious this time. It moved slowly to the center of the square. Harry had Sally moving in circles around Stanford, inching closer and closer as if measuring for an opening. The ax was raised, ready to strike. The crowded chanted, "Kill, kill, kill!"

Suddenly Harry turned and darted toward Stanford. Just as the ax was about to slam into the middle of Sally, she darted right and spun, the extender shooting out and catching Stanford at the corner and putting Stanford on its side but not far enough to flip it over.

Sally's spike shot up and tried to pin Stanford but barely missed. Stanford seemed paralyzed but Sally couldn't take advantage. Belinda watched with growing excitement as the Stanford team shouted at their controller to move the bot away from the spike.

The spike finally made contact, but instead of putting the bot on its back, it flipped Stanford right side up and Stanford was able to back away from the spike which had spent the last several seconds slamming into the concrete tile. A horn sounded and the teams moved their bots back their respective gates. The score was tied up: 1-1. The spike had split the concrete tile and crews rushed out to replace it. Both teams were given time to repair their battlebots and Sal had a replacement spike at the ready. Harry handed the controls to Sal, who looked at Belinda and Harry and smiled.

"We got them," he said. "It's time."

The horn sounded and this time both bots raced directly at each other. The ax popped up and Sally slid right again narrowly escaping the ax. Sally moved behind Stanford as if to use the probe, but Stanford spun in the opposite direction and the ax came crashing into the middle of Sally, barely missing the spike's arm, which it would have severed. The ax unable to remove itself locked the two bots together. Sal turned Sally left and then right as if he was trying to free Sally, but it looked more like he was playing with the Stanford bot, which appeared to be disabled.

The spike shot up and came down hard on the pinned Stanford bot, but despite the damage it was causing, the spike was unable to penetrate the thick steel cover. Sal kept spiking the bot convinced he had the game won. Harry shouted in his ear, "The plan!" but Sal ignored him, his blood lust taking over. Suddenly, the spike stopped. Sal continued to push the button, but it had no effect.

Belinda had just turned to Sal to give him a thumbs up, meaning she had successfully hacked into the Stanford team's operating system and was injecting the virus. But it had no effect. Then a skull and crossbones screen popped up on the computer and with the words, "MIT sucks robot dick! Prepare to die robot whore!" She was stunned. Stanford freed the ax and then Sal knew he had no control of Sally. Sally started moving erratically around the square. Stanford was overjoyed and the team erupted in laughter. It pinned Sally in the corner and battered her repeatedly with the ax finally severing Sally into two pieces. The horn sounded and the Stanford team rushed into the arena, waving its university flag and the Stanford theme played over the loudspeakers.

The announcers from Comedy Central entered the arena with a large trophy and handed it to the Stanford team captain. The announcers invited Sal forward to accept the second-place trophy and interviewed him about how he felt about the sudden turn of events. He congratulated the Stanford captain who said it was a good competition. Belinda, still in shock, remained at her computer and was digging through Sally's code. Then she saw it. A foreign subroutine consisting of about three pages of code. She knew immediately it was not something her team had written, and she went cold. Sal returned.

"We gave it a fight, right?" said Harry.

Sal studied Belinda. She looked at the screen and shut it off.

"Yeah, Harry, we gave it a fight," she said.

Sal said nothing and handed Belinda the second-place trophy.

"We'll get them next year," said Harry and he walked over to the corner where Sally laid in pieces. He collected the pieces and returned to the team.

Sal watched Harry and then turned back to Belinda. He said, "Well, what did we learn?"

"We learned to cheat," she said.

"Yes, we did," he replied, and walked away.

* * *

Van left the meeting with the President conflicted. She told her story and did the best she could to convince the powers in that room that action was needed and quickly. She wanted Belinda and her criminal gangs captured and tried for murder and with the President's support, she was confident that would happen.

But she was not sure that the President was as confident as she was, and she picked up on an ambivalence in the Oval Office around taking decisive action. She met Charlie, who had been waiting in the hallway.

"Is it a go?" he asked her as they made their way back to the black suburban.

"I'm not sure," she replied. "He's a busy guy."

"But she's a danger to the entire world."

"It's complicated," said Van. Charlie stopped.

"It can't be that complicated, Van. She tried to kill you."

"Did she? If she wanted me dead, why not just shoot me?"

"She dumped you drugged in front of a rampaging herd of bulls. You can call it theatrical – she still tried to kill you."

"I don't know, Charlie," Van said sounding resigned. "We'll just have to see what they do."

But Van's mind was churning. Belinda was good at evading capture, and no one knew where she was hiding these days. Perhaps the best option would be to find her again in Pamplona, assuming she couldn't stay away from the San Fermin Festival's Running of the Bulls. The thought brought a chill to Van. She knew how close she had been to becoming another one of Belinda's victims. Even though she wasn't entirely certain why Belinda didn't kill her outright, she found her body shaking as she reflected on what had happened.

Back in Los Angeles, Martin Richard invited Van to the premiere of his movie. She worried that she was leading him on, but she still viewed him as a friend and enjoyed being with him. Her mom wasn't so easy going.

"Does this boy like you?" she asked Van as Van prepared for the night.

"Mom, we are just friends," Van responded.

"He thinks you are just friends?"

"I don't know what he thinks, but he is nice, and I enjoy going out with him."

"My daughter is smarter than that."

"I told him we are just friends."

"You think he is listening?"

Van put her makeup on and gave herself a long look in the mirror. She knew her looks caught men's eyes and she suspected that, when he was with her, Martin enjoyed the feeling of other men's jealousies. But Martin got a lot of attention from girls just because of his connection to Hollywood. Unfortunately for him, that attention was shallow, and she suspected that Martin liked her because she wasn't shallow.

But with all of Van's activities at the Bureau, she had little time for friends and covered up her loneliness by being busy. Martin took the edge off her loneliness and sometimes she wondered if she might have feelings for him.

"We love you and I won't tell you what to do, but you should be careful not to break this boy's heart."

"You tell me what to do all the time."

"Ok, ok. I will stop." They laughed and Mom left for Van to finish her pre-date primping.

The doorbell rang and Martin appeared at the door wearing a colorful tuxedo. He took Van's hand and led her to the waiting white limousine.

The driver held the back door open and as she crawled in ahead of Martin, she glanced back and saw Mom watching her. Van waved but Mom didn't wave back. She just stood there quietly watching and worrying.

Chapter 5.

Murder at the Bureau

Scott Geiringer sat at his new desk organizing his folder system. He didn't like paper and kept most of his research online. Try as he might, he couldn't avoid collecting hard copies and his desk already had stacks of folders and loose papers. His desk had an old-school-style drawer for file folders. Determined to use it, he found a utility cabinet with unused file folders and tonight, after most of the detectives had gone home, he laid out his papers systematically and began stuffing the papers into his desk drawer. The phone rang.

"LAPD."

"Scott!" came a voice slightly inebriated. "What are you doing at the office?"

"Hi, Detective Young. I'm shuffling papers."

"After hours, you call me Paul."

"Ok, Paul."

"Stop whatever you are doing and get down here. We are at Justice Tavern on Los Angeles."

"Sure thing. See you in a bit."

Scott hung up and gazed disappointed at the mess on his desk. He would rather clean it up and go home but he knew it would be smarter to bond quickly with his new boss. He left the building and walked the block and a half over to Los Angeles Street where he could see an old building refashioned as a start-up gastropub called Justice Urban Tavern. Inside at the bar he saw Detective Paul Young with several of his younger team members from Robbery Homicide gathered close by and chatting nonstop like a bevy of chicks around a mother hen. Detective Robert Johnson looked up as he entered.

"New guy!" Robert shouted as Scott walked through the entrance.

"Over here Scott!" Detective Young motioned to a chair he had left for the novice detective.

Young looked at his team with pride. He was especially pleased to have Geiringer as a member of his squad.

"Let me tell you guys about our new friend, Detective Geiringer," he said slightly slurring Scott's last name.

"Come on boss, we already know," said Robert. "Scott here is a bona fide college football all-star."

But they all didn't know, and a host of questions hit Scott rapid fire. Scott had played football at UCLA and, as a walk-on cornerback, started a few games, including in his senior year, a Rose Bowl game. But to Scott, academics had always been more important than sports. He knew early in his college career that he wanted to attend the Police Academy and become a detective.

"Did you think about going pro?" a voice asked.

Scott laughed. "My knees were too important to me."

"Our new man here graduated at the top of his class in the Police Academy," Young managed to say.

A chorus of ohs and wows sounded.

"Yeah, but can he shoot?" said Robert, who had been a police officer in the LAPD Rampart Division before being promoted to detective.

"I did ok," said Scott who downplayed the marksmanship awards he received at the Academy.

Scott was happy to be with Robbery Homicide. He knew Paul Young had a stellar reputation there as the lead detective in the Unit. He was ready to solve crimes and bring perpetrators to justice, but he was tech-savvy and thought he could introduce new tools and systems, like artificial intelligence, to advance the Bureau's efforts. He had seen Van a couple of times, and heard someone say she was the best detective in the Bureau. He thought she seemed young for such acclaim, but he figured there was reason to be impressed.

"What do you all know about the woman detective, the Asian?" he asked.

Detective Paul Young scowled. "Detective Van Eng," he grumbled. "Decent enough. She got lucky a couple times and people talk about her. They are impressed with her because she has a hearing impairment. In my Unit, you can't rely on your disabilities. You must prove yourself."

"She is definitely hot," he heard someone say. "Hot and smart. Doesn't get any better than that."

"Then why don't you ask her out?" Robert Johnson directed at the offending voice.

"Outta my league," came the response. "I know my limits."

Detective Young attempted to redirect the discussion.

"Don't worry about her," Young said. "She came here with marginal policing skills. She is good with computers. Probably the case that she would be better off in forensics, where she came from." He continued. "You, however, have a foundation and I expect great things from you." He smiled. "No pressure."

Scott found the sycophantic setting disturbing. He had respect for Detective Young, but he had no interest in becoming one of Young's followers. He agreed that Van was pretty, but his real interest was in her approach to detective work. He was surprised to learn she was hearing impaired. In every interaction he witnessed, Detective Van Eng seemed confident and comfortable. There was no indication of any sensory challenges. He looked forward to spending time with her in the field and sharing his ideas about artificial intelligence, especially if, as Young had said, she was comfortable with computers.

* * *

Van said good night to Martin and kissed him on the cheek as they stood next to the limousine. He put his arms around her and gave her a bear hug, just a bit too tight.

"You look beautiful tonight," he said.

"You are the star," she said, deflecting and pulling back. "I'm just a lucky girl who got to ride along."

"I don't care about that," he replied. "I know the business and, yes, it pays for my lifestyle. But, as you know, it can be brutal." He grimaced and then gazed at Van with puppy dog eyes.

"Come home with me," he pleaded.

Van pushed back. It had been a very nice night and a part of her wanted to say yes, but she knew it would be a mistake.

"I can't, Martin," she said. "We talked about this."

He looked hurt and she felt bad. "We're friends," she said. "Good friends and I really enjoy spending time with you. I'm just not interested in a relationship."

Martin reacted like he had been stung, but he recovered quickly. "Friends with benefits, I guess." He smiled.

"Friends," Van responded. "Just friends. Thank you for a nice night."

She watched as Martin slid back into the limousine. As the car pulled away, she heard Martin say, "To the club, Jeeves!" She thought she heard in response, "My name is not Jeeves."

As Van entered her parents' house, she noticed the light was on in their bedroom. She peeked in. Her dad was reading. "Did my favorite daughter have a nice night?"

"Your only daughter had a nice night, yes."

She made her way to her room and started to undress. As she was about to crawl into bed, her phone rang.

"Van, this is Charlie." Detective Charles Darling had been instrumental in bringing Van into the Bureau. He was a mentor to her as a junior detective and helped her manage through the challenges she had faced as a female in a Police Department run mostly by old school males.

"Charlie, you need to stop these late-night calls."

"We need you here." Charlie was more brusque than usual.

"Now?"

"Yes, I'm sorry. It's urgent. I will tell you more when you get here."

"Belinda?" Van asked.

"No. You'll learn more when you get here."

When Van arrived at LAPD's downtown headquarters, she was surprised to see the parking lot and front entrance blocked off and covered in police tape. She identified herself and police allowed her to drive into the main parking structure. She walked into the main lobby and toward the elevator bank where she saw Charlie talking to Detective Paul Young.

Young was in bad shape. He looked like he had been sleeping in his car. His shirt tail was hanging out. His tie was loose. His hair was not combed. He was obviously still inebriated. As she walked up to Charlie, she heard him say to Young, "You need to go home. Get some rest. We have this handled." Young glanced at Van as she approached. He looked sad and mumbled, "Good morning." She asked him, "Can I get you some coffee?"

"No," said Charlie. "He needs to go home." Charlie motioned an officer standing near the elevator opening to come over. "Please take Detective Young home."

Van said, "I can take him home, but first tell me what is going on?" She looked the officer and said, "Could you get him some coffee, please?" The officer took off and Charlie pointed to a body crumpled in the corner of the elevator.

Van studied the body. She didn't see the face and her initial reaction was to revert to her forensic expertise and study the details. She could smell beer and the musty staleness of a tap room pub. She had detected the same smell on Young and wasn't sure the odor was coming from the elevator or from Young who was standing next to her. She entered the elevator to move herself away from Young and confirmed the same scent in the elevator coming from the body. The hands of the victim were zip-tied police style. His face was bruised, and his head had a bullet wound fired at close range that blew out part of his skull. The walls of the elevator were splattered with blood, and brains indicating the shooting likely took place in the elevator. There was dirt under his fingernails, which could be blood from the perpetrator. She noticed his building pass hanging from his belt. She looked back at Charlie.

"Is this the new detective?" she asked Charlie who was watching her work. "Scott something?" She studied the pass. "Geiringer?"

Charlie said, "That's him," and Paul Young, standing behind the crowd at the elevator mumbled, "Fucking kid."

"Any witnesses?"

"None yet identified," said Charlie. "His desk is a mess. Possible like someone was looking for something and the kid stumbled onto them."

Dr. Frank Weatherby and Brad Jones from Forensics turned the corner into the elevator bank. Brad had a crush on Van since their time together in the crime lab and a giant smile appeared on his face when he saw her. Van nodded at the team but the impact of the apparent murder of one of her colleagues in the building where they worked was taking over. Frank and Brad's reputation preceded them, and everyone stood back from the elevator to let them begin their work. The officer returned and handed Young the coffee and Young accepted it gratefully. His hand shook as he tried to sip it. Van walked over to Scott's desk and saw the mess of papers. She didn't touch anything but looked at the papers to see if there were any clues. She could see he was studying a couple of new cases, a home robbery and a smash and grab, both in the neighborhood known as Beverly Hills adjacent. Van wanted to stay and study the scene even more closely, but she knew she needed to get Paul Young home. She also wanted to talk to him.

"Let's get out of here," she said to Young, "and let these guys do their job."

"I can drive," he said, but given his state she knew that was a bad idea.

"I can take you," she said. "Robert," she added motioning to Robert Johnson who looked to be in shock himself. "You ok to drive?"

"I think so," he said.

"Can you take the Detective's car home? I will bring you back here."

"Sure, but no need for multiple trips. I can Uber from Paul's."

"Whatever you prefer."

Van held Detective Young's coffee as he slid into the passenger seat. She pulled the car out of the lot. She sat quietly with the senior Detective.

"I know what you are doing," he said as they entered the 101 Freeway north. The coffee was helping. He was still dizzy after too many rounds of Guinness.

"What is that?" she responded.

"Don't be coy. I didn't kill him."

"You taught me never to assume anything."

"I don't think I taught you anything at all."

"Come on Detective. Even drunk you are not one for self-pity. But since you brought it up, what do you think happened?"

"I don't know what happened. A bright new star was lost tonight. Poof! For no good reason."

"Do we know why he was at the office so late?"

"He said something about papers. I called him and told him to drop it and join us at Justice."

"Did he join you?"

"He did but he didn't stay long. Said he wanted to wrap up a couple things before he went home. We tried to get him to hang out, but you could tell something was driving him."

"He was just hired, right?"

"First week on the job."

"Doesn't look good if we can't protect our own."

"No, it doesn't."

Johnson was at the house when they arrived. Young thanked Van for the ride and he and Detective Johnson went into the house together. Van didn't expect to be invited in, and it was late, and she was tired from a long evening. As she drove away, she called Charlie.

"Did you get anything?" he asked.

"Nothing. I've never seen Detective Young this distraught. They were at a bar together tonight, but Scott – the victim – didn't stay long and returned to the Bureau, apparently to finish what he had started." Van was already distancing herself from the crime victim – a skill she learned was essential to being an effective detective.

"Anything yet on your end?"

"No. The only people here were the night cleaning crew who found the body. We asked them and they hadn't heard or seen anything. Forensics is scouring the place for signs of a struggle but nothing yet."

"Did they check the bathroom?"

"The bathroom?"

"There's blood on the victim and someone might have needed to wash up."

"That only works if the perp is someone who works here. No one else would hang around and risk being identified. You think this was internal?"

"I don't know. I'm just freewheeling. Maybe someone with a vendetta wanted to make a point."

"But he was brand new. You think he had enemies?"

"We don't know what we don't know. I think you taught me that one."

"I see. The student has surpassed the master."

"Come on, Charlie," said Van. "We both know that is not true."

"No," said Charlie. "There's where you are wrong. Get home and get some sleep. We have it covered here for now."

Van fell quickly into a deep, troubled sleep. She saw Brian again at the beach, only this time he was struggling in the waves. She tried to reach him but the further she swam out to rescue him the further he drifted away. She woke up early and, even though she was still tired, she dressed and got ready for work. By the time she arrived at work, they had removed the body from the elevator and taken it to the morgue. The elevator was open and covered in police tape. She went over to Scott's desk. It was clean and wiped down.

Van returned to her desk and was surprised to see Paul Young standing there holding a cup of coffee. He extended the cup in her direction.

"Good morning, Detective," he said. "I owe you."

"I'm surprised to see you here this early," she said, graciously accepting the coffee.

"I'm here, but it won't be my best morning."

"It's a tough morning for all of us."

"Time for a chat? I also owe you more than I gave you last night."

"You were in shock last night, and I think most of us are still in shock. It's understandable. But if you feel like talking now, let's find a conference room."

Van didn't find the conversation very helpful. Detective Young admitted that he was intoxicated by the time Scott showed up at the bar and that his awareness of events was muddy. He recalled the scene in the bar as jovial and relaxing. Scott had been friendly but reserved, which made sense given that he was new to the team. Young had been more interested in introducing him to the team than testing his social skills, which were more than adequate. Nothing happened at the bar to presage a later conflict. There were no tense interactions with any team members and no conflicts with drunken patrons who might have followed him out of the bar. It was still twilight when Scott left to return to the office, so Young guessed maybe around 8:30 pm. Downtown Los Angeles can be sketchy at night, even in Little Tokyo. Did anyone leave the bar with Scott? No, not that Young recalled. Was it possible someone followed him from the street and snuck into police headquarters? Sure, but the cameras outside headquarters would have caught an image of anyone entering the building and, at least so far, no one reviewing the video had seen anything unusual. Did Young know much about Scott's past or his experience at the Police Academy? Young said he didn't know for sure but had no reason to suspect anything. Nothing Young said suggested any good leads and Van surmised that Young was genuinely interested in finding the killer and was not attempting to impair the investigation or direct Van toward false leads. She thanked him for taking the time to talk with her and Young offered to help in any way. When she returned to her desk, Charlie was waiting. Young acknowledged him, albeit not too fondly, and walked back to his office. Van watched as Robert Johnson jumped from his desk and made his way to Young's office and closed the door behind him.

"How did that go?" he asked Van.

"Pretty much as expected," she said. "I need to corroborate his statements, but if they hold up, Scott's death has nothing to do with anything that happened at the bar."

"Be careful, partner," said Charlie. "As of now, everyone is a suspect and if we clear someone, let's clear them together."

Chapter 6.

Into the Lion's Den

Belinda stepped from the rolling stairway onto the tarmac at Moffett Federal Airfield adjacent to Google's Mountain View headquarters. The wind was whipping over the southern portion of the San Francisco Bay, and her landing had been rough and bouncy. The crew working the private charter had been professional and calm and as promised, everyone arrived safely. The cool bay wind gave Belinda a slight chill as she stepped onto the metal stairs and reminded her of autumn in Massachusetts even though Boston had been experiencing its hottest summer on record. It was the first time she returned to California since her BattleBot adventures, and the thought gave her some satisfaction. After the first loss to Stanford in her freshman year, Belinda's team had won three consecutive national championships and Comedy Central even flew the team to Hawaii for a celebratory tour and demonstration to an international audience of the latest robotic technology. But once Belinda entered the doctoral program at MIT, she put the robot wars behind her and focused on her thesis, advanced drone weaponry and the tactical use of nuclear weapons. The Pentagon had held several meetings with Belinda, but, in the end, a company in California simply made her a better offer.

Belinda's interest in new inventions went beyond advances in war technology and the company, a lab with a strange name funded by top Silicon Valley companies, gave her exactly the opportunity she sought – freedom to explore and develop new ideas with an unlimited budget that was not hindered by the stilted bureaucracy of the Federal Government. A black Bentley Mulsanne Grand limousine was parked near the staircase. Three attendants met Belinda at the bottom of the stairs, and she watched as the flight crew loaded her luggage into the back of the limousine.

She smiled at the first attendant who introduced himself impressively as so-and-so's executive assistant. "Company car?" she said with a flirty grin. "Or is this yours?" He smiled and picked up on the banter right away. "A rental."

"Classy," she responded and immediately he felt sheepish and quickly held the door for her to slide inside. She rolled down the window, "What was your name?"

"I'm Sam Winters," he responded, trying not to sound too familiar. "The team is waiting for you."

"See you again, Sam Winters," Belinda said as the car sped off toward the airport gate.

Ragnar Willowbrook Laboratories had been around 18 months. It was a jointly owned start-up of the top five Silicon Valley companies, aka the Big Five, and had been built to focus on developing ideas for joint projects. The Labs, as the staff liked to call it, was located in the Santa Cruz Mountains situated to the southwest of the Google Campus. It was a decent looking building from a few decades back but, like many of the Google office buildings, understated. The landscaping was nice but the property on which it was situated was overgrown and not well tended. The idea behind the venture was to keep it as an obscure but well-funded think tank for new ideas. The five partner companies would be allowed to bid on any new ideas emerging out of the Labs, which was a novel way of encouraging innovation and avoiding costly legal battles over patent rights. After a year with nothing to show for their efforts, the Big Five went on a search for a new CEO and found a capable candidate in a strong but young Ph.D. graduate from MIT who had been the first student in this century to win the top academic award in both her junior and senior years.

Belinda's research on biomechanical processing in microscopic organisms had drawn attention at several universities and her name popped up as a candidate in the search for a director of the new lab. Her references from MIT were stellar and it didn't hurt that a majority of the of board members had MIT affiliations. But as she followed her hosts around the lab, she knew instinctively that this Board was looking for a puppet that they could easily manipulate in support of their own agendas. So, despite being wined and dined by top valley chefs and hosted in City penthouses and Marin County mansions, Belinda politely turned down the offer and flew back to Boston.

Billionaire Fred Schmidt knew Belinda was making a mistake. The offer being made to Belinda was unlike any offer she would get, and he wondered if she was playing with the Board or was seriously not interested. He waited for her to land at Logan

International before calling her.

"Hello?"

"Dr. Armendariz."

"Who is this?" she asked climbing into the backseat of a yellow cab.

"Fred Schmidt."

"Yes, Mr. Schmidt."

"Call me Fred, Belinda. I'm not sure if we had a misunderstanding."

"No misunderstanding, Fred. You have assembled a powerful Board and, as interested as I might be, I'm not interested in catering to the whims of newly minted Internet billionaires."

"That's probably a fair concern, but what is it you need?"

"The building is a dump. The lab equipment is cheap. The staff is underqualified. It is obvious your boys are setting up some kind of front or charade to give their half-baked ideas credibility and that is not my game."

"Ok. What is it you need? What would it take to get you on board?"

"More."

"More? What is your price, Belinda?"

"My price? You can start by allowing me to redesign the lab. We need to start from scratch. If that means constructing a new building, so be it. You also need to let me equip the lab. From what I see, your team is simply guessing. I can build a lab to take us through the next five decades. Finally, I want to pick my team. I do not want the Board to pick my team. I know where to go for the best minds that I know will give everything they have to support me. Finally, I do not want repurposed prison inmates as my security team. I want the best ex-military personnel we can find."

"How quickly can you get me a budget?"

"I can put a budget together, Mr. Schmidt, but not for you to approve or reject. If you want me and you want this lab to have the reputation that we both know it needs, then you need to let me build it my way."

"Blank checks are a tough sell. Your directors are not stupid."

"You must trust me, Fred. They must trust me. If you can't, then I am not the right choice."

"I'm listening."

"One more thing. You need to keep the Board off my back."

Fred smiled. Belinda was telling him exactly what he wanted to hear. "I think I can handle that."

The Board grumbled but Fred convinced them to give Belinda a chance. Their only condition was that they name the lab, and the winning name came from two Board members and Belinda made them pay for it. One, a newly minted Norwegian oil baron who wanted to use his first-born son's name, Ragnar, and an English lord and IT billionaire whose English estate was called Willowbrook. No one objected and Belinda, concerned only that the Board fund the new building and lab equipment and give her seed money for her first projects.

She found property on a hill overlooking the south end of the Valley near UC Santa Cruz, installed a gate and guard house at the only entrance. She designed the building with modernist elements, mostly steel and glass with large picture windows overlooking the south end of the Silicon Valley. Construction took two years to complete, and, in the meantime, Belinda studied her Board members closely, immersed herself in their businesses and listened to their ideas on innovation. They were singularly impressed with her capacity to absorb information and her critical eye. She also engaged top universities, identifying and hiring the brightest minds of Stanford, MIT, and Harvard, focusing on engineering, biomedical sciences and law.

The Big Five started feeding projects into Ragnar Willowbrook immediately. The projects ranged from new chip designs and compression technologies in the IT space to genetic engineering models and bioinformatics. Belinda learned very quickly that her team could add tremendous value to the projects by highlighting faulty applications and poor design. She developed a new certification standard, and, with the support of the Big Five's promotional efforts, the certification standard took on a life of its own. Universities began to submit projects destined for the private sector to Ragnar Willowbrook hoping for certification. Most of these projects were rejected, not because they were bad projects but because, given Belinda's deft sense of the market, rejection amplified the value of a Ragnar Willowbrook certification. The Board was delighted.

Robert Jensen, a recent Stanford graduate with a Ph.D. in physics, built a device that he claimed reversed the effects of gravity. Decades of academic research on gravity had failed to support any idea that gravity has a negative form that can be captured in a device and used as a means of propulsion. It seemed that the magic of flying saucers would forever remain science fiction. Jensen based his device on an offshoot theory of quantum mechanics long rejected by mainstream academics. His device, so he claimed, used gravitational waves. He called the device the Jensen anti-graviton. It was a small block that not only would float in the air without any apparent means of propulsion but also could lift as much as two pounds.

Robert Jensen wrote Belinda a dozen letters describing his invention before he got a response. The letter came from Belinda's legal team and told Robert that Ragnar Willowbrook would consider reviewing the project for certification so long as he signed a lengthy waiver. Robert was so excited by the prospect of Ragnar considering his device that he signed and returned the waiver. He waited for two weeks before he received an invitation to exhibit his device, a first step in the process for receiving certification. He bought a new shirt and tie and prepared for the big day. He placed his device in a backpack and rode his scooter up the long steep road to Ragnar Willowbrook's entrance.

He waited for 30 minutes at the entrance before the guard let him through the gate. He sat in the fancy lobby of the glass building for another hour until the time for his appointment was long passed.

He asked the receptionist to check on the delay and she repeated that they would see him shortly. Finally, she handed him a badge and asked him to pass through the metal detectors. He explained that he had a device that would set off the detectors and she told him to hand her the device so it could be inspected before he would be allowed to enter.

Robert complained that he did not want to give the device to anyone who did not understand it and he was asked to wait again. Soon two technicians in lab coats appeared and convinced Robert that they would take appropriate precautions with the device to confirm that it was safe to bring into the lab. He reluctantly handed over the device and waited, upset at himself for handing it over to the technicians.

After another agonizing wait, the receptionist called him back to the front desk where another technician was waiting to take him upstairs. This technician, who happened to be a very attractive young woman, held the elevator door for him and showered him with praise. Robert began to relax as she ushered him into a small room with a desk and a few chairs. In a few minutes, Belinda entered with the original technicians. She handed him his device and sat behind the desk.

"Good morning, Dr. Jensen."

Robert looked across the desk at the CEO. She was no older than him and yet she was running this intimidating lab. Stanford had their share of young geniuses, so he wasn't totally surprised. He had done enough research on her to know about her background with BattleBots and the competition between MIT and Stanford. Still the scene struck him as odd.

"Dr. Armendariz. Pleasure to meet you."

Belinda pointed to an assistant who set the device on the desk. "What is it we have here?"

Robert took a breath and then started. "Anti-gravity is a joke, right?"

Belinda studied him. "I've never found much use for science fiction," she said. "But you got my attention – briefly."

"I'm not much for science fiction myself. But gravity itself is very engaging mostly because no one has been able to advance the discussion beyond Newton. Particle theories of gravity failed. Quantum gravity is long dead in the water. Decades of research and no advances. Even the military gave up. After dumping millions of dollars into anti-gravity research the government simply turned off the tap."

"You think you can turn it back on?"

Robert leaned forward and reached out for the device on the desk. He pressed a small square on the side of the cube, and the bottom of the cube began to glow. The base of the cube glowed blue and then red, and the colors began to flicker red and blue faster until the colors blended into a deep purple, then it appeared to shut off.

Belinda looked at Robert. He did not seem concerned. She looked back at the device which was now emitting a white light and was floating about an inch off the desk. She raised her eyebrows.

"Touch it," Robert said.

Belinda reached out and touched the top of the cube. It felt warm.

"Heat?"

"A by-product," said Robert. "Push it back to the table."

Belinda pushed the cube back to the desk surface. She felt a slight force. As she lifted her hand, the device returned to its position an inch off the table.

"Does the ground surface matter?"

"It's not electromagnetic," said Robert. "It will levitate anywhere."

Belinda stood up. She thanked Robert for his time and left the room.

Robert looked at her assistant.

"Please follow me," she said.

"What's next?" he asked.

"We will be in touch."

The next letter Robert Jenkins received from Ragnar Willowbrook was a legal letter instructing him to cease and desist and identifying a patent number for his device that was owned by Ragnar Willowbrook. Robert called the Labs multiple times with no success. He hired a local patent law firm who told him a challenge would be expensive and fruitless. Ragnar Willowbrook claimed they had identified a scientist who developed a device like Robert's and had patented that device when Robert brought his device to the Labs for review.

Chapter 7.

All in the Family

Van sat down on a concrete garden wall. She set her lunch down next to her and sipped on an energy drink. She meditated on the city skyline imagining its evolution over the past century, back when the City Hall was the tallest building downtown, a trait preserved in an older municipal code. Other officers sat nearby on the same concrete wall. They seemed to be rushing, trying to catch a moment to eat in the sun and then hustle back to a desk stacked with files and loose papers. She glanced down and notice a trail of ants making their way to her lunch. She grabbed it quickly and moved it to her lap but became mesmerized by the ants. They seemed organized, as if one of the ants had issued a verbal command to a specific set of ants who abandoned their existing tasks to join the line making its way toward her lunch. She thought how remarkable it was that such a small insect with the simplest of nervous systems still had an evolved communication system and the ability to respond in a highly organized manner to the opportunities and threats around its nest.

Detective Charles Darling sat down next to her.

"I've warned you about the ants in this garden, haven't I?"

"No. You've never said anything to me about ants."

"Oh. Must have been someone else."

"Charlie."

"I've worked at this Bureau now for 25 years. It's not like cops don't get murdered and sometimes even by their own partners. But I have never

heard of a cop getting murdered at his own precinct."

"I'm new here, so I don't have that perspective. But I find it very hard to imagine that a murder at a police station might be a random event. It's possible a violent inmate might get loose and grab a gun or weapon and attack someone – I'd like to believe most cops are smart enough to prevent that."

"It would be very unusual for someone with a grudge – and a lot of cops have grudges – to think it a good idea to act out the grudge in this setting."

"Not unless it was either well planned and or not planned at all. Remember the bullet? Detective Johnson confessed that it was merely a stupid move on his part. I'm still willing to go with that but I remember very clearly your warning to me when I joined the Bureau. There's a lot of weaponized testosterone in this office. We are taught to manage our authority and ensure that we use our force for good. The lesson doesn't always take."

"Right. There's a kind of mutually assured destruction here that makes us careful. For that reason, I'm not convinced yet this is internal."

"This is going to be hard. And probably dangerous."

"Welcome to the LAPD."

Charlie's cell phone beeped. "Be right there." To Van he said, "Chief's called a briefing. We need to hear this."

The room was crowded and full of buzz when they arrived. A mix of police officers and detectives spoke loudly over the din.

"Quiet down, please," said the deputy chief into a mike at the podium. "Find a seat if you can."

The Chief of Police entered the room with a stern expression. His deputies lined up behind him as if he was about to give a press briefing. The talking continued.

"Quiet!" he started. The room fell silent. "We lost one of our own yesterday. Detective Scott Geiringer was a bright young star from the Academy, and we had great hopes for his success. Unfortunately, he barely had the chance to start his career and was cut down here in our home!"

The crowd erupted with shouts of anger.

"Ok. We are all not only sorry for the loss of Scott but outraged about the circumstances. I have two messages for you. First, there will be a lot of blame thrown around and the risk is that the Department could dissolve into chaos and distrust of our fellow officers. We cannot, I repeat, cannot allow that to happen. Any word of recrimination of any fellow officer will be met with a very harsh response. We are family and we must remain family."

Van watched the nods of assent.

"Second, our Detective Bureau will immediately commence an investigation into Scott's death." Detective Young looked up and started to stand, expecting to be called to the podium.

"We have a very special person on the force who has led us through multiple cases in her short career."

Van had been listening attentively, but this comment confused her. She couldn't imagine about whom the Chief was talking.

"I'm going to ask her to come forward but first let me assure you she is not aware of this decision." Eyes started to turn in Van's direction.

"Would Detective Van Eng please come forward?"

At that point everyone stared at her. There were a handful of supporting faces, beaming with pride. Some, like herself, were simply confused by the decision. It seemed a breach of not only the existing hierarchy, but also of basic Department policy. She was still a first-level detective and, despite her quick successes, had not been promoted. On top of everything, her hearing impairment was not a secret and while some encouraged her in her efforts to overcome the impairment, others still believed she was not suited to the job. She walked to the podium aware of the conflicting vibes but resolute as always despite the circumstances.

The Chief spoke again. "Detective Van Eng will take the lead in this investigation. Everyone in this Department is under strict orders to follow her lead."

He studied Van as she approached. She returned the gaze and saw the same firm resolve in his eyes that she felt in her own heart. Her mind raced. Why her? He was ordering her to lead one of the most complicated and candidly dangerous investigations possible – a murder in their own house most likely committed by one of their own officers. The simplest answer was that the Chief and his leadership team trusted Van's organizational skills, which admittedly outpaced nearly everyone in the Department. She was singlehandedly responsible for taking the jumble of data that made up CHESS, the Cold Case Homicide Special Section filing room and not only modernizing it by putting it online but also compiling the data into a fully interactive database.

The he spoke. "I am not going to ask Detective Eng to address you today. This is as new to her as it is to the rest of you. But let me say this and make it crystal clear. Detective Eng is one of a very few officers to have served in this Department to develop working connections between her own Bureau, the leadership of this Department, the internal review board that guides our department and federal intelligence agencies in the service of justice. She has done so in the shortest time, at least as far as I am aware. We will follow her lead in this investigation." He looked at again. "No pressure, Van, but do you want to say anything?"

Van looked at the crowd and the microphone. She resisted, appreciating the out the Chief was offering but something drew her to speak.

"Thank you, Chief. This is a lot to process but, like the rest of you, I need resolution. We need resolution."

After a short silence, there was a brief smattering of applause led by Detective Darling. The Chief returned to the podium, thanked Van and closed the briefing, but he could hardly be heard over the din that returned.

Charlie quickly made his way to Van, who was shaking the hands of the Chief's team. He whispered in her ear.

"We need to get out of here and chat."

"I'm with you," she responded. "Give me a quick second."

Charlie watched as Van approached the Chief and exchanged a few words. He shook her hand, and she turned and left the building with Detective Darling. As they drove together, Charlie didn't press Van to speak. It had been a big moment for her, and he suspected that she felt overwhelmed. They drove down the 10 freeway toward Santa Monica in their unmarked Acura.

"Where are we going, Detective?" she asked after ten minutes of silence.

"Out of the City," he responded.

"I gathered that," she said.

"Are you hungry?"

"Not at all, but I need to eat something, if you know what I mean."

"I have a place."

They didn't speak again until they arrived. Van watched as Charlie stayed on the freeway until it ended and merged with Pacific Coast Highway. They drove north on PCH past the pier and the beach clubs and turned right onto West Channel Street. At the end of the block, they turned right, drove over a concrete water channel and parked.

"Interesting," said Van. "The Golden Bull?"

"Yes," said Charlie. "It's a good steakhouse and out of the way enough so that it is unlikely we run into our colleagues."

"If you are going to tell me to watch out for myself, I think we have already had that conversation." She smiled.

* * *

Belinda sat at her desk musing on Robert Jenkins' anti-gravity toy. Some part of her wanted to give Jenkins credit, if not for his originality, at least for his ambition. She had spoken to multiple colleges, all of whom claimed to have reached similar conclusions and were applying the same anti-gravity effect to varied applications. Jenkins might have thought he was the first, but he wasn't, and Belinda knew that if he tried to claim she stole his invention, the mountain of data she could assemble to the contrary would bury Jenkins' claims.

The real battle was over patent rights, and Belinda was well on her way to securing those rights as part of an anti-gravity consortium. If Robert wanted to make the claim that his invention was original, he had no choice but to find a unique way to apply it and get that patented on his own. Building a floating box was, in the end, nothing more than a new toy.

Her new iPhone buzzed, and she picked it up to see Christopher Deckwalder Face-timing her. The technology fascinated her. She imagined applying it to a watch and recreating the Dick Tracy science fiction that had fascinated so many of her parents' generation.

"Hi, Christopher."

"I've been talking to the Pentagon."

"And?"

"They asked me to identify the best scientist in the Valley."

"Are you asking me?"

"No. I am telling you. They have some material they want analyzed."

"This is beginning to sound creepy, but then you know how much I like creepy."

"That's on you, Chief Scientist."

"We are not talking alien anti-matter?"

"I don't know what we are talking but I am calling you to let you know that I recommended you. This is a heads up. It's not a choice. It is coming your way."

"Fair enough. Will I get instructions?"

"You might not even know it's arrived. Be on the lookout and make sure you get it into your top scientist's hands immediately."

"I assume you'll cover our expenses."

"As usual. Goodbye."

Christopher Deckwalder hung up or whatever they were calling it with these new phones. He didn't like being cryptic and the Pentagon tended to force his hand on that. General Tom Warner, who seemed to be on the other end of a lot of these conversations, liked giving Deckwalder as little information as possible. He sighed. Belinda was right. The military had a way of being creepy.

Chapter 8.

The Outline of War

When Putin deployed his troops on Ukraine's northern border and called it "war games," the world took note but hardly reacted. China had done the same thing, on occasion, in the Taiwan Strait. But given the United States' support for Taiwan and the strength of Taiwan's own defenses, the Chinese war games never led to an actual invasion. The United States' support for Ukraine had never been tested, but with a new democratically elected leader straight out of Hollywood from a successful movie, it seemed that Ukraine was winning American hearts and therefore unfathomable that Putin's war games might commence an actual war. Besides, in 1994, Russia had signed the Budapest Memorandum on Security Assurances, the result of which was the complete nuclear disarmament of Ukraine, an action Ukraine took in exchange for the assurance of their own border security given by co-signers the United States, Russia and the United Kingdom. Of course, the sentiment was growing that Putin had been planning all along to force Ukraine back into the fold of Mother Russia, a first major step in the reunification of all the republics that once comprised the former USSR.

Putin's military missteps began with his initial expectations. He believed that the surprise attack and a week-long furious bombardment of Kyiv, Kharkiv and other key Ukrainian locations would quickly bring the former republic to its knees. He was wrong, and the fierce resistance by the Ukrainian people and the courage under fire of its new famous leader gave the United States and its NATO allies time to lend military aid and stall the war, though it did not end it. The termination of the war moved into the hands of America's latest new leader, someone who faced his own "courage under fire" moment with remarkable bravery. One conclusion is sure to be drawn: "War games" would never again be mistaken for anything but a prelude to war.

Deep in the bunkers at Muro de Roda in the Pyrenees, Belinda called her leaders together, many of whom were part of the same team that stole the research materials and nanobot samples from the SUMBET lab in the University of Navarra. Belinda's nanobot arsenal had grown but she refused to expand it with conventional weapons, a fact that likely added to the challenge of locating her, buried deep in the Pyrenees. It was time to take her first steps toward the goal of an independent Basque Country. The cabal around her concurred. She arranged to send a small contingent to the Basque Parliament in Vitoria-Gasteiz, the de facto capital of Basque Country known as the Basque Autonomous Region, located just south of Bilbao and west of Pamplona.

She selected Dr. Hadj Arkoun to lead the contingent. Hadj, an Algerian doctor on the medical faculty of the University of Navarra, and a specialist in nanotechnology, had been Belinda's second in command from the moment he joined Belinda after her relocation to Spain. Belinda and Hadj had plotted their next moves as the volume of weaponized nanotechnology in her possession grew. Hadj was a good second in command, but he questioned some of Belinda's decisions, including the decision to kill General Tom Warner. Perhaps General Warner deserved to be terminated. They both questioned his allegiance to Belinda. But murdering an American general in Spain did not seem wise, especially if their lofty goals didn't need the complication. But Hadj never expressed those reservations and was a dutiful second in command and he was rewarded as such.

The plan was simple but elegant. It started out as a top-down plan. Contact the so-called Minister of Defense, Gaston de Bleu and his Chief of Staff. The Minister was known to harbor separatist beliefs and had been granted the title in name only. The Basque Country did not have its own military and the Defense Minister's job was mostly about keeping a lid on separatist pressures that bubbled up now and then. Convince the Minister that he would have access to substantial military resources to establish Basque Country as an independent nation, governed under a parliamentary system, with its own constitution and justice system. Offer the Minister the option to lead the new country until Parliament and the justice system are fully formed. The Minister would report to one person and one person alone, the unidentified leader of the resistance movement.

The plan also called for a grassroots effort that started with an information campaign highlighting the disappearances of activists during prior decades and spontaneous public protests. The protests were designed to start out as small nonviolent gatherings calling the government to accountability for the disappeared. The information campaign would be designed to place the Spanish government in the worst possible light, even if the accuracy of the claims were dubious. Belinda was not concerned about truth. She wanted impact. She also knew that her parents had disappeared when she was a child and therefore that there was enough truth about the claim to give the campaign momentum.

The grassroots campaign gathered steam. Small sporadic outbreaks occurred in Pamplona and Bilboa. Even though they were small, a news-hungry media gave them enough attention to get the Spanish government asking questions. Belinda's team made their way to Vitoria-Gasteiz. They asked to see Minister de Bleu and were told he was away and would return in one week. As they waited, they spread leaflets about the missing protestors, demanding action from Spain. After a week they returned to the Minister's office and were told that he was called away for an emergency meeting in Madrid. This cycle repeated itself for another three weeks until Hadj let the Minister's staff know that he would be exposed as a shill of the Spanish government. Within two days Hadj got his meeting.

"The Minister will see you," said the secretary guarding the door to Minister de Bleu's massive office. She pushed a button and motioned for Hadj to open the door. He obliged as directed and Belinda's front group made their way in.

The Minister stood with his back to the group. He slowly turned to face Hadj.

"You have my brief attention. What is it you want from me?"

Hadj was quick to respond. "You believe in the Basque people, Minister?"

"You think there is another reason I hold this position?"

"Then you believe also in their freedom from Spain."

"We are already free. Franco is long gone and there is no Spanish oppressor."

"You are the Minister of Defense, are you not?"

"You know I am."

"Where is your army?

"There is no need. Spain leaves us alone. We govern ourselves."

"Maybe Spain leaves you alone because you submit to her rule and pay her taxes."

"You haven't told me what you want but I can tell you this – no one wants war with Spain."

"You don't believe that, sir. You hold your position as Defense Minister precisely to keep Spain fearful of a Basque revolt."

"Maybe so, but Spain leaves us alone. We control our own autonomous region."

"We are the poor stepchild of Spain. They take our taxes and give us nothing in return. And the moment they tire of our autonomy will be the moment they remove it and you, sir, have no means to prevent that. We are here to tell you that we can give you the means."

A shadow stepped into the doorway of a small dark room behind the Minister's desk. The light reflected off the medals on his uniform. Minister de Bleu grimaced uncomfortably.

"And who is 'we' exactly?" said the shadow.

Hadj was unmoved. "My meeting is with Minister de Bleu. Whom am I addressing now?"

The shadow smirked. "I would have expected you and your group to be much younger my friend, simple and overly ambitious graduate students. But this is more than a political joyride, isn't it? I smell real treason."

"We have the right to raise concerns about the freedom of the Basque people, sir...I'm sorry I still didn't catch your name."

"You will know my name soon enough."

At that moment, the door burst open and Spanish soldiers entered with guns.

"Arrest the agitators!" the shadow yelled. Minister de Bleu said nothing.

Hadj yelled at the Minister, "You call this freedom?"

The Minister looked up and, without sympathy, said, "I call this stupid." The soldiers led Hadj and the group out of the office in handcuffs.

Belinda waited for news. Hadj had stationed one of the team members outside who watched as Belinda's contingent was led in handcuffs to military vehicles. He jumped on a scooter and left Plaza de la Constitución. Once he was safety outside the city, he found a small country cafe where he stopped, ordered an espresso as cover and called Belinda.

"Is it going to plan?" she asked.

"It is," he responded.

"Fine. We need to know where they have been taken. Can you find out?"

"I have my ways."

"Good for you. Keep me posted."

* * *

Van sat in her new office. It was small but it was her first office and had a window that looked out over the top level of the Department parking structure. The pressure of having been placed in charge of Scott's murder investigation wore on her. She not only had a difficult murder to solve, but she had to manage the reaction of the Bureau to her new appointment and a good number were not happy at the appointment. Charlie poked his head in the door.

"Got a minute, boss?"

"Stop it, Charlie. What's up?"

He sat down on the only chair in the room.

"Henry called. I told him about your appointment, and he says congratulations."

"I'm sure that is not all he said."

"No, of course not. There's a meeting in Denver with the CIA. He wants you to attend."

"Between the FBI and the CIA?"

"Yes."

"This is a tough time for me."

"You'll be fine – I can run things from here for you. You need to go."

"When is it?"

"Tomorrow."

"What?!"

Van called Detective Young and explained her predicament. Young had no difficulty with Van being distracted. He was far from supportive of her new appointment and not opposed to anything that made her seem ill-prepared or unqualified for the new position. "You need to go," he told her.

She rushed home to pack and called FBI Agent Henry Sams on her way home. Sams had organized the FBI assault on Ragnar Willowbrook in the Santa Cruz Mountains.

"Detective Eng," said Henry in response to Van's call.

"What's going on? Charlie told me about the summons to Denver."

"General Tom Warner is missing, and the Pentagon has enlisted us to work the case."

"Wasn't Warner directing black ops?"

"Right. That is what makes it especially challenging."

"Sure, but isn't the military better positioned to investigate their own secrets?"

"Apparently, they have been but to no avail. Warner has been missing for several months."

"Do we think Belinda has something to do with it?"

"She might. We are pulling you in to guide us."

"You and everyone else."

"Excuse me?"

"Never mind. See you in Denver."

Van was not a fan of cold weather. She hated snow and when her friends called her to join them on a skiing trip, she always politely declined. For that reason, she had never travelled to Denver, even in summer, and knew very little about the city. She had not said anything, but she wondered why Denver? Wouldn't Washington DC make more sense? Both FBI and CIA headquarters were there – not in the Rocky Mountains.

The car pulled up to the Four Seasons Hotel Denver at 1111 14th Street. The brisk October air smacked Van in the face. She grumbled under her breath, but Henry had been nice enough to have agents there to attend to her needs and she hustled into the hotel, wondering if she might see someone she recognized. As soon as she got to her room on the 21st floor, she stood by the window and studied her surroundings, including the city's famous opera house and multiple playhouses that made up the Theatre District. The phone rang.

"Welcome to Denver."

"Hi, Henry," Van said, stifling a sniffle.

"Apologies for the cold. You will understand soon enough. In the meantime, enjoy dinner and a show on us. Tickets at the concierge. We'll see you tomorrow at 9:00 am."

"Are we meeting here in the hotel?"

"No, but you are very close. I will send you directions in the morning."

"Thanks."

Van called Charlie.

"Is everything falling apart in my absence?"

"It hasn't yet. Have you started meetings yet?"

"No. They seem to think wining and dining me is an effective use of my time."

"Take advantage. The good life comes and goes like the wind."

"Very wise of you, Charlie. I was going to go to bed, but you've convinced me otherwise."

Van bundled up as best she could. Her car took her to Ruth's Chris around the corner from the hotel and then over to the Ellie Caulkins Opera House. The ticket for her seat placed her on the front of the balcony seating, close enough to have a good view of the performance. She smiled and introduced herself to her neighbors, a salesman from Des Moines and an older woman who said she was in Denver to take care of her nieces while her brother and his wife were traveling.

The performance turned out to be a concert by the Denver Philharmonic Orchestra, a night of Mozart, with guest vocalists and performers. The first half of the concert focused on Mozart's early years. Van enjoyed the music and at intermission was getting ready to stand and wander the lobby when the older woman seated next to her touched her arm.

"I have something for you, my dear." She removed a thick envelope from her purse and handed it to Van. "Don't open it here," she whispered. "Wait until you get back to your room."

Van didn't ask questions. She studied the older woman's face, committing it to memory. She noticed a small dark mole on her left cheek.

"Dear me," said the woman. "Looks like the sitter needs help with my nieces. I'm sorry I can't stay for the second half." She smiled at Van, picked up her items on the chair and left.

It had occurred to Van that something like this might happen, that the invitation had an ulterior purpose, but Van was distracted by the good food and the prospect of a beautiful musical performance and discounted her intuition. Now she sat there holding the brown envelope and her purse, which was too small for the envelope. She thought about leaving, but the second half had begun with a world-famous opera star singing various stanzas in the Magic Flute. She shook her head as she realized that an invitation to a joint meeting of the FBI and the CIA must have some intrigue. It was hard to get her mind off the envelope and as soon as there was a break in the music, she stood and left the Opera House. The car arrived quickly and took her back to the hotel.

As soon as she was back in her room, she opened the envelope. She noticed that it contained a memorandum labeled Top Secret. The memorandum had several attachments, including some photos. She wondered if she would be committing a crime if she read the memorandum, but her curiosity got the best of her, and she started reading.

UNITED STATES DEPARTMENT OF STATE

To: Members of the U.S. Senate Select Committee on Intelligence

From: George Ghantour, Secretary of State

RE: DRAFT TERRORISM ADVISORY, TOP SECRET, FOR YOUR EYES ONLY

The United States and its allies continue to make strides in the fight against global terrorism. Challenges remain and, as has become the new normal, vigilant counter-terrorism efforts must be maintained. A new threat is emerging in the western European Union, where ethnic identity remains strong and ethnicity-based movements develop quickly and without warning. Embassy officials have noted an increase in local protests triggered by what may be a new Basque separatist movement as yet unnamed. To date, the protests have been peaceful but tensions between local officials and protesters are rising. Most of the protests involve graduate level students who are triggered by claims that the Spanish government may have caused the disappearance of Basque supporters of the ETA and other arms of the Basque National Liberation Movement.

It is undisputed that Spain arrested as many as 30,000 alleged militants in the skirmishes that occurred from 1959-2011. New literature on the plight of the detainees now asserts that many of the detained disappeared while incarcerated and efforts to locate the disappeared have proved fruitless. Records also do not account for the children of detainees who were sent into foster care and state-run orphanages. It is believed that the new separatism could be a response by these abandoned children who have matured into adulthood and whose family members have never been recovered.

It is the Department's determination that social unrest in this region can be dangerous for foreign travelers, including Americans. The Department therefore urges caution for all U.S. travelers who intend to visit the northwestern provinces of Spain and the southwestern provinces of France, also known as the Basque Autonomous Region, including the cities of Bilbao, Pamplona and Vitoria-Gasteiz.

To date, none of the protesters have used violent means or triggered violent responses, although police have resorted to tear gas on two occasions in the City of Pamplona. Travelers should stay up to date on developments in the region by following U.S. State Department Advisories.

The memorandum seemed innocuous and hardly worth the label "Top Secret." The draft had not been released, and the State Department must be vetting this version of the advisory with the Senate Select Committee before distributing it. The intelligence community was on edge these days. The current director of the FBI had resigned due to tensions between his staff and the incoming president-elect and for good reason. The president-elect had been the target of two assassination attempts during his campaign, and the intelligence community was engaged in a lot of internal finger-pointing. It would be perfectly understandable for a cabinet position still held by the former administration to confirm policy with Congress before releasing a statement that might have unanticipated impacts.

Van knew this instinctively, but she had very little interest in politics and the *dramatis personae* of the current presidential transition. She found the memorandum interesting but of little consequence until she started perusing the attachments. The first document that struck her was the curriculum vitae of Dr. Belinda Armendariz. She saw no other references to Belinda in any of the written materials except that a news article described the formation of a new chair in the University of Navarra School of Medicine funded by Dr. Armendariz. The Chair oversaw various fields of research including nanotechnology and then Van noticed that the Chair was purportedly named after Dr. Armendariz' late husband, Dr. Leonard Freund.

Assuming it was the same person, Van had no idea that Dr. Freund, whom she had rescued from assault at Ragnar Willowbrook, and Belinda were married.

Leonard didn't act like she was his wife and never described her as such. Then, as she was flipping through the photos depicting various protests, she noticed that a handful of photos showed the Running of the Bulls in Pamplona.

Then she saw it. One of the photos showed a female figure lying on the cobblestoned street, directly in the path of the on-coming bulls. A second photo showed a young male attempting to pull her to safety. She set down the documents. Van knew at once that the photo of the prone figure was her. But why was it in this package? She leaned back and wondered if she might be a topic at the next day's meetings.

Chapter 9.

Running with the Devil

"Can I get you a coffee?"

Detective Paul Young sat as his desk playing with a pencil.

"I don't understand," he said mostly to himself but loud enough for Charlie to pick it up.

"Just coffee. Black, right?"

"Sure, Charles," Young responded.

Detective Charles Darling returned to Young's office, carrying two cups of black coffee. He placed one of the cups in front of Young and sat down.

"You were saying?"

"Saying? I wasn't saying anything."

"What's going on with you, Paul?"

"Shit. Look, I don't have a problem escalating quality people in the Bureau. I do it all the time and I do it because it is the right decision."

"You think the Chief made a bad decision?"

"Far be it from me."

"You know I have a high regard for our deaf detective."

"She's not deaf. Not really."

"I beg to differ. But what you or I think hardly matters. The Police Academy came to that conclusion and kept her out."

"What do you want, Charlie?"

"I want to know what happened at Justice."

"The tavern? I've already told internal affairs too many times. It was a celebration of a new hire, pure and simple."

"Scott didn't leave with you?"

"No. And you shouldn't be asking questions you already know the answer to unless you are just trying to piss me off. As I have said, he told me he was leaving because he wanted to get some work done. You're wasting my time."

"He was a new hire. You just said that. What work did he have to complete?"

"I don't know. I didn't question him. I thought maybe he is trying to look productive. Maybe it was paperwork – maybe he needed to fill out his I-9. I have no idea."

"Ok. Let's view this from a different angle."

"Jesus Christ. You don't give up."

"You know me, Paul. You hired me. Let me do my job."

Young grunted and sipped his coffee. Charlie had always been a pain in the ass, but the Bureau kept him on in part because Charlie was well liked and, regardless, it was difficult to fire somebody from the Bureau unless Internal Affairs had rendered the edict. Young knew Charlie to be persistent, and though he would never say so, he admired it.

"What did you know about Scott?"

"His background?"

"Right. His background."

"He was the top recruit from the Academy."

"What about his background check?"

"We ran it. The Academy ran their own. Nothing remotely interesting. He was a good student, a good athlete, and a good marksman. He was a talented human being, which makes his loss more difficult. I'm sick about it."

"Something is missing, Paul. Does his murder strike you as an accident? Merely bad timing? Or was this planned out in advance. Neither of those scenarios fit here –

Scott hadn't had time to do anything to anyone."

"You're the detective, Detective. Go find out. But as pissed as I am about little miss upstart, I'm on the team. Whatever I can do to help, I will."

"I'm counting on it."

Charlie left the discussion disturbed. Paul had always been ambitious, even as a young detective and not unlike Scott. But over the years, Paul became detached. He seemed to hold a veiled contempt for his superiors driven by what he viewed as a poverty of leadership and unwillingness to promote him. Charlie believed that Paul saw something in Scott that inspired him. He couldn't imagine at this point linking Paul to Scott's murder. But he knew two things now. First, he had to dig deeper into Scott's background. Second, he needed to find out who possibly might hold a grudge so deep to warrant the murder of a young man just starting out.

* * *

After multiple screenings and questions as to why she was there, the FBI's advance team allowed Van access to the empty building across the street from the hotel. FBI Agent Henry Sams walked up to her as soon as she entered a large conference room.

"I am sorry for the hassle," he told her. "The multi-agency meetings are harder to get into than Langley itself."

"I was starting to wonder whether or not I should even be here," Van responded. "But then I remembered this." She held out the package that had been delivered to her the prior evening.

"What is this?" Henry asked.

"You don't know? Huh," exclaimed Van. "The intrigue grows."

"Let's find a seat quickly," said Henry. "You can show me what you have."

"Coffee first," said Van.

For most of the morning, Van felt as if she was attending a breakout session at a convention. Introductions lasted for most of the first hour as agencies tried to one-up each other's level of importance. Henry introduced Van as a detective from LAPD and few in attendance paid any attention. Each agency, CIA, FBI and Homeland Security, among others, had appointed representatives to speak and the presentations focused on efforts to address terrorism, define terrorism, and distinguish domestic terrorism from global terrorism. The speakers all had pictures of alleged terrorists and gruesome images from their despicable acts, but none of the pictures showed Belinda Armendariz or mentioned the destruction of the Tran Lab on Bainbridge Island. There was a brief discussion about the Climate Conference events in Paris and some speculation about the group that launched the attack, but no one drew any connection between Paris and Bainbridge Island. Van had her own questions, but she said nothing, noticing that the audience seemed intentionally passive. She wondered how many times they had to view these same presentations in the past. She looked around for the older woman with the mole who had given her the package but didn't see her.

Henry invited her to join him for lunch. He brought a good friend of his from Homeland Security, Denise Kepler. Henry and Denise attended law school together and even though Denise built her life in Washington, DC, they stayed in touch. Henry took them to a small bistro with private booths. He introduced Denise to Van.

"I've heard of you," said Denise.

"You've heard of me?"

"My director met you at a meeting with the President."

"They called me into the White House and had a couple questions, but I've heard nothing since."

"You are here now, right?"

"I am, but I am not certain why. Nothing we discussed this morning had anything to do with me or my work."

Denise looked at Henry. "I can see why you like her," she said. "She's careful." She looked back at Van. "This morning was all about posturing. Something is going on and I expect they'll break it down this afternoon."

"Do you know why you are here?" Van studied Denise's reaction.

Henry interjected. "There it is. The real reason I like her. Let's hold on that and see what happens this afternoon."

They returned to the conference room. The speaker was walking through a list of "persons of interest." Van leaned over to Henry.

"Do these guys consider Belinda a person of interest?"

"She's on our list."

"Are they aware of her?"

"I'm not sure, Van. Let's see."

It took a couple of hours and a coffee break, but finally Van saw the name Dr. Belinda Armendariz. The speaker quickly brushed over her, noting that there was a possible connection to the incident on Bainbridge Island, but nothing beyond that, including Paris. Van found herself confused on a couple fronts. First, why was she there? Second, who gave her the package with the memorandum and the photos?

When the day was completed, Van asked Henry to introduce her to the CIA. Henry introduced her to Special Agent Vanessa Christian. Vanessa was relatively new to the CIA, having been there just two years. Originally from Des Moines, Iowa, Agent Christian spoke multiple European languages and had been assigned to the Paris office. She had a surprisingly light demeaner for being a CIA agent. Van liked her immediately.

"Special Agent Christian, allow me to introduce you to Detective Van Eng."

Agent Christian smiled. "Are you also a Vanessa?"

"No. Just Van."

"Very nice to meet you, Van."

"I wanted to ask you about one of your persons of interest. Her name is Dr. Belinda Armendariz."

"We've been investigating her."

"Do you know where she is?"

"I'm not sure."

"Are you aware that I ran into her in Pamplona, Spain?"

"Let's take this conversation elsewhere, if you don't mind. Do you have plans for dinner?"

Van looked at Henry. "Do we?"

Henry studied Vanessa. She looked back as if to say, let me take this.

"Maybe you should enjoy dinner with Agent Christian," Henry said to Van.

Van hesitated. She realized that she might be in over her head and, even though Vanessa was nice, she wasn't sure she trusted her.

Henry sensed Van's apprehension. "Call me after dinner," he said.

"Ok." She turned to Vanessa. "I am staying across the street. Can we meet in the lobby?"

Alarms resounded in Van's brain. Something about the situation didn't feel right. She trusted Henry and she felt conflicted about Agent Christian but wanted to think the caricature of the diabolical CIA operative didn't fit. She couldn't understand why Belinda didn't hold their attention. The FBI had expended assets to catch her following the destruction of the Tran Lab on Bainbridge Island and they failed. But when Belinda escaped outside the country, they stopped chasing her, deferring instead on agencies with an international reach, like the CIA, Interpol and MI6. Those agencies had not accomplished anything, as far as Van knew.

She saw Vanessa waiting in the lobby as she exited the elevators and walked directly to meet her. Vanessa smiled her smile as Van approached her.

"Should we try Korean, or do you prefer Vietnamese?"

"Healthy American works for me."

"I know just the place."

They called an Uber. Van assumed there would be a black something or other, like a Lincoln town car or Cadillac SUV. A white Tesla Model Y pulled up.

"Vanessa?" said the driver.

"Yup. Got my address?"

"I do."

They drove for 20 minutes down a remote highway, and, as the drive stretched out, Van felt the fear creeping back in. They turned a corner around a thick grove of pines and found a biker stop called the Roadhouse. The parking lot was full of Gold Wings and Harleys and Van thought about Brian. Inside, the bar and restaurant were loud.

A country western band was playing music by the Marshall Tucker Band. Most of the bikers inside were in their 60s. They wore old bandanas and leather vests and most of them were drinking something that looked like Diet Coke. The hostess recognized Vanessa.

"One of your new recruits?" she asked playfully.

"Depends how well she handles a weapon," Vanessa responded with a wink.

"What did you say?" Van asked as they followed the hostess.

"I told them I'm a secret agent and I need their help protecting my identity," Vanessa responded.

"Good cover," said Van. Vanessa reminded her of Charlie in an odd way. Charlie had taught Van about hiding in plain sight.

The hostess found a table at the back. "The usual?"

"Please."

"And for your friend?"

"Soda and lime."

Van studied Vanessa. "So, what are we doing?"

"We're getting to know each other."

"You brought me to a BBQ joint after I said healthy?"

"Take a look at the menu," said Vanessa with a grin. "This place was built to be a Texas BBQ joint, but things got slow during the pandemic, and they hired a new chef who specializes in Farm-to-Table. You should try the trout."

Van laughed. "You got me. I could have sworn you were taking me into the woods to shoot me."

"Shoot you? I'm a linguist not an assassin."

"That and what else?"

"I'm leading the European investigation into Belinda Armendariz."

"Well, how about that."

"We aren't making progress."

"You admit that?"

"At some point, you have to be honest."

"Are you the reason I am here?"

"I am. I asked Henry to bring you."

"But I approached you."

"That just made it easier. I asked Henry to introduce us."

A waitress returned with drinks.

"Are you ready or do you need time?"

"She'll have the trout," Vanessa said. "I'll do the burnt ends with Memphis style on the side."

"You got it."

Vanessa laughed again. "Farm-to-table BBQ?"

"To each our own."

"Ok, so what can I do?"

"Belinda kidnapped you. Tell me about that."

"Tell me what you know first."

"I know Belinda started as a brilliant scientist who went bad. I know the FBI had reason to believe Belinda was involved in the Bainbridge Island incident and that they brought you in to support a raid on her Silicon Valley lab where they didn't capture her. Then there's Pamplona. I know something happened between you and Belinda and that she tried to kill you and make it look like an accident. Or at least that is what it looks like from the outside."

"Do you have agents in Pamplona looking for her?"

"I can't tell you that."

"Yet somehow you have a picture of me lying in the street. That seems to answer the question."

"And someone who quickly pulled you off the street."

"Your operative?"

"I can't tell you that."

"What do you want to know?"

The food came and the trout was as good as Vanessa promised. But she also felt the pull of good barbecue.

"You want to try some?" Vanessa said smiling and talking with her mouth full. "It's pretty good."

"Ok. Yes. I do."

Vanessa handed her a fork full of burnt ends saturated in Memphis style BBQ sauce.

"Oh, my god," Van said, her own mouth now full of BBQ. "This is so good."

Vanessa waited for Van to finish chewing,

"Where did she take you?"

"I don't know."

"Would you remember anything if we took you back there?"

"I might. I was on some kind of farm. They put a hood on me and drugged me so I have no idea how long I was out, but I could tell it was a farm by the smell of old wood and manure."

"What else? What did she say to you?"

"She didn't say anything to me. She just asked what I was doing there."

"She knew who you were?"

"She seemed to. She referred to me as detective."

"Did you try to talk to her?"

"No. Not at all. I figured she would kill me regardless of what I said."

"The scene at the Running of the Bulls. What was that about?"

"You mean where she dumped me in the street?"

"Yes. That scene."

"I can't make sense of it. Maybe she liked the drama of dumping me drugged in the path of a world-famous stampede. Maybe she liked the macabre and wanted to see me being trampled to death.

Maybe she thought she was sending someone a message. Maybe me. Maybe she expected me to survive. I have run this through multiple times, and it still doesn't make sense."

"What do you know about Bainbridge?"

"You mean what happened in Bainbridge?"

"I know that Bainbridge scientists were working on a batch of nanobots and that the inadvertent release of the nanobots almost killed two of them. I also know that Belinda claimed that the batch, contained in a petri dish, had been stolen from her lab. It was her team's actions that resulted in multiple deaths and the destruction of the lab."

"Do you know if the deaths were caused by the nanobots?"

"I don't. There was a fire and the people who died were burned in the fire. I don't know if the nanobots killed them or the fire. But I do know that the nanobots concerned them and that everyone was wearing gas masks when I reached the scene, me included."

"Did Belinda get the nanobots back or were they destroyed in the fire?

"We looked and did not find any nanobot containers, which would have been kept in a fireproof safe on the premises. Nothing was in the safe."

"Did anyone from the lab survive?"

"Yes, several people got out."

"Anyone you think I should talk to?"

"I would think Agent Sams knows. The most important person in all this is Dr. Brian

Johannsen. He is the chief scientist at Ragnar Willowbrook in the Silicon Valley."

Suddenly Vanessa looked up, distracted, at the band. They were singing "Red Solo Cup" by Toby Keith.

"I love this song!" she exclaimed. "Come on!" She grabbed Van by the arm and pulled her out of her chair and, unfortunately, out of her shoes, which she left scattered under the table.

"Let's dance!"

Chapter 10.

Fibonacci's Gold

The so-called "golden ratio" is a mathematically based ratio that many claim is a foundational element in nature, fine art and architecture. They tell us that this "divine proportion" evokes a sense of balance and harmony that is inherently appealing to the human brain and secretly reveals the existence of God. The golden ratio is given the Greek letter phi, where $\varphi \cong 1.618$ and the ratio is 1:φ. Imagine a rectangle with a width equal to 1 unit and length equal to 1.618 units. Euclid was the first to use geometry to explain the rule of the golden ratio, describing it as two segments of a line the ratio of which is equal to the ratio of the longer segment to the entire length of the line. In the 13th century, Leonardo Fibonacci developed a sequence of numbers that rooted the golden ratio in basic arithmetic. Fibonacci proposed a sequence where the sum of any two consecutive numbers generates a sequence that leads to *phi*. The Fibonacci Sequence follows the pattern: 0, 1, 1, 2, 3, 5, 8, 13, 21, 34, 55, 89, 144, 233... For example, 2+3=5 and 3+5=8 and 8/5=1.6. Continue the sequence and 233/144=1.61805556.

The epic Greek building known as the Parthenon appears to employ this same ratio in its dimensions. Leonardo Da Vinci was captivated by *phi* and used it to depict a balanced human body in his sketch called *The Vitruvian Man*. Supporters of the "golden ratio" assert that this magical balance also appears in the artwork of Sandro Botticelli (*Birth of Venus*), Leonardo Da Vinci (*The Last Supper* and *Mona Lisa*), Salvadore Dali (*The Sacrament of the Last Supper*) and Raphael (*The School of Athens*).

Critics are not so confident. They say the golden ratio pattern can be laid over any image to make it seem like it applies. They acknowledge that certain natural compositions appear to reflect the ratio, such as the spiral pattern of a nautilus shell. But they reject the magical thinking around the golden ratio and claims that the ratio is a divine truth. It would be interesting to calculate the ratio of Fibonacci believers to skeptics only to find that ratio also approximates 1.618.

Dr. Brian Johannsen sat at his desk studying the grounds of Ragnar Willowbrook.

He had kept the landscape crew on salary, not because he felt it necessary to keep the grounds in good shape, but because he didn't want to let go of the crew that Belinda had used for years. He heard a knock.

"Mr. Johannsen?"

"It's doctor, but that's ok. What's up?"

"I'm sorry, Doctor," said the grounds crew manager Stavro. "You need to come see this. We found a body."

Brian followed Stavro down the stairs and outside into the large garden area. They walked to the far corner of the property. Brian saw several crew members standing around a pile of fresh dirt.

"You recall last week's rain?" Stavro said to Brian.

"Yes, it was heavy. I think they called it a Pineapple Express."

"It caused a small mudslide on this hill, nothing to be concerned about, except for this."

Stavro walked Brian over to the pile of dirt and, there, partially exposed, was the decaying body of a young woman.

"Holy shit!" said Brian. "Everyone needs to stop doing what they are doing right now. This looks like a crime scene."

Police identified the victim, later unearthed and taken to the morgue, as Cheryl Brown. The cause of death was a single bullet to the brain. Dr. Leonard Freund, who had seen Cheryl murdered at Belinda's command, knew at once who it was. He told Brian, "I know the FBI searched the grounds but never found the grave. I guess Belinda's team did a good job of hiding it and no one gave up the secret."

"But why kill her?" said Brian.

Leonard turned pale. "I don't know. I was disgusted by it. It. It was too much for me. If the FBI had not raided the Lab, I would have left and probably lived in fear that Belinda would find me and kill me. I still wonder about it."

Brian turned away, thinking now that it was a mistake to take the job at Ragnar Willowbrook. He looked back at Leonard, who was concerned about Brian's reaction.

"We need to do something special to resurrect this girl's memory. I don't know if she was a good person or not, but she did not deserve to be executed in some basement and buried in a field."

"We'll do whatever you think we need to do," said Leonard.

Brian returned to his office and called Bost.

"I heard the news," Bost told Brian.

"Another mess here, but this one is particularly troubling," said Brian. "We live among monsters."

"That is the wonder of the human condition, isn't it – saints and sinners, demons and angels."

"I don't find anything wonderful about it. How was your trip to Spain?"

"We didn't find anything. Warner is still missing, and the University of Navarro was no help, either because they were concerned about liability but possibly protecting their benefactor, Dr. Belinda Armendariz. Professor Echevarria didn't give us any leads, except to tell us that the nanobots that Belinda brought to the University for study were now missing, following a break-in at the laboratory there."

"No idea where she was?"

"If they knew, they were good at hiding it. But I think Belinda knew enough to conceal her location."

"How did Deckwalder take it?"

"He is pissed. No word on General Warner and no location for Armendariz."

"Ok. You are back?"

"What's next with the nanobots?"

"We're still waiting on the FDA's approval of a public use now that the toxicity issue is resolved."

"The new President – can he help us?"

"Maybe, if we can get his or his team's attention. They seem to be busy rebuilding the U.S. government."

"Talk to Deckwalder. Tell him we will do whatever to get this moving. In the meantime, I'm still working on the impact that AI has on nanobot communication. I must think that we are on the edge of something new."

"Deckwalder is getting bored with AI. He wants us to get to the level – they are calling it 'super AI.' Kind of a dumb name but I've never claimed to be a marketing genius."

"How is the nano-chip coming?"

"Deckwalder is putting pressure on. He wants the chip delivered by the end of the quarter. Orders are already piling up and no one knows yet what it can do."

"Do you think it is an advance? Seems just like another fast chip."

"It's a revolution."

"How so?"

"Imagine a computer that syncs with the human brain. You don't just look at it and ask it to answer questions."

"Isn't Musk's company already doing that?"

"Yes, but not this way. Musk's Neuralink implants electrodes into the brain with a surgical robot. This nanochip computer is messenger based. It sends out nanobots, like worker bees, that use carbon dioxide molecules and heat to identify a path through the human nasal cavity into the brain and sends signals back to the computer."

Brian was impressed. "You don't have to turn human beings into cyborgs to gain the advantages of AI."

"Right. Nanobots form the link."

"What about injections?"

"That's part of the testing, but it's indirect and delays the link. With our technology, you connect immediately to the computer by breathing. Imagine the applications. Autonomous planes with a human instinct built into flight patterns. Autonomous vehicles that don't need human drivers as a failsafe."

"The FDA is going to have a field day with this."

"That's where we need help. They could delay this technology for years."

* * *

Charles Darling stared at his notes on Scott Geiringer. The kid was from a middle-class home in the San Fernando Valley. He attended Granada Hills High School before attending UCLA. He loved football but was too small to get a scholarship at a major school, so he had applied to UCLA and then joined the team as a walk-on. The coaches liked Scott for his mental acuity. They offered him the opportunity to join the coaching staff as a student coach, but Scott wanted to keep suiting up and getting whatever playing time he could get. Eventually, in a kind of Rudy-escque fashion, they allowed him to play, and he made several good tackles and an interception as a cornerback. Unfortunately, he was too short to handle the elite receivers from other universities but, for good measure, the staff let him on the field during the one Rose Bowl that the team qualified for during his senior year. As far as Charlie could tell, this kid was bound to be a star somewhere at some point and elected the Police Academy as the opportunity to shine.

And shine he did. He graduated at the top of his recruitment class and, not only was he a top-level student, but he also demonstrated remarkable acuity with weapons and won the Academy's martial arts competition. The more Charlie learned about Scott, the more tragic and incomprehensible was his murder.

He decided to meet with some of Scott's teachers at the Academy. Charlie had done well there himself and, even after several years, the teaching staff still remembered him. His reputation there made it easy to get access to records and personnel. He asked who knew Scott the best and fingers universally pointed to Sergeant Marisa Coldridge, who taught police strategy. Charlie made his way to her office and intercepted her as she was locking the office door and getting ready to leave.

"Sergeant Coldridge?"

She looked up. "Can I help you?"

"Excuse me. I'm Detective Charles Darling, LAPD." Charlie showed her his badge.

"My apologies, Detective, but I am heading to a class of recruits. It would not send the right message if I were late."

"I understand. I can walk and talk with you if you don't mind."

"Sure."

They headed down the hall and several recruits made a point of acknowledging the Sergeant, who happened to be as attractive as she was stern.

"Do you remember a student named Scott Geiringer?"

Charlie saw her hesitate and almost stumble.

"Dammit. They need to fix these walkways," she said and then recovered herself. "Scott? Yes, I remember him. Good student. Recent graduate, wasn't he?"

"Yes, he just joined the LAPD Detective Bureau."

"Good for him. Why do you ask?"

"Scott was murdered two weeks ago."

Coldridge stopped dead in her tracks.

"In the line of duty?"

"No. He was at the Bureau late at night."

"How's that possible?" Charlie could tell this was affecting Sergeant Coldridge more than she was letting on.

"We're still checking into it. It's a tough case. Scott had a lot of natural talent for the job."

"I remember liking Scott. Friendly. Quick witted." She picked up the pace toward her class. Charlie kept up.

"Is there anything you recall about Scott's experience here at the Academy? Anything that might be helpful."

"Like did Scott have enemies?"

"Right."

"No. Not that I was aware of. He was a popular figure here. Some of the recruits that do well here become bullies. They treat their lower achieving classmates with disdain. Scott wasn't like that."

"Was anyone bullying Scott?"

"No one bullied Scott. If anything, Scott interceded when he witnessed that type of behavior. He made bullies feel foolish and incompetent."

"Any one in particular? Are you sure no one in his class had a vendetta?"

"There were a couple students who felt competitive with Scott, but I'm not sure about any vendettas. Leave your card with me. I need to start class. I'll investigate it myself and if I can come up with any names, I'll let you know."

Charlie left the campus and headed back to the Bureau. Sergeant Coldridge's demeanor did not sit well with him. Of course, it was possible that one of Scott's classmates might have held such a grudge that they would find a way to take it out on Scott. But murder? Charlie sat down at his desk and pulled up the list of graduates from Scott's class to see who might have been hired as part of the rookie class along with Scott. A small handful had been admitted onto the force working out of downtown. Scott was the only graduate who came straight to the Detective Bureau. The rest were working as beat cops out of the downtown office. He contacted them, one by one, but it didn't take long for word to get out that the Bureau was focusing on other new recruits, and Charlie could feel the resistance to his inquiries building.

His phone rang.

"Detective Charles Darling."

"Yes, sir," he heard a voice stammering on the other line.

"Can I help you?"

"My name is Officer Ben Bodrogi. I am working out of Rampart."

"Hi, Ben. What can I do for you?"

The Rampart Division of LAPD had suffered many years under the pall of a bad reputation. One of the officers working at Rampart was caught stealing cocaine from an evidence locker and turned state's evidence to reduce his sentence. He claimed that the Rampart CRASH Unit (Community Resources Against Street Hoodlums) had been planting evidence, lying under oath, and falsifying reports to frame gang members. His testimony blew up in the media and implicated more than 70 officers leading to hundreds of overturned convictions. Some believed Rampart itself had been framed to cover up other Department abuses. The officers working out of Rampart were particularly sensitive to any investigations, especially investigations involving Internal Affairs. Charlie knew this and Ben's call signaled to him that word was getting out about his inquiries.

"I heard you were looking into Scott's murder."

"I am."

"I knew Scott at the Academy."

"Ok."

"Can we meet?"

"I'm fine with that. What do you have in mind?"

Charlie heard someone yell in the background.

"Officer! Let's go!"

Ben replied. "I'll call you."

To Charlie, it was good news that another officer had reached out. Ben's call could be the break in the case he was looking for. But he could tell Ben was uncomfortable and he knew that, if Ben had information on Scott's murder, Charlie needed to treat the situation carefully. He didn't want to expose Ben and possibly get him murdered as well. He investigated Ben's record and Ben's performance there was mediocre. He was working vice at Rampart which meant Ben knew how to navigate the politics of that station. He waited to hear back.

Two weeks later he got another call.

"Detective Darling?"

"Yes."

"Are you free to meet today?"

"Ok."

"My shift ends in an hour. I share a space in a house in Coldwater Canyon." He gave Charlie directions to a reservoir near his home that was no longer in use. Charlie parked near a chain link fence with a gate covered in signs. The signs had been ignored, and gate was bent back to create a small opening barely large enough to squeeze through. Charlie waited by the gate. He noticed a couple of cars parked on the road near the gate. He checked his watch. It read 4:10 pm and Ben, who told Charlie to be there at 4 pm was nowhere in sight. He thought Ben might be up the trail and started to crawl through the opening in the gate when he saw a car approaching. The car parked and Ben appeared.

"Charlie!" Ben yelled.

Charlie stopped. He was halfway through the opening in the gate.

Ben seemed nervous. He tried to lighten the moment. "Didn't you read the signs? You're trespassing!"

Charlie got irritated as he tried to pull himself free of the opening. Ben laughed.

"I'm just joking. Follow me."

Ben walked into a small opening in some bushes on the side of the road. He held back a branch and pointed to a wide gap in the fence.

"This way is a little easier," he said and directed Charlie to walk through the gap.

"I'm sorry about being late," Ben said. "I got called into a meeting about some new gang activity."

Charlie started to calm down. "That's okay," he said. "You are here now. Where are we going?"

"There's a cool viewpoint above the reservoir. I thought you would enjoy it."

"I'm here to talk about Scott, not to go sightseeing." Charlie pointed down at his black Oxfords that were already getting dusty from the old road.

Ben studied Charlie. "I know. It's relevant."

They walked for about 30 minutes. Ben described his experience at the Academy, how he and Scott met and occasionally studied together. Ben talked about Scott as if he had adored him. Then Ben pointed up a path on the side of the old road. Charlie grunted as he slipped on the steep path. Ben grabbed his arm and helped Charlie up the path. They turned a corner, and Charlie saw the reservoir about 100 feet below with downtown Hollywood in the distance.

Charlie looked at Ben. "Were you jealous of Scott?"

"I suppose," said Ben. "Scott was the darling of our class. But I didn't need to be Scott. I just wanted him to like me and spend time with me." Ben pointed to a small stone wall that one of the locals built to sit and watch the sunset.

"Scott and I used to come here and relax and talk about our futures."

"Do you know who killed Scott?"

Before Ben could answer, Charlie heard rustling in the bushes behind him. Two men came out of the bushes wearing ski masks. Charlie jumped up from the wall and tried to draw his handgun, but the men were on him too quickly. He tried to push back against their grip, but they were strong and trained in close combat and Charlie was too old to give them much of a fight. He looked over at Ben who had turned away and wasn't looking at Charlie.

"Ben!" Charlie yelled. "What is this?"

"Shut up," he heard and thought he recognized the voice.

"Don't do this," Charlie said. "You don't want to do this!"

But they kept pushing Charlie toward the edge of the overhang. As they reached the edge, Charlie stuck his foot between the legs of one of his attackers who tripped and fell toward the edge. Charlie got free as his other attacker reached to rescue his accomplice. He pulled his handgun and shot the fallen attacker in the leg.

"Stop!" Charlie yelled. "Or I will kill you both." They looked up at Charlie, who was standing near the edge of the cliff trying to maintain his balance as he defended himself with the gun. He didn't see Ben facing him with his arm extended.

"I'm sorry, Charlie," he heard and, as he turned toward Ben, Ben fired a single shot that caught Charlie in the chest and pushed him over the edge. He fell into the empty reservoir, his body bouncing off a large rock projecting from the cliff and then settling motionless on the surface of the empty reservoir below.

Chapter 11.

Hollywoodland

The iconic "HOLLYWOOD" sign erected near the top of Mount Lee in Los Angeles was first erected in 1923 as an advertisement for a new local housing development called "Hollywoodland." The original sign, using the same 30-foot wide by 50-foot-tall block letters, read "HOLLYWOODLAND" and was illuminated by 4,000 light bulbs, timed to flash the words "HOLLY," "WOOD," and "LAND" successively. The elimination of the word "LAND" in 1949 came as a result local opposition to the preservation of the then-deteriorated sign. The Hollywood Chamber of Commerce protested its removal and compromised with the City of Los Angeles by agreeing to remove the last four letters of the sign, leaving the sign emblematic of the local movie industry rather than the development. In the 2006 movie "Hollywoodland," Ben Affleck used the original name to reflect the early days of Hollywood and the dark side of the life of George Reeves, the original Superman of the 1950s. Reeves died in 1959 at the age of 45 by a gunshot to the head. Officially ruled a suicide, Reeves close friends continued to believe that Reeves' death was a contract killing ordered by a studio executive who was jealous of Reeves over an alleged affair between Reeves and the executive's wife.

If the death of Detective Scott Geiringer sent shock waves through the Bureau, the death of Detective Charles Darling hit the Bureau like a nuclear bomb. The media used Darling's death to cast doubt on the Department as a whole and as a reflection of the chaos at the City of Los Angeles. Van found herself caught in the headlights of a brutal media attack. She stood quietly in a row of officers as the Chief approached the array of microphones. Lights flashed.

"Chief! Chief!" Shouts and hands raised to get his attention. "Is the LAPD murdering its own officers?"

"Quiet, please!" said the Chief. "We lost a long time, honorable friend and colleague. Hikers found his body on the dry bed of Franklin Canyon Reservoir near Coldwater

Canyon. Whether or not his death was an accident or intentional is still to be

determined. Detective Charles Darling served this Department and this City for almost three decades. He was one of our very best and we mourn his loss."

"Cause of death?" the Chief heard the question.

"That is still to be determined."

Another voice shouted. "Do you regret placing Detective Eng in charge of the Geiringer murder?"

The Chief grimaced. His wished he could simply throw out the offending voice, but he knew that was not an option with the press and he steadied himself.

"Absolutely not. Detective Eng has proven herself many times over and I have full confidence that she will get to the bottom of Detective Geiringer's murder. That said, don't make the mistake of connecting Detective Darling's death to the Geiringer investigation. We will make that determination ourselves. Now, if you please remain quiet and respectful, I would like to ask Detective Eng to brief you on the status of her investigation."

Van moved to the mikes. Lights flashed.

"Thank you," she said. "Today is a very difficult day. Detective Darling was my close friend. His loss is difficult to bear but we will get to the root cause of his death just as we will find out who murdered Detective Scott Geiringer and bring the perpetrators to justice."

The reporters shouted questions at Van. "Do you have any leads?" "How close were you and Detective Darling?" Isn't the fox guarding the henhouse?" Van measured her words. She did not want to alienate the press, even as she anticipated their desire to uncover the most lurid and sensationalist details.

As Van was heading to the parking structure, Detective Paul Young intercepted her.

"I know how hard this is," he said. "I trusted Charlie completely. I told him to be careful, but he was driven to solve this case and took unnecessary risks."

"Charlie was just doing his job," Van retorted.

"I know that, Van. He was one of our best."

"Did you come here because you wanted to chat about Charlie or was it something else?"

Detective Young looked away, briefly. He had never met such an acute mind and found it difficult to compete with her.

"Just be careful," he said.

"Do you know something I don't?" Van pressed back.

"No, we are in uncharted waters here. It's hard to think someone at the Bureau could be so threatened they would resort to killing a brother detective."

"Brother?"

"You know what I mean, and you know what I don't mean. Just be careful."

As Van drove home, an overwhelming sadness hit her repeatedly like waves on the ocean. For a moment, she would feel a calm acceptance of Charlie's death. Then in a flash, she would visualize a moment between her and Charlie like the time he showed her how to conduct a stakeout in plain view as he sat in the car with her reading one of his favorite books. The tears would well up and she whimpered in the pain of her grief. When she got home, she immediately went to bed and cried some more. After an hour, Mom knocked on the door.

"Are you ok, Daughter?"

Van sat up, her eyes swollen and red. Mom came over and put her arm around Van.

"God has his time for us all, my dear."

"I know Mom. It doesn't make it better. If I had been here, maybe Charlie would still be alive."

"There is no if in our lives, my darling. Everything happens for a reason."

"I miss him, Mom. He was my rock at the Bureau. Now I don't know who to trust and the air there is so heavy."

"Pray to our ancestors. They will watch over you. Talk to Charlie. He will be there by your side, always."

"Thanks, Mom. Do-je. I love you."

"Mo-hat-he."

Van got up and washed her face. She wanted a place where she could reflect on her life and work at the Bureau. She recalled the spot on Mulholland at the top of Runyan Canyon where gang leader Danny Kang took her while she worked him undercover.

She smiled as she recalled him telling her of his dream to be the king of Los Angeles. Van had come as close to falling in love with Danny as any other boy she had dated, even though she knew his criminal history. Something inside of her wanted desperately to see the good in him win out over his criminal side. Van did not entertain that illusion for long, but even if it were possible, Danny did not get his chance to find a better path. A rival gang member killed him in prison. She mourned Danny's death but not like she was mourning Charlie. The pain of Charlie's loss would linger. Right now, she needed a place with a view that reminded her of the bigger picture. She took off for Mulholland Drive. She parked near the trailhead and stared for several moments at the lights of downtown Hollywood below her. Hikers strolled past her, and she was surprised how many there were out there on the hill in the dark. Flashlights bobbed around the hill. She picked up her cell phone and called Agent Vanessa Christian.

"Hello, Van!" Vanessa responded almost shouting. "Are you busy?"

"Yeah, no, I am not in a great place right now."

"Aw honey, do you want to meet up?"

"Thank you, but no. I am calling you to tell you that I need to pull back from the federal investigation of Belinda Armendariz."

Vanessa hesitated. "Why would that be?"

"I'm sorry. It has nothing to do with that investigation. My partner at the LAPD was killed in an investigation that I am supposed to be leading. The Armendariz matter is important to me, but I need to give my full focus to this investigation."

"Yes. Absolutely. And I'll tell you without hesitation, if you need any resources to help you in that effort, call me. We can be very helpful."

"Thank you, Agent Christian. I just may take you up on it."

Van put down the phone. A resolute calm settled over her. She looked at the passenger seat and for a brief instant thought she saw Charlie, sitting next to her, smiling.

Chapter 12.

The Night Brigade

The Kymco AK550 made its way down the tight windy road called Carretera de Francia and designated N-135. The N-135 runs from Pau, France through the Pyrenees to Pamplona, Spain. The rider's destination was not Pamplona, but a small village in the Navarre Province north of Pamplona called Erro. The Basques called the town Erroiberra. Pablo Garcia, the youthful rider of the high-powered scooter bike, ran through the curves of N-135 imagining he was Jorge Lorenzo, the five-time MotoGP world champion from Spain. He saw the crowds rising as he leaned hard into the curves, almost dragging the side of the bike on the asphalt and then whipping down the straightaways. It didn't matter to Pablo that he was transporting bottles of deadly nanobots and the triggers he would set as he followed Belinda's instructions to the tee. The joy of global recognition for his bike handling skills was a fantasy too rich to let go.

Belinda had been of two minds when it came to Pablo. The kid demonstrated absolute loyalty to the cause and cared for nothing more than pleasing his superiors. But when Hadj suggested Pablo for this first mission, Belinda hesitated. She knew it mean entrusting this first critical public display of her power to someone neither refined nor experienced. One the other hand, Belinda knew that this mission did not require perfection. The demand letter that Pablo was carrying would make it clear that her separatist group dubbed the Night Brigade was responsible for the consequences of the release of the nanobots, whatever their impact.

She understood that it would be unfortunate if Pablo were lost in the effort, but the loss would be minor compared to any other member of her leadership team, whom she leaned on to help her accomplish her ultimate goals. If Pablo were successful, and able to return to base camp, he would be given a rank suitable to his accomplishments.

Erro Navarre is a beautiful small town in the foothills of the Pyrenees. In the winter, the snows that come to Erro cause it to glisten like stardust in the night. Like most small towns in the region, the tallest structure is the bell tower of the local church. The bell tower rings twice a day every day. The first ringing of the bell tower is at 12 noon, reminding everyone to prepare to return home for afternoon meal and siesta. The second ringing of the day is at 8:00 p.m. when the shops close and a small evening meal is enjoyed before Erro's residents head to their bedrooms for the night. N-135 skirts the eastern side of the town as it heads south and then turns west and heads through the southern portion of the town before exiting and heading south to Pamplona.

The sun was setting in the West as Pablo sped toward the town. He followed the road as it veered right and placed the setting sun directly in his path. The light of the sun flashed off Pablo's helmet and temporarily obscured his vision. He didn't see a large storage van broken down on the side of the road. The truck had overheated just outside the city and spilled antifreeze across the road. The hood of the truck was open, and a mechanic stood on the bumper reaching into the engine compartment trying to replace the hose.

Pablo jerked his bike hard left and, as he passed the truck, another vehicle emerged from town and headed right in Pablo's path. Pablo jerked the bike back to the right just as he crossed over the spilled antifreeze. His rear tire began to slide carrying Pablo directly into the on-coming vehicle, sparks flying from the exhaust pipe as it dragged on the asphalt.

The oncoming vehicle only now saw Pablo and pulled to its right trying to avoid him. To his fortune, Pablo's rear tire caught some dry asphalt, and the bike lurched upright, allowing Pablo to make the impossibly tight turn between the moving vehicle and the parked truck.

Pablo pulled to the side of the road to catch his breath. He knew that he had just avoided disaster and said a small prayer thanking his Divine Lord for saving his life. The mechanic ran over to him and asked if he was ok. Pablo smiled and said thank you and yes, he would be fine. The mechanic patted him on the shoulder and suggested he take extra care driving his bike in the evening light. He asked if Pablo was planning to stay in Erro for the night. Pablo said no, but that he might catch a late supper. The mechanic told Pablo of his close friend who had the best restaurant in town. He told Pablo to tell the owner that Enrique had sent him, and he was sure the restaurant would treat him well. Pablo said thank you and headed into town just as the bell tower began to ring.

Pablo enjoyed his meal at Bar Zuretzat in downtown Erro and received special treatment after letting the proprietor know of his encounter with Enrique. He smiled and waved good night as he left for his room at a nearby hostel. Before he settled into bed, he set his alarm for 3:00 a.m.

At precisely 3:00 a.m., Pablo arose from a pleasant dream about a girl he dated in school but had not been in touch with. He rolled out of bed, dragged on his clothes, and carried the nanobot duffle to a small desk. He put on his mask and carefully removed the nanobot bottles, checking their lids to be certain they were properly sealed. Then he set out the trigger mechanisms – one for each bottle. He assembled the triggers and attached one trigger to each bottle and placed them back in his satchel and headed to his scooter. A staff member at the desk told him good day and he turned and gave a friendly wave.

As the sun was just rising, he drove his bike to the six preset locations around town and deposited one bottle at each location, covering the bottles with leaves, branches and other detritus laying in the gutters. Before he left, he flicked on the trigger mechanism and checked the detonator to ensure it registered. At the final location, near the eastside entrance to the town, Pablo found the perfect hiding spot in the crevice of a wall. He removed the bottle from his satchel, gently laid it in the crevice, and flipped the switch turning on the trigger. He folded the note from Belinda and the Night Brigade and placed it in the crevice alongside the bottle. A repair truck drove up beside him.

"Pablo!" said Enrique. "It's me, Enrique from the road. Are you ok?"

Pablo turned quickly to see the mechanic he met the day before.

"Oh, uh, good morning, Enrique," he stammered.

"Are you hurt from your accident?" Enrique queried him.

Pablo turned to face Enrique, attempting to hide the bottle in the wall.

"No, no, not at all," he said, somewhat regaining his composure. "I wasn't hurt. Not at all."

"Good news!" Enrique said smiling. "Did you try the restaurant?"

"Loved it," he responded. "Absolutely loved it."

"Good. I'll let them know."

"Thanks. Have a good morning."

"Thanks. I will. What are you putting in the wall?"

Pablo turned toward the wall and, as he did, Enrique could see the bottle.

"Are you passing notes to a girlfriend? Or maybe leaving a secret message for counterintelligence?"

"Uh, well, turns out I'm not really a spy. I have a good friend. We have a secret way of staying in touch and now, thanks to you, it's not so secret."

"Ha! Ha!" Enrique laughed. "I won't touch it, my friend. Very old school, as they say."

"You caught me," Pablo joked and then, inadvertently, turned back to the wall. This time, Enrique saw a small green light and some wires. He squinted attempting to make sense of what he was seeing.

"If it's a message in a bottle, what are the wires?" Now, suspicious, Enrique turned off his truck and climbed out. "What are you doing?" he asked as he went in for a closer look.

Pablo pulled out a knife and flashed it at Enrique. "Leave!" he shouted. "Leave now or you will get hurt!"

"What in God's name! Who are you? What are you doing?"

Enrique ran back to his truck and jumped inside. He reached for his gun and began firing through the window at Pablo. Pablo dove to the side and the bullets, as they careened of the stone wall, all missed him. However, one of the bullets struck the bottle and shattered it. Enrique saw the glass shatter and jumped out of his cab and hid behind the truck anticipating an explosion. Pablo saw the bottle burst and ran to his bike. Even as he reached the bike and pulled out the mask, he felt his throat begin to swell and it became hard to breathe. He fell to his knees and taking quick breaths finally got the mask to seal. Then he passed out.

Enrique felt the same struggle for air but had no idea why he had difficulty breathing. It quickly became worse, and, in a panic, he stood up and saw a black cloud forming out of the bottle. He thought gas! and turned to run. He knew where the town doctor lived, and he only hoped he might make it before choking to death. He didn't make it.

Pablo stirred. His breathing was labored but at least he was getting oxygen. He forced himself to stand and get on the scooter. His vision was blurry, and it was hard to see the N-135 highway as it left town. He started his bike and, weaving back and forth, managed to make it a couple kilometers outside of town. He pulled to the side of the road and turned back to look at Erro. A black cloud was growing and heading south into a dense residential location. Not confident he would live if he removed it, he kept the mask on. He found the detonator. It registered the five remaining nanobot bombs. Pablo was on a mission. Nothing that had happened the day before changed that mission. He flipped the switch detonating all five triggers and waited. He could not hear the small explosions that shattered the bottles and released the deadly nanobots. One of the patrons he met at the restaurant the night before drove past him on a bicycle and smiled and waved at Pablo before riding into the town.

Five small black clouds started reaching to the sky at each of the preset locations. Pablo watched in amazement, then turned and got on his scooter bike and headed north, not looking back.

The town started to get active. More cars, bikes and pedestrians took to the roads. Some were putting out trash cans for pick-up. Many were inside starting a small breakfast of coffee and pastries. Children pulled on clothes to go to school. City laborers were hosing down sidewalks and picking up loose trash. The first sign of a problem occurred when the driver of a small car collided with a bicyclist, killing the young rider.

Shortly thereafter screams broke out across the town. Cars collided with other cars and bikes as they passed out or just attempted to evade bodies that had crumpled to the ground. Parents carrying dead children ran into the streets crying "Help me!" before they themselves succumbed to the deadly rain of bots. The five black clouds merged into a single deadly fog and, within minutes, a thousand bodies, most of the town, lay inert in the streets, in the shops and inside homes.

The town doctor felt his throat swell and recognized it immediately as a kind of anaphylaxis. He gave himself a shot of epinephrin and grabbed a full surgical mask, assuming he was reacting to something in the air. Then he heard the screams and the crashes. A few made it to his door and pounded on it, crying and calling for help. He opened the door as a half dozen people fell in, gagging and reaching for breath. He started administering multiple shots of epinephrin and handed out handfuls of Benadryl. A woman came in with her young child who was turning blue but still breathing. He gave the child a shot and without thinking, pulled off his mask and put it on the child. Within seconds, he passed out and within minutes, many of his patients were dead.

When he came to, his throat was burning but he was breathing. The child with the mask was sitting next to him, staring at him. Some instinct told her to leave the mask on. She coughed but otherwise was not in any pain. Her dead mother lay on the ground beside her. The doctor climbed to his feet. He picked up the child and placed her on a chair, but she slid off and crawled down next to her mother. The doctor understood and left her. He examined the people in his office. He opened a handful of oxygen tanks and told them to share the oxygen masks. Everyone was in shock. No one understood what just happened. The streets were covered with the fine dust of spent nanobots. No one noticed that the air was just a slight bit cleaner.

Within the hour, droves of emergency vehicles entered the town alongside a dozen police cars from Pamplona. All were wearing gas masks of some kind, expecting that the unfortunate events in this innocent town were due to the release of some noxious gas, possibly from a train or an active mine in the nearby mountains. They were devastated by what they saw. Many of the dead were children.

Still many children whose lives were miraculously spared wandered the street, looking for their parents or relatives or even friends. The police and emergency crews handed everyone who was still alive N-95 masks. The toxicity of the nanobots had almost completely dissipated as they performed their carbon-capture duties and fell mostly harmless from the sky. But it didn't matter. The nightmare was real.

Pamplona's hazmat teams tested the air for gas and found nothing. One of the young members of the hazmat team noticed the dust and pointed it out to his superiors. They grabbed plastic bags and began collecting the dust and placing it in protective containers. Police detectives searched the town for explosives and by the end of the day had collected most of the used triggers. They also found a handwritten message stuffed into the wall near the east entrance. The message read: "Freedom for all patriots who rise and take a stand against our capitalist oppressors. Long live the Basque Kingdom!!" It was signed "The Night Brigade."

Chapter 13.

Hannibal's Elephants

Dr. Brian Johannsen had started to regret his decision to run Ragnar Willowbrook. He made it clear to the Board that he was not Dr. Belinda Armendariz and that he would render decisions on underwriting various inventions based on data and not on personal favors. Belinda focused more on increasing her own wealth. Whether or not an invention was perfect mattered very little to her. She had built up the reputation of Ragnar Willowbrook in the Silicon Valley to a point where simply getting an endorsement from the Lab satisfied most of the applicants and made the Board happy as they watched revenues go through the roof. They paid Belinda handsomely for the results.

Brian cared very little for wealth. His goal was to develop projects that enhanced the world and improved the quality of life everywhere. If wealth was a by-product, so be it. Wealth was not the goal. He bore no ill will toward Providia, the value of which was skyrocketing over the development of a new superchip capable of driving artificial intelligence programs and machines to new and unimagined heights. Brian was especially happy for Bost, whom he considered his closest friend and colleague. Bost's stock value was soaring, and Christopher Deckwalder had been generous to his employees, including Bost, as the company's success became the center of attention and envy around the world. Bost tried to convince Brian to buy Providia stock. But Brian was very careful about creating the appearance of favoritism. He had his own mutual funds that invested a small amount in Providia, and his stock value benefitted from the company's success. But the impact was marginal.

The Ragnar Willowbrook Board struggled to get used to Brian's moral code. The Lab was profitable, just not as profitable as it had been under Belinda. Brian started to retreat from the Board, using Fred Schmidt as his go between. Fred's cancer was progressing, and the reality of his ultimate demise added a new introspection to Fred's own thinking. He adjusted his goals accordingly, very much in line with

Brian's goals. Fred understood and respected Brian and defended him often before angry Board members.

The phone rang. Brian saw it was Bost and answered quickly.

"What's up?"

"Deckwalder is having a fit."

"You are looking for a shoulder to cry on?"

"No. He's getting keyed up about the nanobot research. He wants to know where it's going. He thinks it is distracting me and wants goals, cost estimates and a timeline."

"He's not wrong. We solved the toxicity issue, but I don't know exactly where we go from here. AI gave a kind of life to the swarm but what are the real use cases? I want to think about it."

"Well, if we don't come up with something quickly, he is going to pull me off and we might miss a real opportunity."

"I'll think about it. I promise."

Brian hung up but he was troubled by the call. Abandoning a new promising technology just because it didn't produce immediate results was short sighted and irresponsible. He was aware also that blowing millions on a project that was going nowhere was no less myopic. He needed to focus, but nothing revelatory was coming to mind.

His phone rang again.

"Is this Dr. Brian Johannsen?"

"It is."

"Please hold."

"Dr. Johannsen?"

"Yes."

"Just a minute."

Brian almost hung up. He hated phone nonsense.

"Hello, Doctor. This is Sherman Cooke."

"I'm sorry, did you say Sherman Cooke, as in Secretary of Defense?"

"Yes, sir. Thank you for taking a minute to chat. I assume we have a minute."

"Absolutely, Mr. Secretary."

"There are new developments I can't discuss here. But I wanted to confirm. You are an expert in nanotechnology?"

"I don't think that is overstating it."

"Good. How quickly can you get on a plane to Washington, DC?"

"This is a matter of national security, I presume."

"Yes, sir, it is of the utmost importance."

"Then, I can catch a red-eye and be there in the morning."

"That sounds fine. See you tomorrow. Please hold for my assistant."

Brian paused. He'd often wondered if his work might trigger federal interest. To date, he had heard nothing substantive other than his periodic contact with Agent Sams at the FBI.

Cooke's assistant took his contact details and asked that he forward his flight plans. She reminded him that the discussions must be kept confidential. She agreed to meet Brian at Reagan International.

The phone rang again.

"Brian," said Fred Schmidt. "Did Cooke reach you?"

"I'm not supposed to say."

"Good. Meet me at Moffett Field in an hour. We are fueling up for a cross country."

"Washington, DC?"

"The same. Reagan International, right?"

"I'll be there."

The call from Fred relieved Brian. Not only did he not need to worry about booking last minute, but he also would arrive sooner and get some sleep before the morning meeting. Or at least he hoped. He called Leonard who agreed to take him home to grab his gear and then drive him to Moffett. As soon as he was on the plane, he texted Cooke's assistant and told her he would be arriving in DC around midnight and that he would need a place to stay. She agreed to book a room.

A black Lincoln Navigator arrived the next morning as Fred and Brian were finishing their breakfast. Sue Ellen Hasting, the assistant to Secretary Cooke entered the hotel and found them in the dining room.

"Dr. Johannsen?" Sue Ellen directed the question to Fred.

"That would be me," Brian responded, and Sue Ellen blushed.

"My apologies, doctor" she stammered.

"Not at all, my dear," said Fred. "I take it as a compliment. The young man you see before you is one of the sharpest minds on the planet."

Brian laughed and coffee dribbled down his chin. He quickly grabbed a napkin and wiped his face.

"Don't listen to him," he said. "Is that the car out front?" He pointed to the black SUV.

"Yes."

"Ok. Please give me a minute and I will join you."

Fred smiled at the assistant. "It's been a pleasure."

She grinned and went back to the SUV.

Fred had said very little about the reason for the visit. He knew Brian was under strict orders not to discuss the briefing. Still, just as Brian picked up his briefcase and thanked Fred for the meal, Fred found it necessary to comment.

"You will learn some disturbing things today. But it will be up to you to decide how to respond. Don't be bullied by the Pentagon. They need you. You don't necessarily need them. There are many ways to serve your country."

Brian looked at Fred puzzled. "Are you worried about this meeting?"

Fred studied Brian. "I'm not. But gird yourself," he said. "It will be difficult. Just know that I trust you completely, whatever your response." He watched as Brian climbed into the SUV and took off. Then he called a local limo driver whom he trusted and used every time he came to the Capitol. "I feel like seeing the Library of Congress. How soon can you get here?"

Brian had no idea what Fred might be concerned about. But he put it out of his mind and considered what the Pentagon might want to do with nanobots. He determined at the outset that he would not be the one to weaponize nanobots in service of some geopolitical maneuvering.

The SUV, bearing the flags of the Secretary of Defense, pulled up to a gate reserved to foreign dignitaries who were guests of the Pentagon. The guard recognized the Department of Defense insignia on the right front fender and waved them through the gate. Brian followed Sue Ellen along with the security detail that accompanied them on the ride. He submitted himself and his briefcase for a security check and then walked with the detail for what seemed like forever until they reached a special elevator that took them to a situation room underground. He saw a handful of uniformed generals and White House officials. Sue Ellen introduced him immediately to Secretary Cooke.

"Good morning, Dr. Johannsen," he said amiably. "Please have a seat and we will get started."

"It's a pleasure, sir," said Brian, but he felt slightly unnerved by the scene and Fred's words were of little comfort.

The Secretary introduced the generals and officials seated around the table but said nothing about the topics to be discussed. Instead, he pointed to a screen and told Brian, "I'm not sure how comfortable you might be with grisly war scenes, but we recently received details about a terrible event that just occurred in Northen Spain."

Brian nodded. He had seen something about a gas leak in Spain on the news, but he said nothing. The images on the screen were difficult to look at. Handheld videos showed emergency personnel in hazmat suits carrying bodies of villagers, many of whom were the size of small children, to medical vans where bagged bodies were piled like trash. Villagers standing near the vans were weeping. Many fell to their knees as the personnel carefully placed the bodies on top of each other.

The video panned other locations in the village. Several uncovered bodies remained in the streets and on the floors of shops and apartments. Brian could see tears on the faces of many of the first responders. The scene was tragic, and Brian assumed he was being shown the videos because someone had attacked the village with mustard gas or some biological weapon. He did not see any connection to nanobots but assumed he would learn quickly enough. Then he saw one of the first responders in a hazmat suit spooning what looked like dust into vials and taping the vials closed. The picture became clear to him immediately as he recalled the dust in Bainbridge after the explosion.

He looked at the Secretary and asked, "What is the dust?"

"Excellent question, Doctor." Several heads around the table nodded. "But let me put that question back to you. What do you think it may be?"

"Spent nanobots."

"What leads you to that conclusion?"

"Because I am here and you are asking me."

"What can you tell us about spent nanobots?"

"I've been working with carbon capture nanobots for two years. When we first started examining them through a scanning electron microscope, we noticed that once they reached capacity, they fell inert to the ground in the form of dust. In that form, the toxicity level remained low and not harmful to human beings. But as long as they remained potent, meaning able to function, they were highly toxic. My colleague at the Tran Lab in Bainbridge made the mistake of exposing a cartridge to the air, and she and I both almost died. Our bodies went into anaphylactic shock, and it was the quick thinking of our colleagues that saved our lives. These nanobots, meaning the nanobots that I was working with, if untreated have the capacity to kill and I believe that accidental deaths have occurred in locations where they were inadvertently released."

One of the White House staff members cut in.

"What do you mean untreated?"

"I have been working with my colleagues in California, searching for some way to eliminate the toxicity of these nanobots. We are still looking for a good use case, possibly a new form of carbon filter, but we cannot release the nanobots into any public space until we reduce the toxicity to a level that doesn't impact human life."

"Did you develop a treatment?"

"We did."

"You believe it works?"

"I know it works."

The room began buzzing with conjecture about possible military applications. Brian became uneasy.

One of the generals asked, "Is it possible to treat human beings in a way that protects them from the toxicity of these bots?"

"That is not how the treatment works," said Brian. "You treat the nanobots themselves."

He heard grumbling.

Secretary Cooke asked, "Tell us more about the treatment."

Brian responded, "I'd be happy to, but maybe you can enlighten me a bit more on why I am here and what you are looking for."

The general who had pressed Brian before leaned forward toward Brian and stared into Brian's eyes to show strength and resolve. Brian wasn't impressed. "Dr. Johannsen," he began, "what you see before you and what you apparently understand, though I have my doubts, is that we are facing a very real threat to the security of our country. The events that took place in Spain in this innocent village reveal a personality that has no concern for life, American or otherwise."

Secretary Cooke jumped in.

"Thank you, General Sheridan. I'm sure Dr. Johannsen understands the implication of weaponized nanobots in the wrong hands. That would be correct, right?"

"I understand the concern."

The General frowned. Secretary Cooke continued, "I'm sure you do. I'm also sure you understand what it means to introduce a new type of weapon that has no effective defense."

Brian paused. "Hannibal used elephants."

"Oh my god!" shouted the General. "Are we taking this guy seriously?"

"If I have it right," continued Brian, "the shock value alone helped Hannibal's army win many battles against the Romans." He heard several murmurs of assent, and heads turned in his direction that previously had been ignoring him.

"Interesting correlation," responded the Secretary. "Getting back to the present, in most cases, America leads the world in developing new military technologies.

"To your point, we control the shock. But, if these are weaponized nanobots, then we now find ourselves behind the curve, and we do not like being behind the curve. We don't know what exactly we are facing or how to contain it if it spreads."

"I'm not sure how I can help you," said Brian. "I'm not interested in building new weapons."

"You will be," said the General, "if this technology is used against your loved ones."

Brian didn't respond.

This time the Secretary leaned forward. "Do you know where your nanobots came from?"

This statement caught Brian off guard.

"Came from? I'm not sure what you mean."

"Did you invent them?"

"I didn't. I was given a petri dish of an unnamed toxic substance and only after an extensive and dangerous review was I able to determine what they were and what function they served."

"I'm sure you did good work, but it never occurred to you to ask about the source?"

"I was told it was a national security secret. I didn't press."

"Did you know General Tom Warner?"

"Not well, but he attended a demonstration at my Lab in Santa Cruz."

"So, you didn't know General Warner was working with Dr. Belinda Armendariz, your predecessor at Ragnar Willowbrook."

"I know of her, but I am not privy to any details about that relationship."

"Consider yourself under the code of silence. What I am about to disclose to you has the highest security level available and cannot be shared with anyone. To do so would be considered treason. Do you understand?"

"I do."

"Did you know General Tom Warner is missing?"

"I had heard that."

"Really. Can you share how you know?"

"Let's just say I know. He still hasn't been found?"

"No. He is still missing."

"Is that the secret?"

"No. But General Warner gave the nanobots to Dr. Armendariz to study."

This was news to Brian.

"They were stolen from Dr. Armendariz while in her possession."

"If you say so."

"And you received them from Fred Schmidt, correct?"

"You are saying Fred stole the nanobots?"

"I'm not. But rather than return them to Dr. Armendariz, he delivered them to you on Bainbridge Island."

"Are you suggesting the U.S. military destroyed the Tran Lab and killed the team there?"

"I'm not. I am saying that you were working on stolen U.S. Government property."

Secretary Cooke let that news sink in. Brian had been angry at Fred for exposing his teammates on Bainbridge Island to toxic nanobots without telling him. He was not aware that they were stolen from the U.S. Government. He thought about Fred's warning at breakfast. Then he recalled General Warner's attendance at the demonstration at Ragnar Willowbrook.

"Let's say that is the case," Brian responded. "My work on the nanobots at Ragnar Willowbrook had General Warner's blessing. He did not assert a right to my work product and intellectual property. If anything, he wanted me to continue the work."

Secretary Cooke was reflective. "Ok," he said. "Let's agree the situation is complicated and that is especially so given that the General is still missing." He paused for effect and then lowered the temperature. "But I won't force you to produce something you don't want to produce."

The generals coughed and shifted in their chairs, obviously unsettled.

"So, we are done here?" said Brian.

"No," said the Secretary. "Generals, he added. "I think we are done here. Please excuse yourselves so I can talk with Dr. Johannsen."

After the room cleared, Secretary Cooke said to Brian, "Let's talk more about your treatment."

Brian returned to the hotel a few hours later. Fred studied his expressions and didn't press him with questions. Brian was past his early feelings about Fred. If anything, Fred was a means to an end and happened to be the chair of the Ragnar Willowbrook Board and, in that position, was still helpful to Brian. But Brian kept the Pentagon discussions to himself. What the Secretary had requested of Brian and select members of his team at Ragnar Willowbrook, was not unreasonable and, more to the point, inspired Brian to focus on solutions to the problem of weaponized nanobots.

Chapter 14.

Occam's Razor (Part 1)

The principle known as Occam's Razor stands for the proposition that, all else being equal, the simplest answer is usually the correct answer. In the 13th century, when William of Occam developed his thesis, magic and alchemy were both viewed as credible "scientific" explanations of natural events like tides and solar eclipses. William used the idea of a razor to strip the complexities of magic and alchemy down to the simple elegance of a divine creator. Thus, he claimed that God explained heavenly events or the existence of valuable elements like gold better than complex magical incantations or elemental combinations like mice and straw. But it is just as much a mistake to treat Occam's Razor as an absolute as it is to prefer complexity over simplicity just because it is complex. For example, evolution is a complex process that is only detectable following extended periods of time. The fact of its complexity does not render the theory inelegant and the simplicity of the notion of a divine creator does not always render it meaningful.

Most murders are simple. Jealousy, envy, rage and greed can lead one human to devalue the life of another to the point where the elimination of that life appears rational. Detective work and forensics might seem complicated, but in most cases, it is enough to identify the one person who has the motive to kill. Scott Geiringer's murder at the Bureau was not simple. No one knew him. It is possible jealousy played a role. Detective Paul Young had hyped the rookie detective's abilities fresh out of the Academy, but those abilities had not been tested.

It made no sense to kill Scott before he had the chance to fail or, alternatively, to enlist Scott to support the jealous detective's own ambitions. Of the two murders, Charlie's murder at least made sense. Charlie got too close to someone and became a real threat. The question that bothered Van the most was who was that?

Van had worked with Charlie long enough to know that he kept his notes locked in his desk. Luckily, Charlie trusted Van and made a copy of the key to the desk just for her. He insisted that she keep it a secret and no one who pressed her on the investigation seemed to know that she had the key. After Charlie's death, Van told the Chief about the key and asked that she be allowed to search his desk and his office for materials that might be pertinent to the investigation. The Chief agreed. Van opened the locked desk drawer and grabbed a stack of spiral notebooks. As she was stuffing them into a backpack, she heard a knock.

"Need any help?"

She looked up and smiled as she saw Detective Alvin Broad's quirky head peering into the office.

"Please, come on in Alvin."

Alvin pushed the door and walked in slowly, in part due to a bad hip that had gotten worse recently, and out of his natural caution not to disturb possible evidence. Charlie's office had effectively become a crime scene.

"I'm sorry I haven't reached out," Alvin said to Van.

"It's ok," she said. "I know you feel the loss at least as much as I do. You two were close."

Alvin stared at Charlie's desk in silence.

Van respected the silence as they both processed the loss. She was the first to speak.

"Did he share anything with you?"

"About the kid?"

"Yes. About Scott. Did he share any insight or clue with you?"

"No. I think Charlie began to sense that this was bigger than he originally thought. Being bigger, his instinct was to keep whatever he might have known to himself."

"That makes sense. Did he spend any time with you in the file room?"

"No more than usual. He came by to check on me and say hi. We spent more time talking about you and your extra-curriculars than anything. Is anything happening there?"

"I thought I could do it all. It was my mistake to leave Charlie on his own so I could go feel important. I'll never forgive myself."

"Stop that, Van. Charlie was his own man, and Charlie was going to chase whatever clue he had, whether you thought it was a good idea or not."

"I'm sorry," Van replied. "You're right. It's silly. It's a tough loss."

"Do you remember the bullet on your desk? Shortly after you made detective, someone threatened you."

"Of course, I remember. Robert Johnson admitted to doing it. He was jealous and was being stupid and he was reprimanded."

"It was a strange act, right? I've never heard of anything like that happening here in the Bureau or anywhere else in the Department. I think about it sometimes. Who would do that?"

"You think Johnson didn't come up with the idea?"

"Who knows? He took the fall for it. Might be worth digging into. Is there any chance someone did that to Scott or to Charlie?"

"You're a genius, Alvin. Who knows exactly? Maybe it wasn't a bullet. Maybe it was more subtle than that. Or not."

Van and Alvin scanned Charlie's office. Van opened all the drawers of his desk while Alvin scoured the shelves and cabinet tops. She thought there would be a bullet but maybe something that felt like a threat. They didn't see anything in those several minutes that fit the bill, but it was an angle Van wanted to pursue for both Charlie and Scott. She thought maybe it wouldn't be a threat. Maybe it would be a warning.

She said good night to Alvin and took the backpack with her. She wondered if the same might happen to her and as she walked to her car, she was keenly aware of any activity around her. She threw the backpack onto the passenger seat and, as she was starting the car, she saw something in her rear-view mirror that made her freeze. Somebody had written a word in the dust on her back window. It was hardly visible and if Alvin had not suggested something like it, she might have missed it. The word was reversed so she could read it in the mirror. The word was "STOP." She grabbed her phone and popped on the camera and took a picture of the word in her rear-view mirror. She then jumped out of the car and ran to the back and took another picture of the word showing as "POTS" with the letters each reversed. She jumped back in the car and sat for a quick minute before shifting into reverse and squealing out of the police garage. She studied the rear-view mirror to see if anyone was following her. It was hard not to look at the word as various headlights flashed over it. There was nothing she could identify.

When she arrived at home, she parked the car in her parents' garage, grabbed masking tape and Saran wrap and covered the word to prevent any smudging or wiping. In the morning, she would call Forensics. She enjoyed a dinner of leftovers with her parents and went into her room with the backpack. She flipped quickly through the notebooks. Each of them was dated.

She searched until she found the last notebook. It was full. She looked through the notes all of which were dated weeks before his death. Nothing suggested that anyone threatened him or warned him. Then it occurred to her that the last notebook might be in his car or on his body when he died. She stuffed the notebooks back in her backpack and prepared for bed.

Van called Alvin in the morning and together they met Forensics in the parking structure. Van was surprised to see Brad Jones, a forensics specialist she had worked with when she started at LAPD. Brad had changed. He was just as charismatic as he was when they worked together and Van could tell he still had some interest in her, but it was muted.

"Detective!" Brad smiled and reached out to shake Van's hand.

"Good morning," Van responded as professionally as she could muster. "Specialist Jones, let me introduce you to Detective Alvin Broad."

Brad didn't conceal his disappointment at the less than warm welcome. Alvin picked up on the tension and responded warmly to Brad.

"Very nice to meet you. I have heard great things about your department, and I understand you play a major role in that."

Brad smiled again and relaxed, the charm offensive returning.

"That's very nice of you to say. Detective Eng and I go back a bit."

"I'm aware of her forensics background. You probably know what an incredible job she is doing for us."

"I hear rumors," Brad said. "What do we have here?"

The banter helped Van soften. She reached out and removed the tape and Saran wrap from her rear window. The word "POTS" was still visible.

Brad looked at it and then at Van. "POTS?" he said. "Odd."

Van grimaced. "You have to see it from the rear-view mirror."

"Oh, I see. 'STOP'. You think it's a message directed at you."

"Hard to think otherwise. I need you to do your thing. Dust and maybe analyze the handwriting."

Brad took over. "On it," he said. "Can I have your keys?"

Van handed him her keys.

"I'll be in touch when we have something."

Alvin and Van walked over to the Bureau. They stopped by her desk, and she didn't touch anything. Then they went to Alvin's office in CHESS. Alvin's office abutted a large file room and unlike the mess that Van found when she first started working with Alvin, the room was as clean and organized as when she left it to begin her first investigations as an LAPD detective. The process that Van developed of digitizing the files and building the Chess database had worked well and the Bureau had given Alvin the administrative support he needed to keep it going.

Van sat down and Alvin turned on his new laptop and logged in. His assistant configured his system with a docking station and mounted a large monitor on the wall. He pulled up the database capable of collating information from all the files that had moved over to CHESS from individual active investigations that had gone cold.

"What do you suggest?" Alvin asked Van. "Where do we start?"

"Simple is probably a good start," she said. "Look up the word 'Stop.'" She thought for a moment. "That's probably too broad. Let's go with 'Stop < 10 threat.'"

Alvin typed in the query. The computer printed out hundreds of documents, most of which had some form of a victim saying, "Stop threatening me."

"Let's go with something a little different," she said. "Isolate instances where the accused is an LAPD officer."

This time the results were narrower but still voluminous. As they perused the files, the accused officers had tampered with evidence or gone to work under the influence of some substance and been caught. In a few instances, the question was unlawful use of force, but, as Van and Alvin both knew, these crimes were usually addressed by Internal Affairs and, in almost all cases, the officers were excused and place on a short leave. A handful of files mentioned the Rampart Division and the public investigation of abuses out of that Division.

"Ok," said Van, not feeling like the effort had been worth it. "If you have time, can you keep looking and let me know if anything jumps out?"

"Of course," said Alvin. "By the way, I hear we are looking into artificial intelligence. I wonder if that will help."

"AI is interesting," said Van. "I am grateful for you, Detective."

"My honor," said Alvin. "Whatever you need."

When Van returned to her desk, Brad was standing nearby talking to other detectives.

Van saw him and approached.

"Sorry to interrupt, guys. I need this one," she said grabbing Brad by the arm. Brad chuckled and started to say something, but Van hushed him with a wave of her hand. They walked over to Brad's office in the criminal forensics lab.

When they sat down, Van said to Brad, "Frank is gone. Are you running the place yet?"

"Me? No. They brought in a whippersnapper from Chicago to replace him. Maybe someday."

"It'll be you," Van said. "Unless you get a better offer."

Brad chuckled self-consciously.

Van asked, "What do we have?"

"Whoever scrawled stop in your rear window was cautious. There are no fingerprints only a slight bit of talcum residue, probably from rubber gloves."

"That's disappointing."

"We were thorough. Nothing on the inside or in the trunk either. But, Van, be careful. You might want to decide not to drive this car for a while. Maybe Uber or grab an unused squad car for a while. Who knows what these guys might do."

"I appreciate that. Good thought. Any reason you think there are multiple people involved? You said, 'these guys.'"

"Just a hunch, I suppose."

"Ok. If it becomes more than a hunch, let me know. How's life?"

"I'm happy and doing well. I love this lab and the people. Even Chicago is not so bad when you get to know her."

"Her?"

"Yeah. She's good. Kinda reminds me of you."

"Aww."

Van returned to her desk. She studied it looking for further signs of aggression but saw nothing. She called fleet management and asked for an unmarked car. Not a problem. They gave her an unmarked black Ford Interceptor SUV. She told them her personal car had become evidence in the homicide investigation, and she needed it towed and held at the Evidence Vehicle Garage.

Access to the car would be limited to the forensics team. She headed to the morgue to see if they set aside any items that came from Charlie's body. Dr. Gilford Von de Grassy, a former tattoo model turned coroner, met her at the door to the morgue.

"I'm so sorry," he said. "I can't believe this. Charlie was one of the best."

"Thanks, Gil," said Van. "I'm here with a couple questions."

"Please, come on in."

Van wrinkled her nose that strong smell of formaldehyde but otherwise did not react.

"Did Charlie's body have anything on it?"

"Yes, it did."

"Do you recall anything?"

"Sure. Wallet, keys, glasses, handkerchief, and a notebook."

"Did you keep them here?"

"Actually no. Forensics came and bagged them and took them."

"Do you know if they were entered into evidence?"

"I don't know that. I signed the chain of custody form when I turned them over."

"Who from Forensics handled them?"

"You know Brad Jones?"

"Yes, I do. Thanks. Is there anything you can tell me about Charlie's body? Anything unusual?"

"There was a lot of trauma related to the fall from the cliff. But Charlie was

shot in the chest prior to the fall. I believe the shot killed him before he hit the ground."

"Did you pull the bullet fragment?"

"The bullet exploded on impact. There wasn't much left."

"What about the shell casing?"

"You'll have to ask Forensics."

"Thanks, Gil."

"Like I said, Detective."

"By the way, has anyone ever tried to improve the smell of formaldehyde? Seriously." Van made a face.

"What smell?" Gil said and laughed.

Van called Alvin from the car.

"Any luck on your end?"

"Maybe. Nothing at LAPD. I started to explore threats at other PDs. I found internal disputes that escalated to violence. But most of those were efforts to thwart IA investigations. Still looking."

"Ok. Heading back to Forensics. There is more to discuss there."

Van decided not to call Brad. Rather, she headed directly to Evidence Control on Ramirez Street. She showed her badge and informed the attending officer that she led the investigation and needed access to the evidence in the Scott Geiringer and Charles Darling murder cases.

The officer in attendance brought her one box. Inside the box were two plastic bags. One contained items from Scott's desk and items on his body when it was discovered. The second contained the items that Gil had identified that were on Charlie's body.

"Is there a reason the evidence from these two murders is being combined?" she asked the officer.

"Well, as I understand it, they are connected. Wasn't Detective Darling investigating Detective Geiringer's death when he was murdered?"

"True. But they are two separate murders, and it has not been established that they are connected." The attending officer frowned to cover his embarrassment.

"Don't worry about it. It's not an unreasonable assumption. I will keep everything together. If there is a reason to separate these two cases, I will let you know."

The officer handed her the chain of custody form and said, "Please sign this." Van started to sign and looked down at the list. She saw Detective Paul Young's name on it. She took the box to a secure room and reviewed the items. She took care to keep the items separated. In addition to wallets and keys, both bags contained a belt, glasses, a gun and bullets, and a badge. Van studied the pistols. Charlie's gun was more worn than Scott's gun but neither looked to have been fired recently. Unlike Scott's bag, Charlie's bag had a small notebook that had notes on half of the pages. She flipped through the notebook and wrote down names. It was interesting to her that Charlie had contacted the Police Academy where Scott excelled. She took note of the name Sergeant Marisa Coldridge. Toward the end of the written pages, Charlie had written the name Ben but nothing else. Van looked more closely at the notebook. The binder coil was slightly bent, and a small piece of paper was lodged in the coil. It looked like someone had removed a page.

Chapter 15.

The Plan

Pablo arrived at Muro de Roda before sunrise. He had traveled all night replaying in his head the image of Belinda's joy at his success in Erro. But, after he arrived, the guards did not direct him to Belinda's office. Rather, they escorted him to his closet-sized bedroom at the bottom level of the compound and locked the door. He remained in the room for two days without any communication from the team. At first, he thought they might be preparing a parade and honor ceremony for him. But as time passed, he grew concerned. He revisited his actions in Erro with growing concern that he had made a serious mistake, and Belinda was preparing punishment for him. The guards brought him food and didn't say a word.

At the end of the two days, he was escorted to Belinda's office. She was talking to Assad Jazairi when they brought him in. Pablo was shaking. She turned and studied him.

"How are you, Pablo?" she started.

"I'm fine, sir, uh ma'am," he stammered.

"My apologies for the delay," she said. "We needed to be certain no one followed you here."

"I did my best to be careful."

"That was smart. What do you think about the results in Erro?"

"I didn't wait for results. I left as soon as I triggered the canisters."

"That's not entirely true, is it?" asked Assad.

"What do you mean?" said Pablo, growing concerned.

Assad held up Pablo's mask from his scooter.

"You used this?"

"I did. I... someone at the last drop point saw me and started shooting. He hit the canister and released the poison inside. I got to my mask and put it on. It saved me. It didn't save him. As soon as I got it on, I started the scooter and left town, just far enough away to trigger the canisters."

"I see," said Belinda. "You almost got caught but you found a way to complete your mission."

"Yes," said Pablo not sure how to read the moment.

"You did well, Pablo. Go get some food and join us in the conference room."

After Pablo left, Assad looked at Belinda. "He allowed himself to be identified. That could be a problem."

"He'll need to lie low for a while. We don't know if anyone survived who might identify him, but you are right it is possible. It was not an easy mission, and he completed it and made it back here alive. That is a talent I would not quickly dismiss."

The team assembled in the conference room. As Pablo entered, everyone rose and clapped. Pablo had tears in his eyes. Belinda immediately promoted him to lieutenant, which didn't mean much other than as a symbolic reward to Pablo for his accomplishment. But to Pablo the promotion meant he was moving up the chain of command just as he dreamed.

Belinda stood over the conference table. A large map of the Basque Country had been laid out on the table and an X placed over the town of Erro. As she figured, the Spanish government would begin sending troops to Navarre and the other Basque provinces. As those troops settled in, their locations would be identified on the map. The focus of the next attacks would be those troops, but the attacks would be complicated because the troops may be able to protect themselves with gas masks, as they would assume the future attacks must involve the same "gas" that was used in Erro. She expected that and already had a plan. In the meantime, the Minister de Bleu would pressure Hadj to release information on the Erro attack. There would be a grassroots uprising likely coordinated by new splinter groups of the ETA who would build an anti-Spanish insurgency, challenging the military occupation of the Basque Country. But none of this would happen immediately. Belinda needed time to allow the military occupation to take hold. If the Spanish military did not respond, she would detonate more canisters in other locations until they did respond. After the occupation was established, the grassroots campaign would mobilize and then, as attacks on the military mounted, Belinda would capitalize on the confusion created by multiple opponents of the Spanish Government. Only then would Belinda begin her attacks, under the veil of a new Basque insurgency. Meanwhile, she would grow her stockpile.

Belinda returned to her office. Notwithstanding Pablo's minor missteps, the event turned out exactly as planned. She opened the door to a small open porch she had designed adjacent to her underground office. From the porch, she could see the reservoir below and the mountains and meadows sprawled out along the horizon. Her staff knew to leave her alone after conference room meetings. They approached her office only if she called them. This time, she preferred to be alone.

She grabbed a bottle of cognac and a small cigar and enjoyed the evening views as she puffed away on her cigar. As she relaxed, she began to fantasize about the boys in Pamplona risking death in their race with the bulls.

The thoughts made her yearn for her little suite adjacent to the course and the little dalliances she had enjoyed there. She knew it was risky to appear in public. But part of her didn't care about the risk. If nothing else, it had been risk that made the lonely life of an immigrant orphaned girl worth living. Of course, risk and stupidity can be closely aligned, and she was aware that she might make the one dumb mistake that thwarted her bold empire-building plans. It took no time for her to put that out of her mind and she began packing.

* * *

Brian sat at a small table in front of coffee shop on K Street. He sipped his third espresso and enjoyed the morning's *Washington Post* waiting for Fred to call and tell him when the car would arrive. He had forgotten what it was like to read a newspaper and handle the large unmanageable pages as his sipped his coffee and enjoyed his blueberry scone. At one point he bumped his cup, and a little bit of coffee splashed on the paper. He pretended not to care. He noticed an attractive blond woman sitting a few tables down the sidewalk. She was pretending to ignore him but kept peeking in his direction. He laughed and leaned forward.

"Would you like part of the paper?" he said. "It's too large for me to manage."

She smiled. "It's easier if you use your phone."

"I think it's fun to figure out how best to fold it so you can drink your coffee and read at the same time."

"I think it's more fun enjoying my coffee without spilling it."

"Touché," Brian responded.

The woman grabbed her cup and walked over to sit with Brian.

"Do you mind?"

"Not at all, although I am waiting for a car to pick me up and take me to the airport."

"I have a car. I could give you a ride."

"It's a private plane. I have a driver."

"Oh, look at you!" She batted her eyes in a way that looked a bit more sarcastic than flirty.

"Not my plane."

"Not my car," she said as a black SUV screeched up to the curb to pick her up.

"Here's my card," she said. "I know how to reach you, Dr. Johannsen. We have more in common than you might think."

She stood and quickly disappeared into the SUV, which drove off as fast as it had arrived. Brian looked at the card. The card read: Vanessa Christian, Special Advisor, Central Intelligence Agency. Brian felt his phone buzz.

"Fred."

"Car will meet you at the hotel in 15. Plane is fueling now. We leave in 90 minutes. There is much to discuss."

Brian set the paper down and finished his coffee. He noticed an article in the front page section that he missed the first time. The lead was "Tragedy in Pamplona" with the subhead: "Is Basque Nationalism on the Rise?" He folded the paper and left the remainder of the paper behind. As he was walking with the paper tucked under his arm, he pulled his phone out of his pocket, stopped in the middle of the sidewalk, and in the search bar typed "Basque nationalism news." The first entry that popped up was the same *Washington Post* article. He dropped the paper in the next trash bin and took off to the hotel.

As Brian climbed the loading stairs, Fred stepped to the entry door and smiled. When Brian reached the door, Fred extended his hand. Brian grabbed it, and Fred said, "I think that went well."

Brian figured Fred would probably know about the meeting discussion despite the security protocols. Still, he was under strict orders not to discuss the meeting and didn't entertain Fred's unspoken offer to respond. He simply said, "Thanks, Fred."

The flight attendant standing behind Fred motioned him to a seat. "Please fasten your seatbelt. We will be departing shortly." As he stowed his briefcase and fastened his belt, she handed him and Fred a mimosa and then settled into her jump seat. They all sat quietly as the plane taxied and took off. As soon as the plane levelled off, Fred opened his belt and leaned toward Brian.

"You don't need to tell me what you heard, just listen to me," Fred said as Brian waved off a second mimosa. "Belinda is activating some plan of hers and she has taken the first step in a poor unsuspecting Spanish village called Erro."

"You say that with some certainty. How do you know?"

"Christopher Deckwalder went to Spain to find General Warner. No one at the Pentagon and no one in the Spanish military knows where Tom ended up."

"Do you think he is part of Belinda's plan, assuming…?"

"No. I think Belinda used Tom and the Pentagon for her own ends. I think Tom is dead."

"Holy shit."

"You and I know the effect of those nanobots even without being weaponized. If

Belinda has found a way to weaponize them, the world is about to face some serious issues, and it is on us to come up with a response."

"Sound like we need a stronger antidote."

"True. Or a countermeasure or a deterrent. Maybe all three."

"I am not building a nanobot weapon. I can't in good conscience do that, even if we think it might function as a deterrent."

"I understand, Brian. The question you need to ask yourself is would you rather have someone else build those weapons, because I can assure you, someone is going to do it."

"There's got to be another way. You are talking about a new arms race. Based on the way our leaders are talking, people have already forgotten how it felt to destroy entire towns with the flick of switch. Are you kidding me? Mutually assured destruction was a theory, and it turns out it was a 50-year theory. There are real threats being made about the use of nuclear weapons and it is not a crazy Russian dictator who is the only one making the threats. You want me to trigger a new arms race with a weapon that could destroy the world as we know it? I can't do that."

Fred could see Brian was getting agitated.

"I understand. It's ok. What we need, then, is an effective countermeasure, an anti-ballistic weapon."

"Not to say the obvious, but even antiballistics were viewed in the 1970s as another means to escalate the nuclear arms race. But I get it. If Belinda is delivering weaponized nanobots through missiles or other projectiles, then we have an existential problem."

"What is that?"

"You can't destroy weaponized nanobots by blowing up the casing because all you do is release them into the air to self-replicate and rain down death on human populations. Nuclear weapons have a trigger mechanism that is necessary to set off an explosion. You can destroy the trigger mechanism and at least limit the scope of fallout. With weaponized nanobots, blowing up the delivery vehicle has the same effect as if the bombs exploded on impact."

"So, we have a problem we need to solve. You are the right person to lead us in that effort."

"Not sure if I should thank you for that."

"You will." Fred felt tired. He pressed a button, and a nurse approached with an IV bag. Fred reclined his chair and, as she attached the IV, he winced and then smiled at Brian. "I need a nap. You should take time to relax yourself. Take a breath and a moment to get out of your head. It'll do you good." Shortly thereafter, Fred was asleep.

Brian pondered the conversation. He recalled General Sheridan's comments about his loved ones. If he knew someone who hurt a family member, would he stand by his convictions or find some way to rip out their throat? The answer was as obvious as it was painful. The problem was also all too clear: who builds a weapon only to use it in defense?

Chapter 16.

Occam's Razor (Part 2)

Van took the notebook over to Forensics. Brad was in the lab looking through a microscope at some bullet fragments. He looked up and smiled, as he did every time he saw Van. It was nice and this time she appreciated the warm welcome.

"Can you get someone to dust this for prints?" she asked as she handed him the notebook.

"Of course, what is it?"

"Do you recognize it?"

"Now that you say that, was this Charlie's?"

"Yeah, it was. Check the cover and the pages inside."

"All of them?"

"I don't think so. Focus pages near the end of the notes and the first few blanks. How quickly can you get this done?"

"The new system is fast. We are using AI now to help. It's not perfect but it's quick. It basically spits out a list of names and identifies the probability of a match. Occasionally we get 100% but anything in the mid to high nineties warrants further investigation."

"Today?"

"I'll try."

"Thanks, Brad. I'm grateful."

Van went back to her desk, again checking for signs of any messages. She searched Ben and Benjamin in the staff directory and about 30 names popped up. She chuckled as she wondered if Bens happened to like police work, but that said it was a popular name. She searched through the list of Bens, and nothing struck her as unusual. Age wasn't an issue. The Ben who connected with Charlie could have been young or old. He could have been working in downtown LA or at some satellite precinct. Van saved the list for future reference. She noticed in the notebook that Charlie had gone over to the Police Academy in Elysian Park just northwest of downtown Los Angeles and adjacent to Dodger Stadium. She jumped in the Interceptor and took off. She checked to see if anyone from the Department might be following her. At first, she saw nothing. Another black Interceptor appeared behind her and seemed to be following her onto the 110 Freeway. But it quickly moved over and passed her without acknowledgment. She exited off Stadium Way and made her way around the south side of Dodger Stadium before turning onto Academy Road and entering the Academy. She asked for the Commanding Officer and was met with a friendly face.

"You are inquiring about Scott Geiringer?"

"I am, sir."

"Your partner, Darling, was here about the same case. I am terribly sorry about what happened."

"Thank you. I was on another assignment when Charlie came by, and I don't have much detail. Do you recall who spoke with him?"

"I do, but I don't think he got much useful information. Her name is Sergeant Marisa Coldridge, and she teaches police strategy. Scott was one of her top students."

"Thank you."

Van made her way to Sergeant Coldridge's office and knocked. She heard her say, "Enter!" She opened the door and saw numerous awards and shelves stacked with books. The room smelled of air freshener and dust.

"How can I help you?"

"Good afternoon," Van replied. "I am Detective Van Eng. I believe you spoke with my former partner, Detective Darling."

"About Scott Geiringer."

"Yes."

"Seems like that was a dangerous conversation."

"Why do you say that?"

"I understand he was the target of a hit."

"Why do you think it was connected?"

"Everything is connected, my dear," Sergeant Coldridge said, somewhat condescendingly.

"Perhaps in a spiritual sense," Van replied tartly, "but I don't agree forensically."

"That's right," said the Sergeant. "You came in through Forensics. I guess then you would know."

"You know about my past?"

"Let's just say you've made an impression."

"Right. Not everyone was happy about it. Charlie was my advocate."

"Well, you seem to be proving yourself quite well. The Chief put you in charge of this investigation."

"He did, and I need you to tell me what you know about Scott and Charlie's deaths."

"Don't let me mislead you, sweetheart. I don't know anything about either incident."

Van had seen brazen attitudes before in the Department. Something about overseeing jarheads with guns made you hard-nosed, even if all you did was teach. Van wasn't buying it.

"Yet you called it a hit."

"What would you call it? He followed a lead to Coldwater Canyon and ended up face down in a reservoir bed with a bullet in his chest."

"Let me ask you this. Do you think Charlie's murder was an inside job?

"Hard to think otherwise. He was killed investigating another detective's murder."

"Do you think Scott's murder was an inside job?"

"That's a tough call. The best I got there is that Scott's murder took place inside the Department. Unless an outsider was able to sneak into the back office and wait near the elevator, which is possible but seems like a stretch, I would focus my attention internally and not elsewhere."

"Ok, so where would you look if you were investigating these murders?"

"That's your job, isn't it?"

"Entertain me," said Van.

"Now you got my attention," responded the Sergeant. "If I were researching Scott's murder, as your partner was, I would be looking for someone with a grudge, which is exactly what your partner was doing. He asked me if Scott had made any enemies here at school and I said he could have. Scott stood up for other students and faced down some of the recruits who were inclined to be bullies."

"Do you have names?"

"I do, but I think you would be taking a wrong turn if that is the lead you are chasing."

"Why is that?"

"Because your partner's death changes the equation."

"I'll bite."

"Detective Darling's death must have been coordinated. Someone with a grudge is going to take out his or her enemy and then run and hide. They are not going to commit multiple murders simply to thwart an investigation."

"You don't buy that this is evidence of a serial killer."

"Do you?"

"I don't."

"Here is my last thought on it: Detective Darling was led to Coldwater Canyon by someone who planted a clue. He probably met with more than one person even though it was only one person who fired the gun. It is possible that the group intended to threaten him and get him to back down. It is possible that the murder was a reaction to the circumstances and not planned. It is just as possible that it was a hit and very likely that the hit was intended to discourage you from continuing the investigation or at least appearing to be investigating and then allowing the case to go cold."

"That's pretty specific."

"This is what I teach, Detective. I am sorry about your partner."

Van did not drive back to the office. Rather she took a circuitous route home, stopping for dinner and eventually making it home. All the while she replayed the conversation with Sergeant Coldridge over and over in her mind. It gave her chills. It was a remarkable performance if Sergeant Coldridge was involved and used the conversation to ward Van off the case. That did not seem likely. It was possible that the Sergeant was protecting someone. She seemed to be very familiar with the details. But if she were using it as a teaching tool for her students, that would explain it also. Van's gut was telling her to listen to the Sergeant and, as she did, this case took on a completely different hue. But where to go from here?

The next morning Van bypassed her desk and went directly to CHESS to find Alvin. He was at his desk reading the novel, *LA Confidential*.

"Good book?"

"Hell, yeah," said Alvin. "I've read it like five times."

"I saw the movie," said Van. She smiled mischievously. "Young Russell Crowe."

"I'm more of a Guy Pearce fan."

"Oooh," cooed Van. "Nothing like Australian men."

"Isn't Russell a Kiwi?"

"Same thing," said Van. "Yummy."

They laughed. Then Alvin took a breath. "I think we are looking at something sinister."

"Like a plot?"

"Maybe."

"That's the same direction I am going. Sergeant Coldridge at the Academy suggested Charlie's murder was organized."

"What do you know about Rampart?"

"Rampart? I know there was a group of corrupt cops that got nailed."

"It started as part of an anti-gang program called CRASH, Community Resources Against Street Hoodlums. The Rampart unit allegedly took it a step further, planting evidence, framing suspects, even giving perjured testimony. The Department of Justice got involved and reforms were instituted that were supposed to root out corrupt officers before they caused community damage."

"How did that go?"

"Perez and Durden got five years. Scared a lot of officers. I think it went well for a while. But it's been over two decades."

"Do you think the Chief suspects anything? Is that why he chose me to lead the investigation?"

"You should ask him."

"If this is internal, doesn't it strike you as stupid that they would murder somebody inside the Department, I mean, in this building?"

"There are some smart people here. Charlie was one of them. But not all the tools in this shed are as sharp as Charlie."

"That's a concern."

"Be careful, Van."

At the outset, the Chief told Van she did not need to make regular reports on the investigation, only that, as she made progress, he wanted to be kept updated. She notified him that she was ready for a meeting. He asked if she wanted Internal Affairs at the meeting and she replied not yet. They scheduled the meeting for the end of the day. As she made her way to his office, she noticed a variety of reactions from Department officers. People she didn't know smiled and said "Hi, Detective" and "Go get 'em." A few just stared and some turned away as if in disgust. She waited outside the Chief's office until he called her in. The door opened and a group of high-level Assistant Chiefs and Deputy Chiefs emerged, including Van's boss, Detective Paul Young. The others nodded in her direction as they left. Detective Young walked up to her directly.

"Make sure you use your resources," he said. "Whatever you need from the Bureau is yours."

"Thank you," she replied, sincerely, and, when she heard the Chief say, "Come on in, Van," she nodded to Detective Young and made her way into the office.

"Please have a seat," said the Chief.

"I understand you are facing some threats from within."

"Thanks. It would seem to be the case, but it's not confirmed," she replied. "Somebody wrote STOP on my rear window and I had the car impounded as evidence. I'm driving a company car for now."

"Whatever you need," he said. "You have the full resources of the Department."

"For that I am grateful," she replied.

"So where are we at? You called this meeting."

"Still gathering evidence. The Academy will be an important source for us. But I am not inclined to believe that Detective Geiringer's death was a grudge killing."

"You think it was an accident that someone is covering up?"

"No. I don't. Let me ask you something and I need to keep this between us."

"Agreed."

"You are familiar with the phrase 'blue wall of silence.'"

"I am but our anti-gang policies and procedures are supposed to catch that before it starts."

"You have no reason to think it is re-emerging?"

"We got a huge black eye for that activity in the 90s. Hell, Hollywood made a movie about us. It was a very hard time for the Department and not coincidentally, crime rose in the city. But the City government has its own oversight group that works closely with IA and scrutinizes any suggestion of wrongful acts by officers. Finally, our community engagement activities are at an all-time high, something I happen to be very proud of. So, yes, I know the blue wall of silence, but I would be very surprised if it started to reappear."

"But we have two murders in the Department. Not just one. The second officer murdered was investigating the first. You seem more comfortable with the idea that they are two rogue killings."

"I don't have any ideas. I'm counting on you to root this out. Look, I am not prejudging anything. Whether the problem is large or small, we'll deal with it, and you have anything you need to assist you in this effort. But let me be clear about that – you'll have no excuses for failure. Do you understand?"

"I do, sir."

"Good. I am here for you at any time. We are going to need to show progress. The press is impatient."

"Yes, sir."

"Stay in touch then. Here is my personal cell number. Now, I have a stupid dinner to go to with the Mayor. We need to play nice." He rolled his eyes and smiled at Van. "You're dismissed."

Van left the meeting torn. The facts were piling up that these acts involved multiple officers but whether they were a coordinated group or not remained to be seen. She called fleet management and asked for a new car and headed home.

Chapter 17.

Pamplona Redux

Defense Minister Gaston de Bleu was beside himself. He had not taken Hadj's threats seriously and he now knew he should have. At the same time, the "Night Brigade" or whatever they called themselves now were idiots to think that the Basque Autonomous Region needed to separate from Spain. The entire European continent had migrated in exactly the opposite direction, toward unity and away from diversity. They had a European currency, a European court system, and a European government – sort of. The unity preserved the diversity of Europe while it gave Europe a presence on the global stage. The idea that Europe should dissolve itself into a bunch of feudal estates and return to the Middle Ages would do nothing more than weaken Europe and risk subjecting the future of the continent to the aggressions of some superpower.

That said, there was a glimmer of truth to Hadj's accusations. De Bleu did not have access to weapons. He did not have a standing army. He was no more than a conduit to the Spanish government, a beacon in the night that served no greater purpose than sounding an alarm that would bring the Spanish military running into his territory.

His phone rang.

"Hold for the Prime Minister, please."

De Bleu took a breath.

"Minister."

"Yes, sir."

"First, let me tell you how sorry we are that this terrible tragedy has occurred."

"Thank you. It is awful."

"Yes, it is awful, and we need to catch the perpetrators quickly."

"Yes, sir."

"I understand we had some direct interaction with them."

"I believe I did, sir. A representative of the group approached me a few weeks ago and questioned our lack of a Basque military and Basque arsenal. He proposed to deliver weapons to me. He is still in custody"

"Have you questioned him about the terror attack?"

"We have. All we know is that he is from Algeria. He is refusing to disclose anything."

"We will make him talk, Minister."

"Yes."

"Do we think there is an Algerian connection?"

"The Basque people have no affiliation with Algeria, no common heritage or culture."

"I see," responded the Prime Minister, dubious. He turned his head from the phone. "Get me the Algerian ambassador, immediately."

"I have notified CNI. They will be in touch shortly."

"Yes, sir." They hung up.

CNI, the National Intelligence Center, was Spain's equivalent of the CIA. Gordon had mixed feeling about Spanish intelligence. CNI had played a brutal role in the suppression of the Basque nationalist movement and was not liked by the Basque people. For that reason, a major tenet of Basque independence was limiting the role for CNI in the oversight of Basque activities.

CNI had not abandoned the region and maintained a presence there but its involvement in any investigations required approval and was closely monitored. CNI leadership had been careful not to overstep its limited role. They were present at the interrogation of Hadj Arkoun, but they did not have an active role. The moment de Bleu heard what happened in Erro, he expected that limited role to change. The Prime Minister had just now made it clear.

CNI immediately took over the interrogation of Hadj Arjoun. Hadj was being held at a prison south of Vitoria-Gasteiz called Carcel de Zaballa. The facility housed about 725 inmates and included features such as a gymnasium, a library and several workshops. Hadj had never been in prison in Algeria, where he had heard of horrific conditions, but he certainly did not expect the facilities he was in now. Following his incarceration, his interrogations were light. De Blue ordered that he be treated as a high-level military officer and even though he was incarcerated his conditions were tolerable and he was given access to the prison amenities. Following Erro, all that changed. He was immediately placed in solitary confinement and the interrogations got rougher.

But Hadj was not privy to Belinda's plans in Erro, though he was aware that the next step following the failed meeting with De Bleu would be aggressive. The fact that he didn't know those details made it easy for him to deny any knowledge of the incident, but he suffered some harsh beatings for it. Then one night, he was awoken and a black hood placed over his head as a team of CNI agents transported him from the prison to a Pamplona safe house equipped with a cell and torture equipment.

The agents started with waterboarding and electric shock without asking any questions. Hadj was thrown into a concrete cell and subjected to sleep deprivation. This treatment went on for several days and Hadj began to go mad. He started to look for ways to kill himself. Then one morning as he was coming out of a sleep-deprived daze, he saw the agents set up a table in the room adjacent to his cell. He began to cry and pray that he would be executed quickly, but he smelled breakfast meats, sheep's milk cheese, sponge cake, jam and coffee. The agents opened the cell and cuffed Hadj's wrists and ankles. He then helped Hadj to a chair at the table. They offered him a small plate of meat and cheese and a glass of juice. He gobbled the food ravenously but before he finished, they removed it.

"Ok, Mr. Arjoun, or is it Dr. Arjoun?" They looked at each other and laughed.

Hadj was unable to put any thoughts together. He could smell the food, and it was clouding his mind.

"Well," said the principal interrogator, Victor Gomez, "we will call you doctor, as in university professor, someone who understands the theoretical bases for terror, but probably has never fired a gun."

Hadj just stared ahead confused.

"Whom do you work for Dr. Arjoun?"

He spoke slowly and struggled to talk. "I'm uh, I uh work um I'm a professor."

"Really?" said Victor. "What do you teach?"

"I, uh um, I teach, uh, physics."

"So, Professor Arjoun, what do you know about weapons?"

"I don't what you mean."

"Didn't you propose to deliver weapons to Minister De Bleu?"

"Um, I am thirsty. Could you give me some juice?"

Victor waived over an agent who was standing in the background, observing.

"Give the man some juice," he instructed the agent. The agent filled a glass and as he started to hand it to Hadj who was grasping for the glass, he took the glass and poured the juice over his head. The agents in the room laughed. Victor acted angry. "Give the man some juice dammit!" he yelled. The agent refilled the glass and handed it to him.

At this point Hadj was coming to his senses.

"Could you hand me a towel, please?"

The agent looked surprised, but Victor ordered him to bring a towel. He grabbed a cloth bag that was used for waterboarding and handed it to the interrogator, who in turn handed it to Hadj.

"Ok," he said. "You have your juice and your towel."

Hadj wiped his face off and drank the juice. Then, in a flash, he lunged at Victor and wrapped the bag over his head and pulled the draw string before the agents could reach him. He pulled the draw string tighter and could hear the man fighting for breath. He put his arms over the man's head and pulled the handcuffs tight trying to use them to cuff off the man's head and heard shots. They were the last sounds he heard, and he collapsed on the breakfast table and pulled Victor and everything else on the table to the floor just as he died.

Victor fought to get out of Hadj's death grip. He pulled off the bag and, as he was coughing and trying to recover his breath, he yelled at his team of agents. "God dammit!" he said. "Fuck! Did you have to kill him? What the fuck are we supposed to do now? Jesus Christ!"

He looked at Hadj and the bloody mess of food. The agents were standing in shock.

"Would somebody please clean up this mess?!" he yelled and stormed up the staircase and out of the house.

* * *

Belinda looked out her window at the course. She knew not to rent the same apartment as before, but she needed to find some location on the course. Rather than dead man's curve, she chose a location further down the course on Calle Estafeta near La Plaza del Toros. She chuckled to herself as she considered her strategy – this time the runners who made it that far would be too worn out to resist her aggressions. She found a place a No. 72 on the third floor. She cut her hair short and bought different wigs to help conceal her identity.

The races were scheduled to start on July 7 with the opening ceremony on July 6. This year the new American Pope was scheduled to make an appearance on Sunday, July 5, and would hold mass in La Catedral de Santa María la Real de Pamplona. His presence would mark the importance of the Feast of Saint Fermin, but he would also visit Erro and bring peace and healing to the villagers suffering from the attack. The Spanish government welcomed the new pope and asked that he recognize the significant role the Basque people played in the history of Spain.

Not only were they mad about the attack, but they were frightened that it portended a new round of violence which they believed was unnecessary. Under their current leadership, the Basque Autonomous Region was thriving, and the Basque population was experiencing the highest quality of life it had ever known until the attack on Erro threw everything into confusion.

Hopefully, the presence of the Pope in Spain would calm everyone's nerves and discourage additional violence. From Belinda's perspective, the mass of people attending the event would be huge and Belinda was confident her presence would go unnoticed. There were rumors the American President and Vice President might attend the event.

Belinda arrived a week early. She had moved her helicopters to an old World War II bunker complex on the east end of the Pyrenees, adjacent to a small town called Sort near Barcelona. The bunker complex included an old missile silo with a circular lid that still worked. She converted the silo into a landing pad where she could store the helicopters underground. The helicopters were painted to match Spanish Army helicopters, and her pilots wore Spanish military uniforms. The helicopter call signs were altered to Spanish military call signs and the addition of two Army helicopters at an unused military location did not trigger any concerns. When the helicopters landed near Pamplona, carrying Belinda and her vacation gear, no one questioned them.

The local police kept their hands off the Spanish Army in the same manner that they treated the CNI secret service. The police even offered Belinda an escort, but Belinda politely declined. Instead, her team drove her to the Hotel La Perla, where she checked in under a pseudonym and stowed her gear. After the team left, she grabbed a bag and strolled down the Plaza del Castillo and entered 76 Calle de la Estafeta, her secret apartment lair. Her corner room offered a perfect view of the runners making their way to the end of Estafeta and across Cortes de Navarra onto the ramp leading into the bullring and out to the finish line in the middle of the ring. Across from her apartment room was one of her favorite bars in Pamplona, Txirrintxa (pronounced "chirr-in-cha"). She opened the door into 76 Estafeta and climbed the stairs to the third floor. An older couple smiled at her as she climbed past their entrance. She felt relaxed, home again in Pamplona, ready for her new adventures.

That evening, she wandered across the street into the bar. It was filled mostly with older men. She heard them talking about Erro and about the Pope coming to town. She didn't react to either and sat alone at the other end of the bar. Two younger men walked into the bar. She could tell they were foreigners, probably Italian. Their fearlessness and slightly reckless behavior inspired Belinda. She waited, knowing they would eventually approach her. They walked to the bar and pounded on it demanding their drinks. They looked at the old men and said loudly in Italian, "Look at these guys, useless old coots, probably Basque. You come here every day?" The old men ignored them. Then they saw Belinda, seated by herself, sipping her scotch. They wandered over and sat down on the stools next to her.

"So, what do we have here?" they said in broken Spanish.

"What do you see?" she responded in Italian.

"Mio!" they shouted laughing. "Are you Italian?"

"I'm whatever you need me to be," she replied.

"You know what we need," he said, crudely licking his lips. "We need you to be horny."

"Yes, muy horny," said his friend.

"Are you asking me to get out of here? Take you to my place and get laid?"

"Get laid?" he said. "We can do so much more than get laid. We can twist your desert twat into the forests of Amazon. We can make it rain!"

"Well, then," she replied. "Looks like a storm is coming."

The first and more aggressive of the two, turned his head to the old men at the bar.

"Guess what old men!" he shouted. "We have a real cougar here."

The old men looked up annoyed.

"I can be a cougar," Belinda whispered leaning close to the offender, "or a gazelle, ... or a snake!" And just as she said the word 'snake,' her hand flashed forward and grabbed his middle two fingers and snapped them backward until they broke. He grabbed his hand and fell backward over his stool onto the floor. His friend cried out, "Jesu Cristo, you bitch! You broke his hand!"

Belinda stood, and placed her hand in her purse, and revealed a small pistol. The two young men scrambled to their feet and ran out of the bar, knocking over other stools as they fled.

The old men sitting at the bar stood up and applauded, and the bartender offered her a drink on the house. She put the piece back in her purse, snapped up the free drink, slapped cash on the bar, and left, heading to the hotel to bring more gear to her apartment.

Chapter 18.

Countermeasures

The idea that the best defense is a good offense has often been attributed to Sun-Tzu in *The Art of War*. But Sun Tzu didn't say that. Rather, he wrote, "The good fighters of old first put themselves beyond the possibility of defeat, then waited…" In other words, the best offense is a good defense. Still, many have applied the former version as a compelling military strategy. One version of that best defense strategy found its extreme in the 1960s when Robert MacNamara and Henry Kissinger advocated mutually assured destruction as the only feasible solution to the nuclear arms race. Under the apt-acronym MAD, weapons of mass destruction must be developed in volume such that any use of this weapon necessarily means self-annihilation. The problem with the strategy of course was that it justified proliferation of the weapons and, not surprisingly, the discussion shifted to first-strike capabilities. In ecclesiastical terms, the quick had a better shot at surviving than the dead. It seemed the world had abandoned any hope that there was any defense at all to nuclear weapons.

Then in 1983, President Ronald Reagan suggested that a true defense was possible, one that would render nuclear weapons "impotent and obsolete." His Strategic Defense Initiative (SDI) posited that new satellite-borne technologies deployed in space might create a shield against incoming missiles. Critics decried it as Star Wars after the popular George Lucas movies and the program eventually buckled under political pressure and its high cost. But it didn't completely disappear. Rather, ground-based anti-missile systems emerged, one of which proposed a missile intercept system dubbed the Patriot program. Early interceptor success rates were low, but the system kept improving. Israel began deploying Patriots and used them successfully to thwart attempts at missile strikes coming from hostile neighboring countries. The United States now has deployed a midcourse defense system capable of catching intercontinental ballistic missiles in mid-flight and the military has built interceptor silos throughout the Western United States. Unfortunately, the interceptor systems remain imperfect, and the addition of artificial intelligence doesn't solve the problem, it merely raises the arm races discussion to a higher level where the new race is now on to build the smarter AI.

Brian arrived back in California exhausted. He hadn't imagined that running a high-profile laboratory might mean overnight trips to Washington, DC. But he was grateful for Fred's assistance and the use of his plane. It certainly made last-minute long-distance travel more feasible and bypassed public airports and security measures. Fred's driver took him home and he thought about his interaction with Agent Vanessa Christian. He wondered where she might pop up again and what she meant by suggesting their commonality. It didn't surprise him that the CIA might be tracking him, but he wondered what they knew about Erro and how much they might already know about Belinda's whereabouts.

As he was riding home, Bost called him from the Providia lab.

"How's the world traveler?" he started.

"Weary," answered Brian.

"Well, I know you need some rest, but I've been thinking about our AI-infused nanobots, and it occurred to me, what if we ask them how they can be used?"

"I'm game."

"We did it. The first ideas were variations on the themes we have already explored. They suggested different filtering systems and the only interesting idea in that discussion concerned building different kinds of molecule capture systems and expanding beyond carbon dioxide. In other words, manufacture new nanobots that grab molecular complexes like methane, or sulphur dioxide or even larger particles that pollute the air and the water and the human brain."

"Go on."

"Such as microplastics."

"In the brain?"

"In the brain, in the ocean, in the air. I've been reading about dementia and Alzheimer's and there are theories suggesting that human beings are becoming more prone to neurological disorders because of microplastics."

"Ok, now you are making my brain hurt."

"I'm sorry. I know you have a lot on your mind. Relax. Take some gummies. We can chat tomorrow or later this week when you have time."

"Bost, you are the best. Just know I am grateful to have you in my life."

"Shut up," Bost replied and laughed. "Now I know you are exhausted."

Brian didn't need gummies. He dropped into his bed and was asleep within seconds. His dreams were chaotic. He had a meeting with the President at the White House, but he got lost and couldn't find his way around. White House security mistook him as a threat and detained him and when they tried to put a hood on him, he thrashed about and woke himself up, relieved that it was only a dream. Then he rolled back over and quickly fell back asleep.

Brian awoke refreshed but he elected not to go into the office. He heard that surf at Mavericks state beach was breaking big at and thought it might be exciting to ride to Half Moon Bay and watch the large waves. He called his new friend Carl, who had a boat anchored at Pillar Point and confirmed the break. Carl had made money working at Google when it was a start-up and retired young. Brian met Carl at a local bar where Carl liked to play guitar and sings songs from the 70s. Carl had a Harley and a large fishing boat, and he and Brian had gone fishing on a few occasions. Brian always enjoyed it even though he never caught a single fish. Carl had pointed out the Mavericks break and told Brian anytime he wanted, Carl would take him out to watch the surfing.

Today was perfect and Carl offered to take him out. Brian said he would be there in an hour. He then called Leonard and let him know he was reachable but not coming into the office. Leonard wasn't happy but he was starting to fantasize about his old ways with new interns and, well, if the cat was away... Unfortunately for Leonard, the new interns were a much smarter breed, and they made any attempts by Leonard to seduce them look pathetic and foolish. They smiled and pretended to comfort him in his embarrassment. Brian jumped on his bike and took off up Highway 1 through Santa Cruz and past Big Basin Redwoods State Park up to Half Moon Bay. He met his friend at Barbara's Fishtrap, where they shared a beer together. Brian helped carry a chest of ice and drinks to the boat. They climbed in and motored past the breakwaters and quickly caught up with other boats and jet skis carrying surfers to the point break at Sail Rock. The waves were gigantic, larger than any waves Carl had ever seen with sets coming in at 40-50 feet tall. He parked the boat a safe distance from the break, and they kicked back, drank beers and watched the surfing until sunset. Thoughts of a nanobot war never entered Brian's head. Leonard never called.

Brian was back in the office early the following day. Refreshed and exhilarated from the drama at Mavericks, Brian set about addressing the problem of weaponized nanobots. He called the top members of his team together. They met in his office, which Brian used as a signal to them that the discussions were both extremely important and highly confidential. A breach of that trust called for immediate termination. He wanted to bring Bost into the discussion, but he would not do that until he got Bost cleared by the Pentagon. He had the office swept of bugs of any kind. Ragnar Willowbrook rarely this same problem under Belinda because the consequences would be dire. So far under Brian, they found nothing. He started by reminding them of their obligation to preserve the discussion as confidential.

"I've just returned from a meeting with the Secretary of Defense," he told his team. "The meeting was joined by White House staff and top Pentagon brass. It concerned a recent event in Spain."

Dr. Sandra Folsom, recently placed in charge of Ragnar Willowbrook's biological programs, was, as usual, first to respond.

"The Basque terror event? I have been following it on the news. It's horrific."

Brian nodded. "It is horrific. I was told an entity called the Night Brigade claimed responsibility, but we know nothing about them."

Dr. Leonard Freund added, "Why are we talking about chemical weapons? The response should be global condemnation and military action."

"That's the thing," said Brian. "That's not what we are talking about."

Everyone in the room looked puzzled. "That's what the news is reporting," said Leonard.

"Right," said Brian. "Sometimes the news doesn't get it right and, in this case, there is a lot of fear about disclosing what Washington thinks is the actual weapon. We have been working with Providia to eliminate the toxic effects of carbon capture nanobots and we have had some success. It seems someone else has taken the technology in the opposite direction and found a way to weaponize that toxicity and use it in combat or, in the case of Spain, against innocent victims as an act of terror."

The room erupted. Leonard put his hands to his head. "Oh, my god," he said. "Belinda?"

Brian looked at Leonard sternly and said, "We do not know who is doing this and it's not our job to speculate. We have another job to do, and it is delicate, and I want the strictest protocols in place before we start." The team quieted down.

"First, I will repeat myself here – the work we will be doing must stay within this group. No one else at Ragnar, unless authorized by me, can know what we are working on. For that reason, we will be relocating out of the Labs to an undisclosed location, and you need to make arrangements with your families to relocate for at least the next six months. If you choose not to participate, and I cannot force you, then you and your family will be sequestered on one of the military bases nearby until the rest of us complete this mission. You will be compensated well for your time if you elect to join us."

He handed out a short confidentiality agreement and said, "You all must sign this NDA. The agreement identifies a program called "Countermeasures," and says, among other things, that disclosure of any activities associated with the program would be considered an act of treason against the United States of America and you would be subject to criminal prosecution."

Brian continued, "You have 24 hours to decide. Will you join us on what could be one of the most important missions of our time? Or, and I would not judge you for it, does your conscience not allow you to do so?"

Sandra then asked, "Are we building a weapon?"

"I made it very clear to all involved that I would not build a weapon as a countermeasure to these weaponized nanobots. So, my answer is no, definitively. Our job will be to formulate a defense."

Leonard nodded and then added, "Sometimes the best defense…"

Brian interrupted him before he could finish. "No, not that." He collected the signed NDAs. "24 hours," he said. "You are dismissed."

Great Falls, Montana, is an active town with a population of 60,422 split by the Missouri River. Lewis and Clark's famous expedition through Thomas Jefferson's

Louisiana Purchase Territory had specially made river keelboats to simplify the journey, most of which was on the Missouri River. But when they reached the spot that later became Great Falls, they had to portage their boats for 18 miles to get around the five different falls. The bypass took 31 days and was one of the most difficult challenges of the journey. Brian watched his team disembark from the U.S. Air Force's C-130 Super Hercules at Great Falls International Airport. He wondered how difficult the next six months would be and was not confident that it would be successful.

He chose Great Falls because, even though somewhat remote, the Air Force had an active high profile air base that, even though the base was no longer used for fixed wing aircraft, it held a large helicopter squadron that was used to monitor the 150 or so nuclear ICBM silos scattered throughout Montana.

It also held a large empty hangar that the Air Force was authorizing him to use as his lab. He knew it would be easy to get supplies and easy to leave if necessary to attend critical meetings in person. In fact, however, Brian hadn't chosen Great Falls or Malmstrom AFB. The base was proposed to him by the Pentagon and a part of him wondered whether the military intentionally was choosing a remote location in the event of a mishap. He rejected the thought quickly. He needed the effort to go well as did the rest of the world. A large flat-bed semi-truck parked at the rear tail of the plane and cadets from nearby Malmstrom unloaded large pallets and metal containers loaded with lab equipment. An MH-139A Grey Wolf helicopter was parked nearby and cadets directed the team to board the helicopter, which could hold up to 15 people. The airport was located on a mesa on the west end of the town of Great Falls. The helicopter pilot flew low over the edge of the mesa, which dropped about 500 feet down to a golf course called Meadowlark Country Club, then directly over two of the waterfalls on the Missouri River, then over downtown Great

Falls until they reached the east side of town and landed at Malmstrom AFB. The base commander had housing set up for the lab team and the few family members who came along for the journey. Drivers would be available to take them to and from the hangar and into town as needed and only as authorized.

Chapter 19.

Occam's Razor (Part 3)

Van opened her eyes, reflecting on a dream. Once again, she found herself dreaming about Brian. It was a comfortable dream. They were in an apartment she didn't recognize but they were laying on a couch looking out a window. He laid down behind her and started spooning her, kissing the back of her neck and cupping her breasts in his strong hands. She smiled as she opened her eyes and focused on the room. She felt movement behind her and a hand reached up her pajamas. It felt nice and she turned and faced Martin Richard. She smiled.

"I have to go," she cooed.

"Come on, baby, stay with me," Martin pleaded.

"I have work," she said. "You know that."

Martin studied her face and kissed her on the nose. "Let's get married. We can have kids. I'll take care of you."

"What are you talking about?" Van pulled back and laughed. She could sense Martin was hurt by her reaction. She tapped him on the head playfully.

"You're joking, right?"

"No, I'm serious."

"Holy cow," said Van. "If you are going to propose, I would suggest you find a better moment and have some class. But Martin, honestly. I have told you this is fun, and I enjoy you and your family, but I am not ready for anything serious. Marriage? Come on. You can't be serious."

"I am totally serious, Van," he replied. "I understand the art of proposals. I've helped a bunch of friends set them up. I helped a friend organize a proposal on the Dodger Stadium jumbotron."

"Dodger Stadium?! You need to stop right now, dude." Van pulled away and got out of bed.

"I'm just taking the temperature, Van" he insisted.

"Oh, my god," she said and then realized from his shocked look that he needed some reassurance.

"Ok," she said. "Look. Take a breath. This is fun. I can't think about anything like marriage or kids right now. Now I need to get going and you need to get ready for your auditions today."

"Oh crap, that's right. What time is it?"

Maybe because Martin was getting pushy, but for whatever reason, Van decided she needed to see Brad Jones in Forensics. He still hadn't gotten back to her about the fingerprints on the notebook and the handwriting analysis on her car. Rather than head directly to the Bureau, she drove over to the Forensics lab in East LA. As usual, she found Brad working and as usual he greeted her with a smile and a hug.

"I've got news," he said. Before she could respond, he showed her a photograph of him standing next to his girlfriend. "We're engaged."

"Oh, Brad," she said, happy for him. "That's wonderful news! Tell me about it."

They chatted for a bit and turned to business.

"I dusted the book, but prints were hard to make out," he told her. "The only thing I can tell you is there were a lot of partials and nothing complete enough to run."

"A lot?"

"Yeah."

"Could you tell they were different prints?"

"Right. There were variations."

"Did you save what you had?"

"I have screenshots, if that's what you mean."

"Ok. If you don't mind, please don't lose those screenshots."

Van decided to go out on a limb.

"Have you ever been approached here to join an organization?"

"Like the Protective League?"

"Nothing formal. More informal."

Brad studied Van and didn't respond at first. "I don't think so. I have heard some officers say 'You should hang with us,' but I don't think that is what you mean."

"Right. Give it some thought. You might not have recognized it as anything more than that."

"I will."

"Anything on the writing analysis?"

"Your window? Not yet and I doubt it will go anywhere."

"Ok. Give my best to your fiancée. I am truly happy for you."

Van mused on the coincidence as she made her way back to drop off the car at fleet management. She spent time with Alvin and, emboldened by her conversation with Brad, asked him the same question. He told her no, but he added that she needed to be very careful with those kinds of questions. People could get the wrong idea. But Van was on an investigative path and becoming resolute.

She walked over to Internal Affairs. IA was located a few blocks west of central headquarters. IA spent most of their time in the office and Van was confident she would find someone to talk to. She flashed her badge, and security allowed her into the elevators. From there, she found her way to the IA reception area. She announced herself and showed her badge again.

"I'm looking for Captain Chang," said Van to the receptionist.

"I'm sorry," he responded, but Captain Chang is in a meeting right now."

"I'll wait," she said.

"It could be some time."

"I have time."

"Well, ok."

Almost as if on cue, Captain David Chang emerged through the reception door, followed by his deputy.

"Detective Eng," he smiled and extended his hand. "This is a surprise. What can I do for you?"

"I have some questions for you about the Geiringer investigation."

"I figured that much," he said. "Please follow me." He turned to the receptionist. "The Detective has carte blanche here at the Division. Notify me immediately any time she asks for me. Otherwise, you are to provide for her anything she asks."

"Understood, sir."

Van followed Detective Chang into his North Figueroa office. She notices a window lined with awards and multiple photos of movie stars, athletes and famous politicians.

"You seem to know a lot of people."

"I've been lucky enough to meet some people," he said. "It's fun for me. I'm not the kind to shy away from someone just because they are famous."

"I can see that."

"You are becoming famous in your own right."

The comment caught Van off guard.

"I assume that's a compliment."

"Of course it is. You are a young star rising fast."

"I'm not sure I see it that way," she said. "But I'll take the encouragement."

"You should. Just be careful. Success has its pitfalls."

Van ignored the comment. "I'm here," she said, "to find out what you know about police gangs in the Department."

Chang smiled, in the smile way any politician might smile in front of a crowd. "And that is what I mean," he said. "There are a lot a reason certain officers buddy up and not all of them are negative. Some of them experience a shared trauma from a gunfight or the loss of a comrade and they naturally gravitate to each other as a way of managing the trauma. Interfering in those relationships undermines the morale of the force. When it comes to investigating those groups, we need to be careful."

"That makes sense," said Van.

"My problem, and I know my job, is timing. When IA sticks it nose into police business, everyone gets uncomfortable, even the Chief. It's a constant balancing act. You might recall when you first joined the force a couple years back. Several officers questioned your appointment as a detective. They want us to investigate. I made a couple calls and had no reason to look any further."

The comment caught Van off guard. "I didn't know."

"We didn't want you to know, because you were new in the Bureau and showed great potential. Why would we do anything dumb, candidly, to discourage that?"

"You spoke to Charlie?"

"Among others. We followed protocol and that was that."

"Are you asking me to end my investigation?"

"No, not at all. But I am suggesting that you be very cautious and for good reason. I will tell you this. For the record, I am not aware of any malicious groups of officers forming in the Department. That said, I encourage you to continue your investigation and, please, know that you have the full resources of this Division at your disposal."

"Are you saying that I have no reason to believe Charlie's murder was organized?"

"I am not saying anything of the kind."

"Thank you, Captain."

Van left the meeting disturbed. She criticized herself for going into the meeting unprepared. She not only was caught off guard, but she left with nothing beneficial. She had never been concerned about access to resources and yet everyone was telling her she had full access to their resources. It seemed canned.

As she was walking back to HQ, her phone rang.

"Van. This is Alvin."

"Hi Alvin, what's up…"

He interrupted her. "Don't turn around but you are being followed."

"Followed? How do you know?"

"I'm tracking you. You are walking on 1st Street near the Disney Concert Hall. Pick up your pace slowly. Take a right on Grand. Head to the Broad Museum. Duck in there and meet me at Lichtenstein exhibit. I'll find you near *I'm Sorry*."

"*I'm Sorry?*"

"Yes. It's prominent. You will see it."

Van followed Alvin's instructions. She picked up her pace slowly and then headed down Grand. At the Broad there was a line. She went to the front of the line and flashed her badge, and they let her in. She asked a guard where to find the Lichtenstein exhibits. She found the Lichtenstein painting entitled *I'm Sorry* and waited. It seemed a curious choice to her. A modern looking woman apologizing near what looked like the tree of life in the Garden of Eden. Van felt irritated by the painting. Why should a woman be blamed for the sins of a man? Even more so, why should she be compelled to apologize? Or maybe her gender was irrelevant. Was Alvin apologizing for something?

She waited. Alvin didn't show. She was about to call him when someone touched her shoulder.

"Excuse me."

"Excuse me?" She turned quickly toward the voice.

The stranger responded. "I'm sorry," he said, "but I had to be careful."

"Are you pretending to be Alvin?'

"No, Alvin called you but I'm the one who was following you."

"I don't understand. He said he would meet me"

"Alvin knows me. I've done undercover work for the police for the past decade. I must keep my identity secret. If anyone discovers I am meeting with you, my identity could be blown."

"Who are you?"

"Maybe someday I can tell you," he said. "But for right now, you must understand that no one wants you to solve this case."

"Was Charlie close? Is that why they killed him?"

"Charlie was set up, but not because he was close. He was killed as a warning to you."

Van felt sick. "Is Alvin at risk?"

"Everyone is at risk. This is a much bigger matter than you know. You can't trust anyone. Even me."

"You cannot just say that and leave. What do you mean by it's a bigger matter?"

"I can't tell you much right now. This is not the place. Bigger names may be involved."

'What bigger names?"

"I'm not going to say. One last thought."

"What is that?"

"Don't be overly impressed by Hollywood."

"Ok. A little ambiguous but ok. Now I have a question. Are you the one who wrote STOP on my car window?"

He looked away and didn't answer.

"Why? Can you at least tell me what it means?"

"You don't know what you are getting yourself into."

Van was irritated. "So, what do you suggest I do, apart from give up."

"Don't give up. I hope to God you live to expose this. Don't try to reach me. I will reach you."

"And Alvin?"

"Alvin's been around. He knows how to take care of himself."

"So did Charlie."

As quickly as he appeared, the stranger disappeared. Van looked around. No one around her seemed to notice. She looked back at the Lichtenstein and the tear on the woman's face struck her but this time differently. She wasn't confessing some wrongdoing. She was apologizing for telling the truth.

The conversation left Van perplexed. The death of Scott Geiringer seemed meaningless on its face. He was a recruit fresh from the Academy. He had no family connections to the force, no lineage. The simplest answer was that some incident at the Academy followed Scott to the Bureau, and his death was retribution for that incident. But then why kill Charlie? What could Charlie have uncovered about Scott's death that warranted an organized hit on him? Van was stumped. Everyone said they wanted to help her and yet, somehow, if the stranger was to be believed, they were using their positions of power to protect themselves and prevent her from identifying the real culprit. She decided to test the offers, which she knew meant walking directly into the lion's den and staring down some open-mouth snarls. It wasn't the first time.

She started by texting the Chief.

"Need some support from you. I need IA to make inquiries in the Hollywood, North Hollywood and Rampart Divisions."

The response came quickly. "That's all?"

"No. I need a contact in the West Hollywood PD."

"Done."

As expected, she received a call.

"Detective Eng?"

"Yes."

"Captain Chang, here."

"Yes, sir."

"Just received a call from the Chief. What is it exactly that you need?"

Van explained that she needed IA to begin multiple interviews regarding the deaths of Detectives Geiringer and Darling with officers of the three divisions. She wanted the interviews taped and she wanted any relevant comments highlighted so she could review them and decide whether to re-interview those officers.

"As I indicated," said Captain Chang. "Whatever you need."

Chapter 20.

Infiltration

On Sunday, the new Pope made his appearance in Pamplona. He held mass in La Catedral de Santa María and then rode in an electric Mercedes Benz popemobile through the streets of Pamplona. The city was already bustling with tourists for the Running of the Bulls and Belinda found herself enjoying the relative anonymity of the dense crowds. She continued to receive items from her team at the Hotel La Perla under her pseudonym and she was careful to visit the hotel at random times and days. But after a week in Pamplona without recognition or any concerning incidents, she started to relax and enjoy the moment. She wandered to the start of the race where the Pope gave a benediction to the runners and, in the name of his predecessor Pope Francis, reminded the city and the world to treat the animals well. The cameras caught the event live and several videos appeared on YouTube showing the benediction. That same morning, Van was waiting for a follow-up meeting with Captain Chang and noticed that YouTube was showing videos of the Pope in Pamplona at the Feast of San Fermín and the Running of the Bulls. She watched as the camera depicted the benediction and then panned the crowd of Catholic worshippers and interested tourists when she saw a blond woman wearing a hat and sunglasses in the crowd. She stopped the video and took a screenshot of the woman. She texted Agents Henry Sams and Vanessa Christian.

"Take a look." Then she posted her screenshot to the message.

Vanessa was the first to respond.

"Where did you get this?"

"YouTube." She posted the link.

Henry responded. "Is that Belinda?"

Vanessa cut the conversation short.

"Call me."

Right then, Captain Chang appeared. Van stood and followed him into the conference room. As she walked, she texted Henry and Vanessa. "Soon. Busy." Two of Chang's deputies were seated. They stood. Van greeted them and they sat down.

Chang started. "We have conducted several interviews," he said. "As I told you, the temperature is rising. Officers don't like IA inquiries. I have come across some resistance."

"Who is telling you to stop?" Van inquired.

"No one is saying stop. But I have colleagues questioning me about the proper use of police time and resources."

"What are you saying?"

"I'm following orders."

"Names?"

"This is typical for any IA inquiries," Chang said. "The rank and file hate us. This is not a rabbit hole worth chasing."

"What is the Chief saying?"

He says, "Follow your directive."

"Good. What are we finding? Any leads? Anyone willing to talk?"

Chang motioned to his deputies. "For the most part, no," one replied. "From what we can tell, this is not an incident that anyone is bragging about in the

lockers. Most officers are shocked and concerned that this happened under our roof."

"You said, 'for the most part.'"

The other deputy chimed in. "There's a young officer in Rampart named Ben Bodrogi. When we interviewed him, he seemed very anxious. We pressed him and he claimed that he has issues at home. But we don't believe him."

Van recalled the name Ben in Charlie's notebook. She didn't say anything about the notebook. She did say, "Bring him in. I want to talk to him."

The rest of the meeting focused on the plan going forward and timing. Van thanked them and, as she left, she turned back to Captain Chang.

"When it comes to any resistance, I want names."

"Yes, Detective," Chang responded, but his expression made it clear to Van that he was not happy.

"Thank you," she said again, respectfully.

Van left the building. This time she was acutely aware of anyone who might be following her but saw nothing. She called Vanessa.

"Hi, babe," Vanessa answered. "Talk to me."

Van let it pass. "Did you see the video?"

"I did. You think it is Belinda?"

"Don't you have facial recognition software?"

"We do and I have already forwarded it, so this is helpful. Thank you. We suspected she may be there but did not have confirmation. If this proves to be her, then we know for sure."

"Do you have a plan?"

"I thought you were focused on the LAPD."

"I am. My apologies if it's not an appropriate question."

"It's not. But I do look forward to working more closely with you, Detective, when you are ready. Good luck in LA." Vanessa hung up.

Van was satisfied. She took appropriate action and now it was up to the secret services to make it count. Regarding her interaction with Chang, Van wondered if she handled it correctly. She did not want to alienate Chang. She needed to stay close to him for his support in the investigation, but also so she could observe his actions. She wasn't entirely convinced that Chang didn't know something or wasn't somehow involved.

Belinda returned to her apartment after the benediction. She had an odd feeling that she wasn't being smart by wandering the streets. She removed the wig and her sunglasses and trashed both. She wondered if she should wear an N-95 mask. The crowds were dense, especially with the Pope in town, and she wouldn't be the only one wearing a mask. She didn't like masks, though. It would probably be enough to change her appearance, but she needed to be careful. She decided not to go to the hotel. She would find someone to run errands for her. She found a nearby restaurant that delivered and enjoyed her dinner finished with a scotch and a cigar, excited about the race. She sat by an open window and listened to music and watched the fireworks. She imagined dancing and enjoying herself that evening like a common tourist, but she knew her plan was a better plan. She closed the window and went to bed. She had a restless night.

Vanessa called Henry.

"We've confirmed the image was Armendariz in Pamplona."

"What's next?"

"We are working with Interpol to surveil the races. We have actionable intelligence that she attends the races almost every year."

"Be careful. If she is there, she may be planning a major terror event."

"We know. But this may be our last opportunity before she disappears."

That evening, Vanessa jumped on an agency plane carrying a dozen agents. She did her best to sleep but transatlantic red-eye flights were never fun. They landed at a military base in England to re-fuel and then flew to Pamplona. It was 7:00 am Central European Summer Time when they landed.

The traffic into downtown Pamplona was heavy and it was unlikely they would settle in their positions in time for the first encierro or bull run of the week. During the ride in, they were briefed by Interpol. Interpol described the route taken by the bulls and the locations they had staked out. Spanish CNI had been alerted, and they covered other spots. MI-5 was there in place as well. With the addition of the CIA and the help of overhead drones equipped with face and body recognition technology, it seemed impossible that Belinda would be able to evade capture.

Belinda woke in the morning and prepared coffee. She put on a dark wig and dark red lipstick. She could hear noise outside as the crowds gathered four to five persons deep along the end of the route as Estafeta dumped the runners and the bulls together into the Callejon passageway into the bullring. Barricades prevented the crowd from piling up in front of Belinda's doorway. She stood beside her window, careful not to be seen and listened for the whistles of the first fireworks. It sounded and she knew the corral gate was opened.

The first runners would be there in about four minutes. She would let them pass. They were too intent on finishing the race and getting the glory of running into the bullring. Shortly after, a second whistle sounded, and Belinda headed downstairs. She cracked her doorway and felt people pushing against the door.

She yelled and they moved away. Soon the first runners came by. They were the fastest runners and tended to outrun the bulls. The race was easy for them and the crowd inside the bullring erupted as they entered triumphantly.

Soon Belinda saw the bulls racing down Estafeta. Her blood started to boil. She watched as the exhausted runners slammed themselves against the buildings to evade the sharp and deadly bull horns. Adventurous young runners who had already beat the bulls to the bullring turned and ran back headlong into the stampeding bulls. It was one of these young runners that Belinda snagged and pulled into her doorway. The runner looked stunned as she grabbed his belt. Then he took a look and realized his good fortune. He slammed into Belinda's body as she pulled the door shut behind her. She let go of his pants and grabbed his hand, encouraging him to follow her up the stairs and into her apartment. Once inside she threw him down on her bed and he laughed even as he felt paralyzed by her aggression. She pulled off his shoes and pants and climbed on top of him, placing him inside her.

The heat of the moment almost caused her to pass out and she moaned as he grew and responded to her motions. Their ferocity increased until he let out a loud shout and fell back into the bed. Belinda climbed off the runner and went into the bathroom. When she returned to the bed, she had two glasses of scotch, and they sat in bed talking about the race until he finished his drink. She beckoned him toward the door and, now again confused and a bit hurt, he pulled on his pants and shoes and walked with her to the entrance. He turned to kiss her, and she put her hand to her mouth and smiled. She opened the door, and he left. She knew he would get over the hurt and by the end of the day would be bragging about his encounter. She counted on that. Every day the line by her door increased and she had her pick of Pamplona's bravest.

Down the street and the end of the block, two Spanish CNI agents were scanning the crowds. Every so often they would stop a blond woman in a hat and then let her go when the recognition software on their phones failed to confirm it was Belinda. They turned and saw a young runner stumble onto the course, narrowly missing the last bull zigzagging down Estafeta and making its confused way to the bullring. The runner tripped and fell. One of the CNI agents saw him and pointed him out to his partner laughing and saying, "That one is lucky to have lived."

The next morning, Belinda repeated the same steps. This time, the young runner showed up with his friends, but instead of grabbing him, she chose one of his friends and summarily disposed of him in the same manner as she had the first runner. This time, as he emerged from the doorway, he raised his hands. An Interpol agent stationed across the street noticed the reaction and tried to see who was behind the doorway. He raised his camera to take a shot, but it was too late. He reported the incident to command, and they told him she was probably one of several hookers who plied their trade along the route. Vanessa overheard the conversation and asked for details. What evidence did they have that hookers were working the run? They confessed they did not have any evidence but that this seemed more suspicious of that activity than that of a seasoned terrorist. Vanessa pressed harder. She suggested they post a camera in a window across from the entrance. She joined the ops team to set up the stakeout. The rest of the day they saw nothing except the delivery of some food to the entrance. Whoever was behind the door was careful not to reveal herself. They waited all night and saw nothing.

The race started again the next day at 8:00 am with the firing of the first two rounds of fireworks. They roused Vanessa from her sleep and handed her an espresso to wake herself up. *I love being in Europe,* she thought as she sipped the espresso and munched on a croissant.

"They're coming!" the agent at the window shouted to the team and the members all gathered at the windows watching the first runners go by. Then just before the bulls reached the end of Estafeta, five young runners ran to the entrance across the street and knocked. A woman in a shawl with dark hair and wearing sunglasses emerged from the doorway and grabbed one of the runners and pulled him willingly this time inside the entrance. Once she disappeared, Vanessa shouted, get that video analyzed. They sent the video in a secure email back to command. The answer came back shortly – 70% confirmation. No good, thought Vanessa. She turned to the ops team.

"We can't storm the apartment based on that kind of data. We need more certainty."

"We can do whatever we want," said one of the Interpol agents. "If we make a mistake, we make a mistake."

That is idiotic, thought Vanessa but she smiled and said, "Perhaps. But I need something better."

"Maybe we can infiltrate," suggested an MI-5 agent who was running the video.

"Infiltrate how?" asked Vanessa.

"Darren and I," he said referring to another MI-5 agent in the room, "we were top track and field runners at our colleges. We can get down this course ahead of most of these runners and put ourselves by the entrance. If we can wear cams and get inside, we can get you the image you need."

That became the plan. The next morning, Darren and Frederick donned the white and red runner's costumes along with the cams and headed to the group of runners waiting at the corral gate. They knew what to expect. The first whistles sounded, and they took off.

Soon they were at the front of the pack and experienced an exhilaration that they never had before throughout their running careers. This time, they knew that if they were to fall, they might be killed. They loved the feeling and smiled and laughed at each other as they raced down Santa Domingo and around Dead Man's Curve and then down Estafeta. They reached the bottom of Estafeta, and the other agents watched as the two runners ran past the stakeout caught up in the moment and almost forgetting their mission. Darren had the presence of mind to stop, and he grabbed Frederick's arm and quickly turned back up Estafeta. They saw the bulls coming down the narrow street with a couple of runners getting knocked down and trampled. They made their way quickly to the entrance to be certain they were first in line. Before any other runners made it to the entrance, a pretty woman in her thirties appeared out of the doorway and grabbed Darren. Frederick remained standing pressed against the wall at the entrance as she pulled Darren indoors and the bulls raced by him, narrowly missing him with one of their bull horns.

Vanessa and the others watched as Darren let Belinda pull him into the small foyer. They could see her back and the back of her head through the contact cam in Darren's eye and kept waiting for her to turn around. But she didn't. She instructed Darren to close the door behind them, and he reached around and slammed it shut. He followed her up the stairs and into her apartment and just as he expected her to turn and face him, she whipped around and slapped him so hard it knocked the contact off his iris and onto the side of his cornea, cutting off the images being sent to the team. She threw him face down on the bed, popped off his shoes and reached for his pants. He fought to keep his pants on, and she spun him over face up and walloped him again. He shouted, "What the fuck are you doing?!" blinking madly trying to reset the cam.

"Come on, lover," she said, ripping off her blouse and reaching under his pants. Darren couldn't help but get erect and found himself losing control. He let her pull off his pants and spin her around all the while constantly blinking and hoping the lens would right itself. By now Belinda was in a mad fury and grabbed him, pulling him into her. The lens slid back around and then fell out of his eye and on to Belinda's chest. Despite the intensity of the moment, she stopped, picked it up between her fingers and examined it.

"What…" she started to say and then saw the circuits. She immediately crushed the lens and as Darren started to make up a response, she reached for a gun she kept hidden under the bed. Darren saw the gun and grabbed her arm to prevent her from using it and she spun around as they fell together on the floor. The fall knocked the gun loose and Darren let go of Belinda to reach for the gun. Belinda grabbed Darren's hair and slammed her fingers into Darren's eyes. He screamed and she flipped herself over, grabbed the gun, and fired three shots into Darren's chest. The force pushed Darren off her and back on the floor and she scrambled to her feet.

Frederick heard the shots and said, "We have a problem!" The stakeout team ran to the door of their apartment, down the staircase and across the street. Vanessa flipped on her two-way and told the entire team. "We have a problem! Get to the entrance of the 76 Estafeta now! Go! Go! Go!"

They scrambled through the remaining runners. The last two bulls were rambling down Estafeta and the agents almost collided with the bulls as they pushed through the runners. Frederick busted through the building door, but he had no weapon and knew he couldn't just run up the stairs. As the first agents reached him, he waved for them to enter and pointed upstairs. More agents arrived and they pressed their way to the third floor where, because they watched Darren's video, they already knew which apartment to enter.

Belinda was pissed. But she was as mad at herself as she was at the situation. She now knew she had been too reckless. She grabbed her phone and a bathrobe and ran out of the apartment to the rear stairs and down into an alley where she kept her electric scooter. She struggled for a second as she unlocked the bike and jumped on the bike as she heard the ops team scrambling up the stairs. As soon as she started the bike, one of the agents in the apartment looked out the window and saw her take off. He yelled, "On a bike in the alley!" He fired in her direction, and she turned and fired back as she powered the scooter away. Vanessa, who was now in the apartment, called into command and shouted, "Send the drones!"

Belinda, wearing nothing but the bathrobe sped down the narrow Pamplona streets. Within a few minutes, she saw drones above her and did her best to evade them, but they were too quick and seemed to anticipate her every turn. She knew she didn't stand a chance unless she had help. She pinged her team and shouted, "Pick me up. I am being chased by drones." She reached the Arga River Bridge and found a small dirt path that led into a dense grove of trees and raced into the trees and up the river. One of the drones tried to follow her into the trees and she turned and shot it, knocking it to the ground. Then she raced forward down the dirt path. She rode up to a walkway over the river and dumped the bike into the river. She crossed the bridge and sat down hiding her face at a bus stop shelter, pretending to be homeless. A pedestrian asked if they could help and she acted crazy and scared them away. A black SUV showed up and pulled her inside and they sped away.

Chapter 21.

Great Falls

Brian met with the Commanding Officer (CO) at Malmstrom AFB first thing the next morning. They discussed lab preparations and protocol. The CO accepted that brass had chosen his base, but he demanded visibility to the activities and Brian's assurance that strict safety protocols would be in place and strictly adhered to. The last thing Brian wanted was a safety incident. He agreed wholeheartedly with the CO and expressed his confidence both in the base and in his team. He picked up a sense of camaraderie with the CO and he wanted to secure that relationship. He noticed a photograph of the CO standing near a motorcycle.

"Is that yours?"

"It is."

"Indian?"

"A classic. Still runs great, but I don't ride it like I used to."

"I have a Honda Gold Wing. I ride all the time."

"Really? Maybe you should ship it here. A lot of good rides out here."

"Thanks. Maybe. The team needs to see me making the same sacrifices they are making. They need to believe in what they are doing."

"That's honorable, but what they don't need is a boss who overworks himself and expects them to measure up."

"Nice thought, but we are under some pressure here. Time crunch."

"It's more than a nice thought. It's an order from me. Take care of your team and they will take care of you. It's kind of a motto here, and we have a good and effective team." The CO paused. "Tell you what, my bike is in the garage. Been there a couple years now. Come by tomorrow and I will have it here for you. You can use it while you are here."

"I'd be honored, Commander."

"It's my honor. Doctor. From what I hear, we need you and your team to save this country."

"We'll do our best."

"That is all you can do. Now, I suggest you head over to Building H. My design team is there. They will help you prep the hangar for the retrofit."

"Thank you, sir."

The nice thing about working with the military is that cost is never an issue so long as your program is on the docket. Once the shop is closed, everything about you shuts down no matter how much you spent or how close you are to generating deliverables. But so long as the shop is open, so long as the sign is lit up, you will get everything you need. Brian had been developing plans from the moment he was given the directive to proceed. He imagined the scenarios he would need to replicate and what protections would need to be in place before that could happen.

The nanobot research he did with Bost in the Silicon Valley was on a much smaller scale compared to defending against a multiple drone attack or nano-packed RPGs. Malmstrom AFB was famous for its ICBM missile silos maintained both at the base and around the state. Brian knew that he wanted a hangar dedicated to the effort and the base still had empty hangars available for use. He also wanted an empty silo and when he discussed it with the CO, the CO agreed immediately.

"There's an empty silo at the south end of the base. The missile in that silo was decommissioned."

"Ok. We are still formulating how we might use it, but I appreciate it staying in reserve while we are here."

"You got it."

Construction started quickly on the hangar. The entrance to the hangar was set up as office space with conference rooms and individual offices for team leaders including Brian. One conference room contained a large high-definition video wall. At the end of the hall past the offices, doors opened into changing rooms with lockers holding hazmat uniforms and anti-microbial gas masks. Adjacent to the changing rooms was a decontamination chamber that was the only way into and out of the lab. The lab was lined with vacuum chambers equipped with beam scanning electron microscopes with AI-driven pattern recognition and other AI-enabled tools for nanofabrication and 3D imaging. Each chamber contained a large LED monitor that was networked back to the LED video wall in the main conference room. The same conference room had a secured VPN that fed directly to the situation room in the White House and command and control centers in the Pentagon. Brian's team could hold simultaneous video meetings with generals at the Pentagon and White House officials.

In the first couple of weeks, as construction was proceeding, Brian held briefing sessions with the team in the open air at the entrance to the hangar. The air was clear and beautiful cumulus clouds dotted the sky. Brian took to traveling around the base on the Indian motorcycle.

"Where did you get the cool bike?" asked one of the lab techs named Francis.

"It's on loan," said Brian.

"It's beautiful. You and the CO becoming buds?"

Brian might have been irritated, but he'd given some thought to the CO's suggestion and his tone remained soft.

"The CO has been here a long time. We need to show him and every other officer here our utmost respect. Remember that you are on a military base and there is a strict code of conduct that all officers adhere to. So, no, Francis, we are not buds. But I trust him to support us while we are here, and he was kind enough to let me share his ride. And let me tell you," Brian said as he smiled, "it is a nice ride."

"Yes, sir," said Francis. "It is a cool ride." A couple people chuckled and many murmured in assent.

"Ok, people. To the task at hand," said Brian. "Talk to me first. Dr. Folsom."

Dr. Sandra Folsom described the research her team had been doing on toxicity and the body's defenses. She outlined traditional methods of poison management and the treatment of shock and anaphylaxis. In the context of a military engagement, carrying antidotes might be possible and effective but it was a limited tool that could be easily undermined by the exigencies of battle or other circumstances and depended on an adequate supply of the antidote. Brian pressed her on other tools and the only comprehensive alternative she offered was to develop a method of rendering military personnel immune to the toxic effects of the nanobots.

Typically, building immunity meant rigorous long-term engagement with varying levels of exposure, starting with microscopic doses and increasing doses as the immunity developed. The problem was that the immunity might be temporary. Unless the doses continued, the immunity could weaken and, again, in the context of a protracted battle or a remote posting, it would not be an effective solution.

Brian asked Dr. Folsom if a vaccine were possible, and she confirmed that her team had given thought to the idea but agreed that fighting the toxic effects of a nanobot was not the same as attacking a malevolent protein. Still, it was a line of thought worth developing.

Brian turned to his nanotechnology team led by an MIT professor recommended to Brian by Fred Schmidt named Dr. Sal Pinsky. Pinsky began his career in robotics after a successful stint in the now famous Battlebots competitions between Stanford and MIT. Pinsky's MIT team set a record for the most consecutive wins and Pinsky became famous for developing some of the earliest ambulatory robots capable of walking up stairs and balancing on rocky terrain. JPL was exploring using Pinsky robots on missions to Mars. But Pinsky became bored with humanoid robots and started exploring the world of microscopic robots. His work on nanomanufacturing processes was renown and recognized as a baseline for commercial applications.

Brian considered himself lucky to have snagged Sal Pinsky out of academia, and Pinsky was not only delighted to be working with Brian and his AI-infused nanobots, but also to be developing military applications of the science.

"Please, Sal," said Brian, "Go ahead."

"Well," he started, "because of the great work of Dr. Johannsen, we now can detoxify these nanobots. Detoxification is a major accomplishment. We are talking about battle-hardened nanobots – weaponized nanobots that are not only toxic but programmed to kill broadly and quickly. We face a host of issues and there is one solution that seems obvious, but we do not have it at our disposal."

Brian cut in, "Deterrence is not an option."

Sal continued. "Right, we can't simply develop our version of weaponized nanobots and threaten their use as a countermeasure. Our task is to develop alternative countermeasures. Countermeasures work because they recognize patterns in the actions of projectiles. To develop countermeasures, we first need to understand not only the behavior of nanobots, but the delivery systems, how they work, what are their patterns and behavior and effects. The truth is that we do not know a lot about this enemy, and we need to make some assumptions. From what we know, the enemy is not developing new delivery systems. Rather, they are using traditional delivery systems to spread the nanobots. Until we learn otherwise, we will be focusing on traditional delivery systems."

Brian cut in again. "Thank you, Sal. You are correct. We only have limited knowledge of this enemy, and we will be making assumptions until we learn more. That means our job will be to build a wholistic response to the use of weaponized nanobots, with systems that are flexible and can pivot quickly as we discover more about their use. We will start with what we know happened in Erro, Spain."

Brian flashed pictures up on a screen of the devastation in Erro. He showed streets lined with bodies and the bloated faces of dead children. The team groaned, but Brian said, "We need to understand what we are facing not only with the depravity of this enemy but the effects of the weaponized nanobots. We need to attack this scourge from both directions laid out by Drs. Folsom and Pinsky. Our medical teams will work on an antidote and a vaccine. Our technology teams will work on battle-ready countermeasures. The labs will be ready in one week. There is much work for you to do in the meantime. Time to get to it. Thank you for your attention. You are dismissed."

The team dispersed and a few asked Brian logistical questions. After they cleared out, Brian put on his helmet and got on the Indian. He drove the bike around the hangar, inspecting the hangar from the outside for repairs and made a few notes. Then he drove down to the silo and watched as hundreds of cadets worked to add the special protective measures that Brian required for its use. Finally, he headed to the front gate. The guard waved him through, and he took off following Interstate 15 south and then found Old U.S. 91, an older two-lane road that ran directly adjacent to the Missouri River. He stayed on the road all the way to Tower Rock State Park.

The air was clear, and the views of the mighty river and the looming Cascade Mountains were spectacular. The sky seemed to grow, spanning the 360 degrees of horizon around him. He was glad the military chose Malmstrom AFB for his team.

They would work hard, but they would know the joy of working in such a beautiful location.

The first few weeks were tough. It took time to get the residual Erro nanobots collected from Spain and shipped to Brian's team. In the meantime, Brian used the toxic nanobot gel that his team created at Ragnar Willowbrook from the original nanobots recovered from UCLA. The team had no idea whether those nanobots were like the Erro nanobots, but they moved forward anyway, hoping that any progress would be beneficial. Sandra's team seemed to be making the most progress because the directive was clear: Build an immunity platform. The medical community had developed multiple tools for countering the inflammatory effects of anaphylaxis beginning with epinephrine.

Sandra's team had been focused on allergy-based antidotes when one of the cadets working on a remote part of the air force base suffered the bite of a large diamondback rattlesnake. The bite and its treatment caused her to reflect on the potential for facing other toxins in the field and she ordered some of the strongest natural toxins known to be delivered to the base.

Brian reported to the Pentagon on Sandra's progress and the Pentagon immediately began manufacturing the various antidotes in large quantities for military use only. The team also started the complex work of developing a nanobot vaccine and Sandra suggested that they build a large data center on the base both for housing the existing large language models (LLMs) developed during COVID-19 that they needed to assist in formulating the new vaccine and for building new LLMs based on their progress. They learned, among other things, that the scientific community was already experimenting with lipid nanoparticles (LNPs) and nano-delivery vehicles to reach impacted tissues more quickly. They named the vaccine ErroVax after the Spanish town decimated by Belinda's weaponized nanobots.

Brian knew that Sandra's work, as important as it was, could not be the only response to weaponized nanobots. He had no guarantee that new types of toxic nanobots were not in development and no guarantees that the antidotes and vaccines would work against those new nanobots. Unfortunately, Sal was struggling. First, Brian's resistance to developing new delivery vehicles for weaponized nanobots was slowing down his ability to produce an effective countermeasure. Even though AI-generated simulations were helpful in visualizing different classes of responses, the ability to produce a working countermeasure required that some type of weapon to test the effectiveness of the countermeasure. Brian thought about using chemical weapons as a proxy, but the CO was resolute that the United States would not violate treaties forbidding the use and testing of chemical weapons. Several world bodies were already on the verge of classifying weaponized nanobots as a type of chemical weapon to bring its use under the umbrella of existing treaties and, if that happened, Brian's work would stop dead in its tracks. The Pentagon told Brian to ignore those efforts. It was too important to develop an effective response to the use of weaponized nanobots by terrorists.

Sal pressed his case.

"It won't work," he told Brian. "I need to build bombs."

"No bombs," said Brian.

"What about small bombs? IEDs? Nano-grenades?"

"No bombs."

"Bullets?"

"Christ, Sal. I'll think about bullets. But let me ask you this? What are your scenarios? We are not talking about developing the ability to pre-detonate weapons before they reach their targets. Exploding a nanobot missile over a small island in the Pacific could infect everyone in the vicinity of the explosion – islanders, fishermen, vacationers on cruise ships, or military personnel. We can't just destroy these weapons without causing the impacts that our systems need to prevent."

"That's not entirely true," said Sal. "First, we need to focus. Instead of imagining every kind of toxic nanobot and considering how we disable all those nanobots, we need to look at what we have in front of us. We now know the nanobots that were used in Spain are the same carbon-capture nanobots that we worked on at Ragnar Willowbrook and that almost killed you on Bainbridge Island. These nanobots were not built as toxic weapons. They just happened to be toxic to humans. We know that if they are released at high elevations, they will lose their toxicity simply by carrying out their mission, gathering excess CO_2 molecules out of the atmosphere. Similarly, delivery vehicles that are destroyed terrestrially but at distance from populations also lose their effect by the time they reach those populations. I think the effective use of existing antiballistics can work here but we need smart systems that recognize where those measures work and where they do not work."

Brian listened to Sal. He was making good arguments.

"Smart antiballistics is a good place to start and maybe worth discussing with the Pentagon. I agree we need smart antiballistics in the nano space. But terrorists act at close range. What are our solutions for close range engagement? The Secretary got excited about the detoxifying effects of our resonant coatings, but can our coatings work as a countermeasure? It doesn't make any sense to propose spraying a potential terror setting or even a combat setting with fake CO_2 prior to engagement. I don't see it."

"Right," said Sal. "That's where we are stuck."

Chapter 22.

Secrets

Sergeant Marisa Coldridge gathered her lesson plans and headed to the parking lot. Tomorrow's class focused on hostage training. Hostages posed some of the most difficult strategic and tactical issues in police work. The primary goal should be to save the lives of the hostages, but, like conceding to the demands of terrorists, you risk encouraging others to do the same and risk losing even more lives. The true goal was to save lives without making concessions. But were all concessions the same? Marisa took a mental stroll through the lesson. This lesson would be a good one. An SUV pulled up beside her and the driver rolled down the window.

"Sergeant Coldridge?"

"Yes?" She recognized him. "Detective Broad?"

Alvin responded, "Would you mind taking a ride with me?"

"I really need to get home."

"Please. It's important."

Marisa placed her materials in the back and crawled in next to Alvin.

"Do you like sushi?"

"Well, I had other plans, but sure."

Alvin drove through Elysian Park over to Chinatown.

"I'm sorry to catch you off guard like this, but I am concerned about Detective Eng."

"She approached me."

"She told me. Unfortunately, I've seen this scenario before. I'm afraid she is walking into a trap."

"You don't think she can take care of herself?"

"Not this time."

"What do you need me to do?"

They pulled up alongside a food truck called Sushi Sams.

"You like spicy tuna rolls?"

"Sure."

"Wait here."

Alvin jumped out of the car and was back in 10 minutes with three different kinds of rolls, wasabi, ginger and soy sauce and two bottles of Perrier. They drove over to the Los Angeles State Historic Park. Alvin found a table, and they spread out the meal.

"Is this our first date?" Marisa asked Alvin.

Alvin laughed. "Only if you like old police officers past their prime."

Marisa winked, "I can be flexible."

"You got me there. I can't even touch my knees anymore."

"Tai chi."

"I prefer a good book, but enough of this. I am very concerned."

"What do expect from me?"

"I'm not sure if you know but Detective Eng has IA interviewing dozens of police officers about the Scott Geiringer and Charles Darling murders. Not surprisingly no one has willingly come forward yet with any leads. I have doubts that IA is fully engaged in the investigation. Detective Eng pulled rank to force IA's hands."

"IA can be pretty shrewd."

"I need you to talk to your students."

"My students?"

"Scott was one of your students, right?"

"He was."

"Did you consider whether something happened here that followed him to the Bureau?"

"I did. I discussed that with Detective Eng, but I don't think a student killed Scott or Charles."

"I don't either. I want you to ask your students about interactions with active-duty officers."

Marisa sat for a moment without responding. Alvin could see she was processing the question.

"Fine," she said. "Now, unless you want to take me for a drink, I need to get home."

* * *

Van entered IA reception. She flashed her badge.

"No need," said the receptionist. "I know you, Detective. Caption Chang is in interview room B, down the hall and left at the corner."

"Thank you."

Van found the door and knocked. She heard, "Come in, it's not locked," and entered. Captain Chang and Officer Ben Bodrogi were sitting across from each other. One of Chang's deputies stood up and motioned for Van to sit. Van looked at Captain Chang. She turned to Officer Bodrogi.

"One minute, please, officer. Captain?" She motioned for Chang to speak with her outside the door. Chang stood and the deputy opened the door for them and then stayed in the room with Bodrogi. Van let it pass.

"Have you started the interview?" she asked Chang.

"We were just shooting the shit. Like I said, sometimes you need to warm someone up first. IA makes everyone nervous."

"So does the Bureau, but we don't warm up our suspects before interrogating them."

"Right, except our suspects are our employees. We need them to do their jobs. You'll forgive me if our methods are slightly different than yours. Now, shall we conduct the interview?"

"Did you start the tape?"

"The tape will start when you start your questioning."

Van was miffed. She had the sense that Chang was prepping Bodrogi, not just warming him up, but she had no way of knowing for sure.

"Fine."

They returned to the room.

"Officer Ben Bodrogi, correct?"

"Yes."

"Are you aware of the investigation into the murders of two LAPD detectives, Detective Scott Geiringer and Detective Charles Darling?"

Bodrogi shifted nervously and looked at Captain Chang.

"I am aware of the investigation."

"My name is Detective Van Eng and I have been tasked with leading this investigation. I understand that you spoke to IA previously on this matter."

"That's correct."

"Do you recall what you told them?"

"I told them I didn't know anything."

"Do you mean you don't know who might be connected to the murders?"

"I don't know anything, really. I don't know where the murders took place. I don't know how they died. I don't know who shot them."

"Why do you think they were shot?"

Captain Chang shuffled in his chair and Bodrogi once again looked at him and then back at Van.

"I guess that's typical. Right?"

"Of murder?" Van said. "I wouldn't say it is typical."

"I just mean…I guess I assumed they were shot."

"Do you recall anything else you said to IA in the first interview?"

"I think I said something about issues at home."

"Why did you say that?"

"They noticed I was nervous, just like I am here. I explained I was bugged by some personal problems."

"Are you bugged by personal problems today?"

"They haven't gone away if that's what you think."

"Ben," said Van. "Two detectives were murdered. They were both members of our family. You agree that is not acceptable, right?"

"Yes."

"You say you don't know anything, but that is not true, is it?"

"It's true."

"It's not true. You know they were shot. I need you to tell me what you know. You understand that if you lie today and we learn that you were not telling the truth, your career as a police officer is over and your chances of doing anything in your life other than driving for Uber is completely shot."

Van looked at Captain Chang.

"I'm not even sure you can drive for Uber," she added. "You need to come clean now. This is you last shot."

"I really don't know anything," he said. He looked at Chang almost pleading. Chang didn't respond.

Van asked, "Why do you keep looking at him? I'm the one asking the questions. What is he going to do? Do you need him to rescue you?"

Captain Chang stepped in. "Focus on the interview, Detective. Not me."

Van brushed it off. "Where were you the night of Scott Geiringer's death?"

"I was on patrol."

"Alone or with a partner?"

"With my partner?"

"Who is your partner?"

"Officer John Scott." Van took a note.

"Do you recall any specifics?"

"No, but I can check my log."

"What about the day Charles Darling was murdered?"

"I think I was off that day."

"Do you recall what you were doing?"

"Probably watching football."

"Is there anyone who can corroborate that?"

"I tend to spend my off days alone."

"Your answer is no."

Bodrogi was clearly unsettled.

"My answer is no."

"Did you know Detective Darling?"

"I did not."

"Did you call Detective Darling?"

"I don't think so."

Van bluffed. "Then why is your name on his phone?"

Bodrogi looked shocked. "That can't be!" he said.

"Why is that?"

"Uh…because I never called him."

"Fine." Van turned to Captain Chang. "I am terminating this interview." She looked back at Bodrogi. "You should consider getting an attorney, Officer."

She rose and stood at the door. No one moved. She looked at the deputy and he jumped to the door to open it for Van. Officer Bodrogi was fighting back tears. Captain Chang motioned to Officer Bodrogi with his hand to calm down. Then he left the room with Van. They went to Chang's office. He closed the door.

"Kind of rough on him, Detective."

"He's lying," said Van. "He knows something, and he is going to tell us."

Chang took a breath. "Your call, Detective."

The next day, Van returned to the Franklin Canyon Reservoir location where Charlie had died. The reservoir had more water in it now, and as Van looked over the cliff where he fell, she could not see the bottom of the reservoir. She preferred visiting this spot rather than Charlie's grave. The gravesite was the end of Charlie. The reservoir was his last stand, and she could imagine him fighting back even as his assailants got the best of him. Forensics long ago had surveyed the location and found no helpful evidence, not even shoe prints. Whoever killed Charlie knew how to cover up a scene and that fact alone would have caused Van to focus on police suspects despite her conversation with Sergeant Coldridge at the Academy and her discussion with Alvin at CHESS. Still, those interactions hung with her. She might have been inclined to search for a single disgruntled officer who was trying to cover up the first murder by killing Charlie. She had a distaste for conspiracy theories, but she trusted Alvin, and the Sergeant's arguments came across as credible.

Then, out of nowhere, a bullet zipped by her head, barely missing her and lodging in a tree behind her. The noise surprised her, and as she was gathering her senses, a second bullet ripped open her shoulder, and she jumped up to run. The bullets seemed to be coming from across the reservoir, but at this point Van didn't have time to think. She just ran. The path was steep and rocky, and she almost tripped more than once. She opened the driver's side door and dove in as a barrage of bullets hit the side of the car and broke the windows. She pressed the "on" button and hit the gas and almost lost control of the car as she sped away ducking below the steering wheel.

Her heart raced. What was going on? She told no one she was heading to the reservoir. How would they know? She looked at her shoulder. The bullet had torn the skin open, and it was bleeding badly. She entered the term *hospital* in her car's navigation system and found the Hollywood Hospital. She pulled into the ER drop-off and called Alvin and told him what had happened. He agreed to meet her there. She asked him to call Forensics and have them take the car back to SID and search the car for bullet fragments. She jumped out of the car and flashed her detective badge, and the staff escorted her immediately to critical care just as she was about to faint. A physician's assistant helped her into an examining chair and started working on her shoulder until the attending physician entered the room. The doctor determined that there was no damage to the bone and no bullet fragments lodged in the wound. She gave Van some pain medication and a tetanus shot and sutured up the wound before leaving for another patient. The assistant asked Van to relax and wait in the chair until her blood pressure lowered, and to wait until the doctor determined that she was ready to leave.

While Van waited for the doctor to return, she called the Chief on his cell phone.

"Detective."

"Hi, Chief. I am calling to tell you I'm ok, but I've been shot."

"Where are you?" he responded. "Do you need help? What happened?"

"I'm in the ER in Hollywood and I'm fine. I was at the Franklin Canyon Reservoir and barely escaped a hail of bullets. I don't know who fired them

and, more importantly, I don't know how anyone might have known I was there."

"Do you think it is related to the investigation?"

"There is no other plausible explanation."

"Shit. Let me think." He paused, then said, "I need to pull you off the case, Van. It's too dangerous."

"No!" she pled with the Chief. "Please don't. I am getting close, and I think this is proof."

"I'm not going to lose another detective."

Van was quiet for a minute. Then she said, "You can't stop this investigation."

"I agree, but we need to think this through. Maybe IA is better suited to follow through than the Detective Bureau."

Van wasn't in the mood to fight, especially with the Chief.

"Ok," she said. "IA can take over. But I'd like to talk to Captain Chang about it."

"Not a problem," he said. "Chang can call me later if he has questions."

"Thank you, sir."

"Get better quickly. We need you active."

"Yes, sir."

Van called Captain Chang.

"Detective?"

"Yes, Captain, this is Detective Eng."

"Is it important? I'm sorry but now is not a good time. It's my daughter's birthday party and we have guests."

"My apologies, Captain, but I'm at Hollywood Hospital. I've been shot."

"Oh, my god," he said shocked. "Are you ok? I'm so sorry."

"I'm stitched up and yes, thank you, I am ok. Look. I just spoke to the Chief. He is concerned about my safety and is taking me off the case."

"That doesn't seem right," said Chang. "You may be getting close."

"Maybe, maybe not. Perhaps you were right. It is possible my approach is wrong. Maybe I am too aggressive. Ultimately, I agree that this is an internal issue and that perhaps IA should have taken it from the beginning."

"I'm not going to disagree, but decisions were made and no question you are too important to the case to drop out."

"I'll think about that. I want the investigation to continue, but the Chief really wants it handled by your team."

"I will speak with him."

"Thanks. Let me know if you need anything from me. My notes. Anything."

"Will do. God, I am so sorry. I hope you get better quickly."

"I think there's a mandatory leave for something like this. It may be a few weeks before I am back in touch."

"Understood."

"Tell your daughter happy birthday."

Van hung up. While she was waiting, she started to plan. Alvin arrived in a few minutes and flashed his badge so they would allow him into the ICU to see Van. He looked at her bandaged wound.

"You're lucky," he said. "You know I was worried about this. I have great respect for you, Van, but you seemed a bit cavalier in your approach."

"Thanks, Alvin. I know I'm lucky, especially sitting here waiting for a doctor's clearance."

"You scared me. Charlie was a great detective and even he walked into something he should not have."

"The Chief has already told me he is taking me off the investigation and giving it to IA."

"You're better than IA, Van. But I think he is right. I'd rather have you around," said Alvin.

"The Chief will put me on leave until I am healed. Hopefully, IA makes some progress."

"Agreed. I do need to share something with you."

"What?"

"I went to the Academy and spoke to Sergeant Marisa Coldridge."

"You did?"

"Yes. I asked her to talk to her students."

"Why?"

"Just a hunch."

"Will you to tell me what she finds out?"

"Sure, I can do that. But don't be surprised if you get a call from Coldridge."

"I'm off the case, Alvin."

"Right. Don't be surprised."

Chapter 23.

No Vacancy

The Chief placed Van on leave for three months. The first few weeks after the incident she rested at home and recuperated. The doctor suggested she start physical therapy as soon as the stitches were removed. She contacted her best friend Kimmie and, after three weeks, Van was back at the gym, working with Kimmie strengthening her shoulder. Therapy was painful at first. The bullet ripped a part of the muscle and scar tissue began to form. Kimmie worked with Van to preserve her range of motion before starting any strength training. By the sixth week, Van was using her arm with minimal pain and by the eighth week the pain was gone. Kimmie began to press Van into competing again at the Muscle Beach contest in Venice. Van resisted knowing she was not in competition shape as she had been previously, and she wasn't interested in training hard just for a Muscle Beach show. Kimmie was still competing, so she asked Van to join her as a guest. It wasn't the first time Kimmie had asked her, but Van had been consumed by work and couldn't take the time. Now that she was on leave, Van had some extra time, and she loved Kimmie and wanted to support her.

They arrived early, and Kimmie took Van to the registration booth to see big Johnny B, who jumped out of the booth and gave her a bear hug. It hurt her shoulder a little, but she didn't say anything and hugged him back.

"Van! So good to see you!" he said. "You look amazing, better than before. Why are you not competing?"

Then to Kimmie he said, "Hello, darling. Why don't you get Van a bikini? We have extra back here. She should be part of the competition."

Kimmie shrugged her shoulders and Van said, "Thank you, Johnny. Very kind of you, but no, thank you. Not this time. I'm here for Kimmie."

Johnny B laughed and said, "Of course. Kimmie is smoking hot. She will do great!" He walked back to the registration and turned and waved. Kimmie took Van to her seat in the reserved section behind the stage and left to warm up.

Van sat there looking at all the people around her. It was a strange crew, but there was something in the air that she envied. These people all seemed to be ultra fit, whether they were competing or not. It reminded Van of waking early for her runs in the dark and her regular work outs with Kimmie before she became a detective. She examined her arms. She was still in pretty good shape, but nothing like Kimmie and the people around her. The older muscle guys fascinated her. She wondered what it took to be so dedicated to a single activity for so many years just to keep your body in perfect condition. She wandered back to the open workout area and watched as the contestants worked their muscles into show mode. Kimmie seemed relaxed. She had been around this crew so much that she blended in. The competitions no longer concerned her. She used it to have fun and flirt with the audience, who always loved her. Today was the same. Kimmie got second place in her competition and got another big hug from Johnny B. Van grabbed her bag of goodies from the event and walked over to Kimmie.

"Congrats, baby girl!" said Van. "Nice show."

"You should have been out there," she said. "Even without working out, you still would have taken it."

"That's a lie," Van replied laughing. "But it's a nice lie."

"What are you doing now?"

"I was planning on going home. My mom needs some help with dinner."

"No, she doesn't," said Kimmie. "Your mom's the master. But she is cooking for you, right?"

"Yes, she is."

"I have some friends meeting me in West Hollywood later. Why don't you join us after dinner?"

"That does sound nice. Martin is busy on a movie they are filming in Canada somewhere. I'd love to join you."

"Dress up a little," said Kimmie. "We may head to a party."

Mom made pork bellies and crab soup for dinner. Her pork bellies were the best in Southern California – not too crunchy, just the right amount of fat and the spice was perfect. Van loved her pork bellies more than anything else Mom cooked. Van finished her plate.

"Eat more," said Mom. "You are too skinny."

"Come on, Mom. I ate the right amount. I'm full now."

"Your dad is too fat. You need to eat more, or he will finish them."

"What?!" said Dad. "I weigh 145 pounds. How skinny do you want me to be?"

"Skinny," said Mom. "Better for your heart."

Van leaned over and with her chopsticks picked up one more pork belly and forced it down.

"Happy?" she said looking at Mom.

"You must eat, Daughter," she said. "Too skinny and you will not attract a husband. You are getting older."

"Oh, my god, Mom," said Van. "I love you, but that's enough. I am going out tonight. Maybe I will find a man."

"Good girl," said Mom. "Find a good man. That Martin. I am not so sure about him."

"Geez," said Van and left the table. Mom and Dad continued to bicker as Van knew was their manner despite their love for each other.

Van met Kimmie and her friends at Sushi Park. They were laughing and already had their share of sake. Van ordered Nigori and joined in on the fun. Everyone wanted to know about Martin Richard. What was his latest movie? Was she worried about his A-list co-stars working with him? Had he proposed yet? Van responded politely and said nothing about Martin's off-the-cuff proposal. A well-known actor, famous for his role as a detective in several TV series, approached the table.

"You ladies seem to be having fun even without a man."

Kimmie shot back, "You think it takes a man to have fun?"

"No, no, I didn't mean that," he said a bit flustered. The people he was seated with were watching. "I'm just saying you look like a fun group." He pointed to his table. "We were thinking of heading to a party and wondered if you might join us."

"Is this one of those shady parties?" asked Kimmie's friend seated next to her.

"Not at all," he responded.

"That's too bad," she said. "I like shady parties."

"Well, you got me there. I don't know if it qualifies as shady." He leaned closer to her as if to whisper but loud enough for everyone to hear, "You need a password to get in."

Kimmie shouted. "If that's the case, we're all in!" She looked at Van for confirmation. Van was skeptical but not opposed.

"Great!" he responded. "Do you want to ride with us?"

Van said, "Thanks but we will drive ourselves."

Kimmie put on a fake pouty face. Van asked, "Where is it?"

"Not too far from here," he said, walking back to his table. "You familiar with a bar called No Vacancy on Hollywood Boulevard?"

"Of course," said Kimmie. "Everyone knows No Vacancy. You going to tell us the password?"

"Oh, right. Stupid." He walked back over to Kimmie and whispered in her ear. She gave him a quizzical look and said, "Strange, but ok."

After he left, Kimmie's friends pressed in close. "What did he say?" they whispered.

"Virgin."

Van asked Kimmie, "What is No Vacancy?"

Kimmie smiled. "You will love this place. No Vacancy is a house that was converted into a bar/nightclub. It used to be a school for young children, and celebrities like Charlie Chaplin sent their kids there. The house was on Hollywood Boulevard but at some point, it was moved off the street about 100 yards. It is kind of hidden."

"Is it open to the public?"

"If they don't have special events, I think so."

"Do we want to do this?"

Everyone at the table shouted, "Yes! Of course!"

"Ok," said Van, not entirely convinced, "let's do this."

Hollywood Boulevard was busy, and traffic crept along slowly. The sidewalks were packed with people who had found expensive parking and were enjoying the stroll past the Roosevelt Hotel, the Kodak Theatre, Graumann's and the corner at Hollywood and Vine. Hudson was on the east end of the Boulevard, and it took Van and Kimmie more than a half hour to navigate the traffic to Hudson. They valeted the car in front of a three-story house-like structure with a large hotel sign that flashed No Vacancy.

"Even getting into this place is fun," said Kimmie. They walked up stairs to the third level and saw three doors.

"You choose which door you think is right and go in. If you choose incorrectly, the stairs lead you back outside."

While Van waited, Kimmie and her friends ran into door number 1 and took the staircase there back outside. Laughing, they climbed up again and took door number 3 and called Van to join them. As they entered, they met a young woman was sitting in a nightgown on a small bed in a small bedroom. They piled into the bedroom and Kimmie yelled, "Virgin!" The woman smiled knowingly and said, "At least you are honest." Kimmie started to respond, "Isn't that the…" and the woman interrupted her and declared, "Welcome to No Vacancy." She raised a small umbrella she was holding and the bed she was on pulled away from the wall revealing an opening onto another staircase. The group squeezed into the entrance and down the stairs into a beautiful old-fashioned bar.

"That was fun," they told each other and ordered drinks.

Kimmie was still confused. "Did she take the password?" she asked Van.

"It didn't look like it to me," said Van. "I don't know. Maybe."

They found a small patio outside. The bar was not very full yet, but the evening was young. A DJ spun some popular songs, and they decided to dance even though no one was on the dance floor. After a half dozen songs, they all were tired and a little sweaty and took a break. Van was enjoying the evening and started to relax. Her concern about accepting a stranger's invitation to party was lightening up.

Someone tapped her on the shoulder.

"Excuse me, but have we met?"

Van turned and, there he was, the stranger.

"I don't believe so," she said. "Not formally, anyway."

"Weren't you just at Sushi Park in West Hollywood?" She could tell he was questioning his move.

"Yes, and my friends are here with me per your invitation."

"Ahh. Phew. I thought I might be making a mistake."

Kimmie came running from the bar.

"Our friends are here!" she shouted to her crew all of whom were getting another drink.

"Mine too," he said. "My apologies to you, ma'am. My name is Robert Gibbens."

"Gibbens?" Van replied. "I've heard of you. Real estate?"

"That and other things," he replied. "And you are?"

"Van Eng. I'm the third wheel here."

"You are not," said Kimmie. "Van is very special and my very best friend."

"Let me buy you all drinks," said Robert and motioned for his friends to join him.

"I'm fine, thanks," said Van. "Taking a break."

Robert introduced his friends, most of whom had some connection to Hollywood or the music industry or both. Robert seemed to be paying for everything. Kimmie talked about her gym and her involvement with Muscle Beach competitions. Robert was surprised that Muscle Beach was still a thing and Kimmie bragged about Van's win in the competition a couple years back.

Van returned the favor this time showering Kimmie with praise for her dedication.

She also talked about the age range and flattered Robert by suggesting that he seemed to be in good shape and probably could contend. Robert laughed and, as if on cue, so did his friends which cut his laugh short, and he stared at them.

"What? You don't think I could be a contender at Muscle Beach?"

They quickly reversed course. "No. Yes. For sure."

He laughed and Van watch as they relaxed.

"I'm kidding. Me? Are you kidding?"

This group was a strange brew.

Kimmie then said. "Hey, you told us the password was Vir…" Robert immediately put his fingers to his lips.

"Shhh. It's a password guys. It's just for you."

"But…" Kimmie pressed. "I used it at the entrance. Kinda didn't seem necessary."

He smiled. "She'll know it, but it's not a password to get in here."

"What is it?"

Robert looked to his buddies. "You guys ready?"

"Damn straight. Let's do this."

Alarms were going off in Van's brain. But she was also curious.

"What are we talking about?"

"Follow me," said Robert. He gathered everyone together and walked them to a small room behind the bar on the second floor. He motioned to the bartender to come over and whispered in his ear. He pressed a button, and the floor started to move. Robert reached out and pulled Van back a step.

"I wouldn't stand there."

Under the floor was a stairwell. Robert motioned to Van, Kimmie and her friends to follow. Robert's friends waited as if they had been there before. Van could see a kind of greedy look in their eyes and wished she had her gun. But she was committed and whatever this was, she wanted to find out more.

Robert tapped on the door and a red light flashed above the door. Someone opened a peephole, and Van could hear Robert say "Virgin." The red light turned green and the door open into a long narrow hallway.

Van turned to Kimmie.

"This could be dangerous," she whispered. "Are you ok to follow this guy?"

Kimmie looked at Van and leaned up to her ear. "I think it's ok. If they want something we don't want to give them, we can just leave. He's got money and some of these guys are pretty." She smiled.

Van laughed. "Uhh. I don't know. Let's have each other's backs."

"Done," said Kimmie. "Now, my too-serious friend. Let's have some fun!" Then, as she passed the man at the door, she winked at him and whispered, "Virgin." He didn't react.

Robert led them into the hallway. Van could smell the mustiness of an underground tunnel. They walked for several hundred yards. Van tracked their direction as best she could. It seemed they were heading away from Hollywood Boulevard. They walked up a steep stairway and then onto another hall as they turned East. They walked for another several hundred yards before the hallway expanded and Van saw double doors.

She leaned up to Robert as they approached the doors.

"Don't you think we could have driven here?"

He looked at her with a dark expression and then laughed. "There's no parking."

She didn't respond but she thought, *Is there a street?*

Robert knocked on the double doors. They entered and the dank hallway was replaced by over-the-top luxury. The walls were crushed velvet, and the floor had a deep red carpet. Robert led them to a cloak room window with an attendant. He turned back to Van.

"We wear masks here. Part of the fun."

Van walked to the window.

"Your phone, please," said the attendant.

"I think I would rather keep it," she said.

"Your phone or you leave. Now, please."

Robert interceded.

"It's fine. There are famous people here. It's for their protection."

Van hesitated but handed her phone over and got a ticket and a mask. Everyone else did the same. A second set of doors parted into a large dimly lit room where people wearing masks were dancing to what sounded to Van like a famous DJ. Waiters at the door were handing out champagne. Robert grabbed a champagne glass and brought it to Van.

"You need to relax," he said. "This is where the real party starts."

The noise made it hard for her to hear through her hearing aids.

"What did you say?"

Robert smiled and handed her the glass. Then he turned and disappeared.

Van took the glass and sipped it. It tasted good, and she was thirsty from the hike over. Van saw Kimmie moving to the dance floor. A couple of Robert's guys went with her.

Van moved quickly to join Kimmie. She started dancing and could feel her guard coming down. The guy she was with was very handsome and looked silly in a mask. He looked familiar to her, and she leaned close to him and said, "Don't I know you?"

He smiled. "You probably do." She couldn't hear him but smiled and pulled away dancing.

He grabbed her hand and led her off the dance floor. Van felt dizzy but let him lead her. She turned back to see Kimmie getting a bit too close to the guy she was dancing with and Van let it go. Mr. Handsome found a couch on a platform overlooking the dance floor. They sat down and he started kissing her. It felt nice. After a few minutes he stood and led her to a stairway. She started to resist.

"Where are we going?"

"Come on, babe," he said.

"Um, excuse me but not your babe," she replied.

He pulled her to continue up the stairs. She tried to let go. He grabbed harder, and she shouted, "No!" Several people turned and watched her.

"Ok," he said and threw her hand down. "Screw you, anyway," he said as he disappeared.

Van was little shaken up. A couple women near her came over.

"Are you ok, hon?" they asked.

"I'm fine," she said.

"That dude's a jerk. We've seen him here before. He thinks just because he is famous, he can get whatever he wants."

They brought her a glass of water, and she gulped it down. They seemed to want to watch her, but she repeated that she was fine, and they left her alone.

Van looked out over the dance floor for Kimmie. Thankfully she was still there but seemed pretty much into the guy she was with. Van decided she wanted to leave. She walked over to Kimmie and tapped her on the shoulder. Kimmie turned and hugged her.

"Time for me to go," Van said.

"Oh, no, not yet," Kimmie pleaded.

"You can stay," she said, "as long as you feel safe."

"Glenn here's a gem. Totally nice guy. I'm fine," she shouted a little too loud as the music stopped.

"Ok," said Van. She pretended to hold her phone to her ear. "Call me."

Van looked around the room. She remembered where she came in and headed in that direction. She passed some stairs but ignored them and headed for the exit. Something made her stop. She turned back and at the entrance to the stairs she saw a dark figure wearing a mask. He seemed to be guarding access to the staircase. She ducked behind a column to watch. A door behind the staircase opened and she saw what looked to be a group of young pre-teenagers, boys and girls, being shepherded onto the stairway by men and women. They were dressed in Halloween costumes like they were going to a party, but something was odd about the scene. One of the boys pulled away and a woman grabbed him and pushed him up the stairs. Van checked for her phone and remembered that she left it at the entrance. The kids went upstairs but the figure stayed behind. Then, after about 10 minutes, he checked his watch and left.

Van made her way back to the staircase. She looked around. No one seemed interested. She started up the stairs still watching, expecting someone to run over and stop her but no one came.

The top of the stairs opened on to a short hallway. She could hear noises that sounded like girls giggling. Suddenly a figure emerged from a door at the end of the hallway walking with one of the costumed children. Van couldn't tell if it was a boy or a girl, but she had no doubt what was happening. She made her way slowly toward the door. The door opened again and this time she could see people in various stages of undress. A handful of adults were disrobing the children. Most of them seemed oblivious to her presence as if they were in a drug induced haze. She caught a glimpse of Robert with his shirt off stroking the hair of a young girl. As she edged toward the door, a young man appeared in the doorway walking with a young boy. He didn't recognize Van under her mask, and he smiled and said, "Come on in. The water's fine." It was Ben Bodrogi.

Van fell back against the wall. Ben walked down the hall and pulled the boy into a room. She looked back in the large room and recognized several people, a handful of whom were LAPD. She made a quick mental note and then looked over and saw Robert staring at her. He pointed to someone across the room and then pointed at her. She turned and walked back down the hall and quickly down the stairs, feeling nauseated. The dark figure at the foot of the stairs was back, talking into a handset. She walked past him, and he didn't respond. The closer she got to the exit, the faster she moved. The entrance area was crowded. She squeezed her way up to the cloak room attendant.

"My phone, I need it now."

"Ticket, please."

She turned and saw three men in suits making their way through the crowd in her direction. The cloak room attendant took forever but finally handed her a phone. The men had almost reached her. She moved quickly to the exit and out into the hallway. More people were entering the underground club. Van snaked her way past the crowd and into the hallway. As soon as she reached it, she took off running. She reached the long steep stairs when she heard the men behind her. Bullets ricocheted off the concrete walls. She thought she was going to fall but she kept running. When she got to the bottom of the stairs, she saw a hallway on her the right. She figured it wasn't the right route and that she might have to make her way back but, maybe, she hoped, her chasers would assume she went straight. She took off down the right hallway. It seemed to go on forever. When she ran out of breath, she stopped to listen for anyone who might be behind her. She heard nothing. Rather than turn back, she decided to keep walking. The tunnel went on for another mile before she saw a doorway. She tried to open it, but it was locked. She knocked on the door but there was no answer, so she kept walking. Finally, she saw a pair of double doors and a guard.

She ran up to him.

"I'm so sorry but I was trying to get home, and I think I am lost. I have been walking forever."

"You are lucky," he said. "You can get stuck down here for days. Where did you come from?"

"I was looking for No Vacancy. That's where we entered."

"No Vacancy!" he said surprised. "That's almost a mile east of here. You'd have to turn around and go back where you came from."

"I just want to get out of this crazy tunnel system. Can you help me out?"

"I'm not supposed to, but you don't look so well."

"I don't feel so well," said Van.

"You're in the basement of the Roosevelt Hotel. Go in here and turn left. That will take you to the parking garage and you can exit out the back through the garage."

"Thank you so much," said Van. "I am really grateful."

"It's okay, sweetheart. If you get lost, just come back to me. I will help you out."

"I'm so relieved. I won't forget this."

"Happy to help, darling."

Van found her way out of the hotel. They were holding a special event. She felt disheveled and exhausted and wanted to get past the celebrities and looky-loos as fast as she could. She called an Uber as soon as she got outside. The driver picked her up in just a couple minutes. Van didn't care about her loaner car from the Department. She left it at the club and took the Uber straight home. She thought about the children and found it hard not to cry.

Chapter 24.

Drones

Belinda returned in the SUV to Muro de Roda. Her team was careful to watch for tails, including drones, but Belinda had successfully evaded Interpol's efforts to capture her in Pamplona, and it appeared no one saw her get into the SUV. She went directly to her underground loft to clean up and rest when she heard a knock.

"We have news."

Belinda was not in the mood. "It can wait."

"I'm afraid it can't," said Assad Jazairi. "We received word that CNI took over Hadj's interrogation. Hadj was shot and killed."

Belinda steeled herself. "You are certain?" she said without emotion.

"Not entirely."

"What do we know?"

"ETA has contacts in prison."

"We are talking to ETA?"

"No."

"You need to explain."

"Pablo's brother is ETA. He overheard his brother talking about an Algerian named Arjoun killed in prison by security."

It occurred to Belinda the information was suspect, but if CNI was torturing Hadj, she knew he would hold out and probably die in the effort. She thought about her parents and how they probably died.

"Leave me," she said.

The next morning, Belinda called the team leaders together. "What do we know about drones?" she asked. The answer, as she expected, was very little.

"We need a better delivery mechanism, something more effective than glass canisters. Something that can pinpoint a target and then return to base and be reused."

Pablo was present in the meeting. "I've seen drones with cameras in the electronics stores."

"Go to Pamplona tomorrow. Take the back roads and pick up a half dozen camera drones. We need to understand how they work."

Pablo was back the next day with drones ranging in size from a few inches to almost a full meter. Belinda and the team learned how to use them. They were impressed with the quality of the video and the ease with which they maneuvered the drones in very tight spaces even without being able to see the drones. Belinda pulled in the ballistics team and outfitted the drones with miniature nanobot explosives. They worked on the control software, and Belinda knew she missed Hadj and his technical brilliance. She pressed forward regardless, and her team was able to complete the re-engineering. They started testing the drones on the enclosed firing range. They trapped rodents from the nearby fields and set up obstacles. Belinda was pleased with the precision kills but knew something was missing. One of her junior staff members proposed applying artificial intelligence, but Belinda had no one on staff trained in AI who could use it effectively. She also was concerned about a potential security breach if they used the AI tools that were available online, so she scuttled the idea. Besides, she knew that the effect of a few targeted strikes might be sufficient to trigger the uprising she was still counting on. She didn't need super smart weapons.

Her new target was CNI. She wanted the satisfaction of retaliating for Hadj's death but, more importantly, she wanted to prove the vulnerability of the Spanish government. She doubted they had developed an effective countermeasure. Even the drones they used in Pamplona weren't smart enough to follow her back to Roda. She doubted they would recognize an incoming drone attack, especially if the drones were small. She instructed the team to find the parts and build dozens of weaponized mini drones.

She also knew that if she would be going to attack CNI, she needed better intelligence. She called Pablo to her office.

"How exactly did you learn about Hadj's death?"

"I overheard someone talking about it."

"Are you certain they were talking about Hadj?"

"Pretty certain. They were talking about Erro and mentioned an Algerian named Arjoun."

"Did they say what happened?"

"Not specifically. They knew Basque authorities had captured him, but that CNI stepped in after Erro and were interrogating him when he died."

"Did they kill him?"

"They thought they did."

"Who is it you were listening to?"

Pablo hesitated.

"This is important, Pablo. Who was talking about Hadj?"

"My brother is ETA."

"Does your brother know what you are doing?"

"Not at all. He thinks I work at camps for kids."

"You haven't said anything about our operations? Maybe accidentally? Let it slip?"

"No. Never."

"Do you think he was telling you so you would tell me?"

"No one knows who you are."

This time Belinda paused. "That's no longer true. They found me in Pamplona. Someone affiliated with Interpol."

Pablo started to shake. "I promise. I have not said a word. My brother wasn't talking to me. He was talking to his friends at a bar. I just happened to be along for the ride."

"I need something from you, Pablo."

"Anything. I live to serve you."

"I need you to use your brother to help you infiltrate ETA. I need to know what they know about CNI and how they know it. I need to know CNI's plans, and I am guessing ETA has a plant."

"I can do that," said Pablo.

"I'm counting on it, Pablo. I need you to come through just as you did before."

"Yes, sir…ma'am."

The Basque Separatist Movement known as ETA formally dissolved in 2018. Following ETA's dissolution, CNI continued to chase splinter groups to prevent new cells from committing new acts of terror. The Erro incident caught them off guard. There was no intelligence suggesting anything like the Erro mass murder was even possible. During the CNI clean-up of ETA, CNI convinced certain past members of ETA to assist CNI as assets.

Pablo's brother, Antton, was one of these assets who, due to his position, was privy to certain CNI intelligence, such as the torture and death of Hadj Arjoun. Belinda suspected that someone with intimate knowledge of ETA activities might be on the CNI payroll. In fact, when Pablo approached Antton about joining the ETA under the mistaken impression that Antton supported the ETA, Pablo was surprised when Antton tried to discourage Pablo. Pablo persisted, and only after Antton realized his resistance was futile did he help Pablo make contact. But as his did, he warned Pablo that CNI operatives had infiltrated ETA and to be very cautious about his activities.

At this point, ETA was hardly more than a social club. Disarmed, discouraged and mostly disbanded, very few Basque separatists took pride in being a part of ETA, and Pablo found himself at the center of multiple bitch sessions, listening to complaints that ETA no longer served any purpose and had effectively given up. The only benefit of the bitch sessions was that it included complaints about CNI. CNI had made numerous false arrests of alleged splinter group members only to learn that the splinter groups were no more than poker nights with the buddies. These false arrests sowed dissent and mistrust of CNI and, even though ETA had long lost the taste for Spanish blood, the member complaints of CNI were profuse. Pablo reported his discoveries back to Belinda. Belinda wanted to know ETA's impressions of Erro, and to her chagrin, Pablo reported that his ETA contacts were more inclined to believe the incident was caused by a gas leak from a local mine. No one suspected ETA of the heinous act. Belinda told Pablo to focus on identifying the locations of CNI safe houses and agent activities. Pablo began inserting himself into CNI discussions. He asked for details about the death of the Algerian. He asked where it happened and where else the CNI took their suspects for interrogation. He learned about three safe houses in Pamplona that were used as makeshift detention centers and reported the locations back to Belinda.

Belinda used the information to formulate a revenge plan using her new drones. Her team loaded up the SUVs with the weaponized drones and took them to the heliport where Belinda kept her disguised military helicopters. Late at night, they placed a dozen drones into cargo containers ferried by the helicopters. They flew the containers to a location within a few miles of the city. The helicopters set the containers in a field and Belinda's team at Roda remotely opened the lids. The drone operators took over. They started the drones and turned on the cameras. The drones separated into three groups of four and each group headed to a different safe house, including the safe house where Hadj died. The operators hovered the drones near each house and waited. Then, in unison, each group sent in the first drone. That drone was equipped with a device that would explode near an exposed wall creating holes large enough for the drones to penetrate the house. The remaining drones flew through the opening searching for CNI agents. They separated and flew upstairs and downstairs. Each time they identified an agent, they emitted a small burst of toxic nanobots and in minutes the agent was dead.

In the second safe house, Agent Victor Gomez was sleeping, dreaming about a beach vacation with his family. The drone hovered over his head. He heard a buzzing sound and opened his eyes. A red light blinded him, and he shielded his face, uncertain what he was seeing. The drone sent a short burst of nanobots above his head. Victor swung his arm at the drone trying to knock it out of the air. He missed and reached for his gun on the bedside table. Suddenly his throat tightened up and he realized he couldn't breathe. He tried to sit up. He called out for other agents but couldn't speak. He started firing his gun into the ceiling to get their attention, but no one responded. He looked for the drone and fired randomly around the room trying to hit the drone. But the drone was already gone. He stood up choking and then collapsed on the floor.

In a separate safe house, Agent Vanessa Christian was awake in the kitchen waiting for her coffee to brew. She had trouble sleeping ever sense the failed attempt to capture Belinda and a midnight cup of decaf had become a routine. She had expected to be returned to Washington, DC, but agency heads determined that she should stay behind and analyze the failed incident together with representatives of European agencies. Rather than put her up in an expensive hotel, they told her to take a bunk at a safe house. She understood that it was a form of punishment for the failure, and she accepted it like a soldier. She wanted to punish herself, anyway, still upset about Darren's death. As she opened the refrigerator to get cream for her coffee, she heard a blast and felt the house shake. She ran to her bedroom to get her gun. When she returned to the hallway with her gun raised, she saw a drone flying down the hall right at her. She fired but missed the drone which shot a burst of nanobots above her head. She heard the burst and put her arm up to her nose and mouth, but it was ineffective. She tried to shoot the drone again, but it was already gone searching another part of the house. She felt her throat tighten and knew immediately what was next. She dropped the gun and fell to her knees and started to pray just before the oxygen deprivation hit her brain and she passed out.

The drones departed the houses and flew to a second location further from the city where the cargo containers were waiting. They landed in the containers that were remotely sealed and retrieved by the helicopters. The helicopters flew out over the coast and dropped the containers in the ocean. The air traffic controllers who saw the helicopters assumed it was a military operation. By the time they contacted the military to confirm, the helicopters had disappeared from their screens.

Emergency calls from the safe houses had alerted CNI who dispatched active agents to the safe houses. By the time they arrived at the safe houses, the nanobots had gone inert and no one was left alive. The agents put on masks assuming it was another gas attack but there was no indication of gas and all that was left was the nanobot dust on the floors. They collected the dust and returned it to headquarters in Madrid. Forensic scientists were able to confirm that it was the same compound used in the Erro attack.

Minister de Bleu's phone rang. He grumbled and got out of bed to answer the phone.

"It's happened again," said the caller.

"What's happened?"

"Erro."

"Erro? My god."

"This time it was a focused attack in Pamplona. They hit three CNI safe houses with drones and killed everyone present."

Minister de Bleu was silent. "That is impossible," he said.

"Apparently, it's not. They knew who they were targeting, and they were successful."

* * *

"It's the Secretary."

"Put him on," said Brian.

"Drones," said the Secretary.

"Drones, sir?" said Brian trying to follow.

"They beat us to the punch, Dr. Johannsen. There's been another attack in Spain. This time they used drones. You are going to have to speed up your efforts. We need an effective countermeasure against weaponized drones."

"Ok," said Brian. "Can you send us details?"

"Already there."

Brian heard a knock. Sal poked in his head.

"Dr. Pinsky. I was just thinking of you. Please." Brian motioned for Sal to enter and sit.

"Looks like we have a solution to our countermeasure problem," Brian told Sal.

"What's that?" Sal responded.

"I just received a call from the Secretary of Defense."

"He told you about the drones," said Pinsky.

"Yes, he did," said Brian. "How did you know?"

"I just got an encrypted communication from the Pentagon," said Sal. "Pretty sure you were included."

Brian checked his messages. The encrypted subject line read: *Nanobot Drones.*

"It changes the equation," said Sal. "You said we can't pre-detonate the nanobot bombs. We also said we can't just randomly spray the air with our resonant CO_2 coating. What if we outfitted the drones to do both?"

Sal left the office and immediately put in for a shipment of 500 drones of various sizes and designs. The military had been using "first person view" (FPV) drones for over a decade as self-guided delivery systems for missiles and as stealth surveillance. Anti-drone countermeasures were a more recent development, and the technology was still basic. Early versions of drone interceptors used the same heat-seeking technology used by airborne missile countermeasures because the early military drones used modified rocket engines.

This heat-seeking technology was not likely to work well with mini drones. Their evasive capabilities rendered most countermeasures ineffective and, because their electric motors did not run as hot as rocket engines, heat seeking was not an option. It didn't take the team long to realize that, unlike traditional ballistics, drones had eyes. Even the smallest consumer drones had high-definition cameras and, if programmed properly, they should be able to detect and identify objects moving in their field of vision. The federal government had developed rudimentary image recognition software in collaboration with Silicon Valley, and the private sector had advanced it for commercial applications. The military took the more advanced image recognition software for its drones, but even that software would not be smart enough to target the mini drones used in the attacks in Spain. Brian and Sal procured the image recognition software and fed it into the large language models that Brian had been developing for his AI-infused nanobots. The AI tool started spitting out volumes of code, but the code contained glitches, and Brian knew he needed assistance from someone who specialized in LLMs to develop usable code. Besides, he missed Bost.

"Where have you been?" said Bost answering Brian's call. "You tell me how important I am and then disappeared off the planet."

Brian laughed. "I know. I'm sorry. Something came up. But I wasn't lying. You are important to me."

"Wow. Well, that's very reassuring," Bost said sarcastically.

"Ok. Ok. I need you, but I can't tell you what is going on. I need to get you cleared first."

"You realize Providia has billions in government contracts and that I am cleared on everything."

"This one is new and it's terrible. You need a special clearance."

"I'll talk to Deckwalder. I'm sure we can get it done right away."

"Go through the Pentagon. I've already reached out. I need you now. I don't have time to wait."

"Deckwalder can help. What are you doing, building nanobot weapons?"

"No questions," said Brian. Let's get you cleared."

"You are building weapons, you bad boy."

"Be smart, Bost. Talk to you soon."

"Yes, sir."

The Pentagon granted Bost's clearance for the Great Falls project and Deckwalder gave him leave to join Brian in Montana. Brian made it clear that Bost would report to Sal, but he also made it clear to Sal that Bost had a direct line to Brian whenever he wanted. Sal grumbled but once he identified Bost's immediate contributions to the project, he calmed down. Bost was careful not to question Sal's authority, and the team came together. Bost was a code geek and spent hours pouring over the code that the nanobot LLM had spit out. He saw immediately that the code needed drone aeronautics and assembled a team to fly drones in the base's airspace to enhance the LLM.

Residents of Great Falls saw the drones flying at night and a local radio station began reporting sightings of alien space craft. But Bost took the project a step further. He recalled using natural events to program the nanobots and told AI to apply the same swarm technology to the drones. He then identified one of the drones as the queen drone and was able to use the queen to create aerial formations. By using a queen to control a swarm of drones, Bost reduced the number of drone operators from one operator per drone to one operator per 20-50 drones.

The drone operators sent signals from the queen, and the worker drones followed those instructions. Brian used Bost's application to put on a show for the CO and his enlisteds inside one of the hangars. The drones made various formations to country music and even performed a line dance to which several enlisteds rose up and started dancing along. The concluding highlight of the show was a facial image of the CO himself who shouted "Dismissed!" Everyone jumped out of their seats and cheered. Brian brought up his lead team and introduced them. Sal made a point of shaking Bost's hand and then raising it victoriously.

As they were leaving the hanger, Bost turned to Brian. Before he could say anything, Brian said, "Well done."

Bost replied, "I like Montana. I might stay here."

Brian said, "Wait for the winter."

"I've heard," said Bost. "This was fun, but we're not done."

"How so?"

"We can make the queen fully autonomous."

"What are you thinking?"

"The queen should be able to assess battlefield conditions and issue instructions in response to those conditions. She can make those decisions faster than a human operator watching the battle remotely."

"Can we lose control? What if she turns and begins fighting against her own drones?"

"She won't. The swarm technology is bilateral – she recognizes her drones just as they recognize her."

"Show me."

In the meantime, Sal's other team focused on drone-on-drone combat. He honed the image recognition software with AI not only to spot enemy drones but to control drone speed and trajectory. He found it relatively easy to target and hit marked drones with smart attack drones, especially if the targets were human operated drones. He rewarded the most adept of his operators. They forced him to continue improving the attack software. The next and more difficult step was to attack without damaging the target drones. He considered using electronic pulses to disable the drones. The problem with disabling drones equipped with toxic nanobots was that if they fell out of the sky and crashed, they might release the nanobots just as if they were blown out of the sky and the consequences would be the same.

Sal and Brian collaborated closely on a battlefield solution, and they often turned to Bost who continued to feed the LLMs with advanced game theory, cytokine data from Dr. Folsom's work on anaphylaxis and nanobot swarm data from his own experiments. Sal developed a mechanism for grabbing the target drones and for a while, that seemed to be a good solution. They held battlefield scenarios where operators attempted to free their drones from the attack drones. The tactic was marginally successful but often the result was a crash. Then one of the more astute members of Sal's team suggested that as soon as the enemy realized the drones were under attack, they might trigger the detonators on the drones and release the nanobot clouds.

The countermeasure would fail if the focus was only on the drones themselves and not on the nanobots. The attack drones needed to have multiple capabilities. They needed a targeting mechanism, a capture mechanism, a disabling mechanism and an anti-toxin. The latter was proving to be the most difficult to develop but its roots were in the resonant coating that Brian and Bost had developed at Ragnar Willowbrook. The question was how to use the coating to effectively render the weaponized nanobots inert. The process worked fine in an enclosed vacuum chamber. But would it work in the sky in the middle of complex battle scenarios involving hundreds of swarming drones?

The Secretary called again. The Pentagon was concerned that time was running out. They expected another attack and soon.

Chapter 25.

The Elevator

Scott Geiringer left the Justice Tavern. He felt the buzz of a couple beers, but he was glad to get out of the bar and looked forward to spending another hour at his desk before going home. He appreciated Detective Young's enthusiasm for him and felt a mixture of relief and pressure. It was great to have a leg up and have the benefit of not having to prove himself out of the gate, but he knew that he did not have much time before he needed to validate Young's expectations. Failing those expectations might turn out to be worse than having no expectations in the first place.

He entered the Bureau expecting it to be dark and when he saw lights in the darkness, he thought it was the cleaning crew. The lights seemed to be hovering around his desk. He walked over to the light switch and threw it on and what he saw surprised him. Three men in black masks were standing around his desk rifling through his papers.

"What's going on?" he asked. He thought maybe this was a prank being played on him as a new detective. He had been in a fraternity at UCLA, and he knew a prank when he saw it.

The three men looked up.

"Where is it?" one of them said.

"Where is what?"

"The list, asshole."

"The list? What list?" Scott started to think. It wasn't a prank. Moreover, the voice sounded familiar.

"You guys can't be here," Scott said, trying to sound reasonable. "If you want something from me, just ask me."

"We want the list you put together of people you identified at the club," said the voice, raising his gun.

Scott recognized the firearm as a standard issue Glock 22 carried by rank-and-file police officers. "I have no idea what list you are talking about," said Scott but a picture was emerging.

Early in his time at the Academy, Scott had run into cadets who liked to bully other cadets. He'd stood his ground with them, and they started treating him like an equal. He'd always wondered why they acted like bullies to the other cadets. They carried themselves with an arrogance that didn't befit their accomplishments at the Academy. One of them was a young cadet named Ben Bodrogi. Ben was a small guy but strong and especially aggressive. He was good at physical combat and in firearms, but he was not particularly good at academics. He and Scott had a run-in after Scott stepped in to prevent Ben from getting up in another cadet's face and harassing him. They tussled and were taken to the commanding officer who gave them a tongue thrashing and threatened them with expulsion. They were required to take a special ethics course taught by Sergeant Marisa Coldridge. Forced to take the special class, Ben began to appreciate Scott's intelligence as well as his accomplishments at the Academy. He appealed to Scott to help him with his academic work. Sergeant Coldridge took some pride as she witnessed what she thought was their developing friendship.

But Ben had a dark side that he kept hidden from Scott and his colleagues at the Academy. Abused as a child by a neighborhood friend, Ben developed an addiction to sex and pornography, in particular, child pornography. His interest in police work emerged as a complicated cover for his sex addition. He liked guns and he liked physical engagement, and he thought he could legitimize those interests as a well-respected community police officer.

He also carried a lot of shame over his sex addiction, and he reasoned that, as a police officer, he might be better positioned to battle his addiction. At the same time, a darker thought emerged. He began to fantasize that, as a police officer, there was the possibility that he would encounter human trafficking and have certain opportunities presented that he might not otherwise have.

That dark opportunity came sooner than he expected. One late night feeling bored with his studies, Ben took a trip down Hollywood Boulevard and stopped into a strip club there. He immediately felt the rush of sexual thrill as he entered the hazy atmosphere and saw groups of men and a few women gathered around the stages where partially nude dancers performed their pole routines and teased dollar bills from the audience. Ben sat down and immediately was approached by a dancer who sat in his lap and started seducing him. A waitress followed her and asked if he wanted a drink and might buy his new friend a drink. Ben immediately agreed and after a short time the dancer convinced him to go to another room where they could make out for $20. He ended up spending several hundred dollars, and, after he ran out of cash, the couple emerged from the back area and sat down again at a stage. She stayed with him, and, sitting on his lap, she turned to the two men sitting next to them and said, "I got myself a real live police cadet." Ben didn't remember telling her he was a cadet. The two men leaned forward and looked at him and said, "Is that so? Are you a cadet?" Ben replied with a tight smile, "She wasn't supposed to say anything."

It turned out the two men were off duty police officers, and they started engaging Ben. They asked about the Academy and what type of police work he wanted to do. They joked about working in the Vice Unit, but Ben candidly told them, "That's an area I want to explore."

"You need to come with us," they said. "We can give you some lessons in vice."

They took Ben to No Vacancy and down through the tunnel to the underground sex club. Ben didn't stay long that first night. But he soon became a regular visitor and met several police officers who enjoyed the club. They told Ben they would make sure he was given the assignments he wanted and the right beat partners. The encouragement played into Ben's arrogance at the Academy.

But Ben knew none of it would matter if he didn't graduate and become a police officer. When his encounter with Scott presented itself, he knew he needed to take advantage, and he befriended Scott and asked for his help. That relationship grew quickly over the next few weeks, and they stood together at the graduation ceremony. Scott received multiple honors at graduation. Ben was just happy to be graduating, knowing he had been assigned to the Special Enforcement Section at Rampart as a member of the Vice Unit, just as he had hoped.

After graduation, Scott and Ben celebrated at dinner with their parents and, after dinner, Ben, feeling confident in the friendship with Scott, proposed that they continue the celebration at a club. He took Scott to No Vacancy and through the tunnel to the underground sex club. They drank and partied together into the night. Scott chuckled at the stupid sex costumes some people were wearing and viewed the club as a silly experience, a caricature of the seamy side of Los Angeles and the wannabe Hugh Hefners and Larry Flints. But he was having fun. Several women approached him, and he danced but he was not interested in any of them. Soon he was ready to leave.

He couldn't find Ben and started wandering. He found a staircase and explored it, thinking it was just another room for partying. That's when he saw the children and Ben in the room talking to a young boy while other people were touching the children inappropriately. Scott walked into the room and called Ben's name. A couple officers leaned over to Ben and asked him if this was his fellow officer and Ben said yes and bragged about Scott skipping police work and getting hired immediately as a first-year detective. The officers fawned over Scott, and even though Scott was troubled at what he was seeing, he pretended to go along with it, and they exchanged names. Scott told Ben he had been looking for him because was tired and wanted to go home. Ben resisted initially but quickly gave in, and Ben and Scott left the club. Scott didn't say anything about what he saw to Ben on the way back to his car. But, over the next several days, Scott distanced himself from Ben and prepared to join the Detective Bureau. Ben, for his part, got busy with his police work and let it go. He called Scott a couple of times and they had short conversations but never got together.

In the meantime, Scott began to think about how he might be able impress his superiors at the Bureau. He had memorized the names of the officers he met at the sex club and prepared for himself a list of names. He began researching into human trafficking schemes emerging from Mexico and Southeast Asia. He learned that victims of human trafficking enter the country by multiple means including airplanes, boats, trucks and even by foot. Some victims are coached to claim asylum under false pretenses. Other victims are snuck into the country pretending to be part of a legitimate tour group. Some victims are given false job offers as models or domestic workers or factory workers.

Some children of extreme poverty are sold to human traffickers and others are treated as indentured servants, forced to repay the cost of transportation or forged documents. Once they arrive in the United States, or wherever the destination, they are subject to frequent moves between hotel rooms, massage parlors and private homes. Sometimes they are locked in rooms or containers to prevent escape and often they are physically and psychologically abused. Scott started inquiring around the office whether anyone had experience with human trafficking. They told him that concern was part of the Organized Crime and Vice Division – Vice Unit for short. He contacted the Vice Unit and asked for a meeting. Without hesitating, they granted the meeting.

When he arrived for the meeting, Scott was ushered into a small interrogation room. Rather than feeling treated an as invited guest, Scott felt like his interest was being treated as suspect and the questioning felt like an interrogation.

"What can we do for you?" asked the first of the two detectives in the room with him.

"I just wanted to ask you about human trafficking in Los Angeles," he replied. "Is it happening here?"

The two detectives looked at each other as if this rookie detective had no idea what he was asking.

"There are reported incidents of it," said the second detective, holding back a laugh.

"Does it involve children?"

Again, the detectives acted as if this person was wasting their time.

"It can."

Scott persisted. "Are you aware of any specific incidents of it happening?"

This time, rather than answer his question, the detectives began to press Scott.

"What is your concern, Detective?" the first detective asked. "Are you concerned that we are not doing our job, or is this just an academic inquiry?"

"Neither" said Scott. "It is an area that interests me. I find the thought of it troubling, and I wondered whether I might be able to do something helpful or not."

"I see," said the second detective. "You want to be a hero, maybe save some helpless beautiful maiden under the spell of an evil pimp."

"I don't think that's fair," said Scott. "I think we have a problem, and I want to be part of the solution."

"What makes you think we have a problem?" said the first detective.

"Call it a hunch," said Scott. Then he added, "I think we are done here." He pushed back his chair.

"Ok, wait a minute," said the first detective. "You are new here, right?"

"New to the Bureau?" said Scott, still preparing to leave. "I am."

"Our apologies, Detective," he said. "You sound like you know something. What's up?"

Scott thought about standing up and leaving, but he looked at the two detectives gauging their real interest.

"Yes," he said. "I believe I witnessed children being used as sex workers."

"Ok," they responded. "Relax and tell us what you know."

Scott described the setting and the number of children he thought might be involved. He didn't mention any names. He didn't tell the detectives that he had a list of names. He didn't tell them that he thought the LAPD might be complicit. They thanked him and told him they would be in touch. Scott left the interview and went back to his desk. He still felt sickened by the scene he witnessed at the sex club. He was angry at Ben and began to wonder if Ben was just using him at the Academy rather than being a trusted friend. He thought about confronting Ben directly. The truth was he had not decided what action to take when he stumbled onto the intruders after returning from the Justice Tavern.

"Honestly, I have no idea what you are talking about," Scott repeated.

"Did you approach Vice?" came another voice. This one Scott recognized immediately.

"Ben? What the fuck? What are you doing?" said Scott.

"Did you approach Vice about No Vacancy?" Ben asked.

Scott knew he was in trouble.

"Gentlemen," he said. "I think you have the wrong idea. I just wanted to test the waters and see if Vice would be interesting."

"Right," said Ben. "That's why you told them about No Vacancy? I took you there as a friend."

At this point, Scott got angry. "As a friend, Ben? How about as cover for your elicit activities?"

One of the other officers started moving toward Scott. Scott saw him and stepped back. He started to reach for his weapon when the officer rushed him and slammed his pistol into Scott's face. Scott crumpled to the ground.

"We need to get out of here, now," said the other officer. Ben, meanwhile, had walked over to Scott and zip-tied his hands behind him.

"We can't leave him here," said Ben. They grabbed Scott and dragged him to the elevator. They took the elevator to the parking garage ramp entrance and were planning to put Scott in their car and leave when they saw Detective Young and his crew getting out of a car on the same parking lot level. They closed the elevator immediately and took it to another floor. The two officers started to carry Scott out with them, but Ben said, "Leave him." They laid Scott on the elevator floor and, as the door was shutting Ben, who had attached his silencer, put the pistol to Scott's head and pulled the trigger. The other officers looked at each other but said nothing. The elevator door closed and the three took off for the stairwell at the other end of the parking structure where they waited until the coast was clear and then ran to their car and slowly drove out of the structure.

Chapter 26.

Love Story

Van had enough experience with the Department and the Bureau to recognize that her next move would have to be very cautious, but she was worked up. She called Alvin.

"What are you doing?" he asked. "You are supposed to be on leave."

"I am."

"And you are still investigating the murders?"

"I'm not. Not really. Call it a coincidence or divine intervention, but without trying, I stumbled onto something that needs a response, only I genuinely don't know what to do."

"What happened?"

Van knew she had to trust someone with the information. She knew it wasn't David Chang. She doubted it was the Chief, as much as she wanted to trust him. The only person she knew she could trust was Charlie, but he was dead. She felt the same about Alvin Broad, and she hoped like hell that he was the right person to talk to.

"We need to arrest Officer Ben Bodrogi."

"I don't know that person," said Alvin, "but on what charge?"

"Where do I start? Dereliction of duty, child pornography, prostitution, human trafficking."

"You have evidence?"

"I saw him at a sex club with a minor."

"Did you see him in the act?"

"No, but I saw him with a young child."

"You know that's not going to cut it."

"I know, dammit," she said. "I'm just so angry and I can't believe what I saw."

"I believe you," said Alvin. "Sounds like we need to set up a sting and, because human trafficking is a federal crime, we need to get the FBI involved."

"I need a path to Bodrogi," Van responded. "He either is connected to the murders, or he knows who is connected. I am certain of that, and I don't believe IA will follow through with him."

"We can set up the sting around Bodrogi."

"How do we do that?"

"It will take some coordination, but we can do it."

"I love you, Alvin," said Van.

"I'm too old for you, Detective," he responded. They laughed and Van felt a sense of relief.

She hung up and headed out of the house for a run. Within minutes, her phone started buzzing. She slowed her pace.

"Hello?"

"Hi Van. It's Henry."

"Henry! You caught me on a jog. Did Alvin call you?"

"Detective Broad?""

"Yes."

"No. I haven't heard from him. I am calling because I have unfortunate news."

"What happened?"

"We lost Agent Christian."

Van stopped running. She looked for a place to sit down.

"Van? Are you there?"

"Yes, I'm here. You lost her?"

"She was killed in a coordinated attack."

Van didn't respond.

"I am sorry to tell you. It was terrible, from what I understand, and I don't know many details. The CIA knew we were working together. They notified me. They told me she was in Pamplona working with Interpol. She was the victim of a targeted drone attack."

"A drone attack?"

"Yes, crazy. They asked me to notify you. They want you to come to Langley."

Van fought back tears. "Vanessa wanted me with her. I told her no, that I needed to stay here."

"Don't think that you might have been there to help her. A lot has happened since we last saw her. Can you get to Langley? Will the Chief let you off?"

"He put me on leave. I got shot, but I am recovering quickly. A shoulder graze."

"Wow. Sorry to hear."

"Don't be surprised if you get a call from Alvin," said Van. "There are some things going down here also. Please don't say anything. Wait for his call."

"10-4. Can I tell the Feds you are coming?"

"Yes. It works out well. I need to get away from this place for a bit."

"Great. Wait for them to contact you."

Van received an encrypted email later that day. It included a ticket from LAX to Dulles International. She packed her bags and headed to the airport. When she arrived at Dulles, a black SUV was waiting for her. The driver took her bags and opened the rear door. Van looked up and saw Brian. She blinked. Behind Brian in the back seat she noticed Bost and two people whom she didn't recognize. Brian smiled.

"Been a while, Detective." Brian smiled and extended his hand.

Van felt her knees melt just a bit. She didn't expect to see Brian and, try as she might, it was hard for her to suppress her reaction. She let him help her into the SUV and sat next to him. She recognized his scent and fought the urge to hold him. Brian saw the bandage on her shoulder.

"Are you hurt?"

"Long story," she managed to say. "It's well healed. Just keeping it covered."

"Ok," said Brian. "You remember Bost?"

"Of course I do," said Van. She smiled and shook his extended hand. "Good to see you again."

Bost turned to Sal and Sandra. "This is our LA miracle. She is something special."

Van smiled graciously and extended her hand to Sal and then to Sandra. "Detective Van Eng," she said. "LAPD."

"Dr. Sal Pinsky," said Sal. "Nice to meet you."

"Dr. Sandra Folsom," said Sandra.

Brian said, "I assume you are joining us at Langley. Are you read in?"

"Not at all," replied Van. "I heard about Agent Christian, but I don't have any details. Just following orders."

Brian looked at his team. He signaled for them to remain silent. He looked back at Van. "We heard as well. Not good." Then, changing the subject, he said, "You look great, by the way."

Van demurred and said nothing.

Sandra jumped in. "We have a long ride to Langley. Tell us a little about your life. Are you married? Do you have a family?"

They enjoyed the ride to Langley. The conversation was relaxed. Van told Brian and his team about Martin Richard and how she had declined his proposal. She steered away from talking about No Vacancy and the events in the Department. She asked Bost how the nanobot research at Ragnar Willowbrook was going. He told her progress had been slow. He didn't mention Great Falls. Brian was cordial and respectful. If he felt anything deeper toward Van, he didn't show it. Sal was quiet but Sandra was engaging.

They arrived at Langley and were ushered quickly into a large conference room. Several people were already seated. Brian noticed the same generals from the Situation Room at the White House. A side door opened, and the Director of the agency entered alongside the Secretary of Defense.

The Director stood at a podium and started the discussion.

"If you are here, you can assume you are properly cleared. Today's discussion is top secret, and it is not to leave this room. The circumstances we are discussing are highly degraded. We are in a military emergency and anticipate more events in Spain and possibly elsewhere. We are mobilizing forces as we speak and stand at the ready should our assistance be needed. Let me turn it over to the Secretary."

The Secretary rose and walked to the podium.

"The primary purpose of today's meeting is to assess our defensive capabilities even as we get ready to respond. I have asked Dr. Johannsen to brief us on what you may know we are calling the Great Falls Project. He and his team have made remarkable progress on a response to what to the rest of us is an unknown and incomprehensible threat. Dr. Johannsen?"

Brian rose and handed the AV operator a thumb drive. She started the presentation. He spoke about Great Falls and Malmstrom Air Force Base. Then he summarized the attacks in Spain and explained how his team started with the premise that conventional antiballistics would not work against the weaponized nanobots. The generals shifted in their chairs. They had their own plans and weren't confident that Brian and his team could adequately address what was clearly a military concern and needed a military response. Brian explained the impact of releasing toxic nanobots into the air and the self-replication capabilities that allowed the nanobots to spread like a virus. He described how they learned about the use of drones in Spain and his team's efforts to re-engineer the drones to counter the weaponized drones. He then introduced his team and allowed each of them to describe their specific progress, Dr. Sandra Folsom on immunity, Dr. Sal Pinsky on drone-on-drone combat and finally Bost Karnivan on the use of AI to develop swarm capabilities and to render drones autonomous. Brian summarized the presentation by describing a strategic approach to responding to a drone-delivered nanobot attack. He called it a multilayered approach that required all three lines of defense: immunity, incapacity and capture. The audience raised several questions, and Brian handled the questions with ease, but he made it clear the response was not foolproof. The audience was impressed, including Van, and everyone gave the team a standing ovation led by the generals.

After the meeting, the Director invited the team to dinner at his home in West McClean. The driver dropped the team at the McClean Hilton to check in and prepare for dinner, and soon they were on their way to the Director's home. Not surprisingly, the Director lived in a home the size of a small mansion. The driveway was a circular driveway that allowed vehicles to drop passengers off at the front door under a small portico that extended from the front door to the driveway in the event of rain or snow. The home had seven bedrooms and a library room. The library served as the Director's personal office. The Director's children were grown and either away at graduate school or living in their own homes, so the house felt empty. But mom and dad kept the children's rooms in their original state so, when they did visit, they would feel at home. The backyard was expansive and backed up against a small forest. The living room had a large fireplace and a six-foot mantle. Three couches fronted the fireplace, and the Director invited his guests to have a seat as he served pre-dinner drinks.

Van and Brian sat next to each other unintentionally. When they happened to rub arms or touch each other, Van felt something like an electric buzz. Brian felt the same, but they were both careful not to let on to each other or anyone else in the room. The chat around the fireplace was light. The Director was mostly interested in their situations at home. Van described some of the challenges of being hearing impaired and an LAPD detective and the Director was keenly interested. They moved to the dining room. The Director had a personal chef who prepared a five-course French dining experience. The chardonnay came from France. Everyone complimented the chef and carried on the fireplace conversation. Brian spoke about working for a university and the challenge of satisfying wealthy Silicon Valley billionaires. The conversation turned serious when the Director asked if Brian happened to be working at the same Silicon Valley lab that Belinda Armendariz used to lead.

"It is the same lab," Brian said. "I was hesitant to take on the job, but I was assured I could run it my way."

"What way is that?" asked the Director.

"I have my standards. Belinda had hers. Sometimes my customers wish that my standards and hers were more closely aligned. Ragnar Willowbrook is a special place, and that is due in part to Belinda Armendariz. A lab certification is very valuable to someone who is seeking funding of what may be a brilliant concept. But I believe that toward the end, Belinda was taking shortcuts, and her customers relied on her shortcuts to pull investors in more quickly. I have seen proposals where the data is inconclusive, or the product creates negative side effects, and I won't certify those products until the issues are addressed."

"Doesn't the FTC or the EPA act as a backstop to those decisions?"

"Let's just say Belinda had her ways. She was very effective at getting approvals through multiple agencies."

The Director turned to Van.

"You had a discussion with the President about Belinda Armendariz, didn't you?"

"I think you know my situation," Van responded. "I mean, I'm happy to talk about it again but I think you know I had a run-in with her."

"I do," he said. "That's fair. But you lived to tell the tale. That's impressive."

"I got lucky," she answered. "It could have gone very bad for me, just as it did for Agent Christian."

"Indeed," said the Director and everyone nodded.

"Which I suppose leads me to a question for you," said Van. "Why exactly am I here? Brian and his team have developed a remarkable response to the threat in Spain. I'm not sure what I can add to their expertise."

The Director studied Van. Then he smiled and said, "You are here because the President of the United States wants you here. I can see why. Your talents are unique. The people who know you and have worked with you have nothing but praise for you including Agent Vanessa Christian. We have a very complex situation here, and I want the best minds that I can find around me. I include you in that group."

Van felt humbled and a bit embarrassed. Brian reached over and squeezed her hand. She looked at him and she again felt the sparks. It took her a second to realize that she looked at him a bit too long and was embarrassed again when the rest of the table laughed.

"I'm grateful to be here," she said to the Director. "And I will do anything you need of me."

"I don't expect any less of you or anyone else who is here tonight," he said and motioned to everyone at the table. "We will talk more tomorrow," he added. "Anyone up for an aperitif?"

They left the house shortly thereafter and headed back to the hotel. They were impressed with the Director and talked about the experience. Bost tried to joke that Brian and Van needed some time alone and everyone shut him up. But when they arrived at the hotel and exited the SUV, Brian pulled Van aside.

"I feel like you and I should talk. Am I wrong?"

Van looked at Brian. She thought about Martin, but this was different. She wanted to melt into Brian's arms. She knew she had her own career, but her heart was telling her she could follow him anywhere. That he was still available was surprising to her, and she wondered why she knew so little about his life.

Brian for his part, felt guilty about Martin. Here was a guy who had already proposed to Van, and even if she said that was not the proper way to propose, maybe she really did want him to propose. But Brian was so struck by their chemistry, he knew he had to tell her how he felt. He also knew implicitly that the one reason he had not built a relationship with anyone else was that no one could measure up to her and he wasn't willing to accept anything less.

"I'm really tired," said Van. "Besides we both have been drinking. I'm not sure our brains are fully functional." She reached up and kissed him on the cheek. "We'll talk," she reassured him and headed to the stairs and up to her room.

The next day, the group at Langley was decidedly smaller and included the Secretary of Defense and one of his deputies, the general that had given Brian problems in their first encounter, the Great Falls team, and Van. The Director pulled them into a smaller room with clean white boards. There was one large monitor and Brian's presentation was loaded on the monitor. Blank notepads and pens were laid out on the conference table.

"This is our war room," he started. "The American team gathered here this morning is the lead team that we will be sending to Southern France. There you will meet with teams from Great Britain, France and Spain and develop the final strategy for capturing Belinda Armendariz and her new weapons. Our first attempts at flushing her out failed and, unfortunately, we learned just how deadly she can be.

"The work that Brian's team has done will be critical in our engagement and must be handled perfectly. This morning, we will review the Great Falls plan and consider options for addressing the loopholes he raised yesterday. We will present our findings to the Europeans and develop a coordinated strategy around Armendariz."

"Do we know where she is?" Van asked unhesitatingly.

"We do not. Not yet. We believe she is located somewhere north of Pamplona. She could be in Southern France, but we think it is more likely that she is hiding in the Pyrenees. Our domestic teams are coordinating with Europeans digging through satellite images looking for signs of military activity. You asked me yesterday what your role will be. Based on any information we pull from the images, you will be tasked with leading an international team into the mountains to find her and set up our defense. You are the one who has had the closest encounters with Dr. Armendariz, and we are counting on your special talents to guide us in this action."

Brian shuffled in his seat. "If Belinda catches wind of Van's efforts, it could be very dangerous for her and her team."

"That's what we do," said the Director. "Detective Eng understands the situation."

"I'm in," said Van. "I will find her."

"Plus, she will have the benefit of an elite paramilitary team supporting her. That said," added the Director looking at Brian, "your team's role will be to equip them with the defenses they need to protect themselves."

Brian was quiet. The Secretary said, "We can do this."

The Director added, "We don't have any choice. Now, let's discuss the loopholes."

Chapter 27.

The Search

The American team flew to Paris and then down to Bordeaux, where they were driven to a beautiful chateau in Southern France near Saint Emilion called Grand Barrail. The Grand Barrail was a five-star hotel that the French Government had taken over for the coordinated operation. The Americans were introduced to agents from intelligence services including Great Britain's MI6, France's Direction Générale or DGSE, Spain's CNI and Interpol. They gathered in a large ballroom. Spain's CNI was the first to speak and they described the capture and death in captivity of Professor Hadj Arjoun after Arjoun had proposed militarizing the Basque Government. They concluded that Arjoun was representing someone else who carried out the nanobot attack against CNI in Pamplona, the same attack in which an American agent had been killed.

France's DGSE reviewed the investigations of the Dome incident and were now concluding that the tragic events at the Dome were likely tied to the Erro and Pamplona attacks, although the group claiming responsibility for Erro, the Night Brigade, had made no claims on the other events. The CIA Director stood and reported that they had assembled the intelligence gathered from multiple recent nanobot-related events, including destruction of the Duc A. Tran Lab on Bainbridge Island, the FBI's raid on Ragnar Willowbrook, the Dome in Paris, and the Night Brigade attack on Erro and against the CNI in Pamplona.

The CIA Director said evidence suggests that the airport incident in Yerevan, Armenia, might be tied to the same toxic nanobots. According to the CIA, those events all pointed to the same person as the primary suspect, Dr. Belinda Armendariz, the former CEO at Ragnar Willowbrook Labs in California. Armendariz had led the attack on Bainbridge and Armendariz had taken the toxic nanobots from that lab before killing its top scientists. Interpol also had learned that Armendariz had bribed officials at the University of Navarra to conduct secret research on nanobots and then, for no reason that was apparent to the University,

Armendariz stole the nanobots in a night raid and disappeared. Considering all these details, the Saint Emilion group agreed that Armendariz should be targeted as Suspect No. 1, the principal behind the nanobot attacks.

The next step would be to locate her. The CIA long suspected that Armendariz had escaped the United States and moved to Spain. The failed attempt to capture her in Pamplona confirmed that, whether she was presently residing in Spain, she was spending time in the country and in the Navarra region. He introduced Detective Van Eng, who was on special assignment from the President to lead the U.S team and any others who might join her in another effort to capture Armendariz. He asked Van to introduce herself and Van chose to say very little other than she looked forward to working with all the agencies in a coordinated effort to put this international criminal away.

The European team was prepared to start the search for the Night Brigade and Armendariz immediately. Now that the Americans had joined the discussion, the Director suggested that the European search be placed on hold. He introduced Dr. Brian Johannsen, who started by describing his original work as a lab technician on the nanobots and his nearly fatal accident in the lab on Bainbridge. He learned, because of that experience, not to take the threat of toxic nanobots lightly. Then he walked through the Great Falls project and described the work his team had done to build a viable counteroffensive against weaponized nanobots. Brian concluded that the teams needed to work together to formulate a comprehensive strategic approach to any assault on the Armendariz compound or they might risk a tragic outcome.

Van, after discussions with the Director and Brian, proposed to the entire group that she would assemble a scouting party comprised of the best research and detective minds from each country. She told each of the countries to identify the appropriate personnel and bring them to Saint Emilion. The French Government had already built a new data center adjacent to the Chateau with secure high-speed connections to intelligence and military data centers. Van quickly identified a team to dig through and organize the data. She pulled Brian and Bost aside to discuss building a new large language model based on the search data and a specialized AI chatbot that would allow them to apply artificial intelligence to the search. Langley acquired and shipped dozens of servers to France. The servers were equipped with the latest AI-enabled GPUs and Bost had his existing LLMs in California transferred to France and went to work building the enhanced LLM using satellite imagery, military data, heat sensory imagery, traffic patterns and population or demographic changes. Within a couple weeks, the new AI bot was working. Bost called it the Belinda Bot. Once Van's team had the Belinda Bot, they very quickly isolated a dozen different locations where Belinda might be hiding out, all of which were at various locations in the Pyrenees.

During this time in Southern France, Van and Brian spent many hours together. They explored dozens of chateaus and enjoyed French wine and food and went on many strolls under the stars. Van knew she was falling in love with Brian, and, for Brian's part, that had never been a question. He was happier than he had ever been, and it didn't matter to him that Van's primary focus in France was on Belinda and not on Brian. For that reason, Van repeatedly told Brian that she was not interested in a relationship of any kind outside of being colleagues. Brian, though, was frightened for Van. The scouting party would be leaving soon to begin their search for Belinda's compounds. Van was participating on maneuvers that included elite counterterrorism units from each of the countries. These units knew the Pyrenees and were specialized in mountain-based missions. Brian fought his urge to ask Van to remain behind and lead the units remotely. He knew that was not practical. He asked the Director if he could join her team. The Director knew there was chemistry between them and that chemistry threatened the mission. He didn't oppose them spending down time together in Saint Emilion, but Van had a different job than Brian and Van needed to focus on her job. Brian needed to focus on preparing the team for a direct assault on the Night Brigade compounds once they were found using the techniques developed in Great Falls to face attack by weaponized nanobots. He refused Brian's request.

The day came when it was time to leave on the first scouting party mission. Van was re-packing a backpack when Brian peeked into her room.

"Leaving soon, I see," he said.

"Tomorrow morning, at 0400."

"How's the shoulder?" asked Brian, looking for something to say.

"I'm good," said Van and she smiled. "You must trust me. I know what I am doing."

"I know. I'm just concerned."

Van set down her backpack. She walked over to Brian, still standing in the doorway.

"Come in here, you big oaf."

She pulled Brian into the room and closed and locked the door behind him. She put her arms around his neck.

"I think it's time."

"Time for what?" Brian asked but he knew he didn't need to ask. His lifted her in his arms and carried her to the bed. Van pulled off her tee shirt and Brian buried his face in her chest feeling the sweetness that he had dreamed about on so many nights. He stood and pulled off his shirt and shoes. Van slid out of her khakis and reached up to undo Brian's pants. They both felt a rush of desire and urge to be together, and Van pulled Brian down on top of her. Right then they heard a knock on the door. It was Bost.

"Brian, are you in there?"

Van put her finger up to her lips and Brian said nothing.

"Come on, Brian, I know you are in there. I saw you go in."

The couple could hardly restrain their laughter.

"Oh, shit," said Bost. "Look if you are in there, the Director is looking for you. I don't know why, but he is." He waited and when he heard nothing he left.

Van burst out laughing but Brian was already back in action. He pressed down on her and kissed her hard. Van flipped him over and the passion of the moment took over. Neither of them had known such joy.

The intensity of the moment was long overdue and, after concluding, they laughed and joked with each other before starting again, both feeling that it could go on forever and still not be enough. But it made the morning harder. Brian left her room at midnight and promised to be there when her team left at 4 am. He didn't sleep the rest of the night and was in the kitchen adjacent to the ballroom at 3:30 am making coffee. Van's team was gathering in the ballroom. Van showed up at 3:45 am carrying her full backpack and immediately walked over to Brian and took a sip of coffee from his mug. "There's more," he said, pointing to the counter. "You want your own?"

"I'm fine," said Van and she started to leave the kitchen and then turned back and kissed Brian hard on the mouth. She whispered, "I love you," and then turned and walked out.

Van addressed the team in the ballroom. She made a few comments about the importance of the mission and turned it over to the pre-designated lead of the joint counterterrorism unit. He spoke with the seriousness befitting any military operation:

"As you have been told repeatedly but I must remind you again, the mountains we are entering today are dangerous and unpredictable. Weather changes occur in this mountain range without warning. A bright summer day can become dense fog, heavy rain can cause rockslides, and sudden drops in temperature can cause hypothermia and possibly death. Be careful of snow bridges. They may appear stable but may hide deep ravines and they can collapse without warning. We will be taking helicopters to a landing zone several miles outside the first identified target. At that point, we will be releasing surveillance drones to search the area. If we see evidence of paramilitary activity, we will hold and begin reporting back to the base teams. You know what to do if we face a nanobot attack. We are prepared for this. Each of you has been outfitted with gas masks, EpiPens and anti-toxins. Any questions?"

Brian stood at the door watching Van and the escort units climb into the NH90 Caiman helicopters waiting in the Chateau parking lot. He muttered a short prayer as they took off and turned and went back to the kitchen for another coffee. Van watched him through the window. She knew it was hard for him to see her go on a mission so dangerous as this one. Van knew there was a chance she would not return, but she knew there was no alternative. Belinda needed to be captured.

The helicopters headed to the westernmost spot identified by the Belinda Bot. This spot, in the heart of the Basque country was the site of a mansion built a century before on a mountaintop in the heart of Basque Country. The mansion, the Palacio de Aizkolegi, had been abandoned long ago. The AI bot showed some traffic increase and had the feel of an ancient palace perfect for someone with grandiose ambitions. It was also adjacent to the Infernuko Errota or "Devil's Mill," about three kilometers down the mountain. The helicopters crossed the border into Spain. They landed first in Elizondo, a small village at the foot of the national park where the Palacio was located and set up a camp.

Van took a team into town and the rest of the party set up the surveillance drones and sent them at high levels into the park. Van wandered the town with interpreters who asked about unusual activity. No one had anything to report. The drones used heat sensitive imaging software that showed two hikers around the Palacio and the Devil's Mill but no other activity. The team hiked up to the Devil's Mill and then up to the Palacio. Van began to relax, more like she was on vacation than hunting the world's number 1 terrorist. The base team back at the Chateau was tracking their movements and was capturing the drone footage. Van reported "Nothing here," and the Director told her, "Move to point two."

The team made it to two additional locations that day and then flew back to the Chateau. Van was exhausted but she hugged Brian and went to sleep. The scouting team rested for a day and discussed moving on the other locations further east. These locations were far more rugged than the locations at the western end of the Pyrenees. The teams noticed that each of the locations identified by the Belinda Bot had small villages that were popular with tourists, and they wondered how it might be possible for Belinda to set up operations in the middle of populated locations, albeit remote. Van told the story of her first stakeout with Charlie, how she learned that it is possible to hide in plain sight. Bost suggested that for Belinda to carry out her nanobot experiments and weapons construction, she probably needed a large underground facility. That discussion had two effects. First, the team realized that the surveillance drones needed to be equipped with ground penetrating radar, and they needed to fly at lower elevations. Second, of the remaining locations identified by the Belinda Bot, only two were in locations where the terrain might allow for a large underground installation. The first location was outside of a small town called Sort where abandoned World War II bunkers and armories might easily be refashioned into a large underground base. The second was an abandoned monastery and ancient settlement called Muro de Roda built on a hillside overlooking a large reservoir called Embalse de Mediano.

The team decided to split up and cover both locations at the same time. The first team would go to Sort and the bunkers and the second team to Muro de Roda and the monastery. Van went with the second team. They agreed to maintain radio contact with each other and with the base in Saint Emilion.

Van's team landed near the town of Ainsa, at the head of the Mediano reservoir. The drone team set up the drones and sent them flying over the reservoir and up the hill to Muro de Roda. Van took a unit into town.

They stopped in several restaurants with photos of Belinda. No one recognized the photos, but something seemed strange to Van. The more places they went, the more hostile the reception. Once they had walked into the first few restaurants, the owners approached them immediately and warned them not to ask stupid questions. After a couple more restaurants, the patrons would leave as soon as they entered, and the owners threatened to call the police. The team, sensing the hostility, didn't press the issue and left and returned to the landing zone. The drone team came up to them excitedly.

"You need to see this," said the leader of the drone team. He showed Van a video of a drone flying over the monastery using ground penetrating radar.

The GPR video revealed large bunkers buried underneath the monastery with a complex of tunnels linking the bunkers. On the back side of the mountain a small road led to a concrete entrance with a large steel door painted to look like brush. "Holy shit," thought Van. "We found her."

The first team that had gone to Sort initially thought they had another dud. No one in Sort claimed to know anything and the search around the bunkers revealed very little, other than a hangout for drug addicts. They sent up a drone to surveil the area and seeing nothing more than the empty bunkers, they called the drone back to their LZ. As it was coming back, the drone spotted a large steel disc painted to look like brush. The team brought the drone back and took off hiking in search of the disc. As they were approaching the disc, they heard the noise of a helicopter. They hid in the brush and watched as the helicopter descended toward the disc, hovered, and then disappeared.

They hustled up to the hilltop and were examining the disc when over the ridge five drones appeared. The drones flew directly at the team and emitted puffs of what looked like smoke. The smartest team members pulled their masks on immediately, but a handful were not so fortunate.

Mesmerized by the drones, they stood and watched only to be hit by the nanobot clouds emerging from the drones. A few got their masks on, but they had already inhaled the nanobots and were struggling to catch their breaths. The protected team members pulled the exposed team members back down the hillside and hid in the brush. They popped them in their thighs with EpiPens and anti-toxins to stop the anaphylactic reactions. The nanobots seemed to be penetrating the masks and they injected themselves, feeling the rush of epinephrine that cleared their tightening throats. Two members of the team never got their masks on. As the team pulled back from the drones and down the hill toward the LZ, the drones followed them and continued to pepper them with the nanobot clouds. They dragged themselves and the injured teammates onto the helicopter and took off. They radioed Van at Ainsa.

"She knows we are here," they spoke into the mike. "We found a hidden helicopter landing pad and immediately were attacked by drones. We are heading back to the Chateau."

"Don't go to the Chateau," Van insisted. "Tell Command that you need to take your injured to the nearest military base where they can be treated. Do not under any circumstances lead Belinda to the Chateau."

Chapter 28.

The Nanobot Wars

Belinda called the team together in the Roda conference room, satisfied with the initial results of her plan.

"The drone plan was brilliant. Well done, Assad. Now they fear us, and they should. We can hit entire towns, and we can hit individual targets. The Spanish government is mobilizing the military and taking its first steps to occupy the Basque Country. We need to stop them in their tracks. It is time to show them their conventional weapons are no match for our nanotechnology. Pablo?"

Pablo stood and pointed at the screen. The screen displayed a satellite image of the Basque Country.

"There are two military bases in Basque Country that are still active. The largest is Loiola in San Sebastian and the second base is called Araca in Vitoria-Gasteiz. We expect that the additional regiments will be stationed at these two bases and anticipate that a third regiment will be stationed around Pamplona. We believe they will settle near the Pamplona airport and take over two heliports, Grupo Rescate on the west side of Pamplona and the old eastside heliport next to Siemens that we have used before. These bases will be out next principal targets."

"What is happening with ETA," asked Belinda.

"ETA is formally distancing itself from the attacks, but splinter groups that recognize the opportunity are starting to mobilize. The Spanish government knows the risk of sending troops to this region, but they are saying they have no choice and need to protect the Basque people from the terror group called the Night Brigade. Given the history, there is very little trust in the Spanish government and that is beginning to spark dissent. I predict that the arrival of Spanish troops will trigger some early protests. Your plan is working."

"Good," said Belinda. "Send a team to the locations you identified and plant canisters. We can throw the whole military into chaos with a few targeted detonations. Be cautious. No doubt they are already preparing to defend these locations before they move the troops, but they are not ready for us. We still have the element of surprise on our side."

The speaker on the conference table buzzed.

"There's been an incident at Sort," said the detached voice on the speaker. "We have video."

"Show us," said Belinda.

The map image on the screen flipped to a video taken from a fixed remote camera near the heliport at Sort. It showed a Spanish military helicopter descending into the silo opening.

"Not unusual," said Belinda.

"Wait a couple minutes."

Soon the video showed movement around the circular entrance. A team in fatigues was exploring the entrance.

"Stop the video," said Belinda. "What are those uniforms?"

"They look French," said Assad.

"Zoom in," said Belinda. "That helmet is Interpol."

"They responded," said the voice. Soon the five drones appeared and began deploying nanobots over the team. Belinda watched as they put on gas masks and began injecting each other. They dragged each other down the hillside and disappeared into the bushes. The drones lost contact and returned to the base.

"This is a problem," said Belinda. "Get me command."

The speaker went silent and then buzzed again.

"Command here."

"You should have alerted me before you fired on that Interpol team."

"We didn't have time. They were getting too close."

"But you've exposed us by using the bots!"

"We didn't have a choice."

"You did. You just didn't exercise it. Mierda."

There was a pause.

"What are your orders?"

Belinda controlled her rage. "You have to scuttle the base."

"What?"

"You need to destroy everything, including the drones. Kill the electronics. Rig a trap with the remaining bots. Anyone who decides to explore further does it at their peril. Do it now. Get everyone out and make your way to Ainsa. Scratch that. Put on your Spanish fatigues and take a chopper to the base at Pamplona. Park it there. You are Spanish soldiers coming to protect Pamplona from the Night Brigade. Then make your way back here, slowly, and be cautious. Rent bikes or something."

Pablo looked at Belinda. "Anything you need from me?"

"I need you and your team to move fast. Set the traps at the bases and get back here. We can't be certain Roda is not on the radar. If they found Sort, they might have found Roda. We need to prep."

Pablo took his team and went into the laboratory's freezer vault where they stored the nanobots. They put on their hazmat suits and entered the vault and began building explosive canisters and filing them with chunks of grey goo. They packed the canisters in sealed containers and transported them to an underground parking lot where Belinda kept a fleet of trucks and military vehicles she had acquired over time. Pablo took two trucks and two bikes and drove down the tunnel to the concrete rear exit. From there they took the convoy into Pamplona. Spanish soldiers were beginning to arrive, and he noticed a handful waiting alongside the road. They waved at him as he passed, and he waved back. He drove to a location near the first heliport, parked out of sight. He called Belinda and told her he was in position at what they called Checkpoint A. She agreed he should sit tight until nightfall. They waited.

Just as the sun began to set, a young boy on a bike rode up to the truck. He banged on the door. Pablo looked down.

"Hey, mister," said the boy.

Pablo rolled down his window.

"Are you a soldier?"

Pablo smiled at the boy.

"Do you like soldiers?"

"Not really," said the boy.

"Why not?" said Pablo.

"My dad said you are here to take away our land."

"That's not true," said Pablo. "We're here to protect you."

"Why are you protecting us? What are you protecting us from?" said the boy.

"You are a very smart boy," replied Pablo. "You need to run along. We have important work to do."

"I don't think you are protecting us," said the boy. He pressed on his pedal and rode away. He turned and shouted, "You're a liar!"

Pablo shook his head. He wished the boy knew that Pablo was there to restore the boy's land. He climbed out of the truck. He loaded canisters onto the two bikes and rode over to the heliport. He saw soldiers climbing out of trucks at the heliport. Pablo was glad he moved quickly. The soldiers were still in the early stages of setting up the base. He and his partner on the other bike found strategic locations along the perimeter fence and hid the canisters. Then they rode back to the truck. They drove up and noticed the other truck was missing. He radioed his teammates. There was no response. He told his partner to wait while he investigated the truck. He walked to the rear of the truck and looked onto the truck bed. The canisters were gone. He radioed Belinda to confirm that the other truck had moved on to Checkpoint B. Belinda had heard nothing. Then she heard an explosion. The truck lifted 10 feet in the air before turning and landing on its side in in a large crater in flames. Pablo's body disintegrated. Pablo's partner watched in horror as a missile hit the truck from an overhead drone. He felt the blast and fell backwards off the bike. The bike tipped over and crashed to the asphalt. Dazed, he picked up the bike and rode off. He started back toward the Roda base camp. His radio crackled. Belinda was yelling

Pablo's name. He stopped the bike and answered, "Pablo's gone."

"Gone?" she asked.

"Dead," he replied.

"What happened?" she yelled.

"I don't know," he answered. "Everything exploded."

"What happened to the canisters?"

"We placed some of them. They are at the heliport. The rest are missing with the other truck."

"You need to find it," she said. "Don't come back. Find the truck and the canisters and report in."

"Understood," he responded.

"Do you have the detonator?"

"I have a back-up."

"Don't wait. Get your mask on and blow the charges. Confirm with me directly when it's done."

"Will do."

He rode back to the heliport. The soldiers were racing around the base. They must have seen the explosion because they were acting like they were under attack. He pulled the back-up detonator out of his jacket and put the mask on, hiding behind a wall where he could see the smoke from the canisters as they blew. He pressed the detonator. Nothing happened. He pressed it again. Still nothing. He radioed Belinda. "Nothing is happening."

"What do you mean?"

"I am blowing the canisters, but I don't see anything."

"Did you check to see that they were hot?"

"Yes, all of them."

"Nothing?"

"Nothing."

"Go find the truck." She clicked off.

Belinda's mind was racing. She readied the team for an assault. She thought it unlikely they would bomb the compound. Releasing that many of her nanobots into the atmosphere would cause a catastrophe that reached from Lisbon to Rome. It would destroy Spain completely. But if they were that foolish, she was already dead. She armed her team members and placed them in strategic locations around the base. She also armed her weapon drones and released surveillance drones and waited in the command center for signs of an assault.

* * *

Brian overheard the discussion between Van and the Sort team leader. He approached the Director, who was engaged with directors from other agencies.

The Director looked back at Brian.

"Are we ready?"

"We could be readier," Brian said. "But if this is the moment, this is the moment."

"This is the moment. The Roda team believes they found the compound."

"We need a final briefing on nanobot protections," said Brian. "The team needs to be assured that we will do everything we can to defend them but, if they are attacked, they must protect themselves. If they freeze up, they imperil not only their own lives, but the lives of those around them."

Brian took a breath. He had never been the military type. Even with all the work done in Great Falls, the reality of combat felt like something entirely new. He thought about Van and how utterly fearless she seemed to be. The thought of Van gave Brian the resolve he needed.

A half-dozen semi-trucks were loaded with drones. Each truck carried over 500 drones the vast majority of which were attack drones. Behind the semis, four mobile launchers carried missile interceptors. Behind them, Brian had fire trucks loaded with the resonant CO_2 spray in the event of a ground-level nanobot release.

At a signal from Command, the trucks left on their five-hour journey to Ainsa. Meanwhile, Van moved her team out of the town of Ainsa and back to the LZ. She decided she wanted a better look at the compound. Along with her team, Van boarded the Caiman helicopter and took off.

"Come around from behind," she said to the pilot through the mike. Command was listening. The pilot took a wide swath over the adjacent mountains, flying at 15,000 feet, well above the tallest peaks. He swung back at the Aragon border heading southwest and dropped to 2,000 feet. At Formigales, he took a beeline for Muro de Roda. Halfway up the hill they noticed a new dirt road leading to a rear vehicle entrance.

"Are you seeing this?" Van said to Command.

"Confirmed," they responded.

Just as the helicopter moved past the entrance, a swarm of drones lifted out of an opening above the entrance.

"Drones," shouted someone.

"Abort" yelled Van. "Get us out of here."

The pilot did a quick pivot and headed away. The drone swarm followed. Those with guns fired at the drones. Brian yelled in the mic, "Don't shoot the drones!"

"Masks!" yelled Van and everyone put on their modified gas masks.

The pilot took the helicopter up to 20,000 feet and the drones began to fall away but a couple managed the elevation and fired RPGs at the helicopter. One RPG hit the tail of the helicopter and knocked it sideways. The pilot fought to get control. A black cloud enveloped the helicopter, and the drones fell back unable to sustain the loft. As good as the masks were, Van still felt her throat start to clinch up and she saw members of the unit start to cough.

"Get your pens out!" she directed. She grabbed her EpiPen and stabbed her thigh. Everyone followed suit. The helicopter righted and flew out of the cloud. Van felt her symptoms subside.

Brian shouted into the mike, "Everyone all right?"

"We're good! We're good," said Van.

"We need a new LZ," she told Command. "Where do you want us?"

"Give us a second," Command responded. "Head to Zaragoza Air Base. We will alert them."

"10-4."

Brian assembled his team for a pre-briefing.

"It's clear now their drones not only spray nanobots but also have firing capability. Get yourselves ready because it's time. Our team is the head of the spear."

Bost chuckled, "Head of the spear?"

"Whatever," said Brian. "We are the advance group. It's our job to deplete Belinda's drone army. Van's team will make their way as close to the compound as possible. They will plant mesh routers around the compound, so we have the bandwidth we need for the AI swarm to work. Our back-up will be operator controlled for targets that evade the swarm. We don't know how smart Belinda's drones are. We also don't know the size of her drone army. This could be a very long day. Be ready for it."

They joined the main group assembled in the field near the helicopter squadron. Units from each country were receiving instructions in their home language. Brian and the Director walked together to the podium.

"Brian's team will lead the assault. Everything will be monitored here at the Chateau. I can't tell you how important our mission is. Nanobot warfare is an entirely new kind of battle. We don't know the full capabilities of our enemy. But we have prepared well. The world is counting on you to end this reign of terror before it spreads. I have believed in you all along. It is time now for you to believe in yourselves."

The assembled units shouted an assent in multiple languages. The Director laughed.

"How about a simple hoo-rah!" said the Director and raised his fist.

"Hoo-rah!" they said in unison and raised their fists.

"Now Brian has a few words."

Brian knew he didn't need to repeat any instructions. He told them to be aware of the enemy. He explained that their protection and the protection of their fellow soldiers demanded that they follow protection protocol. Their gas masks were specially outfitted for the nanobots and each of them carried pens and antitoxins to protect against the anaphylactic reactions.

"You will need everything you have." He concluded.

The squads boarded the helicopters and took off. Brian and the leadership returned to Command.

Van checked in with Command.

"Status?"

"We're coming," said the Director. "How is the team?"

"Team A is mostly recovered. Two are still with the medical unit here. They need to remain. The rest of us are go."

"Good. We believe in you, Van," he said. "You got this."

"What's the drones' ETA?"

"Two hours."

Van gathered her remaining team members and boarded the helicopters. She spoke to both teams. "You heard Brian. We'll mask up immediately. Be ready with your EpiPens. We know she has cameras. We'll use sensors to locate any active electronics and take them out. Be on the lookout for nanobot traps."

The helicopters dropped off the teams in a field next to Fumenal, a small hamlet that served as an outpost in medieval times in the Kingdom of Aragon when Muro de Roda was an active military fort. The helicopters disappeared and Van and her team began the climb up to Muro de Roda. The drones were still an hour away. As Van's teammates made their way up the hill, they spread out and set up tripods with battery operated routers and cams capable of communicating with the drones. Suddenly Van heard a pop. She looked up and saw a small puff of smoke about 100 yards in front of her. She ran up the trail to the puff of smoke and a team member was on the ground writhing. The blast tore open his pants and his leg was bleeding.

The smoke looked as if it was trying to enter the wound. He jerked and shouted, "They're in me!" Van pulled an EpiPen and jammed it in his leg.

"You are ok. You are going to be ok." She felt her own throat tighten as the cloud started to grow and enveloped the team. "Your pens!" she shouted and stabbed her thigh. They all did the same. The wounded soldier started to cough and choke. Van injected him with the anti-toxin and within seconds he relaxed. They wrapped the wound and carried him down the trail away from the blast site and told him to rest.

"How many cams have we set?" Van asked her crew. Different voices popped off.

"Three here."

"I got five."

"Two over here."

"Two over here also."

"Ok. I need a team to come with me to the rear entrance. Who's in?"

The names came flying in. No one wanted to be left behind.

"Someone needs to stay with Bret." One person who happened to be a trained medic agreed to stay and help the injured soldier down to the LZ.

"The rest of you make your way here," said Van. "We will wait for the drones before moving further."

The trucks arrived in Ainsa just as the helicopter squadron arrived. The soldiers jumped off the choppers and ran to the trucks, assisting the existing crew in setting up the basecamp and preparing the drones for battle.

"Get them in the air," said Brian from Command. "As the signals from each drone turned green, operators at Command hit the flight switches and the drones lifted to 25 feet and hovered. Five trucks carried attack drones. Each truck operated as a separate swarm and had an individual operator. Soon the sky was filled with 2,500 attack drones. At Brian's command, the operators hit a button labeled autopilot and the queen drones for each swarm rose above the rest and moved toward Muro de Roda.

Brian radioed Van. "They're coming."

Van replied, "No activity from the compound. We've seen nothing."

* * *

Belinda watched with her leads from the underground operations room for signs of an attack.

"Helicopters approaching from the south."

"How many?"

"Two."

"Landing at Fumenal."

"Hold," said Belinda.

"It is a small group," said Assad. "They don't stand a chance."

"It's a lead group," said Belinda. "Don't be distracted. We will hit them when it's time."

"They are setting up some kind of network."

A red light blinked. "They tripped a canister. Someone is down."

"That should hold them for now," said Belinda.

"Activity in Ainsa!" someone yelled. "A lot of it!"

"What do you see?"

"Drones. Hundreds of drones. Maybe a couple thousand. They look small."

Belinda was not surprised by the idea of a drone attack on the compound. The good news was that she and her team were underground in a fortified compound. A full-on assault of the compound by bunker busters would release cataclysmic volumes of nanobots into the air, the consequences of which would, as she thought previously, spread across the entire country and beyond. The small drones were not intended to do that kind of damage. So, thought Belinda, what were they thinking?

"The drones are separating into swarms. They are five clicks out."

"Open the shields."

The doors of multiple bunkers situated on the hillsides below the fort parted and a landing pad containing dozens of drones armed with nanobot-filled RPGs and guns with nano-bullets on each pad slid into place. Above the bunker doors, smaller windows appeared in the hillside with armed and masked fighters ready for combat.

"Go!" said Belinda. "Now!"

Belinda's terror drones lifted in unison and waited until the attack drones were within a few hundred yards, close enough for the shooters to reach. They began firing and the drone swarms followed the queen drone zipping left and right and up and down, evading most of the bullets. The terror drones began firing at the attack drones and the grenades that missed flew down the hillside and exploded, sending plumes of nanobot clouds into the air. Belinda then watched as something happened that at first, she could not comprehend. Several of the attack drones surrounded the nanobot clouds and began spraying the clouds with a mist that within seconds caused the clouds to dissipate. The attack drones that ignored the clouds began what looked like a mating ritual or comical dance with the terror drones. The fighters kept shooting and were able to take down several attack drones, but the volume of drones was more than they could handle. The attack drones were latching onto the terror drones and carrying them away from the compound.

"What the hell is going on?" Belinda cried. "Stop them!"

Assad responded, "The entire team is firing high speed rounds, but they can't hit them all."

"They are not hitting any of them. We are just firing randomly in the air.

"We hit about 10 percent," said Assad.

"We need something else," said Belinda. She was beginning to realize she wasn't prepared for this assault. Any scenario that she had imagined would have no defense against the weaponized nanobots. But this attack was working. She needed to escalate and fast.

"Launch the spikes!"

Assad looked at her like she was crazy. The precision strike missiles called spikes were not intended as a defense of the compound.

"Launch the spikes? Where?"

Belinda yelled, "You are idiots! Open the main entrance and get the launchers on the road. Target Ainsa! Target Zaragoza! Target Pamplona! They'll pay for this. They won't know what hit them."

Assad looked at Belinda. For a minute he thought she was losing control and doubted her sanity. This is the horror of war, he thought. She must have a plan. We've been here too long for it to come apart so quickly. He turned to his team.

"Do as she says!" he shouted. "Launch the spikes. They won't reach Pamplona or Zaragosa, but they will reach the base at Ainsa. We need to destroy the source."

* * *

"Here we go," said Brian.

"We got this," said Bost, although he had no idea what was about to happen.

The cam and mesh network set up by Van's team popped on the main monitor. Command leadership watched as the drone swarms rose off their landing pads and formed around the queens. The queens separated and moved in different directions with their swarms tailing behind them. They watched as the first wave of drones clashed with Belinda's drone army.

"Beautiful," said Bost.

"They are shooting at them," said Brian. "But they're missing."

The attack drones began arriving back at the Ainsa base with the captive terror drones and deposited the disabled drones on the ground. Soldiers sprayed the terror drones with resonant CO_2 and carefully disassembled the drones.

From the Command Center, Sal directed his team, "Ready the interceptors. We don't know what to expect." Brian heard Sal and the military commanders discussing an air attack.

The drone battle continued for well over an hour and the attack drones were able to capture over 80 percent of the terror drones. The remaining drones launched their weapons and returned to the compound. The nanobot clouds had dissipated and the queens pulled back the swarms.

"Bring them home," said Brian and the operators took control of the queens and led the attack drones back to basecamp.

Van used the drone mêlée to advance her team toward the concrete rear entrance. They moved slowly up the hill and used the bushes for cover as much as possible.

They looked for trip wires and where they found them and the rigged canisters, they carefully disassembled them to clear out their path of escape. When they reached the entrance, they notified Command and Command steered the battle to the opposite side of the compound. Brian let her know that the drone strategy was working and they were successfully disabling Belinda's drone army. Then the rear doors parted. Van hid with her crew on both sides of the entrance and watched as two large missile launchers drove out of the compound.

The trucks were moving fast. Van radioed into Command that the launchers had just exited the compound. As the doors started to close, Van and her team were able to sneak in through doors and into a large tunnel that disappeared under the mountain. They moved quietly through the tunnel with their weapons at the ready, but they saw no one. Van tried her radio to see if it worked and Command could hear her, but the connection was patchy. She was able to communicate by text.

As they moved through the tunnel, they saw vaults filled with army vehicles and weapons including crates of machine guns and surface to air missiles. They saw a double doorway leading into a large walk-in freezer chamber. Inside the chamber were dozens of large five-foot cylinders with temperature gauges on the lids. Van assumed that was where Belinda stored the weaponized nanobots. They wandered further and found more freezer vaults. Van texted the findings back to Command. Brian read the texts and told the Director, "You must tell the military that they cannot bomb the compound. It would be a disaster."

* * *

Belinda pulled the team into the conference room.

"We are not done," she said. "This little skirmish is not over. Thoughts?"

The first deputy started, "They can't think that their drones are enough to secure this compound. The batteries will die. The drones won't last forever."

Belinda responded, "We don't know the battery life or their charging capabilities. We can't trust that the drones will die."

Assad pulled a map up on the monitor. "The drone camp is on the north end of Ainsa," he said. "Wait until dark and send RPG squads to hit the camp. We might be able to steal some of their drones and bring them back here."

"Right," said another deputy. "We can soften the camp with RPGs and then hit them with the spikes. The spikes will destroy the camp."

Belinda responded, "The spikes will set them back on their heels and give us time. The bottom line is that this compound is compromised.

Even if the drone problem is addressed, their military knows where we are. They still may try to bomb the compound, but they will send an invasion force. I'm not interested in a Masada or Alamo-type end to this battle. We need an escape plan and route."

"We bomb the base camp and leave the compound while they are dealing with the bombings."

"That, but more," said Belinda. "They made a mistake by not evacuating Ainsa or the other villages around here. Take the drones we have left and hit every small town we can. The distraction will force them to redirect their efforts to save the lives of the villagers. Once distracted, we can take our helicopters and leave. It won't be easy, but we can escape."

Belinda told Assad to ready the RPG squads and to target the helicopters. She had her team reload the remaining drones. She readied the helicopters and loaded them with enough frozen nanobots to be able to start over at a new location.

* * *

Brian texted Van: "Well done. Fighting has stopped. TIME TO LEAVE." But Van worried that they might not get another shot at Belinda. She was in the compound and didn't want to leave. She texted back. "Send a team with the spray. We will get the back door open. Need to DISABLE the nanobots."

"Shit," said Brian, loud enough for others to hear. He looked at Bost. "Send a truck with a team and the spray. Van thinks she can get us into the compound."

Van heard voices. They broke through a side door and into an armory and hid. A dozen of Belinda's fighters came down the tunnel in jeeps and drove into the armory. They busted open the crates containing handheld rocket launchers and tossed them into the back of the jeeps. They found crates containing the RPGs and loaded them on a flatbed cart and rolled them out of the armory and into the freezer vaults. They drove the jeeps back into the tunnel and locked the armory.

Van's team remained hidden in the armory and were never discovered. After the fighters left, she texted Command that the enemy was readying a ground incursion. She told them to watch for movement near the base camp and soldiers with RPGs. She waited until the jeeps drove away, and they broke out of the armory. She told three of her team members to go back to the entrance and find some way to get the rear doors to open and lock in an open position. Then she and the rest of the team made their way deeper into the tunnel.

The other team reached the entrance. They studied the electronics and looked for a switch that would override the mechanism and allow them to lock the rear doors in an open position. The doors were too heavy to force open, and they texted Van. "We are at the doors. Unclear how to open."

"Look for a bypass switch," she texted. "Find a circuit breaker box."

"Got it," they texted. "Can't just kill the electrical. Doors are too heavy to move."

"Keep looking."

Van's team reached the end of tunnel. There was an elevator and a staircase. On the right was another doorway. Van looked carefully through the window. She saw the helicopter bay and noticed some of Belinda's team members were loading the helicopters. She left two of her team hiding by the helicopter bay entrance and pointed for them to move in when clear. Then she and three remaining members went up the stairs.

At the first level they carefully investigated a lit hall and saw sleeping quarters that looked like dorm rooms. They kept climbing and heard footsteps. They went back to the hallway and ducked into the nearest dorm. Someone walked out of the bathroom and started to yell but the squad silenced him and pulled his body back in the bathroom. They waited for the footsteps to pass and re-entered the staircase. The next level was the operations center, and Van caught a glimpse of Belinda making her way to the elevator. They rushed back down the stairs and waited near the helicopter bay, but the elevator went up and stopped. The helicopter bay had emptied, and Van watched the elevators until it started down. She moved the team into the helicopter bay and waited again. Belinda and her deputies entered the bay. Van and her team started shooting and they hit two of the deputies. Belinda turned and ran out of the bay. Fighters that had been following her came through the door and started firing toward the shots coming from Van's team. They pinned Van and her team down and allowed the deputies to make their way behind the fighters to one of the helicopters and scramble on. The fighters kept firing but backed out toward the same helicopter. A large port above the helicopter parted and the helicopters rotors began to turn. Van's team hit one of the fighters sitting on the edge of the helicopter door and he tumbled to the ground as the helicopter lifted toward the open port. Van's team kept firing and hit the main rotor engine. The helicopter lurched forward into the steel door that had been opening and exploded. The helicopter crashed onto the bay as Van's team raced out of the bay and back into the tunnel.

Meanwhile Belinda made her way to the RPG team and climbed into one of the two jeeps they had outfitted with RPGs.

"Go!" she said, and the jeeps took off down the tunnel toward to entrance. As they approached the rear doors, they saw Van's team members at the circuit box and began firing. The doors parted as the jeeps approached and

Belinda yelled, "Keep driving!" As soon as the doors opened, Van's team hit the circuit breaker, and the doors stopped moving.

As soon as the shooting stopped and the helicopter was gone, Van and her team ran down to the armory. They grabbed a couple of jeeps and chased Belinda out of the compound and down the dirt road. Van could see her well below as the road wound down the steep grade of the mountain. They reached a fork and Belinda sent part of the team toward Ainsa and the base camp and she took a jeep herself down the other road. Van radioed in that she was in pursuit of Belinda and that a team of fighters was making their way toward the basecamp. She told her team to follow the fighters, and she went in pursuit of Belinda.

Belinda took a long road north around the back of Muro de Roda. Van got close enough to follow her. She headed around the base of the mountains and over to the western end of the Mediano reservoir right next to the dam. Van saw her pull off the road and jump out of the jeep and run. She pulled up beside Belinda's jeep and took off after her on a footpath. The footpath started to go uphill, and the river below fell away from the path. Van turned a corner and the view puzzled her. A large, tall cliff several hundred feet high ran from a couple hundred feet above her down to the river below. Instead of a footpath, the forestry service or some mining company had cut out a notch about four feet into the cliff.

Van looked ahead and saw Belinda moving down the notch. She jumped into the notch and ran. The notch went on for miles. Van kept running and looking for Belinda. After every corner she paused to peek and be sure Belinda wasn't waiting there to shoot her and then she ran on.

There was nowhere for Belinda to go except forward. There were no hiding places and no way to climb up the cliff. Van reached a sharp turn in the notch and looked around the corner and there was Belinda. A large boulder had fallen into the notch and blocked it. Belinda was trying to climb around the boulder on the outside, but her grip was tentative.

"Stop!" yelled Van. "Stop and surrender! I won't shoot."

Belinda looked at Van.

"Of course, it's you," she said. She turned at Van and smiled. "I thought I killed you when I left you on the road in Pamplona."

"Surrender, Belinda. You can't get around the boulder."

"Shoot me," said Belinda. She momentarily lost her grip, and her bag fell off her shoulder and plummeted down into the river. She almost fell but got her grip back. "Whoa, that was close," she said as if she didn't care. She looked at Van. "Americans," she said. "You think you're doing all of us a favor, but you forget why you are there in the first place. You forget the people, and you think it's your job to protect the world. Doesn't it strike you as odd that we, the ones who make up the world, think we need to protect ourselves from you?"

"I'm not the one who kills innocent children, Belinda. You are. Surrender or I'll shoot."

"Then shoot," said Belinda and suddenly, for no apparent reason, let go of the boulder. Her body seemed suspended in the air for an instant, and she stared at Van as she dropped out of sight and down into the river below. Van waited and watched the splash and then saw Belinda's body pop up and float unmoving down the river and then over a 100-foot waterfall at the end of the gorge. She turned and headed back to the jeep. As she walked back through the notch, she hadn't realized how far she had run. It took forever to get to the jeep and when she got there, she radioed Command.

"Belinda's dead."

"What happened? Do you have her body?"

"I don't. She fell several hundred feet into a river. I saw the body float unmoving down the river and go over a large waterfall. I don't have any reason to believe she survived. I'm heading to the falls to confirm. I'll detail when I get back to base."

The drone team at Ainsa got Van's earlier texts about the RPG attack and set up a dragnet around the camp waiting for Belinda's fighters. The jeep carrying the RPGs came flying around a corner and directly into a blockade filled with masked soldiers. The driver veered and the jeep slid sideways to avoid the blockade and turned over, spilling the fighters and the rocket launchers onto the road. A couple launchers fired indiscriminately, and the RPGs exploded sending plumes of nanobots into the air. Drones that had been hovering above the blockade targeted the plumes and sprayed the nanobots sending them falling harmlessly to the ground. Van's team came upon the crash scene and rushed the fighters who were injured from the crash and bound them and took them into custody. A couple fighters tried to run and the soldiers at the blockade cut them down.

Back at Command, surveillance drones that caught up with the mobile launchers captured images of them preparing to launch. The military redirected a high-altitude strike drone that initially was sent to hit Muro de Roda. It hit the launchers before they could launch. Large plumes of nanobots emerged out of the strike and Brian directed dozens of attack drones to contain the plumes. On the ground, the team carrying the resonant CO_2 spray saw the explosion and the plume and raced to the blast site where they sprayed the nanobot cloud at its base and the combination melted the cloud and it too fell harmlessly to the ground.

Troops moved out from the Ainsa base camp and headed to the Muro de Roda compound. They entered through the concrete entrance that Van's team had frozen open. At first, it seemed no one was there. They searched to the end of the tunnel and up the stairs and found a group of fighters in the main conference room on their knees with a white flag.

The Command Center erupted in cheers, jumping and hugging each other. The Director came over to Brian with a huge smile. He grabbed Brian's hand and said, "You did it, you fucking genius." Brian laughed and said, "Not without this team, and not without Detective Eng." He looked down at the floor and had to fight back the tears of relief. Then he looked up, "Where is she, anyway?"

Chapter 29.

Consequences

Van waited in her room at the Chateau. The exhaustion of the past week caught up with her, and she wanted nothing to do with anyone. The Director threw a party for the team, but Van begged off and asked politely to be excused. The Director was understanding but requested that she make an appearance, so she took time to dress up and walked into the ballroom. The entire room stood and applauded Van. She bowed her head in appreciation and immediately pointed out Brian and his team, and the applause continued. The Director grabbed a microphone and expressed to everyone how their cooperation, bravery and ingenuity made the difference. He pointed to a large screen on the wall and the President of the United States appeared. He told them how grateful the country was for their efforts and for ridding the world of this insane terrorist. He introduced the Secretary of Defense who played a video and, noting that all the weaponized nanobots had been destroyed, described the destruction of the bunker complex that Belinda built under Muro de Roda. The video showed a pair of bunker busters hitting the hilltop and leaving a giant crater where Muro de Roda once stood. The room erupted and Van, noting the moment, slipped out and went back to her room. She laid down and tried to rest. There was a knock on the door.

"Are you ok?" asked Brian through the door.

"I'm fine," said Van. "Don't talk through the door. Come on in. It's open."

Brian poked his head into the room, and Van sat up on the edge of her bed. She patted the spot next to her, and he came over sat down.

"I was so worried about you."

"I know," she said. "I'm sorry."

"No. Don't be sorry. You are a hero."

"I don't feel like a hero," said Van.

Brian hugged her. She felt soft and accepting. "How do you feel about a little love?"

She looked up at him and Brian kissed her. She wrapped her arms around him and kissed him back and pulled him down onto the bed.

"I'm so tired," she said.

"Let's find a way to put you to sleep." He looked into her eyes and smiled. They were speaking to him, and they said yes, and he kissed her again.

"Lock the door," she whispered. He crawled over to the edge and pushed himself up, his pants dragging around his knees. He locked the door and kicked off his pants and jumped back into bed. Van laughed at him and kissed her, and he helped her pull off her dress. They crawled under the sheets and then heard a knock.

"Everyone ok in there?" asked Bost.

"Go away, Bost," said Van and laughed again. Bost disappeared and Brian slid on top of Van and smothered her in his love. This is exactly what I needed, she thought to herself, and before the sky turned dark, they both passed out.

Two days later, Van arrived in Los Angeles. She contacted the Chief and let him know she would be home if he wanted to chat. He had heard on the news and through various channels what had happened in Spain. The President had commended the team for their accomplishments and world leaders talked about the importance of the collaboration and the contribution of multiple countries.

The Chief knew of Van's involvement and followed it closely. He invited her to the morning briefing where he called her up and commended her again for her work in Europe. The Mayor showed up to the meeting and handed Van a special award. She spoke for a minute thanking them and talked about the importance of teamwork on the international front and at home. The Chief handed her badge and gun and made a show of welcoming her back from her leave. Then he continued the briefing.

Van sat down. The other officers all smiled at her and made her feel that they knew how important she had become. The briefing went forward, but there was no mention of the investigation into Scott or Charles' murders and no mention of the child prostitution ring at the underground sex club.

Van left and returned to her desk. She could tell someone rifled through the desk and then tried to make it look as it was previously but had acted hastily. She wandered over to CHESS and found Alvin.

"What's going on?"

Alvin looked dishevelled. His skin was dry and flaky, and his suit was covered with the flakes. He didn't want to look at her.

"Alvin?" she said.

"I'm glad you are back."

"Me too," Van replied. "I think. The murders? Did they get resolved?"

"We should talk," said Alvin. "But not here. Meet me at Angelico's at 3 pm. Can you do that?"

"Of course," she said. Angelico's had been a popular lunch spot for the Bureau back in the 1950s. The Bureau had long since moved on to other dining establishments and only a few of the old guard ever went back. It was a decent Italian restaurant and survived by the skin of its teeth and by the bar regulars.

Van looked in a couple minutes late. Alvin was standing at the bar talking with the bartender. He saw her and smiled, and they grabbed a booth in the back.

"You got me concerned," said Van. "What's going on?"

"Do you want a drink?" said Alvin and motioned to the bartender. He came over.

"We'll have a couple old fashioneds," he said. He looked at Van for her to confirm and she nodded.

"House?"

"No," said Alvin. "I've heard wonderful things about a Kentucky bourbon called Angel's Envy. Do you have that?"

"Of course."

"Awesome," said Alvin, "because I am sitting with someone right now who is exactly that, the envy of the angels."

Van didn't respond. Alvin was being very strange, and the compliment came off as tacky and inauthentic. She looked at the bartender and said, "Thank you."

"Something happened to you," she said.

"They shut it down, Van," said Alvin. "I tried to put a sting together and they shut it down. Not only that, but they threatened me with firing and the loss of my pension if I pursued it. I'm sorry."

Van was shocked. "Who shut it down?" she asked. "The Chief?"

"IA," he replied. "IA concluded there was no evidence to charge any officers."

"Did you mention the tunnel and the sex club?"

"I did and no one wanted to talk about it. They called it a cheesy night club."

"What about Scott and Charles? What about me?"

"You need to watch out for yourself. With all this international stuff, maybe you should join the FBI or the CIA."

"That's not a response, Alvin. Did IA put the cases in the freezer?"

Alvin didn't want to talk anymore.

"What about the FBI?"

"How's the old fashioned?" he asked innocently.

"Alvin!" Van let her frustration show and then took a breath.

"Ok," she said. "You need to protect yourself. I get it. I understand."

Alvin looked down. "I've never been so disappointed in myself."

"You're brilliant, Alvin. Don't forget that." Van slammed down the remainder of her old fashioned and stood. "I love you, Alvin," she said as she turned to leave the restaurant. "You've been there for me."

When she got to her car, she called Agent Sams at the FBI.

"Did Detective Broad contact you?"

"I don't believe so," said Sams. "Wait. I did get a call but not from Broad. It came from someone named Coldridge and I tried but haven't been able to reach her."

"Do you have time?"

"For you? Of course."

"Meet me in Franklin Canyon Reservoir in 45 minutes. Can you do that?"

"I'll be there."

Van started her Ford Interceptor and took off. She parked at the entrance to the reservoir. No one had followed her. She felt the trauma of her last visit there but steeled herself. She waited for Sams and in about ten minutes he showed up.

"Good to see you, Van," he said. "I heard about Europe. I was worried."

"It was not easy," she said. "But I have come home to something just as disturbing."

"What is this place?" asked Henry.

"This is where Charlie was killed investigating the murder of a young detective names Scott Geiringer. It is also a place where I was ambushed and barely escaped."

"Is it safe?"

"I can't guarantee that," said Van. "Follow me."

She drew her pistol and Sams did the same. They walked up the path to the ledge overlooking the reservoir.

"What was Charlie looking for?"

"He wasn't looking for anything. He was meeting an officer named Ben Bodrogi."

"You know that?"

"I have Charlie's notebook. It was the last note he took before he was killed. So, I believe that."

"Sounds like it's not in our jurisdiction."

"I understand but I need your help."

"What can I do?"

"Right now, help me look for bullet fragments." She handed him gloves and a bag.

Henry and Van and crawled through the bushes and studied the trees. Van kept hearing sounds that seemed like bullets coming at her again, but it was just Henry crunching over the stems and scraping through the bushes. After about 30 minutes, they had bagged a handful of fragments and shell casings. Van gave them to Henry.

"Can you take these to your forensics team and have them analyzed?"

"I can."

"I'll find the fragments from Charlie and Scott. They may be in Evidence or with the coroner, but I will find them. I need you to compare these fragments and casings with those fragments."

"We can do that. But you still are not telling me something."

"Right. I stumbled onto a child prostitution ring while I was on leave."

"I see. Wow. Now that is interesting."

"It is something the FBI needs to investigate. But I think the LAPD is involved and I think it is connected to Scott's murder and probably Charlie's murder and I can't do anything. Internal Affairs has closed the case prematurely. I think they are protecting officers, including this officer named Ben Bodrogi. If I try to reopen the case, they will probably kill me also."

Van walked through her experience with tunnel out of No Vacancy and the sex club. She told Henry that she saw officers there and Bodrogi with a young child. She wanted Bodrogi detained but she was told that what she saw did not constitute credible evidence of actual prostitution.

"And you want him detained and connected to the murders."

"If he is guilty, I do."

"I got it," said Henry. "Let me take it from here. You lay low."

"You don't have to ask me twice," said Van.

Agent Sams pulled his team together and strategized about the sex club. They pulled in a couple of agents who were unknowns from out of state and planted them as guests at the club. They wore wires and found the secret room and recorded multiple conversations. They found alternative entrances to the club and then they set up the sting.

"You might want to come along," Henry told Van. "You said Ben didn't recognize you before. We can keep it that way."

The FBI's undercover unit outfitted Van with makeup, a wig and a padded suit to make her look heavier. She and Henry drove to No Vacancy. The FBI had questioned No Vacancy and determined that staff was aware of underground shenanigans at what they viewed as an underground club but not anything as nefarious as child prostitution. Many Hollywood actors seemed to enjoy the intrigue of an underground club, and No Vacancy had found an offshoot to the main tunnel near its location. They build a connecting link to the tunnel system from their night club and used it as an attraction for customers.

No Vacancy was in on the sting. The undercover agents identified the LAPD officers who were paid to watch over the operation, and those officers, like Ben, who took part in the activities. They were in the secret room as Henry and Van and a team of agents made their way through the tunnel to the club. When they arrived at the club, they ordered the doors locked and blocked the staircase to the secret room.

Within minutes they had arrested everyone up in the secret room including, Van noticed with satisfaction, Robert Gibbens and his buddies and Officer Ben Bodrogi. Child Services arrived and shepherded the children out of the room and out of the club through the same rear entrance that the prostitution ring had been using to bring the children into the club.

When Henry and Van got to the surface, Van turned and said, "I can't thank you enough."

"I can't thank you enough," he responded. "This is a just a beginning. These arrests are likely to lead to a hunt for ringleaders that we don't have yet. But it is a good start."

"Let me know where Bodrogi goes," said Van. "I want to talk to him out of earshot of IA and the LAPD."

When Van returned to the Bureau the next day, the Chief called her into his office.

"Seems you have been busy," he said.

"Not really," Van responded. "I am looking for new cases."

"Really," he said. "Did you hear about the bust in Hollywood?"

"Was it on the news?" she asked.

"The FBI nabbed some child prostitution ringers."

"That's a good thing, right?"

"Definitely. If you haven't heard, there will be some news regarding us."

"What do you mean?"

"Unfortunately, some of our guys got themselves involved. It's too bad. Not going to look good for us."

"Sorry to hear that Chief. Let me know if there is anything I can do."

"As a matter of fact, there is," he said. "IA closed your partner's murder case and now I am thinking they might have closed it prematurely."

"Do you want me to dig in again?"

"I do. I know it's dangerous, but you are the only one who can solve it."

"I can do that, Chief. Thanks."

"Be careful."

The discussion with the Chief surprised Van, but then again it didn't. The Chief was a politician. If the sex club bust made him look bad, he needed something else that made him look good like solving a tough murder case. That he was using her for his own ends didn't bother Van. All she cared about was getting Bodrogi and those involved in the Bureau murders and the Chief had re-opened the door for those investigations.

"Where is he being held?" Van asked Henry.

"In the main detention center," Henry said. "Just asked for him. Tell them I sent you."

They found Van an interrogation room at the FBI detention center and got her coffee. After a few minutes, they led Officer Ben Bodrogi into the room and cuffed him to the table and left him with Van.

She studied him. She remembered him crying but this time he seemed arrogant and unremorseful.

"Hi Ben," she said. "Remember me?"

"Hi fuckface," he said dismissively. "I remember you. I remember you well."

"Where are your IA buddies? I don't see them here."

"Fuck you," he said.

Van was unmoved. "You have some problems, officer. It would serve you better to get your shit together and talk to me."

"Yah," he said looking down at the table. "About what?"

"Well, let's start with Detective Scott Geiringer. You knew him, didn't you?"

"I don't think so."

"Really?"

"If he was with the LAPD, I probably ran into him."

"Well, there's somebody here I think you do know."

Van motioned to the two-way mirror and an agent opened the door for Sergeant Marisa Coldridge.

Ben eyes opened wide and then he put his head in his hands. "I want an attorney," he said.

"Of course," said Van. "We have an attorney here for you right now." She motioned again and a public defender appeared.

"No, I want my attorney."

"That's fine, Ben. You make a phone call to whomever you want."

The agent led Ben out of the interrogation room to a phone on the wall. Van and Marisa sat in the interrogation room. Ben called Captain David Chang at Internal Affairs.

"David," he said. "This is Ben Bodrogi. I need some help."

"Hi, Ben," said David. "I'm really sorry but I can't help you right now."

"David," said Ben. "Is there an attorney there who can help me?"

"Not here," said David. "Maybe call the Police Union."

"Yeah, right, ok," said Ben, who started to shake. "Can you give me the number?"

"Sure, Ben," said David.

Ben clicked to hang up the phone. He tried to dial but his hand was shaking so badly he kept missing the numbers. The agent said, "Let me help you," and Ben gave him the number.

"Police Union," someone answered. "Hi," said Ben. "This is officer Ben Bodrogi. I have been detained by the FBI and need help from the Union."

"I see," said the voice. "What help do you need?"

"I need an attorney."

"There's no one here. Did you try the City Attorney's office?"

That call proved just as fruitless when the City Attorney recommended that Ben call a public defender. The agent pointed out the public defender still waiting by the interrogation room.

"Let me talk to him," said Ben to the agent.

"Of course," she responded.

The public defender took Ben into another room and asked for the recording devices to be turned off. They sat down and spoke. A few minutes later, they appeared. Ben looked defeated.

The agent led Ben and the attorney back to the room where Van and Marisa were sitting and chatting.

"Welcome back, Ben," said Van. "Now I am going to ask you again, did you know Detective Scott Geiringer?"

"I plead the fifth amendment," said Ben.

"Fine," said Van. "Let's get to it, then. Did you shoot Detective Scott Geiringer?"

"Plead the fifth."

"Ok. Did you know Detective Charles Darling?"

"Plead the fifth."

"Did you shoot Detective Charles Darling?"

"Plead the fifth."

"Do you know who I am?"

"You are Detective Van something. Eng or something like that."

"Ok, good. Did you shoot at me when I was at Franklin Canyon Reservoir?"

"Plead the fifth."

"Ok, I would like to ask Sergeant Coldridge a few questions."

The public defender interceded. "Detective, my client has asserted his Miranda rights. You know you are walking a fine line here. I can get the discussion thrown out in court."

"You certainly can try, counsellor. State your objections and I would like to question Sergeant Coldridge."

"So objected."

Van looked at Marisa. "For the record, please identify yourself." She did.

"Do you know Officer Ben Bodrogi?"

"I do. Ben was a student of mine at the Los Angeles Police Academy."

"How would you describe your interactions with Ben?"

"Ben was rough at the start and not a great student. I heard rumors he picked on other cadets."

Ben shouted, "That's a lie!"

His attorney stopped him and said, "Objection, hearsay." He whispered to Ben. "Don't say a word."

"Did students complain to you about Ben?"

"No, but they did complain to other instructors."

"Objection."

"Was he disciplined?"

"Yes, he was, and he was ordered to take my special police ethics course."

"You taught Ben ethics?"

"Yes."

"Did anyone else attend that course?"

"Yes. Scott Geiringer."

"Ben and Scott took that course together?"

"They did after both were disciplined for an incident on the grounds."

"Did Ben and Scott know each other?"

"Ben and Scott became friends. Scott told me he was helping Ben with his academics, and it was showing. Ben started to improve."

"Same objection."

"Ok, thank you,' Van said to Marisa. Turning back to Ben, Van asked, "Why did you tell me that you didn't know Scott Geiringer? You did know him, didn't you?"

Ben grabbed his fingers that were shaking and clenched them.

"Ben, you are a cop, or at least you were a cop."

"Harassing, Detective. If you do it again, we will leave."

Van ignored the attorney. "You want to be a cop, don't you. You like being a cop. Gives you power, doesn't it?"

"Detective."

"Power over friends, power over enemies, power over the public, power over children."

Ben raised his eyes and stared at Van. She stared back.

"That's enough," said the attorney. "This session is over."

"Ben," said Van earnestly. "You are in a lot of trouble. We can help you but only if you work with us."

The agent removed the table cuffs and re-cuffed Ben and led him to the door.

"First degree, Ben! First degree!" she shouted as the door closed behind him.

"Thanks, Sergeant," said Van to Marisa.

"Thank you," she responded. "I wish I would have seen this coming. We think we can screen but Ben seemed to be doing so well with Scott. I'm sorry, Detective. I'm sorry about your partner."

The agent started to lead Ben back to his cell, but Ben's attorney said, "Give us a minute." He took Ben back to the other room and they sat and talked for almost an hour. They came back out, and Ben pulled the agent who was handling him over to Van. The move felt aggressive to Van, and she readied herself, but as soon as Ben was a few feet away, he said, "I want a deal."

"If you want a deal, you have to give us something."

Ben repeated his words, "I want a deal."

Van said, "Take him in, and pointed to the interrogation room."

Officer Ben Bodrogi ultimately pled guilty under California Penal Code 192 to two counts criminal voluntary manslaughter and one count under Penal Code 245 for assault with a deadly weapon. He also pled guilty to a felony charge for violating of Penal Code 647, soliciting a minor for prostitution. Due to his cooperation, Ben's sentence was reduced from 34 years without parole to 20 years with an opportunity for parole within 10 years. Ben also was required to register as a sex offender. In exchange, Ben identified two police officers who assisted him in the murders of Scott and Charlie and an additional 10 police officers who also engaged in soliciting minors for sex. Ben was placed on suicide watch and, for the first two years in prison, he was held in isolation. But he survived.

Back in Spain, after seeing Belinda fall to her death, Van did hike down the Rio Cinca River that emerged from the Mediano spillway looking for Belinda. She walked from the point of the fall all the way to the foot of the waterfall she saw Belinda go over. She never saw Belinda's body. The waterfall dropped into a deep hole. It seemed plausible to Van that Belinda's body was still down there and maybe eventually it would be discovered.

Captain David Chang stepped down from his role as director of internal affairs. He joined a popular consulting firm that works with elected local officials.

The Chief of Police managed to navigate the child prostitution blemish on his otherwise stellar record. Van's help in solving the two Detective Bureau murders was an important part of the Chief's recovery. As soon as he qualified for retirement, he took it and moved into a cabin on a lake in Montana not too far from Great Falls.

Martin Richard went on to a successful career as an actor. He was nominated for an Oscar, but he didn't win. Still, he felt satisfied in his own accomplishments and as proud as he was of his Oscar-winning parents, he knew he was no longer standing in their shadow but casting his own shadow. His only regret in life was a woman named Van Eng, the one that got away.

Detective Alvin Broad retired shortly after his conversation with Van. She visited him on a regular basis, and they would play chess together and talk literature.

* * *

Van sat with her parents eating dinner, pork bellies and fried rice with chicken and udon soup with carrots, scallops and bok choy. After everything that had happened, Van requested another leave of absence. This time it was her choice, and she willingly left her badge and her gun with the Chief. She looked out the front door.

The sun was near the horizon and the shadows stretched toward darkness. Van heard a bike and saw the shadow of a helmet pass through the doorway. The bike stopped and the horn beeped. Van came to the doorway.

"What do you think?" said Brian.

"What do you mean what do I think?"

"I replaced the Gold Wing."

"You know I don't know anything about motorcycles," Van said and smiled. She studied the bike. "Does it make you happy?"

"The only thing that makes me happy is seeing you," Brian replied and winked. "And this BMW 1250. So, yes, I'm very happy." He reached back and pulled out a black bike jacket and helmet and held out the helmet. "Get on."

"Get on?" Van said acting shocked. Mom came to the door and handed her a bag.

"Go, Daughter," she said. "Go with Brian. Bring me back a son-in-law."

"Mom!" Van said. "Don't be ridiculous."

To Brian, she said, "Where are we going?"

"Up the coast," he said.

"We need to talk, pardner. Get off your new ride and give me ten minutes. Mom has soup. Bok choy, your favorite."

"Yum," said Brian, forcing a smile, and walked up the stairs to the front door.

Van climbed on the back of the BMW. "This is nice," she said into the microphone on her helmet.

"Yes, it is," said Brian. He grabbed her hands and pulled them around his waist. They took off and headed to Santa Monica where they spent the night and woke up early the next morning to meet Jaward and the Brothers of Sobriety for their motorcycle trip up the California coast.

"This is the one, isn't it?" Jaward said to Brian.

Brian hugged Jaward and patted him on the back. Brian smiled at Van blushing with deep pride. She smiled back and looked up at Jaward.

"Van," she said and extended her hand.

"Van Eng."

POSTSCRIPT

Various species of trout, some native, some not, swim in the deep pools of the Rio Cinca River in Northern Spain and many grow to 10-15 pounds. Francis and his dad Benny spent many hours on the river just below the waterfall where spawning fish would get trapped. Rarely did they take the drive to the river and return home empty-handed. Today was one of those days. Francis and Benny wandered the shallow parts of the river, the inlets where the current stalled and fish tended to congregate. But whatever fish they saw were not interested in their lures. Francis sat down frustrated and cut off his lure, looking for an alternative lure in his tackle box. Benny kept casting. Francis set down his pole and took off walking down the river just to enjoy the day.

After a few minutes of trudging along the shoreline, he looked at the middle of the river and noticed clothing caught on a rock. He complained to God why do people throw their trash into the river? But as he looked more closely, he saw an arm and realized he was looking at the body of a woman. He yelled to his dad to come over and Benny came running. The force of the river at the rock scared them. Benny held out a long branch from the shallows and Francis made his way carefully to the body. The woman was pretty, but her body was blue and severely bruised. She wasn't moving, and Francis thought she must be dead. He put his arm around her chest and lifted her off the rock as he hung onto the branch. Benny coaxed Francis back across the fast current, and they were able to bring the body to shore. They laid her down on a sand bank and were about to call the police they heard her cough and saw her spit up water and blood. Francis ran to her side.

"Are you ok, sweetheart?"

Belinda looked around dazed. "I hurt," she mumbled to the stranger.

"You need a hospital," said Francis.

"No," said Belinda, slowly regaining her senses. "Please. No hospital. I will be ok."

"You are not ok," said Benny. "If you don't want to go to a hospital, let us take you home. I know a doctor who will help you."

Belinda whispered, "Thank you," and passed out.

"Get the truck," said Benny. Francis ran to the vehicle and pulled it as close to the river as he could. He and Benny carried Belinda to the truck and laid her across the back seat. They packed their gear and drove home. When they got home, Benny's wife came to the front door and saw Belinda lying in the back.

"What is this?" she asked. "You are supposed to bring home fish, not strange women."

"She's hurt," said Benny. "Call the doctor."

* * *

After rounding up the remaining fighters inside Belinda's compound, the troops who came with the drone regiment wandered around through the complex of tunnels and underground warehouses.

"Be careful," said the sergeant leading the unit. "They have some weird shit in this place. Could be booby-trapped." The troops saw the wrecked helicopter and found the armories with vehicles and weapons and crates of bullets and RPGs.

"What do we do with this stuff?"

The CO radioed back to Command, who responded, "Send the semis in. Let's collect as much as we can."

Brian heard the discussion and said, "We need to destroy the nanobots before we do anything."

The Director asked, "How do we destroy the nanobots?"

Brian replied, "If they are frozen, they are inert. The squad can open the canisters and spray them with the resonant CO_2 spray. But be sure they are wearing masks and are ready with the antidote if anyone has a reaction."

The tankers filled with resonant spray made their way up the dirt road and into the compound through the rear entrance. Inside the compound, soldiers directed the tankers to the freezer vaults where they opened the canisters and began soaking the frozen remnants of the nanobots in the resonant spray. The Director called the Secretary of Defense to report on the status of the incursion. He described the clean-up efforts.

"Switch to private," said the Secretary.

The Director took the call off the central speaker system.

"Get me the nanobots," said the Secretary. "Do not destroy them."

"There are multiple militaries and countries represented here, sir," he responded. "How do you propose I get you the nanobots?"

"If you can't get them all, then just get me something. Send someone in whom you trust and get me some nanobots."

"Yes, sir," said the Director, and he hung up the phone.

[End of Book 3]

ROBERT JYSTAD

Kindle and Amazon Reviews of *The Nanobot Trilogy*

"What an amazing debut novel!"

"I was on the edge of my seat the whole time. A great thriller and a very enjoyable read."

"Resonating Reading."

"Fabulous read."

"Is this Tom Clancy?"

"For those of you that live in Southern California.....this is a MUST READ since a lot of the story takes place in detail in areas that you know well! For the rest of you, it's a great novel with twists and turns that is a great page turner similar to other crime novelists that you enjoy!"

"Engaging characters, a well thought out plot, and an oh so very good MacGuffin makes me wait with anticipation for the second and third novels in this trilogy."

"Very neat subject matter that will entertain you with modern Silicone Valley intrigue. Takes you on a roller coaster ride as Detective Van and the LAPD tract murders past and present."

"Jystad has taken seemingly unrelated threads and woven them into a fast-paced thriller that penetrates the world of greed, intrigue and espionage among scientists and investors pursuing high stakes, lucrative, but controversial, biomedical advances...advances that can save lives.... or end them."

"5 Stars. An exciting, fast-paced page turner. I love the main character, Van Eng. She is such a role model with her spunk, tenaciousness and commitment to purpose. The technical details surrounding nanobots and their creation would fascinate readers. The story takes you on twists and turns while uncovering the truth. In addition, the details regarding the Silicon Valley Hi Tech industry and how it impacts society is so relevant to today's circumstances. It was great how it all came together at the end but does leave you wanting more. Love that this series is a trilogy. Looking forward to Book 2."